Alexander Adam

The Rudiments of Latin and English Grammar

designed to facilitate the study of both languages, by connecting them together

Alexander Adam

The Rudiments of Latin and English Grammar
designed to facilitate the study of both languages, by connecting them together

ISBN/EAN: 9783337392642

Printed in Europe, USA, Canada, Australia, Japan

Cover: Foto ©Andreas Hilbeck / pixelio.de

More available books at **www.hansebooks.com**

O F

LATIN AND *ENGLISH*

GRAMMAR;

DESIGNED

TO FACILITATE THE STUDY OF BOTH LANGUAGES, BY CONNECTING THEM TOGETHER.

BY

ALEXANDER ADAM, LL. D.

Rector of the High School of Edinburgh.

Grammatice eft ars, neceffaria pueris, jucunda fenibus, dulcis fecretorum comes, et
quæ vel fola omni ftudiorum genere plus habet operis quam oftentationis. Ne
quis igitur tanquam parva faftidiat Grammatices elementa ; quia interiora velut
facri hujus adeuntibus, apparebit multa rerum fubtilitas, quæ non modo acuere
ingenia puerilia, fed exercere altiffimam quoque eruditionem ac fcientiam poffit.
Quinctilian i. 4, 5.

First American from the Fifth English Edition, with
Improvements.

Recommended by the Univerfity at *Cambridge* (Maff.)
to be ufed by thofe who are intended for that Seminary.

BOSTON:
Printed by MANNING & LORING,
For S. HALL, W. SPOTSWOOD, J. WHITE,
THOMAS & ANDREWS, D. WEST,
E. LARKIN, W. P. & L. BLAKE,
and J. WEST.

DECEMBER, 1799.

ADVERTISEMENT of *CAMBRIDGE UNI-VERSITY.*

WHEREAS the *Univerſity* in *Cambridge* for ſeveral years paſt has ſuffered much inconvenience, and the intereſt of Letters no ſmall detriment, from the variety of Latin and Greek Grammars uſed by the ſtudents, in conſequence of that diverſity, to which, under different inſtructors, they have been accuſtomed in their preparatory courſe; to promote, ſo far as may be, the cauſe of Literature, by preventing thoſe evils in future, the Government of the Univerſity, on due conſideration of the ſubject, has thought it expedient to requeſt all inſtructors of Youth, who may reſort to Cambridge for education, to adopt " *Adam's Latin Grammar,*" and the " *Glouceſter Greek Grammar,*" with reference to ſuch pupils, as Books ſingularly calculated for the improvement of ſtudents in theſe languages. The Univerſity has no wiſh to recommend, much leſs to dictate, to any other inſtitution, but only to facilitate the acquiſition of Literature by promoting uniformity within itſelf. Theſe being the Grammars which will be uſed at this College by all claſſes, admitted after the preſent year, it ſeems neceſſary, to prevent future difficulty, by giving this public and timely notice; for though a knowledge of the Grammar is not at preſent made indiſpenſably neceſſary to admiſſion into the Univerſity, yet every Scholar, who may be accepted after the preſent Commencement without ſuch knowledge, will be required immediately to form a radical and intimate acquaintance with them, as no ſtudent will be permitted at the claſſical exerciſes to uſe any other Grammar.

Cambridge, July 7, 1799.

P R E F A C E

TO THE

FIRST EDITION.

MAN enjoys the fingular advantage of being able to communicate his thoughts by articulate founds. Different nations employ very different verbal figns for the expreffion of thought ; but with refpect to the nature and ufe of the feveral parts of fpeech in general, they uniformly agree. Hence the Principles of Grammar in all languages are much the fame.

The ftudy of Grammar has been confidered as an object of great importance by the wifeft men in all ages. But, like other fciences, it has often been involved in myftery, and perplexed with needlefs difficulties. Inftead of facilitating the acquifition of languages, which was its original defign, it has frequently ferved to render that more laborious.

As language is regular in its general ftructure, rules muft no doubt be ufeful to affift us in underftanding it. We firft learn to fpeak from imitation. We ufe the expreffions which we hear from others. But when we have once gained a certain ftock of words, we employ them according to general rules. When a child, for inftance, has occafion to fpeak of two perfons, he will fay, "two mans," inftead of "two men ;" becaufe he learns the general method of forming the plural, before he attends to particular exceptions. The fame may be obferved of a perfon who endeavours to acquire any foreign language. Memory furnifhes us with proper terms to exprefs our thoughts,

but

but judgment muſt be exerted in adapting theſe to particular circumſtances.

Every ſcience may be reduced to principles. The principles of Grammar may be traced from the progreſs of the mind in the acquiſition of language. Children firſt expreſs their feelings by motions and geſtures of the body, by cries and tears. This is the language of nature, and therefore univerſal. It fitly repreſents the quickneſs of ſentiment and thought, which are as inſtantaneous as the impreſſion of light on the eye. Hence we always expreſs our ſtronger feelings by theſe natural ſigns. But when we want to make known to others the particular conceptions of the mind, we muſt repreſent them by parts, we muſt divide and analyze them. We expreſs each part by certain ſigns, and join theſe together according to the order of their relations. Thus words are both the inſtrument and ſigns of the diviſion of thought. But as words are only artificial ſigns of thought, and their connection with what they repreſent, merely arbitrary; the ſame thought may be expreſſed by different ſigns, and theſe ſigns variouſly arranged: Hence the diverſity of languages and idioms. All languages, however, muſt conſiſt of the ſame eſſential parts. There muſt be ſome words to mark the ſubject of diſcourſe, and others to expreſs what we affirm concerning it. The former excite our curioſity, and by the latter it is gratified. In this manner muſt language have been originally invented, if it be a human invention; and in this manner do children always acquire the uſe of ſpeech. We are firſt taught the names of objects; and then we learn the words, which expreſs their qualities and actions. As we grow up, we become acquainted with the uſe of Prepoſitions, Adverbs, and Conjunctions, together with the different variations of Verbs employed to mark time, number, and perſon. By joining theſe together, we form ſentences, which we compound and arrange variouſly, according to the ſentiments we want to expreſs. Thus we come to analyze our thoughts, and repreſent them by parts, ſo as to convey them properly to others, with all their circumſtances and relations.

Grammar

Grammar is founded on common fenfe. Every fentiment expreffed by words exemplifies its rules, and the ignorant obferve them, as well as the learned. The Principles of Grammar are the firft abftract truths which a young mind can comprehend. Children difcover their capacity for underftanding the rules of Grammar, by putting them in practice. It is indeed difficult to make young people attend to what paffes in their own minds. But perhaps this is partly owing to the abftrufe manner in which it is laid before them. The Principles of Grammar will be moft fuccefsfully taught by arranging and explaining them according to the order of nature. Every art is more or lefs involved in obfcurity by the hard terms peculiar to it. In no art is this more remarkably the cafe than in Grammar. The terms it employs are fo abftract, that, unlefs they be properly explained, even perfons of advanced years cannot underftand them. Could this inconvenience be thoroughly removed, the Principles of Grammar might be adapted to the meaneft capacity: For were the nature of the different parts of fpeech, and their ufe in fentences properly explained, the mind would recognife its own operations, and perceive that Grammar is nothing elfe than a delineation of thofe rules which we obferve in every expreffion of thought by words. Thus the ftudy of Grammar would not only improve the memory, but ferve in a high degree to ftrengthen and enlarge all the faculties of the mind.

Whatever we learn firft, is the moft familiar to us. For this reafon children will moft eafily apprehend the Principles of Grammar, when explained and exemplified in that language which is natural to them. Hence it feems proper to begin in Grammar, as in reading, with the language of our own country. But as moft of the modern languages in Europe are in a great meafure founded on the Latin, and as a very confiderable part of our knowledge, with regard both to fcience and tafte, is derived from Latin authors, the ftudy of Latin Grammar has generally been preferred to that of the Grammar of the mother tongue. This has particularly been the practice in this country. Till of late very little attention has been paid to the ftudy of

A 2

Englifh

Englifh Grammar ; in confequence of which many irregularities have crept into the language, which might otherwife have been prevented. Were the importance of the two languages to come into competition, that would no doubt deferve the preference which we have the moft frequent occafion to ufe. But to fuch as aim at polite literature, the ftudy of both feems neceffary : and the knowledge of the one will be found highly conducive to that of the other. The Englifh language has received its greateft improvements from thofe who were mafters of claffical learning ; and perhaps it cannot be thoroughly underftood, without fome acquaintance with the Latin. It is certain, no one can properly tranflate from the one language into the other, without underftanding the idioms of both. In order therefore to teach Latin Grammar with fuccefs, we fhould always join with it a particular attention to the rudiments of Englifh. This is the defign of the following attempt. And as in writing upon Grammar, materials entirely new cannot be expected, the compiler has with freedom borrowed from all hands whatever he judged fit for his purpofe. He acknowledges himfelf particularly indebted to Mr Harris's Hermes with regard to the principles of univerfal Grammar ; to Wallis and Dr Lowth, for moft of his obfervations concerning the Englifh ; and to Gerard Voffius, and Ruddiman, with refpect to the Latin.

The merit of any performance on this fubject muft in a great meafure depend upon the method of illuftration and arrangement. In the prefent effay that arrangement has been obferved, which appeared moft natural. The feveral parts of Grammar are reduced to general principles ; and after thefe are fubjoined particular obfervations and exceptions. The moft effential rules and remarks are printed in larger characters ; and the committing of thefe to memory, together with the examples, will to a learner at firft, it is thought, be found fufficient. A careful perufal of the particular obfervations, afterwards, joined with the reading of the claffics, and the practice of writing and fpeaking Latin, will fuperfede the ufe of any other Grammar rules. If a further exercife for the memory be be wanted, beautiful paſſages ſelected from the Claſſics ſeem much more proper for this purpoſe, than Latin verſes about words and phraſes, however accurately compoſed.

Whatever other Grammar may have formerly been taught, the peruſal of the following, it is hoped, will be attended with advantage. The compiler has done every thing in his power to prepare it for the public. He has examined with care the method of education, and the ſeveral Grammars made uſe of both at home and abroad. He has communicated his own plan to many perſons of the firſt character for letters in this kingdom ; and the attention which they have been pleaſed to pay to it, and the many uſeful obſervations which he has received from them, he will always remember with gratitude. He is ſtill afraid, that notwithſtanding all his care, ſome defects may be found in the execution ; but hopes that his deſign at leaſt will meet with approbation, and earneſtly entreats the aſſiſtance of the encouragers of learning, to enable him to bring his ſcheme to greater perfection.

EDINBURGH,
May, 1772.

PREFACE

FOURTH EDITION.

—————

THE compiler was first led, at an early period of life, to think of composing this Book, by observing the hurtful effects of teaching boys Grammar Rules in Latin verse, which they did not understand; while they were ignorant, not only of the principles of that language, but also of those of their mother tongue. Experience has since afforded him the most convincing proofs of the impropriety of this practice; and his opinion has been still further confirmed by perusing the writings of the old Grammarians, and of the most eminent among the moderns. The old Grammarians, *Charisius, Diomedes, Priscianus, Probus, Donatus, Servius, Victorinus, Augustinus, Cassiodorus, Macrobius, Beda, Alcuinus,* * *&c.* have no verse rules; and so in latter times *Perotte, Manutius, Erasmus, Valerius, Buchanan, Milton, &c.:* Nicolaus Perotte was one of the chief restorers of learning in the fifteenth century. He died Archbishop of Siponto in 1480. The compiler has a copy of the first edition of his Grammar, printed at Brescia anno 1474.— It is composed by way of question and answer; but without any verse rules.— Soon after the invention of printing, and perhaps before, for the compiler has not been able to ascertain the precise period, the custom was introduced of expressing the principles

—————

* TERENTIANUS MAURUS, a learned Grammarian, by birth an African, who is supposed to have lived under Trajan, and wrote in verse, treats only of poetry.

ples of almost every art and science in Latin and Greek verse. The rules of Logic, and even the aphorisms of Hippocrates, were taught in this manner. Among the versifiers of Latin Grammar *Despauter* and *Lily* were the most conspicuous. The first complete edition of Despauter's Grammar was printed at Cologne, anno 1522; his *Syntax* had been published anno 1509. Lily was made first Master of St Paul's school in London, by Dr. Colet, its founder, anno 1510; so that he was contemporary with Despauter. His Grammar was appointed, by an act which is still in force, to be taught in the established schools of England. Various attempts were afterwards made by different authors; as, *Sanctius*, *Alvarus*, *Scioppius*, *Kirkwood*, *Watt*, *Ruddiman*, &c. to improve on the plan of Despauter and Lily; but with little success. The truth is, it seems impracticable to express with sufficient perspicuity the Principles of Grammar in Latin verse; and it appears strange, that when scholastic jargon is exploded from elementary books on other sciences, it should be retained by public authority, where it ought never to have been admitted, in Latin Grammars for children. But such is the force of habit and attachment to established modes, that we go on in the use of them, without thinking whether they be founded in reason or not. When there are a great many exceptions from a general rule, whatever can assist the memory is no doubt useful. On this account the principal rules for the genders of nouns, &c. are here subjoined, for local reasons, from Ruddiman's Grammar; although many of them are by no means adapted to the capacity of boys; and more of them are inserted, in compliance with the opinion of others, than the compiler judges necessary. They are printed at the end of the book; and such as choose it, may have Lily's rules, Watt's rules, or any other, substituted in their place.

The authors of the *Nouvelle Methode*, or *Port Royal Grammar* in France, judging it as absurd to teach Latin by rules in Latin verse, as to teach Greek, by rules in Greek verse, or Hebrew by rules in Hebrew, composed the rules of Latin Grammar, in French verse. Some authors in England, as, *Clarke*, *Phillips*, &c. have imitated their
example.

example. But this plan has not in either country been much followed. Nothing can be more uncouth than such verſification. So that Latin rules, on the whole, ſeem preferable.—However this may be, the following remarks concerning the method of teaching Latin, it is hoped, will not be deemed improper.

When the learner is once maſter of the inflexion of nouns and verbs, he ſhould be exerciſed in getting by heart words and phraſes, while at the ſame time he is employed in reading ſome eaſy author; and in turning plain ſentences from Engliſh into Latin. The ſooner he can be brought to write part of his exerciſes, the better; but he ſhould never be obliged to get Grammar rules in Latin verſe, till he is capable of underſtanding them by himſelf; becauſe although the teacher may explain them, the ſcholar will ſoon forget the interpretation, and repeat the words merely by rote, without attending to their meaning : Nor ſhould he be forced to get rules in Latin verſe, which may be remembered equally well in Engliſh proſe. Rules in verſe are only uſeful when they aſſiſt the memory ; as when there is a number of exceptions from a general rule, where alone they are indeed of advantage : and even here, perhaps, any chime of words might anſwer the purpoſe as well as Latin hexameters. It is of importance, when the rule is long, that the learner be accuſtomed to repeat no more of it than is ſtrictly applicable to the word or phraſe in queſtion. The repetition of the whole is an uſeleſs waſte of time. The great object ought to be, to bring the learner, in as ſhort time as poſſible, to join without heſitation an adjective with a ſubſtantive in any caſe, number, or degree of compariſon ; and in like manner to touch upon any part of a verb, and tell readily by what caſe any adjective, verb, or prepoſition is followed. This facility practice alone can teach, and the method of acquiring it muſt in all languages be much the ſame.

The niceties of conſtruction, the figures of Syntax, and the other parts of Grammar, ſhould be occaſionally taught, as the learner proceeds in reading the more difficult authors.

As

As the ancient Romans joined the Grammar of their own language with that of the Greek ; fo we ought to connect the ftudy of Englifh Grammar with that of the Latin ; and when the learner properly underftands Latin Grammar, he ought to join with it the ftudy of the Greek; the knowledge of both thefe languages being requifite for the thorough underftanding of the Englifh. This is the practice in England, and other countries, where the beft Greek and Latin fcholars are formed. It is particularly neceffary in Scotland to pay attention to the Englifh in conjunction with the Latin, as by neglecting it boys at fchool learn many improprieties in point of Grammar, as well as of pronunciation, which it is difficult in after life to correct. This attention is lefs requifite in England ; though even there, in the opinion of Dr. Lowth, to ufe his own words, "the connection of the Englifh with the Latin " Grammar, if it could be introduced into fchools, might " be of good fervice."*

EDINBURGH,
Oct. 25, 1793.

In the prefent edition the Appendix to Etymology has been omitted, becaufe a larger work on that fubject is intended, and will probably foon be fent to the prefs.

EDINBURGH,
Jan. 23. 1798.

* In a letter concerning this book, after having read the manufcript, dated, Cuddefdon, Sept. 27, 1771.

CONTENTS.

CONTENTS.

VERBS

B   II. COMPOUND

CONTENTS.

THE

GRAMMAR is the art of speaking and writing correctly.

Latin or English Grammar is the art of speaking and writing the Latin or the English language correctly.

The *Rudiments* of Grammar are plain and easy instructions, teaching beginners the first principles and rules of it.

Grammar treats of sentences, and the several parts of which they are compounded.

Sentences consist of words; Words consist of one or more syllables; Syllables of one or more letters. So that Letters, Syllables, Words, and Sentences, make up the whole subject of grammar.

LETTERS.

A Letter is the mark of a sound, or of an articulation of sound.

That part of Grammar which treats of letters, is called *Orthography*.

The letters in Latin are twenty-five : A, a; B, b; C, c; D, d; E, e; F, f; G, g; H, h; I, i; J, j; K, k; L, l; M, m; N, n; O, o; P, p; Q, q; R, r; S, s; T, t; U, u; V, v; X, x; Y, y; Z, z;

In English there is one letter more, namely, *W, w.*

Letters

Letters are divided into *Vowels* and *Consonants*.

Six are vowels; *a, e, i, o, u, y.* All the reft
are confonants.

A vowel makes a full found by itſelf; as, *a, e.*

A confonant cannot make a perfect ſound
without a vowel; as, *b, d.*

A vowel is properly called a *ſimple ſound;* and the
ſounds formed by the concourſe of vowels and confonants,
articulate ſounds.

Confonants are divided into *Mutes, Semi-vowels,* and
Double Confonants.

A mute is ſo called, becauſe it entirely ſtops the paſſage
of the voice; as, *p* in *ap.*

The mutes are, *p, b; t, d; c, k, q,* and *g;* but *b, d,* and
g, perhaps may more properly be termed *Semi-mutes.*

A ſemi-vowel, or half vowel, does not entirely ſtop the
paſſage of the voice; thus, *al.*

The ſemi-vowels are, *l, m, n, r, s, f.* The firſt four of
theſe are alſo called *Liquids,* particularly *l* and *r;* becauſe
they flow ſoftly and eaſily after a mute in the ſame ſyllable; as, *bla, ſtra.*

The mutes and ſemi-vowels may be thus diſtinguiſhed.
In naming the mutes, the vowel is put after them; as, *pe,
be,* &c. but in naming the ſemi-vowels, the vowel is put
before them; as, *el, em,* &c.

The double confonants are, *x, z,* and *j.* *X* is made up
of *cs, ks,* or *gs.* *Z* ſeems not to be a double confonant
in Engliſh. It has the ſame relation to *s,* as *v* has to *f,*
being ſounded ſomewhat more ſoftly.

In Latin *z,* and likewiſe *k* and *y,* are found only in
words derived from the Greek.

Y in Engliſh is ſometimes a confonant, as in *youth.*

H by ſome is not accounted a letter, but only a breathing.

DIPHTHONGS.

A diphthong is two vowels joined in one found.

If

If the sound of both vowels be distinctly heard, it is called a *Proper Diphthong;* if not, an *Improper Diphthong.*

The proper diphthongs in Latin are commonly reckoned three; *au, eu, ei;* as in *aurum, Eurus, omneis.* To these, some, not improperly, add other three, namely, *ai;* as in *Maia; oi,* as in *Troia :* and *ui,* as in *Harpuia,* or in *cui* and *huic,* when pronounced as monosyllables.

The improper diphthongs in Latin are two, *ae,* or when the vowels are written together, *æ;* as *aetas,* or *ætas; oe,* or *œ;* as *poena* or *pœna;* in both of which the sound of the *e* only is heard. The ancients commonly wrote the vowels separately, thus, *aetas, poena.*

The English language abounds with improper diphthongs, the just pronunciation of which practice alone can teach. In some words derived from the French, there are three vowels in the same syllable, but two of them only are sounded; as in *beauty, lieutenant.*

SYLLABLES.

A syllable is the sound of one letter, or of several letters pronounced by one impulse of the voice; as *a, to, strength.*

In every word there are as many syllables as there are distinct sounds; as, *in-fal-li-bi-li-ty.*

In Latin there are as many syllables in a word as there are vowels or diphthongs in it; unless when *u* with any other vowel comes after *g, q,* or *s,* as in *lingua, qui, sua-deo;* where the two vowels are not reckoned a diphthong, because the sound of the *u* vanishes, or is little heard.

Words consisting of one syllable, are called *Monosyllables;* of two, *Dissyllables;* and of more than two, *Polysyllables.* But all words of more than one syllable are commonly called *Polysyllables.*

In dividing words into syllables, we are chiefly to be directed by the ear. Compound words should be divided into the parts of which they are made up; as, *up-on, with-out,* &c. and so in Latin words, *ăb-ūtor, ĭn-ops, proptĕr-ea, et-ĕnim, vel-ut,* &c. In like manner, when a syllable is added in the formation of the English verb, as, *lov-ed, lov-ing, lov-eth, will-ing,* &c.

Observe, A long syllable is thus marked [-]; as, *amāre;*

or

or with a circumflex accent thus, [ˆ] ; as, *amáris.* A
ſhort ſyllable is marked thus [˘] ; as, *omnĭbus.*

What pertains to the quantity of ſyllables, to accent,
and verſe, will be treated of afterwards.

WORDS.

Words are articulate ſounds ſigniſicant of thought.

That part of Grammar which treats of words, is called
Etymology, or *Analogy.*

All words may be divided into three kinds ; namely, 1. ſuch as
mark the names of things; 2. ſuch as denote what is affirmed concerning
things ; and 3. ſuch as are ſigniſicant only in conjunction with other
words ; or what are called *Subſtantives, Attributives,* and *Connectives.*
Thus in the following ſentence, " *The diligent boy reads the leſſon care-*
" *fully in the ſchool, and at home,*" the words *boy, leſſon, ſchool, home,*
are the names we give to the things ſpoken of ; *diligent, reads, care-*
fully, expreſs what is affirmed concerning the boy ; *the, in, and, at,*
are only ſigniſicant when joined with the other words of the ſentence.

All words whatever are either *ſimple* or *compound, pri-*
mitive or *derivative.*

The diviſion of words into ſimple and compound, is
called their *Figure ;* into primitive and derivative, their
Species or kind.

A ſimple word is that which is not made up of more than
one ; as, *pius,* pious ; *ĕgo,* I ; *dŏceo,* I teach.

A compound word is that which is made up of two or
more words ; or of one word, and ſome ſyllable added, as,
impius, impious ; *dēdŏceo,* I unteach ; *ĕgŏmet,* I myſelf.

A primitive word is that which comes from no other ;
as, *pius,* pious ; *diſco,* I learn ; *dŏceo,* I teach.

A derivative word is that which comes from another
word ; as, *piĕtas,* piety ; *doctrīna,* learning.

The different claſſes into which we divide words, are
called *Parts of Speech.*

PARTS OF SPEECH.

[The parts of ſpeech in Latin are eight ;
1. *Noun, Pronoun, Verb, Participle ;* declined :
2. *Adverb, Prepoſition, Interjection,* and *Con-*
junction ; undeclined.]

In

In Englifh the adjective and participle are not declined.

Thofe words or parts of fpeech are faid to be *declined* which receive different changes, particularly on the end, which is called the *Termination* of words.

The changes made upon words are by grammarians called *Accidents*.

Of old, all words which admit of different terminations were faid to be declined. But *Declenfion* is now applied only to nouns. The changes made upon the verb are called *Conjugation*.

The Englifh language has one part of fpeech more than the Latin, namely, the ARTICLE.

The *article* is a word put before fubftantive nouns, to point them out, and to fhew how far their fignification extends.

There are two articles, *a* and *the* : *a* becomes *an* before a vowel, or a filent *h*.

A is called the *Indefinite*; *The* the *Definite Article*.

A is ufed to point out one fingle thing of a kind, without fixing precifely what that thing is : *The* determines what particular thing is meant.

A man means fimply fome one or other of that kind : *the man* fignifies that particular man who is fpoken of.

The want of the article is a defect in the Latin tongue, and often renders the meaning of nouns undetermined : thus, *filius regis*, may fignify, either, *a fon of a king*, or *a king's fon* ; or *the fon of the king*, or *the king's fon*.

The placed before certain common names, marks either a whole kind, or fome individual of that kind, with which we are acquainted ; as, *the lion*, *the ox*, &c.

A can only be joined to fubftantive nouns in the fingular number : *the* may alfo be joined to plurals. *A* is likewife ufed before adjectives which exprefs number, when many are confidered as one whole ; as, *a thoufand men*, *a few*, *a great many men*.

The is likewife applied to adjectives and adverbs in the comparative or fuperlative degree, to mark their fenfe more ftrongly ; as, " *the* wifer," " *the* better ;" " *the* more I think of it, *the* better I like it."

NOUN.

N O U N.

A noun is either fubftantive or adjective.

The adjective feems to be improperly called *noun* : it is only a word *added to* a fubftantive or noun, expreffive of its quality ; and therefore fhould be confidered as a different part of fpeech. But as the fubftantive and adjective together exprefs but one object, and in Latin are declined after the fame manner, they have both been comprehended under the fame general name.

S U B S T A N T I V E.

A Subftantive, or Noun, is the name of any perfon, place, or thing ; as, *boy, fchool, book.*

Subftantives are of two forts ; *proper* and *common* names.

Proper names are the names appropriated to individuals ; as the names of perfons and places ; fuch are, *Cæfar, Rome.*

Common names ftand for whole kinds, containing feveral forts ; or for forts, containing many individuals under them ; as, *animal, man, beaft, fifh, fowl,* &c.

Every particular being fhould have its own proper name ; but this is impoffible, on account of their innumerable multitude : men have therefore been obliged to give the fame common name to fuch things as agree together in certain refpects. Thefe form what is called a *genus,* or kind ; a *fpecies,* or fort.

A proper name may be ufed for a common, and then in Englifh it has the article joined to it ; as, when we fay of fome great conqueror, " He is *an* Alexander ;" or, " *The* Alexander of his age."

To proper and common names may be added a third clafs of nouns, which mark the names of qualities, and are called *abftract nouns ;* as, *hardnefs, goodnefs, whitenefs,* virtue, juftice, piety, &c.

When we fpeak of things, we confider them as one or more. This is what we call *Number.* When one thing is fpoken of, a noun is faid to be of the *fingular number ;* when two or more, of the *plural.*

Things confidered according to their kinds, are either male or female, or neither of the two. Males are faid to be of the *mafculine gender ;* females of the *feminine ;* and all other things, of the *neuter gender.*

Such

Such nouns as are applied to signify either the male or the female, are said to be of the *common gender,* that is, either masculine or feminine.

Various methods are used, in different languages, to express the different connexions or relations of one thing to another. In the English, and in most modern languages, this is done by prepositions, or particles placed before the substantive: in Latin, by declension, or by different cases; that is, by changing the termination of the noun; as, *rex,* a king, *or* the king; *regis,* of a king, or of the king.

ENGLISH NOUNS.

In English, nouns have only one case, namely, the genitive, or possessive case, which is formed from the noun, by adding an *s,* with an apostrophe, or mark to separate it; as, *John's book,* the same with, *the book of John.* It was formerly written *Johnis book.*

Some have thought the *'s* a contraction for *his;* but improperly; because, instead of *the woman's book,* we cannot say, *the woman his book.* Others have imagined, and with more justness, that by the addition of the *'s* the substantive is changed into a possessive adjective. When the noun ends in *s,* the sign of the possessive case is sometimes not added; as, *for righteousness sake;* and never to the plural number ending in *s;* as, *on eagles wings.* Perhaps it would be better in the plural, when it ends in *s,* always to use the particle, and not the possessive form; as, *on the wings of eagles.* Both the sign and the preposition seem sometimes to be used; as, *a soldier of the king's:* but here there are two possessives; for it means, *one of the soldiers of the king.*

A singular noun, in English, is made plural by adding to it *s,* or, for the sake of sound, *es;* as, *king, kings; church, churches; brush, brushes; witness, witnesses; fox, foxes; leaf, leaves;* in which last, and in many others, *f* is also turned into *v,* to make the pronunciation easier.

Several plurals are formed by adding *en;* as *ox, oxen.* Of these some are contracted, or interpose a letter on account of sound; as, *brethren, children, swine, kine, women, men,* &c. *for brotheren, sowen,* &c. Instead of *kine* we now commonly say *cows;* and we seldom use *brethren* but in solemn discourse.

Nouns in *y* change *y* into *ie;* as, *cherry, cherries; city, cities. Cherry's, city's,* &c. are in the possessive case. ·····

Some

Some nouns form the plural more irregularly; as, *mouse, mice; louse, lice; tooth, teeth; foot, feet; goose, geese, &c.*

The words *sheep, deer,* are the same in both numbers. Some nouns, from the nature of the things which they express, are used only in the singular, or in the plural form; as, *wheat, pitch, gold, sloth, pride,* &c. and *bellows, scissars, lungs, bowels,* &c.

Several nouns in English are changed in their termination, to express gender; as *prince, princess; actor, actress; lion, lioness; hero, heroine; duke, duchess,* &c.

The English language has a peculiar advantage over most other languages, in making all words whatever, except the names of males and females, to be of the neuter gender: unless when inanimate beings are personified, or considered as persons; as, when we say of the sun, *he shines;* or of the moon, *she shines.*

LATIN NOUNS.

[A Latin noun is declined by *Genders, Cases,* and *Numbers.*]

[There are three genders, *Masculine, Feminine,* and *Neuter.*]

[The cases are six, *Nominative, Genitive, Dative, Accusative, Vocative,* and *Ablative.*]

[There are two numbers, *Singular* and *Plural.*]

[There are five different ways of varying or declining nouns, called, the *first, second, third, fourth,* and *fifth declensions.*]

Cases are certain changes made upon the termination of nouns, to express the relation of one thing to another.

They are so called, from *cădo,* to fall; because they fall, as it were, from the nominative; which is therefore named *cāsus rectus,* the straight case; and the other cases, *cāsus obliqui,* the oblique cases.

The different declensions may be distinguished from one another by the termination of the genitive singular. The first declension has *æ* diphthong; the second has *i;* the

third

third has *is;* the fourth has *ús;* and the fifth has *ei* in the genitive.

Although Latin nouns be said to have six cases, yet none of them have that number of different terminations, both in the singular and plural.

GENERAL RULES *of Declension.*

1. Nouns of the neuter gender have the Accusative and Vocative like the Nominative, in both numbers; and these cases in the plural end always in *a.*

2. The Dative and Ablative plural end always alike.

3. The Vocative for the most part in the singular, and always in the plural, is the same with the Nominative.

Greek nouns in *s* generally lose *s* in the Vocative; as, *Thomas, Thoma; Anchises, Anchise; Păris, Pari; Panthus, Panthu; Pallas, -antis; Palla,* names of men. But nouns in *es* of the third declension oftener retain the *s;* as, *ô Achilles,* rarely *-e; O Socrătes,* seldom *-e:* and sometimes nouns in *is* and *as;* as, *O Thais, Mysis, Pallas, -ădis,* the goddess Minerva, &c.

4. Proper names for the most part want the plural:

Unless several of the same name be spoken of; as, *duŏdecim Cæsăres,* the twelve Cæsars.

The cases of Latin nouns are thus expressed in English;
1. With the indefinite article, *a king.*

	Singular.			Plural.	
Nom.		*a king,*	Nom.		*kings,*
Gen.	*of*	*a king,*	Gen.	*of*	*kings,*
Dat.	*to* or *for*	*a king,*	Dat.	*to* or *for*	*kings,*
Acc.		*a king,*	Acc.		*kings,*
Voc.	*O*	*king,*	Voc.	*O*	*kings,*
Abl.	*with, from, in, by, a king,*		Abl.	*with, from, in, by, kings.*	

2. With

2. With the definite article, *the king*.

<table>
<tr><td colspan="2">Singular.</td><td colspan="2">Plural.</td></tr>
<tr><td>Nom.</td><td>*the king*,</td><td>Nom.</td><td>*the kings*,</td></tr>
<tr><td>Gen. *of*</td><td>*the king*,</td><td>Gen. *of*</td><td>*the kings*,</td></tr>
<tr><td>Dat. *to* or *for*</td><td>*the king*,</td><td>Dat. *to* or *for*</td><td>*the kings*,</td></tr>
<tr><td>Acc.</td><td>*the king*,</td><td>Acc.</td><td>*the kings*,</td></tr>
<tr><td>Voc. *O*</td><td>*king*,</td><td>Voc. *O*</td><td>*kings*,</td></tr>
<tr><td>Ab. *with, from, in, by,* the king :</td><td></td><td>Ab. *with, from, in, by,* the kings.</td><td></td></tr>
</table>

GENDER.

Nouns in Latin are faid to be of different genders, not merely from the diſtinction of ſex; but chiefly from their being joined with an adjective of one termination, and not of another. Thus, *penna*, a pen, is faid to be feminine, becauſe it is always joined with an adjective in that termination which is applied to females; as, *bŏna penna*, a good pen, and not *bŏnus penna*.

The gender of nouns which fignify things without life, depends on their termination, and different declenſion.

To diſtinguiſh the different genders, grammarians make uſe of the pronoun *hic*, to mark the maſculine ; *hæc*, the feminine ; and *hoc*, the neuter.

GENERAL RULES *concerning Gender*.

1. Names of males are maſculine ; as, *Hŏmērus*, Homer ;) *păter*, a father ; *poēta*, a poet.

2. Names of females are feminine ; as, *Hĕlĕna*, Helen ;) *mŭlier*, a woman ; *uxor*, a wife ; *māter*, a mother ; *sŏror*, a fifter ; *Tellŭs*, the goddefs of the earth.

3. Nouns which fignify either the male or female, are of the common gender ; that is, either maſculine or feminine ; as, Hic *bos*, an ox ; hæc *bos*, a cow ; hic *părens*, a father ; hæc *părens*, a mother.)

The following liſt comprehends moſt nouns of the common gender.

Adŏleſcens,

dŏlescens, ⎱ a young

Jŭvĕnis, ⎰ man, or woman.

Affīnis, *a relation by marriage.*

Antiftes, *a prelate.*

Auctor, *an author.*

Augur, *a foothfayer.*

Cănis, *a dog or bitch.*

Cīvis, *a citizen.*

Cliens, *a client.*

Cŏmes, *a companion.*

Conjux, *a husband or wife.*

Convīva, *a guest.*

Cuftos, *a keeper.*

Dux, *a leader.*

Hæres, *an heir.*

Hoftis, *an enemy.*

Infans, *an infant.*

Interpres, *an interpre- [ter.*

Jūdex, *a judge.*

Martyr, *a martyr.*

Mīles, *a foldier.*

Mūnĭceps, *a burgefs.*

Nēmo, *no body.*

Obfes, *an hoftage.*

Patruēlis, *a coufin-ger- man by the father's [fide.*

Præs, *a furety.*

Princeps, *a prince or princefs.*

Săcerdos, *a prieft or priefiefs.*

Sus, *a fwine.*

Teftis, *a witnefs.*

Vātes, *a prophet.*

Vindex, *an avenger.*[*]

But *antiftes, cliens,* and *hofpes,* alfo change their termination to exprefs the feminine, thus, *antiftita, clienta, hofpita:* in the fame manner with *leo,* a lion; *leæna,* a lionefs; *equus, equa; mulus, mula;* and many others.

There are feveral nouns, which, though applicable to both fexes, admit only of a mafculine adjective; as, *advena,* a ftranger; *agricŏla,* a hufbandman; *affecla,* an attendant; *accŏla,* a neighbour; *exul,* an exile; *latro,* a robber; *fur,* a thief; *ŏpĭfex,* a mechanic; &c. There are others, which, though applied to perfons, are, on account of their termination, always neuter; as, *fcortum,* a courtefan; *mancĭpium, fervĭtium,* a flave, &c.

In like manner *ŏpĕræ,* flaves or day-labourers; *vigĭliæ, excŭbiæ,* watches; *noxæ,* guilty perfons; though applied to men, are always feminine.

OBSERVATIONS.

OBS. 1. The names of brute animals commonly follow the gender of their termination.

Such are the names of wild beafts, birds, fifhes, and infects, in which the diftinction of fex is either not eafily difcerned, or feldom attended to. Thus, *paffer,* a fparrow, is mafculine, becaufe nouns in *er* are mafculine; fo *ăquila,*

* *Conjux,* atque *parens, infans, patruelis,* et *hæres.*
 Affinis, vindex, judex, dux, miles, et *hoftis,*
 Augur, et *antiftes, juvenis, conviva, facerdos,*
 Muniqueceps, vates, adolefcens, civis, et *auctor,*
 Cuftos, nemo, comes, teftis, fus, bofque, canifque,
 Interpr.fque, cliens, princeps, præs, martyr, et *obfes.*

C

Aquĭla, an eagle, is feminine, becauſe nouns in *a* of the firſt declenſion are feminine. Theſe are called *Epicene* or promiſcuous nouns. When any particular ſex is marked, we uſually add the word *mas* or *femĭna*; as, *mas paſſer*, a male ſparrow; *femĭna paſſer*, a female ſparrow.

OBS. 2. A proper name, for the moſt part, follows the gender of the general name under which it is comprehended.

Thus, the names of months, winds, rivers, and mountains, are maſculine; becauſe *menſis*, *ventus*, *mons*, and *fluvius*, are maſculine; as, hic *Aprīlis*, April; hic *Aquĭlo*, the north wind; hic *Afrĭcus*, the ſouth-weſt wind; hic *Tĭbĕris*, the river Tiber; hic *Othrys*, a hill in Theſſaly. But many of theſe follow the gender of their termination; as, hæc *Matrŏna*, the river Marne in France; hæc *Ætna*, a mountain in Sicily; hoc *Sōraĉte*, a hill in Italy.

In like manner, the names of countries, towns, trees, and ſhips, are feminine, becauſe *terra* or *rĕgio*, *urbs*, *arbor*, and *nāvis*, are feminine; as, hæc *Ægyptus*, Egypt; *Sămos*, an iſland of that name; *Cŏrinthus*, the city Corinth; *pōmus*, an apple-tree; *Centaurus*, the name of a ſhip: Thus alſo the names of poems, hæc *ilĭas*, *-ados*, and *Odyſſēa*, the two poems of Homer; hæc *Ænēis*, *-idos*, a poem of Virgil's; hæc *Eunŭchus*, one of Terence's comedies.

The gender, however, of many of theſe depends on the termination; thus, hic *Pontus*, a country of that name: hic *Sulmo*, *-ōnis*; *Peſſīnus*, *-untis*; *Hydrus*, *-untis*, names of towns; hæc *Perſis*, *-ĭdis*, the kingdom of Perſia; *Carthāgo*, *-ĭnis*, the city Carthage: hoc *Albion*, Britain: hoc *Cære*, *Reāte*, *Præneſte*, *Tĭbur*, *ilium*, names of towns. But ſome of theſe are alſo found in the feminine; as, *Gelĭda Præneſte*, Juvenal. iii. 190.; *Alta Ilion*, Ovid. Met. xiv. 466.

The following names of trees are maſculine, *ŏleaſter*, *-tri*, a wild olive tree; *rhamnus*, the white bramble.

The following are maſculine or feminine; *cўtĭſus*, a kind of ſhrub; *rŭbus*, the bramble-buſh; *larix*, the larch-tree; *lōtus*, the lot-tree; *cupreſſus*, the cypreſs-tree. The firſt two however are oftener maſculine; the reſt oftener feminine.

Thoſe in *um* are neuter; as, *buxum* the buſh, or box-tree; *liguſtrum*, a privet; ſo likewiſe are *ſūber*, *-ĕris* the
cork-

cork-tree ; *siler, -eris,* the osier ; *robur, -oris,* oak of the hardest kind ; *acer, -eris,* the maple-tree.

The place where trees or shrubs grow is commonly neuter ; as, *Arbustum, quercetum, esculetum, salictum, fruticetum,* &c. a place where trees, oaks, beeches, willows, shrubs, &c. grow : Also the names of fruits and timber, as, *pomum,* or *malum,* an apple ; *pirum,* a pear ; *ebenum,* ebony, &c. But from this rule there are various exceptions.

Obs. 3. Several nouns are said to be of the *doubtful gender ;* that is, are sometimes found in one gender, and sometimes in another ; as, *dies,* a day, masculine or feminine ; *vulgus,* the rabble, masculine or neuter.

FIRST DECLENSION.

Nouns of the first declension end in *a, e, as, es.* Latin nouns end only in *a,* and are of the feminine gender.

The terminations of the different cases are ; Nom. and Voc. Sing. *a* ; Gen. and Dat. *æ* diphthong ; Acc. *am* ; Abl. *â :* Nom. and Voc. Plur. *æ* ; Gen. *ārum ;* Dat. and Abl. *is ;* Acc. *as :* Thus,

Penna, *a pen,* fem.

	Singular.		Plural.		Terminations.
N.	penna, *a pen ;*	*N.*	pennæ, *pens ;*	*a, æ,*
G.	pennæ, *of a pen ;*	*G.*	pennārum, *of pens ;*	*æ, arum,*
D.	pennæ, *to a pen ;*	*D.*	pennis, *to pens ;*	*æ, is,*
A.	pennam, *a pen ;*	*A.*	pennas, *pens ;*	*am, as,*
V.	penna, *O pen ;*	*V.*	pennæ, *O pens ;*	*a, æ,*
A.	pennâ, *with a pen :*	*A.*	pennis, *with pens.*	*â, is.*

In like manner decline,

Acerra, *a censer.*	Aluta, *tanned leather.*	Ancilla, *an handmaid.*
Acta, *the shore.*	Ambrosia, *the food of*	Anchora, *an anchor.*
Æra, *a period of time.*	*the gods.*	Anguilla, *an eel.*
Ærumna, *toil.*	Amita, *an aunt, the*	Ansa, *a handle.*
Agricola, *a husbandman.*	*father's sister.*	Antenna, *a sail-yard.*
Ala, *a wing.*	Amphora, *a cask.*	Antlia, *a pump.*
Alapa, *a blow.*	Ampulla, *a jug.* plur.	Aqua, *water.*
Alauda, *a lark.*	*bombast.*	Aquila, *an eagle.*
Alga, *sea-weed.*	Amurca, *the lees of oil.*	Ara, *an altar.*

Arena,

Aranea, _a spider._
Arca, _a chest._
Ardea, & -eola, _a heron._
Area, _an open place._
Arena, _sand._
Argilla, _potter's earth._
Arista, _an ear of corn._
Arrha, _an earnest penny._
Arvina, _fat._
Ascia, _an axe._
Athleta, m. _a wrestler._
Aula, _a hall._
Aura, _a breeze._
Auriga, m. _a charioteer._
Avia, _a grandmother._
Axilla, _the arm-pit._
Balæna, _a whale._
Barba, _a beard._
Belua, _any large beast,_
and Bellua, _the same._
Beta, _beet, an herb._
Bibliopola, _a bookseller._
Bibliotheca, _a library._
Blatta, _a moth._
Bractea, _a thin leaf of gold._
Brassica, _collyflower._
Bruma, _winter._
Bulla, _a bubble, a ball or boss._
Byrsa, _an ox-hide._
Caliga, _a kind of shoe set with nails._
Caltha, _marygold._
Calva & calvaria, _a skull._
Calumnia, _slander._
Camena, _a muse, a song._
Camera, _a vault._
Campana, _a bell._
Canna, _a cane_ or _reed._
Candela, _a candle._
Capra, _a she-goat._
Capsa, _a coffer._
Carina, _the keel of a ship._
Casa, _a cottage._
Castanea, _a chesnut._

Catapulta, _an engine to cast darts._
Catena, _a chain._
Caterva, _a body of men._
Cathedra, _a chair, a pulpit._
Cauda, _the tail._
Caula, _a sheep-cote._
Causa, _a cause._
Caverna, _a cavern._
Cavilla, _a banter._
Cella, _a cell._
Cera, _wax._
Ceremonia, _a ceremony._
Cervisia, _ale, beer._
Cerussa, _white lead, paint._
Cetra, _a square target._
Charta, _paper._
Chorda, _a string._
Cicada, _a kind of insect._
Ciconia, _a stork._
Cicuta, _hemlock._
Cinara, _an artichoke._
Cista, _a chest._
Cisterna, _a cistern._
Cithara, _a harp._
Clava, _a club._
Clepsydra, _an hour-glass._
Cloaca, _a sink._
Cochlea, _a snail._
Cœna, _a supper._
Columba, _a pigeon._
Coma, _the hair._
Comœdia, _a comedy._
Concha, _a shell._
Copia, _plenty._
Copula, _a bond._
Corrigia, _a shoe latchet._
Corona, _a crown, a circle._
Cortina, _a cauldron._
Costa, _a rib._
Coxa, _the haunch._
Crapula, _a surfeit._
Cratera, _a cup._
Craticula, _a gridiron._
Crena, _a notch._

Crepida, _a slipper._
Creta, _chalk._
Crista, _a crest._
Crumena, _a purse._
Crusta, & -um, _a morsel._
Culcita, _a cushion._
Culina, _a kitchen._
Culpa, _a fault._
Cumera, _a corn basket._
Cupa, _a tun._
Cura, _care._
Curia, _a senate-house._
Curruca, _a hedge sparrow._
Cymba, _a boat._
Decempeda, _a pole of ten feet._
Diæta, _diet, food._
Dolabra, _an axe._
Drachma, _a drachm, a weight or coin._
Epistola, _a letter._
Esca, _a bait._
Faba, _a bean._
Fabula, _a fable._
Fama, _fame._
Farina, _meal._
Fascia, _a bandage._
Favilla, _embers._
Fenestra, _a window._
Fera, _a wild beast._
Ferula, _a rod._
Festuca, _the shoot of a tree._
Fibra, _a fibre._
Fibula, _a clasp._ [fol.
Fidelia, _an earthen vessel._
Fimbria, _a fringe._
Fiscina, _a bag, or basket._
Fistuca, _a rammer._
Fistula, _a pipe._
Flamma, _a flame._
Fœmina, _a woman._
Forma, _a form._
Formica, _an ant._
Fossa, _a ditch._
Fovea, _a pit._
Framea, _a short spear._
Fulica, _a sea-fowl._

Funda,

Funda, *a sling.*
Furca, *a fork.*
Fuscīna, *a trident.*
Gălĕa, *an helmet.*
Gallīna, *a hen.* [*ulcer.*
Gangræna, *an eating*
Gaza, *a treasure.*
Gemma, *a gem.*
Gĕna, *the cheek.*
Gĕnista, *broom.*
Gingīva, *the gum.*
Glārea, *gravel.*
Glēba, *a clod.*
Gŭla, *the gullet.*
Gutta, *a drop.*
Hăbēna, *a rein.*
Hăra, *a hog-sty.*
Hărūga, *a sacrifice.*
Hasta, *a spear.*
Hĕdĕra, *ivy.*
Herba, *an herb.*
Herma, *v. -es, m. a statue of Mercury.*
Hernia, *a rupture.*
Hilla, *a sausage.*
Hōra, *an hour.*
Hostia, *a victim.*
Hydria, *a water-pot.*
Jactūra, *loss.*
Jānua, *a gate.*
Idea, *a form, an idea.*
Idiōta, *m. an illiterate person.*
Igrōmĭnia, *an affront.*
Illĕcebra, *an allurement.*
Impensa, *expense.*
Indĭgĕna, *m. a native.*
Inĕdia, *hunger.*
Infŭla, *a mitre.*
Injūria, *a wrong.*
Inŏpia, *want.*
Instĭta, *a fringe.*
Insŭla, *an island.*
Inŭla, *elecampane, an herb.*
Invĭdia, *envy.*
Ira, *anger.*
Juba, *the mane.*

Lăcerna, *a riding coat.*
Lăcerta, *a lizard.*
Lăcinia, *a fringe.*
Lacrȳma, *a tear.*
Lactūca, *lettuce.*
Lăcūna, *a ditch.*
Lăgēna, *a flagon.*
Lāma, *a ditch.*
Lămia, *a sorceress.*
Lāmĭna, *a plate.*
Lāna, *wool.*
Lancea, *a lance or spear.*
Lănista, *m. a fencing-master.*
Larva, *a mask.*
Lāterna, *a lantern.*
Latrīna, *a house of office.*
Lectīca, *a sedan or chair.*
Lēna, *a bawd.*
Lepra, *the leprosy.*
Libra, *a pound.*
Lĭgŭla, *a latchet.*
Līma, *a file.*
Līnea, *a line.*
Lingua, *the tongue.*
Līra, *a ridge or furrow.*
Lĭtĕra, *a letter.*
Lŏcusta, *a locust.*
Lūcerna, *a light.*
Lūna, *the moon.*
Luscĭnia, *a nightingale.*
Lympha, *water.*
Lyra, *a lyre.*
Māchĭna, *a machine.*
Mactra, *a kneading trough.*
Măcŭla, *a stain.*
Māla, *the cheek-bone.*
Mălācia, *a calm.*
Malva, *a mallow.*
Mamma, *a pap.*
Mănĭca, *a sleeve.*
Mantĭca, *a wallet.*
Mappa, *a napkin.*
Margărīta, *a pearl.*
Marra, *a mattock.*
Massa, *a lump.*

Matĕria, *matter, stuff, timber.*
Matertĕra, *the mother's sister.* [*stress.*
Matta, *a mat or mat-*
Matŭla, *a chamber-pot.*
Mĕdulla, *marrow.*
Membrāna, *a thin skin, a film; parchment.*
Mĕmŏria, *memory.*
Mensa, *a table.*
Mensūra, *a measure.*
Merda, *dung.*
Merga, *a pitch-fork.*
Mĕrŭla, *a black bird.*
Mēta, *a goal.*
Mĕtăphŏra, *a trope.*
Mīca, *a crumb.*
Mitra, *a mitre.*
Mŏla, *a mill.*
Mŏnēdŭla, *a jack-daw.*
Mŏnēta, *money.*
Mŏra, *a delay.*
Multa, *a fine.*
Mūræna, *a lamprey.*
Mūria, *pickle, brine.*
Mūsa, *a muse.*
Musca, *a fly.*
Mustēla, *a weasel.*
Myrrha, *myrrh.*
Myrīca, *a tamarisk.*
Mysta, *v. -es, m. a priest.*
Nassa, *a net.*
Nausea, *sea-sickness.*
Nauta, *m. a mariner.*
Nītēdŭla, *a field mouse.*
Nœnia, *a funeral song.*
Norma, *a rule.*
Nŏvācŭla, *a razor.*
Nŏverca, *a step-mother.*
Nympha, *a nymph.*
Occa, *an harrow.*
Ocrea, *a boot.*
Ōda, *v. -e, an ode or song.*
Offa, *a morsel.*
Ŏlea, *an olive.*
Olla, *a pot.*

Ōra.

Ōra, a coaſt.
Orbĭta, a path.
Ōrca, a jar.
Orcheſtra, the ſtage, or the place next it, where the nobles ſat.
Oſtrea, an oyſter.
Pænŭla, a riding coat.
Pāgĭna, a page.
Pāla, a ſhovel.
Pălæſtra, a wreſtling, or place for it.
Pălea, chaff.
Palinōdia, a recantation.
Palla, a large gown.
Palma, the palm.
Palpebra, the eye lid.
Pāpilla, the nipple.
Pāpŭla, a pimple.
Părăbŏla, comparing things together.
Parma, a ſhield.
Parra, a jay.
Pătĕra, a goblet.
Pauſa, a ſtop or pauſe.
Pĕdĭca, a fetter.
Pēnŭla, a mantle.
Pēnūria, want.
Pĕra, a purſe.
Perca, a perch.
Perſūga, m. a deſerter.
Pergămēna, ſc. charta, parchment.
Perna, a gammon of bacon.
Perſōna, a maſk.
Pertĭca, a pole.
Petra, a rock.
Phălārĭca, a long ſpear.
Phăretra, a quiver.
Phăſiāna, ſc. avis, a pheaſant.
Phiăla, a vial.
Philŏmēla, a nightingale.
Philȳra, the linden tree, a leaf of paper.
Phōca, a ſea-calf.

Pīca, a magpy.
Pīla, a ball.
Pila, a pillar.
Pincerna, m. a butler.
Pinna, a fin, a wing.
Pīrāta, m. a pirate.
Piſcīna, a fiſh-pond.
Pītuīta, phlegm.
Plăcenta, a cake.
Plāga, a climate.
Plāga, a blow.
Planta, a plant.
Plătēa, or Plătĕa, a broad ſtreet.
Plūma, a feather.
Plŭvia, rain.
Pŏdagra, the gout.
Pœna, a puniſhment.
Pŏēta, m. a poet.
Poetria, a poeteſs.
Pŏlenta, malt.
Pŏlītia, policy.
Pompa, a proceſſion.
Pŏpa, m. a prieſt who ſlew the ſacrifice.
Pŏpīna, a tavern.
Porta, a gate.
Præda, plunder.
Prærŏgātīva, ſc. tribus, v. centuria, that voted firſt.
Prŏcella, a ſtorm.
Prōra, the prow.
Prōſa, proſe.
Prōſapia, a race.
Pruīna, hoar froſt.
Prūna, a burning coal.
Pſaltria, a muſic girl.
Puella, a girl.
Pugna, a battle.
Pulpa, the pulp.
Pūpĭla, the apple of the eye.
Purpŭra, purple.
Puſtŭla, a bliſter.
Pyra, a funeral pile.
Quadra, & -um, a ſquare.
Răbŭla, m. a wrangler.

Rāna, a frog.
Rĕpulſa, a refuſal.
Resīna, roſin.
Rhēda, a chariot.
Rīma, a chink.
Rīpa, a bank.
Rīxa, a ſcold.
Rŏſa, a roſe.
Rŏta, a wheel.
Rūga, a wrinkle.
Ruīna, a downfall.
Runcīna, a ſaw or
Rūta, rue. [plane.
Săburra, ballaſt.
Sāga, a ſorcereſs.
Săgīna, cramming.
Săgitta, an arrow.
Sălebra, a rugged way.
Săliunca, lavender.
Sālīva, ſpittle.
Salpa, ſtock fiſh.
Sambūca, an harp, or engine of war.
Sanctĭmōnia, devotion.
Sandăpĭla, a bier.
Sanna, a ſcoff.
Sarcĭna, a burden.
Săriſſa, a long ſpear.
Satrăpa, v. -es, m. a Perſian governor.
Sătyra, a ſatyr.
Scāla, a ladder.
Scandŭla, a lath to cover houſes.
Scăpha, a boat.
Scăpŭla, the ſhoulder.
Scēna, a ſtage.
Schĕda, a ſheet or ſcroll.
Schŏla, a ſchool.
Scintilla, a ſpark.
Scrīblīta, a tart or wafer.
Scrofŭla, the king's evil.
Scurra, m. a buffoon.
Scŭtĭca, a ſcourge.
Scytŭla, a kind of ſerpent, or round ſtaff.
Sēlibra, half a pound.
Sēmihōra, half an hour.
Sēmĭta,

Sēmīta, *a path.*
Sententia, *an opinion.*
Sentīna, *a sink.*
Sĕra, *a lock.*
Serra, *a saw.*
Sesquihōra, *an hour and a half.*
Sēta, *a bristle.*
Sĭbylla, *a prophetess.*
Sīca, *a dagger.*
Sĭlīqua, *an husk.*
Silva, *a wood.*
Sīmia, *an ape.*
Sīmĭla, *flour.*
Sĭtŭla, *a bucket.*
Sŏcordia, *sloth.*
Sōlea, *a sole.*
Sŏphĭsta, & -es, m. *a sophist.*
Spĕcŭla, *a watch tower.*
Spēlunca, *a cave.*
Sphæra, *a sphere.*
Spīca, *an ear of corn.*
Spīna, *the back bone.*
Spīra, *a wreath.*
Sponda, *a bedstead.*
Spongia, *a sponge.*
Sponsa, *a bride.*
Sporta, *a basket.*
Spūma, *foam.*
Squāma, *a scale.*
Squilla, *a prawn or shrimp.*
Stătēra, *a balance,*
Stătua, *a statue.*
Stella, *a star.*
Stĭpŭla, *stubble.*
Stīria, *an icicle.*
Stīva, *the plough-tail.*
Stōla, *a gown.*
Strangūria, *the making of water with great pain.*
Strēna, *a new year's gift.*
Strūma, *a botch.*
Stūpa, *tow.*

Sublīca, *a pile.*
Sŭbūcŭla, *a shirt.*
Sŭbŭla, *an awl.* [con.
Succīdia, *a flitch of ba-*
Summa, *a sum, the whole.*
Sŭperbia, *pride.*
Sūra, *the calf of the leg.*
Sutrīna, sc. taberna, *a shoemaker's shop.*
Sūtūra, *a seam.*
Sycŏphanta, m. *a sharper.*
Syllăba, *a syllable.*
Symbŏla, *a club, a share of a reckoning.*
Symphōnia, *harmony.*
Syngrăpha, *a bill or bond.*
Tăberna, *a shop.*
Tăbŭla, *a table.*
Tæda, *a torch.*
Tænia, *a ribbon.*
Techna, *a trick or wile.*
Tēgŭla, *a tile.*
Tēla, *a web.*
Térebra, *a wimble.*
Terra, *the earth.*
Tessĕra, *a dye.*
Testa, *an earthern pot.*
Textrīna, *a weaver's shop.*
Thēca, *a case.*
Tībia, *a pipe, the leg.*
Tĭlia, *the linden tree.*
Tīnea, *a moth.*
Tonstrīna, *a barber's shop.*
Trăgœdia, *a tragedy.*
Trāgŭla, *a javelin with a barbed head.*
Trahea, *a sledge or dray.*
Trāma, *the woof.*
Trochlea, *a pulley.*
Trulla, *a trowel.*
Trŭtīna, *a balance.*

Tŭba, *a trumpet.*
Tŭnīca, *a waistcoat.*
Turba, *a crowd.*
Turma, *a troop.*
Ulna, *an ell.*
Ŭlŭla, *an owl.*
Ulva, *sedge.*
Umbra, *a shade.*
Unda, *a wave.*
Ungŭla, *a nail, the hoof.*
Ŭpŭpa, *the houpe, a bird.*
Ūrīna, *urine.*
Urna, *an urn.*
Urtīca, *a nettle.*
Ŭva, *a grape.*
Vacca, *a cow.*
Vāgīna, *a scabbard.*
Vappa, *palled wine, a spendthrift.*
Vena, *a vein.*
Vénia, *leave.*
Verna, m. *an home-born slave.*
Verrūca, *a wart.*
Vēsīca, *the bladder.*
Vespa, *a wasp.*
Via, *a way.*
Vīcia, *a vetch or tare.*
Victĭma, *a victim.*
Victōria, *a conquest.*
Villa, *a country seat.*
Vindēmia, *vintage.*
Vindicta, *vengeance: a rod laid on the head of slaves when freed.*
Vĭŏla, *a violet.*
Vīpĕra, *a viper.*
Virga, *a rod.*
Vīta, *life.*
Vitta, *a fillet.*
Vīverra, *a ferret.*
Vōla, *the palm of the hand.*
Zōna, *a girdle, a zone.*

EXCEPTIONS.

EXCEPTIONS.

EXC. 1. The following nouns are masculine : *Hadria*, the Hadriatic sea ; *cŏmeta*, a comet ; *planēta*, a planet ; and sometimes *talpa*, a mole ; and *dāma*, a fallow-deer. *Pascha*, the passover, is neuter.

EXC. 2. The ancient Latins sometimes formed the genitive singular in *āi* ; thus, *aula*, a hall, gen. *aulāi* ; and sometimes likewise in *as* ; which form the compounds of *fāmilia* usually retain ; as, *māter-fāmilias*, the mistress of a family ; genit. *matris-familias* ; nom. plur. *matres-familias*, or *matres-familiarum*.

EXC. 3. The following nouns have more frequently *ābus* in the dative and ablative plural, to distinguish them in these cases from masculines in *us* of the second declension :

Ănĭma, *the soul, the life*.	Filia, & Nāta, *a daughter*.
Dea, *a goddess*.	Lībĕrta, *a freed woman*.
Ĕqua, *a mare*.	Mūla, *a she-mule*.
Fămŭla, *a female servant*.	

Thus *deābus*, *fĭliābus*, rather than *filiis*, &c.

GREEK NOUNS.

Nouns in *as*, *es*, and *e*, of the first declension, are Greek. Nouns in *as* and *es* are masculine : nouns in *e* are feminine.

Nouns in *as* are declined like *penna* ; only they have *am* or *an* in the accusative ; as, *Æneas*, Æneas, the name of a man ; gen. *Ænēæ* ; dat. -*æ* ; acc. -*am* or *an* ; voc. -*a* ; abl. *ā*. So *Bŏreas*, -*eæ*, the north wind ; *Tiāras*, -*æ*, a turban. In prose they have commonly *am*, but in poetry oftener *an*, in the accusative. Greek nouns in *a* have sometimes also *an* in the acc. in poetry ; as *Ossa*, -*am*, or -*an*, the name of a mountain.

Nouns in *es* and *e* are thus declined,

Anchīses, *Anchises*, the name of a man.
Singular.

Nom. Anchīses,	*Acc.* Anchīsen,
Gen. Anchīsæ,	*Voc.* Anchīse,
Dat. Anchīsæ,	*Abl.* Anchīse.

Pĕnĕlŏpe, *Penelope*, the name of a woman.
Singular.

Nom. Pĕnĕlŏpe,	*Acc.* Penelopen,
Gen. Penelopes,	*Voc.* Penelope,
Dat. Penelope,	*Abl.* Penelope.

These

These nouns, being proper names, want the plural, unless when several of the same name are spoken of, and then they are declined like the plural of *penna*.

¶ The Latins frequently turn Greek nouns in *es* and *e* into *a*; as, *Atrida*, for *Atrides*; *Persa*, for *Perses*, a Persian; *Geometra*, for *-tres*, a Geometrician; *Circa*, for *Circe*; *Epitoma*, for *-me*, an abridgment; *Grammătĭca*, for *-ce*, grammar; *Rhětŏrĭca*, for *-ce*, oratory. So *Clinia*, for *Clinias*, &c. The accusative of nouns in *es* and *e* is found sometimes in *em*.

Note. We sometimes find the genit. plur. contracted; as, *Cælĭcŏlûm*, for *Cælicolarum*; *Æneădûm*, for *-arum*.

SECOND DECLENSION.

¶ Nouns of the second declension end in *er*, *ir*, *ur*, *us*, *um*; *os*, *on*. ¶

¶ Nouns in *um* and *on* are neuter; the rest are masculine. ¶

Nouns of the second declension have the gen. sing. in *i*; the dat. and abl. in *o*; the acc. in *um*; the voc. like the nom. (But nouns in *us* make the vocative in *e*:) The nom. and voc. plur. in *i*, or *a*; the gen. in *orum*; the dat. and abl. in *is*; and the acc. in *os*, or *a*; as,

¶ Gĕner, *a son in law*, masc.

Sing.	*Plur.*	Terminations.
Nom. gĕner,	*Nom.* gĕnĕri, .	er, ir, us, i,
Gen. genĕri,	*Gen.* generōrum,	i, orum,
Dat. genero,	*Dat.* generis,	o, is,
Acc. generum,	*Acc.* generos,	um, os,
Voc. gener,	*Voc.* generi,	er, ir, e, i,
Abl. genero.	*Abl.* generis. ¶	o, is.

After the same manner decline *sŏcer*, *-ĕri*, a father-in-law; *puer*, *-ĕri*, a boy: So *Furcĭfer*, a villain; *Lucĭfer*, the morning star; *ădulter*, an adulterer; *armĭger*, an armour bearer; *presbўter*, an elder; *Mulcĭber*, a name of the god Vulcan; *vesper*, the evening; and *Iber*, *-ĕri*, a Spaniard, the only noun in *er* which has the gen. long, and its compound *Celtĭber*, *-ēri*: Also, *vir*, *vĭri*, a man, the only noun in *ir*; and its compounds, *Lĕvir*, a brother-in-law; *Semĭvir*, *duumvir*, *triumvir*, &c. And likewise *Sătur*, *-ŭri*, full, (of old *satŭrus*,) an adjective.

But

But most nouns in *er* lose the *e* in the genitive; as,
Ager, *a field,* masc.

	Sing.		Plur.
Nom.	ăger,	*Nom.*	agri,
Gen.	agri,	*Gen.*	agrōrum,
Dat.	agro,	*Dat.*	agris,
Acc.	agrum,	*Acc.*	agros,
Voc.	ager,	*Voc.*	agri,
Abl.	agro.	*Abl.*	agris.

In like manner decline,

Aper, *a wild boar.*
Arbiter, (& -tra,) *a judge.*
Auster, *the south-wind.*
Cancer, *a crab fish.*
Colüber, & -bra, *a serpent.*
Culter, *the coulter of a plough, a knife.*
Făber, *a workman.*
Măgister, *a master.*
Minister, *a servant.*
Onăger, *a wild ass.*
Scalper, *a lancet.*

Also *liber,* the bark of a tree, or a book, which has *libri;* but *liber,* free, an adjective, and *Liber,* a name of Bacchus, the God of wine, have *liberi.* So likewise proper names, *Alexander, Evander, Periander, Menander, Teucer, Meleager,* &c. gen. *Alexandri, evandri,* &c.

Dŏmĭnus, *a lord,* masc.

	Sing.		Plur.
Nom.	dŏminus,	*Nom.*	dŏmini,
Gen.	domini,	*Gen.*	dominōrum,
Dat.	domino,	*Dat.*	dominis,
Acc.	dominum,	*Acc.*	dŏminos,
Voc.	domine,	*Voc.*	domini,
Abl.	domino.	*Abl.*	dominis.

In like manner decline,

Abăcus, *a table or desk.*
Acervus, *a heap.*
Acūleus, *a sting.*
Agnus, *a lamb.*
Alnus, f. *an alder tree.*
Alveus, *the channel of a river.*
Angŭlus, *a corner.*
Anĭmus, *the mind.*
Annus, *a year.*
Annŭlus, *a ring.*
Anus, *a circle.*
Archĭtectus, *a master-builder.*
Argentārius, *a banker.*
Arnius, *the shoulder of a beast; also of a man.*
Asĭnus, & -a, *an ass.*
Autumnus, *the autumn.*
Avus, *a grandfather.*
Avuncŭlus, *the mother's brother.*
Bajŭlus, *a porter.*
Barrus, *an elephant.*
Bōlus, *a morsel.*
Bombus, *a buzz.*
Căballus, *a pack-horse.*
Cŏcăbus, *a kettle.*
Căchinnus, *a loud laugh.*
Cădūceus, *a wand.*
Cādus, *a cask.*
Călămus, *a reed.*
Călăthus, *a basket.*
Callus, & -um, *hard flesh.*
Cămīnus, *a chimney.*
Campus, *a plain.*
Canthărus, *a cup or jug.*
Carduus, *a thistle.*
Carpus, *the wrist.*
Carrus, & -um, *a cart.*

Caseus;

Căseus, *cheese.*
Cătălŏgus, *a roll.*
Cătīnus, *a platter.*
Caurus, *a west wind.*
Cēdrus, f. *a cedar tree.*
Cervus, *a stag.*
Cētus, *a whale,* pl. cē-
 te, n. *indecl.*
Chīrurgus, *a surgeon.*
Chŏrus, *a choir.*
Cibus, *meat.*
Cincinnus, *a curl.*
Cinnus, *a medley.*
Cippus, *a grave-stone.*
Circĭnus, *a pair of*
 compasses. (*circle.*
Circus & circŭlus, *a*
Cirrus, *a tuft, or curl.*
Citrus, f. *a citron tree.*
Clathrus, *a grate.*
Clāvus, *a nail.*
Clībănus, *a portable*
 oven.
Clīvus, *a hill.*
Clypeus, *a round shield.*
Coccus, v. -um. *scarlet.*
Cŏlăphus, *a box on the*
 ear.
Condus, *a butler.*
Condylus, *the knuckle.*
Congius, *a gallon.*
Consŏbrīnus, *a cousin-*
 german by the mother's
 side.
Contus, *a long pole.*
Conus, *a cone.*
Cophīnus, *a basket.*
Cŏquus, *a cook.*
Cornus, f. *the cornel*
 tree.
Corvus, *a raven.*
Cŏrylus, f. *a hasel-tree.*
Corymbus, *a bunch of*
 ivy berries.
Cŏryphæus, *a ring-*
 leader.
Cŏrȳtus, *or -os, a bow-*
 case.
Cŏthurnus, *a buskin.*

Cŭbĭtus, *a cubit.*
Cŭcullus, *a hood.*
Cŭcŭlus *vel* cŭcŭlus, *a*
 cuckow.
Cūleus, *a leathern bag.*
Culmus, *a stalk.*
Cŭlullus, *a pot or jug.*
Cŭmŭlus, *an heap.*
Cúneus, *a wedge.*
Cŭnīcŭlus, *a rabbit.*
Cyăthus, *a cup or glass.*
Cygnus, *a swan.*
Cylindrus, *a roller.*
Diălŏgus, *a discourse*
 between two or more.
Dĭgĭtus, *a finger.*
Difcus, *a quoit.*
Dīvus, *a god.*
Dŏlus, *deceit,*
Dūmus, *a bush.*
Echīnus, *an urchin.*
Elĕgus, *an elegy.*
Ephēbus, *a youth.*
Epĭlŏgus, *a conclusion.*
Epiſcŏpus, *an overseer,*
 a bishop.
Equŭleus, *an instru-*
 ment of torture.
Equus, *an horse.*
Erĕbus, *hell.*
Eurus, *the east wind.*
Fāgus, f. *a beech-tree.*
Fămŭlus, *a man ser-*
 vant.
Făvōnius, *the west wind.*
Făvus, *an honeycomb.*
Fĭgŭlus, *a potter.*
Fiſcus, *the exchequer.*
Floccus, *a lock of wool.*
Flŭvius, *a river.*
Fŏcus, *a hearth.*
Fraxĭnus, f. *an ash tree.*
Frĭtillus, *a dice-box.*
Fūcus, *a drone bee,*
 paint.
Fūmus, *smoke.* [*dancer.*
Fūnambŭlus, *a rope-*
Fundus, *a farm.*
Fungus, *a mushroom.*

Furnus, *an oven.*
Fūſus, *a spindle.*
Gallus, *a cock.*
Gĕrŭlus, *a porter.*
Gibbus, *a swelling.*
Glădius, *a sword.*
Glŏbus, *a globe.*
Grăbātus, *a couch.*
Grācŭlus, *a jackdaw.*
Grūmus, *a hillock.*
Guttus, *a cruet or vial.*
Gȳrus, *a circle.*
Hædus, *a kid.*
Hāmus, *a hook.*
Hāriŏlus, *a diviner.*
Hĕrus, *a master.*
Heſpĕrus, *the evening.*
Hinnŭleus, *a young*
 hind or fawn.
Hinnŭs, *a mule.*
Hircus, *a goat.*
Hortus, *a garden.*
Hŭmĕrus, *a shoulder.*
Hydrus, *a water-ser-*
 pent.
Internuncius, *a go be-*
 tween.
Iſthmus, *a neck of land*
 between two seas.
Juncus, *a bulrush.*
Jŭvencus, *a bullock.*
Lăbȳrinthus, *a maze.*
Lăcertus, *the arm.*
Lănius, *a butcher.*
Lăqueus, *a noose.*
Lectus, *a couch.*
Lēgātus, *an ambassador.*
Lēgŭleius, *an ignorant*
 lawyer, a pettifogger.
Lēthargus, *the lethargy.*
Limbus, *a selvedge.*
Līmus, *slime.*
Lĭtuus, *a crooked staff.*
Lūcus, *a sacred grove.*
Lumbrīcus, *an earth*
 worm.
Lumbus, *the loin.*
Lŭpus, *a wolf.*
Lychnus, *a lamp.*
 Măgus,

Măgus, *a magician.*
Malleus, *a mallet.*
Mālus, *the maſt of a ſhip.*
Mālus, f. *an apple-tree.*
Mannus, *a little horſe.*
Măthēmăticus, *a mathematician.*
Mēdiaſtīnus, *a ſlave, a drudge.*
Mĕdicus, *a phyſician.*
Mendīcus, *a beggar.*
Mergus, *a cormorant.*
Milvus, *a kite.*
Mīmus, *a mimic.*
Mŏdius, *a buſhel.*
Mŏdus, *a manner.*
Mœchus, *an adulterer.*
Mōrus, f. *a mulberry tree.*
Mūcus, *the filth of the noſe, ſnot.*
Mullus, *a mullet fiſh.*
Mūlus, & -a, *a mule.*
Mŭrus, *a wall.*
Muſcus, *moſs.*
Myrtus, f. *a myrtle tree.*
Nævus, *a ſpot.*
Nānus, *a dwarf.*
Nāſus, *the noſe.*
Nervus, *a ſtring.*
Nīdus, *a neſt.*
Nimbus, *a cloud.*
Nŏdus, *a knot.*
Nŏthus, *a baſtard.*
Nŏtus, *the ſouth wind.*
Nucleus, *a kernel.*
Nŭmĕrus, *a number.*
Nummus, *a piece of money.*
Nuntius, *a meſſenger.*
Obŏlus, *a farthing.*
Ōcĕănus, *the ocean.*
Ocŭlus, *the eye.*
Orcus, *hell.*
Ornus, f. *a wild aſh.*
Oſtrăciſmus, *a voting with ſhells.*
Pædăgōgus, *a ſervant who attended boys.*

Pāgus, *a canton or village.*
Pālus, *a ſtake.*
Pannus, *cloth.*
Părăsītus, *a flatterer.*
Pardus, *a panther.*
Părŏchus, *an entertainer.*
Patruus, *the father's brother.*
Patrōnus, *a patron.*
Pĕdīcŭlus, *a louſe.*
Peſsŭlus, *a bolt.*
Pĕtăsus, *a broad brimmed hat.*
Phărus, or -os, *a watch-tower.*
Phĭlŏsŏphus, *a lover of wiſdom.*
Phœbus, poet. *the ſun.*
Physicus, *an inquirer into nature.*
Pīcus, *a wood-pecker.*
Pīleus, *a hat.*
Pĭlus, *a hair.*
Pĭrus, f. *a pear-tree.*
Plăgiarius, *a plagiary, a man-ſtealer; or one who ſteals from others books.*
Plānus, *a vagrant, a beggar.*
Plŭteus, *a pent-houſe, a preſs for books.*
Pŏlus, *the pole, heaven.*
Pontus, *the ſea.*
Pŏpŭlus, *a people.*
Pŏpŭlus, f. *a poplar-tree.*
Porcus, *a hog.*
Porrus, *a leek.*
Primipīlus, *the chief centurion.*
Prīvignus, *a ſtepſon.*
Prŏcus, *a ſuitor.*
Prōmus, *a ſteward.*
Prūnus, f. *a plumb-tree.*
Pſittăcus, *a parrot.*
Pugnus, *the fiſt.*
Pullus, *a chicken.*

Pulvīnus, *a pillow.*
Pūpillus, *an orphan.*
Pūpus, *a young child, a babe.*
Pŭteus, *a well.*
Quālus & quăsillus, *a basket.* [grapes.
Răcēmus, *a cluſter of*
Rădius, *a ray.*
Rāmus, *a branch.*
Rēmus, *an oar.*
Rhombus, *a turbot.*
Rhonchus, *a ſnorting.*
Riſcus, *a trunk.*
Rīvus, *a rivulet.*
Rŏgus, *a funeral pile.*
Rythmus, *metre, rhyme.*
Saccus, *a ſack.*
Sarcŏphăgus, *a ſtone, in which dead bodies were incloſed.*
Sătyrus, *a ſatyr, a kind of demigod.*
Scalmus, *a boat; a piece of wood where the oars hang.*
Scăpus, *a ſtalk, a ſhaft or ſhank.*
Scărus, *the ſcar, a fiſh.*
Scirpus, *a ruſh.*
Sciūrus, *a ſquirrel.*
Scŏpŭlus, *a rock.*
Scŏpus, *a mark.*
Scrŭpŭlus, *a doubt or ſcruple.*
Scrūpus, *a little ſtone.*
Scyphus, *a bowl.*
Servus, *a ſlave.*
Seſtertius, *two pounds and a half; a ſeſterce, a Roman coin.*
Sīcarius, *an aſſaſſin.*
Sīmius, & -a, *an ape.*
Sīrius, *the dog ſtar.*
Soccus, *a kind of ſhoe.*
Somnus, *ſleep.*
Sŏnus, *a ſound.*
Spărus, *a ſpear.*
Sponſus, *a bridegroom.*

Stĭmŭlus,

Stĭmŭlus, *a sting, a spur.*
Stŏmăchus, *the stomach.*
Strŭpus, *a thong, a strap.*
Stўlus, *a style,* or *iron pen to write with on waxen tables.*
Sŭbulcus, *a swine herd.*
Succus, *juice.*
Sulcus, *a furrow.*
Surcŭlus, *a young twig.*
Sŭsurrus, *a whisper.*
Tālus, *the ancle, a die.*
Taurus, *a bull*
Taxus, f. *the yew tree.*
Termĭnus, *a bound.*
Thălămus, *a marriage bed-chamber.*
Thĕolŏgus, *a divine.*
Thĕsaurus, *a treasure.*
Thŏlus, *the roof of a temple.*

Thrōnus, *a royal seat.*
Thyăsus, *a chorus in honour of Bacchus.*
Thyrsus, *a spear wrapt with ivy.*
Titŭlus, *a title.*
Tŏmus, *a volume.*
Tŏnus, *a note in music.*
Tŏphus, *a gravel stone.*
Tornus, *a turner's wheel.*
Tŏrus, *a couch.*
Trĭbulus, *a thistle.*
Triumphus, *a triumph.*
Trŏchus, *a top.*
Truncus, *the trunk.*
Tūbus, *a tube* or *pipe.*
Tŭmŭlus, *a hillock.*
Turdus, *a thrush.*
Tўrannus, *a tyrant.*

Tўpus, *a figure* or *type.*
Ulmus, f. *an elm tree.*
Umbĭlīcus, *the navel.*
Uncus, *a hook.*
Urceus, *a pitcher.*
Ursus, *a bear.*
Ūrus, *a buffalo.*
Ŭtĕrus, *the womb.*
Vallus, *a stake.*
Vĕnĕfĭcus, *a sorcerer.*
Ventus, *the wind.*
Vīcus, *a village, a street.*
Villĭcus, & -a, *an overseer of a farm.*
Villus, *shaggy hair.*
Vitellus, *the yolk of an egg.*
Vitrĭcus, *a stepfather.*
Vītŭlus, *a calf* [*wind.*
Zĕphўrus, *the west-*

(Regnum, *a kingdom,* neut.

	Sing.		Plur.
Nom.	regnum,	*Nom.*	regna,
Gen.	regni,	*Gen.*	regnōrum,
Dat.	regno,	*Dat.*	regnis,
Acc.	regnum,	*Acc.*	regna,
Voc.	regnum,	*Voc.*	regna,
Abl.	regno :	*Abl.*	regnis.)

In like manner decline,

Acētum, *vinegar.*
Acŏnītum, *wolfs-bane, a poisonous plant.*
Adăgium, *a proverb.*
Admĭnĭcŭlum, *a prop.*
Adytum, *the most secret part of a temple.*
Album, *a register.*
Allium, *garlick.*
Āmentum, *a thong.*
Ămŭlētum, *a charm.*
Anēthum, *anise.*
Antīcum, *a fore-door.*
Antrum, *a cave.*
Ăpium, *parsley.*
Argentum, *silver.*

Armentum, *an herd.*
Arvum, & -us, *a field.*
Astrum, *a star.*
Asўlum, *a sanctuary.*
Atrium, *a court* or *hall.*
Aulæum, *tapestry.*
Aurum, *gold.*
Auxĭlium, *assistance.*
Aviārium, *a cage.*
Balsămum, *balm.*
Bărathrum, *an abyss.*
Băsium, *a kiss.*
Bellum, *war.*
Bīduum, *two days.*
Biennium, *two years.*
Brāchium, *an arm.*

Būtўrum, *butter.*
Cælum, *a graving tool.*
Cæmentum, *materials for building.*
Cănistrum, *a basket.*
Căpistrum, *a halter* or *muzzle.*
Castrum, *a castle.*
Centrum, *the centre.*
Cĕrebrum, *the brain.*
Chīrogrăphum, *a hand-writing.*
Cilium, *the eye-lashes.*
Citrum, *citron wood.*
Classĭcum, *a trumpet.*
Cœlum, pl. -i, *heaven.*
Cœnum.

D

Cœnum, *mire, dirt.*
Collŏquium, *a con-ference.*
Collum, *the neck.*
Commŏdum, *advan-tage.*
Confīnium, *a bound or limit.*
Congiārium, *a largess.*
Convīcium, *a reproach.*
Cŏrium, *a hide.*
Coftum, *spikenard.*
Crĕmium, *a dry stick.*
Crĕpufcŭlum, *the twi-light.*
Cribrum, *a sieve.*
Cŭbĭcŭlum, *a bed-chamber.*
Cumīnum, *cumin, an herb.*
Cymbălum, *a cymbal.*
Damnum, *loss.*
Dĕlūbrum, *a temple.*
Dĕmenfum, *an allow-ance of meat.*
Detrīmentum, *damage.*
Diārium, *a day's wages.*
Dīlūcŭlum, *the dawn-ing of day.*
Dium, poet. *the open air.*
Dōlium, *a cask.*
Dŏmĭcīlium, *an abode.*
Dōnum, *a gift.*
Dorfum, *the back.*
Effŭgium, *or escape.*
Flectrum, *amber.*
Ĕlĕmentum, *an element, a letter.*
Ĕlŏgium, *a brief say-ing, a testimonial in one's praise.*
Ĕmŏlŭmentum, *profit.*
Emplaftrum, *a plafter.*
Empŏrium, *a mart or market town.*
Ephippium, *a faddle.*
Epĭtăphium, *an in-fcription on a tomb.*
Ergaftŭlum, *a work-houfe.*

Ervum, *vetches.*
Efsēdum, *a chariot.*
Everrĭcŭlum, *a drag-net.*
Exemplum, *an example.*
Exĭtium, *deftruction.*
Exordium, *a beginning.*
Fānum, *a temple.*
Fafcĭnum, *witchcraft.*
Faftĭgium, *the top.*
Fercŭlum, *a dish of meat.*
Ferrum, *iron.*
Fīlum, *a thread.*
Flăbellum, *a fan.*
Flagrum & flăgellum, *a whip.*
Flammeum, *a veil.*
Fœnum, *hay.*
Fŏlium, *a leaf.*
Fŏrum, *a market-place.*
Frāgum, *a ftrawberry.*
Frĕtum, *a narrow fea.*
Frūmentum, *corn.*
Fruftum, *a bit or piece.*
Fulcrum, *a prop.*
Furtum, *theft.*
Grānārium, *a granary.*
Grānum, *a grain.*
Grăphium, *a pencil.*
Grĕmium, *the bofom.*
Gymnāfium, *a place of exercife.*
Gynæcēum, *the wo-men's apartment.*
Gypfum, *plafter.*
Hauftrum, *a bucket.*
Hellĕbōrum, & -us, *hellebore, a plant.*
Hōrŏlŏgium, *any thing that tells the hours.*
Idōlum, *an image.*
Idyllium, *a paftoral poem.*
Impĕrium, *command.*
Inceptum, *an enter-prife.*
Indĭcium, *a difcovery.*
Indūfium, *a fhirt.*
Ingĕnium, *wit, genius.*

Initium, *a beginning.*
Intervallum, *diftance between.*
Jūdĭcium, *judgment.*
Jŭgŭlum, *the throat.*
Jŭgum, *a yoke, the ridge of a hill.*
Jurgium, *a quarrel.*
Juffum, *an order.*
Juftĭtium, *a vacation.*
Lăbium, *the lip.*
Lardum, *bacon.*
Lăsănum, *a chamber-pot.*
Libum, *a fweet-cake.*
Līcium, *the woof.*
Lignum, *wood.*
Līlium, *a lily.*
Linteum, *a fheet.*
Linum, *lint.*
Lōrum, *a thong.*
Lŭcrum, *gain.*
Lūdĭbrium, *a laugh-ing ftock.*
Luftrum, *a furvey.*
Lūteum, *the yolk of an egg.*
Lŭtum, *clay.*
Macellum, *the fhambles.*
Mănŭbrium, *a hilt or handle.*
Matrĭmōnium, *mar-riage.*
Mausōlæum, *any fump-tuous monument.*
Membrum, *a member.*
Mendācium, *a lie.*
Mentum, *the chin.*
Mĕtallum, *metal, a mine.*
Mĭlium, *millet, a kind of grain.*
Minium, *vermilion.*
Mōmentum, *weight, importance.*
Mŏnŏpōlium, *the fole right of felling any thing.*
Monftrum, *a monfter, any *

any thing againſt the common courſe of nature.

Mortārium, *a mortar.*

Mūsēum, *a study or library.*

Muſtum, *new wine.*

Myſterium, *a myſtery, a thing not eaſily comprehended.*

Naſturtium, *creſſes.*

Naulum, *freight.*

Nauſrāgium, *ſhipwreck.*

Nĕgōtium, *a thing, buſineſs.*

Nitrum, *nitre.*

Obſēquium, *compliance.*

Ōdium, *hatred.*

Ŏmāſum, *the paunch.*

Omentum, *the caul, or ſkin which covers the bowels.*

Oppĭdum, *a town.*

Opprobrium, *a reproach.*

Opſōnium, *fiſh, or any thing eaten with bread.*

Orgănum, *any inſtrument.* [*the lips.*

Oſcŭlum, *a kiſs;* pl.

Oſtrum, *purple.*

Ōtium, *repoſe.*

Oſtium, *the door.*

Ōvum, *an egg.*

Pābŭlum, *fodder.*

Pactum, *an agreement.*

Pălātium, *a palace.*

Pălātum, *the palate.*

Pallium, *a cloak.*

Pălūdāmentum, *a general's robe.*

Pănārium, *a breadbaſket.*

Pătĭbŭlum, *a gibbet.*

Penſum, *a taſk.* [*robe.*

Peplum, *a woman's*

Perjūrium, *perjury, taking a falſe oath.*

Perpendĭcŭlum, *a straight line upwards or downwards.*

Pĕtorītum, *a waggon.*

Pīlentum, *a chariot.*

Pīlum, *a javelin.*

Piſtillum, *the peſtle of a mortar.*

Pīſum, *peaſe.*

Plauſtrum, *a waggon.*

Plectrum, *a quill or bow to play with on a muſical inſtrument.*

Plumbum, *lead.*

Pōmārium, *an orchard.*

Pōmœrium, *a void ſpace on each ſide of a town-wall.*

Pōmum, *an apple.*

Poſtīcum, *a back-door.*

Poſtlīmĭnium, *a return to one's country.*

Prædium, *a farm.*

Prejūdĭcium, *a forejudging.*

Prælium, *a battle.*

Præmium, *a reward.*

Præſĭdium, *a defence, a garriſon.*

Prandium, *a dinner.*

Prātum, *a meadow.*

Prēlum, *a press.*

Prĕtium, *a price.*

Prīmordium, ? *a begin-*

Princĭpium, } *ning.*

Prīvĭlēgium, *a private law or ſpecial right.*

Probrum, *a diſgrace.*

Prōdĭgium, *a prodigy, any thing preternatural.*

Prōmiſſum, *a promiſe.*

Prōpŏſĭtum, *a purpoſe.*

Prōpugnācŭlum, *a bulwark.* [*ſaying.*

Prōverbium, *an old*

Pulpĭtum, *a pulpit.*

Rāmentum, *a chip or ſhaving.*

Raſtrum, *a rake.*

Rĕfūgium, *a ſhelter.*

Rĕmĕdium, *a cure.*

Rĕmulcum, *a towbarge.*

Rĕpāgŭlum, *a bar.*

Rĕpūdium, *a divorce.*

Reſponſum, *an anſwer.*

Rĕtīnacŭlum, *a cable.*

Roſtrum, *the bill of a bird, the beak of a ſhip.*

Rŭdīmentum, *pl.* -a, *the firſt principles of any art.*

Rutrum, *a pick-ax.*

Sabbātum, *the ſabbath.*

Săbŭlum, *gravel.*

Sacchārum, *ſugar.*

Săcellum, *a chapel.*

Săcerdōtium, *the prieſthood.*

Sacrāmentum, *a military oath.*

Sacrĭfĭcium, *a ſacrifice.*

Sacrĭlĕgium, *ſtealing ſacred things.*

Săgum, *a ſoldier's cloak.*

Sălārium, *a ſalary.*

Sălīnum, *a ſalt-cellar.*

Salſāmentum, *ſalt-meat.*

Sălum, *the ſea.*

Sandālium, *a ſlipper.*

Sarcŭlum, *a weeding-hook, a ſpade.*

Sarmentum, *a twig.*

Sătiſdătum, *a bond of ſecurity.*

Saxum, *a large ſtone.*

Scalprum, *dim.* Scalpellum, *a knife.*

Scamnum, *dim.* Scabellum, *a bench or form.*

Sceptrum, *a ſceptre, a mace.*

Scītum, *a decree.*

Scortum, *an harlot.*

Scrinium, *a coffer.*

Scriptum,

Scriptum, *a writing.*
Scrupulum, *a scruple, a certain weight.*
Scutum, *a shield.*
Seculum, *an age.*
Seminarium, *a nursery.*
Senaculum, *a senate-house.*
Senatus consultum, *a decree of the senate.*
Sericum, *silk.*
Servitium, *slavery.*
Serpyllum, *wild thyme.*
Sertum, *a garland.*
Serum, *whey.*
Sestertium, *a thousand sesertii.*
Sevum, *tallow.*
Signum, *a sign, a standard.*
Sigillum, *a seal.*
Silicernium, *a funeral supper, an old man.*
Sinum, *a milk pail.*
Sistrum, *a timbrel.*
Sodalitium, *a company, a corporation.*
Solarium, *a sun-dial.*
Solatium, *comfort.*
Solium, *a throne.*
Solum, *the ground.*
Somnium, *a dream.*
Spatium, *a space.*
Spectaculum, *a shew.*
Spectrum, *a phantom, or apparition.*
Speculum, *a looking glass.*
Spelæum, *a den.*
Spicilegium, *a gleaning.*
Spiculum, *a dart.*
Spiraculum, *a breathing hole.*
Spolium, *spoil.*
Sputum, *spittle.*
Stabulum, *a stable.*
Stadium, *a furlong.*
Stagnum, *a pond.*
Stannum, *tin.*

Sterquilinium, *a dung-hill.*
Stipendium, *pay.*
Stragulum, *a blanket.*
Stratum, *a couch.*
Strigmentum, *a scraping.*
Studium, *desire, study.*
Stuprum, *debauchery.*
Suavium, *a kiss.*
Subsellium, *a bench.*
Subsidium, *help.*
Suburbanum, *a house near the town.*
Suburbium, *the suburbs, the part of a town without the walls.*
Sudarium, *a handkerchief.*
Suffragium, *a vote.*
Suggestum, & -us, ûs, *a place raised above others.*
Summarium, *an abridgment.*
Supercilium, *the brow, pride.*
Suspirium, *a sigh.*
Symbolum, *a sign or token.*
Symposium, & -on, *a banquet.*
Tabernaculum, *a tent.*
Tabulatum, *a story.*
Tabum, *black gore.*
Tædium, *weariness.*
Talentum, *a talent.*
Tectum, *the roof, a house.*
Telum, *a weapon.*
Templum, *a church.*
Tergum, *the back.*
Testimonium, *an evidence.*
Theatrum, *a theatre.*
Thuribulum, *a censer, a vessel to burn incense in.*

Tintinnabulum, *a little bell.*
Tirocinium, *an apprenticeship.*
Tormentum, *an engine, a torment.*
Toxicum, *poison.*
Tributum, *tax or custom.*
Triclinium, *a dining-room.*
Triduum, *three days.*
Triennium, *three years.*
Tripudium, *a dancing.*
Trivium, *a place where three ways meet.*
Tropæum, *a trophy, a token of victory.*
Tugurium, *a cottage.*
Tympanum, *a drum.*
Vaccinium, *a berry.*
Vadimonium, *bail; a promise to appear in court.*
Vadum, *a ford, the sea.*
Vallum, *a rampart.*
Velum, *a veil, a sail.*
Venabulum, *a hunting pole.*
Venenum, *poison.*
Ventilabrum, *a fan.*
Verbum, *a word.*
Vestibulum, *a porch.*
Vestigium, *the print of the foot.*
Vexillum, *a banner.*
Viaticum, *money, or provisions for a journey.*
Vinculum, *a chain.*
Vinum, *wine.*
Vitium, *vice, a fault.*
Vitrum, *glass.*
Vivarium, *a place to keep beasts in, a warren or fish-pond.*
Vocabulum, *a name or word.*
Votum, *a vow.*

Ex-

Exceptions *in Gender.*

Exc. 1. The following nouns in *us* are feminine, *hŭmus,* the ground ; *alvus,* the belly ; *vannus,* a sieve.

And the following, derived from Greek nouns in *os :*

Abyssus, *a bottomless pit.*

Antĭdŏtus, *a preserva- tive against poison.*

Arctos, *the Bear, a constellation near the north pole.*

Carbăsus, *a sail.*

Diălectus, *a dialect, or manner of speech.*

Diämetros, *the diame- ter of a circle.*

Diphthongus, *a diph- thong.*

Erēmus,*-a desert.*

Mĕthŏdus, *a method.*

Pĕriŏdus, *a period.*

Pĕrímetros, *the cir- cumference.*

Phărus, *a watch tower.*

—Sÿnŏdus, *an assembly.*

To these add some names of jewels and plants, because *gemma* and *planta* are feminine ; as,

Amĕthÿstus, *an ame- thyst.* [*folite.*

Chrÿsŏlĭthus, *a chry-*

Chrÿsŏphĭălus, *a kind of topaz.*

Chrÿstallus, *crystal.*

Leucŏchrÿsus, *a jacinth.*

Sappīrus, *a sapphire.*

Tŏpazius, *a topaz.*

Biblus,

Păpyrus, { *an Egyptian reed of which pa- per was made.*

Byssus, *fine flax or li- nen.*

Costus, *costmary.*

Crŏcus, *saffron.*

Hÿssōpus, *hyssop.*

Nardus, *spikenard.*

Other names of jewels are generally masculine ; as, *Bĕryllus,* the beryl ; *carbuncŭlus,* a carbuncle ; *Pÿrōpus,* a ruby ; *Smăragdus,* an emerald.: And also names of plants ; as, *Aspărăgus,* asparagus, *or* sparrowgrass ; *ellebŏrus,* elle- bore ; *raphănus,* radish *or* colewort ; *intÿbus,* endive *or* succory, &c.

Exc. 2. The nouns which follow, are either masculine or feminine :.

Atŏmus, *an atom.*

Balănus, *the fruit of the palm-tree, ointment.*

Barbītus, *a harp:*

Cămēlus, *a camel.*

Cŏlus, *a distaff.*

Grossus, *a green fig.*

Pēnus, *a store-house.*

Phasēlus, *a little ship.*

Exc. 3.. *Vīrus,* poison ; *pĕlăgus,* the sea, are neuter.

Exc. 4. *Vulgus,* the common people, is either masculine. or neuter, but oftener neuter..

Exceptions *in Declension.*

Proper names in *ius* lose *us* in the vocative ; as,

Hŏrātius, Horāti ;) Virgĭlius, Virgĭli ; Georgius, Georgi, names of men ; *Lārius, Lāri ; Mincius, Minci,* names of lakes. *Fīlius,* a son, also hath *fĭli :* *gĕnius,* one's guar- dian angel, *gĕni ;* and *deus,* a god, hath *deus,* in the voc..

and in the plural more frequently *dii* and *diis*, than *dëi* and *dëis*. *Meus*, my, an adjective pronoun, hath *mi*, and sometimes *meus* in the vocative.

Other nouns in *ius* have *e*; as, *tăbellārius*, *tabellarie*, a letter-carrier; *pius*, *pie*, &c. So these epithets, *Dēlius*, *Dēlie*; *Tĭrynthĭus*, *Tirynthie*; and these possessives, *Laertius*, *Laertie*; *Saturnius*, *Saturnie*, &c. which are not considered as proper names.

The poets sometimes make the voc. of nouns in *us* like the nom. as, *fluvius*, *Latinus*, for *fluvie*, *Latine*, Virg. This also occurs in prose, but more rarely. Thus, *Audi tu pŏpŭlus*, for *pŏpŭle*. Liv. i, 24.

The poets also change nouns in *er* unto *us*; as *Evandir*, or *Evandrus*, voc. *Evander*, or *Evandre*: So *Maander*, *Leander*, *Tymber*, *Teucer*, &c. and so anciently *puer* in the voc. had *puere* from *puerus*.

Note, When the gen. sing. ends in *ii*, the latter *i* is sometimes taken away by the poets, for the sake of quantity; as, *tugŭri*, for *tugurii*; *ingĕni*, for *ingenii*, &c. And in the gen. plur. we find *deûm*, *libeûm*, *fabrûm*, *duûm virûm*, &c. for *deorum*, *librorum*, &c. and in poetry, *Teucrûm*, *Graiûm*, *Argivûm*, *Dănaûm*, *Pĕlasgûm*, &c. for *Teucrorum*, &c.

Greek Nouns.

(Os and on are Greek terminations; as, *Alphëos*, a river in Greece; *Ilion*, the city Troy; and are often changed into *us* and *um*, by the Latins; *Alphëus*, *Ilium*, which are declined like *dominus* and *regnum*.)

Nouns in *eos* or *ios* are sometimes contracted in the genitive; as, *Orphëos*, gen. *Orphëi*, *Orphei* or *Orphi*. So *Thesëus*, *Promethëus*, &c. But nouns in *eus*, when the *eu* is a diphthong, are of the third declension.

Some nouns in *os* have the gen. sing. in *o*; as, *Androgeos*, gen. *Androgeo*, or *-ii*, the name of a man; *Athos*, *Atho*, or *-i*, a hill in Macedonia: both which are also found in the third decl. thus, nom. *Androgeo*, gen. *Androgeonis*: So *Atho* or *Athon*, *-onis*, &c. Anciently nouns in *os*, in imitation of the Greeks, had the gen. in *u*; as, *Menandru*, *Apollodoru*, for *Mĕnandri*, *Apollodori*, Ter.

Nouns in *os* have the acc. in *um* or *on*; as, *Delus* or *Delos*, acc. *Delum* or *Delon*, the name of an island.

Some neuters have the gen. plur. in *ōn*; as, *Georgĭca*, gen. pl. *Georgicōn*, books which treat of husbandry, as, Virgil's *Georgicks*.

(THIRD DECLENSION.)

There are more nouns of the third declension than of all the other declensions together. The number of its final syllables is not ascertained. Its final letters, are thirteen, *a*, *c*, *i*, *o*, *y*, *c*, *d*, *l*, *n*, *r*, *s*, *t*, *x*. Of these, eight are peculiar to this declension, namely, *i*, *o*, *y*, *c*, *d*, *l*, *t*, *x*; *a* and *e* are common to it with the first declension; *n* and *r*,

with

with the second; and *s*, with all the other declensions. *A*, *i*, and *y*, are peculiar to Greek nouns.

The terminations of the different cases are these: nom. sing. *a*, *e*, &c.; gen. *is*; dat. *i*; acc. *em*; voc. *the same with the nominative*; abl. *e*, or *i*: nom. acc. and voc. plur. *es*, *a*, or *ia*; gen. *um*, or *ium*; dat. and abl. *ibus*; thus,

Sermo, *speech*, masc.		Căput, *the head*, neut.	
Sing.	Plur.	Sing.	Plur.
N. sermo,	N. sermōnes,	N. căput,	N. capíta,
G. sermōnis,	G. sermōnum,	G. capitis,	G. capitum,
D. sermoni,	D. sermonĭbus,	D. capiti,	D. capitibus,
A. sermonem,	A. sermōnes,	A. caput,	A. capita,
V. sermo,	V. sermones,	V. caput,	V. capita,
A. sermone.	A. sermonibus.	A. capite.	A. capitibus.

Rupes, *a rock*, fem.		Sedile, *a seat*, neut.	
Sing.	Plur.	Sing.	Plur.
N. rūpes,	N. rupes,	N. sedile,	N. sedilia,
G. rupis,	G. rupium,	G. sedilis,	G. sedilium,
D. rupi,	D. rupibus,	D. sedili,	D. sedilibus,
A. rupem,	A. rupes,	A. sedile,	A. sedilia,
V. rupes,	V. rupes,	V. sedile,	V. sedilia,
A. rupe.	A. rupibus.	A. sedili.	A. sedilibus.

Lapis, *a stone*, masc.		Iter, *a journey*, neut.	
Sing.	Plur.	Sing.	Plur.
N. lăpis,	N. lăpides,	N. ĭter,	N. itinĕra,
G. lapĭdis,	G. lapidum,	G. itinĕris,	G. itinĕrum,
D. lapidi,	D. lapdibus,	D. itineri,	D. itinĕribus,
A. lapidem,	A. lapides,	A. iter,	A. itinera,
V. lapis,	V. lapides,	V. iter,	V. itinera,
A. lăpide.	A. lapidibus.	A. itinere.	A. itineribus.

Of the GENDER and GENITIVE of Nouns of the Third Declension.

A, E, I, and *Y.*

1. Nouns in *a, e, i,* and *y,* are neuter.

Nouns in *a* form the genitive in *ătis*; as, *diadēma, diademătis,* a crown; *dogma, -ătis,* an opinion. So,

Ænigma, *a riddle.*	Diplōma, *a charter.*	Poēma, *a poem.*
Apŏthegma, *a short pithy saying.*	Epigramma, *an inscription.*	Schēma, *a scheme or figure.*
Arōma, *sweet spices.*	Numisma, *a coin.*	Sophisma, *a deceitful argument.*
Axiōma, *a plain truth.*	Phasma, *an apparition.*	

Stemma,

Stemma, *a pedigree.*
Stigma, *a mark or brand, a disgrace.*
Strătāgēma, *an artful contrivance.*
Thēma, *a theme, a* subject *to write or speak on.*
Tŏreuma, *a carved vessel.*

Nouns in *e* change *e* into *is;* as, *rēte, retis,* a net. So,

Ancīle, *a shield.*
Aplustre, *the flag of a ship.*
Campestre, *a pair of drawers.*
Cochleāre, *a spoon.*
Conclāve, *a room.*
Crīnāle, *a pin for the hair.*
Cŭbīle, *a couch.*
Equīle, *a stable for horses.*
Làqueāre, *a ceiled roof.*
Mantīle, *a towel.*
Mónīle, *a necklace.*
Nāvāle, *a dock or place for shipping.*
Ŏvīle, *a sheep-fold.*
Præsēpe, *a stall; a bee-hive.*
Sĕcāle, *rye.*
Suīle, *a sow-cote.*
Tibiāle, *a stocking.*

Nouns in *i* are generally indeclinable; as, *gummi,* gum: *zingĭbĕri,* ginger: but some Greek nouns add *tis;* as, *hydrŏmĕli, hydromelitis,* water and honey sodden together, mead.

Nouns in *y* add *os;* as, *moly, molyos,* an herb; *myfy, -yos,* vitriol.

O.

2. (Nouns in *o* are masculine, and form the genitive in *ōnis;*) as,

Sermo, sermōnis, speech; *draco, drăcōnis,* a dragon.———So,

Agāso, *a horse-keeper.*
Aquīlo, *the north wind.*
Arrhăbo, *an earnest-penny, a pledge.*
Bălatro, *a pitiful fellow.*
Bambălio, *a stutterer.*
Bāro, *a blockhead.*
Būbo, *an owl.*
Būfo, *a toad.*
Cīlo, *a soldier's slave.*
Cāpo, *a capon.*
Carbo, *a coal.*
Caupo, *an innkeeper.*
Cerdo, *a cobler, or one who follows a mean trade.*
Cĭnĭflo, *a frizler of hair.*
Crabro, *a wasp, or hornet.*
Cūrio, *the chief of a ward or curia.*
Equīso, *a groom or ostler.*
Erro, *a wanderer.*
Fullo, *a fuller of cloth.*
Helluo, *a glutton.*
Histrio, *a player.*
Latro, *a robber.*
Lēno, *a pimp.*
Lūdio, *&* -ius, *a player.*
Lurco, *a glutton.*
Mango, *a slave-merchant.*
Mirmillo, *a fencer.*
Mōrio, *a fool.*
Mucro, *the point of a weapon.*
Mulio, *a muleteer.*
Nĕbŭlo, *a knave.*
Pāvo, *a peacock.*
Pēro, *a kind of shoe.*
Præco, *a common crier.*
Prædo, *a robber.*
Pulmo, *the lungs.*
Pūsio, *a little child.*
Salmo, *a salmon.*
Sannio, *a buffoon.*
Sāpo, *soap.*
Sipho, *a pipe or tube.*
Spādo, *an eunuch.*
Stŏlo, *a shoot or scion.*
Străbo, *a goggle-eyed person.*
Tēmo, *the pole or draught-tree.*
Tīro, *a raw soldier.*
Umbo, *the boss of a shield.*
Ūpĭlio, *a shepherd.*
Volo, *a volunteer.*

Exc.

Exc. 1. Nouns in *io* are feminine, when they signify any thing without a body; as, *ratio, rationis*, reason.——So,

Captio, *a quirk.*
Cautio, *caution, care.*
Concio, *an assembly, a speech.*
Cessio, *a yielding.*
Dictio, *a word.*
Deditio, *a surrender.*
Lectio, *a lesson.*
Legio, *a legion, a body of men.*
Mentio, *mention.*
Notio, *a notion or idea.*
Opinio, *an opinion.*
Optio, *a choice.*
Oratio, *a speech.*
Pensio, *a payment.*

Perduellio, *treason.*
Portio, *a part.*
Potio, *drink.*
Proditio, *treachery.*
Proscriptio, *a proscription, ordering citizens to be slain, and confiscating their effects.*
Quæstio, *an inquiry.*
Rebellio, *rebellion.*
Regio, *a country.*
Relatio, *a telling.*
Religio, *religion.*
Remissio, *a slackening.*
Sanctio, *a confirmation.*

Sectio, *the confiscation or forfeiture of one's goods.*
Seditio, *a mutiny.*
Sessio, *a sitting.*
Statio, *a station.*
Suspicio, *mistrust.*
Titillatio, *a tickling.*
Translatio, *a transferring.*
Usucapio, *the enjoyment of a thing by prescription.*
Vacatio, *freedom from labour, &c.*
Visio, *an apparition.*

But when they mark any thing which has a body, or signify numbers, they are masculine; as,

Curculio, *the throat-pipe, the weasand.*
Papilio, *a butterfly.*
Pugio, *a dagger.*
Pusio, *a little child.*

Scipio, *a staff.*
Scorpio, *a scorpion.*
Septentrio, *the north.*
Stellio, *a lizard.*
Titio, *a firebrand.*

Unio, *a pearl.*
Vespertilio, *a bat.*
Ternio, *the number three.*
Quaternio, —— *four.*
Senio, —— *six.*

Exc. 2. Nouns in *do* and *go* are feminine, and have the genitive in *ĭnis*; as, *ărundo, arundĭnis*, a reed; *ĭmāgo, imagĭnis*, an image.——So,

Ærūgo, *rust,* (of brass.)
Cālīgo, *darkness.*
Cartĭlāgo, *a gristle.*
Crĕpīdo, *a crack, a bank.*
Farrāgo, *a mixture.*
Ferrūgo, *rust,* (of iron.)
Formīdo, *fear.*
Fūligo, *soot.*
Grando, *hail.*
Hĭrūdo, *a horse-leech.*

Hīrundo, *a swallow.*
Intercăpēdo, *a space between.*
Lānūgo, *down.*
Lentīgo, *a pimple.*
Orīgo, *an origin.*
Porrīgo, *scurf,* or *scales in the head; dandruff.*
Prŏpago, *a lineage.*
Rūbīgo, *rust, mildew.*

Sartāgo, *a frying-pan.*
Scātūrigo, *a spring.*
Teſtūdo, *a tortoise.*
Torpēdo, *a numbness.*
Ūlīgo, *the natural moisture of the earth.*
Vālētūdo, *health.*
Vertīgo, *a dizziness.*
Virgo, *a virgin.*
Vŏrāgo, *a gulf.*

But the following are masculine:

Cardo, -ĭnis, *a hinge.*
Cūdo, -ōnis, *a leather cap.*
Harpăgo, -ōnis, *a drag.*
Līgo, -ōnis, *a spade.*

Margo, -ĭnis, *the brink of a river;* also fem.
Ordo, -ĭnis, *order.*
Tendo, -inis, *a tendon.*
Udo, -ōnis, *a linen or woollen sock.*

Cūpīdo, desire, is often masc. with the poets; but in prose always fem.

Exc.

Exc. 3. *. The following nouns have *inis*,

Apollo, -inis.* *the god Apollo*   Nēmo, -inis, m. or f. *no body.*
Homo, -inis, *a man* or *woman.*   Turbo, -inis, m. *a whirlwind.*

Caro, *flesh*, fem. has *carnis :* Anio, masc. the name of a river, *Anie-*
nis : Neris, *Neirienis*, the wife of the god Mars; from the obsolete
nominatives *Maier, Nerien.* Turbo, the name of a man, has *ōnis.*

Exc. 4. Greek nouns in *o* are feminine, and have *us* in
the genitive, and *o* in the other cases singular; as, *Dido,*
the name of a woman; genit. *Didūs;* dat. *Didō,* &c.
Sometimes they are declined regularly; thus, *Dido, Didō-*
nis : so *echo, -ūs,* f. the resounding of the voice from a rock
or wood; *Argo, -ūs,* the name of a ship; *halo, -onis,* f.
a circle about the sun or moon.

C, D, L.

3. Nouns in *c* and *l* are neuter, and form the
genitive by adding *is*; as,

Animal, *animalis*, a living creature; *toral, -ālis,* a bed-
cover; *halec, halecis,* a kind of pickle.——So,

Cervical, *a bolster.*   Minerval, *entry-money.*   Puteal, *a well cover.*
Cubital, *a cushion.*   Minutal, *minced meat.*   Vectigal, *a tax.*

Except. Conful, -ūlis, m *a conful.*   Mugil, -ilis, m. *a mullet-fish.*
      Fel, fellis, n. *gall.*   Sal, sălis, m. or n. *falt.*
      Lac, lactis, n. *milk.*   Sāles, -ium, pl. m. *witty fayings.*
      Mel, mellis, n. *honey.*   Sol, sōlis, m. *the fun.*

D is the termination only of a few proper names, which
form the genitive by adding *is*; as, *David, Davidis.*

N.

4. Nouns in *n* are masculine, and add *is* in
the genitive; as,

Canon, -ōnis, *a rule.*   Physognōmon, -ōnis, *one who*
Dæmon, -ōnis, *a spirit.*   *guesses at the dispositions of men*
Delphin, -inis, *a dolphin.*   *from the face.*
Gnōmon, -ōnis, *the cock of a dial.*   Ren, rēnis, *the reins.*
Hymen, -ĕnis, *the god of marriage.*   Splen, splēnis, *the spleen.*
Lien, -ĕnis, *the milt.*   Syren, -ēnis, f. *a Syren.*
Pæan, -ānis, *a song.*   Titan, -ānis, *the fun.*

Exc. 1. Nouns in *men* are neuter, and make their genitive in *inis*; as *flūmen, flumĭnis,* a river.——So,

Abdōmen, *the paunch.* Agmen, *an army on* Alūmen, *alum.*
Acūmen, *sharpness.*   *march.*   Bitūmen, *a kind of clay.*
Cacūmen,

Căcŭmen, *the top.*
Carmen, *a song, a poem.*
Cognōmen, *a surname.*
Cŏlŭmen, *a support.*
Crīmen, *a crime.*
Discrīmen, *a difference.*
Exāmen, *a swarm of bees.*
Fŏrāmen, *a hole.*

Germen, *a sprout.*
Grāmen, *grass.*
Lĕgūmen, *all kind of pulse.*
Lūmen, *light.*
Nōmen, *a name.*
Nūmen, *the deity.*
Ōmen, *a presage.*
Pŭtāmen, *a nut-shell.*

Sagmen, *vervain, an herb.*
Sēmen, *a seed.*
Spĕcimen, *a proof.*
Stāmen, *the warp.*
Subtēmen, *the woof.*
Tegmen, *a covering.*
Vīmen, *a twig.*
Vŏlūmen, *a folding.*

The following nouns are likewise neuter :

Glūten, -ĭnis, *glue.*
Unguen, -ĭnis, *ointment.*
Inguen, -ĭnis, *the groin.*
Pollen, -ĭnis, *fine flour.*

Exc. 2. The following masculines have *ĭnis ; pecten*, a comb ; *tūbĭcen*, a trumpeter ; *tībĭcen*, a piper ; and *oscen, v. oscĭnis*, sc. *ăvis*, f. a bird, which foreboded by singing.

Exc. 3. The following nouns are feminine : *Sindon, -ŏnis*, fine linen ; *aëdon, -ŏnis*, a nightingale ; *Halcyon, -ŏnis*, a bird called the King's fisher ; *icon, -ŏnis*, an image.

Exc. 4. Some Greek nouns have *ontis* ; as, *Laŏmĕdon, -ontis*, a king of Troy. So *Achĕron, Chamæleon, Phaĕthon, Chăron*, &c.

AR and *UR.*

5. | Nouns in *ar* and *ur* are neuter, and add *is* to form the genitive ; as,

Calcar, calcāris, | a spur ; *murmur, murmŭris*, a noise.—So,
Guttur, -ŭris, *the throat.*
Jūbar, -ăris, *a sun-beam.*
Lăcūnar, -āris, *a ceiling.*
Except, Ĕbur, -ŏris, n. *ivory.*
Far, farris, n. *corn.*
Fĕmur, -ŏris, n. *the thigh.*
Furfur, -ŭris, m. *bran.*
Fur, fūris, m. *a thief.*
Hĕpar, -ătis, *or* ătos, n. *the liver.*
Nectar, -ăris, *drink of the gods.*
Pulvīnar, -āris, *a pillow.*
Sulphur, -ŭris, *sulphur.*
Jĕcur, -ŏris, *or* jecĭnŏris, n. *the liver.*
Rōbur, -ŏris, n. *strength.*
Sălar, -aris, m. *a trout.*
Turtur, -ŭris, m. *a turtle-dove.*
Vultur, -ŭris, m. *a vulture.*

ER and *OR.*

6. | Nouns in *er* and *or* are masculine, and form the genitive by adding *is* ; as,

Anser, ansĕris, | a goose *or* gander ; *agger, -ĕris*, a rampart ; *āer, -ĕris*, the air ; *carcer, -ĕris*, a prison ; *asser, -ĕris, & assis, -is*, a plank ; *dŏlor, -ōris*, pain ; *cŏlor, -ōris*, a colour.——So,

Actor,

Actor, *a doer, a pleader.*
Creditor, *he that trusts or lends.*
Cruor, *gore.*
Debitor, *a debtor.*
Fœtor, *an ill smell.*
Honor, *honour.*
Lector, *a reader.*
Lictor, *an officer among the Romans who attended the magistrates.*
Livor, *paleness, malice.*
Nidor, *a strong smell.*

Odor, & -os, *a smell.*
Olor, *a swan.*
Prædor, *filth.*
Pastor, *a shepherd.*
Prætor, *a commander.*
Pudor, *shame.*
Rubor, *blushing.*
Rumor, *a report.*
Sapor, *a taste.*
Sartor, *a cobler or tailor.*
Sutor, *a sewer, a father.*

Sopor, *sleep.*
Splendor, *brightness.*
Sponsor, *a surety.*
Squalor, *filthiness.*
Stupor, *dulness.*
Sutor, *a sewer.*
Tepor, *warmth.*
Terror, *dread.*
Timor, *fear.*
Tonsor, *a barber.*
Tutor, *a guardian.*
Vapor, *a vapour.*
Venator, *a hunter.*

Rhetor, a rhetorician, has *rhetoris ; castor*, a beaver, *-oris.*

Exc. 1. The following nouns are neuter:

Acer, -eris, *a maple-tree.*
Ador, -oris, *fine wheat.*
Æquor, -oris, *a plain, the sea.*
Cadaver, -eris, *a dead carcass.*
Cicer, -eris, *vetches.*
Cor, cordis, *the heart.*
Iter, itineris, *a journey.*

Marmor, oris, *marble.*
Papaver, -eris, *poppy.*
Piper, -eris, *pepper.*
Spinther, -eris, *a clasp.*
Tuber, -eris, *a swelling.*
Uber, -eris, *a pap, or fatness.*
Ver, veris, *the spring.*

Arbor, -oris, a tree, is fem. *Tuber*, -eris, the fruit of the tuber tree, is masc. but when put for the tree, fem.

Exc. 2. Nouns in *ber* have *bris* in the genitive ; as, hic *imber*, *imbris*, a shower. So *Insuber, October*, &c.

Nouns in *ter* have *tris ;* as *venter*, *ventris*, the belly ; *pater*, *patris*, a father ; *frater*, *-tris*, a brother ; *accipiter*, *-tris*, a hawk ; but *crater*, a cup, has *crateris ; soter*, *-eris*, a saviour ; *later*, a tile, *lateris ; Jupiter*, the chief of the Heathen gods, has *Jovis ; linter*, *-tris*, a little boat, is masc. or fem.

A S.

7. | Nouns in *as* are feminine, and have the genitive in *atis ;* as, *ætas, ætatis,* | an age.——So,

Æstas, *the summer.*
Pietas, *piety.*
Potestas, *power.*
Probitas, *probity.*
Satietas, *a glut or disgust.*

Simultas, *a feud, a grudge.*
Tempestas, *a time, a tempest.*
Ubertas, *fertility.*

Veritas, *truth.*
Voluntas, *will.*
Voluptas, *pleasure.*
Anas, *a duck, has anatis.*

Except. 1. As, assis, m. *a piece of money, or any thing which may be divided into twelve parts.*

Mas, maris, m. *a male.*
Vas, vadis, m *a surety.*
Vas, vasis, n. *a vessel.*

Note.

Note. All the parts of *es* are likewife mafculine, except *uncia*, an ounce, fem.; as *fextans*, 2 ounces; *quadrans*, 3; *triens*, 4; *quincunx*, 5; *femis*, 6; *feptunx*, 7; *bes*, 8; *dodrans*, 9; *dextans*, or *dēcunx*, 10; *deunx*, 11 ounces.

Exc. 2. Of Greek nouns in *as*, fome are mafculine; fome feminine; fome neuter. Thofe that are mafculine have *antis* in the genit. as, *gīgas, gigantis,* a giant; *ădămas, -antis,* an adamant; *ělěphas, -antis,* an elephant. Thofe that are feminine have *ădis,* or *ădos;* as, *lampas lampă-dis,* or *lampădos,* a lamp; *drŏmas, -ădis,* f. a dromedary: likewife *Arcas,* an Arcadian, though mafculine, has *Ar-cădis,* or *-ados.* Thofe that are neuter have *ătis;* as, *bū-cĕras, -ătis,* an herb; *artocrcas, -ătis,* a pie.

E S.

8. Nouns in *es* are feminine, and in the genitive change *es* into *is*; as,

rūpes, rupis, a rock; *nūbes, nubis,* a cloud.———So,

Ædes, or -is, *temple;* plur. *a houfe.*	Lues, *a plague.*	Sēpes, *a hedge.*
Cautes, *a rugged rock.*	Mōles, *a heap.*	Sōbŏles, *an offspring.*
Clādes, *an overthrow, deftruction.*	Nātes, *the buttock.*	Strāges, *a flaughter.*
	Pālumbes, m. or f. *a pigeon.*	Strues, *a heap.*
Crātes, *a hurdle.*	Prōles, *an offspring.*	Sūdes, *a ftake.*
Fames, *hunger*	Pūbes, *youth.*	Tābes, *a confumption.*
Fides, *a fiddle.*		Vulpes, *a fox.*

Exc. 1. The following nouns are mafculine, and moft of them likewife excepted in the formation of the genitive:

Ales, -ĭtis, *a bird.*	Palmes, -ĭtis, *a vine-branch*
Ames, -ĭtis, *a fowler's ftaff.*	Pāries, -ĕtis, *a wall.*
Āries, -ĕtis, *a ram.*	Pes, pĕdis, *the foot.*
Bes, beffis, *two thirds of a pound.*	Pĕdes, -ĭtis, *a footman.*
Cefpes, -ĭtis, *a turf.*	Poples, -ĭtis, *the ham of the leg.*
Eques, -ĭtis, *a horfeman.*	Præfes, -ĭdis, *a prefident.*
Fomes, -ĭtis, *fuel.*	Sătelles, -ĭtis, *a life-guard.*
Gurges, -ĭtis, *a whirlpool.*	Stīpes, -ĭtis, *the ftock of a tree.*
Hēres, -ēdis, *an heir.*	Termes, -ĭtis, *an olive bough.*
Indĭges, -ĕtis, *a man deified.*	Trāmes, -ĭtis, *a path.*
Interpres, -ĕtis, *an interpreter.*	Vēles, -ĭtis, *a light-armed foldier.*
Līmes, -ĭtis, *a limit or bound.*	Vātes, vatis, *a prophet.*
Mīles, -ĭtis, *a foldier.*	Verres, verris, *a boar-pig.*
Obfes, -ĭdis, *a hoftage.*	

But *ales, miles, beres, interpres, obfes,* and *vates,* are alfo ufed in the feminine.

E

Exc.

Exc. 2. The following feminines are excepted in the formation of the genitive :

Ābies, -ĕtis, *a fir-tree.*
Cĕres, -ĕris, *the goddess of corn.*
Merces, -ēdis, *a reward, hire.*
Merges, -ĭtis, *a handful of corn.*
Quies, -ētis, *rest.*

Rĕquies, -ētis ; *or* requiēi, (*of the fifth declension,*) *rest.*
Sĕges, -ĕtis, *growing corn.*
Tĕges, -ĕtis, *a mat* or *coverlet.*
Tūdes, ·is, *or* -ĭtis, *a hammer.*

To these add the following adjectives.

Āles, -ĭtis, *swift.*
Bīpes, -ĕdis, *two-footed.*
Quadrŭpes, -ĕdis, *four-footed.*
Dĕses, -ĭdis, *slothful.*
Dīves, -ĭtis, *rich.*
Hĕbes, -ĕtis, *dull.*
Perpes, -ĕtis, *perpetual.*

Præpes, -ĕtis, *swift-winged.*
Rĕses, -ĭdis, *idle.*
Sospes, -ĭtis, *safe.*
Sŭperstes, -ĭtis, *surviving.*
Tĕres, -ĕtis, *round and long, smooth.*
Lŏcuples, -ētis, *rich.*
Mansues, -ētis, *gentle.*

Exc. 3. Greek nouns in *es* are commonly masculine ; as hic ăcīnăces, -is, a Persian sword, a scimitar ; but some are neuter ; as, hoc căcoēthes, an evil custom, hippŏmănes, a kind of poison which grows in the forehead of a foal ; pănăces, the herb all-heal ; nēpenthes, the herb kill-grief. Diffyllables, and the monosyllables *Cres*, a Cretan, have *ētis* in the genitive, as, hic magnes, magnētis, a load-stone ; tāpes, -ētis, tapestry ; lēbes-ētis, a cauldron. The rest follow the general rule. Some proper nouns have either *ētis* or *is* ; as, *Dăres, Darētis, or Daris* ; which is also sometimes of the first declension ; *Achilles,* has *Achillis* ; or *Achilli* contracted for *Achillēi* or *Achillei,* of the second decl. from *Achillēus :* So *Ŭlysses, Pĕricles, Verres, Arif-tŏtĕles, &c.*

I S.

9. Nouns in *is* are feminine, and have their genitive the same with the nominative ; as,

auris, auris, *the ear* ; ă̄vis, avis, *a bird.*——So,

Āpis, *a bee.*
Bīlis, *the gall, anger.*
Claffis, *a fleet.*
Felis, *a cat.*
Fŏris, *a door* ; *oftener* plur. fores, -ium.

Meffis, *a harvest or crop.*
Nāris, *the nostril.*
Neptis, *a niece.*
Ŏvis, *a sheep.*
Pellis, *a skin.*
Peftis, *a plague.*

Rătis, *a raft.*
Rŭdis, *a rod.*
Vallis, *a valley.*
Veftis, *a garment*
Vītis, *a vine.*

Exc. 1. The following nouns are masculine, and form the genitive according to the general rule :

Axis,

Axis, axis, *an axle-tree.*
Aqualis, *a water-pot, an ewer.*
Callis, *a beaten road.*
Caulis, *the stalk of an herb.*
Collis, *a hill.*
Cenchris, *a kind of serpent.*

Ensis, *a sword.*
Fascis, *a bundle.*
Fecialis, *a herald.*
Follis, *a pair of bellows.*
Fustis, *a staff.*
Mensis, *a month.*
Mugilis, or -il, *a mullet fish.* [*world.*
Orbis, *a circle, the*

Patruēlis, *a cousin-german.*
Piscis, *a fish.*
Postis, *a post.*
Sodalis, *a companion.*
Torris, *a fire-brand.*
Unguis, *the nail.*
Vectis, *a lever.*
Vermis, *a worm.*

To these add Latin nouns in *nis;* as, *pānis,* bread; *crinis,* the hair; *ignis,* fire; *fūnis,* a rope, &c. But Greek nouns in *nis* are feminine, and have the genitive in *ĭdis;* as *tȳrannis, tȳrannĭdis,* tyranny.

EXC. 2. The following nouns are also masculine, but form their genitive differently:

Cĭnis, -ĕris, *ashes.*
Cŭcŭmis, -is, or -ĕris, *a cucumber.*
Dis, dītis, *the god of riches,* or *rich,* an adj.
Glis, glīris, *a dormouse, a rat.*
Impūbis, or impūbes, -is or -ĕris, *not marriageable.*
Lăpis, -ĭdis, *a stone.*

Pŭbis or pūbes, -is, or oftener -ĕris, *marriageable.*
Pulvis, -ĕris, *dust.*
Quiris, -ītis, *a Roman.*
Samnis, -ītis, *a Samnite.*
Sanguis, -ĭnis, *blood.*
Sēmis, -issis, *the half of any thing.*
Vōmis, or -er, -ĕris, *a ploughshare.*

Pulvis and *cinis* are sometimes feminine. *Semis* is also sometimes neuter, and then it is indeclinable. *Pubis* and *impubis* are properly adjectives; thus, *Puberibus caulem foliis,* a stalk with downy leaves, *Virg. Æn.* xii. 413. *Impube corpus,* the body of a boy not having yet got the down (*pubes,* -is, f) of youth, *Herat. epod.* 5. 13. *Exsanguis,* bloodless, an adj. has *exsanguis* in the gen.

EXC. 3. The following are either masc. or feminine, and form the genitive according to the general rule.

Amnis, *a river.*
Anguis, *a snake.*
Cănālis, *a conduit-pipe.*
Clūnis, *the buttock.*
Corbis, *a basket.*

Finis, *the end:* fines, *the boundaries of a field, or territories, is always masc.*
Scrōbis, or scrobs, *a ditch.*
Torquis, *a chain.*

EXC. 4. These feminines have *ĭdis:* Cassis, -ĭdis, a helmet; *cuspis,* -ĭdis, the point of a spear; *capis,* -ĭdis, a kind of cup; *prōmulsis,* -ĭdis, a kind of drink, metheglin. *Lis,* strife, f. has *lītis.*

EXC. 5. Greek nouns in *is* are generally feminine, and form the genitive variously: Some have *eos* or *ios;* as, *hærēsis,* -eos, or -ios or -is, a heresy; so, *bāsis,* f. the foot of a pillar; *phrăsis,* a phrase; *phthĭsis,* a consumption: *poēsis,* poetry: *metrŏpŏlis,* a chief city, &c. Some have *ĭdis,* or *ĭdos;*

ĭdos ; as, *Păris*, -*ĭdis*, or -*ĭdos*, the name of a man ; *aspis*, -*ĭdis*, f. an afp ; *ĕphēmĕris*, -*ĭdis*, f. a day book ; *īris*, -*ĭdis*, f. the rainbow ; *pyxis*, -*ĭdis*, f. a box. So, *Ægis*, the fhield of Pallas ; *canthăris*, a fort of fly ; *pĕrifcēlis*, a garter ; *prolofcis*, an elephant's trunk ; *pўrămis*, a pyramid ; and *tigris*, a tiger, -*ĭdis*, feldom *tīgris :* all fem. Part have *īdis* ; as, *Pfophis*, -*ĭdis*, the name of a city : others have *īnis* ; as, *Eleufis*, -*īnis*, the name of a city ; and fome have *entis* ; as, *Simois*, *Simoentis*, the name of a river, *Chăris*, one of the graces, has, *Chărĭtis*.

O S.

10. Nouns in *os* are mafculine, and have the genitive in *ōtis* ; as,

nĕpos, -*ōtis*, a grandchild ; *săcerdos*, -*ōtis*, a prieft, alfo fem.

Exc. 1. The following are feminine :

Arbos, *or* -or, -ŏris, *a tree.*	Eos, eōis, *the morning.*
Cos, cōtis, *a whetftone.*	Glos, glōris, *the hufband's fifter, or*
Dos, dōtis, *a dowry.*	*brother's wife.*

Exc. 2. The following mafculines are excepted in the genitive :

Flos, flōris, *a flower.*	Cuftos, -ōdis, *a keeper ;* alfo fem.
Honos, *er -or*, -ōris, *honour.*	Hĕros, herōis, *a hero.*
Labos, *or -or*, -ōris, *labour.*	Mīnos, -ōis, *a king of Crete.*
Lĕpos, *er -or*, -ōris, *wit.*	Tros, Trōis, *a Trojan.*
Mos, mōris, *a cuftom.*	Bos, bŏvis, m. or f. *an ox or cow.*
Ros, rōris, *dew.*	

Exc. 3. *Os, offis*, a bone ; and *ōs, oris*, the mouth, are neuter.

Exc. 4. Some Greek nouns have -*ōis* ; as *hēros*, -*ōis*, a hero, or great man : So *Mīnos*, a king of Crete ; *Tros*, a Trojan ; *thos*, a kind of wolf.

U S.

11. Nouns in *us* are neuter, and have their genitive in *ŏris* ; as,

pĕctus, *pĕctŏris*, the breaft ; *tempus*, *temporis*, time. So,

Corpus, *a body.*	Frīgus, *cold.*	Pĕnus, *provifions.*
Dĕcus, *honour.*	Littus, *a fhore.*	Pignus, *a pledge.*
Dĕdĕcus, *difgrace.*	Nĕmus, *a grove.*	Stercus, *dung.*
Facīnus, *a great action.*	Pĕcus, *cattle.*	Tergus, *a hide.*
Fœnus, *ufury.*		

Exc. 1.

Exc. 1. The following neuters have *ĕris*.

Acus, *chaff.*
Fūnus, *a funeral.*
Fœdus, *a covenant.*
Génus, *a kind,* or *kin-
dred.*
Glŏmus, *a clew.*
Lătus, *the side.*
Mūnus, *a gift,* or *office.*
Ŏlus, *pot-herbs.*
Ŏnus, *a burden.*
Ŏpus, *a work.*
Pondus, *a weight.*
Rūdus, *rubbish.*
Scĕlus, *a crime.*
Sīdus, *a star.*
Vellus, *a fleece of wool.*
Vīscus, *an entrail.*
Ulcus, *a bile.*
Vulnus, *a wound.*

Thus *acĕris, funĕris,* &c. *Glŏmus,* a clew, is sometimes masculine, and has *glŏmi,* of the second declension. *Vĕnus,* the goddess of love, and *vĕtus,* old, an adjective, likewise have *ĕris*.

Exc. 2. The following nouns are feminine, and form the genitive variously :

Incus, -ūdis, *an anvil.*
Pălus, -ūdis, *a pool or morass.*
Pĕcus (*not used*), -ūdis, *a sheep.*
Subscus, -ūdis, *a dove-tail.*
Tellus, -ūris, *the earth,* or *goddess
of the earth.*
Jŭventus, -ūtis, *youth.*
Sălus, -ūtis, *safety.*
Sĕnectus, -ūtis, *old age.*
Servĭtus, -ūtis, *slavery.*
Virtus, -ūtis, *virtue.*
Intercus, -ŭtis, *an hydropsy.*

Intercus is properly an adjective, having *aqua* understood.

Exc. 3. Monosyllables of the neuter gender have *ūris* in the genitive ; as,

Crus, crūris, *the leg.*
Jus, jūris, *law or right ;* also *broth.*
Pus, pūris, *the corrupt matter of any
sore.*
Rus, rūris, *the country.*
Thus, thūris, *frankincense.*
So Mus, mūris, masc. *a mouse.*

Ligus, or *-ur,* a Ligurian, has *Ligŭris ; lĕpus,* masc. a hare, *lĕpŏris ; sus,* masc. or fem. a swine, *suis ; grus,* mas. or fem. a crane, *gruis.*

OEdipus, the name of a man, has *OEdipŏdis :* sometimes it is of the second declension, and has *OEdipi.* The compounds of *pus* have *ŏdis ;* as, *tripus,* masc. a tripod, *tripŏdis ;* but *lăgōpus,* -ŏdis, a kind of bird, or the herb hares-foot, is fem. Names of cities have *untis ;* as, *Trăpezus, Trapezuntis ; Ŏpus, Opuntis.*

Y S.

12. Nouns in *ys* are all borrowed from the Greek, and are for the most part feminine. In the genitive, they have sometimes *yis* or *yos ;* as hæc *chĕlys, chelyis,* or *-yos,* a harp ; *Căpys, Capyis,* or *-yos ;* the name of a man : sometimes they have *ўdis,* or *ўdos ;* as, hæc *chlămys, chlămÿdis* or *chlamÿdos,* a soldier's cloak ; and sometimes *ўnis,* or *ўnos ;* as, *Trăchys, Trachÿnis,* or *Trachÿnos,* the name of a town.

ÆS, AUS, EUS.

13. The nouns ending in *æs* and *aus* are,

Æs, æris, n. *brass,* or *money.*
Fraus, fraudis, f. *fraud.*
Laus, laudis, f. *praise.*
Præs, prædis, m. or f. *a surety.*

Substantives ending in the syllable *eus* are all proper names, and

 have

have the genitive in *eos*; as, *Orpheus, Orpheos*; *Tereus, Tereos*. But these nouns are also found in the second declension, where *eus* is divided into two syllables: thus, *Orpheus*, genit. *Orphei*, or sometimes contracted *Orphei*, and that into *Orphi*.

S with a consonant before it.

14. ❘ Nouns ending in *s* with a consonant before it, are feminine; and form the genitive by changing the *s* into *is* or *tis*; as,

trabs, trăbis, ❘ a beam; *scobs, scŏbis,* saw-dust; *hiems, hiĕmis,* winter; *gens, gentis,* a nation; *stips stĭpis,* alms; *pars, partis,* a part; *sors, sortis,* a lot; *mors, -tis,* death.

Exc. 1.   The following nouns are masculine:

Chălybs, -ўbis, *steel.*　　　Mĕrops, -ŏpis, *a wood-pecker.*
Dens, -tis, *a tooth.*　　　Mons, -tis, *a mountain.*
Fons, -tis, *a well.*　　　Pons, -tis, *a bridge.*
Gryps, grўphis, *a griffin.*　　Seps, sĕpis, *a kind of serpent;* but,
Hydrops, -ōpis, *the dropsy.*　Seps, sĕpis, *a hedge,* is fem.

Exc. 2.   The following are either masc. or feminine:

Adeps, adĭpis, *fatness.*　　Serpens, -tis, *a serpent.*
Rudens, -tis, *a cable.*　　　Stirps, stirpis, *the root of a tree.*
Scrobs, scrŏbis, *a ditch.*　　Stirps, *an offspring,* always fem.

Animans, a living creature, is found in all the genders, but most frequently in the feminine or neuter.

Exc. 3.   Polysyllables in *eps* change *e* into *i*; as, hæc *forceps, forcĭpis,* a pair of tongs; *princeps, -ĭpis,* a prince or princess; *particeps, -cĭpis,* a partaker; so likewise *cælebs, cælĭbis,* an unmarried man or woman. The compounds of *căput* have *cipĭtis*; as, *præceps, præcipĭtis,* headlong; *anceps, ancipĭtis,* doubtful; *biceps, -cipĭtis,* two-headed. *Auceps,* a fowler, has *aucŭpis.*

Exc. 4.   The following feminines have *dis*:

Frons, frondis, *the leaf of a tree.*　　Juglans, dis, *a walnut.*
Glans, glandis, *an acorn.*　　Lens, lendis, *a nit.*

So, *librĭpens, libripendis,* m. a weigher; *nefrens, -dis,* m. or f. a grice, or pig; and the compounds of *cor*; as, *concors, concordis,* agreeing; *discors,* disagreeing; *vĕcors,* mad, &c. But *frons,* the forehead, has *frontis,* fem. and *lens,* a kind of pulse, *lentis,* also fem.

Exc. 5. *Iens,* going; and *quiens,* being able, participles from the verbs *eo* and *queo,* with their compounds, have *euntis*: thus, *iens, euntis*; *quiens, queuntis*; *rĕdiens, redĕuntis*; *nĕquiens, nequeuntis*: but *ambiens,* going round, has *ambientis.*

Exc. 6.

Exc. 6. *Tiryns*, a city in Greece, the birth-place of Hercules, has *Tirynth's*.

T.

15. (There is only one noun in *t*, namely, *căput, capĭtis*, the head, neuter.) In like manner, its compounds, *sincĭput, sincĭpĭtis*, the forehead: and *occĭput, -ĭtis*, the hind-head.

X.

16. Nouns in *x* are feminine, and in the genitive change *x* into *cis*; as,

vox, vōcis, the voice; *lux, lūcis*, light.——So,

Appendix, -ĭcis, an addition; dim. -ĭcŭla.
Arx, arcis, a castle.
Cĕlox, -ōcis, a pinnace.
Cervix, -ĭcis, the neck.
Cĭcātrix, -īcis, a scar.
Cornix, -īcis, a crow.
Cŏturnix, -īcis, a quail.
Coxendix, -īcis, the hip.
Crux, crŭcis, a cross.
Fæx, -cis, dregs.
Falx, -cis, a scythe.
Fax, -ăcis, a torch.
Filix, -īcis, a fern.
Lanx, -cis, a plate.
Lōdix, -īcis, a sheet.
Mēretrix, -īcis, a courtesan.
Merx, -cis, merchandise.
Nutrix, -īcis, a nurse.
Nux, nŭcis, a nut.
Pax, -ācis, peace.
Pix, pĭcis, pitch.
Rādix, -īcis, a root.
Sălix, -īcis, a willow.
Vibix, or -ex, -īcis, the mark of a wound.

Exc. 1. Polysyllables in *ax* and *ex* are masculine; as, *thōrax, -ācis*, a breast-plate; *Cŏrax, -ăcis*, a raven. *Ex* in the genitive is changed into *ĭcis*; as, *pollex, -ĭcis*, m. the thumb.——So the following nouns, also masculine,

Apex, the tuft or tassel on the top of a priest's cap, the cap itself, or the top of any thing.
Artifex, an artist.
Carnifex, an executioner.
Caudex, the trunk of a tree.
Cimex, a bug.
Codex, a book.
Cŭlex, a gnat, a midge.
Frŭtex, a shrub.
Index, an informer.
Lātex, any liquor.
Mūrex, a shell-fish, purple.
Pōdex, the breech.
Pontĭfex, a chief priest.
Pūlex, a flea.
Rūmex, a rupture.
Sōrex, a rat.
Vertex, the crown of the head.
Vortex, a whirlpool.

Vervex, a wedder sheep, has *vervēcis*; *fænisex*, a mower of hay, *fænisēcis*: *Rēsex*, m. -ĕcis, a vine-branch cut off.

To these masculines add,

Călix, -ĭcis, a cup.
Călyx, -ȳcis, the bud of a flower.
Coccyx, -ȳgis, vel -ȳcis, a cuckow.
Fornix, -īcis, a vault.
Oryx, -ȳcis, a wild goat.
Phœnix, -īcis, a bird so called.
Trādux, -ūcis, a graff, or off-set of a vine; also fem.

But

But the following polysyllables in *ax* and *ex* are feminine.

Fornax, -ācis, *a furnace*.
Panax, -ācis, *the herb all-heal*.
Clūnax, -ācis, *a ladder*.
Forfex, -ĭcis, *a pair of scissars*.
Hālex, -ēcis, *a herring*.

Smilax, -ăcis, *the herb rope-weed*.
Cārex, -ĭcis, *a sedge*.
Supellex, supellectilis, *houshold-furniture*.

Exc. 2. A great many nouns in *x* are either masculine or feminine; as,

Calx, -cis, *the heel, or the end of any thing, the goal; but calx, lime, is always fem.*
Cortex, -ĭcis, *the bark of a tree*.
Hyſtrix, -ĭcis, *a porcupine*.
Imbrex, -icis, *a gutter* or *roof-tile*.
Lynx, -cis, *an ounce, a beaſt of a very quick fight*.

Limax, -ăcis, *a snail*.
Obex, -ĭcis, *a bolt or bar*.
Perdix, -ĭcis, *a partridge*.
Pūmex, -ĭcis, *a pumice-ſtone*.
Rūmex, -ĭcis, *sorrel, an herb*.
Sandix, -icis, *a purple colour*.
Silex, -ĭcis, *a flint*.
Vārix, -ĭcis, *a ſwoln vein*.

Exc. 3. The following nouns depart from the general rule in forming the genitive:

Aquĭlex, -ĕgis, *a well-maker*.
Conjunx, *or* -ux, -ūgis, *a huſband* or *wife*.
Frux, *(not uſed)*, frūgis, f. *corn*.
Grex, grĕgis, m. *or* f. *a flock*.
Lex, lēgis, f. *a law*.

Phălanx, -angis, f. *a phalanx*.
Rēmex -ĭgis, *a rower*.
Rex, rēgis, *a king*.
Nix, nĭvis, f. *ſnow*.
Nox, noctis, f. *night*.
Sēnex, sĕnis, (an adj.), *old*.

Exc. 4. Greek nouns in *x*, both with reſpect to gender and declenſion, are as various as Latin nouns: thus, *bombyx, bombȳcis*, a ſilk-worm, maſc. but when it ſignifies ſilk, or the yarn ſpun by the worm, it is feminine; *ŏnyx*, maſc. or fem. *onychis*, a precious-ſtone; and ſo *sardŏnyx; lărynx, laryngis*, fem. the top of the wind-pipe; *Phryx, Phrȳgis*, a Phrygian; *ſphinx, -ngis*, a fabulous hag; *ſtrix, -ĭgis*, f. a ſcreechowl; *Styx, -ȳgis*, f. a river in hell; *Hȳlax, -ctis*, the name of a dog; *Bibrax, Bibractis*, the name of a town, &c.

DATIVE SINGULAR.

The Dative ſingular anciently ended alſo in *e*; as, *Eſurĭente leoni ex ore exculpere prædam*, To pull the prey out of the mouth of a hungry lion, Lucil. *Hæret pede pes*, Foot ſticks to foot. Æn. x. 361. for *eſurienti* and *pedi*.

Ex-

Exceptions in the Accusative Singular.

Exc. 1. The following nouns have the accusative in *im* :

Amuſſis, f. *a maſon's rule.*
Būris, f. *the beam of a plough.*
Gummis, f. *gum.*
Mēphitis, f. *a damp or ſtrong ſmell.*
Rāvis, f. *hoarſeneſs.*
Sınāpis, f. *muſtard.*

Cannăbis, f. *hemp.*
Cŭcŭmis, m. *a cucumber.*
Sĭtis, f. *thirſt.*
Tuſſis, f. *the cough.*
Vis, f. *ſtrength.*

To theſe add proper names, 1. of cities, and other places ; as, *Hiſpălis*, Seville, a city in Spain ; *Syrtis*, a dangerous quickſand on the coaſt of Libya ;—2. of rivers ; as, *Tĭbĕris*, the Tiber, which runs paſt Rome ; *Bætis*, the Guadalquiver in Spain: So *Athĕſis, Arăris, Albis, Liris*, &c.—3. Of gods ; as, *Anūbis, Apis, Oſiris, Serāpis*, deities of the Egyptians. But theſe ſometimes make the accuſative alſo in *in* ; thus, *Syrtim* or *Syrtin*, *Tiberim* or *-in*, &c.

Exc. 2. Several nouns in *is* have either *em* or *im* ; as,

Clāvis, f. *a key.*
Cŭtis, f. *the ſkin.*
Febris, f. *a fever.*
Nāvis, f. *a ſhip.*

Pelvis, f. *a baſon.*
Puppis, f. *the ſtern of a ſhip.*
Reſtis, f. *a rope.*

Sĕcūris, f. *an ax.*
Sēmentis, f. *a ſowing.*
Strigĭlis, f. *a horſe-comb.*
Turris, f. *a tower.*

Thus *navem*, or *navim* ; *puppem*, or *puppim*, &c. The ancients ſaid *avim, aurim, ovim, peſtim, vallim, vitim*, &c. which are not to be imitated.

Exc. 3. GREEK NOUNS form their accuſative variouſly:

1. Greek nouns, whoſe genitive increaſes in *is* or *os* impure, that is, with a conſonant going before, have the accuſative in *em* or *a*, as, *lampas, lampădis*, or *lampădos, lampădem*, or *lampăda*. In like manner, theſe three, which have *is* pure in the genitive, or *is* with a vowel before it : *Tros, Trōis, Troem*, and *Troa*, a Trojan ; *hēros*, a hero ; *Mīnos*, a king of Crete. The three following have almoſt always *a* : *Pan*, the god of ſhepherds ; *æther*, the ſky ; *delphin*, a dolphin ; thus, *Pāna, æthĕra, delphīna.*

2. Maſculine Greek nouns in *is*, which have their genitive in *is* or *os* impure, form the accuſative in *im* or *in* ; ſometimes in *ĭdem*, never *ĭda*, as, *Păris, Paridis* ; or *Parĭdos* ; *Parim*, or *Parin*, ſometimes *Parĭdem*, never *Parĭda*.—So *Daphnis*.

3. Feminines in *is*, increaſing impurely in the genitive, have commonly *ĭdem* or *ĭda*, but rarely *im* or *in* ; as, *Tlis, Elĭdis* or *Elĭdos, Elĭdem* or *Elĭda* ; ſeldom *Elim* or *Elin* ; a city in Greece. In like manner feminines in *ys, ўdos*, have *ўdem*, or *ўda*, not *ym* or *yn* in the accuſative ; as, *chlamys, -ўdem*, or *-ўda*, not *chlamyn*, a ſoldier's cloak.

4. But all Greek nouns in *is* or *ys*, whether maſculine or feminine, having *is* or *os* pure in the genitive, form the accuſative by changing *s* of the nominative into *m* or *n* ; as, *metamorphōſis, -eos*, or *-ios, metamorphōſim* or *-in*, a change : *Tēthys, -yos*, or *-yis, Tēthym*, or *-yn* ; the name of a goddeſs.

5. Nouns ending in the diphthong *eus*, have the accuſative in *ea* : as, *Thēſeus, Thēſea* ; *Tydeus, Tydea*.

EXCEPTIONS in the ABLATIVE SINGULAR.

EXC. 1. Neuters in *e*, *al*, and *ar*, have *i* in the ablative; as, *sedile*, *sedili*; *animal*, *animali*; *calcar*, *calcari*. Except proper names; as, *Praeneste*, abl. *Praeneste*, the name of a town; and the following neuters in *ar*:

Far, farre, *corn*.	Nectar, -are, *drink of the gods*.
Hépar, -ate, *the liver*.	Par, pare, *a match, a pair*.
Jûbar, -are, *a sun beam*.	Sal, sale, *salt*.

EXC. 2. Nouns which have *im* or *in* in the accusative, have *i* in the ablative; as, *vis*, *vim*, *vi*: but *canalis*, *Betis*, and *tigris*, have *e* or *i*.

Nouns which have *im* or *in* in the accusative, make their ablative in *e* or *i*; as, *turris*, *turre*, or *turri*; but *restis*, a rope; and *cutis*, the skin, have *e* only.

Several nouns which have only *em* in the accusative, have *e* or *i* in the ablative; as, *finis*, *supellex*, *vectis*; *pugil*, a champion; *strigil* or *mugilis*; so, *rus*, *occiput*: Also names of towns, when the question is made by *ubi*; as *habitat Carthagine* or *Carthagini*, he lives at Carthage. So, *civis*, *classis*, *fors*, *imber*, *anguis*, *avis*, *postis*, *fustis*, *amnis*, and *ignis*; but these have oftener *e*. *Canalis* has only *i*. The most ancient writers made the ablative of many other nouns in *i*; as, *aetati*, *muni*, *lapidi*, *ovi*, &c.

EXC. 3. Adjectives used as substantives have commonly the same ablative with the adjectives; as, *bipennis*, -*i*, an halbert; *molaris*, -*i*, a millstone; *quadriremis*, -*i*, a ship with four banks of oars. So names of months, *Aprilis*, -*i*; *December*, -*bri*, &c. But *rudis*, f. a rod given to gladiators when discharged; *juvenis*, a young man, have only *e*; and likewise nouns ending in *il*, *x*, *ceps*; or *ns*; as,

Adolescens, *a young man*.	Princeps, *a prince*.	Torrens, *a brook*.
Infans, *an infant*.	Senex, *an old man*.	Vigil, *a watchman*.

Thus, *adolescente*, *infante*, *sene*, &c.

EXC. 4. Nouns in *ys*, which have *yn* in the accusative, make their ablative in *ye* or *y*; as, *Atys*, *Atye*, or *Aty*, the name of a man.

NOMINATIVE PLURAL.

1. The nominative plural ends in *es*, when the noun is either masculine or feminine; as, *sermones*, *rupes*.

Nouns in *is* and *es* have sometimes in the nominative plural also *eis* or *is*, as, *puppes*, *puppeis*, or *puppis*.

2. Neuters

2. Neuters which have *e* in the ablative singular, have *a* in the nominative plural; as, *capĭta, itinĕra:* but those which have *i* in the ablative, make *ia;* as, *sedīlia, calcāria.*

Genitive Plural.

Nouns which in the ablative singular have *i* only, or *e* and *i* together, make the genitive plural in *ium;* but if the ablative be in *e*, the genitive plural has *um;* as, *sedile, sedili, sedilium; turris, turre* or *turri, turrium; caput, capĭte, capĭtum.*

Exc. 1. Monosyllables in *as* have *ium*, though their ablative end in *e;* as, *mas*, a male, *măre, marium; vas*, a surety, *vădium;* but polysyllables have rather *um;* as, *civĭtas*, a state or city, *civitātum*, and sometimes *civitatium.*

Exc. 2. Nouns in *es* and *is*, which do not increase in the genitive singular, have also *ium;* as *hostis*, an enemy, *hostium.* So likewise nouns ending in two consonants; as, *gens*, a nation, *gentium; urbs*, a city, *urbium.*

But the following have *um: parens, vātes, pānis, jŭvĕnis,* and *cănis.*

Exc. 3. The following nouns form the ablative plural in *ium*, though they have *e* only in the ablative singular:

Caro, carnis; f. *flesh.*
Cohors, -tis, f. *a company.*
Cor, cordis, n. *the heart.*
Cos, cotis, f. *a hone or whetstone.*
Dos, dōtis, f. *a dowry.*
Faux, faucis, f. *the jaws.*
Glis, glīris, m. *a rat.*
Lar, laris, m. *a household-god.*
Linter, -tris, m. or f. *a little boat.*

Lis, litis, f. *strife.*
Mus, mūris, m. *a mouse.*
Nix, nivis, f. *snow.*
Nox, noctis, f. *the night.*
Os, ossis, n. *a bone.*
Quīris, -ĭtis, *a Roman.*
Samnis, -ītis, m. or f. *a Samnite.*
Uter, utris, m. *a bottle.*

Thus *Samnitium, lintrium, litium, &c.* Also the compounds of *uncia* and *as;* as, *septunx*, seven ounces, *septuncium; bes*, eight ounces, *bessium. Bes*, an ox or cow, has *boum*, and in the dative, *bōbus* or *būbus.*

Greek nouns have generally *um;* as, *Măcĕdo*, a Macedonian; *Arabs*, an Arabian; *Æthiops*, an Ethiopian; *Mŏnŏcĕros*, an unicorn; *Lynx*, a beast so called; *Thrax*, a Thracian: *Macedŏnum, Arăbum, Æthiŏpum, Monocerōtum, Lyncum, Thracum.* But those which have *a* or *sis* in the nominative singular, sometimes form the genitive plural in *on;* as, *Epigramma, epigrammătum*, or *epigrammatōn*, an epigram; *metamorphosis, -ium*, or *-eōn.*

Obs. 1. Nouns which want the singular, form the genitive plural as if they were complete; thus *mānes*, m. souls departed, *manium; caestes,*

m. inhabitants of heaven, *cælitum;* because they would have had in the sing. *manis* or *manes,* and *cœles.* But names of feasts often vary their declension; as, *Saturnalia,* the feasts of Saturn, *Saturnalium* and *Saturnaliorum.* So, *Bacchanalia, Compitalia, Terminalia,* &c.

Obf. 2. Nouns which have *ium* in the genitive plural, are, by the poets, often contracted into *um;* as, *nocentûm* for *nocentium:* and sometimes, to increase the number of syllables, a letter is inserted; as, *cælituum* for *cælitum.* The former of these is said to be done by the figure *Syncope;* and the latter by *Epenthesis.*

EXCEPTIONS in the DATIVE PLURAL.

Exc. 1. Greek nouns in *a* have commonly *tis* instead of *tibus;* as, *poëma,* a poem, *poematis,* rather than *poematibus,* from the old nominative *poëmatum* of the second decl.

Exc. 2. The poets sometimes form the dative plural of Greek nouns in *si,* or when the next word begins with a vowel, in *sin;* as, *Troäsi* or *Troäsin,* for *Troädibus,* from *Troas, Troadis,* a Trojan woman.

EXCEPTIONS in the ACCUSATIVE PLURAL.

Exc. 1. Nouns which have *ium* in the genitive plural, make their accusative plural in *es, eis,* or *is;* as, *partes, partium,* acc. *partes, parteis,* or *partis.*

Exc. 2. If the accusative singular end in *a,* the accusative plural also ends in *as;* as, *lampas, lampädem,* or *lampäda, lampädes* or *lampädas.* So *Tros, Troas; heros, heroas; Æthiops, Æthiopas,* &c.

(GREEK NOUNS through all the Cases.

Lampas, a lamp, f. *lampädis,* or *-ädos; -ädi, -ädem,* or *-äda; -as; -äde:* Plur. *-ädes; -ädum; -ädibus; -ädes,* or *-ädas; -ädes, -ädibus.*)

Troas, f. *Troädis,* or *-ädos; -i; em* or *a; as; e:* Pl. *Troädes; -um; ibus, si* or *sin; es* or *as, es; ibus.*

Tros, m. *Trois; Troï; Troëm* or *-a; Tros; Troë,* &c.

Phillis, f. *Phillidis* or *-dos, di, dem,* or *da; i* or *is; de.*

Paris, m. *Paridis* or *-dos; di; dem, Parim* or *in; i; de.*

Chlamys, f. *Chlamydis* or *-ydos, ydi, ydem* or *yda, ys, yde,* &c.

Capys, m. *Capyis,* or *-yos; yi; ym* or *yn; y; ye* or *y.*

Metamorphosis, f. *-is* or *-eos, i, em* or *in, i, i,* &c.

Orpheus, m. *-eos, ëi* or *ei, ea, eu,* abl. *eo* of the second decl.

Dido, f. *Didûs* or *Didonis, Dido* or *Didoni,* &c.

FOURTH

Nouns of the fourth declenſion end in *us* and *u*.

Nouns in *us* are maſculine; nouns in *u* are neuter, and indeclinable in the ſingular number.

The terminations of the caſes are; nom. ſing. *us*; gen. *ûs*; dat. *ui*; acc. *um*; voc. *like the num.*; nom. acc. voc. plur. *us* or *ua*; gen. *uum*; dat. and abl. *ibus*; as,

Fructus, *fruit, maſc.*		Cornu, *a horn, neut.*	
Sing.	Plur.	Sing.	Plur.
N. fructus,	*N.* fructus,	*N.* cornu,	*N.* cornua,
G. fructûs,	*G.* fructuum,	*G.* cornu,	*G.* cornuum,
D. fructui,	*D.* fructibus,	*D.* cornu,	*D.* cornibus,
A. fructum,	*A.* fructus,	*A.* cornu,	*A.* cornua,
V. fructus,	*V.* fructus,	*V.* cornu,	*V.* cornua,
A. fructu.	*A.* fructibus.	*A.* cornu.	*A.* cornibus.

In like manner decline,

Aditŭs, *an acceſs.*

Anfractus, *a winding.*

Auditus, *the ſenſe of hearing.* [ſong.

Cautus, *a ſinging* or

Caſus, *a fall, an accident or chance.*

Cæſtus, *a gauntlet.*

Ceſtus, *a marriage-girdle.*

Cœtus, *an aſſembly.*

Cultus, *worſhip, dreſs.*

Currus, *a chariot.*

Curſus, *a race.*

Deceſſus, *a departure.*

Eventus, *an event.*

Exercitus, *an army.*

Exitus, *an iſſue.*

Faſtus, *pride.*

Flātus, *a blaſt.*

Flētus, *weeping.*

Fluctus, *a wave.*

Fœtus, *an offspring.*

Gĕlu, *ice.*

Gĕmitus, *a groan.*

Gradus, *a ſtep, a degree.*

Guſtus, *the taſte.*

Habitus, *a habit, the ſtate of mind or body.*

Halitus, *breath.*

Hauſtus, *a draught.*

Ictus, *a ſtroke.*

Impetus, *an attack.*

Inceſſus, *a ſtately gate.*

Luctus, *grief.*

Luxus, *luxury, riot.*

Metus, *fear.*

Miſſus, *a throw; a turn or beat in races.*

Mōtus, *a motion.*

Nexus, *ſervitude for debt.*

Nŭrus, *a daughter-in-* [law.

Nūtus, *a nod.*

Obtūtus, *a look.*

Ödōrătus, *the ſenſe of ſmelling.*

Paſſus, *a pace.*

Principātus, *pre-eminence.*

Prōceſſus, *a progreſs.*

Progreſſus, *an advancement.*

Proſpectus, *a view.*

Prōventus, *an increaſe, revenue.*

Quæſtus, *gain.*

Queſtus, *a complaint.*

Reditus, *a return; an income.*

Rictus, *a grinning.*

Ritus, *a rite, a ceremo-* [ny.

Riſus, *laughter.*

Ructus, *a belching.*

Saltus, *a leap, a foreſt.*

Sĕnātus, *the ſenate, the ſupreme council among the Romans.*

Senſus, *a ſenſe, feeling, meaning.*

Sexus, *a ſex.*

Sinus, *a boſom.*

Singultus, *a ſob, the hickup.*

Situs, *a ſituation.*

Stătus, *a poſture.*

Socrus, *a mother-in-law.*

Spīrĭtus, *a breathing, ſpirit.*

Succeſſus, *ſucceſs.*

Sumptus, *expenſe.*

Tactus, *the touch.*

Tŏnitru, *thunder.*

Transitus, *a paſſage.*

Tŭmultus, *an uproar.*

Vēnātus, *hunting.*

Viſus, *the ſight.*

Victus, *food.*

Vultus, *the countenance.*

Exc.

Exc. 1. The following nouns are feminine:

Ācus, *a needle.*   Ficus, *a fig.*   Portĭcus, *a gallery.*
Ănus, *an old woman.*   Mănus, *the hand.*   Spĕcus, *a den.*
Dŏmus, *a house.*   Pĕnus, *a storehouse.* Trĭbus, *a tribe.*

Penus and *specus* are sometimes masc. *Ficus, penus,* and *domus,* with several others, are also of the second declension. *Caprĭcornus,* m. the sign Capricorn, although from *cornu,* is always of the second decl. and so are the compounds of *manus; unĭmănus,* having one hand; *centĭmănus,* &c. adj. *Domus* is but partly of the second declension, thus,

(**Dŏmus,** *a house, fem.*

<table>
<tr><td colspan="2">Sing.</td><td colspan="2">Plur.</td></tr>
<tr><td>Nom.</td><td>domus,</td><td>Nom.</td><td>domus,</td></tr>
<tr><td>Gen.</td><td>domûs, or -mi,</td><td>Gen.</td><td>domorum, or -uum,</td></tr>
<tr><td>Dat.</td><td>domui, or -mo,</td><td>Dat.</td><td>domibus,</td></tr>
<tr><td>Acc.</td><td>domum,</td><td>Acc.</td><td>domos, or -us,</td></tr>
<tr><td>Voc.</td><td>domus,</td><td>Voc.</td><td>domus,</td></tr>
<tr><td>Abl.</td><td>domo.</td><td>Abl.</td><td>domibus.)</td></tr>
</table>

Note. Domûs, in the genit. signifies, of a house; and *domi,* at home, or of home; as, *memineris domi.* Terent. iv. 7. 45.

Exc. 2. The following nouns have *ŭbus,* in the dative and ablative plural.

Ācus, *a needle.*   Lăcus, *a lake.*   Spĕcus, *a den.*
Arcus, *a bow.*   Partus, *a birth.*   Trĭbus, *a tribe.*
Artus, *a joint.*   Portus, *a harbour.*   Vĕru, *a spit.*
Gĕnu, *the knee.*

Portus, genu, and *veru,* have likewise *ĭbus;* as, *portĭbus* or *portŭbus.*

Exc. 3. Iɛsus, the venerable name of our Saviour, has *um* in the accusative, and *u* in all the other cases.

Nouns of this declension anciently belonged to the third, and were declined like *grus, gruis,* a crane; thus *fructus, fructuis, fructui, fructuem, fructue; fructues, fructuum, fructuibus, fructues, fructues, fructuibus.* So that all the cases are contracted, except the dative singular, and genitive plural. In some writers, we still find the genitive singular in *uis;* as, *Ejus anuis causâ,* for *anûs.* Terent. Heaut. ii. 3. 46. and in others, the dative in *u;* as, *Resistere impetu,* for *impetui,* Cic. Fam. x. 24. *Esse usu sibi,* for *usui,* Ib. xiii. 71. The gen. plur. is sometimes contracted; as, *currûm* for *curruum.*

FIFTH

FIFTH DECLENSION.

Nouns of the fifth declenfion end in *es*, and are of the feminine gender : as,

Res, *a thing, fem.*

Sing.	Plur.	Terminations.	
Nom. res,	*Nom.* res,	*es*,	*es*,
Gen. rëi,	*Gen.* rērum,	*ëi*,	*erum*,
Dat. rëi,	*Dat.* rēbus,	*ëi*,	*ebus*,
Acc. rem,	*Acc.* res,	*em*,	*es*,
Voc. res,	*Voc.* res,	*es*,	*es*,
Abl. re.	*Abl.* rēbus.	*e*.	*ebus*.

In like manner decline,

Acies, *the edge of a thing, or an army in order of battle.*
Caries, *rottenneſs.*
Cæsaries, *the hair.*
Facies, *the face.*
Glacies, *ice.*

Ingluvies, *gluttony.*
Macies, *leanneſs.*
Materies, *matter.*
Pernicies, *deſtruction.*
Proluvies, *a looſeneſs.*
Rabies, *madneſs.*
Sanies, *gore.*

Scabies, *the ſcab, or itch.*
Series, *an order.*
Species, *an appearance.*
Superficies, *the ſurface.*
Temperies, *temperateneſs:*

Except *dies*, a day, maſc. or fem. in the ſingular, and always maſc. in the plural; and *meridies*, the mid-day, or noon, maſc.

The poets ſometimes make the genitive, and more rarely the dative, in *e*.

The nouns of this declenfion are few in number, not exceeding fifty, and ſeem anciently to have been comprehended under the third declenfion. Moſt of them want the genitive, dative, and ablative plural, and many the plural altogether.

All nouns of the fifth declenfion end in *ies*, except three, *fides*, faith; *ſpes*, hope; *res*, a thing: and all nouns in *ies* are of the fifth, except theſe four, *abies*, a fir-tree; *aries*, a ram; *paries*, a wall; and *quies*, reft; which are of the third declenſion.

IRREGULAR NOUNS.

Irregular nouns may be reduced to three claſſes, *Variable*, *Defective*, and *Redundant*.

I. VARIABLE NOUNS.

Nouns are variable, either in gender, or declenfion, or in both.

I. Thoſe which vary in gender are called *heterogeneous*, and may be reduced to the following claſſes :

1. *Maſculine*

1. *Masculine in the singular, and neuter in the plural:*

Avernus, *a lake in Campania, hell.*
Dindўmus, *a hill in Phrygia.*
Ismărus, *a hill in Thrace.*
Massĭcus, *a hill in Campania, fa-mous for excellent wines.*
Mænălus, *a hill in Arcadia.*
Pangæus, *a promontory in Thrace.*
Tænărus, *a promontory in Laconia.*
Tartărus, *hell.*
Taygĕtus, *a hill in Laconia.*

Thus, *Averna, Avernorum; Dindyma, -orum, &c.* These are thought by some to be properly adjectives, having *mons* understood in the singular, and *juga* or *cacumĭna*, or the like, in the plural.

2. *Masc. in the sing. and in the plur. masc. and neuter.* Jŏcus, a jest, pl. *joci* and *joca;* lŏcus, a place, pl. *loci* and *loca.* When we speak of passages in a book, or topics in discourse, *loci* only is used.

3. *Feminine in the singular, and neuter in the plural:* Carbăsus, a sail, pl. *carbăsa; Pergămus,* the citadel of Troy, pl. *Pergama.*

4. *Neuter in the singular, and masculine in the plural:* Cælum, pl. *cœli,* heaven; Elўsium, pl. *Elysii,* the Elysian fields; *Argos,* pl. *Argi,* a city in Greece.

5. *Neuter in the sing. in the plur. masc. or neuter:* Rastrum, a rake, pl. *rastri* and *rastra;* frēnum, a bridle, pl. *freni* and *frena.*

6. *Neuter in the singular, and feminine in the plural:* Dēlĭcium, a delight, pl. *deliciæ;* Ěpŭlum, a banquet, pl. *ěpŭla; Balneum,* a bath, pl. *balnea* and *balnea.*

II. Nouns which vary in declension are called *heteroclites;* as, *vas, vāsis,* a vessel, plur. *vāsa, vasorum; jūgĕrum, jugĕri,* an acre, plur. *jūgĕra, jūgĕrum, jugerĭbus,* which has likewise sometimes *jugĕris* and *jugĕre* in the singular, from the obsolete *jugus,* or *juger.*

II. Defective Nouns.

Nouns are defective, either in cases or in number.
Nouns are defective in cases different ways.)

1. Some are altogether indeclinable; as, *pondo,* a pound or pounds; *fas,* right; *něfas,* wrong; *sināpi,* mustard; *māne,* the morning; as *clārum māně,* Pers. *A mane ad vesperam,* Plaut. *Multo mane,* &c.; *cēpe,* an onion; *gau-sāpe,*

sāga, a rough coat, &c.; all of them neuter. We may rank among indeclinable nouns, any word put for a noun; as, *velle suum*, for *sua voluntas*, his own inclination, *Perf.* *Istud cras*, for *iste crastinus dies*, that to-morrow. *Mart.* *O magnum Græcorum*, the *Omĕga*, or the large O of the Greeks; Infīdus *est compositum ex* in *et* fīdus; *infidus* is compounded of *in* and *fidus*. To these add foreign or barbarous names; that is, names which are neither Greek nor Latin, as *Job, Elisabet, Jerusalem*, &c.

2. ❙ Some are used only in one case, and therefore called *mŏnoptōta:* as, *inquies*,❙ want of rest, in the nominative singular; *dīcis*, and *nauci*, in the genit. sing.; thus, *dicis gratiâ*, for form's sake; *res nauci*, a thing of no value; *infĭcias*, and *incĭta* or *incĭtas*, in the acc. plur.; thus *ire infĭcias*, to deny; *ad incitas redactus*, reduced to a strait or non-plus; *ingrātiis*, in the abl. plur. in spite of one; and these ablatives singular, *noctu*, in the night-time; *diu, interdiû*, in the day-time; *promptu*, in readiness; *nātu*, by birth; *injussu*, without command or leave: *ergô* for the sake, as, *ergo illius*, Virg. *Ambāge*, f. with a winding or a tedious story; *Compĕde*, m. with a fetter; *Casse*, m. with a net; *veprem*, m. a briar: Plur. *Ambāges, -ĭbus; compedes, -ĭbus; casses, -ium; vepres, -ium*, &c.

3. ❙ Some are used in two cases only, and therefore called *diptōta*;❙ as, *nĕcesse* or *-um*, necessity; *vŏlŭpe* or *volup*, pleasure; *instar*, likeness, bigness; *astu*, a town; *hir*, the palm of the hand; in the nom. and acc. sing.; *vesper*, m. abl. *vespĕre* or *vespĕri*, the evening; *siremps*, the same, all alike, abl. *sirempse; spontis*, f. in the genitive, and *sponte* in the ablative. of its own accord: so *impĕtis*, m. and *impĕte*, force; *verbĕris*, n. genit. and *verbĕre*, abl. a stripe; in the plural entire; *verbĕra, verberum, verberĭbus*, &c. *rĕpĕtundarum*, abl. *repetundis*, sc. *pecuniis*, money unjustly taken in the time. of one's office, extortion; *suppĕtiæ*, nom. plur. *suppĕtias*, in the acc. help; *infĕriæ, inferias*, sacrifices to the dead.

4. ❙ Several nouns are only used in three cases, and therefore called *triptōta*;❙ as, *prĕcī, precem, prece*, f. a prayer, from *prex*, which is not used: in the plural it is entire, *preces, precum, precibus*, &c. *Fĕmĭnis*, gen. from the obsolete *femen*, the thigh; in the dat. and abl. sing.; in the

nom.

nom. acc. and voc. plur. *femina*. *Dīca*, a procefs, acc. fing. *dicam*, pl. *dicas*; *tantundem*, nom. and acc. *tantīdem*, genit. even as much. Several nouns in the plural want the genitive, dative, and ablative; as, *hiems*, *rus*, *thus*, *mĕtus*, *mel*, *far*, and moft nouns of the fifth declenfion.

To this clafs of defective nouns may be added thefe neuters, *mĕlos*, a fong; *mĕle*, fongs; *ĕpos*, a heroic poem; *cacoēthes*, an evil cuftom; *cēte*, whales; *Tempe*, plur. a beautiful vale in Theffaly, &c. ufed only in the nom. acc. and voc.; alfo *grātes*, f. thanks.

5. [The following nouns want the nominative, and of confequence the vocative, and therefore are called *tetraptōta* :] *vĭcis*, f. of the place or ftead of another; *pĕcŭdis*, f. of a beaft; *fordis*, f. of filth; *ditiōnis*, f. of dominion, power; *ŏpis*, f. of help. Of thefe *pĕcŭdis* and *fordis* have the plural entire: *ditiōnis* wants it altogether :: *vĭcis* is not ufed in the genitive plural; *ŏpis* in the plural, generally fignifies wealth, or power, feldom help. To thefe add *nex*, flaughter; *daps*, a difh of meat; and *frux*, corn; hardly ufed in the nominative fingular, but in the plural moftly entire.

6. [Some nouns only want one cafe, and are called *periptōta* :] thus, *os*, the mouth; *lux*, light; *fax*, a torch, together with fome others, want the genitive plural. *Chaos*, n. a confufed mafs, wants the genit. fing. and the plural entirely; dat. fing. *chao*. So *sătias*, i. e. *satietas*, a glut or fill of any thing. *Sĭtus*, a fituation, naftinefs, of the fourth decl. wants the gen. and perhaps the dat. fing. alfo the gen. dat. and abl. plur.

Of nouns defective in number there are various forts.

1. Several nouns want the plural, from the nature of the things which they exprefs. Such are the names of virtues and vices, of arts, herbs, metals, liquors, different kinds of corn, moft abftract nouns, &c. as, *juftītia*, juftice; *ambītus*, ambition; *aftus*, cunning; *mūsĭca*, mufic; *ăpium*, parfley; *argentum*, filver; *aurum*, gold; *lac*, milk; *trītĭcum*, wheat; *hordeum*, barley; *ăvēna*, oats; *jŭventus*, youth, &c. But of thefe we find feveral fometimes ufed in the plural.

2. The

2. The following masculines are hardly ever found in the plural :

Aër, aëris, *the air.*
Æther, -ëris, *the sky.*
Fĭmus, -i, *dung.*
Hespĕrus, -i, *the evening star.*
Limus, -i, *slime.*
Mĕridies, -iëi, *mid-day.*
Mundus, *a woman's ornaments.*
Muſcus, -i, *moss.*

Nēmo, -ĭnis, *no body.*
Pĕnus, -i, *or* -ūs, *all manner of provisions.*
Pontus, -i, *the sea.*
Pulvis, -ĕris, *dust.*
Sanguis, -ĭnis, *blood.*
Sŏpor, -ōris, *sleep.*
Viſcus, -i, *bird-lime.*

3. The following feminines are scarcely used in the plural :

Argilla, -æ, *potters earth.*
Fāma, -æ, *fame.*
Hŭmus, -i, *the ground.*
Lues, -is, *a plague.*
Plebs, plēbis, *the common people.*
Pūbes, -is, *the youth.*
Quies, -ētis, *rest.*

Sălus, -ūtis, *safety.*
Sĭtis, -is, *thirst.*
Sŭpellex, -ĕtilis, *household-furniture.*
Tābes, -is, *a consumption.*
Tellus, -ūris, *the earth.*
Vespĕra, -æ, *the evening.*

4. These neuters are seldom used in the plural :

Album, -i, *a list of names.*
Dilūcŭlum, -i, *the dawning of day.*
Ebur, -ōris, *ivory.*
Gĕlu, *ind. frost.*
Hīlum, -i, *the black speck of a bean, a trifle.*
Juſtītium, -i, *a vacation, the time when courts do not sit.*
Lēthum, *death.*

Lūtum, -i, *clay.*
Nihil, nihĭlum, *or* nil, *nothing.*
Pĕlăgus, -i, *the sea.*
Pĕnum, -i, *and* penus, -ŏris; *all kind of provisions.*
Sal, sălis, *salt.*
Sĕnium, -ii, *old age.*
Ver, vēris, *the spring.*
Vīrus, -i, *poison.*

5. Many nouns want the singular; as the names of feasts, books, games, and several cities; thus,

Apollĭnāres, -ium, *games in honour of Apollo.*
Bacchānālia, -ium, & -iorum, *the feasts of Bacchus.* [*erals.*
Būcŏlĭca, -orum, *a book of pastorals.*

Ōlympia, -orum, *the Olympic games.*
Syracūſæ, -arum, *Syracuse.*
Hierŏsŏlyma, -orum, *Jerusalem;* or, Hierŏsŏlyma, -æ, *of the first declension.*

6. The following masculines are hardly used in the singular :

Cancelli, *lattices, or windows, made with cross bars like a net; a rail or balustrade round any place; bounds or limits.*
Cāni, *grey hairs.*
Casses, -ium, *a hunter's net.*

Cĕlĕres, -um, *the light-horse.*
Cōdĭcilli, *writings.*
Druĭdes, -um, *the Druids, priests of the ancient Britons and Gauls.*
Fasces, -ium, *a bundle of rods, carried before the chief magistrates of Rome.*

Fasti,

Faſti, -orum, *or* faſtus, -uum, *ca-*
lendars, in which were marked
feſtival days, the names of magi-
ſtrates, &c.
Fines, -ium, *the borders of a coun-*
try, or a country.
Föri, *the gang-ways of a ſhip, ſeats*
in the Circus, or the cells of a bee-
hive.
Furfüres, -um, *ſcales in the head.*
Inféri, *the gods below.*

Lēmŭres, -um, *hobgoblins, or ſpi-*
rits in the dark.
Lībĕri, *children.*
Majōres, -um, *anceſtors.*
Mïnōres, -um, *ſucceſſors.*
Nātāles, -ium, *parentage.*
Poſtĕri, *poſterity.*
Prōcĕres, -um, *the nobles.*
Pŭgillāres, -ium, *writing-tables.*
Sentes, -ium, *thorns.*
Sŭpĕri, *the gods above.*
Vepres, -ium, *briars.*

7. The following feminines want the ſingular number :

Alpes, -ium, *the Alps.*
Anguſtiæ, *difficulties.*
Ăpinæ, *gewgaws.*
Argūtiæ, *quirks, wit-*
ticiſms.
Bīgæ, *a chariot drawn*
—by two horſes.
Trīgæ, —— *by three.*
Quadrigæ, ——*by four.*
Braccæ, *breeches.*
Branchiæ, *the gills of*
a fiſh.
Charites, -um, *the three*
graces.
Cūnæ, *a cradle.*
Dĕcĭmæ, *tithes.*
Dīræ, *imprecations, the*
furies.
Dīvitiæ, *riches.*
Dryădes, -um, *the*
nymphs of the woods.
Excŭbiæ, *watches.*
Exŏquiæ, *funerals.*
Exŭviæ, *ſpoils.* [*ings.*
Făcĕtiæ, *pleaſant ſay-*
Făcultates, -ium, *one's*
goods and chattels.

Fēriæ, *holidays.*
Gādes, -ium, *Cadiz.*
Gerræ, *trifles.*
Hyădes, -um, *the ſeven*
ſtars.
Indŭciæ, *a truce.*
Indŭviæ, *cloaths to put*
on.
Ineptiæ, *ſilly ſtories.*
Insīdiæ, *ſnares.*
Kălendæ, Nōnæ, Ĭ-
dus, -uum, *names*
which the Romans
gave to certain days
in each month.
Lăpĭcīdīnæ, *ſtone-*
quarries.
Lĭtĕræ, *an epiſtle.*
Lactes, -ium, *the ſmall*
guts.
Mănūbiæ, *ſpoils taken*
in war.
Mĭnæ, *threats.*
Mĭnŭtiæ, *little niceties.*
Nūgæ, *trifles.*
Nundĭnæ, *a market.*
Nuptiæ, *a marriage.*

Offūciæ, *cheats.*
Ŏpĕræ, *workmen.*
Părĭĕtĭnæ,   *ruinous*
walls.
Partes, -ium, *a party.*
Phălĕræ, *trappings.*
Plăgæ, *nets.*
Pleiădes, -um, *the ſe-*
ven ſtars.   [*ments.*
Preſtigiæ,   *enchant-*
Prīmĭtiæ, *firſt fruits.*
Quiſquĭliæ, *ſweepings.*
Rĕlĭquiæ, *a remainder.*
Sălebræ, *rugged places.*
Sălīnæ, *ſalt-pits.*
Scālæ, *a ladder.*
Scătebræ, *a ſpring.*
Scōpæ, *a beſom.*
Tĕnebræ, *darkneſs.*
Thermæ, *hot baths.*
Thermŏpўlæ, *ſtraits of*
mount Oeta.
Trīcæ, *toys.*
Valvæ, *folding doors.*
Vergĭliæ, *the ſeven ſtars.*
Vindĭciæ, *a claim of*
liberty, a defence.

8.   The following neuter nouns want the ſingular :

Acta, *public acts or records.*
Æſtīva, ſc. caſtra, *ſummer quarters.*
Arma, *arms.*
Bellāria, -orum, *ſweet meats.*
Bona, *goods.*
Brĕvia, -ium, *ſhelves.*

Caſtra, *a camp.*
Chăriſtia, -orum, *a peace-feaſt.*
Cĭbāria, *victuals.*
Cōmĭtia, *an aſſembly of the people,*
to make laws, elect magiſtrates,
or hold trials.

Crĕpundia,

Crĕpundia, *children's baubles.*
Cūnābŭla, *a cradle, an origin.*
Dictĕria, *scoffs, witticisms.*
Exta, *the entrails.*
Februa, -orum, *purifying sacrifices.*
Flabra, *blasts of wind.*
Frāga, *strawberries.*
Hỹberna, sc. castra, *winter quarters.*
Ilia, -ium, *the entrails.*
Incūnābŭla, *a cradle.*
Insecta, *insects.*
Justa, *funeral rites.*
Lāmenta, *lamentations.*
Lautia, *provisions for the entertain-*
  ment of foreign ambassadors.
Lustra, *dens of wild beasts.*
Māgālia, -ium, *cottages.*
Mœnia, -ium, *the walls of a city.*
Mūnia, -iorum, *offices.*
Orgia, *the sacred rites of Bacchus.*
Ōvīlia, -ium, *an inclosure, where the*
  people went to give their votes.
Pāleāria, -ium, *the dew-lap of a beast.*
Pārāpherna, *all things the wife*
  brings her husband except her
  dowry.
Pārentālia, -ium, *solemnities at the*
  funeral of parents.
Philtra, *love potions.*
Præcordia, *the bowels.*
Princĭpia, *the place in the camp*
  where the general's tent stood.
Pỹthia, *games in honour of Apollo.*
Rostra, *a place in Rome made of the*
  beaks of ships, from which orators
  used to make orations to the people.
Scrūta, *old cloaths.*
Sponsālia, -ium, *espousals.*
Stătīva, sc. castra, *a standing camp.*
Suŏvĕtaurīlia, -ium, *a sacrifice of*
  a swine, a sheep, and an ox.
Tālāria, -ium, *winged shoes.*
Tesqua, *rough places.*
Transtra, *the seats where the rowers*
  sit in ships.
Ūtensília, -ium, *utensils.*

Several nouns in each of the above lists are found also in the fingular, but in a different fenfe; thus, *caftrum*, a caftle; *litera*, a letter of the alphabet, &c.

III. REDUNDANT NOUNS.

Nouns are redundant in different ways: 1. In termination only; as, *arbos* and *arbor*, a tree. 2. In declenfion only; as, *laurus*, genit. *lauri*, and *laurûs*, a laurel tree, *sĕquefter*, -tri, or -tris, a mediator. 3. Only in gender; as, hic or hoc *vulgus*, the rabble. 4. Both in termination and declenfion; as, *mătĕria*, -æ, or, *materies*, -iēi, matter; *plebs*, -is, the common people, or *plebes*, -is, -ēi, or contracted, *plebi*. 5. In termination and gender; as, *tŏnitrus*, -ûs, mafc. *tonitru*, neut. thunder. 6. In declenfion and gender; as, *pĕnus*, -i, and -ûs, m. or f. or *penus*, -ŏris, neut. all kind of provifions. 7. In termination, gender, and declenfion; as, *æther*, -ĕris, mafc. and *æthra*, -æ, fem. the fky. 8. Several nouns in the fame declenfion are differently varied; as, *tigris*, -is, or *ĭdis*, a tyger: to which may be added, nouns which have the fame fignification in different numbers; as, *Fĭdēna*, -æ; or *Fidenæ*, -arum, the name of a city.

The moft numerous clafs of redundant nouns confifts of thofe which exprefs the fame meaning by different terminations; as, *menda*, -æ; and *mendum*, -i, a fault; *caffis*, -ĭdis; and *cafsĭda*, -dæ, a helmet.——So,

Acĭnus,

Acĭnus, & -um, *a grape-ſtone.*
Alvear, & -e, & -ium, *a bee-hive.*
Amărăcus, & -um, *ſweet mar-
joram.*
Ancīle, & -ium, *an oval ſhield.*
Angĭportus, -ûs, & -i, & -um,
a narrow lane.
Aphractus, & -um, *an open ſhip.*
Apluſtre, & -um, *the flag, colours.*
Băcŭlus, & -um, *a ſtaff.*
Balteus, & -um, *a belt.*
Bătillus, & -um, *a fire-ſhovel.*
Căpŭlus, & -um, *a hilt.*
Căpus, & -o, *a capon.*
Cēpa, & -e, indec. *an onion.*
Clypeus, & -um, *a ſhield.*
Collŭvies, & -io, *filth, dirt.*
Compāges, & -go, *a joining.*
Conger, & -grus, *a large eel.*
Crŏcus, & -um, *ſaffron.*
Cŭbĭtus, & -um, *a cubit.*
Dilŭvium, & -es, *a deluge.*
Ĕlĕphantus, & Ĕlephas, -antis, *an
elephant.*
Ĕlĕgus, & -ëia, *an elegy.*
Eſsĕda, & -um, *a chariot.*
Eventus, & -um, *an event.*
Fulgetra, & -um, *lightning.*
Gălērus, & -um, *a hat.*
Gibbus, & -a; & -er, -ĕris, or
-ĕri, *a bunch, a ſwelling.*
Glūtĭnum, & -en, *glue.*

Hebdŏmas, & -ăda, *a week.*
Intrīta, & -um, *fine mortar, mixed
meat.*
Librārium, & -a, *a book-caſe.*
Mācĕria, & -es, iĕi, *a wall.*
Milliāre, & -ium, *a mile.*
Mŏnĭtum, & -us, -ûs, *an admo-
nition.*
Muria, & -es, -iĕi, *brine* or *pickle.*
Nāſus, & -um, *the noſe.*
Obsĭdio, & -um, *a ſiege.*
Oeſtrus, & -um, *a gad bee.*
Oſtrea, & -um, *an oyſter.*
Peplus, & -um, *a veil, a robe.*
Piſtrīna, & -um, *a bake-houſe.*
Prætextus, -us, & -um, *a pretext.*
Rāpa, & -um, *a turnip.*
Rūma, & -men, *the cud.*
Ruſcus, & -um, *a bruſh.*
Seps, & sēpes, f. *an hedge.*
Segmen, & -mentum, *a piece* or
paring.
Sĭbĭlus, & -um, *a hiſſing.*
Sīnus, & -um, *a milk-pail.*
Spurcĭtia, & -es, *naſtineſs.*
Strāmen, & -tum, *ſtraw.*
Suffīmen, & -tum, *a perfume.*
Tignus, & -um, *a plank.*
Tŏral, & -āle, *a bed-covering.*
Torcŭlar, & -are, *a wine-preſs.*
Viſcus, & -um, *bird lime.*
Vĕternus, and -um, *a lethargy.*

Note. The nouns which are called variable and defective, ſeem
originally to have been redundant: thus *vāſa, -orum,* properly comes
from *vaſum,* and not from *vas;* but cuſtom, which gives laws to all
languages, has dropt the ſingular, and retained the plural; and ſo
of others.

*Diviſion of Nouns according to their ſignification and deriva-
tion.*

1. ❙ A ſubſtantive which ſignifies many in the ſingular
number, is called a *Collective* noun; as, *pŏpŭlus,* a people;
exercĭtus, an army.

2. ❙ A ſubſtantive derived from another ſubſtantive proper, ſignifying one's extraction, is called a *Patronymic*
noun; as, *Priămĭdes,* the ſon of Priamus; ❙ *Æëtias,* the
daughter

daughter of Æëtes ; *Nērīnē*, the daughter of Nereus. Patronymics are generally derived from the name of the father ; but the poets, by whom they are chiefly ufed, derive them alfo from the grandfather, or from fome other remarkable perfon of the family ; fometimes likewife · from the founder of a nation or people ; as, *Æăcĭdes*, the fon, grandfon, great-grandfon, or one of the pofterity of *Æăcus* ; *Rŏmŭlīdæ*, the Romans, from their firft king Romulus.

/ Patronymic names of men end in *des* ; of women, in *is*, *as*, or *ne*. Thofe in *des* and *ne* are of the firft declenfion, and thofe in *is* and *as*, of the third ; as, *Priamides*, *dæ*, &c. pl. *-dæ*, *darum*, &c. ; *Nērīne*, *es* : *Tyndăris*, *-ĭdis* or *-ĭdos* ; *Æëtias*, *-ădis*, &c.)

3. / A noun derived from a fubftantive proper, fignifying one's country, is called a *Patrial* or *Gentile* noun ; as, *Tros*, *Trois*, a man born at Troy ;) *Troas*, *-ădis*, a woman born at Troy. *Sicŭlus*, *-i*, a Sicilian man ; *Sicĕlis*, *-ĭdis*, a Sicilian woman : fo, *Măcĕdo*, *-ŏnis* ; *Arpīnas*, *-ātis*, a man born in Macedonia, Arpinum ; from *Troja*, *Sicilia*, *Măcedonia*, *Arpinum*. But patrials for the moft part are to be confidered as adjectives, having a fubftantive underftood, as, *Romānus*, *Athēnienfis*, &c.

4. / A fubftantive derived from an adjective, expreffing fimply the quality of the adjective, without regard to the thing in which the quality exifts, is called an *Abftract* ;/ as *juftitia*, juftice ; *bŏnĭtas*, goodnefs ; *dulcēdo*, fweetnefs : from *juftus*, juft ; *bonus*, good ; *dulcis*, fweet. The adjectives from which thefe abftracts come, are called *Concretes* ; becaufe, befides the quality, they alfo fuppofe fomething · to which it belongs. Abftracts commonly end in *a*, *as*, or *do*, and are very numerous, being derived from moft adjectives in the Latin tongue.

5. I A fubftantive derived from another fubftantive, fignifying a diminution or leffening of its fignification, is called a *Diminutive*/; as, *libellus*, a little book ; *chartŭla*, a little paper ; *ŏpufculum*, a little work ; *corcŭlum*, a little heart ; *rētĭculum*, a fmall net ; *fcăbellum*, a fmall form ; *lăpillus*, a little ftone ; *cultellus*, a little knife ; *păgella*, a little

little page : from *liber, charta, ŏpus, cor, rēte, scamnum, lă-pis, culter, pāgĭna.* Several diminutives are sometimes formed from the same primitive ; as, from *puer, pucrŭlus, puellus, puellŭlus ;* from *cifta, cifiŭla, cifiella, cifiellŭla ;* from *hŏmo, hŏmuncio, hŏmunculus.* Diminutives for the moft part end in *lus, la, lum ;* and are generally of the fame gender with their primitives. When the fignification of the primitive is increafed, it is called an *Amplificative,* and ends in o*, as, *Căpĭto, -ōnis,* having a large head : So, *nāfo, lăbeo, bucco,* having a large nofe, lips, cheeks.

6. A fubftantive derived from a verb is called a *Verbal* noun ; as, *ămor,* love ; *doărĭna,* learning : from *ămo,* and *dŏceo.* Verbal nouns are very numerous, and commonly end in *io, or, us,* and *ura ;* as, *lĕĕio,* a leffon ; *ămātor,* a lovér ; *luĕus,* grief, *creātūra,* a creature.

ADJECTIVE.

An adjective is a word *added* to a fubftantive, to exprefs its quality ; as, *hard, foft.*

We know things by their qualities only. Every quality muft belong to fome fubjeĕ. An adjeĕive therefore always implies a fubftantive expreffed or underftood, and cannot make full fenfe without it.

An adjeĕive may be thus diftinguifhed from a fubftantive : If the word *thing* be joined to an adjeĕive, it will make fenfe ; but if it be joined to a fubftantive, it will make nonfenfe : thus we can fay, " a good thing ;" but we cannnot fay, " a book thing."

Adjeĕives in Englifh admit of no variation, except that of the degrees of comparifon.

LATIN ADJECTIVES.

Adjeĕives in Latin are varied by gender, number, and cafe, to agree with fubftantives in all thefe accidents.

An adjeĕive properly hath neither genders, numbers, nor cafes; but certain terminations anfwering to the gender, number, and cafe of the fubftantive with which it is joined.

Adjeĕives are varied like three fubftantives of the fame termination and declenfion.

All adjeĕives are either of the firft and fecond declenfion, or of the third only.

Adjeĕives of three terminations are of the firft and fecond declenfion ; but adjeĕives of one or two terminations are of the third.

Exc.

Exc. The following adjectives, though they have three terminations, are of the third declension.

Ācer, *sharp.*
Ālācer, *cheerful.*
Campester, *belonging to a plain.*
Cĕlĕber, *famous.*
Cĕler, *swift.* [*horse.*
Ĕquester, *belonging to a*
Păluster, *marshy.*
Pĕdester, *on foot.*
Sălŭber, *wholesome.*
Sylvester, *woody.*
Vŏlŭcer, *swift.*

Adjectives of the First and Second Declension.

(Adjectives of the first and second declension have their masculine in *us* or *er*, their feminine always in *a*, and their neuter always in *um*; as, *bŏnus*, for the masc. *bona*, for the fem. *bonum*, for the neut. good : thus,)

	Sing.				Plur.		
N. bŏn-us,	-a,	-um,		*N.* bon-i,	-æ,	-a,
G. bon-i,	-æ,	-i,		*G.* bon-orum,	-arum,	-orum,
D. bon-o,	-æ,	-o,		*D.* bon-is,	-is,	-is,
A. bon-um,	-am,	-um,		*A.* bon-os,	-as,	-a,
V. bon-e,	-a,	-um,		*V.* bon-i,	-æ,	-a,
A. bon-o,	-â,	-o.		*A.* bon-is,	-is,	-is.

In like manner decline,

Acerbus, *unripe, bitter.*
Acĭdus, *sour, tart.*
Acūtus, *sharp.*
Adultĕrīnus, *counterfeit.*
Ægrōtus, *sick.*
Æmŭlus, *vying with.*
Æquus, *equal, just.*
Ahēnus, *of brass.*
Albus, *white.*
Altus, *high.*
Amārus, *bitter.*
Amœnus, *pleasant.*
Ambĭguus, *doubtful.*
Amīcus, *friendly.*
Amplus, *large.*
Annuus, *yearly.*
Angustus, *narrow.*
Antīquus, *ancient.*
Aprīcus, *sunny.*
Aptus, *fit.*
Arcānus, *secret.*

Arctus, *strait.*
Arduus, *lofty.*
Argūtus, *quick, shrill.*
Assus, *roasted, hot, pure.*
Astūtus, *cunning.*
Avārus, *covetous.*
Avĭdus, *greedy.*
Augustus, *venerable.*
Austĕrus, *harsh, rough.*
Balbus, *stammering.*
Barbărus, *savage.*
Bardus, *dull, slow.*
Beātus, *blessed.*
Bellus, *pretty.*
Bĕnignus, *kind.*
Bimus, *two years old.*
Blæsus, *lisping.*
Blandus, *flattering.*
Brūtus, *brutish, senseless.*
Cădūcus, *fading.*

Cæcus, *blind.*
Callĭdus, *cunning.*
Calvus, *bald.*
Cămŭrus, *crooked.*
Candĭdus, *fair, sincere.*
Cānus, *hoary.*
Cārus, *dear.*
Cassus, *void.*
Castus, *chaste.*
Cautus, *wary.*
Căvus, *hollow.*
Celsus, *high, lofty.*
Cernuus, *stooping.*
Certus, *certain, sure.*
Clārus, *famous.*
Claudus, *lame.*
Cœrŭlus, *or* -ĕus, *azure, sky coloured.*
Commŏdus, *convenient.*
Concinnus, *fine, neat.*
Cŏruscus, *glittering.*
Crassus, *thick.*

G

Crĕpĕrus,

Crĕpĕrus, *doubtful.*
Crĭſpus, *curled.*
Crŭdus, *raw.*
Cunctus, *all.*
Curtus, *ſhort.*
Curvus, *crooked.*
Cўnĭcus, *churliſh.*
Dædălus, poet. *curiouſly made.*
Dĕcōrus, *graceful.*
Denſus, *thick.*
Dignus, *worthy.*
Dīrus, *direful.*
Dīſertus, *eloquent.*
Diŭturnus, *laſting.*
Doctus, *learned.*
Dŭbius, *doubtful.*
Dūrus, *hard.*
Ebrius, *drunk.*
Effætus, *paſt having young.*
Egēnus, *poor.*
Egrĕgius, *remarkable.*
Elixus, *boiled.*
Exĭguus *ſmall.*
Exĭmius, *excellent.*
Exōtĭcus, *from a foreign country.*
Externus, *outward.*
Făcētus, *witty.*
Fācundus, *eloquent.*
Falſus, *falſe, lying.*
Fămēlĭcus, *famiſhed.*
Fătuus, *fooliſh.*
Fauſtus, *lucky.*
Fĕrus, *wild, ſavage.*
Feſſus, *weary.*
Feſtīnus, *haſtening.*
Feſtus, *feſtival.*
Fīdus, *faithful.*
Finítĭmus, *neighbouring.*
Firmus, *firm, ſteady.*
Flaccus, *flap-eared.*
Flāvus, *yellow.*
Fœdus, *ugly.*
Fœtus, *big with young.*
Formōſus, *fair.*

Frētus, *truſting.*
Frīvŏlus, *trifling.*
Fulvus, *yellow.*
Furvus, *ſwarthy.*
Fuſcus, *brown.*
Garrŭlus, *prattling.*
Gĕlĭdus, *cold as ice.*
Gĕmĭnus, *double.*
Germānus, *of the ſame ſtock, real.*
Gibbus, *convex.*
Gilvus, *fleſh-coloured.*
Glaucus, *grey.*
Gnārus, *ſkilful.*
Gnāvus, *active.*
Grātus, *thankful.*
Hirſūtus, hirtus, *rough.*
Hiſpĭdus, *rugged.*
Hŏneſtus, *honourable, honeſt.*
Hornus, *of this year.*
Hūmānus, *human, belonging to a man: humane, polite.*
Hūmĭdus, *moiſt.*
Idōneus, *fit.*
Jejūnus, *faſting.*
Ignārus, *ignorant.*
Ignāvus, *ſlothful.*
Imprŏbus, *wicked.*
Inceſtus, *unchaſte.*
Inclўtus, *renowned.*
Indĭgus, *needy.*
Induſtrius, *diligent.*
Ineptus, *unfit.*
Infīdus, *unfaithful.*
Ingĕnuus, *free-born.*
Inĭmīcus, *unfriendly.*
Inīquus, *unever, unjuſt.*
Intentus, *intenſe, ſtrait.*
Invĭdus, *envious.*
Invītus, *unwilling.*
Irācundus, *paſſionate.*
Irātus, *angry*
Irrĭtus, *fruitleſs, vain.*
Jūcundus, *pleaſant.*
Lætus, *joyful.*
Lævus, *on the left hand.*

Largus, *large.*
Laſcīvus, *wanton.*
Laſſus, *weary.*
Lātus, *broad.*
Laxus, *looſe, ſlack.*
Lentus, *ſlow, pliant.*
Lĕpĭdus, *pretty, witty.*
Limpĭdus, *clear, pure.*
Limus, *ſquinting.*
Lippus, *blear-eyed.*
Longinquus, *far off.*
Longus, *long.*
Lubrĭcus, *ſlippery.*
Lūcĭdus, *bright.*
Lūridus, *pale, ghaſtly.*
Luſcus, *blind of one eye.*
Măcĭlentus, *lean.*
Mălignus, *ſpiteful.*
Mancus, *maimed, lame.*
Mănĭfeſtus, *evident.*
Marcĭdus, *rotten.*
Mĕdius, *mid or middle.*
Mendīcus, *beggar-like.*
Menſtruus, *monthly.*
Mĕrācus, *without mixture.*
Mĕrus, *pure.*
Mīrus, *wonderful.*
Mŏdeſtus, *modeſt.*
Mœſtus, *ſad.*
Mŏleſtus, *troubleſome.*
Mōrōſus, *ſurly.*
Mōrus, *fooliſh.*
Mūcĭdus, *muſſy.*
Mundus, *neat.*
Mŭtĭlus, *maimed, without horns.*
Mūtus, *dumb.*
Mūtuus, *mutual, lent or borrowed.*
Nĭmius, *too much.*
Noxius, *hurtful.*
Nūdus, *naked.*
Nuntius, *bringing news*
Obēſus, *fat, dull.*
Oblīquus, *crooked.*
Obſcænus, *obſcene, ominous.*

Obſcūrus, *dark, mean.*
Obſolētus, *old, out of uſe.*
Obſtīpus, *ſtiff, wry.*
Obtūſus, *blunt.*
Odiōſus, *hateful.*
Opācus, *dark, ſhady.*
Opīmus, *rich, fat.*
Opīpărus, *coſtly, dainty.*
Opportūnus, *ſeaſonable.*
Opŭlentus, v.-ens, *rich.*
Orbus, *deſtitute.*
Otiōſus, *at leiſure.*
Pætus, *pink-eyed.*
Pallĭdus, *pale.*
Parcus, *ſparing.*
Patrīmus, } *having father and*
Matrīmus, } *mother alive.*
Pătŭlus, *wide, ſpreading.*
Paulus, *little.*
Pauci, -cæ, -ca, *few.*
Pĕrītus, *ſkilful.*
Perfĭdus, *treacherous.*
Perpĕtuus, *continual.*
Perſpĭcuus, *evident.*
Pius, *pious.*
Plānus, *plain.*
Plēnus, *full.*
Plērīque, -æque, -ăque, *the moſt part:* ſing. fem. plerăque.
Poſticus, *on the back part of a houſe.*
Præditus, *endued with.*
Prāvus, *wicked.*
Prĕcārius, *at another's pleaſure.*
Priſcus, *old, out of uſe.*
Priſtĭnus, *ancient.*
Prīvātus, *private, retired.*
Prīvus, *ſingle, peculiar.*
Prŏbus, *good, honeſt.*
Prōcērus, *high, tall.*
Prŏfānus, *profane, unholy.*

Prŏfundus, *deep.*
Prōmiſcuus, *confuſed.*
Promptus, *ready.*
Prōnus, *with the face downward.*
Prŏpĕrus, *haſty.*
Prŏpinquus, *near.*
Proprius, *proper.*
Prŏtervus, *ſaucy.*
Pŭblĭcus, *public.*
Pŭdĭcus, *chaſte.*
Pullus, *blackiſh.*
Pūrus, *pure, clean.*
Pūtus, *without mixture.*
Quantus, *how great.*
Quadrīmus, *four years old.*
Quŏtīdiānus, *daily.*
Rābĭdus, *mad.*
Rancĭdus, *rank, ſtale.*
Rārus, *rare, thin.*
Raucus, *hoarſe.*
Rectus, *right, ſtraight.*
Reus, *impeached.*
Rĭgĭdus, *cold, ſtiff, ſevere.*
Rĭguus, *moiſt, well watered.*
Rōbuſtus, *ſtrong.*
Roſcĭdus, *dewy.*
Rŏtundus, *round.*
Rŭbĭcundus, *bluſhing.*
Rūfus, *reddiſh.*
Ruſſus, *of a carnation colour.*
Rŭtĭlus, *fiery, red.*
Sævus, *cruel.*
Sāgus, *knowing.*
Salſus, *ſalted, ſmart.*
Salvus, *ſafe.*
Sanctus, *holy.*
Sānus, *ſound.*
Saucius, *wounded.*
Scævus, *left.*
Scambus, *bow-legged.*
Scaurus, *club-footed.*
Sĕcūrus, *ſecure, out of danger.*
Sēdŭlus, *careful.*

Sentus, *rough.*
Sĕrēnus, *clear.*
Sĕrius, *earneſt.*
Sērus, *late.*
Sĕvērus, *ſevere, harſh.*
Siccus, *dry.*
Sīmus, *flat-noſed.*
Sincērus, *ſincere, pure.*
Situs, *ſituate, placed.*
Sobrius, *ſober, temperate.*
Sŏcius, *in alliance, a companion.*
Sŏlĭdus, *ſolid.*
Sordidus, *dirty.*
Spīnōſus, *prickly.*
Spiſſus, *thick.*
Splendĭdus, *bright.*
Spŭrius, *baſe-born, not genuine.*
Squālĭdus, *naſty.*
Stŏlĭdus, *fooliſh.*
Strēnuus, *active, ſtout.*
Strĭgōſus, *lean, lank.*
Stultus, *fooliſh.*
Stŭpĭdus, *ſtupid, dull.*
Sŭbĭtus, *ſudden.*
Subſĕcīvus, *cut off, or taken from other buſineſs.*
Sūdus, *fair, without clouds.*
Sŭperbus, *proud.*
Sŭpīnus, *lying on the back.*
Surdus, *deaf.*
Tăcĭtus, *ſilent.*
Tantus, *ſo great.*
Tardus, *ſlow.*
Tĕmĕrārius, *raſh.*
Tempeſtīvus, *ſeaſonable.*
Tĕmŭlentus, *drunken.*
Tĕpĭdus, *lukewarm.*
Tĭmĭdus, *fearful.*
Torvus, *ſtern.*
Tranquillus, *calm.*
Trĕpĭdus, *trembling for fear.*

Trŭcŭlentus,

Trŭcŭlentus, *cruel.*	Văcuus, *empty, void.*	Verbofus, *talkative.*
Truncus, *maimed, wanting.*	Văgus, *wandering.*	Vĭrēcundus, *bafhful.*
Túmĭdus, *fwollen.*	Vălgus, *bow-legged.*	Vernăcŭlus, *born in one's houfe.*
Turbĭdus, *muddy.*	Vălĭdus, *ftrong.*	Vērus, *true.*
Tūtus, *fafe.*	Vānus, *vain, empty.*	Vefcus, *fit for eating.*
Udus, *wet.*	Vărius, *various, dif-ferent.*	Vicīnus, *neighbouring.*
Uncus, *crooked.*	Vărus, *bandy-legged.*	Vĭduus, *deprived.*
Unĭcus, *only.*	Vaftus, *huge.*	Viētus, *withered.*
Urbānus, *courteous.*	Vēgĕtus, *vigorous.*	Vīvĭdus, *lively.*
Văcĭvus, *at leifure.*	Venuftus, *comely.*	Vīvus, *alive.*

Tĕner, tenĕra, tenĕrum, *tender.*

	Sing.				*Plur.*	
N. ten-er,	-ĕra,	-ĕrum,	*N.* ten-ĕri,	-ĕræ,	-ĕra,
G. ten-ĕri,	-ĕræ,	-ĕri,	*G.* ten-eroum,	-erarum,	-erorum,
D. ten-ero,	-eræ,	-ero,	*D.* ten-eris,	-eris,	-eris,
A. ten-erum,	-eram,	-erum,	*A.* ten-eros,	-eras,	-era,
V. ten-er,	-era,	-erum,	*V.* ten-eri,	-eræ,	-era,
A. ten-ero,	-erâ,	-ero.	*A.* ten-eris,	-eris,	-eris.

In like manner decline,

Afper, *rough.*	Lăcer, *torn.*	Mĭfer, *wretched.*
Ceter, *(hardly ufed) the reft.*	Liber, *free.*	Profper, *profperous.*
Gibber, *crook-backed.*		

Alfo the compounds of *gero* and *fero* ; as, *lānĭger,* bearing wool : *ŏpĭfer,* bringing help, &c. Likewife, *sătur, fŏtŭra, fatŭrum,* full. But moft adjectives in *er* drop the *e ;* as, *āter, atra, atrum,* black : gen, *atri, atræ, atri ;* dat, *atro, atræ, atro,* &c.——So,

Æger, *fick.*	Măcer, *lean.*	Săcer, *facred.*
Crĕber, *frequent.*	Nĭger, *black.*	Scăber, *rough.*
Glăber, *fmooth.*	Pĭger, *flow.*	Tēter, *ugly.*
Intĕger, *entire.*	Pulcher, *fair.*	Văfer, *crafty.*
Lūdĭcer, *ludicrous.*	Rŭber, *red.*	

Dexter, *right,* has -tra, trum, *or* -tĕra, -tĕrum.

Obf. I. (The following adjectives have their genitive fin-gular in *ius,* and the dative in *i,* through all the genders : in the other cafes like *bonus* and *tener.*

Unus, -a, -um ; *gen.* unius, *dat.* uni, *one.*)	Alter, altĕrĭus, *one of two, the other.*
Alius, -ĭus, *one of many, another.*	Neuter, -trius, *neither.*
Nullus, nullius, *none.*	Uter, utrius, *whether of the two.*
Solus, -ius, *alone.*	Uterque, utriufque, *both.*
Tōtus, -ius, *whole.*	Uterlĭbet, -triuflĭbet, } *which of*
Ullus, -ius, *any.*	Utervis, -triufvis, } *the two you pleafe*

Alterŭter, *the one or the other*, alterutrius, alterutri, *and ſometimes* alterius utrius, alteri utri, &c.

Theſe adjectives, except *totus*, are called *Partitives*; and ſeem to reſemble, in their ſignification as well as declenſion, what are called pronominal adjectives. In ancient writers we find them declined like *bonus*.

Obſ. 2. To decline an adjective properly, it ſhould always be joined with a ſubſtantive in the different genders; as *bonus liber*, a good book; *bona penna*, a good pen; *bonum ſedile*, a good ſeat. But as the adjective in Latin is often found without its ſubſtantive joined with it, we therefore, in declining *bonus*, for inſtance, commonly ſay, *bonus* a good man, underſtanding *vir* or *homo*; *bona*, a good woman, underſtanding *fæmina*; and *bonum*, a good thing, underſtanding *negotium*.

ADJECTIVS of the THIRD DECLENSION.

1. Adjectives of one termination; as *felix*, for the maſc. *felix*, for the fem. *felix*, for the neut. happy; thus,

	Sing.				*Plur.*		
N.	fēl-ix,	-ix,	-ix,	*N.*	fel-ices,	-ices,	-icia,
G.	fel-īcis,	-īcis,	-īcis,	*G.*	fel-icium,	-icium,	-icium,
D.	fel-ici,	-ici,	-ici,	*D.*	fel-icibus,	-icibus,	-icibus,
A.	fel-icem,	-icem,	-ix,	*A.*	fel-ices,	-ices,	-icia,
V.	fel-ix,	-ix,	-ix,	*V.*	fel-ices,	-ices,	-icia,
A.	fel-ice, *or* -ici, &c.			*A.*	fel-icibus,	-icibus,	-icibus.

In like manner decline,

Āmens, -tis, *mad.*	Fallax, *deceitful.*	Prūdens, *prudent.*
Atorx, -ōcis, *cruel.*	Fĕrax, *fertile.*	Rĕcens, *freſh.*
Audax, -ācis, & -ens, -tis, *bold.*	Fĕrox, *fierce.*	Rĕpens, *ſullen.*
Bĭlix, -īcis, *woven with a double thread.*	Frequens, *frequent.*	Sāgax, -ācis, *ſagacious.*
Cāpax, *capacious.*	Ingens, *huge.*	Sălax, -acis, *luſtful.*
Cĭcur, -ŭris, *tame.*	Iners, -tis, *ſluggiſh.*	Sāpiens, *wiſe.*
Clēmens, -tis, *merciful.*	Infons, *guiltleſs.*	Sōlers, *ſhrewd.*
Contŭmax, *ſtubborn.*	Mendax, *lying.* [cal.	Sons, *guilty.*
Dēmens, *mad.*	Mordax, *biting, ſatiri-*	Tĕnax, *tenacious.*
Edax, *gluttonous.*	Pernix, -īcis, *ſwift.*	Trux, -ŭcis, *cruel.*
Efficax, *effectual.*	Pervĭcax, *wilful.*	Ūber, -ĕris, *fertile.*
Elĕgans, *handſome.*	Pĕtŭlans, *forwards, ſaucy.*	Vehemens, *vehement.*
	Prægnans, *with child.*	Vēlox, -ōcis, *ſwift.*
		Vŏrax, *devouring.*

2. Adjectives of two terminations; as, *mitis*, for the maſc. and fem. *mite*, for the neut. meek; ſo, *mitior*, *mitior*, *mitius*, meeker) thus,

Sing.

	Sing.			*Plur.*		
N.	mītis,	mitis,	mite,	*N.*	mītes,	mites,	mitia,
G.	mitis,	mitis,	mitis,	*G.*	mitium,	mitium,	mitium,
D.	miti,	miti,	miti,	*D.*	mitibus,	mitibus,	mitibus,
A.	mitem,	mitem,	mite,	*A.*	mites,	mites,	mitia,
V.	mitis,	mitis,	mite,	*V.*	mites,	mites,	mitia,
A.	miti,	miti,	miti.	*A.*	mitibus,	mitibus,	mitibus.)

In like manner decline;

Agĭlis, *aſtive.*	Ignōbĭlis, *of mean pa-*	Rŭdis, *raw.*
Ămābĭlis, *lovely.*	*rentage.*	Sagax, *ſhrewd.*
Biennis, *of two years.*	Immānis, *huge, cruel.*	Segnis, *ſlow.*
Brĕvis, *ſhort.*	Inānis, *empty.*	Sōlennis, *annual, ſo-*
Cīvīlis, *courteous.*	Incŏlŭmis, *ſafe.*	*lemn.*
Cœleſtis, *heavenly.*	Infāmis, *infamous.*	Stĕrīlis, *barren.*
Cōmis, *mild, affable.*	Inſignis, *remarkable.*	Suāvis, *ſweet.*
Crūdēlis, *cruel.*	Jūgis, *perpetual.*	Sublīmis, *lofty.*
Dehĭlis, *weak.*	Lævis, *ſmooth.*	Suhtīlis, *ſubtile, fine.*
Dēformis, *ugly.*	Lēnis, *gentle.*	Tālis, *ſuch.*
Dŏcĭlis, *teachable.*	Lĕvis, *light.*	Tĕnuis, *ſmall.*
Dulcis, *ſweet in taſte.*	Mĕdiocris, *middling.*	Terreſtris, *earthly.*
Exīlis, *ſlender.*	Mīrābĭlis, *wonderful.*	Terribĭlis, *dreadful.*
Exſanguis, *bloodleſs.*	Mollis, *ſoft.*	Triſtis, *ſad.*
Fortis, *brave.*	Omnis, *all.*	Turpis, *baſe.*
Frăgĭlis, *brittle.*	Pernix, *ſwift, fleet.*	Ūtĭlis, *uſeful.*
Grandis, *great.*	Putris, *rotten.*	Vīlis, *worthleſs.*
Grăvis, *heavy.*	Pinguis, *fat.*	Vĭrĭdis, *green.*
Hĭlăris, *cheerful.*	Quālis, *of what kind.*	Vītĭlis, *pliant.*

	Sing.			*Plur.*		
N.	mīti-or,	-or,	-us,	*N.*	miti-ōres,	-ōres,	-ŏra,
G.	miti-ōris,	-ōris,	-ōris,	*G.*	miti-orum,	-orum,	-orum,
D.	miti-ori,	-ori,	-ori,	*D.*	miti-oribus,	-oribus,	-oribus,
A.	miti-orem,	-orem,	-us,	*A.*	miti-ores,	-ores,	-ora,
V.	miti-or,	-or,	-us,	*V.*	miti-ores,	-ores,	-ora,
A.	miti-ore, *or* -ori, *&c.*			*A.*	miti-oribus,	-oribus,	-oribus.)

In this manner all comparatives are declined.

3. Adjectives of three terminations; as, *ācer*, or *acris*, for the maſc. *acris*, for the fem. *acre*, for the neut. ſharp; thus,

	Sing.			*Plur.*		
N.	ā-cer *or* ācris,	acris,	acre,	*N.*	a-cres,	-cres,	-cria,
G.	a-cris,		-cris,	-cris,	*G.*	a-crium,	-crium,	-crium,
D.	a-cri,		-cri,	-cri,	*D.*	a-crĭbus,	-cribus,	-cribus,
A.	a-crem,		-crem,	-cre,	*A.*	a-cres,	-cres,	-cria,
V.	a-cer, *or* acris,	-cris,	-cre,	*V.*	a-cres,	-cres,	-cria,
A.	a-cri,		-cri,	-cri.	*A.*	a-cribus,	-cribus,	-cribus)

In

In like manner *ălăcer* or *alacris*, *cĕler* or *celĕris*, *cĕlĕber* or *celebris*, *sălūber* or *falūbris*, *volŭcer* or *volucris*, &c.

RULES.

1. Adjectives of the third declension have *e* or *i* in the ablative singular: but if the neuter be in *e*, the ablative has *i* only.

2. The genitive plural ends in *ium*, and the neuter of the nominative, accusative, and vocative, in *ia :* except comparatives, which have *um* and *a.*

EXCEPTIONS.

EXC. 1. *Dīves, hofpes, fofpes, sŭperfles, jŭvĕnis, sĕnex,* and *pauper,* have *e* only in the ablative singular, and consequently *um* in the genitive plural.

EXC. 2. The following have also *e* in the abl. sing, and *um*, not *ium*, in the genit. plur. *Compos, -ŏtis,* master of, that hath obtained his defire; *impos, -ŏtis,* unable; *inops, -ŏpis,* poor; *fupplex, -ĭcis,* suppliant, humble; *uber, -ĕris,* fertile; *confors, -tis,* sharing, a partner; *dĕgĕner, -ĕris,* degenerate, *or* degenerating; *vĭgil,* watchful; *pūber, -ĕris,* of age, marriageable; and *celer :* Also compounds in *ceps, fex, pes,* and *corpor ;* as, *partĭceps,* partaking of; *artĭfex, -ĭcis,* cunning, an artift ; *bĭpes, -pĕdis,* two-footed; *bĭcorpor, -ŏris,* two-bodied, &c. All thefe have feldom the neut. sing. and almoft never the neut. plur. in the nominative and accusative. To which add *mĕmor,* mindful, which has *memŏri,* and *memŏrum :* also *dīses, rĕjes, bĭbes, perpes, prăpes, tĕres, concŏlor, versĭcŏlor,* which likewife for the moft part want the genitive plural.

EXC. 3. *Par,* equal, has only *pări :* but its compounds have either *e* or *i;* as *compăre,* or *-ri. Vetus,* old, has *vetĕra,* and *vetĕrum : plus,* more, which is only ufed in the neut. sing. has *plure :* and in the plural, *plūres, plura,* or *pluria, plurium.*

EXC. 4. *Exfpes,* hopelefs; and *pŏtis, -e,* able, are only ufed in the nominative. *Potis* has alfo fometimes *potis* in the neuter.

REMARKS.

1. Comparatives, and adjectives in *ns,* have *e* more frequently than *i;* and participles in the ablative called abfolute have generally *e;* as, *Tiberio regante,* not *reganti,* in the reign of Tiberius.

2. Adjectives joined with fubstantives neuter for the moft part have *i;* as, *victrici ferro,* not *victrice.*

3. Different words are fometimes ufed to exprefs the different genders; as, *victor,* victorious, for the mafc. *victrix,* for the fem. *Victrix,* in the plur. has likewife the neuter gender; thus, *victrices, victricia :* fo alfo; and *ultrix,* revengeful. *Victrix* is alfo neut. in the fingular.

4. Several

4. Several adjectives compounded of *clivus*, *frenum*, *bacillum*, *arma*, *jugum*, *limus*, *somnus*, and *animus*, end in *is* or *us*; and therefore are either of the first and second declension, or of the third; as, *declivis*, *-is*, *-e*; and *declivus*, *-a*, *-um*, steep; *imbecillis*, and *imbecillus*, weak; *semisomnis*, and *semisomnus*, half-asleep; *exanimis*, and *exanimus*, lifeless. But several of them do not admit of this variation; thus we say *magnanimus*, *flexanimus*, *effrenus*, *levisomnus*, not *magnanimis*, &c. On the contrary, we say, *pusillanimis*, *injugis*, *illimis*, *insomnis*, *exsomnis*; not *pusillanimus*, &c. So *semianimis*, *inermis*, *sublimis*, *acclivis*, *declivis*, *proclivis*; rarely *semianimus*, &c.

5. Adjectives derived from nouns are called *Denominatives*; as *cordatus*, *moratus*, *cœlestis*, *adamantinus*, *corporius*, *agrestis*, *æstivus*, &c. from *cor*, *mos*, *cœlum*, *adamas*, &c. Those which diminish the signification of their primitives are called *Diminutives*; as, *misellus*, *parvulus*, *duriusculus*, &c. Those which signify a great deal of a thing are called *Amplificatives*, and end in *osus* or *entus*; as, *vinosus*, *vinulentus*, given to much wine; *operosus*, laborious; *plumbosus*, full of lead; *nodosus*, knotty, full of knots; *corpulentus*, corpulent, &c. Some end in *tus*; as, *auritus*, having long or large ears; *nasutus*, having a large nose; *literatus*, learned, &c.

6. An adjective derived from a substantive or from another adjective, signifying possession or property, is called a *Possessive adjective*; as, *Scoticus*, *paternus*, *herilis*, *alienus*, of or belonging to Scotland, a father, a master, another: from *Scotia*, *pater*, *herus*, and *alius*.

7. Adjectives derived from verbs are called *Verbals*; as, *amabilis*, amiable; *capax*, capable; *docilis*, teachable: from *amo*, *capio*, *doceo*.

8. When participles become adjectives, they are called *Participials*; as, *sapiens*, wise; *acutus*, sharp; *disertus*, eloquent. Of these many also become substantives; as, *adolescens*, *animans*, *rudens*, *serpens*, *advocatus*, *sponsus*, *natus*, *legatus*; *sponsa*, *nata*, *serta*, sc. *corona*, a garland; *prætexta*, sc. *vestis*; *debitum*, *decretum*, *præceptum*, *fatum*, *tectum*, *votum*, &c.

9. Adjectives derived from adverbs, are called *Adverbials*; as, *hodiernus*, from *hodie*; *crastinus*, from *cras*; *binus*, from *bis*; &c. There are likewise adjectives derived from prepositions; as, *contrarius*, from *contra*; *anticus*, from *ante*; *posticus*, from *post*.

NUMERAL ADJECTIVES.

Adjectives which signify number, are divided into four classes, *Cardinal*, *Ordinal*, *Distributive*, and *Multiplicative*.

1. The *Cardinal* or *Principal* numbers are:

Unus,	*one.*	Septem,	*seven.*
Duo,	*two.*	Octo,	*eight.*
Tres,	*three.*	Novem,	*nine.*
Quatuor,	*four.*	Decem,	*ten.*
Quinque,	*five.*	Undecim,	*eleven.*
Sex,	*six.*	Duodecim,	*twelve.*

Tredecim,

Trĕdĕcim,	*thirteen.*	Nōnaginta,	*ninety.*
Quatuordecim,	*fourteen.*	Centum,	*a hundred.*
Quindecim,	*fifteen.*	Dŭcenti,	*two hundred.*
Sexdecim;	*sixteen.*	Trecenti,	*three hundred.*
Septendecim,	*seventeen.*	Quadr̆ingenti,	*four hundred.*
Octŏdĕcim,	*eighteen.*	Quĭngenti,	*five hundred.*
Nŏvemdecim,	*nineteen.*	Sexcenti,	*six hundred.*
Vīginti,	*twenty.*	Septingenti,	*seven hundred.*
Viginty unus, or }		Octingenti,	*eight hundred.*
Unus & viginti, } *twenty-one.*		Nongenti,	*nine hundred.*
Viginti duo, or }		Mille,	*a thousand.*
Duo & viginti, } *twenty-two.*		Duo millia, or } *two thousand.*	
Trĭginta,	*thirty.*	bis mille, }	
Quadrāginta,	*forty.*	Dĕcem millia, or } *ten thousand.*	
Quinquāginta,	*fifty.*	dĕcies mille, }	
Sexāginta,	*sixty.*	Viginti millia, or } *twenty thousand.*	
Septuāginta,	*seventy.*	vicies mille, }	
Octŏginta,	*eighty.*		

The Cardinal numbers, except *unus* and *mille*, want the singular.

Unus is not used in the plural, unless when joined with a substantive which wants the singular; as, *in unis ædibus*, in one house, *Terent. Eun.* ii. 3. 75. *Unæ nuptiæ*, Id. *And.* iv. 1. 51. *In una mœnia convenêre*, Sallust; *Cat.* 6. or when several particulars are considered as one whole; as, *una vestimenta*, one suit of cloaths, *Cic. Flacc.* 29.

Duo and *tres* are thus declined:

	Plur.				*Plur.*	
N. duo,	duæ,	duo,		N. tres,	tres,	tria;
G. duōrum,	duārum,	duōrum,		G. trium,	trium,	trium,
D. duōbus,	duābus,	duōbus,		D. tribus,	tribus,	tribus,
A. duos *or* duo,	duas,	duo,		A. tres,	tres,	tria,
V. duo,	duæ,	duo,		V. tres,	tres,	tria,
A. duobus,	duabus,	duobus.		A. tribus,	tribus,	tribus.

In the same manner with *duo*, decline *ambo*, both.

All the Cardinal numbers from *quatuor* to *centum*, including them both, are indeclinable; and from *centum* to *mille*, are declined like the plural of *bonus*; thus, *ducenti*, *-tæ*, *-ta*; *ducentorum*, *-tarum*, *-torum*, &c.

Mille is used either as a substantive or adjective; when taken substantively it is indeclinable in the singular number; and in the plural has *millia*, *millium*, *millibus*, &c.

Mille, an adjective, is commonly indeclinable, and to express more than one thousand, has the numeral adverbs joined with it; thus, *mille homines*, a thousand men; *mille hominum*, of a thousand men, &c. *Bis mille homines*, two thousand men; *ter mille homines*, &c. But with *mille*, a substantive, we say *mille hominum*, a thousand men: *duo millia hominum*, *tria millia*, *quatuor millia*, *centum* or *centena millia hominum*; *Decies centena millia*, a million; *Vicies centena millia*, two millions, &c.

2. The

2. *The Ordinal numbers are, primus, firſt; sĕcundus,
second, &c. declined like bonus.*

3. *The diſtributive are, fingŭli, one by one; bĭni, two
by two, &c. declined like the plural of bonus.*

The following Table contains a liſt of the Ordinal and Diſtributive
Numbers, together with the Numeral Adverbs, which are often
joined with the Numeral Adjectives.

	Ordinal.	*Diſtributive.*	*Numeral Adverbs.*
1	Primus, a, um.	Singŭli, æ, a.	Semel, once.
2	sĕcundus.	bĭni.	bis, twice.
3	tertius.	terni.	ter, thrice.
4	quartus.	quaterni.	quater, four times.
5	quintus.	quĭni.	quinquies, &c.
6	fextus.	seni.	fexies.
7	septĭmus.	septēni.	septies.
8	octāvus.	octōni.	octies.
9	nōnus.	nŏvēni.	novies.
10	dĕcĭmus.	dēni.	dĕcies.
11	undĕcimus.	undēni.	undecies.
12	duodecimus.	duodēni.	duodecies.
13	decimus tertius.	trĕdēni, terni deni.	tredecies.
14	decimus quartus.	quaterni deni.	quatuordecies.
15	decimus quintus.	quindeni.	quindecies.
16	decimus fextus.	feni deni.	fexdecies.
17	decimus feptimus.	septeni deni.	decies ac fepties.
18	decimus octavus.	octoni deni.	decies ac octies.
19	decimus nonus.	noveni deni.	decies et novies.
20	vīgefimus, vīcefimus.	vīcēni.	vicies.
21	vīgefimus primus.	vīcēni finguli.	vicies femel.
30	trigefimus, tricefimus.	trĭceni.	trīcies.
40	quadrāgefimus.	quadrāgēni.	quadrāgies.
50	quinquagefimus.	quinquāgeni.	quinquagies.
60	fexagefimus.	fexāgeni.	fexagies.
70	feptuagefimus.	feptuāgeni.	feptuagies.
80	octogefimus.	octogeni.	octōgies.
90	nonagefimus.	nonageni.	nonagies.
100	centefimus.	centeni.	centies.
200	dŭcentefimus.	dŭcēni.	dūcenties.
300	trĕcentefimus.	trĕcenteni.	trĕcenties.
400	quadringentefimus.	quāter centeni.	quadringenties.
500	quingentefimus.	quinquies centeni.	quingenties.
600	fexcentefimus.	fexies centeni.	fexcenties.
700	feptingentefimus.	fepties centeni.	feptingenties.
800	octingentefimus.	octies centeni.	octingenties.
900	nongentefimus.	novies centeni.	nōningenties.
1000	millefimus.	millēni.	millies.
2000	bis millefimus.	bis milleni.	bis millies.

4. The

4. The multiplicative numbers are *fimplex*, fimple ; *duplex*, double, *or* two-fold ; *triplex*, triple, *or* three-fold ; *quadruple*, four-fold, &c. ; all of them declined like *felix* ; thus, *fimplex*, *-icis*, *&c.*

The interrogative words, to which the above numerals anfwer, are *quot*, *quŏtus*, *quŏtēni*, *quŏties*, and *quŏtŭplex.*

Quot, how many ? is indeclinable : So *Tot*, fo many ; *tŏtīdem*, juft fo many ; *quotquot*, *quotcunque*, how many foever ; *aliquot*, fome.

To thefe numeral adjectives may be added fuch as exprefs divifion, proportion, time, weight, &c. as, *bĭpartītus*, *trĭpartītus*, *&c. duplus*, *triplus*, *&c. bimus*, *trīmus*; *&c. biennis*, *triennis*, *&c. bīmeſtris*, *trimeſtris*, *&c. bilibris*, *trilibris*, *&c. bīnārius*, *ternarius*, *&c.* which laft are applied to the number of any kind of things whatever ; as *verfus ſēnārius*, a verfe of fix feet ; *dēnārius nummus*, a coin of ten affes ; *octogenarius senex*, an old man eighty years old ; *grex centenarius*, a flock of an hundred, &c.

COMPARISON of ADJECTIVES.

The comparifon of adjectives exprefſes the quality in different degrees ; as, *hard, harder, hardeſt.*

Thofe adjectives only are compared, whofe fignification admits the diftinction of *more* and *lefs.*

The degrees of comparifon are three, the *Pofitive, Comparative*, and *Superlative.*

The *Pofitive* feems improperly to be called a degree. It fimply fignifies the quality : as, *durus*, hard : and ferves only as a foundation for the other degrees. By it we exprefs the relation of equality ; as *he is as* tall *as I.*

The *Comparative* exprefſes a greater degree of the quality, and has always a reference to a lefs degree of the fame ; as, *ſtronger, wifer.*

The *Superlative* exprefſes the quality carried to the greateft degree ; as, *ſtrongeſt, wifeſt.*

Comparifon of ENGLISH Adjectives.

In Englifh the comparative is formed from the pofitive, by adding to the end of the word *r* or *er*; and the fuperlative by adding *ſt* or *eſt* ; as, *wife, wifer, wifeſt* ; *cold, colder, coldeſt.* The adverbs *more* and *moſt*, put before the adjective, have the fame effect ; as *brave, more brave, moſt brave.*

Monofyllables for the moft part are compared by *er* and *eſt* ; as, *fair, fairer, faireſt* ; and polyfyllables by *more* and *moſt* ; as, *beautiful, more beautiful, moſt beautiful.*

In fome few adjectives, the fuperlative is formed by adding *moſt* ; as, *undermoſt, uttermoſt, or utmoſt, uppermoſt, nethermoſt, foremoſt.*

Comparifon

Comparison of LATIN Adjectives.

The comparative degree is formed from the first case of the positive in *i*, by adding the syllable *or*, for the masculine and feminine, and *us* for the neuter: The superlative is formed from the same case, by adding *ssĭmus*; as, *Altus*, high, genit. *alti* : Comparative *altior*, for the masc. *altior*, for the fem. *altius*, for the neut. higher; Superlative, *altissĭmus*, *-a*, *-um*, highest. So *mītus*, meek; dat. *miti* : *mitior*, *-or*, *-us*, meeker : *mitissĭmus*, *-a*, *-um*, meekest.

If the positive end in *er*, the superlative is formed by adding *rĭmus*; as, *pauper*, poor ; *pauperrĭmus*, poorest.

The comparative is always of the third declension : The superlative of the first and second ; as, *altus*, *altior*, *altissĭmus* ; *alta*, *altior*, *altissĭma* ; *altum*, *altius*, *altissĭmum* ; gen. *alti*, *altiōris*, *altissĭmi*, &c.

Irregular and defective Comparison.

1.
Bonus,	mělior,	optĭmus,	good,	better,	best.
Mălus,	pejor,	pessĭmus,	bad,	worse,	worst.
Magnus,	major,	maxĭmus,	great,	greater,	greatest.
Parvus,	mĭnor,	minĭmus,	small,	less,	least.
Multus,	———	plurĭmus,	much,	more,	most.

Fem. Multa, plurima ; *neut.* multum, plus, plurimum ; *plur.* multi, plures, plurimi ; multæ, plures, plurimæ, &c.

In several of these, both in English and Latin, the comparative and superlative seem to be formed from some other adjective, which in the positive has fallen into disuse : in others, the regular form is contracted ; as, *maximus*, for *magnissimus* ; *most*, for *morest* ; *least*, for *lessest* ; *worst*, for *worsest*.

2. These five have their superlative in *lĭmus* ;

Făcĭlis, facilior, facillĭmus, *easy*.
Grăcĭlis, gracilior, gracillĭmus, *lean*.
Hŭmĭlis, humilior, humillĭmus, *low*.
Imbēcillis, imbecillior, imbecillĭmus, *weak*.
Sĭmĭlis, similior, simillĭmus, *like*.

3. The following adjectives have regular comparatives, but form the superlative differently ;

Cĭter, citerior, citimus, *near*.
Dexter, dexterior, dextĭmus, *right*.
Sĭnister, sinisterior, sinistĭmus, *left*.
Exter, -erior, extimus, *or* extrēmus, *outward*.
Infĕrus, -ior, infĭmus *or* imus, *below*.
Intĕrus, intĕrior, intĭmus, *inward*.
Mātūrus, -ior, maturrĭmus, *or* maturissĭmus, *ripe*.
Postĕrus, posterior, postremus, *behind*.
Sŭpĕrus, -rior, suprēmus, *or* summus, *high*.
Vĕtus, vĕtĕrior, vĕterrĭmus, *old*.

4. Compounds

4. Compounds in *dicus*, *loquus*, *ficus*, and *volus*, have *entior*, and *entissimus*; as, *maledicus*, railing, *maledicentior*, *maledicentissimus*: So *magniloquus*, one that boasteth; *beneficus*, beneficent; *malevolus*, malevolent; *mirificus*, wonderful; *-entior*, *-entissimus*, or *mirificissimus*. *Nequam*, indecl. worthless, vicious, has *nequior*, *nequissimus*.

There are a great many adjectives, which, though capable of having their signification increased; yet either want one of the degrees of comparison, or are not compared at all.

1. The following adjectives are not used in the positive:
Deterior, *worse*, deterrimus. Propior, *nearer*, proximus; *nearest*
Ocior, *swifter*, ocissimus. or *next*.
Prior, *former*, primus. Ulterior, *farther*, ultimus.

2. The following want the comparative:
Inclytus, inclytissimus, *renowned*. Nuperus, nuperrimus, *late*.
Meritus, meritissimus, *deserving*. Par, parissimus, *equal*.
Novus, novissimus, *new*. Sacer, sacerrimus, *sacred*.

3. The following want the superlative:
Adolescens, adolescentior, *young*. Pronus, pronior, *inclined down-*
Diuturnus, diuturnior, *lasting*. *wards*.
Ingens, ingentior, *huge*. Satur, saturior, *full*.
Juvenis, junior, *young*. Senex, senior, *old*.
Opimus, opimior, *rich*.

To supply the superlative of *juvenis* or *adolescens*, we say, *minimus natu*, the youngest; and of *senex*, *maximus natu*, the oldest.

Adjectives in *ilis*, *alis*, and *bilis*, also want the superlative; as *civilis*, *civilior*, civil; *regalis*, *regalior*, regal; *flebilis*, *-ior*, lamentable. So, *juvenilis*, youthful; *exilis*, small, &c.

To these add several others of different terminations: Thus, *arcanus*, *-ior*, secret; *declivis*, *-ior*, bending downwards; *longinquus*, *-ior*, far off; *propinquus*, *-ior*, near.

Anterior, former; *sequior*, worse; *satior*, better; are only found in the comparative.

4. Many adjectives are not compared at all: such are those compounded with nouns or verbs; as, *versicolor*, of diverse colours; *pestifer*, poisonous: also adjectives in *us* pure, in *ivus*, *inus*, *orus*, or *imus*, and diminutives; as, *dubius*, doubtful; *vacuus*, empty; *fugitivus*, that flieth away; *matutinus*, early; *canorus*, shrill; *legitimus*, lawful; *tenellus*, somewhat tender; *majusculus*, &c.: together with a great many others of various terminations; as, *almus*, gracious; *praecox*, *-ocis*, soon er early ripe; *mirus*, *egenus*, *lacer*, *memor*, *sospes*, &c.

This defect of comparison is supplied by putting the adverb *magis* before the adjective, for the comparative degree; and *valde* or *maxime*

for

for the superlative; thus, *egēnus*, needy; *magis egenus*, more needy; *valde* or *maxime egenus*, very *or* most needy. Which form of comparison is also used in those adjectives which are regularly compared.

PRONOUN.

(A Pronoun is a word which stands instead of a Noun.)

Thus, *I* stands for the name of the person who speaks; *thou* for the name of the person addressed.

Pronouns serve to point out objects, whose names we either do not know, or do not want to mention. They also serve to shorten discourse, and prevent the too frequent repetition of the same word; thus, instead of saying, *When Cæsar had conquered Gaul, Cæsar turned Cæsar's arms against Cæsar's country*, we say, When Cæsar had conquered Gaul, *he* turned *his* arms against *his* country.

ENGLISH PRONOUNS.

In English there are five substantive pronouns, *I, thou, he, she,* and *it.*

The first is used, when one speaks of himself; as, *I love:* the second, when the person spoken to is the subject of the discourse; as, *thou lovest:* and the last three, in speaking of any other person or thing; as, *he, she,* or *it falls.*

I is said to be of the first person; *thou,* of the second; and *he, she,* or *it,* together with all other words, of the third : and so in the plural number, *we, ye, they.* Hence these are called *Personal Pronouns.*

The person speaking, and the person spoken to, do not need the distinction of gender; because they are supposed to be present, and therefore their sex is commonly known. But the third person, or thing spoken of, being frequently absent, and often unknown, requires to be distinguished by different genders; thus, *he, she, it.*

Substantive pronouns in English have three cases, the *nominative,* the *genitive* or *possessive,* and the *objective* or *accusative* case, which follows the verb active, or the preposition.

Substantive Pronouns, according to their Cases, Numbers, and Persons.

	Singular. Persons.			Plural. Persons.		
Cases.	1.	2.	3.	1.	2.	3.
Nom.	I,	thou,	he, she, it ;	we,	ye *or* you,	they.
Gen.	mine,	thine,	his, hers, its ;	ours,	yours,	theirs.
Acc.	me,	thee,	him, her, it :	us,	you,	them.

All other pronouns are adjectives; as, *this, that, our, your*, &c.
A pronominal adjective differs from a common adjective in this, that
it does not expreſs quality.

Several adjective pronouns do not admit the article before them,
becauſe they very much reſemble it in their ſignification; as, *that*
man, &c.

From the perſonal pronouns are formed theſe pronominal adjectives,
my, thy, his, her, our, your, their. Mine and *thine* are often uſed as
adjectives for *my* and *thy*, when the ſubſtantive following them begins
with a vowel.

Some adjective pronouns are varied to mark number; as, *this,
theſe; that, theſe.* To theſe add the adjectives *other; one*, which,
when their ſubſtantive is not expreſſed, have in the plural *others, ones;*
as, *many others, great ones;* in which caſe they ſeem to be uſed as ſubſtantives.

Who, which, that, are called RELATIVES, becauſe they refer to ſome
ſubſtantive going before, which is therefore called the ANTECEDENT.
Who is varied by caſes, thus, *who, whoſe, whom. His* and *whoſe* ſeem
to be contractions for *him's* and *whom's*, the poſſeſſive caſe being formed from the objective; as *hers* from *her; mine* from *me*, &c.

Who, which, what, whether, are called INTERROGATIVES, when
uſed in aſking queſtions; when uſed otherwiſe, they are called
INDEFINITES.

Own, and *ſelf*, in the plural *ſelves*, are joined to the poſſeſſives,
my, our, thy, your, his, her, their; as, my, or *mine own hand, myſelf,
yourſelves. Self* is likewiſe joined to the ſubſtantive pronoun *it*, as
itſelf. Himſelf, themſelves, ſeem to be uſed by corruption for *hiſſelf,
theirſelves.*

LATIN PRONOUNS.

The ſimple pronouns in Latin are eighteen; *ĕgo, tu,
ſui; ille, ipſe, iſte, hic, is, quis, qui; meus, tuus, ſuus, noſter,
veſter; noſtras, veſtras*, and *cujas.*

Three of them are ſubſtantives, *ego, tu, ſui;* the other
fifteen are adjectives.

Ego, I.

Sing.		*Plur.*	
Nom. ĕgo, *I,*		*Nom.* nos, *we,*	
Gen. mei, *of me.*		*Gen.* noſtrûm *or* noſtri, *of us,*	
Dat. mihi, *to me,*		*Dat.* nōbis, *to us,*	
Acc. me, *me,*		*Acc.* nos, *us,*	
Voc. ———		*Voc.* ———	
Abl. me, *with me.*		*Abl.* nobis, *with us.*	

Tu,

Tu, *thou.*

Sing.	Plur.
N. tu, *thou,*	*N.* vos, *ye* or *you,*
G. tui, *of thee,*	*G.* veſtrûm *or* veſtri, *of you,*
D. tĭbi, *to thee,*	*D.* vōbis, *to you,*
A. te, *thee,*	*A.* vos, *you,*
V. tu, *O thou,*	*V.* vos, *O ye* or *you.*
A. te, *with thee,*	*A.* vobis, *with you.*

or *you.*

Sui, *of himſelf, of herſelf, of itſelf.*

Sing.	Plur.
N. ————	*N.* ————
G. ſui, *of himſelf, of herſelf, of itſelf,*	*G.* ſui, *of themſelves,*
D. sĭbi, *to himſelf, to herſelf,* &c.	*D.* ſibi, *to themſelves,*
A. ſe, *himſelf,* &c.	*A.* ſe, *themſelves,*
V. ————	*V.* ————
A. ſe, *with himſelf,* &c.	*A.* ſe, *with themſelves.*

Obſ. 1. *Ego* wants the vocative, becauſe one cannot call upon himſelf, except as a ſecond perſon: thus, we cannot ſay, *O ego,* O I; *O nos,* O we.

Obſ. 2. *Mihi* in the dative is ſometimes by the poets contracted into *mî.*

Obſ. 3. The genitive plural of *ego* was anciently *noſtrorum* and *noſtrarum;* of *tu, veſtrorum* and *veſtrarum,* which were afterwards contracted into *noſtrûm* and *veſtrûm.*

We commonly uſe *noſtrûm* and *veſtrûm* after partitives, numerals, comparatives, or ſuperlatives; and *noſtri* and *veſtri* after other words.

The Engliſh ſubſtantive pronouns, *he, ſhe, it,* are expreſſed in Latin by theſe pronominal adjectives, *ille, iſte, hic,* or *is;* as,

Ille, for the maſc. *Illa,* for the fem. *illud,* for the neut. that; or, *ille,* he; *illa,* ſhe; *illud,* it, or that; thus,

	Sing.			Plur.		
N.	ille,	illa,	illud,	*N.* illi,	illæ,	illa,
G.	illius,	illius,	illius,	*G.* illorum,	illarum,	illorum,
D.	illi,	illi,	illi,	*D.* illis,	illis,	illis,
A.	illum,	illam,	illud,	*A.* illos,	illas,	illa,
V.	ille,	illa,	illud,	*V.* illi,	illæ,	illa,
A.	illo,	illâ,	illo.	*A.* illis,	illis,	illis.

Ipſe,

Ipse, he himfelf, *ipfa*, fhe herfelf, *ipfum*, itfelf; and *ifte, ifta, iftud*, that, are declined like *ille*; only *ipfe* has *ipfum* in the nom. acc. and voc. fing. neut.

Ipfe is often joined to *ego, tu, fui*; and has in Latin the fame force with *felf* in Englifh, when joined with a pofſeſſive pronoun; as, *ego ipfe*, I myfelf.

Hic, hæc, hoc, this.

	Sing.			*Plur.*	
N. hic,	hæc,	hoc,	*N.* hi,	hæ,	hæc,
G. hujus,	hujus,	hujus,	*G.* horum,	harum,	horum,
D. huic,	huic,	huic,	*D.* his,	his,	his,
A. hunc,	hanc,	hoc,	*A.* hos,	has,	hæc,
V. hic,	hæc,	hoc,	*V.* hi,	hæ,	hæc,
A. hoc,	hac,	hoc.	*A.* his,	his,	his.

Is, ea, id; he, ſhe, it; or that

	Sing.			*Plur.*	
N. is,	ea,	id,	*N.* ii,	eæ,	ea,
G. ejus,	ejus,	ejus,	*G.* eorum,	earum,	eorum,
D. ei,	ei,	ei,	*D.* iis *or* eis, &c.		
A. eum,	eam,	id,	*A.* eos,	eas,	ea,
V. ———	———		*V.* ———		
A. eo,	eâ,	eo,	*A.* iis *or* eis, &c.		

Quis, qua, quod, or *quid?* which, what? Or *Quis?* who? *or* what man? *quæ?* who? *or* what woman? *quod* or *quid?* what? which thing? *or* what thing? thus,

	Sing.			*Plur.*	
N. quis,	quæ,	quod *or* quid,	*N.* qui,	quæ,	quæ,
G. cujus,	cujus,	cujus,	*G.* quorum,	quarum,	quorum,
D. cui,	cui,	cui,	*D.* queis *or* quibus,	&c.	
A. quem,	quam,	quod *or* quid,	*A.* quos,	quas,	quæ,
V. ———	———		*V.* ———		
A. quo,	qua,	quo;	*A.* queis *or* quibus, &c.		

Qui, quæ, quod, who, which, that; Or vir *qui*, the man *who* or *that*; fœmina *quæ*, the woman *who* or *that*; negotium *quod*, the thing *which* or *that:* genit. vir *cujus*, the man *whofe* or *of whom*; mulier *cujus*, the woman *whofe* or *of whom*; negotium *cujus*, the thing *of which*, feldom *which, &c.* thus,

H 2

Sing.

	Sing.				*Plur.*	
N. qui,	quæ,	quod,	*N.* qui,	quæ,	quæ,
G. cujus,	cujus,	cujus,	*G.* quorum,	quarum,	quorum,
D. cui,	cui,	cui,	*D.* queis *or* quibus, &c.
A. quem,	quam,	quod,	*A.* quos,	quas,	quæ,
V. ————	————	————	*V.* ————	————	————
A. quo,	qua,	quo.	*A.* queis *or* quibus, &c.

The other pronouns are derivatives, coming from *ego,* *tu,* and *sui.* *Meus,* my or mine; *tuus,* thy or thine; *suus,* his own, her own, its own, their own, are declined like *bonus,* -a, -um; and *noster,* our; *vester,* your, like *pulcher,* -chra, -chrum, of the first and second declension.

Nostras, of our country; *vestras,* of your country; *cujas,* of what *or* which country, are declined like *felix,* of the third declension: gen. *nostrātis,* dat. *nostrāti,* &c.

Pronouns as well as nouns, that signify things, which cannot be addressed, or called upon, want the vocative.

Meus hath *mi,* and sometimes *meus,* in the voc. sing. masc.

The relative *qui* has frequently *qui* in the ablative, and that, which is remarkable, in all genders and numbers.

Qui is sometimes used for *quis:* and instead of *cujus,* the gen. of *quis,* we find an adjective pronoun, *cujus,* -a, -um.

Simple pronouns, with respect to their signification, are divided into the following classes:

1. *Demonstratives,* which point out any person or thing present, or as if present: *Ego, tu, hic, iste,* and sometimes *ille, is, ipse.*

2. *Relatives,* which refer to something going before: *ille, ipse, iste, hic, is, qui.*

3. *Possessives,* which signify possession: *meus, tuus, suus, noster, vester.*

4. *Patrials,* or *Gentiles,* which signify one's country: *nostras, vestras, cujas.*

5. *Interrogatives,* by which we ask a question: *quis? cujas?* When they do not ask a question, they are called *Indefinites,* like other words of the same nature.

6. *Reciprocals,* which again call back or represent the same object to the mind: *sui,* and *suus.*

COMPOUND LATIN PRONOUNS.

Pronouns are compounded variously:

1. With other pronouns; as, *isthic, isthæc, isthoc, isthuc,* or *istuc.* Acc. *isthunc, isthanc, isthoc,* or *isthuc.* Abl. *Isthoc, isthac, isthoc.* Nom. and acc. plur. neut. *isthæc,* of *iste* and *hic.* So *illic,* of *ille* and *hic.*

2. With some other parts of speech; as *hujusmodi, cujusmodi,* &c. *mecum, tecum, secum, nobiscum, vobiscum, quocum* or *quicum* and *quibus-*
cum:

tum : eccum, eccam ; eccos, eccas, and sometimes ecca, in the nom. sing. of *ecce* and *is.* So *ellum,* of *ecce* and *ille.*

3. With some syllable added; as, *tute* of *tu* and *te,* used only in the nom. egomet, tutemet, suimet, through all the cases, thus, memet, tuimet, &c. of *ego, tu, sui,* and *met.* Instead of *tumet* in the nom. we say, tutemet : hiccine, hæccine, &c. in all the cases that end in *C* ; of *hic* and *cine :* Meapte, tuapte, suapte, nostrapte, vestrapte, in the ablat. fem. and sometimes meopte, tuopte, &c. of *meus,* &c. and *pte :* hicce, hæcce, hocce : hujusce, huic, hisce, hosce : of *hic* and *ce :* whence hujuscemodi, ejuscemodi, cujuscemodi. So *IDEM,* the same, compounded of *is* and *dem,* which is thus declined :

	Sing.			Plur.	
N. idem,	eadem,	idem,	*N.* iidem,	eædem,	eadem,
G. ejusdem,	ejusdem,	ejusdem,	*G.* eorundem,	earundem,	eorundem,
D. eidem,	eidem,	eidem,	*D.* eisdem *or* iisdem, &c.		
A. eundem,	eandem,	idem,	*A.* eosdem,	easdem,	eadem,
V. idem,	eadem,	idem,	*V.* iidem,	eædem,	eadem,
A. eodem,	eadem,	eodem,	*A.* eisdem *or* iisdem, &c.		

The pronouns which we find most frequently compounded, are *quis* and *qui.*

Quis in composition is sometimes the first, sometimes the last, and sometimes likewise the middle part of the word compounded : but *qui* is always the first.

1. The compounds of *quis,* in which it is put first, are, *quisnam,* who ? *quispiam, quisquam,* any one ; *quisque,* every one ; *quisquis,* whosoever ; which are thus declined.

	Nom.			Gen.	Dat.
Quisnam,	quænam,	quodnam *or* quidnam ;		cujusnam,	cuinam,
Quispiam,	quæpiam,	quodpiam *or* quidpiam ;		cujuspiam,	cuipiam,
Quisquam,	quæquam,	quodquam *or* quidquam ;		cujusquam,	cuiquam,
Quisque,	quæque,	quodque *or* quidque ;		cujusque,	cuique.
Quisquis,	———	quidquid *or* quicquid ;		cujuscujus,	cuicui.

And so in the other cases, according to the simple *quis.* But *quisquis* has not the feminine at all, and the neuter only in the nominative and accusative. *Quisquam* has also *quicquam* for *quidquam.* Accusative, *quenquam,* without the feminine. The plural is scarcely used.

2. The compounds of *quis,* in which *quis* is put last, have *qua* in the nominative sing. fem. and in the nominative and accusative plur. neut. as, *aliquis,* some ; *ecquis,* who ? of *et* and *quis* ; also *nequis, siquis, numquis,* which for the most part are read separately, thus, *ne quis, si quis, num quis.* They are thus declined.

	Nom.		Gen.	Dat.
Aliquis, aliqua,	aliquod *or* aliquid,		alicujus,	alicui,
Ecquis, ecqua *or* ecquæ,	ecquod *or* ecquid,		eccujus,	eccui,
Si quis, si qua,	si quod *or* si quid,		si cujus,	si cui,
Ne quis, ne qua,	ne quod *or* ne quid,		ne cujus,	ne cui,
Num quis, num qua,	num quod *or* num quid,		num cujus,	num cui.

3. The

3. The compounds which have *quis* in the middle, are, *ecquifnam*, who? *unufquifque*, gen. *uniufcujufque*, every one. The former is ufed only in the nom. fing. and the latter wants the plural.

4. The compounds of *qui* are *quicunque*, whofoever; *quidam*, fome; *quilibet*, *quivis*, any one, whom you pleafe; which are thus declined.

	Nom.		*Gen.*	*Dat.*
Quicunque,	quæcunque,	quodcunque,	cujufcunque,	cuicunque,
Quidam,	quædam,	quoddam *or* quiddam,	cujufdam,	cuidam,
Quilibet,	quælibet,	quodlibet *or* quidlibet,	cujuflibet,	cuilibet,
Quivis,	quævis,	quodvis *or* quidvis,	cujufvis,	cuivis.

Obf. 1. All thefe compounds have feldom or never *queis*, but *quibus*, in their dat. and abl. plur.; thus, *aliquibus*, &c.

Obf. 2. *Quis*, and its compounds in comic writers, have fometimes *quis* in the feminine gender.

Obf. 3. *Quidam* has *quendam*, *quandam*, *quoddam* or *quiddam*, in the acc. fing. and *quorundam*, *quarundam*, *quorundam*, in the gen. plur. *n* being put inftead of *m*, for the better found.

Obf. 4. *Quod*, with its compounds, *aliquod*, *quodvis*, *quoddam*, &c. are ufed, when they agree with a fubftantive in the fame cafe; *quid*, with its compounds, *aliquid*, *quidvis*, &c. for the moft part have either no fubftantive expreffed, or govern one in the genitive. For this reafon they are by fome reckoned fubftantives.

VERB.

A verb is a word which expreffes what is affirmed of things; as, The boy *reads.* The fun *fhines.* The man *loves.* (Or, *A verb is that part of fpeech which fignifies to be, to do, or to fuffer.*)

It is called *Verb* or *Word*, by way of eminence, becaufe it is the moft effential word in a fentence, without which the other parts of fpeech can form no complete fenfe. Thus, *the diligent boy reads his leffon with care*, is a perfect fentence; but if we take away the affirmation, or the word *reads*, it is rendered imperfect, or rather becomes no fentence at all: thus, *the diligent boy his leffon with care.*

A verb therefore may be thus diftinguifhed from any other part of fpeech: Whatever word expreffes an affirmation or affertion is a verb; or thus, Whatever word, with a fubftantive noun or pronoun before or after it, makes full fenfe, is a verb; as, *ftones fall, I walk, walk thou.* Here *fall* and *walk* are verbs, becaufe they contain an affirmation; but when we fay, *a long walk, a dangerous fall*, there is no affirmation expreffed; and the fame words *walk* and *fall* become fubftantives or nouns. We often find likewife in Latin the fame word ufed as a verb, and alfo as fome other part of fpeech; thus, *amor, -oris, love*, a fubftantive; and *amor, I am loved*, a verb.

(Verbs, with respect to their signification, are divided into three different classes, *Active*, *Passive*, and *Neuter*; because we consider things either as acting, or being acted upon; or as neither acting, nor being acted upon; but simply existing, or existing in a certain state or condition; as in a state of motion or rest,) &c.

1. An *Active* verb expresses an action, and necessarily supposes an agent, and an object acted upon, as, *amāre*, to love; *amo te*, I love thee.

2. A verb *Passive* expresses a passion or suffering, or the receiving of an action; and necessarily implies an object acted upon, and an agent, by which it is acted upon; as, *amāri*, to be loved; *tu amāris a me*, thou art loved by me.

3. A *Neuter* verb properly expresses neither action nor passion, but simply the being, state, or condition of things; as, *dormio*, I sleep; *sedeo*, I sit.

The verb *Active* is also called *Transitive*, when the action *passeth over* to the object, or hath an effect on some other thing; as, *scribo literas*, I write letters; but when the action is confined within the agent, and *passeth not over* to any object, it is called *Intransitive*; as, *ambūlo*, I walk; *curro*, I run, which are likewise called *Neuter Verbs*. Many verbs in Latin and English are used both in a transitive and in an intransitive or neuter sense; as, *sistere*, to stop; *incipĕre*, to begin; *durāre*, to endure, or to harden, &c.

Verbs which simply signify *being*, are likewise called *Substantive* verbs; as, *esse* or *existere*, to be or to exist. The notion of existence is implied in the signification of every verb; thus, *I love*, may be resolved into, *I am loving*.

When the meaning of a verb is expressed without any affirmation, or in such a form as to be joined to a substantive noun, partaking thereby of the nature of an adjective, it is called a *Participle*; as, *amans*, loving; *amatus*, loved. But when it has the form of a substantive, it is called a *Gerund*, or a *Supine*; as, *amandum*, loving; *amatum*, to love; *amatu*, to love, *or* to be loved.

A verb is varied or declined by *Voices, Modes, Tenses, Numbers,* and *Persons*.

There are two voices; the *Active* and *Passive*.

The

[The modes are four; *Indicative*, *Subjunctive*, *Imperative*, and *Infinitive*.]

[The tenses are five; the *Present*, the *Preter-imperfect*, the *Preter-perfect*, the *Preter-pluperfect*, and the *Future*.]

[The numbers are two; *Singular* and *Plural*.

The persons are three; *First*, *Second*, *Third*.]

1. *Voice* expresses the different circumstances in which we consider an object, whether as acting, or being acted upon. The *Active voice* signifies action; as, *amo*, I love; the *Passive*, suffering, or being the object of an action; as, *amor*, I am loved.

2. *Modes* or *Moods* are the various *manners* of expressing the signification of the verb.

The *Indicative* declares or affirms positively; as, *amo*, I love; *amábo*, I shall love; or asks a question; as, *an tu amas?* dost thou love?

The *Subjunctive* is usually joined to some other verb, and cannot make a full meaning by itself; as, *si me obsecret, redibo*, if he entreat me, I will return. *Ter.*

The *Imperative* commands, exhorts, or entreats; as, *ama*, love thou.

The *Infinitive* simply expresses the signification of the verb, without limiting it to any person or number; as, *amáre*, to love.

3. *Tenses or Times* express the time when any thing is supposed to be, to act, or to suffer.

Time in general is divided into three parts, the present, past, and future.

Past time is expressed three different ways. When we speak of a thing, which was doing, but not finished at some former time, we use the *Preter-imperfect*, or past time not completed; as, *scribēbam*, I was writing.

When we speak of a thing now finished, we use the *Preter-perfect*, or past time completed; as, *scripsi*, I wrote, or have written.

When we speak of a thing finished at or before some past time, we use the *Preter-pluperfect*, or past time more than completed; as, *scripsēram*, I had written.

Future time is expressed two different ways. A thing may be considered either as simply about to be done, or as actually finished, at some future time; as, *scribam*, I shall write, or, I shall [then] be writing; *scripsēro*, I shall have written.

4. *Number* marks *how many* we suppose to be, to act, or to suffer.

5. *Person* shews to what the meaning of the verb is applied, whether to the person speaking, to the person addressed, or to some other person or thing.

Verba

Verbs have two numbers and three perfons, to agree with fubftantive nouns and pronouns in thefe refpects: for a verb properly hath neither numbers nor perfons, but certain terminations anfwering to the perfon and number of its nominative.

A verb is properly faid to be *conjugated*, when all its parts are properly claffed, or, as it were, yoked together, according to Voice, Mode, Tenfe, Number, and Perfon.

English Verbs.

Englifh verbs change their termination to exprefs only the prefent and the paft time of the Active voice; and in regular verbs, the Perfect participle is always the fame with the perfect or paft time, both of them ending in *ed* or *'d*. The prefent participle always ends in *ing*. The Englifh has no future participle, which defect is fupplied by a circumlocution; as, *about to love*.

An Englifh Verb is thus varied;

To LOVE.

Active Voice.

Indicative Mode.

Prefent Time.		*Paft Time.*	
Sing.	*Plur.*	*Sing.*	*Plur.*
1. I love,	We love,	1. I loved,	We loved,
2. Thou loveft,	Ye *or* you love,	2. Thou lovedft,	Ye *or* you loved,
3. He loveth *or* loves;	They love.	3. He loved;	They loved.

Subjunctive Mode,		*Imperative Mode.*	
Prefent Time.			
Sing.	*Plur.*	*Sing.*	*Plur.*
1. I love,	We love,	2. Love thou, Love ye, *or* love you,	
2. Thou love,	Ye *or* you love,	*Infinitive Mode.*	
3. He love;	They love.	*Prefent,* To love.	

Participle Prefent, Loving; *Perfect,* Loved.

The feveral remaining parts of the Englifh verb are formed by the affiftance of other verbs, called therefore *Auxiliaries* or *Helpers*. The chief of thefe are *have*, *be*, *fhall*, and *will*, which are thus varied,

To HAVE.

Indicative Mode.

Prefent Time.		*Paft Time.*	
Sing.	*Plur.*	*Sing.*	*Plur.*
1. I have,	We have,	1. I had,	We had,
2. Thou haft,	Ye have,	2. Thou hadft,	Ye had,
3. He hath, *or* has;	They have.	3. He had,	They had.

Subjunctive

Subjunctive Mode.		*Imperative Mode.*	
Present.			
Sing.	*Plur.*	*Sing.*	*Plur.*
1. I have,	We have,	2. Have thou ;	Have ye.
2. Thou have,	Ye have,	*Infinitive Mode.*	
3. He have ;	They have.	*Present*, To have.	

Participle Present, Having ; *Perfect*, Had.

To BE.

Indicative Mode.

Present Time.		*Past Time.*	
Sing.	*Plur.*	*Sing.*	*Plur.*
1. I am,	We are,	1. I was,	We were,
2. Thou art,	Ye are,	2. Thou wast,	Ye were,
3. He is ;	They are.	3. He was ;	They were.

Subjunctive Mode.

Present.		*Past Time.*	
Sing.	*Plur.*	*Sing.*	*Plur.*
1. I be,	We be,	1. I were,	We were,
2. Thou be,	Ye be,	2. Thou wert,	Ye were,
3. He be ;	They be.	3. He were ;	They were.

Imperative Mode.		*Infinitive Mode.*	
Sing.	*Plur.*	*Present*, To be.	
2. Be thou ;	Be ye.		

Participle.

Present, Being. *Perfect*, Been.

SHALL.		WILL.	
Sing.	*Plur.*	*Sing.*	*Plur.*
1. I shall,	We shall,	1. I will,	We will,
2. Thou shalt,	Ye shall,	2. Thou wilt,	Ye will,
3. He shall ;	They shall.	3. He will ;	They will.

The terminations of these auxiliary verbs seem to be irregular. Most of them however are only contractions of the regular form. Thus, *hast* is contracted for *havest*; *hath*, for *haveth*; *has*, for *haves*; and *wilt* for *willest*; which last is likewise used from the regular verb, *to will*; thus, *I will, thou willest, he willeth*, or *wills*, &c.

The tenses of the subjunctive mode are expressed by *may* or *can*, *might, could, would*, and *should*, together with the other auxiliary verbs.

Would, wouldst, comes from *will*; and *should, shouldst*, from *shall*. *Might* and *could* seem to be the past time of *may* and *can*.

To express with greater force the present and past time of the indicative Mode, we use the auxiliary verb *do*; as, *I do love*; *I did love*. And so in the Imperative, *do thou love, do ye love*. In the third person of the Imperative, we always use *let*, which being an active verb, has always an accusative after it ; as, *let him love ; let them love*.

When we speak of present time indeterminately, we use the simple
form ;

form; as, *I love, I loved:* but when we speak of it with some particular limitation, we use an auxiliary; as, *I am loving* just now; I *was* (then) *loving.* The termination *th*, in the third person of the present of the Indicative, properly belongs to solemn discourse; as, *he hath, he doth,* &c.

The whole of the passive voice in English is formed by the auxiliary verb *to be,* and the participle perfect; as, *I am loved, I was loved,* &c. In many verbs the present participle also is used in a passive sense; as, *These things are doing, were doing,* &c.; *The house is building, was building,* &c.

When an auxiliary is joined to a verb, the auxiliary is varied according to number and person, and the verb itself always continues the same. When there are two or more auxiliaries joined to the verb, the first of them only is varied according to person and number. The auxiliary *must* admits of no variation.

Shall and *will* are always employed to express future time. *Will,* in the first person singular and plural, promises or threatens; in the second and third persons, only foretels: *shall,* on the contrary, in the first person, simply foretels; in the second and third persons, promises, commands, or threatens. But the contrary of this holds, when we ask a question: thus, " I *shall* go;" " you *will* go;" express event only; but " *will* you go?" imports intention: and " *shall* I go?" refers to the will of another.

The neuter verb is varied like the active; but sometimes it assumes the passive form; as, *I had fallen,* or *I was fallen.*

IRREGULAL ENGLISH VERBS.

The English language abounds in irregular verbs.

A verb in English is said to be irregular, which has not the Past Time and the Participle Perfect in *ed.*

Most English verbs are liable to some irregularity from contraction. To this we are led by the nature of the language, and the manner of pronouncing it. Thus, instead of *loved, lovedst,* we say, *lov'd, lov'dst.* Hence in many verbs *ed* is changed into *t;* as *snatcht, checkt, rapt, mixt, dwelt, past, meant, felt, left, bereft,* &c. for *snatched, checked,* &c. In such words, however, the entire form is also used, and in general to be preferred. They are not therefore commonly ranked among irregular verbs.

Irregular verbs in English, properly so called, are all monosyllables, unless compounded; and may be reduced to the three following cases, in which those marked thus*, are likewise used in the regular form.

I. Irregulars by contraction.

These commonly end in *d* or *t,* and have the Present, the Past Time, and the Participle Perfect, all alike, without any variation: , *beat, burst, cast, cost, cut, bit, hurt, knit, let, list*, light*, put, it*, read, rent, rid, set, shed, shred, shut, slit, split, spread, thrust, wet*;* all of which are contracted for *beated, bursted, casted,* &c.

I

The

The following in the Paſt Time, and Participle Perfect, vary a little from the Preſent; as, *lead, led; ſweat, ſwet*; meet, met; breed, bred; feed, fed; ſpeed, ſped; bend, bent*; lend, lent; rend, rent; ſend, ſent; ſpend, ſpent; build, built*; geld, gelt*; gild, gilt*; gird, girt*; loſe, loſt.*

Sold, told, had, made, fled, ſtood, clad; from *ſell, tell, have, make, flee, ſhoe, clothe*; are contracted for *ſelled, telled,* &c.   *Stand* has *ſtood; ſmell, ſmelt; dare, durſt,* in the participle *dared.*

2.   *Irregulars in* ght.

Theſe are few in number, and have the Paſt Time and Participle in *ght*; as, *bring, brought; buy, bought; catch, caught; fight, fought; teach, taught; think, thought; ſeek, ſought; work, wrought.*

3.   *Irregulars in* en.

This is by far the moſt numerous claſs of irregular verbs. They have commonly the Participle perfect in *en*, and form the Paſt Time by changing the vowel or diphthong of the Preſent. Some form the Paſt Time regularly.

Preſent.	*Paſt.*	*Participle.*
Fall,	fell,	fallen.
Awake,	awoke *,	(awaked).
Forſake,	forſook,	forſaken.
Shake,	ſhook,	ſhaken.
Take,	took,	taken.
Draw,	drew,	drawn.
Slay,	ſlew,	ſlain.
Get,	gat *or* got,	gotten.
Help,	(helped)	holpen *.
Melt,	melted,	molten *.
Swell,	ſwelled,	ſwollen *.
Eat,	ate,	eaten.
Bear,	bare, *or* bore,	born.
Break,	brake, *or* broke,	broken.
Cleave,	clave, *or* clove *,	cloven.
Speak,	ſpake, *or* ſpoke,	ſpoken.
Swear,	ſware, *or* ſwore,	ſworn.
Tear,	tare *or* tore,	torn.
Wear,	ware, *or* wore,	worn.
Heave,	hove *,	hoven *.
Shear,	ſhore,	ſhorn.
Steal,	ſtole,	ſtolen.
Tread,	trod,	trodden.
Weave,	wove,	woven.

Preſent.	*Paſt.*	*Participle.*
Creep,	crope *,	crept *.
Freeze,	froze,	frozen.
Seethe,	ſod,	ſodden.
See,	ſaw,	ſeen.
Bite,	bit,	bitten.
Chide,	chid,	chidden.
Hide,	hid,	hidden.
Slide,	ſlid,	ſlidden.
Abide,	abode,	
Climb,	clomb,	(climbed).
Drive,	drove,	driven.
Ride,	rode,	ridden.
Riſe,	roſe,	riſen.
Shine,	ſhone *,	ſhined.
Strive,	ſtrove *,	ſtriven *.
Smite,	ſmote,	ſmitten.
Stride,	ſtrode,	ſtridden.
Shrive,	ſhrove,	ſhriven.
Thrive,	throve,	thriven.
Write,	wrote,	written.
Strike,	ſtruck,	ſtricken *or* ſtrucken.
Bid,	bade,	bidden.
Give,	gave,	given.
Sit,	ſat,	ſitten.
Spit,	ſpat,	ſpitten.
Dig,	dug *,	digged.
Lie,	lay,	lain *or* lien.
Chuſe,	choſe,	choſen.
Hold,	held,	holden.

Do.)

Present.	Past.	Participle.
Do,	did,	done.
Blow,	blew,	blown.
Crow,	crew,	(crowed).
Grow,	grew,	grown.
Know,	knew,	known.
Throw,	threw,	thrown.
Fly,	flew,	flown.
Bake,	(baked),	baken *.
Grave,	(graved),	graven *.
Hew,	(hewed),	hewen or hewn.
Lade,	(laded),	laden.
Load,	(loaded),	loaden *.
Mow,	(mowed),	mown *.

Present.	Past.	Participle.
Rive,	(rived),	riven.
Saw,	(ſawed),	ſawn *.
Shave,	(ſhaved),	ſhaven *.
Shew,	(ſhewed),	ſhewn *.
Show,	(ſhowed),	ſhown.
Sow,	(ſowed),	ſowen *.
Straw, ſtrew, or ſtrow,	(ſtrawed, &c.)	ſtrown *.
Waſh,	(waſhed),	waſhen *.
Wax,	(waxed),	waxen *.
Wreath,	(wreathed),	wreathen *.
Writhe,	(writhed),	writhen.

Several verbs ſeem to have dropt the termination *en* in the Participle; as,

Present.	Past.	Participle.
Begin,	began,	begun.
Cling,	clung or clung,	clung.
Drink,	drank,	drunk or drunken.
Fling,	flung,	flung.
Ring,	rang or rung,	rung.
Shrink,	ſhrank or ſhrunk,	ſhrunk.
Sing,	ſang or ſung,	ſung.
Sink,	ſank or ſunk,	ſunk.
Sling,	ſlang or ſlung,	ſlung.
Slink,	ſlunk,	ſlunk.
Spin,	ſpan or ſpun,	ſpun.
Spring,	ſprang or ſprung,	ſprung.
Sting,	ſtung,	ſtung.

Present.	Past.	Participle.
Stink,	ſtank or ſtunk,	ſtunk.
String,	ſtrung,	ſtrung.
Swim,	ſwam or ſwum,	ſwum.
Swing,	ſwung,	ſwung.
Wring,	wrung,	wrung.
Bind,	bound,	bound or bounden.
Find,	found,	found.
Grind,	ground,	ground.
Wind,	wound,	wound.
Hang,	hung *,	hung *.
Shoot,	ſhot,	ſhot.
Stick,	ſtuck,	ſtuck.
Come,	came,	come.
Run,	ran,	run.
Win,	won,	won.

Frequent miſtakes are committed with regard to thoſe verbs which make the Participle Perfect different from the Paſt Time; thus it is ſaid, *he begun*, for *he began*; *he run*, for *he ran*; the Participle being uſed inſtead of the Paſt Time: and much more frequently the Paſt Time inſtead of the Participle; as, *I had wrote*, for *I had written*; *it was wrote*, for *it was written*; ſo *bore* for *borne*; *choſe* for choſen; *bid*, for *bidden*; *drove*, for *driven*; *broke*, for *broken*; *rode*, for *ridden*, &c.

Several verbs are either defective, or made up of parts derived from different verbs of the ſame ſignification; as, *go*, *went*, *gone*, *weet*, *wit* or *wot*, *wot*; *wis*, *wiſt*; *aught*, *quoth*, *muſt*, together with moſt of the auxiliary verbs.

Latin

The Latins have four different ways of varying verbs, called the *First*, the *Second*, the *Third*, and the *Fourth Conjugation.*

The Conjugations are thus diftinguifhed:

The Firft has *a* long before *re* of the Infinitive; the Second has *e* long, the Third has *e* fhort, and the Fourth has *i* long, before *re* of the Infinitive.

Except *dăre*, to give, which has *ă* fho:t, and alfo its compounds; thus, *Circundăre*, to furround; *circundămus, -dătis, -dăbam, -dăbo*, &c.

The different conjugations are likewife diftinguifhed from one another by the different terminations of the following tenfes:

ACTIVE VOICE.
Indicative Mode.
Prefent Tenfe.

	Singular. Perfons.			Plural. Perfons.		
	1.	2.	3.	1.	2.	3.
1.	-o,	-as,	-at;	-āmus,	-ātis,	-ant.
2.	-eo,	-es,	-et;	-ēmus,	-ētis,	-ent.
3.	-o,	-is,	-it;	-ĭmus,	-ĭtis,	-unt.
4.	-io,	-is,	-it;	-īmus,	-ītis,	-iunt.

Imperfeft.

1.	-ābam,	-ābas,	-ābat;	-ābāmus,	-ābātis,	-ābant.
2.	-ēbam,	-ēbas,	-ēbat;	-ēbāmus.	-ēbātis,	-ēbant.
3.	-ēbam,	-ēbas,	-ēbat;	-ēbāmus,	-ēbātis,	-ēbant.
4.	-iēbam,	-iēbas,	-iēbat;	-iēbāmus,	-iēbātis,	-iēbant.

Future.

1.	-ābo,	-ābis,	-ābit;	-ābĭmus,	-ābĭtis,	-ābunt.
2.	-ēbo,	-ēbis,	-ēbit;	-ēbĭmus,	-ēbĭtis,	-ēbunt.
3.	-am,	-es,	-et;	-ēmus,	-ētis,	-ent.
4.	-iam,	-ies,	-iet;	-iēmus,	-iētis,	-ient.

Subjunctive Mode.
Prefent Tenfe.

1.	-em,	-es,	-et;	-ēmus,	-ētis,	-ent.
2.	-eam,	-eas,	-eat;	-eāmus,	-eātis,	-eant.
3.	-am,	-as,	-at;	-āmus,	-ātis,	-ant.
4.	-iam,	-ias,	-iat;	-iāmus,	-iātis,	-iant.

Imperfeft.

Imperfect.

1. -ārem, -āres, -āret ; -ārēmus, -ārētis, -ārent.
2. -ērem, -ēres, -ēret ; -ērēmus, -ērētis, -ērent.
3. -ĕrem, -ĕres, -ĕret ; -ĕrēmus, -ĕrētis, -ĕrent.
4. -īrem, -īres, -īret ; -īrēmus, -īrētis, -īrent.

Imperative Mode.

2.	3.	2.	3.
1. -a *or* -āto,	-āto ;	-āte *or* -ātōte,	-anto.
2. -e *or* -ēto,	-ēto ;	-ēte *or* -ētōte,	-ento.
3. -e *or* -ĭto,	-ĭto ;	-ĭte *or* -ĭtōte,	-unto.
4. -i *or* -īto,	-īto ;	-īte *or* -ītōte,	-iunto.

PASSIVE VOICE.

Indicative Mode.
Present Tense.

1. -or, -āris *or* -āre, -ātur ; -āmur, -āmĭni, -antur.
2. -eor, -ēris *or* -ēre, -ētur ; -ēmur, -ēmĭni, -entur.
3. -or, -ĕris *or* -ĕre, -ĭtur ; -ĭmur, -ĭmĭni, -untur.
4. -ior, -īris *or* -īre, -ītur ; -īmur, -īnĭni, -iuntur.

Imperfect.

1. -ābar, -ābāris *or* -ābāre, -ābātur ; -ābāmur, -ābāmĭni, -ābantur.
2. -ĕbar, -ēbāris *or* -ēbāre, -ēbātur ; -ēbāmur, -ēbāmĭni, -ēbantur.
3. -ēbar, -ēbāris *or* -ēbāre, -ēbātur ; -ēbāmur, -ēbāmĭni, -ēbantur.
4. -iēbar, -iēbāris *or* -iēbāre, -iēbātur ; -iēbāmur, -iēbāmĭni, -iēbantur.

Future.

1. -ābor, -ābĕris *or* -abĕre, -ābĭtur ; -ābĭmur, -ābĭmĭni, -ābuntur.
2. -ēbor, -ēbĕris *or* -ēbĕre, -ēbĭtur ; -ēbĭmur, -ēbĭmĭni, -ēbuntur.
3. -ar, -ēris *or* -ēre, -ētur ; -ēmur, -ēmĭni, -entur.
4. -iar, -iēris *or* -iēre, -iētur ; -iēmur, -iēmĭni, -ientur.

Subjunctive Mode.
Present Tense.

1. -er, -ēris *or* -ēre, -ētur ; -ēmur, -ēmĭni, -entur.
2. -ear, -eāris *or* -eāre, -eātur ; -eāmur, -eāmĭni, -eantur.
3. -ar, -āris *or* -āre, -ātur ; -āmur, -āmĭni, -antur.
4. -iar, -iāris *or* -iāre, -iātur ; -iāmur, -iāmĭni, -iantur.

Imperfect.

1. -ārer, -ārēris *or* -ārēre, -ārētur ; -ārēmur, -ārēmĭni, -ārentur.
2. -ērer, -ērēris *or* -ērēre, -ērētur ; -ērēmur, -ērēmĭni, -ērentur.
3. -ĕrer, -ĕrēris *or* -ĕrēre, -ĕrētur ; -ĕrēmur, -ĕrēmĭni, -ĕrentur.
4. -īrer, -īrēris *or* -īrēre, -īrētur ; -īrēmur, -īrēmĭni, -īrentur.

Imperative

Imperative Mode.

	2.	3.	2.	3.
1.	-āre *or* -ātor,	-ātor ;	-āmĭni,	-āntor.
2.	-ēre *or* -ētor,	-ētor ;	-ēmĭni,	-ēntor.
3.	-ĕre *or* -ĭtor,	-ĭtor ;	-ĭmĭni,	-untor.
4.	-īre *or* -ītor,	-ītor ;	-īmĭni,	-iuntor.

Obſerve, Verbs in *io* of the third conjugation have *iunt* in the third perſon plur. of the preſent indic. active, and *iuntur* in the paſſive; and ſo in the imperative, *iunto* and *iuntor*. In the imperfect and future of the indicative they have always the terminations of the fourth conjugation, *iēbam* and *iam ; iēbar* and *iar*, &c.

The terminations of the other tenſes are the ſame through all the Conjugations. Thus,

ACTIVE VOICE.

Indicative Mode.

Sing.   Plur.

	1.	2.	3.	1.	2.	3.
Perf.	-i,	-iſti,	-it ;	-ĭmus,	-iſtis,	-ērunt *or* -ēre.
Plu.	-ĕram,	-ĕras,	-ĕrat ;	-ĕrāmus,	-ĕrātis,	-ĕrant.

Subjunctive Mode.

Perf.	-ĕrim,	-ĕris,	-ĕrit ;	-ĕrĭmus,	-ĕrĭtis,	-ĕrint.
Plu.	-iſſem,	-iſſes,	-iſſet ;	-iſsēmus,	-iſsētis,	-iſſent.
Fut.	-ĕro,	-ĕris,	-ĕrit ;	-ĕrĭmus,	-ĕrĭtis,	-ĕrint.

Theſe Tenſes, in the Paſſive Voice, are formed by the Participle Perfect, and the auxiliary verb *ſum*, which is alſo uſed to expreſs the Future of the Infinitive Active.

SUM is an irregular verb, and thus conjugated :

Principal Parts.

Preſ. Indic.   Perf. Indic.   Preſ. Infin.
Sum,   fui,   eſſe,   *To be.*

Indicative Mode.

Preſent Tenſe.   *am.*

Sing.   Plur.

	Sing.		*Plur.*
1.	Sum, *I am,*		Sŭmus, *We are,*
2.	Es, *Thou art,* or *you are,*		Eſtis, *Ye* or *you are,*
3.	Eſt, *He is ;*		Sunt, *They are.*

Imperfect.

Imperfect.   *was.*

1. Eram, *I was,*   Erāmus, *We were,*
2. Eras, *Thou waft, or you were,*   Erātis, *Ye were,*
3. Erat, *He was;*   Erant, *They were.*

Perfect.   *have been or was.*

1. Fui, *I have been,*   Fuĭmus, *We have been,*
2. Fuifti, *Thou haft been,*   Fuiftis, *Ye have been,*
3. Fuit, *He hath been;*   Fuērunt, *or* -ēre, *They have been.*

Plu-perfect.   *had been.*

1. Fuĕram, *I had been,*   Fuĕrāmus, *We had been,*
2. Fueras, *Thou hadft been,*   Fueratis, *Ye had been,*
3. Fuerat, *He had been;*   Fuerant, *They had been.*

Future.   *fhall or will.*

1. Ero, *I fhall be,*   Erĭmus, *We fhall be,*
2. Eris, *Thou fhalt be,*   Erĭtis, *Ye fhall be,*
3. Erit, *He fhall be;*   Erunt, *They fhall be.*

Subjunctive Mode.
Prefent Tenfe.   *may or can.*

1. Sim, *I may be,*   Sīmus, *We may be,*
2. Sis, *Thou mayeft be,*   Sītis, *Ye may be,*
3. Sit, *He may be;*   Sint, *They may be.*

Imperfect.   *might, could, would, or fhould.*

1. Effem, *I might be,*   Efsēmus, *We might be,*
2. Effes, *Thou mighteft be,*   Effetis, *Ye might be,*
3. Effet, *He might be;*   Effent, *They might be.*

Perfect.   *may have.*

1. Fuĕrim, *I may have been,*   Fuĕrĭmus, *We may have been,*
2. Fueris, *Thou mayeft have been,* Fueritis, *Ye may have been,*
3. Fuerit, *He may have been;*   Fuerint, *They may have been.*

Plu-perfect.   *might, could, would, or fhould have; or had.*

1. Fuiffem, *I might have been,*   Fuifsēmus, *We might have been,*
2. Fuiffes, *Thou mighteft have   Fuiffetis, *Ye might have been,*
   been,*
3. Fuiffet, *He might have been;*   Fuiffent, *They might have been.*

Future.   *fhall have.*

1. Fuĕro, *I fhall have been,*   Fuĕrĭmus, *We fhall have been,*
2. Fueris, *Thou fhalt have been,*   Fueritis, *Ye fhall have been,*
3. Fuerit, *He fhall have been;*   Fuerint, *They fhall have been.*

Imperativ:

Imperative Mode.

2. Es *vel* esto,   *Be thou,*   Este *vel* estōte,   *Be ye,*
3. Esto,   *Let him be ;*   Sunto,   *Let them be.*

Infinitive Mode.

Pref. Esse,   *To be.*
Perf. Fuisse,   *To have been.*
Fut. Esse futurus, -a, -um, *To be about to be.*
    Fuisse futurus, -a, -um, *To have been about to be.*

Participle.

Future.   Fŭtūrus, -a, -um, *About to be.*

Obf. 1. The perfonal pronouns, which in Englifh are, for the moft part, added to the verb, in Latin are commonly underftood ; becaufe the feveral perfons are fufficiently diftinguifhed from one another by the different terminations of the verb, though the perfons themfelves be not expreffed. The learner however at firft may be accuftomed to join them with the verb ; thus, *ego fum,* I am ; *tu es,* thou art, *or* you are ; *ille eft,* he is ; *nos fumus,* we are, *&c.* So *ego ămo,* I love ; *tu amas,* thou loveft, *or* you love ; *ille amat,* he loveth *or* loves ; *nos amamus,* we love, *&c.*

Obf. 2. In the fecond perfon fingular in Englifh, we commonly ufe the plural form, except in folemn difcourfe ; as, *tu es,* thou art, *or* much *oftener,* you are ; *tu eras,* thou waft, *or* you were ; *tu fis,* thou mayeft be, *or* you may be, *&c.* So *tu amas,* thou loveft, *or* you love ; *tu amabas,* thou lovedft, *or* you loved, *&c.*

Verbs are thus varied in the different Conjugations.

FIRST CONJUGATION.

ACTIVE VOICE.

Principal Parts.

Pref. Indic.	*Perfect.*	*Supine.*	*Pref. Infinit.*
Amo,	ămāvi,	ămātum,	ămāre, *To love.*

Indicative Mode.

Prefent Tenfe. *love, do love,* or *am loving.*

Sing. 1.	AM-o,	*I love,*
	2. Am-as,	*Thou loveft,* or *you love ;*
	3. Am-at,	*He loveth,* or *he loves ;*
Plur. 1.	Am-āmus,	*We love,*
	2. Am-atis,	*Ye* or *you love,*
	3. Am-ant,	*They love.*

Imperfect.

Imperfect.   *loved, did love,* or *was loving.*

Sing.	1. Am-ābam,	*I loved,*
	2. Am-abas,	*Thou lovedst,*
	3. Am-abat,	*He loved;*
Plur.	1. Am-abamus,	*We loved,*
	2. Am-abatis,	*Ye* or *you loved,*
	3. Am-abant,	*They loved.*

Perfect.   *loved, have loved,* or *did love.*

Sing.	1. Am-āvi,	*I have loved,*
	2. Am-avisti,	*Thou hast loved,*
	3. Am-avit,	*He hath loved;*
Plur.	1. Am-āvĭmus,	*We have loved,*
	2. Am-avistis,	*Ye have loved,*
	3. Am-avērunt, v.-avēre,	*They have loved.*

Plu-perfect.   *had.*

Sing.	1. Am-āvĕram,	*I had loved,*
	2. Am-averas,	*Thou hadst loved,*
	3. Am-averat,	*He had loved;*
Plur.	1. Am-averamus,	*We had loved,*
	2. Am-averatis,	*Ye had loved,*
	3. Am-averant,	*They had loved.*

Future.   *shall* or *will.*

Sing.	1. Am-ābo,	*I shall love,*
	2. Am-abis,	*Thou shalt love,*
	3. Am-abit,	*He shall love;*
Plur.	1. Am-abĭmus,	*We shall love,*
	2. Am-abitis,	*Ye shall love,*
	3. Am-abunt.	*They shall love.*

Subjunctive Mode.

Present Tense.   *may* or *can.*

Sing.	1. Am-em,	*I may love,*
	2. Am-es,	*Thou mayest love,*
	3. Am-et,	*He may love;*
Plur.	1. Am-ēmus,	*We may love,*
	2. Am-etis,	*Ye may love,*
	3. Am-ent,	*They may love.*

Imperfect.

Imperfect.   *might, could, would, or should.*

Sing. 1. Am-ārem,   *I might love,*
   2. Am-ares,   *Thou mightest love,*
   3. Am-aret,   *He might love;*
Plur. 1. Am-arēmus,   *We might love,*
   2. Am-aretis,   *Ye might love,*
   3. Am-arent,   *They might love.*

Perfect.   *may have.*

Sing. 1. Am-āvĕrim,   *I may have loved,*
   2. Am-averis,   *Thou mayest have loved,*
   3. Am-averit,   *He may have loved;*
Plur. 1. Am-averĭmus,   *We may have loved,*
   2. Am-averitis,   *Ye may have loved,*
   3. Am-averint,   *They may have loved.*

Plu-perfect.   *might, could, would, or should have; or had.*

Sing. 1. Am-avissem,   *I might have loved,*
   2. Am-avisses,   *Thou mightest have loved,*
   3. Am-avisset,   *He might have loved;*
Plur. 1. Am-avissemus,   *We might have loved,*
   2. Am-avissetis,   *Ye might have loved,*
   3. Am-avissent,   *They might have loved.*

Future.   *shall have.*

Sing. 1. Am-āvĕrò,   *I shall have loved,*
   2. Am-averis,   *Thou shalt have loved,*
   3. Am-averit,   *He shall have loved;*
Plur. 1. Am-averĭmus,   *We shall have loved,*
   2. Am-averitis,   *Ye shall have loved,*
   3. Am-averint,   *They shall have loved.*

Imperative Mode.

Sing. 2. Am-a, *vel* am-āto,   *Love thou,* or *do thou love,*
   3. Am-ato,   *Let him love;*
Plur. 2. Am-āte, *vel* amatōte, *Love ye,* or *do ye love,*
   3. Am-anto,   *Let them love.*

Infinitive Mode.

Pref. Am-āre,   *To love.*
Perf. Am-avisse,   *To have loved.*
Fut. Esse amaturus, -a, -um,   *To be about to love.*
   Fuisse amaturus, -a, -um, *To have been about to love.*

Participle.

Participle.

Prefent, Am-ans, Loving.
Future, Am-aturus, -a, -um, About to love.

Gerunds.

Nom. Am-andum, Loving,
Gen. Am-andi, Of loving,
Dat. Am-ando, To loving,
Acc. Am-andum, Loving,
Abl. Am-ando, With loving.

Supine.

Former. Am-ātum, To love,
Latter. Am-atu, To love, or to be loved.

PASSIVE VOICE.

Prefent Indicative. *Perfect Participle.* *Infinitive.*
Amor, amātus, amāri, to be loved.

Indicative Mode.

Prefent Tenfe. am.

Sing. 1. Am-or, I am loved,
2. Am-āris, vel -āre, Thou art loved,
3. Am-atur, He is loved;
Plur. 1. Am-amur, We are loved,
2. Am-amĭni, Ye or you are loved,
3. Am-antur, They are loved.

Imperfect. was.

Sing. 1. Am-ābar, I was loved,
2. Am-abāris vel -abāre, Thou waft loved,
3. Am-abatur, He was loved;
Plur. 1. Am-abamur, We were loved,
2. Am-abamĭni, Ye were loved,
3. Am-abantur, They were loved.

Perfect. am; have been, or was.

Sing. 1. Amatus fum, vel fui, I have been loved,
2. Amatus es, v. fuifti, Thou haft been loved,
3. Amatus eft, v. fuit, He hath been loved;
Plur. 1. Amati fumus, v. fuimus, We have been loved,
2. Amati eftis, v. fuiftis, Ye have been loved,
3. Amati funt, fuĕrunt, v fuēre, They have been loved.

Plu-perfect.

Plu-perfect. *had been, or was.*

Sing.	1. Amatus eram *vel* fueram,	*I had been loved,*
	2. Amatus eras *v.* fueras,	*Thou hadst been loved,*
	3. Amatus erat *v.* fuerat,	*He had been loved;*
Plur.	1. Amati eramus *v.* fueramus,	*We had been loved,*
	2. Amati eratis *v.* fueratis,	*Ye had been loved,*
	3. Amati erant *v.* fuerant,	*They had been loved.*

Future. *shall, or will be.*

Sing.	1. Am-ābor,	*I shall be loved,*
	2. Am-abĕris *vel* -abĕre,	*Thou shalt be loved,*
	3. Am-abĭtur,	*He shall be loved;*
Plur.	1. Am-ābĭmur,	*We shall be loved,*
	2. Am-abimini,	*Ye shall be loved,*
	3. Am-abuntur,	*They shall be loved.*

Subjunctive Mode.

Present Tense. *may or can be.*

Sing.	1. Am-er,	*I may be loved,*
	2. Am-ēris *vel* -ēre,	*Thou mayst be loved,*
	3. Am-etur,	*He may be loved;*
Plur.	1. Am-ēmur,	*We may be loved,*
	2. Am-emini,	*Ye may be loved,*
	3. Am-entur,	*They may be loved.*

Imperfect. *might, could, would, or should be.*

Sing.	1. Am-ārer,	*I might be loved,*
	2. Am-arēris *vel* -arēre,	*Thou mightest be loved,*
	3. Am-aretur,	*He might be loved;*
Plur.	1. Am-ārēmur,	*We might be loved,*
	2. Am-aremini,	*Ye might be loved,*
	3. Am-arentur,	*They might be loved.*

Perfect. *may have been.*

Sing.	1. Amatus sim *vel* fuerim,	*I may have been loved,*
	2. Amatus sis *v.* fueris,	*Thou mayst have been loved,*
	3. Amatus sit *v.* fuerit,	*He may have been loved;*
Plur.	1. Amati simus *v.* fuerimus,	*We may have been loved,*
	2. Amati sitis *v.* fueritis,	*Ye may have been loved,*
	3. Amati sint *v.* fuerint,	*They may have been loved.*

Plu-perfect. *might, could, would, or should have been; or had been.*

Sing.	1. Amatus essem *vel* fuissem,	*I might have been loved,*
	2. Amatus esses *v.* fuisses,	*Thou mightest have been loved,*
	3. Amatus esset *v.* fuisset,	*He might have been loved;*

Plur.

Plur. 1. Amati essemus *v.* fuissemus,   *We might have been loved,*
      2. Amati essetis *v.* fuissetis,   *Ye might have been loved,*
      3. Amati essent *v.* fuissent,   *They might have been loved.*

Future. *shall have been.*

Sing. 1. Amatus fuero,   *I shall have been loved,*
      2. Amatus fueris,   *Thou shalt have been loved,*
      3. Amatus fuerit,   *He shall have been loved;*
Plur. 1. Amati fuerimus,   *We shall have been loved,*
      2. Amati fueritis,   *Ye shall have been loved,*
      3. Amati fuerint,   *They shall have been loved.*

Imperative Mode.

Sing. 2. Am-are *vel* am-ator,   *Be thou loved,*
       3. Am-ator,   *Let him be loved;*
Plur. 2. Am-amini,   *Be ye loved,*
       3. Am-antor,   *Let them be loved.*

Infinitive Mode.

Pres. Am-ari,   *To be loved.*
Perf. Esse *v.* fuisse amatus, -a, -um,   *To have been loved.*
Fut. Am-atum iri,   *To be about to be loved.*

Participle.

Perf. Am-atus, -a, -um,   *Loved.*
Fut. Am-andus, -a, -um,   *To be loved.*

SECOND CONJUGATION.

ACTIVE VOICE.

Doceo,   docui,   doctum,   docere,   *To teach.*

Indicative Mode.

	Sing.			Plur.		
	1.	2.	3.	1.	2.	3.
Pres.	Doc-eo,	-es,	-et ;	-emus,	-etis,	-ent.
Imp.	Doc-ebam,	-ebas,	-ebat ;	-ebamus,	-ebatis,	-ebant.
Perf.	Doc-ui,	-uisti,	-uit ;	-uimus,	-uistis,	-uerunt, *v.* uere.
Plu.	Doc-ueram,	-ueras,	-uerat ;	-ueramus,	-ueratis,	-uerant.
Fut.	Doc-ebo,	-ebis,	-ebit ;	-ebimus,	-ebitis,	-ebunt.

Subjunctive Mode.

	1.	2.	3.	1.	2.	3.
Pres.	Doc-eam,	-eas,	-eat ;	-eamus,	-eatis,	-eant.
Imp.	Doc-erem,	-eres,	-eret ;	-eremus,	-eretis,	-erent.
Perf.	Doc-uerim,	-ueris,	-uerit ;	-uerimus,	-ueritis,	-uerint.
Plu.	Doc-uissem,	-uisses,	-uisset ;	-uissemus,	-uissetis,	-uissent.
Fut.	Doc-uero,	-ueris,	-uerit ;	-uerimus,	-ueritis,	-uerint.

                          Imperative,

Imperative Mode.

	2.	3.	2.	3.
Pref.	Doc-e *vel* -ēto,	-ēto ;	-ēte *vel* -etote,	-ento.

Infinitive. *Participles.* *Gerunds.* *Supines.*

Pref. Doc-ēre. *Pr.* Doc-ens, Doc-endŭm, 1. Doc-tŭm,
Perf. Doc-uiffe. *Fut.* Doc-tūrus. Doc-endi, 2. Dóc-tu.
Fut. Effe-doĉturus, -a, -um. Doc-endo, &c.
      Fuiffe doĉturus, -a, -um.

PASSIVE VOICE.

Dŏceor, doĉtus, dŏcēri, *To be taught.*

Indicative Mode.

       Sing.   *Plur.*

Pref. Doc-eor, -ēris, *vel* -ēre, -etur ; -emur, -emĭni, -entur.

Imp. Doc-ēbar, -ebāris, *vel* -ebare, -ebatur ; -ebamur, -ebamini, -ebantur.

Perf. Doĉtus fum *vel* fui, doĉtus es *vel* fuifti, &c.

Plu. Doĉtus eram *v.* fueram, doĉtus eras *v.* fueras, &c.

Fut. Doc-ebor, -ēbĕris, *vel* -ebere, -ebĭtur ; -ebĭmur, -ebimini, -ebuntur.

Subjunctive Mode.

Pref. Doc-ear, -cāris, *vel* -eare, -catur ; -eamur, -eamĭni, -eantur.

Imp. Doc-erer, -erēris, *vel* -erēre, -eretur ; -eremur, -eremini, -erentur.

Perf. Doĉtus fim *vel* fuerim, doĉtus fis *vel* fueris, &c.
Plu. Doĉtus effem *v.* fuiffem, doĉtus effes *v.* fuiffes, &c.
Fut. Doĉtus fuero, doĉtus fueris, doĉtus fuerit, doĉti fuerimus, &c.

Imperative Mode.

	2.	3.	2.	3.
Pref.	Doc-ēre *vel* -ētor,	-etor ;	-emĭni,	-entor.

Infinitive.   *Participles.*

Pref. Doc-eri,   *Perf.* Doc-tus, -a, -um.
Perf. Effe *vel* fuiffe doĉtus, -a, -um, *Fut.* Doc-endus, -a, -um.
Fut. Doĉtum iri.

THIRD

THIRD CONJUGATION.

ACTIVE VOICE.

Lĕgo,   lēgi,   lĕctum,   lĕgĕre;   *To read.*

Indicative Mode.

	Sing.			Plur.		
	1.	2.	3.	1.	2.	3.
Pref.	Leg-o,	-is,	-it ;	-ĭmus,	-ĭtis,	-unt.
Imp.	Leg-ēbam,	-ebas,	-ebat ;	-ebamus,	-ebatis,	-ebant.
Perf.	Lēg-i,	-ĭsti,	-it ;	-ĭmus,	-ĭstis,	-ērunt, -ēre.
Plu.	Lēg-ĕram,	-eras,	-erat ;	-eramus,	-eratis,	-erant.
Fut.	Lĕg-am,	-es,	-et ;	-ēmus,	-etis,	-ent.

Subjunctive Mode.

Pref.	Lĕg-am,	-as,	-at ;	-amus,	-atis,	-ant.
Imp.	Lĕg-ĕrem,	-eres,	-cret ;	-ērēmus,	-eretis,	-erent.
Perf.	Lēg-ĕrim,	-eris,	-erit ;	-erĭmus,	-eritis,	-erint.
Plu.	Lēg-ĭssem,	-ĭsses,	-ĭsset ;	-ĭssemus,	-ĭssetis,	-ĭssent.
Fut.	Lēg-ĕro,	-eris,	-erit ;	-erĭmus,	-eritis,	-erint.

Imperative Mode.

	2.	3.	2.	3.
	Lĕg-e, *vel* -ĭto,	-ĭto ;	-ĭte, *vel* -ĭtōte;	-unto.

Infinitive.	*Participles.*	*Gerunds.*	*Supines.*
Lĕg-ĕre,	*Pr.* Leg-ens.	Lĕg-endum.	1. Lec-tum.
Perf. Lĕg-ĭsse,	*Fut.* Lec-tūrus.	Leg-endi.	2. Lec-tu.
Fut. Esse lectūrus, -a, -um,		Leg-endo, &c.	
Fuisse lectūrus, -a, -um.			

PASSIVE VOICE.

Lĕgor,   lĕctus,   lĕgi,   *To be read.*

Indicative Mode.

	Sing.			Plur.		
Pref.	Leg-or,	-ĕris, *vel* -ĕre,	-ĭtur ;	-ĭmur,	-imĭni,	-ŭntur.
Imp.	Leg-ēbar,	-ebaris, *vel* -ebāre,	-ebatur;	-ebamŭr,	-ebamini,	-ebantur.
Perf.	Lectus sum *vel* fui, lectus es *vel* fuisti, &c.					
Plu.	Lectus eram *vel* fueram, lectus eras *vel* fueras, &c.					
Fut.	Leg-ar,	-ēris, *vel* -ēre,	-ētur ;	-ēmur,	-emini,	-entur.

Subjunctive

Subjunctive Mode.

Pref. Lĕg-ar, -āris, *vel* āre, -atur ; -amur, -amini, -antur.

Imp. Leg-ĕrer, -erēris, *vel* -erēre, -eretur ; -eremur, -eremini, -erentur.

Perf. Lĕctus fim *vel* fuerim, lĕctus fis *vel* fueris, &c.

Plu. Lĕctus effem *v.* fuiffem, lĕctus effes *v.* fuiffes, &c.

Fut. Lĕctus fuero, lĕctus fueris, lĕctus fuerit, &c.

Imperative Mode.

   2.   3.   2.   3.

Pref. Leg-ĕre, *vel* -ĭtor, -ĭtor ; -imĭni, -untor.

   Infinitive.   *Participles.*

Pref. Lĕg-i.   *Perf.* Lec-tus, -a, -um.

Perf. Effe *v.* fuiffe lĕctus, -a, -um. *Fut.* Leg-endus, -a, -um.

Fut. Lĕctum iri.

FOURTH CONJUGATION.
ACTIVE VOICE.

Audio, audīvi, audītum, audīre, *To hear.*

Indicative Mode.

  Sing.   *Plur.*

   1. 2. 3. 1. 2. 3.

Pr. Aud-io, -is, -it ; -īmus, -ītis, -iunt.

Imp. Aud-iēbam, -iebas, -iebat ; -iebamus, -iebatis, -iebant.

Per. Aud-īvi, -ivifti, -ivit ; -ivĭmus, -iviftis, -ivērunt, *vel* -ivēre.

Plu. Aud-ivĕram, -iveras, -iverat ; -iveramus, -iveratis, -iverant.

Fut. Aud-iam, -ies, -iet ; -iemus, -ietis, -ient.

Subjunctive Mode.

Pr. Aud-iam, -ias, -iat ; -iamus, -iatis, -iant.

Imp. Aud-īrem, -ires, -iret ; -irēmus, -iretis, -irent.

Per. Aud-iverim, -iveris, -iverit ; -iverĭmus, -iveritis, -iverint.

Plu. Aud-iviffem, -iveffes, -iveffet ; -iviffemus, -iviffetis, -iviffent.

Fut. Aud-ivero, -iveris, -iverit ; -iverimus, -iveritis, -iverint.

Imperative Mode.

   2.   3.   2.   3.

Pr. Aud-i, *vel* -īto ; -īto ; -īte, *vel* -itōte, -iunto.

                Infinitive.

Infinitive.	*Participles.*	*Gerunds.*	*Supines.*
Pr. Aud-īre.	*Pr.* Aud-iens.	Aud-iendum.	1. Auditum.
Per. Aud-iviſſe.	*Fu.* Aud-iturus.	Aud-iendi.	2. Auditu.
Fut. Eſſe auditūrus, -a, -um;		Aud-iendo, &c.	
Fuiſſe auditurus, -a, -um.			

PASSIVE VOICE.

Audior,   Audītus,   Audīri;   *To be heard.*

Indicative Mode.

	Sing.		*Plur.*	
Preſ. Aud-ior,	-īris, *vel* -īre,	-ītur;	-īmur, -īmĭni, -iuntur.	
Imp. Aud-iēbar,	-iebaris, *vel* -iebare,	-iebatur;	-iebāmur, -iebamini, -iebantur.	
Perf. Auditus ſum, *vel* ſui, Auditus es *v.* fuiſti, &c.				
Plu. Auditus eram *v.* fueram, Auditus eras *v.* fueras, &c.				
Fut. Aud-iar,	-ieris, *vel* -iere,	-ietur;	-iemur, -iemini, -ientur.	

Subjunctive Mode.

Preſ. Aud-iar,	-iaris, *vel* -iare,	-iatur;	-iamur, -iamini, -iantur.	
Imp. Aud-irer,	-ireris, *vel* -irere,	-iretur;	-iremur, -iremini, -irentur.	
Perf. Auditus ſim *vel* fuerim, Auditus ſis *v.* fueris, &c.				
Plu. Auditus eſſem *v.* fuiſſem, Auditus eſſes *v.* fuiſſes, &c.				
Fut. Auditus fuero, Auditus fueris, &c.				

Imperative Mode.

	2.	3.	2.	3.
Preſ. Aud-īre, *vel* -ītor,		-ītor;	-īmĭni,	-iuntor.

Infinitive.	*Participles.*
Pr. Aud-iri,	*Per.* Audī-tus, -a, -um.
Per. Eſſe *vel* fuiſſe aud-itus, -a, -um;	*Fut.* Aud-iendus, -a, -um.
Fut. Aud-ītum iri.	

FORMATION OF VERBS.

There are four principal parts of a verb, from which all the reſt are formed; namely, *o* of the preſent, *i* of the perfect, *um* of the ſupine, and *re* of the infinitive; according to the following rhyme.

K 2

1. From

X 1. From *o* are formed *am* and *em*.

 2. From *i; ram, rim, ro, ſſe,* and *ſſem*.

 3. *U, us,* and *rus,* are formed from *um*.

 4. All other parts from *re* do come ; as, *bam, bo, rem ;
a, e,* and *i ; ns* and *dus ; dum, do,* and *di ;* X as,

AM-o, em ; AM-AVI, -eram, -erim, -iſſem, -ero, -iſſe ; AMAT-UM,
   -u, -urus, -us ; AM-ARE, -abam, -abo, -arem, -a, -ans, -andum,
   di, do; -andus.
Doc-EO, -eam ; Doc-UI, -ueram, &c. ; DOCT-UM, -u, -urus, -us ;
   Doc-ERE, -ebam, -ebo, -erem, -e, -ens, -endum, di, do, -endus.
LEG-o, -am ; LEG-I, -eram, &c.; LECT-UM, -u, -urus, -us ; LEG-
   ĕRE, -ebam, -ĕrem, -e, -ens, -endum, &c.
AUD-IO, -iam ; AUD-IVI, -iveram, &c. ; AUDIT-UM, -u, -urus, -us :
   AUD-IRE, -iebam, -irem, -i, -iens, -iendum, di, do, -iendus.——So
   verbs of the third conjugation in *io ;* as, CAP-IO, -iam ; CEP-I,
   -eram, &c.; CAPT-UM, -u, &c.; CAP-ĕRE, -iebam, -ĕrem, -e, -iens,
   -iendum, di, do, -iendus.

The paſſive voice is formed from the active, by adding *r* to *o,* or
changing *m* into *r*.

But it is much more eaſy and natural to form all the
parts of a verb from the preſent and perfect of the indicative, and from the ſupine ; thus,

AM-o, -ābam, -ābo, -em, -ārem, -a *or* -āto, -āre, -ans, -andum, di,
   do, &c. -andus :
AMAV-I, -ĕram, -ĕrim, -iſſem, -ĕro, -iſſe : AMĀT-UM, -us, -ūrus.
So Doc-EO, -ēbam, -ēbo, -eam, -ĕrem, -e *or* -eto, ēre, -ens,
   -endum, di, &c. -endus ; Docu-I, ĕram, -ĕrim, -iſſem, -ĕro, -iſſe :
   DOCT-UM, -us, -ūrus.
LĔG-o, -ēbam, -am, es, et, &c. -am, as, at, &c. -ĕrem, -e *or* -Ito,
   -ĕre, -ens, -endum, &c. -endus :
LĔG-I, -ĕram, &c. LECT-UM, -us, -urus :
CĂP-IO, -iēbam, -iam, ies, iet, &c. -iam, ias, &c. -ĕrem, -e *or*
   -Ito, -ĕre, -iens, -iendum, -iendus : CĔP-I, -ĕram, &c. CAPT-UM,
   -us, -ūrus.
AUD-IO, -iēbam, &c. AUDĪV-I, -ĕram, &c.

A verb is commonly ſaid to be conjugated, when only
its principal parts are mentioned, becauſe from them all
the reſt are derived.
The firſt perſon of the Preſent of the Indicative is called
the *Theme* or the *Root* of the verb, becauſe from it the
other three principal parts are formed.

The letters of a verb which always remain the ſame, are
called *Radical* letters ; as, *am* in *am-o*. The reſt are called the *Termination ;* as, *abamus* in *am-abamus*.

All

All the letters which come before -*āre*, -*ēre*, -*ĕre*, or *ire*, of the infinitive, are radical letters. By putting these before the terminations, all the parts of any regular verb may be readily formed, except the compound tenses.

SIGNIFICATION *of the* TENSES *in the various Modes.*

The tenses formed from the present of the indicative or infinitive signify in general the continuance of an action or passion, or represent them as present at some particular time : the other tenses express an action or passion completed ; but not always so absolutely, as entirely to exclude the continuance of the same action or passion ; thus, *Amo*, I love, do love, *or* am loving ; *amabam*, I loved, did love, *or* was loving, &c.

Amavi, I loved, did love, *or* have loved, *that is*, have done with loving, &c.

In like manner, in the passive voice ; *Amor*, I am loved, I am in loving, *or* in being loved, &c.

Past time in the passive voice is expressed several different ways, by means of the auxiliary verb *sum*, and the participle perfect ; thus,

Indicative Mode.

Perfect. *Amatus sum*, I am, *or* have been loved, *or oftener*, I was loved.
    Amatus fui, I have been loved, *or* I was loved.
Plu-perfect. *Amatus eram*, I was *or* had been loved.
    Amatus fueram, I had been loved.

Subjunctive Mode.

Perfect. *Amatus sim*, I may be *or* may have been loved.
    Amatus fuerim, I may have been loved.
Plu-perfect. *Amatus essem*, I might, could, would, *or* should be *or* have been loved.
    Amatus fuissem, I might, could, would, *or* should have been loved ; *or* I had been loved.
Future. *Amatus fuero*, I shall have been loved.

The verb *sum* is also employed to express future time in the indicative mode, both active and passive ; thus,
    Amaturus sum, I am about to love, I am to love, I am going to love, *or* I will love. We chiefly use this form, when some purpose or intention is signified.
    Amatus ero, I shall be loved.

Obs. 1. The participles *amatus* and *amaturus* are put before the auxiliary verb, because we commonly find them so placed in the classics.

Obs. 2. In these compound tenses the learner should be taught to vary the participle like an adjective noun, according to the gender and number of the different substantives to which it is applied ; thus, *amatus est*, he is *or* was loved, when applied to a man ; *amata est*, she was loved, when applied to a woman ; *amatum est*, it was loved, when applied to a thing ; *amati sunt*, they were loved, when
applied

applied to men, &c. The connecting of syntax, so far as is necessary, with the inflection of nouns and verbs, seems to be the most proper method of teaching both.

Obs. 3. The past time and participle perfect in English are taken in different meanings, according to the different tenses in Latin which they are used to express. Thus, "I loved," when put for *amabam*, is taken in a sense different from what it has when put for *amavi*: so *amor*, and *amatus sum*, I am loved ; *amabar*, and *amatus eram*, I was loved ; *amer*, and *amatus sim*, &c. In the one, *loved* is taken in a present, in the other, in a past sense. This ambiguity arises from the defective nature of the English verb.

Obs. 4. The tenses of the subjunctive mode may be variously rendered, according to their connection with the other parts of a sentence. They are often expressed in English as the same tenses of the indicative, and sometimes one tense apparently put for another.

Thus, *Quasi intelligant, qualis sit*: As if they understood, what kind of person he is, Cic. *In facinus jurasse putas*, You would think, &c, Ov. *Eloquar an sileam?* Shall I speak out, or be silent? *Nec vos arguerim, Teucri*, for *arguam*, Virg. *Si quid te fugerit, ego perierim*, for *peribo*, Ter. *Hunc ego si potui tantum sperare dolorem ; Et perferre, soror, petero:* for *potuissem* and *possem*, Virg. *Singula quid referam?* Why should I mention every thing? Id. *Prædiceres mihi*, You should have told me before hand, Ter. *At tu dictis, Albane, maneres*, Ought to have stood to your word, Virg. *Citius crediderim*, I should sooner believe, Juv. *Hauserit ensis*, The sword would have destroyed, Virg. *Fuerint irati*, Grant or suppose they were angry. *Si id fecisset*, If he did or should do that, Cic. The same promiscuous use of the tenses seems also to take place sometimes in the indicative and infinitive ; and the indicative to be put for the subjunctive ; as, *Animus meminisse horret, luctuque refugit*, for *refugit*, Virg. *Fuerat melius*, for *fuisset*, Id. *Invidiæ dilapsa erat*, for *fuisset*, Sall. *Quamdiu in portum venis?* for *venisti*, Plaut. *Quam mox navigo Ephesum*, for *navigabo*, Id. *Tu si hic sis, aliter sentias*, Ter. for *esses* and *sentires*. *Cato affirmat, se vivo, illum non triumphare*, for *triumphaturum esse*, Cic. *Persuadet Castico, ut occuparet*, for *occupet*, Cæs.

Obs. 5. The future of the subjunctive, and also of the indicative, is often rendered by the present of the subjunctive in English ; as, *nisi hoc faciet*, or *fecerit*, unless he do this, Ter.

Obs. 6. Instead of the imperative we often use the present of the subjunctive ; as, *valeas*, farewell ; *huc venias*, come hither, &c. And also the future both of the indicative and subjunctive ; as, *non occides*, do not kill ; *ne feceris*, do not do it ; *valebis*, *meque amabis*, farewell, and love me. Cic.

The present time and the preter-imperfect of the infinitive are both expressed under the same form. All the varieties of past and future time are expressed by the other two tenses. But in order properly to exemplify the tenses of the infinitive mode, we must put an accusative, and some other verb, before each of them ; thus,

Dicit

Dicit me scribere; he says *that* I write, do write, *or* am writing.
Dixit me scribere; he said *that* I wrote, did write, *or* was writing.
Dicit me scripsisse; he says *that* I wrote, did write, *or* have written.
Dixit me scripsisse; he said *that* I had written.
Dicit me scripturum esse; he says *that* I will write.
Dixit nos scripturos esse; he said *that* we would write.
Dicit nos scripturos fuisse; he says *that* we would have written.
Dicit literas scribi; he says *that* letters are written, writing, a-writing, or in writing.
Dixit literas scribi; he said *that* letters were writing, *or* written.
Dicit literas scripta esse; he says *that* letters are *or* were written.
Dicit literas scriptas fuisse; he says *that* letters have been written.
Dixit literas scriptas fuisse; he said *that* letters had been written.
Dicit literas scriptum iri; he says *that* letters will be written.
Dixit literas scriptum iri; he said *that* letters would be written.

The future, *scriptum iri,* is made up of the former supine, and the infinitive passive of the verb *eo,* and therefore never admits of any variation.

The future of the infinitive is sometimes expressed by a periphrasis or circumlocution; thus, *scio fore* vel *futurum esse ut scribant,—ut literæ scribantur,* I know that they will write,—that letters will be written. *Scivi fore* vel *futurum esse ut scriberent,—ut literæ scriberentur;* I knew that they would write, &c. *Scivi futurum fuisse, ut literæ scriberentur;* I knew that letters would have been written. This form is necessary in verbs which want the supine.

Obs. 7. The different tenses, when joined with any expediency or necessity, are thus expressed:

Scribendum est mihi, puero, nobis, &c. *literas;* I, the boy, we, &c. must write letters.
Scribendum fuit mihi, puero, nobis, &c. I must have written, &c.
Scribendum erit mihi; I shall be obliged to write.
Scio scribendum esse mihi literas; I know that I must write letters.
——*Scribendum fuisse mihi;*——that I must have written.
Dixit scribendum fore mihi; He said that I would be obliged to write.

Or with the participle in *dus,*

Literæ sunt scribendæ mihi, puero, hominibus, &c. or *a me, puero,* &c.; Letters are to be, *or* must be written by me, by the boy, by men, &c. So *literæ scribendæ erant, fuerunt, erunt,* &c. *Si literæ scribendæ sint, essent, forent,* &c. *Scio literas scribendas esse;* I know *that* letters are to be, *or* must be written. *Scivi literas scribendas fuisse;* I knew *that* letters ought to have been, *or* must have been written.

Note. Most of the simple tenses of a verb in Latin may be expressed, as in English, by the participle and the auxiliary verb *sum;* as, *Sum amans,* for *amo,* I am loving; *eram amans,* for *amabam, &c. Fui te carens,* for *carui,* Plaut. *Ut sis sciens,* for *ut scias,* Ter. Only the tenses in the active which come from the preterite, and those in the passive which come from the present, cannot be properly expressed in this manner; because the Latins have no participle perfect active, nor participle present passive. This manner of expression however does not often occur.

FORMATION

FORMATION OF THE PRETERITE AND SUPINE.

GENERAL RULES.

1. Compound and simple verbs form the preterite and supine in the same manner; as,

Voco, vŏtāvi, vŏcātŭm, to call : so *rĕvŏco, revŏcāvi, revŏcātŭm*, to recall.

Exc. 1. When the simple verb in the preterite doubles the first syllable of the present, the compounds lose the former syllable; as, *pello, pĕpŭli*, to beat; *rĕpello, nĕpŭli*, never *repĕpŭli*, to beat back. But the compounds of *do, sto, disco*, and *posco*, follow the general rule; thus, *ēdisco, ēdĭdici*, to get by heart; *dēposco, dēpŭposci*, to demand: So, *præcurro, præcŭcurri; rĕpungo, rĕpŭpŭgi*.

Exc. 2. Compounds which change *a* of the simple verb into *i*, have *e* in the supine; as, *făcio, fēci, făctum*, to make; *perfĭcio, perfēci, perfĕctum*, to perfect. But compound verbs ending in *do* and *go*; also the compounds of *habeo, placeo, sapio, salio*, and *statuo*, observe the general rule.

2. Verbs which want the preterite, want likewise the supine.

SPECIAL RULES.

First Conjugation.

Verbs of the first conjugation have *āvi* in the preterite, and *ātŭm* in the supine; as,

Creo, creāvi, creātum, to create; *păro, părāvi, părātum*, to prepare.—So,

Abundo, *to abound.*
Accūfo, *to charge with a crime.*
Adumbro, *to shade, to delineate.*
Ædĭfico, *to build.*
Æstĭmo, *to value.*
Ambŭlo, *to walk.*
Amplio, *to enlarge, to put off a cause.*
Anĭmo, *to encourage.*
Antĭcipo, *to anticipate.*
Antīquo, i. e. antiqua probo, *to reject a law.*
Appello, *to call.*
Apprŏpinquo, *to approach.*

Arĭĕto, *to push like a ram.*
Apto, *to fit.*
Ăro, *to plough.*
Ascio, *to cut or hew.*
Afsĕvēro, *to affirm.*
Aufculto, *to listen.*
Auctōro, *to engage for service.*
Autŭmo, *to suppose.*
Averrunco, *to avert.*
Bajŭlo, *to carry.*
Bālo, *to bleat.*
Bāfio, *to kiss.*
Bello, *to war.*
Beo, *to bless.*
Blătĕro, *to babble.*
Boo, *to bellow.*

Būlĭlo, *to hoot like an owl.*
Căco, *to go to stool.*
Cæco, *to blind or dazzle.*
Cælo, *to carve.*
Calceo, *to put on shoes, to shoe.*
Calcĭtro, *to kick.*
Calco, *to tread.*
Cālīgo, *to be dark or dim-sighted.*
Carmino, *to card wool.*
Castīgo, *to chastise.*
Castro, *to cut off.*
Cĕlebro, *to make famous.*
Cēlo, *to conceal.*
Centŭrio, & concen-
        tŭrio,

tūrio, *to divide into companies.*
Certo, *to strive, to fight.*
Cesso, *to ceafe.*
Clamo, *to cry.*
Claudico, *to limp.*
Coagulo, *to curdle.*
Cōgito, *to think.*
Collineo, *to aim at, to hit the mark.*
Cōlo, *to strain.*
Communico, *to impart.*
Comparo, *to compare.*
Compenso, *to make amends.*
Comprehendino, *to put off a caufe to the day after to-morrow.*
Compilo, *to pile up, to pillage.*
Concilio, *to gain, to reconcile.*
Concordo, *to agree.*
Confuto, refuto, *to difprove.*
Congelo, *to freeze.*
Considero, *to consider.*
Contamino, *to pollute.*
Copulo, *to couple.*
Corrugo, *to wrinkle.*
Corrufco, *to brandifh.*
Cremo, *to burn.*
Creo, *to create.*
Cribro, *to fift.*
Crispo, *to curl.*
Crucio, *to torment.*
Curo, *to care.*
Damno, *to condemn.*
Decimo, *to take the tenth part, or punifh every tenth man.*
Declaro, *to declare.*
Decollo, *to loofe a thing from off the neck, to behead.*
Decoro, *to adorn.*
Decurio, *to divide foldiers into files or fmall companies, or citizens into wards.*

Dedico, *to dedicate.*
Delecto, *to delight.*
Delibero, *to deliberate.*
Delineo, *to trace, to chalk out.*
Deliro, *to doat, to rave.*
Delumbo, *to weaken.*
Desidero, *to defire.*
Desolo, *to lay wafte.*
Destino, *to defign.*
Dico, *to dedicate.*
Difcepto, difputo, *to debate.*
Difsipo, *to fcatter.*
Dolo, *to hew or cut.*
Dono, *to prefent.*
Duplico, *to double.*
Educo, *to bring up.*
Ejulo, *to wail, to weep.*
Emancipo, *to free a fon from the power of his father.*
Emendo, *to amend.*
Enucleo, *to take out the kernel, to explain.*
Enodo, *to unknit, to explain.*
Equito, *to ride.*
Erro, *to wander.*
Examino, *to examine, to try.*
Exantlo, *to empty, to endure.*
Exaro, *to plough up, to fcrawl, to write firft.*
Exentero, *to take out the guts.*
Exiftimo, *to think.*
Exploro, *to fearch.*
Extrico, *to difentangle.*
Fabrico, *to frame.*
Fafcino, *to bewitch.*
Fatigo, *to weary.*
Fermento, *to leaven with dough, to ferment.*
Festino, *to haften.*
Flagito, *to dun.*
Flagro, *to be on fire.*

Flo, *to blow.*
Focillo, refocillo, *to cherifh, to warm.*
Fodico, *to pierce or pufh.*
Foro, *to bore.*
Fortuno, *to profper.*
Fragro, *to fmell fweetly.*
Fraudo, *to defraud.*
Frio, *to crumble.*
Fruftro, & -or, *to difappoint.*
Fuco, *to colour, to paint.*
Fugo, *to put to flight.*
Fundo, *to found.*
Genero, *to beget.*
Gravo, *to weigh down.*
Guberno, *to govern.*
Gufto, *to tafte.*
Habito, *to dwell.*
Hæsito, *to doubt.*
Halo, *to breathe.*
Hio, *to gape.*
Honoro, *to honour.*
Jacto, *to boaft, to brag.*
Jento, *to breakfaft.*
Ignoro, *to be ignorant.*
Immolo, *to facrifice.*
Impero, *to command.*
Impetro, *to obtain.*
Inauro, *to gild.*
Inchoo, *to begin.*
Inclino, *to incline.*
Indago, *to trace out.*
Indico, *to fhew.*
Inquino, *to pollute.*
Infpico, *to fharpen at the end.*
Inftauro, *to renew.*
Inftigo, *to pufh on.*
Intercalo, *to infert one or more days, to make the year agree with the courfe of the fun.*
Intro, *to enter.*
Invito, *to invite.*
Irradio, *to fhine upon.*
Irrito, *to provoke.*
Itero, *to do again.*
Jubilo, *to fhout for joy.*
Jurgo,

Jurgo, & -or, *to chide or scold.*
Juro, *to swear.*
Laboro, *to labour.*
Lacero, *to tear.*
Lachrymo, & -or, *to weep.*
Lævigo, *to smooth or polish.*
Lallo, *to sing as a nurse to a child.*
Lanio, *to tear.*
Latro, *to bark.*
Laxo, *to loose.*
Lego, *to send as an ambassador, to bequeath.*
Levo, *to lighten.*
Libo, *to taste.*
Libero, *to free.*
Ligo, *to bind.*
Liquo, *to melt.*
Litigo, *to quarrel.*
Lito, *to appease by sacrifice.*
Lucubro, *to sit up late, to study.*
Lustro, *to survey.*
Luxo, *to put out of joint.*
Macto, *to slay, to sacrifice.*
Mando, *to command, to commit.*
Mano, *to flow.*
Maturo, *to hasten.*
Medico, & -or, *to cure.*
Memoro, *to tell.*
Meo, *to go or pass.*
Meridio, & -or, *to sleep at noon.*
Migro, *to remove.*
Milito, *to be a soldier.*
Ministro, *to serve.*
Mitigo, *to pacify.*
Monstro, *to shew or tell.*
Mulco, *to beat.*
Multo, & -cto, *to fine.*
Musso, & -ito, *to mutter.*
Mutilo, *to maim.*
Muto, *to change.*

Narro, *to tell.*
Nauseo, *to be sea-sick.*
Navigo, *to sail.*
Navo, *to act vigorously.*
Nego, *to deny.*
Nicto, *to wink.*
No, *to swim.*
Nodo, *to knot,* rar. act.
Nomino, *to name.*
Noto, *to mark.*
Novo, *to renew.*
Nudo, *to make bare.*
Numero, *to count.*
Nuncupo, *to call.*
Nuntio, *to tell.*
Nuto, *to nod.*
Obsecro, *to beseech.*
Obsero, *to lock.*
Obtempero, *to obey.*
Obtrunco, *to kill.*
Obturo, *to stop up.*
Occo, *to harrow.*
Odoro, *to perfume.*
Onero, *to load.*
Opto, *to wish.*
Orbo, *to deprive.*
Ordino, *to put in order.*
Orno, *to deck, to adorn.*
Oro, *to beg.*
Oscito, & -or, *to yawn, to be listless.*
Paco, *to subdue.*
Palpito, *to beat or throb.*
Palpo, *to stroke, to gain by flattery.*
Parento, *to perform funeral rites, to revenge.*
Paro, *to prepare.*
Patro, *to perform.*
Pecco, *to sin.*
Penetro, *to pierce.*
Persevero, *to continue constant.*
Pio, *to expiate.*
Placo, *to appease.*
Ploro, *to bewail.*
Porto, *to carry.*
Postulo, *to demand.*
Privo, *to deprive.*

Probo, *to approve.*
Procrastino, *to delay.*
Profligo, *to rout.*
Promulgo, *to publish.*
Propago, *to propagate.*
Propero, *to hasten.*
Propino, *to drink to.*
Protelo, *to chase away.*
Publico, *to publish, to confiscate.*
Pugno, *to fight.*
Pullulo, *to bud.*
Purgo, *to cleanse.*
Puto, *to think.*
Quadro, *to square.*
Recupero, *to recover.*
Recuso, *to refuse.*
Refrigero, *to cool.*
Regelo, *to thaw.*
Reparo, *to repair.*
Repræsento, *to resemble, to shew; to pay money in advance.*
Resero, *to unlock.*
Rigo, *to water.*
Rogo, *to ask.*
Roto, *to wheel about.*
Ructo, & -or, *to belch.*
Rumino, *to chew the* [cud.
Runco, *to weed.* [cud.
Sacro, *to consecrate.*
Sagino, *to fatten.*
Salivo, *to spit or slaver.*
Salto, *to dance.*
Saluto, *to salute.*
Sano, *to heal.*
Satio, *to satisfy.*
Saturo, *to fill, to glut.*
Scarifico, *to lance or open.*
Screo, *to hawk or retch in spitting.*
Secundo, *to prosper.*
Sedo, *to allay.*
Separo, *to sever.*
Servo, *to keep.*
Sibilo, *to hiss.*
Sicco, *to dry.*
Signo, *to mark out.*
Significo,

Significo, *to mean, to give notice.*
Simulo, *to pretend.*
Socio, *to match, to join.*
Solicito, *to stir up, to disquiet.*
Somnio, *to dream.*
Specto, *to behold.*
Spero, *to hope.*
Spiro, *to breathe.*
Spolio, *to rob.*
Spumo, *to foam.*
Stagno, *to stand as water.*
Stillo, *to drop.*
Stimulo, *to goad, to vex.*
Stipo, *to stuff, to guard.*
Strangulo, *to stifle.*
Strigo, *to breathe, or rest in work, as oxen, or horses do.*
Sudo, *to sweat.*
Suffoco, *to strangle.*
Suffico, *to burn incense.*
Sugillo, *to taunt or jeer.*

Sulco, *to furrow.*
Supero, *to overcome.*
Suppedito, *to afford.*
Susurro, *to whisper.*
Tardo, *to stop.*
Taxo, *to rate, to reprove.*
Temero, *to defile.*
Tempero, *to temper.*
Tenuo, *to make small.*
Terebro, *to bore.*
Termino, *to bound.*
Titillo, *to tickle.*
Titubo, *to stagger.*
Tolero, *to bear.*
Trano, *to swim over.*
Tripudio, *to caper.*
Triumpho, *to triumph.*
Trucido, *to kill.*
Turbo, *to disturb.*
Ululo, *to howl.*
Umbro, *to shade.*
Vacillo, *to waver.*
Vaco, *to want, to be at leisure.*

Vasto, *to lay waste.*
Vellico, *to pluck, twitch or pinch; to taunt or rail at.*
Velo, *to cover.*
Ventilo, *to fan.*
Verbero, *to whip.*
Vestigo, *to search for.*
Vibro, *to brandish, to shake.*
Viduo, *to deprive.*
Vigilo, *to watch.*
Vindico, *to claim, to revenge.*
Violo, *to violate.*
Vitio, *to spoil.*
Vito, *to shun.*
Vitupero, *to blame.*
Voco, *to call.*
Volo, *to fly.*
Voro, *to devour.*
Vulgo, *to spread abroad.*
Vulnero, *to wound.*

EXC. 1. *Do, dedi, datum, dare,* to give : so, *venundo,* to sell ; *circundo,* to surround ; *pessundo,* to overthrow ; *satisdo,* to give surety ; *venundedi, venundatum, venundare, &c.* The other compounds of *do* are of the third conjugation.

Sto, steti, statum, to stand. Its compounds have *stiti, stitum,* and oftener *statum ;* as, *præsto, præstiti, præstitum,* or *præstatum,* to excel, to perform. So *ad-, ante-, con-, ex-, in-, ob-, per-, pro-, re-sto.*

EXC. 2. *Lavo, lavi, lotum, lautum, lavatum,* to wash.

Poto, potavi, potum, or *potatum,* to drink.

Juvo, juvi, jutum, to help ; fut. part. *juvaturus.* So *adjuvo.*

EXC. 3. *Cubo, cubui, cubitum,* to ly. So, *ac-, ex-, oc-, re-cubo.* The other compounds insert an *m,* and are of the third conjugation.

Demo, domui, domitum, to subdue. So *e-, per-domo.*

Sono, sonui, sonitum, to sound. So *af-, circum-, con-, dif-, ex-, in-, per-, præ-, re-sono.*

Tono, tonui, tonitum, to thunder. So *at-, circum-, in-, superin-, re-tono.* Horace has *intonatus.*

Veto, vetui, vetitum, to forbid.

L

Crepo,

Crĕpo, crĕpui, crĕpĭtum, to make a noise. So *con-, in-, per-, rĕ-crĕpo : difcrĕpo* has rather *difcrĕpāvi.*

Exc. 4. *Frĭco, frĭcui, friĉtum,* to rub. So *af-, circum-, con-, de-, ef-, in-, per-, re-frĭco.* But fome of thefe have alfo *atum.*

Sĕco, sĕcui, feĉtum, to cut. So *circum-, con-, dē-, dif-, ex-, in-, inter-, per-, præ-, rĕ-, fub-sĕco.*

Nĕco, nĕcui, or *nĕcavi, nĕcātum,* to kill. So *inter-, ē-nĕco :* but thefe have oftener *eĉtum ; eneĉtum, interneĉtum.*

Mĭco, mĭcui, ——— to glitter, to fhine. So *inter-, prō-mĭco. Emĭco,* has *ēmĭcui, ēmĭcātum : dĭmĭco, dimĭcāvi, dimĭcātum,* rarely, *dimĭcui,* to fight.

Exc. 5. Thefe three want both pret. and fup. *lăbo,* to fall or faint ; *nexo,* to bind ; and *plĭco,* to fold.

Plĭco, compounded with a noun, or with the prepofitions *re, fub,* has *āvi, ātum ;* as, *duplĭco, duplĭcavi, duplĭcatum,* to double. So *multi-, fup-, re-plĭco.*

The other compounds of *plĭco* have either *āvi* and *ātum,* or *ui* and *ĭtum ;* as *applĭco, applĭcui, applĭcĭtum,* or *-āvi, ātum,* to apply. So *im-, com-plĭco. Explĭco,* to unfold, has commonly *explĭcui, explĭcitum ;* but when it fignifies to explain or interpret, *explĭcāvi, explĭcātum.*

Second Conjugation.

(Verbs of the fecond conjugation have *ui* and *ĭtum ;* as *hăbeo, habui, habitum,*) to have.—So,

Adhĭbeo, *to admit, to ufe.*
Cohibeo, inhibeo, *to reftrain.*
Exhibeo, *to fhew, to give.*
Pĕrhibeo, *to fay, to give out.*
Prohibeo, *to hinder.*
Pofthabeo, *to value lefs.*
Præbeo, *to afford.*
Rĕdhibeo, *to return or take back a thing that was fold for fome fault.*

Dēbeo, *to owe.*
Mĕreo, *to deferve :* Com-, de-, e-, per-, pro-mĕreo, *or* mereor.
Mŏneo, *to admonifh :* Ad-, com-, præ-mŏneo.
Terreo, *to terrify :* Abf-, con-, de-, ex-, per-terreo.
Dīrĭbeo, *to count over, to diftribute.*

Neuter verbs which have *ui* want the fupine ; as, *āreo, ārui,* to be dry : So,

Aceo, &-fco, *to befour.*
Albeo, *to be white.*
Candeo, *to be white.*
Calleo, *to be hard.*
Cāneo, *to be hoary.*
Clāreo, *to be bright.*
Egeo, indĭgeo, *to want.*
Emĭneo, *to ftand above others.*
Flacceo, *to wither.*
Flōreo, *to flourifh.*
Fœteo, *to ftink.*
Frendeo, *to gnafh the teeth.*
Frondeo, *to bear leaves.*
Horreo, *to be rough.*
Hūmeo, *to be wet.*
Immĭneo, *to hang over.*

Langueo,

Langueo, *to languish.*	Pāteo, *to be open.*	Stŭdeo, *to favour.*
Līqueo, licui, *to melt,*	Fūteo, *to stink.*	Stŭpeo, *to be amazed.*
to be clear.	Putreo, *to rot.*	Splendeo, *to shine.*
Măceo, *to be lean.*	Ranceo, *to be mouldy.*	Tĕpeo, *to be warm.*
Mădeo, *to be wet.*	Rĭgeo, *to be stiff.*	Torpeo, *to be benumbed.*
Marceo, *to wither.*	Rŭbeo, *to be red.*	Tŭmeo, *to swell.*
Mūceo, *to be mouldy.*	Squāleo, *to be foul.*	Vĭgeo, *to be strong.*
Nĭteo, *to shine.*	Sordeo, *to be nasty.*	Vĭreo, *to be green.*
Palleo, *to be pale.*		

But the neuter verbs which follow, together with their compounds, have the supine, and are regularly conjugated : *Văleo*, to be in health ; and *æqui-, con-, e-, in-, præ-valeo* : *Plăceo*, to please ; and *com-, per-placeo* : *displiceo*, to displease :· *Căreo*, to want : *Pāreo*, to appear, to obey ; and *ap-, com-pāreo* : *Jăceo*, to lie ; and *ad-, circum-, inter-, ob-, præ-, sub-, super-jăceo* : *Caleo*, to be warm ; and *con-, in-, ob-, per-, re-căleo* : *Nŏceo*, to hurt ;· *Dŏleo*, to be grieved ; and *con-, de-, in-, per-dŏleo* : *Coaleo*, to grow together : *Lĭceo*, which in the active signifies, to be lawful, to be valued ; and, what is singular, in the passive, to bid a price : *Lăteo*, to lurk, the compounds of which want the supine, *delĭteo, inter-, sub-lateo* : as likewise do those of *Tăceo, -cui, -cĭtum*, to be silent, *con-, ob-, rĕ-tĭceo.*

These three active verbs likewise want the supine : *Tĭmeo, -ui*, to fear ; *Sĭleo, -ui*, to conceal ; *Arceo, -cui*, to drive away : But the compounds of *arceo* have the supine ; as, *exerceo, exercui, exercĭtum*, to exercise. So *co-erceo*, to restrain.

Exc. 1. The following verbs in *BEO* and *CEO* :

Jŭbeo, jussi, jussum, to order. So *fidĕ-jŭbeo*, to bail, or be surety for.

Sorbeo, sorbui, sorptum, to sup. So *ab-sorbeo*, to suck in ; *ex-, rĕ-sorbeo.* We also find *absorpsi, exsorpsi* : *Exsorptum, rĕsorptum*, are not in use.

Dŏceo, dŏcui, doctum, to teach. So *ad-, con-, de-, e-, per-, sub-dŏceo.*

Mĭsceo, miscui, mistum, or *mixtum*, to mix. So *ad-, com-, im-, inter-, per-, rĕ-misceo.*

Mulceo, mulsi, mulsum, to stroak, to soothe. So *ad-, circum-, com-, de-, per-, rĕ-mulceo.*

Lūceo, luxi, —— to shine. So *al-, circum-, col-, di-, ē-, il-, inter-, per-*, or *pel-, præ-, pro-, re-, sub-, trans-lūceo.*

Exc.

Exc. 2. The following verbs in *DEO*:

Prandeo, prandi, pranfum, to dine.

Video, vīdi, vīfum, to fee. So *in-, per-, præ-, pro-, rĕ-video.*

Sĕdeo, sēdi, feffum, to fit. So *af-, con-, de-, dif-, in-, ob-, per-, pof-, præ-, rĕ-, fub-sĭdeo :* Circumsĭdeo, or *circum-sĕdeo, fupersĕdeo.* But *dē-, dif-, per-, præ-, rĕ-, fub-fideo,* feem to want the fupine.

Strīdeo, ftrĭdi, ⸺ to make a noife.

Pendeo, pĕpendi, penfum, to hang. So *de-, im-, pro-, fuper-pendeo.*

Mordeo, mŏmordi, morfum, to bite. So *ad-, com-, de-, ob-, præ-, re-mordeo.*

Spondeo, fpŏpondi, fponfum, to promife. So *de-, re-fpondeo.*

Tondeo, tŭtondi, tonfum, to clip. So *at-, circum-, de-tondeo.* But the compounds of thefe verbs do not double the firft fyllable ; thus, *dependi, remordi, refpondi, attondi, &c.*

Rīdeo, rīfi, rīfum, to laugh. So *ar-, de-, ir-, fub-rīdeo.*

Suādeo, fuāfi, fuāfum, to advife. So *dif-, per-fuādeo.*

Ardeo, arfi, arfum, to burn. So *ex-, in-, ob-ardeo.*

Exc. 3. The following verbs in *GEO*:

Augeo, auxi, auctum, to increafe. So *ad-, ex-augeo.*

Lūgeo, luxi, ⸺ to mourn. So *e-, pro-, fub-lugeo.*

Frīgeo, frixi, ⸺ to be cold. So *per-, re-frīgeo.*

Tergeo, terfi, terfum, to wipe. So *abs-, circum-, de-, ex-, per-tergeo.*

Mulgeo, mulfi, mulfum, or *mulctum,* to milk. So *e-, im-mulgeo.*

Indulgeo, indulfi, indultum, to grant, to indulge.

Urgeo, urfi, ⸺ to prefs. So *ad-, ex-, in-, per-, fub-, fuper-urgeo.*

Fulgeo, fulfi, ⸺ to fhine. So *af-, circum-, con-, ef-, inter-, præ-, re-, fuper-fulgeo.*

Turgeo, turfi, ⸺ to fwell. *Algeo, alfi,* ⸺ to be cold.

Exc. 4. The following verbs in *IEO* and *LEO*:

Vieo, viēvi, victum, to bind with twigs, to hoop a veffel.

Cieo, (cīvi) cītum, to ftir up, to roufe. So *ac-, con-, ex-, in-, per-cieo.* *Cīvi* comes from *cio* of the fourth conjugation.

Fleo, flēvi, flētum, to weep. So *af-, de-fleo.*

Compleo, complēvi, complētum, to fill. So the other compounds of *pleo ; de-, ex-, im-, adim-, op-, re-, fup-pleo.*

Dēleo,

Dēleo, dēlēvi, dēlētum, to deſtroy, to blot out.

ŏleo, to ſmell, has *ŏlui, ŭlĭtum.*   So likewiſe its compounds which have a ſimilar ſignification ; *ob-, per-, red-, ſub-ŏleo.*   But ſuch of the compounds as have a different ſignification make *ēvi* and *ētum ;* thus *exŏleo, exŏlēvi, exŏlētum,* to fade.   So *inŏleo, -ēvi, -ētum,* or *-ĭtum,* to grow into uſe ; *obsŏleo, -ēvi, -ētum,* to grow out of uſe.   *Abŏleo,* to aboliſh, has *abŏlēvi, abŏlĭtum ;* and *adŏleo,* to grow up, to burn, *adŏlēvi, adultum.*

Exc. 5.   Several verbs in *NEO, QUEO, REO,* and *SEO,.*

Mǎneo, manſi, manſum, to ſtay.   So *per-, rĕ-mǎneo.*

Neo, nēvi, nētum, to ſpin.   So *per-neo.*

Tĕneo, tĕnui, tentum, to hold.   So *con-, de-, dis-, ob-, re-, ſuſ-tĭneo.*   But *attĭneo, pertĭneo,* are not uſed in the ſupine ; and ſeldom *abſtĭneo.*

Torqueo, torſi, tortum, to throw, to whirl, to twiſt.   Thus, *con-, de-, dis-, ex-, in-, ob-, re-torqueo.*

Hæreo, hæſi, hæſum, to ſtick.   Thus, *ad-, con-, in-, ob-, ſub-hæreo.*

Torreo, torrui, toſtum, to roaſt.   So *extorreo.*

Cenſeo, cenſui, cenſum, to judge.   So *ac-, per-, re-cenſeo,* to review ; *ſuccenſeo,* to be angry.

Exc. 6.   Verbs in *VEO* have *vi, tum ;* as, *mŏveo, mōvi, mōtum,* to move ; *Fŏveo, fŏvi, fōtum,* to cheriſh.   So *con-, rĕ-foveo.*   So *vŏveo,* to vow, or wiſh, and *dēvŏveo.*

Fǎveo, to favour ; has *fāvi, fautum ;* and *cǎveo,* to beware of ; *cāvi, cautum.*   So *præ-cǎveo.*

Neuter verbs in *veo* want the ſupine ; as, *pǎveo, pāvi,* to be afraid.

Ferveo, to boil, to be hot, makes *ferbui.*   So *de-, ef-, in-, per-, rĕ-ferveo.*

Connīveo, to wink, has *connīvi* and *connixi.*

Exc. 7.   The following verbs want both preterite and ſupine : *Lacteo,* to ſuck milk, *līveo,* to be black and blue ; *ſcăteo,* to abound ; *renĭdeo,* to ſhine ; *mæreo,* to be ſorrowful ; *ǎveo,* to deſire ; *polleo,* to be able ; *flāveo,* to be yellow ; *denſeo,* to grow thick ; *glabreo,* to be ſmooth or bare.   To theſe add *calveo,* to be bald ; *cēveo,* to wag the tail, as dogs do when they fawn on one ; *hĕbeo,* to be dull ; *ūveo,* to be moiſt ; and ſome others.

L 2

Third

[Verbs of the third conjugation form their preterite and supine variously, according to the termination of the present.]

10.

1. *Făcio, fēci, factum,* to do, to make. So the compounds which retain *a*: *lucri-, magni-, āre-, căle-, măde-, tĕpĕ-, bĕnĕ-, măle-, sătis-făcio, &c.* But those which change *a* into *i* have *ectum*; as, *afficio, affēci, affectum.* So, *con-, de-, ef-, in-, inter-, of-, per-, præ-, pro-, re-, suf-ficio. Note;* FACIO, compounded with a noun, verb, or adverb, retains *a*; but when compounded with a preposition, it changes *a* into *i.*

Some compounds of *facio* are of the first conjugation; as, *Amplifico, sacrifico, terrifico, magnifico; gratificor,* to gratify, or do a good turn, to give up; *lūdificor,* to mock.

Jacio, jēci, jactum, to throw. So *ab-, ad-, circum-, con-, de-, dif-, e-, in-, inter-, ob-, pro-, re-, sub-, super-, superin-, tra-jicio;* in the supine *-ectum.*

The compounds of *spĕcio* and *lăcio,* which themselves are not used, have *exi,* and *ectum;* as, *aspĭcio, aspexi, a-spectum,* to behold. So *circum-, con-, de-, dif-, in-, intro-, per-, pro-, re-, retro-, su-spĭcio.*

Allĭcio, allexi, allectum, to allure. So *il-, pel-lĭcio;* but *ēlĭcio,* to draw out, has *elĭcui, elĭcĭtum.*

2. *Fŏdio, fŏdi, fossum,* to dig, to delve. So *ad-, circum-, con-, ef-, in-, inter-, per-, præ-, re-, suf-, transf-fŏdio.*

Fŭgio, fūgi, fŭgĭtum, to fly. So *au-,* (for *ab-,*) *con-, de-, dif-, ef-, per-, pro-, re-, suf-, subter-, transf-fŭgio.*

3. *Căpio, cēpi, captum,* to take. So *ac-, con-, de-, ex-, in-, inter-, oc-, per-, præ-, re-, suf-cĭpio,* (in the supine *-ceptum;*) and *ante-căpio.*

Răpio, răpui, raptum, to pull or snatch. So *ab-, ar-, cor-, de-, di-, e-, præ-, pro-, sur-rĭpio-, -rĭpui, -reptum.*

Săpio, săpui, —— to favour, to be wise. So *consĭpio,* to be well in one's wits; *desĭpio,* to be foolish; *resĭpio,* to come to one's wits.

Cŭpio, cupīvi, cupĭtum, to desire. So *con-, dif-, per-cŭpio.*

4. *Părio, tĕpĕri, parĭtum,* or *parium,* to bring forth a child, to get. Its compounds are of the fourth conjugation.

Quătio,

Quătio, quaſſi, quaſſum, to ſhake ; but *quaſſi* is hardly uſed. Its compounds have *cuſſi, cuſſum*, as, *concŭtio, concuſſi concuſſum.* So *de-, diſ-, ex-, in-, per-, re-, reper-, ſuc-cŭtio.*

UO has *ui, ūtum* ; as,

Arguo, argui, argūtum, to ſhew, to prove, or argue, to reprove. So *co-, red-arguo*, to confute.—So,

Acuo, Exăcuo, *to ſharpen.*

Batuo, *vel* battuo, *to beat, to fight, to fence with foils.*

Induo, *to put on cloaths.*

Exuo, *to put off cloaths.*

Imbuo, *to wet* or *imbrue, to ſeaſon or inſtruct.*

Minuo, *to leſſen :* Com-, de-, di-, im-minuo.

Spuo, *to ſpit :* Con-, de-, ex-, in-ſpuo.

Stătuo, *to ſet* or *place, to ordain.* Con-, de-, in-, præ-, pro-, re-, ſub-ſtĭtuo.

Sternuo, *to ſneeze.*

Suo, *to ſew* or *ſtitch, to tack together :* Aſ-, circum-, con-, diſ-, in-, præ-, rĕ-, ſuo.

Tribuo, *to give, to divide :* At-, con-, diſ-, re-trĭbuo.

Exc. 1. *Fluo, fluxi, fluxum*, to flow. So *aſ-, circum-, con-, de-, diſ-, ef-, in-, inter-, per-, præter-, pro-, re-, ſubter-, ſuper-, tranſ-fluo.*

Struo, ſtruxi, ſtructum, to put in order, to build. So *aſ-, circum-, con-, de-, ex-, in-, ob-, præ-, ſub-, ſuper-ſtruo.*

Exc. 2. *Luo, lui, luĭtum*, to pay, to waſh away, to ſuffer puniſhment. Its compounds have *ūtum ;* as, *abluo, -ui, -ūtum*, to waſh away, to purify. So *al-, circum-, col-, de-, di-, e-, inter-, per-, pol-, pro-, ſub-luo.*

Ruo, rui, ruĭtum, to ruſh, to fall. Its compounds have *ūtum ;* as *diruo, dirui, dirūtum*, to overthrow. So *ē-, ob-, prō-, ſub-ruo.* *Corruo*, and *irruo*, want the ſupine ; as likewiſe do *mĕtuo*, to fear ; *pluo*, to rain ; *ingruo*, to aſſail ; *congruo*, to agree ; *reſpuo*, to reject, to ſlight ; *annuo*, to aſſent ; and the other compounds of the obſolete verb *nuo ; abnuo*, to refuſe ; *innuo*, to nod or beckon with the head ; *rĕnuo*, to deny : all which have *ui* in the preterite.

BO has *bi, bĭtum* ; as,

Bĭbo, bĭbi, bibĭtum, to drink. So *ad-, com-, e-, im-, per-, præ-bĭbo.*

Exc. 1. *Scrībo, ſcripſi, ſcriptum*, to write. So *ad-, circum-, con-, de-, ex-, in-, inter-, per-, poſt-, præ-, pro-, re-, ſub-, ſuper-, ſupra-, tranſ-ſcrībo.*

Nūbo,

Nūbo, nupsi, nuptum, to veil, to be married. So *de-, e-, in-, ob-nubo.* Instead of *nupsi,* we often find *nupta sum.*

Exc. 2. The compounds of *cŭbo* in this conjugation insert an *m* before the last syllable ; as, *accumbo, accŭbui, accŭbĭtum,* to recline at table. So *con-, de-, dis-, in-, oc-, pro-, re-, suc-, superin-cumbo, -cŭbui, -cubĭtum.*

These two verbs want the supine ; *scābo, scābi,* to scratch ; *lambo, lambi,* to lick. So *ad-, circum-, dē-, pre-lambo.*

Glūbo and *deglūbo,* to strip, to flay, want both pret. & sup.

CO.

1. *Dīco, dixi, dĭctum,* to say. So *ab-, ad-, con-, contra-, e-, in-, inter-, præ-, pro-dīco.*

Dūco, duxi, ductum, to lead. So *ab-, ad-, circum-, con-, de-, di-, e-, in-, intro-, ob-, per-, præ-, pro-, re-, se-, sub-, tra-,* or *transf-dūco.*

2. *Vinco, vīci, victum,* to overcome. So *con-, de-, e-, per-, rĕ-vinco.*

Parco, pĕperci, parsum, seldom *parsi, parsĭtum,* to spare. So *comparco,* or *comperco,* which is seldom used.

Ico, īci, ĭctum, to strike.

SCO has *vi, tum ;* as,

Nosco, nōvi, nōtum, to know ; fut. part. *nosciturus.* So

Dignosco, *to distinguish ;* ignosco, *to pardon ; also* inter-, per-, præ-nosco.

Cresco, -ēvi, -ētum, *to grow :* Con-de-, ex-, re-, *and without the supine,* ac-, in-, per-, pro-, suc-, super-cresco.

Quiesco, -ēvi, -ētum, *to rest :* Ac-, con-, inter-, rĕ-quiesco.

Scisco, -īvi, -ītum, *to ordain ;* ad-, or ascisco, *to take, to associate ;* concisco, *to vote, to commit ; also* præ-, re-cisco ; descisco, *to revolt.*

Suesco, *to be accustomed :* As-, con-de-, in-suesco, -ēvi, -ētum.

Exc. 1. *Agnosco, agnōvi, agnĭtum,* to own ; *cognosco, cognōvi, cognĭtum,* to know. So *rĕcognosco,* to review.

Pasco, pāvi, pastum, to feed. So *com-, dē-pasco.*

Exc. 2. The following verbs want the supine.

Disco, dĭdĭci, to learn. So *ad-, con-, de-, e-, per-, præ-disco, dĭdĭci.*

Posco, pŏposci, to demand. So *ap-, dē-, ex-, rĕ-posco.*

Compesco, compescui, to stop, to restrain. So *dispesco, dispescui,* to separate.

Exc. 3. *Glisco,* to grow ; *fatisco,* to be weary ; and
likewise

likewise inceptive verbs, want both preterite and supine ; as *aresco*, to become dry. But these verbs borrow their preterite and supine from their primitives ; as *ardesco*, to grow hot, *arsi*, *arsum*, from *ardeo*.

DO has *di*, *sum* ; as,

Scando, *scandi*, *scansum*, to climb ; *edo*, *edi*, *esum*, to eat. So,

Ascendo, *to mount.*	Cūdo, *to forge, to stamp*	Mando, *to chew :* Præ-,
Descendo, *to go down :*	*or coin :* Ex-, in-,	re-mando.
Con-, e-, ex-, in-;	per-, pro-, re-cūdo.	Prehendo, *to take hold*
tran-scendo.	Defendo, *to defend.*	*of :* Ap-, com-, de-
Accendo, *to kindle :*	Offendo, *to strike a-*	prehendo.
In-, suc-cendo.	*gainst, to offend, to find.*	

Exc. 1. *Divido*, *divisi*, *divisum*, to divide.

Rado, *rasi*, *rasum*, to shave. So *ab-*, *circum-*, *cor-*, *de-*, *e-*, *inter-*, *præ*, *sub-rado*.

Claudo, *clausi*, *clausum*, to close. So *circum-*, *con-*, *dis-*, *ex-*, *in-*, *inter-*, *præ-*, *re-*, *se-clūdo*.

Plaudo, *plausi*, *plausum*, to clap hands for joy. So *ap-*, *circum-plaudo :* also *com-*, *dis-*, *ex-*, *sup-plōdo*, *-plosi*, *-plosum*.

Lūdo, *lūsi*, *lūsum*, to play. So *ab-*, *al-*, *col-*, *de-*, *e-*, *il-*, *inter-*, *ob-*, *præ-*, *pro-*, *re-lūdo*.

Trūdo, *trūsi*, *trūsum*, to thrust. So *abs-*, *con-*, *de-*, *ex-*, *in-*, *ob-*, *pro-*, *re-trūdo*.

Lædo, *læsi*, *læsum*, to hurt. So *al-*, *col-*, *e-*, *il-līdo*, *-līsi*, *-līsum*.

Rōdo, *rosi*, *rōsum*, to gnaw. So *ab-*, *ar-*, *circum-*, *cor-*, *de-*, *e-*, *ob-*, *per-*, *præ-rōdo*.

Vādo, to go, wants both preterite and supine : but its compounds have *si*, *sum* ; as *invādo*, *invāsi*, *invāsum*, to invade, or fall upon. So *circum-*, *e-*, *super-vādo*.

Cēdo, *cessi*, *cessum*, to yield. So *abs-*, *ac-*, *antē-*, *con-*, *de-*, *dis-*, *ex-*, *in-*, *inter-*, *præ-*, *pro-*, *rē-*, *retrō-*, *se-*, *suc-cēdo*.

Exc. 2. *Pando*, *pandi*, *passum*, and sometimes *pansum*, to open, to spread. So *dis-*, *ex-*, *op-*, *præ-*, *rē-pando*.

Cŏmĕdo, *comēdi*, *comēsum*, or *comēstum*, to eat. But *edo* itself and the rest of its compounds have always *ēsum* ; as, *ad-*, *amb-*, *ex-*, *per-*, *sub-*; *super-ĕdo*, *-ēdi*, *-ēsum*.

Fundo, *fūdi*, *fūsum*, to pour forth. So *af-*, *circum-*, *con-*, *de-*, *dif-*, *ef-*, *in-*, *inter-*, *of-*, *per-*, *pro-*, *re-*, *suf-*, *super-*, *superin-*, *trans-fundo*.

- *Scindo,*

Scindo, *scĭdi*, *scissum*, to cut. So *af-*, *circum-*, *con-*, *ex-*, *inter-*, *per-*, *præ-*, *pro-*, *re-*, *tran-scindo*.

Findo, *fĭdi*, *fissum*, to cleave. So *con-*, *dif-*, *in-findo*.

Exc. 3. *Tundo*, *tŭtŭdi*, *tunsum*, and sometimes *tūsum*, to beat. The compounds have *tŭdi*, *tūsum*; as, *contundo*, *contŭdi*, *contūsum*, to bruise. So *ex-*, *ob-*, *per-*, *re-tundo*.

Cădo, *cĕcĭdi*, *cāsum*, to fall. The compounds want the supine; as, *ac-*, *con-*, *de-*, *ex-*, *inter-*, *pro-*, *succĭdo*, *-cĭdi*, ———: except, *incĭdo*, *incĭdi*, *incāsum*, to fall in; *recĭdo*, *recĭdi*, *recāsum*, to fall back; and *cĕcĭdo*, *occĭdi*, *occāsum*, to fall down.

Cædo, *cĕcīdi*, *cæsum*, to cut, to kill. The compounds change *æ* into *i* long; as, *accīdo*, *accīdi*, *accīsum*, to cut about. So *abf-*, *con-*, *circum-*, *de-*, *ex-*, *in-*, *inter-*, *oc-*, *per-*, *præ-*, *rĕ-*, *suc-cīdo*.

Tendo, *tĕtendi*, *tensum*, or *tentum*, to stretch out. So *at-*, *con-*, *de-*, *dif-*, *ex-*, *ob-*, *præ-*, *pro-tendo*, *-tendi*, *-tensum* or *-tentum*. But the compounds have rather *tentum*, except *ostendo*, to shew; which has commonly *ostensum*.

Pēdo, *pĕpēdi*, *pedĭtum*, to break wind backwards. So *op-pēdo*.

Pendo, *pĕpendi*, *pensum*, to weigh. So *ap-*, *de-*, *dif-*, *ex-*, *im-*, *per-*, *re-*, *fus-pendo*, *-pendi*, *-pensum*.

Exc. 4. The compounds of *do* have *dĭdi*, and *dĭtum*; as, *abdo*, *abdĭdi*, *abdĭtum*, to hide. So *ad-*, *con-*, *de-*, *dī-*, *ē-*, *ob-*, *per-*, *pro-*, *red-*, *fub-*, *trado*: also *decon-*, *recon-do*: and *coad-*, *fupperad-do*; and *dsper-*, *difper-do*. To these add *crēdo*, *crēdĭdi*, *crēdĭdum*, to believe; *vendo*, *vendĭdi*, *vendĭtum*, to sell. *Abfcondo*, to hide, has *abfcondi*, *abfcondĭtum*, rarely *abfcondĭdi*.

Exc. 5. These three want the supine: *strīdo*, *strīdi*, to creak; *rŭdo*, *rŭdi*, to bray like an afs; and *sīdo*, *sīdi*, to sink down. The compounds of *sīdo* borrow the preterite and supine from *sĕdeo*; as, *consīdo*, *consēdi*, *confessum*, to sit down. So *af-*, *circum-*, *de-*, *in-*, *ob-*, *per-*, *rĕ-*, *sub-sīdo*.

Note, Several compounds of verbs in *do* and *deo*, in some respects resemble one another, and therefore should be carefully distinguished; as, *concĭdo*, *concēdo*, *concīdo*; *consīdo* and *consĭdeo*; *confcindo*, *confcendo*, &c.

GO, GUO, has *xi*, *ctum* ; *æ*,

Rĕgo, *rexi*, *rectum*, to rule, to govern ; *dirĭgo*, *-exi*, *-ectum*, to direct ; *arrigo*, & *ērigo*, *-exi*, *-ectum*, to raife up : *corrĭgo*, to correct ; *porrĭgo*, to ftretch out ; *fubrĭgo*, to raife up. So

Cingo, cinxi, cinctum, *to gird, to furround:* Ac-, dif-, circum-, in-, præ-, re-, fuc-cingo.

Fligo, *to dafh* or *beat upon :* Af-, con-, in-fligo : alfo profligo, *to rout,* of the firft conj.

Jungo, *to join ;* abjungo, *to feparate :* Ad-, con-, de-, dif-, in-, inter-, fe-, fub-jungo.

Lingo, *to lick :* de-, e-lingo ; & pollingo, *to anoint a dead body.*

Mungo, *to wipe* or *clean the nofe.*

Emungo, *to wipe, to cheat.*

Plango, *to beat, to lament.*

Stingo, *or* Stinguo, *to dafh out, to extinguifh :* Di-, ex-, in-, inter-, præ-, re-ftinguo.

Tĕgo, *to cover :* Circum-, con-, de-, in-, ob-, per-, præ-, pro-, re-, fub-, fuper-tĕgo.

Tingo, *or* Tinguo, *to dip* or *dye :* Con-, in-tingo.

Ungo, *or* Unguo, *to anoint :* ex-, in-, per-, fuper-ungo.

Exc. 1.   *Surgo*, to rife, has *furrexi, furrectum.* So *af-, circum-, con-, de-, ex-, in-, re-furgo.*

Pergo, *perrexi*, *perrectum*, to go forward.

Stringo, *ftrinxi*, *ftrictum*, to bind, to ftrain, to lop. So *ad-, con-, de-, dif-, ob-, per-, præ-, re-, fub-ftringo.*

Fingo, *finxi*, *fictum*, to feign. So *af-, con-, ef-, re-fingo.*

Pingo, *pinxi*, *pictum*, to paint. So *ap-, de-pingo.*

Exc. 2. *Frango*, *frēgi*, *fractum*, to break. So *con-, de-, dif-, ef-, in-, per-, præ-, re-, fuf-fringo, -frēgi, -fractum.*

Ăgo, *ēgi*, *actum*, to do, to drive. So *ab-, ad-, ex-, red-, fub-, tranf-, tranfad-ĭgo ;* and *circum-, per-ăgo : cōgo,* for *coăgo, coēgi, coactum,* to bring together, to force.

Thefe three compounds of *ăgo* want the fupine : *fătăgo, fatēgi,* to be bufy about a thing.; *prōdĭgo, prodēgi,* to lavifh, or fpend riotoufly ; *dēgo,* for *deăgo ; dēgi,* to live or dwell. *Ambĭgo,* to doubt, to difpute, alfo wants the preterite.

Lĕgo, *lēgi*, *lectum*, to gather, to read. So *al-, per-, præ-, re-, fub-lĕgo :* alfo *col-, de-, e-, recol-, fe-lĭgo,* which change *e* into *i.*

Dīlĭgo, to love, has *dilexi, dilectum.* So *neglĭgo,* to neglect ; and *intellĭgo,* to underftand ; but, *negligo* has fometimes *neglēgi,* Sall. Jug. 40.

Exc. 3. *Tango*, *tĕtĭgi*, *tactum*, to touch. So *at-, con-, ob-, per-tingo ;* thus, *attingo, attigi, attactum,* &c.

Pungo, pŭpŭgi, punctum, to prick or sting. The compounds have *punxi;* as, *compungo, compunxi, compunctum.* So *dif-, ex-, inter-pungo:* but *repungo* has *repunxi,* or *repŭpŭgi.*

Pango, panxi, pactum, to fix, to drive in, to compose:: or *pĕpĭgi,* which comes from the obsolete verb *pago,* to bargain, for which we use *pacifcor.* The compounds of *pango,* have *pēgi;* as, *compingo, compēgi, compactum,* to put together. So *im-, ob-, sup pingo.*

Exc. 4. *Spargo, sparsi, sparsum,* to spread. So *ad-, circum-, con-, di-, in-, inter-, per-, pro-, re-spergo.*

Mergo, mersi, mersum, to dip, or plunge. So *de-, e-, im-, sub-mergo.*

Tergo, tersi, tersum, to wipe, or clean. So *abf-, de-, ex-, per-tergo.*

Figo, fixi, fixum, to fix or fasten. So *af-, con-, de-, in-, of-, per-, præ-, re-, suf-, transf-figo.*

Frīgo, frixi, frixum, or *frictum,* to fry.

Exc. 5. These three want the supine: *clango, clanxi,* to sound a trumpet; *ningo,* or *ninguo, ninxi,* to snow; *ango, anxi,* to vex. *Vergo,* to incline, or lie towards, wants both preterite and supine. So *e-, de-, in-vergo.*

HO, JO.

1. *Trăho, traxi, tractum,* to draw. So *alf-, at-, circum-, con-, de-, dif-, ex-, per-, pro-, re-, sub-trăho.*

Veho, vexi, vectum, to carry. So *a-, ad-, circum-, con-, di-, e-, in-, per-, præ-, præter-, pro-, re-, sub-, super-, trænf-vĕho.*

2. *Mejo,* or *mingo, minxi, mictum,* to make water. So *immejo.*

LO.

1. *Cŏlo, cŏlui, cultum,* to adorn, to inhabit, to honour, to till. So *ec-, circum-, ex-, in-, per-, præ-, re-cŏlo:* and likewise *occŭlo, occului, occultum,* to hide.

Consŭlo, consului, consultum, to advise or consult.

Alo, ălui, alitum, or contracted *altum,* to nourish.

Mŏlo, molui, molitum, to grind. So *com-, e-, per-mŏlo.* The compounds of *cello,* which itself is not in use, want the supine; as, *ante-, ex-, præ-cello, -cellui,* to excel. *Percello,* to strike, to astonish, has *percŭli, percuisum.*

Pello,

Pello, pĕpŭli, pulsum, to thrust. So *ap-, as-, com-, de-, dif-, ex-, im-, per-, pro-, re-pello ; appŭli, appulsum,* &c.

Fallo, fĕfelli, falsum, to deceive.   But *rĕfello, refelli,* to confute, wants the supine.

3. *Vello, velli,* or *vulsi, vulsum,* to pull *or* pinch. So *a-, con-, e-, inter-, præ-, re-vello.*   But *de-, di-, per-vello,* have rather *velli.*

Sallo, salli, salsum, to falt.   *Pfallo, pfalli,* ——— to play *on* a musical instrument, wants the supine.

Tollo, to lift up, to take away, in a manner peculiar to itself, makes *sustuli,* and *sublatum ; Extollo, extŭli, elātum ;* but *attollo,* to take up, has neither preterite nor supine.

MO has *ui, ĭtum ;* as,

Gĕmo, gĕmui, gemĭtum, to groan.   So *ad-,* or *ag-, circum-, con-, in-, re-gĕmo.*

Frĕmo, fremui, fremitum, to rage or roar, to make a great noise.   So *af-, circum-, con-, in-, per-frĕmo.*

Vŏmo, ēvŏmo, -ui, -itum, to vomit or spew, to cast up.

Exc. 1.   *Dēmo, dempsi, demptum,* to take away.

Prŏmo, prompsi, promptum, to bring out.   So *de-, ex-promo.*

Sūmo, sumpsi, sumptum, to take.   So *ab-, as-, con-, de-, in-, præ-, re-, tran-sūmo.*

Cōmo, compsi, comptum, to deck or dress.

These verbs are also used without the *p.;* as *demsi, demtum ; sumsi, sumtum,* &c.

Exc. 2.   *Emo, ēmi, emptum,* or *emtum* to buy. So *ad-, dir-, ex-, inter-, per-, red-ĭmo* and *co-ĕmo, -emi, -emptum* or *-emtum.*

Prĕmo, pressi, pressum, to press.   So *ap-, com-, de-, ex-, im-, op-, per-, re-, sup-prĭmo.*

Trĕmo, trĕmui, to tremble, to quake for fear, wants the supine.   So *at-, circum-, con-, in-trĕmo.*

NO.

1. *Pōno, pŏsui, pŏsitum,* to put or place.   So *ap-, ante-, circum-, com-, de-, dif-, ex-, im-, inter-, ob-, post-, præ-, pro-, re-, se-, sup-, super-, superim-, trans-pōno.*

Gigno, gĕnui, gĕnitum, to beget.   So *con-, e-, in-, ter-, pro-, re-gigno.*

Cāno, cĕcĭni, cantum, to sing. But the compounds have *inui* and *centum ;* as, *accino, accĭnui, accentum,* to sing

M

in

in concert. So *con-*, *in-*, *præ-*, *suc-căno*; *oc-ĉino*, and *oc-căno*: *re-ĉino* and *re-căno*. But *occanui*, *recanui*, are not in ufe.

Temno, to defpife, wants both preterite and fupine: but its compound *Contemno*, to defpife, to fcorn, has *contempfi*, *contemptum*; or whithout the *p*, *contemfi*, *contemtum.*

2. *Sperno*, *fprēvi*, *fprētum*, to difdain or flight. So *defperno*.

Sterno, *ftrāvi*, *ftrātum*, to lay flat, to ftrow. So *ad-*, *con-*, *in-*, *præ-*, *pro-*, *fub-fterno*.

Sĭno, *sĭvi*, or *fii*, *sĭtum* to permit. So *desĭno*, *desĭvi*, oftener *defii*, *desĭtum*, to leave off.

Lĭno, *lĭvi*, or *lēvi*, *lĭtum*, to anoint or daub. So *al-*, *circum-*, *col-*, *de-*, *il-*, *inter-*, *ob-*, *per-*, *præ-*, *re-*, *fub-*, *fubter-*, *fuper-*, *fuperil-lino*.

Cerno, *crēvi*, feldom *crētum*, to fee, to decree, to enter upon an inheritance. So *de-*, *dif-*, *ex-*, *in-*, *fe-cerno*.

PO, QUO.

Verbs in *po* have *pfi* and *ptum*; as, *Carpo*, *carpfi*, *carptum*, to pluck or pull, to crop, to blame.——So *con-*, *de-*, *dif-*, *ex-*, *præ-cerpo*, *-cerpfi*, *-cerptum*.

Clĕpo, *-pfi*, *-ptum*, *to fteal.*	*Scalpo*, *to fcratch* or *engrave*. So *circum-*, *ex-fcalpo*.
Rēpo, *to creep:* Ad-, v. ar-, cor-, de-, di-, e-, ir-, intro-, ob-, per-, pro-, *fub-rēpo*, *-pfi*, *-ptum*.	*Sculpo*, *to grave* or *carve*. So *ex-*, *in-fculpo*.
	Serpo, *to creep as a ferpent.*

Exc. 1. *Strĕpo*, *ftrĕpui*, *ftrĕpĭtum*, to make a noife. So *ad-*, *circum-*, *in-*, *inter-*, *ob-*, *per-ftrepo*.

Exc. 2. *Rumpo*, *rūpi*, *ruptum*, to break. So *ab-*, *cor-*, *di-*, *e-*, *inter-*, *intro-*, *ir-*, *ob-*, *per-*, *præ-*, *pro-rumpo*.

There are only two fimple verbs ending in *QUO*; viz.

Cŏquo, *coxi*, *coctum*, to boil. So *con-*, *de-*, *dis-*, *ex-*, *in-*, *per-*, *re-còquo*.

Linquo, *līqui*, ————, to leave. The compounds have *lictum*; as, *rĕlinquo*, *reliqui*, *relictum*, to forfake. So *de-*, and *dĕrĕ-linquo*.

RO.

1. *Quæro* makes *quæsīvi*, *quæsītum*, to feek. So *ac-*, *an-*, *con-*, *dis-*, *ex-*, *in-*, *per-*, *re-quīro*, *-quisīvi*, *-quisītum*.

Tĕro, *trīvi*, *trītum*, to wear, to bruife. So *al-*, *con-*, *de-*, *dif-*, *ex-*, *in-*, *ob-*, *per-*, *pro-*, *fub-tĕro*.

Verro, *verri*, *verfum*, to fweep, brufh, or make clean. So *ā-*, *con-*, *de-*, *e-*, *præ-*, *re-verro*.

Ser.

Ūro, uſſi, uſtum, to burne. So ad-, amb-, comb-, de-, ex-, in-, per-, ſub-ūro.

Gĕro, geſſi, geſtum, to carry. So ag-, con-, di-, in-, prō-, rĕ-, ſug-gĕro.

2. Curro, cŭcurri, curſum, to run. So ac-, con-, dĕ-, diſ-, ex-, in-, oc-, per-, præ-, prō-curro, which ſometimes double the firſt ſyllable, and ſometimes not; as, accurri, or accŭcurri, &c. Circum-, rĕ-, ſuc-, tranſ-curro, hardly ever redouble the firſt ſyllable.

3. Sĕro, ſēvi, ſătum, to ſow. The compounds which ſignify planting or ſowing, have ſēvi, ſĭtum; as, conſĕro conſēvi, conſĭtum, to plant together. So aſ-, circum-, dĕ-, diſ-, in-, intĕr-, ob-, pro-, rĕ-, ſub-, tran-ſĕro.

Sĕro, ——— to knit, had anciently ſĕrui, ſertum, which its compounds ſtill retain; as, aſſĕro, aſſĕrui, aſſertum, to claim. So con-, circum-, dĕ-, diſ-, ēdiſ-, ex-, in-, inter-ſĕro.

4. Fŭro, to be mad, wants both preterite and ſupine.

SO has ſīvi, ſĭtum; as,

Arceſſo, arceſſīvi, arceſſītum, to call or ſend for. So că-peſſo, to take; ficeſſo, to do, to go away; lăceſſo, to provoke.

Exc. 1. Viſo, viſi, ——— to go to ſee, to viſit. So in-, rĕ viſo. Inceſſo, inceſſi, ——— to attack, to ſeize.

Exc. 2. Depſo, depſui, depſtum, to knead. So con-, per-depſo.

Pinſo, pinſui, or pinſi, pinſtum, piſtum, or pinſĭtum, to bake.

TO.

1. Flecto, has flexi, flexum, to bow. So circum-, de-, in-, re-, retro-flecto.

Plecto, plexi, and plexui, plexum, to plait. So implecto.

Necto, nexi, and nexui, nexum, to tie or knit. So ad-, vel an-, con-, circum-, in-, ſub-necto.

Pecto, pexi, and pexui, pexum, to dreſs or comb. So de-, ex-, re-pecto.

2. Mĕto, meſſui, meſſum, to reap, mow, or cut down. So de-, e-, præ-mĕto.

3. Pĕto, pĕtīvi, pĕtītum, to ſeek, to purſue. So af-com-, ex-, in-, op-, re-, ſup-pĕto.

Mitto, miſi, miſſum, to ſend. So a-, ad-, com-, circum-, dĕ-, dē-, dī-, ē-, im-, inter-, intro-, ō-, per-, præ-, præter-, prō-, rĕ-, sub-, super-, transf-mitto.

Verto, verti, versum, to turn. So a-, ad-, animad-, ante-, circum-, con-, de-, di-, e-, in-, inter-, ob-, per-, præ-, præter-, re-, sub-, transf-verto.

Sterto, stertui, —— to snore. So de-sterto.

4. Sisto, an active verb, to stop, has stiti, statum: but sisto, a neuter verb, to stand still, has stĕti, statum, like sto. The compounds have stiti, and stitum: as, assisto, astiti, astitum, to stand by. So ab-, circum-, con-, de-, ex-, in-, inter-, ob-, per-, re-, sub-sisto. But the compounds are seldom used in the supine.

VO, XO.

There are three verbs in vo, which are thus conjugated:

1. Vivo, vixi, victum, to live. So ad-, cin-, per-, prō-, re-, super-vivo.

Solvo, solvi, sŏlūtum, to loose. So absolvo, to acquit, dif-, ex-, per-, re-solvo.

Volvo, volvi, vŏlūtum, to roll. So ad-, circum-, con-, de-, ē-, in-, ob-, per-, prō-, rĕ-, sub-volvo.

2. Texo, to weave, (the only verb of this conjugation ending in xo), has texui, textum. So at-, circum-, con-, de-, in-, inter-, ob-, per-, præ-, pro-, re-, sub-texo.

Fourth Conjugation.

Verbs of the fourth conjugation make the preterite in īvi, and the supine in ītum;) as,

Mūnio, mūnīvi, mūnītum, to fortify. So,

Balbūtio, to stammer, to lisp, to flutter.
Bullio, to boil or bubble.
Condio, to season.
Crŏcio, to croak.
Custōdio, to keep.
Dormio, to sleep.
Effūtio, to babble or blab out.
Erūdio, to instruct.
Expĕdio, to disentangle, to free.
Gannio, to yelp, or whine.
Garrio, to prate.
Glūtio, to swallow.
Grunnio, to grunt.
Hinnio, to neigh.
Impĕdio, to entangle, to hinder.
Insāno, to be mad.
Irrĕtio, to ensnare.
Lascīvio, to be wanton.
Lēnio, to ease or mitigate.
Ligūrio, to eat deliciously, to slabber up.
Lippio, to be dim-sighted.
Mollio, to soften.
Mūgio, to bellow.
Mūtio, to mutter.
Nutrio, to nourish.
Obēdio, to obey.
Păvio, to beat.
Pīpio, to peep, like a chicken.
Pŏlio, to polish.
Prūrio, to itch, to tickle.
Pūnio, to punish.
Rĕdĭmio, to bind.
Rūgio, to roar like a lion.
Sævio, to rage.

Săgio.

Sāgio, præsāgio, *to*   Servio, *to serve.*   Tinnio, *to tinkle, y*
  guess, to foresee.   Sītio, *to thirst.*   Tussio, *to cough.*
Sarrio, *to weed, to rake.*   Sōpio, *to lull asleep.*   Vāgio, *to cry or squeal*
Scio, *to know.*   Stabīlio, *to establish.*   *as a child.*
Nescio, *not to know.*   Sŭperbio, *to be proud.*   Vestio, *to clothe.*
Scăturio, *to gush out.*   Suffio, *to perfume.*

Exc. 1. *Singultio, singultīvi, singultum,* to sob.

Sĕpĕlio, sĕpĕlīvi, sepultum, to bury.

Vĕnio, vĕni, ventum, to come. So *ad-, ante-, circum-, con-, contra-, de-, e-, in-, inter-, intro-, ob-, per-, post-, præ-, re-, sub-, super-venio.*

Vēneo, vēnii, —— to be sold.

Sàlio, sălui, and *sălii, saltum,* to leap. The compounds have commonly *sĭlui,* sometimes *sĭlii,* or *sĭlīvi,* and *sultum;* as, *transĭlio, transĭlui, transĭlii,* and *transĭlīvi, transultum,* to leap over. So *ab-, as-, circum-, con-, de-, dis-, ex-, in-, re-, sub-, super-silio.*

Exc. 2. *Amĭcio,* has *amĭcui, amictum,* seldom *amixi,* to cover or clothe.

Vincio, vinxi, vinctum, to tie. So *circum-, de-, e-, re-vincio.*

Sancio, sanxi, sanctum; and *sancīvi, sancītum,* to establish or ratify.

Exc. 3. *Cambio, campsi, campsum,* to change money.

Sēpio, sepsi, septum, to hedge or inclose. So *circum-, dis-, inter-, ob-, præ-sēpio.*

Haurio, hausi, haustum, rarely *hausum,* to draw out, to empty, to drink. So *de-, ex-haurio.*

Sentio, sensi, sensum, to feel, to perceive, to think. So *as-, con-, dis-, per-, præ-, sub-sentio.*

Raucio, rausi, rausum, to be hoarse.

Exc. 4. *Sarcio, sarsi, sartum,* to mend or repair. So *ex-, re-sarcio.*

Farcio, farsi, fartum, to cram. So *con-fercio, ef-fercio,* or *ef-farcio; in-fercio,* or *in-farcio; re-fercio.*

Fulcio, fulsi, fultum, to prop or uphold. So *con-, ef-, in-, per-, suf-fulcio.*

Exc. 5. The compounds of *părio,* have *pĕrui, pertum;* as, *apĕrio, apĕrui, apertum,* to open. So *opĕrio,* to shut, to cover. But *compĕrio,* has *compĕri, compertum,* to know a thing for certain. *Rĕpĕrio, repĕri, repertum,* to find.

M 2

Exc.

Exc. 6. The following verbs want the supine. *Cæcutio, cæcutivi*, to be dim-sighted. *Gestio, gestivi*, to shew one's joy by the gesture of his body. *Glocio, glocivi*, to cluck or keckle as a hen. *Dementio, dementivi*, to be mad. *Ineptio, ineptivi*, to play the fool. *Prosilio, prosilui*, to leap forth. *Ferocio, ferocivi*, to be fierce.

Ferio, to strike, wants both preterite and supine. So *referio*, to strike again.

DEPONENT and COMMON VERBS.

A deponent verb is that which, under a passive form, has an active or neuter signification; as, *Loquor*, I speak; *morior*, I die.

A common verb, under a passive form, has either an active or passive signification; as, *Criminor*, I accuse; or I am accused.

Most deponent verbs of old were the same with common verbs. They are called *Deponent*, because they have laid aside the passive sense.

Deponent and common verbs form the participle perfect in the same manner as if they had the active voice; thus, *Lætor, lætatus, lætari*, to rejoice; *vereor, veritus, vereri*, to fear; *fungor, functus, fungi*, to discharge an office; *potior, potitus, potiri*, to enjoy, to be master of.

The learner should be taught to go through all the parts of deponent and common verbs, by proper examples in the several conjugations; thus, *lætor*, of the first conjugation, like *amor* :

Indicative Mode.

Pref. *Lætor*, I rejoice; *lætaris*, vel *-are*, thou rejoicest, &c.

Imp. *Lætabar*, I rejoiced, or did rejoice; *lætabaris*, &c.

Perf. *Lætatus sum* vel *fui*,* I have rejoiced, &c.

Plu-perf. *Lætatus eram* vel *fueram*, I had rejoiced, &c.

Fut. *Lætabor*, I shall or will rejoice; *lætaberis*, or *-abere*, &c.

   Lætaturus sum, I am about to rejoice, *or* I am to rejoice, &c.

Subjunctive.

Pref. *Læter*, I may rejoice; *læteris*, or *-ere*, &c.

Imp. *Lætarer*, I might rejoice; *lætareris*, or *-rere*, &c.

Perf. *Lætatus sim* vel *fuerim*, I may have rejoiced, &c.

Plu-perf. *Lætatus essem* vel *fuissem*, I might have rejoiced, &c.

Fut. *Lætatus fuero*, I shall have rejoiced, &c.

   Imperative.

---

* *Fui, fueram*, &c. are seldom joined to the participles of deponent verbs; and not so often to those of passive verbs as *sum, eram*, &c.

Imperative.

Pref. *Lætare,* vel *-ator,* rejoice thou ; *lætator,* let him rejoice, &c.

Infinitive.

Pref. *Lætari,* to rejoice.

Perf. *Lætatus esse* vel *fuisse,* to have rejoiced.

Fut. *Lætaturus esse,* to be about to rejoice.

Lætaturus fuisse, to have been about to rejoice.

Participles.

Pref. *Lætans,* rejoicing.

Perf. *Lætatus,* having rejoiced.

Fut. *Lætaturus,* about to rejoice.

Lætandus, to be rejoiced at.

In like manner conjugate, in the First Conjugation,

Abŏmĭnor, *to abhor.*

Adŭlor, *to flatter.*

Æmŭlor, *to vie with, to envy.*

Altercŏr, *to dispute, to make a repartee.*

Apricor, *to bask in the sun.*

Arbitror, *to think.*

Aſpernor, *to despiſe.*

Averſor, *to diſlike.*

Auctiōnor, *to ſell by auction.*

Aucŭpor, & -o, *to hunt after.*

Augŭror, & -o, *to forebode, or preſage by augury.*

Auſpĭcor, *to take an omen, to begin.*

Auxilior, *to aſſiſt.*

Bacchor, *to rage, to revel, to riot.*

Calumnior, *to accuſe falſely.*

Cavillor, *to ſcoff.*

Caupōnor, *to huckſter, to retail.*

Cauſor, *to plead in excuſe, to blame.*

Circŭlor, *to meet in companies, to ſtroll, to talk.*

Cŏmeſſor, *to revel.*

Cŏmĭtor, *to accompany.*

Commentor, *to meditate on, or write what one is to ſay.*

Conciōnor, *to harangue.*

Conflictor, *to ſtruggle.*

Cōnor, *to endeavour.*

Conſpĭcor, *to ſpy, to ſee.*

Contemplor, *to view.*

Convĭvor, *to feaſt.*

Cornĭcor, *to chatter like a crow.*

Crīmĭnor, *to blame.*

Cunctor, *to delay.*

Deteſtor, *to abhor.*

Dŏmĭnor, *to rule.*

Epŭlor, *to feaſt.*

Exſecror, *to curſe.*

Fămŭlor, *to ſerve.*

Fērior, *to keep holy-day.*

Fruſtror, *to diſappoint.*

Fūror, *to ſteal.*

Glōrior, *to boaſt.*

Grātŭlor, *to rejoice, to wiſh one joy.*

Grăvor, *to grudge.*

Hărĭŏlor, *to conjecture.*

Helluo, *to guttle or gormandize, to waſte.*

Hortor, *to encourage.*

Hallūcĭnor, *to ſpeak at random, to err.*

Imāgĭnor, *to conceive.*

Imĭtor, *to imitate.*

Indignor, *to diſdain.*

Inſĭcior, *to deny.*

Inſector, *to purſue, to inveigh againſt.*

Inſĭdior, *to lie in wait.*

Interprĕtor, *to explain.*

Jăcŭlor, *to dart.*

Jŏcor, *to jeſt.*

Lāmentŏr, *to bewail.*

Lucror, *to gain.*

Luctor, *to wreſtle.*

Māchĭnor, *to contrive.*

Mĕdĭcor, *to cure.*

Mĕdĭtor, *to muſe or ponder.*

Mercor, *to purchaſe.*

Mētor, *to meaſure.*

Mĭnor, *to threaten.*

Mīror, *to wonder.*

Mĭſĕror, *to pity.*

Mŏdĕror, *to rule.*

Mŏdŭlor, *to play a tune.*

Mŏrĭgĕror, *to humour.*

Mŏror, *to delay.*

Mūnĕror, *to preſent.*

Mūtuor, *to borrow.*

Nūgor, *to trifle.*

Obteſtor, *to beſeech.*

Ŏdōror, *to ſmell.*

Ŏpĕror, *to work.*

Ŏpīnor, *to think.*

Ŏpĭtŭlor, *to help.*

Oſcŭlor, *to kiſs.*

Ōtior, *to be at leiſure.*

Pālor, *to ſtroll or ſtraggle.*

Palpor,

Palpor, or -o, to stroke or soothe.
Patrocinor, to patronise.
Percontor, to inquire.
Peregrinor, to go abroad.
Periclitor, to be in danger.
Pigneror, to pledge.
Piscor, to fish.
Populor, & -o, to lay waste.
Prædor, to plunder.
Prælior, to fight.
Præstolor, to wait for.
Prævaricor, to go crossed, to shuffle or prevaricate.

Precor, to pray.
Deprecor, to entreat, to pray against.
Procor, to ask, to woo.
Recordor, to remember.
Refragor, to be against.
Rimor, to search.
Rixor, to scold or brawl.
Rusticor, to dwell in the country.
Scrutor, to search.
Solor, to comfort.
Spatior, to walk abroad.
Speculor, to view, to spy.
Stipulor, to stipulate or agree.

Stomachor, to be angry.
Suavior, to kiss.
Suffragor, to vote for one, to favour.
Suspicor, to suspect.
Tergiversor, to boggle, to put off.
Testor, to witness.
Tutor, to defend.
Vador, to give bail, to force to give bail.
Vagor, to wander.
Vaticinor, to prophesy.
Velitor, to skirmish.
Veneror, to worship.
Venor, to hunt.
Versor, to be employed.
Vociferor, to bawl.

In the Second Conjugation,

Mereor, meritus, *to deserve.*　　Polliceor, pollicitus, *to promise.*
Tueor, tuitus, or tutus, *to defend.*　　Liceor, licitus, *to bid at an auction.*

In the Third Conjugation,

Amplector, amplexus; *and* complector, complexus, *to embrace.*
Revertor, reversus, *to return.*

In the Fourth Conjugation,

Blandior, *to soothe, to flatter.*　　Partior, *to divide.*
Mentior, *to lie.*　　Sortior, *to draw or cast lots.*
Molior, *to attempt something difficult.*　　Largior, *to give liberally.*

Part. perf. *Blanditus, mentitus, molitus, partitus, sortitus, largitus.*

There are no exceptions in the *First Conjugation.*

EXCEPTIONS *in the Second Conjugation.*

Reor, ratus, to think.

Misereor, misertus, or not contracted *miseritus,* to pity.

Fateor, fassus, to confess.　The compounds of *fateor*
have *fessus;* as, *profiteor, professus,* to profess.　So *con-
fiteor,* to confess, to own *or* acknowledge.

EXCEPTIONS *in the Third Conjugation.*

Labor, lapsus, to slide.　So *al-, col-, de-, di-, e-, il-, inter-,
per-, præter-, pro-, re-, sub-, subter-, super-, trans-labor.*

Ulciscor, ultus, to revenge.

Utor, usus, to use.　So *ab-, de-utor.*

Loquor,

Lŏquor, lŏquūtus, or *locūtus,* to speak. So *al-, col-, circum-, e-, inter-, ob-, præ-, pro-lŏquor.*

Sĕquor, sĕquutus, or *sĕcutus,* to follow. So *af-, con-, ex-, in-, ob-, per-, pro-, re-, sub-sĕquor.*

Quĕror, questus, to complain. So *con-, inter-, præ-quĕror.*

Nītor, nīsus, or *nixus,* to endeavour, to lean upon. So *ad-* vel *an-, con-, e-, in-, ob-, re-, sub-nītor:* but the compounds have oftener *nixus.*

Păciscor, pactus, to bargain. So *de-peciscor.*

Grădior, gressus, to go. So *ag-, ante-, circum-, con-, de-, di-, e-, in-, intro-, præ-, præter-, pro-, re-, retro-, sug-, super-, transf-gredior.*

Prōficiscor, profectus, to go a journey.

Nanciscor, nactus, to get.

Pătior, passus, to suffer. So *per-pĕtior.*

Apiscor, aptus, to get. So *adipiscor, adeptus,* and *in-dipiscor, indeptus.*

Commĭniscor, commentus, to devise or invent.

Fruor, fruitus, or *fructus,* to enjoy. So *per-fruor.*

Oblīviscor, oblitus, to forget.

Expergiscor, experrectus, to awake.

Mŏrior, mortuus, to die. So *com-, de-, e-, in-, inter-, præ-mŏrior.*

Nascor, nātus, to be born. So *ad-, circum-, de-, e-, in-, inter-, re-, sub-nascor.*

ŏrior, ortus, ŏrīri, to rise. So *ab-, ad-, co-, ex-, ob-, sub-ŏrior.*

The three last form the future participle in *ĭtūrus;* thus *mŏrĭtūrus, nascĭtūrus, ŏrĭtūrus.*

EXCEPTIONS *in the Fourth Conjugation.*

Mētior, mensus, to measure. So *ad-, com-, di-, e-, præ-, re-mētior.*

Ordior, orsus, to begin. So *ex-, red-ordior.*

Expĕrior, expertus, to try.

Oppĕrior, oppertus, to wait or tarry for one.

The following verbs want the participle perfect:

Vescor, vesci, *to feed.*   Mĕdeor, mederi, *to heal.*

Līquor, liqui, *to melt* or *be dis-*   Rĕmĭniscor, reminisci, *to remember.*
  selves.   Irascor, irasci, *to be angry.*

Ringor,

Ringor, ringi, *to grin like a dog.*
Praevertor, praeverti, *to get before,*
  to outrun.
Diffiteor, diffiteri, *to deny.*

Divertor, diverti, *to turn aside, to*
  take lodging.
Defetiscor, defetisci, *to be weary,*
  or faint.

The verbs which do not fall under any of the foregoing rules are called *Irregular.*

I. Irregular Verbs.

The irregular verbs are commonly reckoned eight; *sum, eo, queo, volo, nolo, malo, fero,* and *fio,* with their compounds.

But properly there are only six; *nolo* and *malo* being compounds of *volo.*

SUM has already been conjugated. After the same manner are formed its compounds, *ad-, ab-, de-, inter-, prae-, ob-, sub-, super-sum,* and *insum,* which wants the preterite; thus, *adsum, adfui, ad-esse, &c.*

PROSUM, to do good, has a *d* where *sum* begins with *e;* as,

Ind. *Pr.* Pro-sum, · prod-es, prod-est ; pro-sumus, *&c.*

  Im. Prod-eram, prod-eras, prod-erat ; prod-eramus, *&c.*
Sub. *Im.* Prod-essem, prod-esses, prod-esset ; prod-essemus, *&c.*
Imperat. Prod-esto, prod-este.   Infinit. *Pref.* Prod-esse.

In the other parts it is like *sum : Pro-sim, -sis, &c. Pro-fui, -fueram,* &c.

POSSUM is compounded of *potis,* able, and *sum ;* and is thus conjugated :

   Possum, potui, posse, *To be able.*

Indicative Mode.

Pr. Possum,   potes,   potest ; possumus, potestis, possunt.
Im. Pot-eram, -eras,   -erat ;   -eramus,   -eratis,   -erant.
Per. Pot-ui,   -uisti,   -uit ;   -uimus,   -uistis,   -uerunt, -uere.
Plu. Pot-ueram, -ueras, -uerat ; -ueramus, -ueratis, -uerant.
Fut. Pot-ero,   -eris,   -erit ;   -erimus,   -eritis,   -erunt.

Subjunctive Mode.

Pr. Pos-sim,   -sis,   -sit ;   -simus,   -sitis,   -sint.
Im. Pos-sem,   -ses,   -set ;   -semus,   -setis,   -sent.
Per. Pot-uerim, -ueris, -uerit ; -uerimus, -ueritis, -uerint.
Plu. Pot-uissem, -uisses, -uisset ; -uissemus, -uissetis, -uissent.
Fut. Pot-uero, -ueris, -uerit ; -uerimus, -ueritis, -uerint.

Infinitive.

Pref. Posse.   ·Per. Potuisse.   *The rest wanting.*

Indicative Mode.

Pr. Eo,	is,	it ;	īmus,	ītis,	eunt.
Imp. Ibam,	ības,	ibat ;	ibamus,	ibatis,	ibant.
Per. Ivi,	ivisti,	ivit ;	ivimus,	ivistis,	iverunt, iverē.
Plu. Iveram,	iveras,	iverat ;	iveramus,	iveratis,	iverant.
Fut. Ibo,	ibis,	ibit ;	ibimus,	ibitis,	ibunt.

Subjunctive Mode.

Pr. Eam,	eas,	eat ;	eamus,	eatis,	eant.
Im. Irem,	ires,	iret ;	iremus,	iretis,	irent.
Per. Iverim,	iveris,	iverit ;	iverimus,	iveritis,	iverint.
Plu. Ivissem,	ivisses,	ivisset ;	ivissemus,	ivissetis,	ivissent.
Fut. Ivero,	iveris,	iverit ;	iverimus,	iveritis,	iverint.

Imperative.

Pres. { I, — Ito ; { ite, — itote, eunto.
{ Ito, — ito ;

Infinitive.

Pres. Ire.
Perf. Ivisse.
Fut. Esse iturus, a, um.
Fuisse iturus.

Participles.	Gerunds.	Supines.
Pr. Iens, *Gen.* euntis.	Eundum.	1. Itum.
Fut. Iturus, -a, -um.	Eundi.	2. Itu.
	Eundo, &c.	

The compounds of *eo* are conjugated after the same manner ; ăd-, ăb-, ex-, ŏb-, rĕd-, sŭb-, pĕr-, cŏ-, ĭn-, prǣ-, ante-, prōd-eo : only in the perfect and the tenses formed from it, they are usually contracted ; thus, *Adeo, adii*, seldom *adivi, aditum, adire*, to go to ; perf. *Adii, adiisti* or *adisti, &c. adieram, adierim, &c.* So likewise *vēneo, venii*, —— to be sold, (compounded of *venum* and *eo*.) But *Ambio, -īvi, -ītum, -īre*, to surround, is a regular verb of the fourth conjugation.

Eo, like other neuter verbs, is often rendered in English under a passive form : thus, *it*, he is going ; *ivit*, he is gone ; *iverat*, he was gone ; *iverit*, he may be gone, or shall be gone. So *venit*, he is coming ; *venit*, he is come ; *venerat*, he was come; &c. In the passive voice these verbs for the most part are only used impersonally ; i.e. *itur ab illo*, he is going ; *ventum est ab illis*, they are come. We find some of the compounds of *eo*, however, used personally : as, *pericula adeuntur*, are undergone. Cic. *Libri similiter aditi sunt*, were looked into. Liv. *Flamen pedibus transiri potest*. Quef. *Inimicitiæ subeuntur*. Cic.

QUEO, I can, and *NEQUEO*, I cannot, are conjugated the same way as *eo*; only they want the imperative and the gerunds ; and the participles are seldom used.

VOLO,

VOLO, vŏlui, velle, *To will,* or *to be willing.*

Indicative Mode.

Pr. Vŏl-o,   vis;   vult ; volŭmus, vultis, volunt.
Im. Vol-ebam, -ebas,   -ebat ; -ebamus, -ebatis, -ebant.
Per. Vol-ui;   -uisti,   -uit ; -uimus,   -uistis, -uerunt, -uere.
Pl. Vol-ueram, -ueras, -uerat;-ueramus,-ueratis, -uerant.
Fu. Vol-am,   -es,   -et ; -emus,   -etis,   -ent.

Subjunctive Mode.

Pr. Velim,   velis,   velit ; velimus, velitis, velint.
Im. Vellem;   velles, vellet ; vellemus, velletis, vellent.
Per. Vol-uerim, -ueris, -uerit ; -uerimus, -ueritis, -uerint.
Plu. Vol-uissem, -uisses, -uisset ; -uissemus, -uistetis, -uissent.
Fut. Vol-uero,   -ueris, -uerit ; -uerimus, -ueritis, -uerint.

Infinitive.		*Participle.*
Pref. Velle.	Perf. Voluisse.	Pref. Volens.

The rest not used.

NOLO, nolui, nolle, *To be unwilling.*

Indicative Mode.

Pr. Nolo,   non-vis, non-vult ; nolŭmus, non-vultis, nolunt.
Im. Nol-ebam; -ebas, -ebat ;   -ebamus, -ebatis,   -ebant.
Per. Nol-ui,   -uisti, -uit ;   -uimus, -uistis,   -uerunt, -uere.
Plu. Nol-ueram, -ueras, -uerat ; -ueramus, -ueratis, -uerant.
Fut. Nolam,   noles, nolet ; nolemus, noletis,   nolent.

Subjunctive Mode.

Pr. Nolim,   nolis, nolit ; nolimus, nolitis, nolint.
Im. Nollem,   nolles, nollet ; nollemus, nolletis, nollent.
Per. Nol-uerim, -ueris, -uerit ; -uerimus, -ueritis, -uerint.
Plu. Nol-uissem, -uisses, -uisset ; uissemus, -uistetis, -uissent.
Fut. Nol-uero, -ueris, -uerit ; -uerimus, -ueritis, -uerint.

Imperative.		*Infinitive.*	*Participle.*
2. Sing.	2. Plur.		
Pr. { Noli, *vel*	{ nolite, *vel*	Pr. Nolle.	Pr. Nolens.
{ Nolito;	{ nolitote.	Per. Noluisse.	*The rest wanting.*

MALO

MALO, malui, malle, *To be more willing.*

Indicative Mode.

Pr. Māl-o,   mavis, mavult ; malŭmus, mavultis, malunt.
Im. Mal-ebam, -ebas, -ebat ;   -ebamus, -ebatis, -ebant.
Per. Mal-ui,   -uifti, -uit ;   -uimus, -uiftis,   -uerunt.
                                                    -uere.
Plu. Mal-ueram, -ueras, -uerat ; -ueramus, -ueratis, -uerant.
Fut. Mal-am,   -es,   -et : &c. *This is fcarcely in ufe.*

Subjunctive Mode.

Pr. Malim,   malis, malit ; malīmus, malitis,   malint.
Im. Mallem,   malles, mallet ; mallemus, malletis, mallent.
Per. Mal-uerim, -ueris, -uerit ; -uerimus, -ueritis,   -uerint.
Plu. Mal-uiffem, -uiffes, -uiffet ; -uiffemus, -uiffetis, -uiffent.
Fut. Mal-uero, -ueris, -uerit ; -uerimus, -ueritis,   -uerint.

Infinitive Mode.

Pref. Malle.   *Perf.* Maluiffe.   *The reft not ufed.*

FERO, tŭli, lātum, ferre, *To carry, to bring* or *fuffer.*

A C T I V E   V O I C E.

Indicative Mode.

Pr. Fĕro,   fers,   fert ;   ferĭmus, fertis,   ferunt.
Im. Fer-ebam, -ebas, -ebat ; -ebamus, -ebatis, -ebant.
Per. Tuli,   tulifti, tulit ;   tulimus, tuliftis, tulerunt, -ere
Plu. Tul-eram, -eras, -erat ; -eramus, -eratis, -erant.
Fut. Feram,   feres, feret ; feremus, feretis, ferent.

Subjunctive Mode.

Pr. Feram,   feras, ferat ; feramus, feratis,   ferant.
Im. Ferrem,   ferres, ferret ; ferremus, ferretis, ferrent.
Per. Tul-erim,   -eris,   erit ;   -erimus,   -eritis,   -erint.
Plu. Tul-iffem, -iffes, -iffet ; -iffemus, -iffetis, -iffent.
Fut. Tul-ero,   -eris,   -erit ;   -erimus,   -eritis,   -erint.

Imperative.   Infinitive.

Pr. { Fer,   ferto : { ferte,   ferunto.   *Pr.* Ferre.
      { Ferto,   { fertote,   *Per.* Tuliffe.
                                         Fut. Effe laturus, a, um.
                                           Fuiffe laturus, a, um.

Participles.	*Gerunds.*	*Supines.*
Pref. Fĕrens,	Ferendum.	1. Lātum.
Fut. Laturus, -a, -um.	Ferendi.	2. Latu.
	Ferendo, &c.	

                                                PASSIVE

PASSIVE VOICE.
Fĕror, lātus, ferri, *To be brought.*
Indicative Mode.

Pr. Fĕror,   ferris,   sertur;   ferĭmur, ferimĭni, feruntur.
                vel ferre,

Im. Fer-ebar,   -ebaris,   -batur;   -ebamur, -ebamĭni, -ebantur.
                   vel -ebare,

Perf. Latus fum, &c. latus fui, &c.
Plu. Latus eram, &c. latus fueram, &c.

Fut. Ferar,   ferĕris,   feretur;   feremur, feremĭni, ferentur.
                 vel ferĕre,

Subjunctive Mode.

Pr. Ferar,   feraris,   feratur;   feramur, feramini, ferantur.
                vel ferare,

Im. Ferrer,   ferreris,   ferretur;   ferremur, ferremini, ferrentur.
                 vel ferrere,

Per. Latus fim, &c. latus fuerim, &c.
Plu. Latus effem, &c. latus fuiffem, &c.
Fut. Latus fuero, &c.

Imperative Mode.

Pref. Ferre *vel* fertor,   fertor;   ferimini,   feruntor.

Infinitive.   #### Participles.

Pref. Ferri.   *Perf.* Latus,   -a, -um.

Perf. Effe *vel* fuiffe latus, -a, -um.   *Fut.* Ferendus, -a, -um.

Fut. Latum iri.

In like manner are conjugated the compounds of *fĕro;* as, *affĕro, attŭli, allatum; aufĕro, abftuli, ablatum; diffĕro, diftuli, dilatum; confĕro, contuli, collatum; infĕro, intuli, illatum; offĕro, obtuli, oblatum; effĕro, extuli, elatum.* So *circum-, per-, tranf-, de-, pro-, ante-, prefĕro.* In fome writers we find *adfĕro, adtuli, adlatum; conlatum, inlatum; obfero,* &c. for *affĕro,* &c.

Obf. 1. Moft part of the above verbs are made irregular by contraction. Thus, *nolo* is contracted for *non volo; malo,* for *magis volo; fero, fers, fert,* &c. for *feris, ferit,* &c. *Feror, fĕrris,* v. *ferre, fertur,* for *ferĕris,* &c.

Obf. 2. The imperatives of *dīce, dūco,* and *fácio* are contracted in the fame manner with *fer:* thus we fay, *die, duc, fac,* inftead of *dice, duce, face.* But thefe often occur likewife in the regular form.

FIO, factus, fĭĕri, *To be made* or *done, to become.*
Indicative Mode.

Pr. Fīo,   fis,   fit;   fimus.   .   fiunt.
Im. Fiebam,   fiebas, fiebat;   fiebamus,   fiebatis,   fiebant.
Per. Factus fum, &c. factus, fui, &c.
Plu. Factus eram, &c. factus fuerom. &c.
Fut. Fiam.   fies,   fiet;   fiemus,   fietis,   fient.

Subjunctive Mode.

P. Fiam, fias, fiat ; fiamus, fiatis, fiant.
Im. Fiĕrem, fieres, fieret ; fieremus, fieretis, fierent.
Per. Factus sim, &c. factus fuerim, &c.
Pl. Factus essem, &c. factus fuissem, &c.
Fut. Factus fuero, &c.

Imperative.   Infinitive.

Pr. { Fi,   fito : { ste,   fiunto.   *Pr.* Fieri.
     { Fito,   { sitote,   *Per.* Esse *vel* fuisse factus, a, um.
                                       Fut. Factum iri.

Participles.   Supine.

Per. Factus,   -a,   -um.   Factu.
Fut. Faciendus, -a,   -um.

The compounds of *făcio* which retain *a*, have also *fio* in the passive, and *fac* in the imperative active ; as, *calefacio*, to warm, *calefio*, *calefac* : but those which change *a* into *i*, form the passive regularly, and have *fice* in the imperative ; as, *conficio*, *confice* ; *conficior*, *confectus*, *confici*. We find, however, *confit*, it is done, and *confieri* ; *defit*, it is wanting ; *infit*, he begins.

To irregular verbs may properly be subjoined what are commonly called NEUTER PASSIVE *Verbs*, which, like *fio*, form the preterite tenses according to the passive voice, and the rest in the active. These are, *sŏleo*, *solĭtus*, *solēre*, to use ; *audeo*, *ausus*, *audēre*, to dare ; *gaudeo*, *gavisus*, *gaudēre*, to rejoice ; *fido*, *fisus*, *fidĕre*, to trust : So *confido*, to trust ; and *diffido*, to distrust ; which also have *confidi*, and *diffidi*. Some add *mæreo*, *mæstus*, *mærere*, to be sad ; but *mæstus* is generally reckoned an adjective. We likewise say *juratus sum* and *cænatus sum*, for *juravi* and *cænavi*, but these may also be taken in a passive sense.

To these may be referred verbs, wholly active in their termination, and passive in their signification ; as, *vāpŭlo*, *-avi*, *-atum*, to be beaten *or* whipped ; *vēneo*, to be sold ; *exŭlo*, to be banished, &c.

DEFECTIVE VERBS.

Verbs are called *Defective*, which are not used in certain tenses, numbers, and persons.

These three, *ōdi*, *cœpi*, and *mĕmĭni*, are only used in the preterite tenses ; and therefore are called *Preteritive Verbs* ; though they have sometimes likewise a present signification : thus,

Odi, I hate, or have hated, *oderam*, *oderim*, *odissem*, *odero*, *odisse*. Participles, *osus*, *osurus* : *exosus*, *perosus*.

Cœpi, I begin *or* have begun, *cœperam*, *-erim*, *-issem*, *-ero*, *-isse*. Supine, *cœptu*. Participles, *cœptus*, *cœpturus*.

Mĕmini,

Mĕmĭni, I remember, or have remembered, *memineram, -erim, -iſſem, -ero, -iſſe :* Imperative, *memento, mementote.*

Inſtead of *odi*, we ſometimes ſay, *oſus ſum* ; and always *exoſus, peroſus ſum*, and not *exodi, perodi.* We ſay, *opus cœpit fieri*, or *cœptum eſt.*

To theſe ſome add *nŏvi*, becauſe it frequently has the ſignification of the preſent. *I know*, as well as, *I have known*, though it comes from *neſco*, which is complete.

Fŭro, to be mad, *dor*, to be given, and *for*, to ſpeak, as alſo, *der* and *fer*, are not uſed in the firſt perſon ſingular ; thus, we ſay, *daris, datur ;* but never *dor.*

Of verbs which want many of their chief parts, the following moſt frequently occur : *Aio*, I ſay, *inquam*, I ſay, *fŏrem*, I ſhould be ; *auſim*, contracted for *auſus ſim*, I dare ; *faxim*, I'll ſee to it, *or* I will do it ; *ăve* and *ſalve*, ſave you, hail, good-morrow ; *cedo*, tell thou, *or* give me ; *quæſo*, I pray.

Ind. Pr. Aio,	ais,	ait :	——	——	aiunt.
Im. Aiebam,	-ebas,	-ebat :	-ebamus,	-ebatis,	-ebant.
Per. ——	aiſti,	——	——	——	——
Sub. Per. ——	aias,	aiat :	——	aiatis,	aiant.

Imperat. Ai.   *Particip. Preſ.* Aiens.

Ind. Pr. Inquam,	-quis,	-quit :	-quĭmus,	-quĭtis,	-quiunt.
Im. ——	——	inquiebat :	——	——	inquiebant.
Per. ——	inquiſti,	——	——	——	——
Fut. ——	inquies,	inquiet :	——	——	——

Imperat. Inque, inquĭto.   *Particip. Pr.* Inquiens.

Sub. Im.
Plu. } Fŏrem, fores, foret : foremus, foretis, forent.

Inf. Fore, *to be hereafter*, or *to be about to be*, the ſame with *eſſe futurus.*

Sub. Pr. Auſim,	auſis,	auſit :	——	——	——
Per. Faxim,	faxis,	faxit :	——	——	faxint.
Fut. Faxo,	faxis,	faxit :	——	faxĭtis,	faxint.

Note. *Faxim* and *faxo* are uſed inſtead of *fecerim* and *fecero.*

Imper. Ave *vel* aveto ; *plur.* avĕte *vel* avetote.   *Inf.* avere.

—— Salve *v.* ſalvēto ; — ſalvēte *v.* ſalvetote.   — ſalvere.

Indic. Fut. —— Salvebis.

Imperat. ſecond perſ. ſing. Cedo, *plur.* cedite.

Indic. Preſ. firſt perſ. ſing. Quæſo, *plur.* quæsŭmus.

Moſt of the other Defective verbs are but ſingle words, and rarely to be found, but among the poets ; as, *infit*, he begins ; *deſt*, it is wanting. Some are compounded of a verb and the conjunction *ſi* ; as, *ſis*, for *ſi vis*, if thou wilt ; *ſultis*, for *ſi vultis* ; *ſodes*, for *ſi audes*, equivalent to *quæſo*, I pray ; *capſis*, for *cape ſi vis.*

IMPERSONAL

A verb is called *Imperfonal*, which has only the terminations of the third perfon fingular, but does not admit any *perfon* or nominative before it.

Imperfonal verbs in Englifh, have before them the neuter pronoun *it*, which is not confidered as a perfon; thus, *delectat*, it delights; *decet*, it becomes; *contingit*, it happens; *evenit*, it happens:

		1ft Conj.	2d Conj.	3d Conj.	4th Conj.
Ind.	Pr.	Delectat,	Decet,	Contingit,	Evenit,
	Im.	Delectabat,	Decebat,	Contingebat,	Eveniebat,
	Per.	Delectavit,	Decuit,	Contigit,	Evenit,
	Plu.	Delectaverat,	Decuerat,	Contigerat,	Evenerat,
	Fut.	Delectabit.	Decebit.	Continget.	Eveniet.
Sub.	Pr.	Delectet,	Deceat,	Contingat,	Eveniat,
	Im.	Delectaret,	Deceret,	Contingeret,	Eveniret,
	Per.	Delectaverit,	Decuerit,	Contigerit,	Evenerit,
	Plu.	Delectaviffet,	Decuiffet,	Contigiffet,	Eveniffet,
	Fut.	Delectaverit.	Decuerit.	Contigerit.	Evenerit.
Inf.	Pr.	Delectare,	Decere,	Contingere,	Evenire,
	Per.	Delectaviffe.	Decuiffe.	Contigiffe.	Eveniffe.

Moft Latin verbs may be ufed imperfonally in the paffive voice, efpecially Neuter and Intranfitive verbs which otherwife have no paffive; as, *pugnatur, favetur, curritur, venitur;* from *pugno,* to fight; *faveo,* to favour; *curro,* to run; *venio,* to come:

Ind.	Pr.	Pugnatur,	Favetur,	Curritur,	Venitur;
	Im.	Pugnabatur,	Favebatur,	Currebatur,	Veniebatur,
	Per.	Pugnatum eft,	Fautum eft,	Curfum eft,	Ventum eft,
	Plu.	Pugnatum erat,	Fautum erat,	Curfum erat,	Ventum erat,
	Fut.	Pugnabitur.	Favebitur.	Curretur.	Venietur.
Sub.	Pr.	Pugnetur,	Faveatur,	Curratur,	Veniatur,
	Im.	Pugnaretur,	Faveretur,	Curreretur,	Veniretur,
	Per.	Pugnatum fit,	Fautum fit,	Curfum fit,	Ventum fit,
	Plu.	Pugnatum effet,	Fautum effet,	Curfum effet,	Ventum effet.
	Fut.	Pugnatum fuerit.	Fautum fuerit.	Curfum fuerit.	Ventum fuerit.
Inf.	Pr.	Pugnari,	Faveri,	Curri,	Veniri,
	Per.	Pugnatum effe,	Fautum effe,	Curfum effe,	Ventum effe,
Fut.		Pugnatum iri.	Fautum iri.	Curfum iri.	Ventum iri.

Obf. 1. Imperfonal verbs are fcarcely ufed in the imperative, but inftead of it we take the fubjunctive: as, *delectet*, let it delight, &c.; nor in the fupines, participles, or gerunds, except a few; as, *pœni-*

tens,

tens, -*dum*, -*dus*, &c. *Induci ad pudendum et pigendum*, Cic. In the preterite tenfes of the paſſive voice, the participle perfect is always put in the neuter gender.

Obſ. 2. Grammarians reckon only ten real imperſonal verbs, and all in the ſecond conjugation ; *dĕcet*, it becomes ; *pœnĭtet*, it repents ; *oportet*, it behoves ; *miſĕret*, it pities ; *pĭget*, it irketh ; *pŭdet*, it ſhameth ; *lĭcet*, it is lawful ; *lĭbet* or *lŭbet*, it pleaſeth ; *tædet*, it wearieth ; *lĭquet*, it appears. Of which the following have a double preterite ; *miſeret*, *miſeruit*, or *miſertum eſt* ; *piget*, *piguit*, or *pigitum eſt* ; *pudet*, *puduit*, or *puditum eſt* ; *licet*, *licuit*, or *licitum eſt* ; *libet*, *libuit*, or *libitum eſt* ; *tædet*, *tæduit*, *tæſum eſt*, oftener *pertæſum eſt*. But many other verbs are uſed imperſonally in all the conjugations:

In the firſt, *Jŭvat*, *ſpĕctat*, *văcat*, *ſtat*, *conſtat*, *præſtat*, *reſtat*, &c.

In the ſecond, *Appāret*, *attĭnet*, *pertĭnet*, *dēbet*, *dōlet*, *nŏcet*, *lătet*, *lĭquet*, *pătet*, *plăcet*, *diſplĭcet*, *sĕdet*, *sŏlet*, &c.

In the third, *Accĭdit*, *incĭpit*, *desĭnit*, *ſuffĭcit*, &c.

In the fourth, *Convĕnit*, *expĕdit*, &c.

Alſo Irregular verbs, *Eſt*, *obeſt*, *prŏdeſt*, *pŏteſt*, *intĕreſt*, *ſupĕreſt* ; *fit*, *prætĕrit*, *nequit*, and *nequitur*, *ſubit*, *confert*, *refert*, &c.

Obſ. 3. Under imperſonal verbs may be comprehended thoſe which expreſs the operations or appearances of nature ; as, *Fulgŭrat*, *fulmĭnat*, *tŏnat*, *grandĭnat*, *gĕlat*, *pluit*, *ningit*, *luceſcit*, *adveſperaſcit*, &c.

Obſ 4. Imperſonal verbs are applied to any perſon or number, by putting that which ſtands before other verbs, after the imperſonals, in the caſes which they govern ; as, *placet mihi*, *tibi*, *illi*, it pleaſes me, thee, him ; *or* I pleaſe, thou pleaſeſt, &c. *pugnatur a me*, *a te*, *ab illo*, I fight, thou fighteſt, he fighteth, &c. So *Curritur*, *venitur a me*, *a te*, &c. I run, thou runneſt, &c. *Favetur tibi a me*, Thou art favoured by me, *or* I favour thee, &c.

Obſ. 5. Verbs are uſed perſonally or imperſonally, according to the particular meaning which they expreſs, or the different import of the words with which they are joined : Thus we can ſay, *ego placeo tibi*, I pleaſe you ; but we cannot ſay, *ſi places audire*, if you pleaſe to hear, but *ſi placet tibi audire*. So, we can ſay, *multa homini contingunt*, many things happen to a man : but inſtead of *ego contigi eſſe domi*, we muſt either ſay, *me contigit eſſe domi*, or *mihi contigit eſſe domi*, I happened to be at home. The proper and elegant uſe of Imperſonal verbs can only be acquired by practice.

REDUNDANT VERBS.

Thoſe are called *Redundant Verbs*, which have different forms to expreſs the ſame ſenſe : thus, *aſſentio* and *aſſentior*, to agree ; *fabrico* and *fabricor*, to frame ; *mereo* and *mereor*, to deſerve, &c. Theſe verbs, however, under the paſſive form have likewiſe a paſſive ſignification.

Several verbs are uſed in different conjugations.

1. Some are uſually of the firſt conjugation, and rarely of the third ; as, *lavo*, *lavas*, *lavāre* : and *lavo*, *lavis*, *lavĕre*, to waſh.

2. Some are uſually of the ſecond, and rarely of the third ; as, Ferveo, ferves, *and* fervo, fervis, *to boil.*

Fulgeo, fulges, *and* fulgo, fulgis, *to ſhine.*

Strideo,

Strīdeo, strides, *and* strido, stridis, *to make a hissing noise, to creak.*

Tueor, tuēris, *and* tuor, tuēris, *to defend.*

To these add *tergeo, terges*; and *terga, tergis,* to wipe, which are equally common.

3. Some are commonly of the third conjugation, and rarely of the fourth; as,

Fodio, fodis, fodĕre, *and* fodio, fodis, fodīre, *to dig.*

Sallo, fallis, fallĕre, *and* fallio, fallis, fallīre, *to falt.*

Arceffo, -is, arceffere, *and* arceffio, arcefsire, *to fend for.*

Morior, morĕris, mori, *and* morior, morīris, morīri, *to die.*

So Orior, orĕris, *and* orior, orīris, orīri, *to rife.*

Potior, potĕris, *and* potior, potīris, potīri, *to enjoy.*

There is likewife a verb, which is ufually of the fecond conjugation, and more rarely of the fourth, namely, *cieo, cies, ciēre*; and *cio, cis, cīre,* to roufe; whence *accīre* and *accītus.*

To thefe we may add the verb *EDO,* to eat, which though regularly formed, alfo agrees in feveral of its parts with *fum*; thus,

Ind. Pref. *Edo, edis or es, edit or eft;* ———— *editis or eftis* ————

Sub. Imperf. *Ederem or effem, ederes or effes, &c.*

Imp. *Ede or es, edito or efto; edite or efte; efitote or eftote.*

Inf. Pref. *Edare or effe.*

Paffive Ind. Pref. *Editur or eftur.*

It may not be improper here to fubjoin a lift of thofe verbs which refemble one another in fome of their parts, though they differ in fignification. Of thefe fome agree in the prefent, fome in the preterite, and others in the fupine.

1. The following agree in the prefent, but are differently conjugated:

Aggĕro, -as, *to heap up.*	Aggĕro, -is, *to bring together.*
Appello, -as, *to call.*	Appello, -is, *to drive to, to arrive.*
Compello, -as, *to addrefs.*	Compello, -is, *to drive together.*
Collĭgo, -as, *to bind.*	Collĭgo, -is, *to gather together.*
Confterno, -as, *to aftonifb.*	Confterno, -is, *to ftrew.*
Effĕro, -as, *to enrage.*	Effĕro, -fers, *to bring out.*
Fundo, -as, *to found.*	Fundo, -is, *to pour out.*
Mando, -as, *to command.*	Mando, -is, *to chew.*
Obsĕro, -as, *to lock.*	Obsĕro, -is, *to befet.*
Vŏlo, -as, *to fly.*	Vŏlo, vis, *to will.*

Of this clafs fome have a different quantity; as,

Cōlo, -as, *to ftrain.*	Cŏlo, -is, *to till.*
Dīco, -as, *to dedicate.*	Dīco, -is, *to fay.*
Edūco, -as, *to train up.*	Edūco, -is, *to lead forth.*
Lēgo, -as, *to fend on an embaffy.*	Lĕgo, -is, *to read.*
Vădo, -as, *to wade.*	Vădo, -is, *to go.*

2. The following verbs agree in the preterite :

Aceo, acui, *to be sour.*	Acuo, acui, *to sharpen.*
Crefco, crēvi, *to grow.*	Cerno, crēvi, *to see.*
Frīgeo, frixi, *to be cold.*	Frīgo, frixi, *to fry.*
Fulgeo, fulfi, *to shine.*	Fulcio, fulfi, *to prop.*
Lūceo, luxi, *to shine.*	Lūgeo, luxi, *to mourn.*
Pāveo, pāvi, *to be afraid.*	Pafco, pāvi, *to feed.*
Pendeo, pĕpendi, *to hang.*	Pendo, pĕpendi, *to weigh.*

3. The following agree in the fupine :

Crefco, crētum, *to grow.*	Cerno, cretum, *to behold.*
Māneo, manfum, *to stay.*	Mando, manfum, *to chew.*
Sto, ftatum, *to ftand.*	Sifto, ftatum, *to ftop.*
Succenfeo, cenfum, *to be angry.*	Succendo, -cenfum, *to kindle.*
Téneo, tentum, *to hold.*	Tendo, tentum, *to ftretch out.*
Verro, verfum, *to fweep.*	Verto, verfum, *to turn.*
Vinceo, victum, *to overcome.*	Vīvo, victum, *to live.*

The OBSOLETE CONJUGATION.

This chiefly occurs in old writers, and only in particular conjugations and tenfes.

1. The ancient Latins made the imperfect of the indicative active
of the fourth conjugation in *IBAM*, without the *e* ; as, *audibam, fci-
bam*; for *audiebam, fciebam.*

2. In the future of the indicative of the fourth conjugation, they
ufed *IBO* in the active, and *ibor* in the paffive voice : as, *dormibo,
dormibor*, for *dormiam, dormiar.*

3. The prefent of the fubjunctive anciently ended in *IM* : as, *edim*,
for *edam* ; *duim* for *dem.*

4. The perfect of the fubjunctive active fometimes occurs in *SSIM*,
and the future in *SSO* ; as, *levaffim, levaffo*, for *levaverim, levavero* ;
capfim, capfo, for *ceperim cepero* : Hence the future of the infinitive
was formed in *ASSERE* ; as, *levaffere* for *levaturus effe.*

5. In the fecond perfon of the prefent of the imperative paffive, we
find *MINO* in the fingular, and *minor* in the plural ; as *famino*, for
fare ; and *progrediminor* for *progredimini.*

6. The fyllable *ER* was frequently added to the prefent of the infinitive paffive ; as, *farier*, for *fari* ; *dicier* for *dici.*

7. The participles of the future time active, and perfect paffive,
when joined with the verb *effe*, were fometimes ufed as indeclinable :
thus, *credo inimicos dictarum effe*, for *dicturos*, Cic. *Cohortes ad me miffum
facias*, for *miffas*, Cic. ad Attic. viii. 12.

DERIVATION and COMPOSITION of VERBS.

1. Verbs are derived either from nouns or from other verbs.

Verbs derived from nouns are called *Denominative* ; as, *Cæno*, to
fup ; *laudo*, to praife ; *fraudo*, to defraud ; *lapido*, to throw ftones ;
operor, to work ; *frumentor*, to forage ; *lignor*, to gather fuel, &c.
from *cæna, laus, fraus*, &c. But when they exprefs imitation or refemblance,

ſemblance, they are called *Imitative* ; as, *Patriſſo, Græcor, būbŭlo, cor‑nĭcor, &c.* I imitate or reſemble my father, a Græcian, a crow, &c. from *pater, Græcus, cornix.*

Of thoſe derived from other verbs, the following chiefly deſerve attention ; namely, *Frequentatives, Inceptives,* and *Deſideratives.*

1. *FREQUENTATIVES* expreſs frequency of action, and are all of the firſt conjugation. They are formed from the laſt ſupine, by changing *ātu* into *ĭto,* in verbs of the firſt conjugation ; and by changing *u* into *o,* in verbs of the other three conjugations ; as, *clamo,* to cry, *clamĭto,* to cry frequently : *terreo, terrĭto ; verto, verſo ; dormio, dormĭto.*

In like manner, Deponent verbs form Frequentatives in *or* ; as, *minor,* to threaten ; *minĭtor,* to threaten frequently.

Some are formed in an irregular manner ; as, *nato* from *no ; noſcito* from *noſco ; ſcitor,* or rather *ſciſcĭtor,* from *ſcio ; pavĭto,* from *paveo ; ſector,* from *ſequor, loquĭtor,* from *loquor.* So *quærĭto, fundĭto, agĭto, fluĭto, &c.*

From Frequentative verbs are alſo formed other Frequentatives ; as, *curro, curſo, curſito ; pello, pulſo, pulsĭto,* or by contraction *pulto ; capio, capto, captĭto ; cano, canto, cantĭto ; defendo, defenſo, defenſito ; dico, dicto, dictĭto ; gero, geſto, geſtĭto ; jacio, jacto, jactĭto ; venio, ventito ; mutio, muſſo,* (for *mutito*) *muſsĭto, &c.*

Verbs of this kind do not always expreſs frequency of action. Many of them have much the ſame ſenſe with their primitives, or expreſs the meaning more ſtrongly.

2. *INCEPTIVE Verbs* mark the beginning or continued increaſe of any thing. They are formed from the ſecond perſon ſing. of the preſent of the indicative, by adding *co* : as, *caleo,* to be hot, *cales, caleſco,* to grow hot. So in the other conjugations, *labaſco,* from *labo : tremiſco,* from *tremo ; obdormiſco,* from *obdormio. Hiſco,* from *hio,* is contracted for *hiaſco.* Inceptives are likewiſe formed from ſubſtantives and adjectives ; as, *pueraſco,* from *puer ; dulceſco,* from *dulcis ; juveneſco,* from *juvenis.*

All Inceptives are Neuter verbs, and of the third conjugation. They want both the preterite and ſupine ; unleſs very rarely, when they borrow them from their primitives

3. *DESIDERATIVE Verbs* ſignify a deſire or intention of doing a thing. They are formed from the latter ſupine, by adding *rio,* and ſhortening the *u* ; as, *cænātŭrio,* I deſire to ſup, from *cænatu.* They are all of the fourth conjugation ; and want both preterite and ſupine, except theſe three, *eſŭrio, -ivi, -ītum,* to deſire to eat ; *partŭrio, -ĭvi, —,* to be in travail ; *nuptŭrio, -ivi, —,* to deſire to be married.

There are a few verbs in LLO, which are called *Diminutive* ; as, *cantillo, ſorbillo, -are,* I ſing, I ſup a little : To theſe ſome add *albĭco* and *candĭco, -are,* to be or to grow whitiſh ; alſo *nigrĭco, fodĭco,* and *vellĭco.* Some verbs in SSO are called *Intenſive* ; as *capeſſo, faceſſo, petĭſſo* or *petiſſo,* I take, I do, I ſeek earneſtly.

Verbs are compounded with nouns, with other verbs, with adverbs, and chiefly with prepoſitions. Many of theſe ſimple verbs are not in uſe ; as, *Fuo, fendo, ſpecio, gruo,* &c. The component parts uſually
remain

remain entire. Sometimes a letter is added; as *prodeo*, for *pro-eo*: or taken away; as, *asporto*, *omitto*, *trado*, *pejero*, *pergo*, *debeo*, *præbeo*, &c. for *absporto*, *obmitto*, *transdo*, *perjuro*, *perrego*, *debibeo*, *prælibeo*, &c. So *demo*, *promo*, *sumo*, of *de*, *pro*, *sub*, and *emo*, which anciently signified *to take*, or *to take away*. Often the vowel or diphthong of the simple verb, and the last consonant of the preposition, is changed: as, *damno*, *condemno*; *calco*, *conculco*; *lædo*, *collido*; *audio*, *obedio*, &c. *Affero*, *aufero*, *collaudo*, *implico*, &c. for *adfero*, *abfero*, *conlaudo*, *implico*, &c.

PARTICIPLE.

A Participle is a kind of adjective formed from a verb, which in its signification implies time.

It is so called, because it partakes both of an adjective and of a verb, having *in Latin* gender and declension from the one, time and signification from the other, and number from both. Participles *in English*, like adjectives, admit of no variation.

Participles in Latin are declined like adjectives; and their signification is various, according to the nature of the verbs from which they come; only participles in *dus* are always passive, and import not so much future time, as obligation or necessity.

Latin verbs have four Participles, the present and future active; as, *Amans*, loving; *amātūrus*, about to love; and the perfect and future passive; as, *amātus*, loved, *amandus*, to be loved.

The Latins have not a participle perfect in the active, nor a participle present in the passive voice; which defect must be supplied by a circumlocution. Thus, to express the perfect participle active in English, we use a conjunction, and the plu-perfect of the subjunctive in Latin, or some other tense, according to its connection with the other words of a sentence; as, he having loved, *quum amavisset*, &c.

Neuter verbs have commonly but two Participles; as, *Sedens*, *sessurus*; *stans*, *stātūrus*.

From some Neuter Verbs are formed Participles of the perfect tense; as, *Erratus*, *festinatus*, *juratus*, *laboratus*, *vigilatus*, *cessatus*, *sudatus*, *triumphatus*, *regnatus*, *decursus*, *desitus*, *emeritus*, *emersus*, *obitus*, *placĭtus*, *peccatus*, *cœnatus*, &c. and also of the future in *dus*; as, *Jurandus*, *vigilandus*, *regnandus*, *carendus*, *dormiendus*, *erubescendus*, &c. Neuter passive verbs are equally various. *Veneo* has no participle: *Fido*, only *fidens* and *fisus*; *soleo*, *solens* and *solĭtus*; *vapulo*, *vapulans* and *vapulaturus*; *Gaudeo*, *gaudens*, *gavisus*, and *gavisurus*; *Audeo*, *audens*, *ausus*, *ausurus*, *audendus*. *Ausus* is used both in an active and passive sense; as, *Ausi omnes immane nefas, ausique potiti*. Virg. Æn. vi. 624.

Deponent and Common verbs have commonly four Participles; as,

Loquens,

Loquens, speaking ; *locuturus,* about to speak ; *locutus,* having spoken ; *loquendus,* to be spoken : *Dignans,* vouchsafing ; *dignaturus,* about to vouchsafe ; *dignatus,* having vouchsafed, being vouchsafed, *or* having been vouchsafed ; *dignandus,* to be vouchsafed. Many participles of the perfect tense from Deponent verbs have both an active and passive sense ; as, *Abominatus, conatus, confessus, adortus, amplexus, blanditus, largitus, mentitus, oblitus, testatus, veneratus,* &c.

There are several Participles compounded with *in* signifying *not,* the verbs of which do not admit of such composition : as, *Insciens, insperans, indicens,* for, *non dicens, inopinans,* and *necopinans, immerens ; Illæsus, impransus, inconsultus, incustoditus, immutatus, impunitus, imparatus, incomitatus, incomptus, indemnatus, indotatus, incorruptus, interritus,* and *imperterritus, intestatus, inausus, inopinatus, inultus, incensus,* for *non census,* not registered ; *infectus,* for *non factus, invisus,* for *non visus, indictus,* for *non dictus,* &c. There is a different *incensus* from *incendo ; infectus,* from *inficio ; invisus* from *invideo ; indictus* from *indico,* &c.

If from the signification of a Participle we take away *time,* it becomes an adjective, and admits the degrees of comparison ; as,

Amans, loving, *amantior, amantissimus ; | doctus,* learned, *doctior, doctissimus :* or a substantive ; as, *Præfectus,* a commander or governor ; *consonans,* s. sc. *litera,* a consonant ; *continens,* s. sc. *terra,* a continent ; *confluens,* m. a place where two rivers run together ; *oriens,* m. sc. *sol,* the east ; *occidens,* m. the west ; *dictum,* a saying ; *scriptum,* &c.

There are many words in *ATUS, ITUS,* and *UTUS,* which although resembling participles are reckoned adjectives, because they come from nouns, and not from verbs ; as, *alatus, barbatus, cordatus, caudatus, cristatus, auritus, pellitus, turritus ; astutus, cornutus, nasutus,* &c. winged, bearded, discreet, &c. But *auratus, æratus, argentatus, ferratus, plumbatus, gypsatus, calceatus, clypeatus, galeatus, tunicatus, larvatus, palliatus, lymphatus, purpuratus, prætextatus,* &c. covered with gold, brass, silver, &c. are accounted participles, because they are supposed to come from obsolete verbs. So perhaps *calamistratus,* frizzled, crisped or curled, *crinitus,* having long hair, *peritus,* skilled, &c.

There are a kind of Verbal adjectives in *BUNDUS,* formed from the imperfect of the indicative, which very much resemble Participles in their signification, but generally express the meaning of the verb more fully, or denote an abundance or great deal of the action ; as, *vitabundus,* the same with *valde vitans,* avoiding much ; *Sall. Jug.* 60. and 101.; *Liv.* xxv. 13. So *errabundus, ludibundus, populabundus, moribundus,* &c.

GERUNDS and SUPINES.

GERUNDS are participial words, which bear the signification of the verb from which they are formed ; and are declined like a neuter noun of the second declension, through all the cases of the singular number, except the vocative.

There are, both in Latin and English, substantives derived from

the

the verb, which so much resemble the Gerund in their signification, that frequently they may be substituted in its place. They are generally used, however, in a more undetermined sense than the Gerund, and in English have the article always prefixed to them. Thus, with the gerund, *Delector legendo Ciceronem*, I am delighted with reading Cicero. But with the substantive, *Delector lectione Ciceronis*, I am delighted with the reading of *Cicero*.

The Gerund and Future Participle of verbs in *io*, and some others, often take *u* instead of *e*; as, *faciundum, di, do, dus; experiundum, potiundum, gerundum, petundum, dicundum*, &c. for *faciendum*, &c.

SUPINES have much the same signification with Gerunds; and may be indifferently applied to any person or number. They agree in termination with nouns of the fourth declension, having only the accusative and ablative cases.

The former Supine is commonly used in an active, and the latter in a passive sense, but sometimes the contrary; as, *coctum non vapulatum, dudum conductus fui*, i. e. *ut vapularem*, v. *verberarer*, to be beaten, Plaut.

ADVERB.

An adverb is an indeclinable part of speech, *added to a verb*, adjective, or other adverb, to express some circumstance, quality, or manner of their signification.

All adverbs may be divided into two classes, namely, those which denote *Circumstance*; and those which denote *Quality, Manner*, &c.

I. Adverbs denoting CIRCUMSTANCE are chiefly those of *Place, Time*, and *Order*.

1. Adverbs of *Place*, are fivefold, namely, such as signify,

1. Motion or rest in a place.

Ubi ?	*Where ?*
Hic,	*Here.*
Illic,	
Isthic,	*There.*
Ibi,	
Intus,	*Within.*
Föris,	*Without.*
Übique,	*Every where.*
Nusquam,	*No where.*
Alicubi,	*Some where.*
Alibi,	*Else where.*
Übivis,	*Any where.*
Ibidem,	*In the same place.*

2. Motion to a place.

Quo ?	*Whither ?*
Huc,	*Hither.*
Illuc,	*Thither.*
Isthuc,	
Intro,	*In.*
Föras,	*Out.*
Eô,	*To that place.*
Aliô,	*To another place.*
Aliquô,	*To some place.*
Eôdem,	*To the same place.*

3. Motion towards a place.

Quorsum ?	*Whitherward ?*
Versus,	*Towards.*
Horsum,	*Hitherward.*
Illorsum,	*Thitherward.*
Sursum,	*Upward.*
Deorsum,	*Downward.*
Antrorsum,	*Forward.*
Retrorsum,	

Retrorſum,	Backward.	Sicunde,	If from any place.
Dextrorſum,	Towards the right.	Utrinque,	On both ſides.
Siniſtrorſum,	Towards the left.	Sŭperne,	From above.

4. Motion from a place.

Unde ?	Whence ?	Inferne,	From below.
Hinc,	Hence.	Cœlĭtus,	From heaven.
		Fundĭtus,	From the ground.

Illinc,	} Thence.		
Iſthinc,			
Inde,			

5. Motion through or by a place.

Indĭdem,	From the ſame place.	Quâ ?	Which way ?
Aliunde,	From elſewhere.	Hâc,	This way.
Alĭcunde,	From ſome place.	Illac,	} That way.
		Iſthac,	
		Aliâ,	Another way.

2. Adverbs of *Time* are threefold, namely, ſuch as ſignify,

1. Some particular time, either preſent, paſt, future, or indefinite.

Nunc,	Now.	Nunquam,	Never.
Hŏdie,	To day.	Intĕrim,	In the mean time.
		Quŏtĭdie,	Daily.

Tunc,	} Then.	
Tum,		
Hĕri,	Yeſterday.	

2. Continuance of time.

Dŭdum,	} Heretofore.	Dĭu,	Long.
Prĭdem,		Quamdĭu ?	How long ?
Prĭdie,	The day before.	Tamdiu,	So long.
Nŭdius tertius,	Three days ago.		

		Jamdiu,	} Long ago.
		Jamdŭdum,	
		Jamprĭdem,	

Nŭper,	Lately.

3. Viciſſitude or repetition of time.

Jamjam,	} Preſently.	Quŏties ?	How often ?
Mox,	} Immediately.	Sæpe,	Often.
Stătim,	} By and by.	Rārò,	Seldom.
Prōtĭnus,	Inſtantly.	Tŏties,	So often.
Illĭco,	Straightway.	Alĭquŏties,	For ſeveral times.
Cras,	To-morrow.		

		Vĭciſſim,	} By turns.
		Alernātim,	

Poſtridie,	The day after.	Rurſus,	} Again.
Pĕrendie,	Two days hence.	Itĕrum,	
Nondum,	Not yet.		
Quando ?	When ?	Sŭbinde,	} Ever and anon, now
		Identĭdem,	and then.

Alĭquando,	} Sometimes.	Sĕmel,	Once.
Nonnunquam,		Bis,	Twice.
Interdum,		Ter,	Thrice.
Semper,	Ever, always.	Quăter,	Four times, &c.

3. Adverbs of *Order.*

Inde,	Then.	Dĕnĭque,	Finally.
Deinde,	After that.	Poſtrēmò,	Laſtly.
Dehinc,	Henceforth.	Prĭmò, -ùm,	Firſt.
Porro,	Moreover.	Sĕcundò, -ùm,	Secondly.
Deinceps,	So forth.	Tertiò, -ùm,	Thirdly.
Dĕnuo,	Of new.	Quartò, -ùm,	Fourthly, &c.

II. Adverb

II. Adverbs denoting QUALITY, MANNER, &c. are either *Absolute* or *Comparative.*

Those called *Absolute* denote,

1. QUALITY, simply ; as, *bene*, well ; *male*, ill ; *fortiter*, bravely ; and innumerable others that come from adjective nouns or participles.

2. CERTAINTY ; as, *profecto*, *certe*, *sane*, *plane*, *næ*, *utique*, *ita*, *etiam*, truly, verily, yes ; *quidni*, why not ? *omnino*, certainly.

3. CONTINGENCE ; as, *forte*, *forsan*, *fortassis*, *fors*, haply, perhaps, by chance, peradventure.

4. NEGATION ; as, *non haud*, not ; *nequaquam*, not at all ; *neutiquam*, by no means ; *minime*, nothing less.

5. PROHIBITION ; as, *ne*, not.

6. SWEARING ; as, *hercle*, *pol*, *edepol*, *mecastor*, by Hercules, by Pollux, &c.

7. EXPLAINING ; as, *utpote*, *videlicet*, *scilicet*, *nimirum*, *nempe*, to wit, namely.

8. SEPARATION ; as, *seorsum*, apart ; *separatim*, separately ; *sigillatim*, one by one ; *viritim*, man by man ; *oppidatim*, town by town, &c.

9. JOINING TOGETHER ; as, *simul*, *una*, *pariter*, together : *generaliter*, generally ; *universaliter*, universally ; *plerumque*, for the most part.

10. INDICATION *or* POINTING out ; as, *en*, *ecce*, lo, behold.

11. INTERROGATION ; as, *cur*, *quare*, *quamobrem*, why, wherefore ? *num*, *an*, whether ? *quomodo*, *qui*, how ? To which add, *Ubi*, *quo*, *quorsum*, *unde*, *qua*, *quando*, *quamdiu*, *quoties.*

Those Adverbs which are called *Comparative* denote,

1. EXCESS ; as, *Valde*, *maxime*, *magnopere*, *maximopere*, *summopere*, *admodum*, *oppido*, *perquam*, *longe*, greatly, very much, exceedingly ; *nimis*, *nimium*, too much ; *prorsus*, *penitus*, *omnino*, altogether, wholly ; *magis*, more ; *melius*, better ; *pejus*, worse ; *fortius*, more bravely : and *optime*, best ; *pessime*, worst ; *fortissime*, most bravely ; and innumerable others of the comparative and superlative degrees.

2. DEFECT ; as, *Ferme*, *fere*, *propemodum*, *pene*, almost ; *parum*, little : *paulo*, *paululum*, very little.

3. PREFERENCE ; as, *potius*, *satius*, rather ; *potissimum*, *præcipue*, *præsertim*, chiefly, especially ; *imo*, yes, nay, nay rather.

4. LIKENESS *or* EQUALITY ; as, *ita*, *sic*, *adeo*, so ; *ut*, *uti*, *sicut*, *sicuti*, *velut*, *veluti*, *ceu*, *tanquam*, *quasi*, as, as if ; *quemadmodum*, even as ; *satis*, enough ; *itidem*, in like manner ; *juxta*, alike, equally.

5. UNLIKENESS *or* UNEQUALITY ; as, *aliter*, *secus*, otherwise ; *alioqui* or *alioqvin*, else ; *nedum*, much more *or* much less.

6. ABATEMENT ; as, *sensim*, *paulatim*, *pedetentim*, by degrees, piecemeal ; *vix*, scarcely ; *ægre*, hardly, with difficulty.

7. EXCLUSION ; as, *tantum*, *solum*, *modo*, *tantummodo*, *duntaxat*, *demum*, only.

DERIVATION,

Adverbs are derived, 1. from Substantives, and end commonly in TIM or TUS; as, *Partim*, partly, by parts; *nominatim*, by name; *generatim*, by kinds, generally; *speciatim, vicatim, gregatim; radicitus*, from the root, &c. 2. From Adjectives: and these are by far the most numerous. Such as come from Adjectives of the first and second declension usually end in E; as, *libere*, freely; *plene*, fully: Some in O, UM, and TER; as, *falso, tantum, graviter:* A few in A, ITUS, and IM; as, *recta, antiquitus, privatim.* Some are used two or three ways, as, *primum*, v. -ò; *pure*, -iter; *certò*, -ò; *cautò*, -tim; *humane*, -iter, -itus; *publice, publicitus*, &c. Adverbs from Adjectives of the third declension commonly end in TER, seldom in E; as, *turpiter, feliciter, acriter; pariter; facile, repente:* one in O, *omnino.* The neuter of Adjectives is sometimes taken Adverbially; as, *recens natus*, for *recenter; perfidum ridens*, for *perfide*, Hor: *multa reluctans*, for *multum* or *valde*, Virg. So in English we say, *to speak loud, high*, &c. for *loudly, highly*, &c. In many cases a Substantive is understood; as, *primò*, sc. *loco, optatò advenis.* sc. *tempore; hâc*, sc. *viâ*, &c.

3. From each of the pronominal adjectives, *ille, ist, hic, is, idem*, &c. are formed adverbs, which express all the circumstances of place; as from *ille, illic, illuc, illorsum, illinc*, and *illac.* So from *quis, ubi, quo, quorsum, unde*, and *quâ.* Also of time: thus, *quando, quamdiu, &c.*

4. From verbs and participles; as, *caesim*, with the edge: *punctim*, with the point; *strictim*, closely; from *caedo, pungo, stringo: amanter, properanter, dubitanter; distinctè, emendatè; meritò, inopinato*, &c. But these last are thought to be in the ablative, having *ex* understood, which is also sometimes expressed.

5. From prepositions; as, *intus, intro*, from *in; clanculum*, from *clam; subtus*, from *sub*, &c.

[Adverbs derived from adjectives are commonly compared like their primitives. The *positive* generally ends in *e*, or *ter*; as, *dure, facile, acriter:* The *comparative*, in *ius*; as, *durius, facilius, acrius:* The *superlative*, in *ime*; as, *durissime, facillime, acerrime.* [

If the comparison of the adjective be irregular or defective, the comparison of the adverb is so too: as, *bene, melius, optime; male, pejus, pessime; parum, minus, minime, & -um; multum, plus, plurimum; prope, propius, proxime; ocyus, ocyssime; prius, primò, -um; nuper, nuperrime; novè, & noviter, novissime; meritò, meritissimò*; &c. Those adverbs also are compared whose primitives are obsolete; as, *sæpe, sæpius, sæpissime; penitùs, penitius, penitissime; satis, setius; secus, secius*; &c. *Magis, maxime*; and *potius, potissimùm*, want the positive.

Adverbs in English are not varied by comparison, except some few of them, particularly irregulars; as, *often, oftener, oftenest; well, better, best; much, more, most*, &c.

Adverbs are variously compounded with all the different parts of speech; thus, *postridie, magnopere, maximopere, summopere, tantopere, multimodis*, *multimŏdis, omnimŏdis, quomŏdo, quare* ; of *poſtero die* ; *magno opere*, &c. Iſi-*cet*, *ſcilĭcet*, *videlĭcet*, of *ire*, *ſcire*, *videre*, *licet* ; *illĭco*, of *in loco* : *quor-ſum*, of *quo verſum* ; *commĭnus*, hand to hand, of *cum* or *con* and *manus* ; *emĭnus*, at a diſtance, of *e* and *manus* ; *quorſum*, of *quo verſum* ; *denuo*, anew, of *de novo* ; *quin*, why not, but, of *qui ne* ; *cur*, of *cui rei* ; *pede-tentim*, ſtep by ſtep, as it were *pedem tendendo* ; *perendie*, for *perempto die* ; *nimĭrum*, of *ne*, i. e. *non* and *mirum* ; *antea*, *poſtea*, *præterea*, &c. of *ante* and *ea*, &c. *Ubivis*, *quovis*, *undelĭbet*, *quouſque*, *ſicut*, *ſicŭti*, *velut*, *velŭti*, *deſŭper*, *inſuper*, *quamobrem*, &c. of *ubi*, and *vis*, &c. *nudiuſter-tius*, of *nunc dies tertius* : *identĭdem*, of *idem et idem* ; *impræſentiarum*, i. e. *in tempore rerum præſentium*, &c.

Obſ. 1. The Adverb is not an eſſential part of ſpeech. It only ſerves to expreſs ſhortly, in one word, what muſt otherwiſe have required two or more ; as, *ſapienter*, wiſely, for *cum ſapientia* ; *hic*, for *in hoc loco* ; *ſemper*, for *in omni tempore* ; *ſemel*, for *una vice* ; *bis*, for *duabus vicibus* ; *Mehercule*, for *Hercules me juvet*, *&c.*

Obſ. 2. Some adverbs of time, place, and order, are frequently uſed the one for the other : as, *ubi*, where *er* when ; *inde*, from that place, from that time, after that, next ; *hactēnus*, hitherto, thus far, with reſpect to place, time, or order, &c.

Obſ. 3. Some adverbs of time are either *paſt*, *preſent* or *future* ; as, *jam*, already, now, by and by ; *olim*, long ago, ſome time, hereafter. Some adverbs of place are equally various ; thus, *eſſe peregrè*, to be a-broad ; *ire peregrè*, to go abroad ; *redire peregrè*, to return from abroad.

Obſ. 4. Interrogative adverbs of time and place doubled, or com-pounded with *cunque*, anſwer to the Engliſh adjection *ſo ever* ; as, *ubi-ubi*, or *ubicunque*, whereſoever ; *quoquò*, *quocunque*, whitherſoever, &c. The ſame holds alſo in other interrogative words ; as, *quotquot*, or *quot-cunque*, how many ſoever ; *quantuſquantus*, or *quantaſcunque*, how great ſoever ; *utut* or *utcunque*, however *or* howſoever, &c. In Engliſh, the adverbs *here*, *there*, and *where*, when joined to certain participles or prepoſitions, as, *to*, *of*, *by*, *with*, *in*, &c. have the ſignification of pronouns ; as, *hereof*, the ſame with *of this* ; *thereof*, the ſame with *of that* ; *whereof*, *of which*, *&c.*

PREPOSITION.

A Prepoſition is an indeclinable word which ſhews the relation of one thing to another.

There are twenty-eight Prepoſitions in Latin, which govern the accuſative ; that is, have an accuſative after them.

Ad,	To.	Cis,	On this ſide.
Apud,	At.	Citra,	
Ante,	Before.	Circa,	About.
Adverſus,	Againſt, towards.	Circum,	
Adverſum,		Erga,	Towards.
Contra,	Againſt.	Extra,	Without.

Inter,

Inter,	Between, among.	Pĕnes,	In the power of.
Intra,	Within.	Poſt,	After.
Infra,	Beneath.	Pōne,	Behind.
Juxta,	Nigh to.	Sĕcus,	By, along.
Ob,	For.	Sĕcundum,	According to.
Propter,	For, hard by.	Supra,	Above.
Per,	By, through.	Trans,	On the farther ſide.
Præter,	Beſides, except.	Ultra,	Beyond.

The Prepoſitions which govern the ablative are fifteen ; namely,

A;		De;	Of, concerning.
Ab,	} From, or by.	E,	} Of, out of.
Abs,		Ex,	
Abſque,	Without.	Pro,	For.
Cum,	With.	Præ,	Before.
Clam,	{ Without the knowledge of.	Pălam,	With the knowledge of.
		Sine,	Without.
Cōram,	{ Before, in the preſence of.	Tĕnus,	Up to, as far as.

Theſe four govern ſometimes the accuſative, and ſometimes the ablative :

In, *In, into,* Sub, *Under.* Sŭper, *Above.* Subter, *Beneath.*

Obſ. 1. Prepoſitions are ſo called, becauſe they are generally *placed before* the word with which they are joined. Some, however, are put after ; as, *cum,* when joined with *me, te, ſe,* and ſometimes with *quo, qui,* and *quibus :* thus, *mecum, tecum,* &c. *Tenus* is always placed after ; as, *mento, tenus,* up to the chin. So likewiſe are *verſus* and *uſque ;* and *ward,* in Engliſh ; as, *toward, eaſtward,* &c.

Obſ. 2. Prepoſitions, both in Engliſh and Latin, are often compounded with other parts of ſpeech, particularly with verbs ; as, *ſubire,* to undergo. In Engliſh they are frequently put after verbs ; as, *to go in, to go out, to look to,* &c.

Prepoſitions are alſo ſometimes compounded together ; as, *Ex adverſus eum locum,* Cic. *Ex adverſum Athenas,* C. Nep. *In ante diem quartum Kalendarum Decembris diſtulit,* i. e. *uſque in eum diem,* Cic. *Supplicatio indicta eſt ex ante diem quintum idus Octob.* i. e. *ab eo die,* Liv. *Ex ante pridie Idus Septembris,* Plin. But prepoſitions compounded together commonly become adverbs or conjunctions ; as, *propălam, protinus, inſuper,* &c.

Obſ. 3. Prepoſitions in compoſition uſually retain their primitive ſignification : as, *adeo,* to go to : *præpono,* to place before. But from this there are ſeveral exceptions. 1. IN joined with adjectives generally denotes privation ; as, *inſīdus,* unfaithful : but when joined with verbs, increaſes their ſignification ; as, *indūro,* to harden greatly. In ſome words *in* has two contrary ſenſes ; as, *invŏcātus,* called upon, or not called upon. So *infrēnātus, immŭtātus, inſuetus, impenſus, inhumatus, intentātus,* &c. 2. PER commonly increaſes the

ſignification ;

fignification ; as, *Percārus, pertōler, percōmis, percuriōfus, perdifficilis, perelegans, pergrātus, pergrāvis, perhofpitālis, perilluftris, perlætus,* &c. very dear, very fwift, &c.   3. PRÆ fometimes increafes ; as, *Prȇclārus, prædīvec, prædulcis, prædūrus, præpinguis, prævalidus ; prævāleo, præpolleo ;* and alfo Ex ; as, *Exclāmo, exaggēro, exaugeo, excalefacio, extenuo, exhilāro ;* but EX fometimes denotes privation, as, *Exfanguis,* bloodlefs, pale : *excors, exanimis, -mo,* &c.   4. SUB often diminifhes ; as, *Subalbidus, fubabfurdus, fubamārus, fubdulcis, fubgrandis, fubgrāvis, fubniger ;* &c. a little white or whitifh, &c.   DE often fignifies downward ; as, *Decīdo, decurro, degrāvo, defpicio, delābor :* fometimes increafes ; as, *Deāmo, demīror ;* and fometimes expreffes privation ;. as, *Demens, decōlor, deformis,* &c.

Obf. 4.   There are five or fix fyllables, namely, *am, di* or *dif, re, fe, con,* which are commonly called, *Infepurable Prepofitions,* becaufe they are only to be found in compound words :   however they generally add fomething to the fignification of the words with which they are compounded ; thus,

Am,	round about.			Ambio,	to furround.
Di,		afunder.		Divello,	to pull afunder.
Dis,			as,	Diftrāho,	to draw afunder.
Re,	again.			Rĕlĕgo,	to read again.
Se,	afide or apart.			Sēpono,	to lay afide.
Con,	together.			Concrefco,	to grow together.

INTERJECTION.

| An Interjection is an indeclinable word *thrown in between* the parts of a fentence, to exprefs fome paffion or emotion of the mind. |

Some Interjections are natural founds, and common to all languages ; as, *Oh ! Ah !*

Interjections exprefs in one word a whole fentence, and thus fitly reprefent the quicknefs of the paffions.

The different paffions have commonly different words to exprefs them ; thus,

1. JOY ; as, *evax,* hey, brave, io !
2. GRIEF ; as, *ah, hei, heu, eheu !* ah, alas, woes me !
3. WONDER ; as, *papæ !* O ftrange ! *vah !* hah !
4. PRAISE ; as, *euge !* well done !
5. AVERSION ; as, *apāge !* away, begone, avaunt, off, fy, tufh !
6. EXCLAIMING ; as, *Oh, proh !* O !
7. SURPRISE or FEAR ; as, *atat !* ha, aha !
8. IMPRECATION ; as, *væ !* wo, pox on't !
9. LAUGHTER ; as, *ha, ha, he !*
10. SILENCING ; as, *au, 'ft, pax !* filence, hufh, 'ft !
11. CALLING ; as, *eho, ehodum, io, he !* fo, ho, ho, O !

12. DERISION ; as, *bui !* away with !
13. ATTENTION ; as, *bem !* ha !.

Some interjections denote several different passions : thus, *Vab* is used to express joy, and sorrow, and wonder, &c.

Adjectives of the neuter gender are sometimes used for interjections ; as, *Malum !* with a mischief ! *Infandum !* O shame ! fy, fy ! *Miserum,* O wretched ! *Nefas !* O the villany !.

CONJUNCTION.

/ A conjunction is an indeclinable word, which serves to join sentences together. */*

Thus, *You* and *I,* and *the boy, read Virgil,* is one sentence made up of these three, by the conjunction *and* twice employed ; *I read Virgil ; You read Virgil ; The boy reads Virgil.* In like manner, "You *and* I read Virgil, *but* the boy reads Ovid," is one sentence, made up of three, by the conjunctions *and* and *but.*

Conjunctions, according to their different meaning, are divided into the following classes :

1. COPULATIVE ; as, *et; ac, atque, que,* and ; *etiam, quŏque, item,* also ; *cum, tum,* both, and. Also their contraries, *nec, nĕque, neu, neve,* neither, nor.

2. DISJUNCTIVE ; as, *aut, ve, vel, seu, sive,* either, or.

3. CONCESSIVE ; as, *etsi, etiamsi, tametsi, licet, quanquam, quamvis,* though, although, albeit.

4. ADVERSATIVE ; as, *sed, verum, autem, at, ast, atqui,* but ; *tamen, attamen, veruntamen, verumenimverò,* yet, notwithstanding, nevertheless.

5. CAUSAL ; as, *nam, namque, enim,* for ; *quia, quippe, quoniam,* because ; *quòd,* that, because.

6. ILLATIVE or RATIONAL ; as, *ergo, ideo, igitur, idcirco, ităque,* therefore ; *quapropter, quocirca,* wherefore ; *proinde,* therefore ; *eum, quum,* seeing, since ; *quandoquĭdem,* forasmuchas.

7. FINAL or PERFECTIVE ; as, *ut, uti,* that, to the end that.

8. CONDITIONAL ; as, *si, sin,* if ; *dum, modo, dummŏdo,* provided, upon condition that ; *siquĭdem,* if indeed.

9. EXCEPTIVE or RESTRICTIVE ; as, *ni, nisi,* unless, except.

10. DIMINUTIVE ; as, *saltem, certe,* at least.

11. SUSPENSIVE or DUBITATIVE ; as, *an, anne, num,* whether ; *ne, annon,* whether, not ; *necne,* or, not.

12. EXPLETIVE ; as, *autem, vero,* now, truly ; *quidem, equĭdem,* indeed.

13. ORDINATIVE ; as, *deinde,* thereafter ; *denique,* finally ; *insuper,* moreover ; *cætĕrum,* moreover, but, however.

14. DECLARATIVE ; as, *videlĭcet, scilicet, nempe, nimīrum,* &c. to wit, namely.

Obs. 1. The same words, as they are taken in different views, are both *adverbs* and *conjunctions.* Thus, *an, anne,* &c. are either *interrogative*

ative adverbs: as, *An scribit?* Does he write? or, *suspensive conjunc-tions;* as, *Nescio an scribat,* I know not if he writes.

Obf. 2. Some conjunctions, according to their natural order, stand first in a sentence; as, *Ac, atque, nec, neque, aut; vel, sive, at, sed, verum, nam, quandoquidem, quocirca; quare, sin, siquidem, præterquam,* &c.: some stand in the second-place; as, *Autem, vero, quoque, quidem, enim:* and some may indifferently be put either first or second; as *Etiam, equidem, licet, quamvis, quanquam, tamen, attamen, namque, quod, quia, quoniam, quippe, utpöte, ut, uti, ergo, ideo, igitur, idcirco, itaque, proinde, propterea, si, ni, nisi,* &c. Hence arose the division of them into *Prepositive, Subjunctive,* and *Common.* To the subjunctive may be added these three, *que, ve, ne,* which are always joined to some other word; and are called *Enclitics,* because, when put after long syllables, they make the accent incline to the foregoing syllable; as in the following verse,

> *Indoctusque pilæ, discive, trochive, quiescit.* Horat.

But when these enclitic conjunctions come after a short vowel, they do not affect its pronunciation; thus,

> *Arbuteos fœtus montanäque fraga legebant.* Ovid.

SENTENCES.

SENTENCES.

A SENTENCE is any thought of the mind expressed by two or more words put together ; as, *I read. The boy reads Virgil.*

That part of grammar which teaches to put words rightly together in sentences, is called *Syntax* or *Construction*.

Words in sentences have a twofold relation to one another ; *namely*, that of *Concord* or Agreement ; and that of *Government* or Influence.

Concord, is when one word agrees with another in some accidents ; as, in gender, number, person, or case.

Government, is when one word requires another to be put in a certain case, or mode.

General Principles of SYNTAX.

1. In every sentence there must be a verb and a nominative expressed or understood.

2. Every adjective must have a substantive expressed or understood.

3. All the cases of Latin nouns, except the nominative and vocative, must be governed by some other word.

4. The genitive is governed by a substantive noun expressed or understood.

5. The dative is governed by adjectives and verbs.

6. The accusative is governed by an active verb, or by a preposition ; or is placed before the infinitive.

7. The vocative stands by itself, or has an interjection joined with it.

8. The ablative is governed by a preposition expressed or understood.

9. The infinitive is governed by some verb or adjective.

10. The genitive or possessive case in English always depends on some noun ; and the objective or accusative case is put after a verb active or a preposition.

All

All Sentences are either SIMPLE or COMPOUND.

Syntax therefore may be divided into two parts, according to the general division of sentences.

SIMPLE SENTENCES.

A Simple Sentence is that which has but one nominative; and one finite verb, *that is,* a verb in the indicative, subjunctive, or imperative mode.

In a simple sentence, there is only one *Subject* and one *Attribute.*

The SUBJECT is the word which marks the person or thing spoken of.

The ATTRIBUTE expresses what we affirm concerning the subject, as,

The boy reads his lesson : Here, " the boy," is the *Subject* of discourse, or the person spoken of ; " reads his lesson," is the *Attribute,* or what we affirm concerning the subject. *The diligent boy reads his lesson carefully at home.* Here we have still the same subject, " the boy," marked by the character of " diligent," added to it ; and the same attribute, " reads his lesson," with the circumstances of manner and place subjoined, " carefully," " at home."

CONCORD.

The following words agree together in sentences, 1. A substantive with a substantive. 2. An adjective with a substantive. 3. A verb with a nominative.

1. Agreement of one Substantive with another.

RULE I. Substantives signifying the same thing, agree in case ; as,

Cicero orator, Cicero the Orator ; *Cicerōnis oratōris,* Of Cicero the Orator.
Urbs Athēnæ, The city Athens ; *Urbis Athēnārum,* Of the city Athens.

2. Agreement of an Adjective with a Substantive.

II. An Adjective agrees with a Substantive, in gender, number, and case ; as,

Bonus vir, a good man ;   *Boni viri,* good men.
Femina casta, a chaste woman ;   *Feminæ castæ,* chaste women.
Dulce pomum, a sweet apple ;   *Dulcia poma,* sweet apples.

And so through all the cases and degrees of comparison.

This

This rule applies alſo to Adjective pronouns and participles ; as *Meus liber*, my book ; *ager colendus*, a field to be tilled : Plur.`Mei libri, agri, colendi*, &c.

Obſ. 1. The ſubſtantive is frequently understood, or its place ſupplied by an infinitive ; and then the adjective is put in the neuter gender ; as, *triſte*, ſc. *negotium*, a ſad thing, Virg. ; *Tuum ſcire*, the ſame with *tua ſcientia*, thy knowledge, Perſ. We ſometimes however find the ſubſtantive underſtood in the feminine ; as, *Non poſteriores feram*, ſup. *partes*, Ter.

Obſ. 2. An adjective often ſupplies the place of a ſubſtantive ; as, *Certus amicus*, a ſure friend : *Bona ferīna*, Good veniſon ; *Summum bonum*, The chief good : *Homo* being underſtood to *amicus*, *caro* to *ferīna*, and *negotium* to *bonum*. A ſubſtantive is ſometimes uſed as an adjective ; as, *incola turba vocant*, the inhabitants, *Ovid Faſt.* 3. 582.

Obſ. 3. Theſe adjectives, *primus, medius, ultimus, extremus, infimus, imus, ſummus, ſupremus, reliquus, cætera*, uſually ſignify *the firſt part, the middle part*, &c. of any thing ; as, *Media nox*, the middle part of the night ; *Summa arbor*, the higheſt part of a tree.

Obſ. 4. In Engliſh, the adjective generally goes before the noun ; as, *a wiſe man, a good horſe* ; unleſs ſomething depend upon the adjective ; as, *food convenient for me* ; or the adjective be emphatical ; as, *Alexander the Great*. And the article goes before the Adjective : except the adjectives *all, ſuch*, and *many*, and others ſubjoined to the adverbs *ſo, as*, and *how* ; as, *all the men ; many a man, ſo good a man ; as good a man ; how beautiful a proſpect !* or when there are two or more adjectives joined to the noun ; as, *a man learned and religious*.

Obſ. 5. Whether the adjective or ſubſtantive ought to be placed firſt in Latin, no certain rule can be given. Only if the ſubſtantive be a monoſyllable, and the adjective a polyſyllable, the ſubſtantive is elegantly put firſt ; as, *vir claſiſſimus, res præſtantiſſima, &c.*

Obſ. 6. A ſubſtantive in Engliſh, ſometimes ſupplies the place of an adjective ; as, *ſea-water, land-fowl, foreſt-trees, a ſtone-arch*, &c. and even when no hyphen is marked ; as, *the London Chronicle, the Edinburgh Magazine*.

Obſ. 7. Nouns of meaſure, number, and weight, are ſometimes joined in the ſingular with Numeral Adjectives plural ; as, *fifty foot ; ſix ſcore ; ten thouſand fathom ; a hundred head ; an hundred weight*. We ſay, *by this means, by that means* ; for, *by theſe means, by thoſe means* ; or, *by this mean, by that mean*, as it was uſed anciently : So, *This ſer-*

ty years, for *these*; *these* and *those kind of things*, for *this* and *that*. *Each*, *every*, *either*, are always joined with the fingular number, unlefs the plural noun convey a collective idea; as, *every twelve years*.

3. *Agreement of a Verb with a Nominative.*

III. A Verb agrees with its Nominative in number and perfon; as,

Ego lego, I read;   *Nos legimus*, We read.
Tu fcribis, Thou writeft or you write; *Vos fcribitis*, Ye or you write;
Præceptor docet, the mafter teaches; *Præceptores docent*, Mafters teach.

 And fo through all the modes, tenfes, and numbers.

Obf. 1. *Ego* and *nos* are of the firft perfon; *tu* and *vos* of the fecond perfon; *ille* and all other words, of the third. The nominative of the firft and fecond perfon in Latin is feldom exprefled, unlefs for the fake of emphafis or diftinction; as, *Tu es patronus, tu pater*, Ter. *Tu legis, ego fcribo*.

Obf. 2. An infinitive, or fome part of a fentence, often fupplies the place of a nominative; as, *Mentiri eft turpe*, to lie is bafe; *Diu non perlitatum tenuit dictatorem*; The facrifice not being attended wih favourable omens detained the dictator for a long time, Liv. 7. 8. Sometimes the neuter pronoun *id* or *illud* is added, to exprefs the meaning more ftrongly; as, *Facere quæ libet*, id *eft effe regem*, Salluft.

Obf. 3. The infinitive mode often fupplies the place of the third perfon of the imperfect of the indicative; as, *Milites fugēre*, the foldiers fled, for *fugiebant* or *fugere cæperunt*. *Invidēre omnes mihi*, for *invidebant*.

Obf. 4. A collective noun may be joined with a verb either of the fingular or of the plural number; as, *Multitudo ftat*, or *ftant*; The multitude ftands, *or* ftand.

 A collective noun, when joined with a verb fingular, exprefles many confidered as one whole; but when joined with a verb plural, fignifies many feparately, or as individuals. Hence, if an adjective or participle be fubjoined to the verb, when of the fingular number, they will agree both in gender and number with the collective noun; but if the verb be plural, the adjective or participle will be plural alfo, and of the fame gender with the individuals of which the collective noun is compofed; as, *Pars erant cæfi*; *Pars obnixe trudunt*, fc. *formicæ*, Virg. Æn. iv. 406. *Magna pars raptæ*, fc. *virgines*, Liv. i. 9.
fometimes

Sometimes, however, though more rarely, the adjective is thus uſed in the ſingular ; as, *Pars arduus*, Virg. Æn. vii. 624.

Obſ. 5. The neuter pronoun *it* in Engliſh, is often the nominative to the verb when we ſpeak either of perſons or things ; as, *It is I ; it is he ; it was they ; it appears ;* in Latin, *Ego ſum, ille eſt, &c.* It is ſometimes underſtood ; as, *may be,* for, *it may be ; as follows,* for, *as it follows ; as is thought,* for, *as it is thought.*

Obſ. 6. We often ſay in Engliſh, *You was,* inſtead of *You were ;* which is a great inaccuracy in grammar ; but ſo frequently uſed, particularly in common converſation, that it ſeems to be in a manner eſtabliſhed by cuſtom. So *there's two or three of us,* for *there are ; There was more Sophiſts,* for *were ; great pains has been taken,* for *have,* &c.

Accuſative before the Infinitive.

¶ IV. The infinitive mode has an accuſative before it ; as,

Gaudeo te valere,   I am glad that you are well.

Obſ. 1. The participle *that* in Engliſh, is the ſign of the accuſative before the infinitive in Latin, when it comes between two verbs, without expreſſing intention or deſign. Sometimes the participle is omitted ; as, *Aiunt regem adventare,* They ſay the king is coming, *that* being underſtood.

Obſ. 2. The accuſative before the infinitive always depends upon ſome other verb, commonly on a neuter or ſubſtantive verb ; but ſeldom on a verb taken in an active ſenſe.

Obſ. 3. The infinitive, with the accuſative before it, ſeems ſometimes to ſupply the place of a nominative ; as, *Turpe eſt militem fugere,* That a ſoldier ſhould fly is a ſhameful thing.

Obſ. 4. The infinitive *eſſe* or *fuiſſe,* muſt frequently be ſupplied, eſpecially after participles ; as, *Hoſtium exercitum cæſum faſumque cognovi,* Cic. Sometimes both the accuſative and infinitive are underſtood ; as, *Pollicitus ſuſcepturum,* ſcil. *me eſſe,* Ter.

Obſ. 5. The infinitive may frequently be otherwiſe rendered by the conjunctions, *quod, ut, ne,* or *quin ;* as, *Gaudeo te valere,* i. e. *quod valeas,* or *propter tuam bonam valetudinem : Jubeo vos bene ſperare,* or *ut bene ſperetis ; Prohibeo eum exire,* or *ne exeat : non dubito eum feciſſe,* or much better, *quin fecerit. Scio quod filius amet,* Plaut. for *filium amare. Miror, ſi potuit,* for *eum potuiſſe,* Cic. *Nemo dubitat, ut populus Romanus omnes virtute ſuperârit,* for *populum Romanum ſuperaſſe,* Nep. *Ex animi ſententia juro, ut ego rempublicam non deſeram,* for *me non deſerturum eſſe,* Liv. xxii. 53.

P

The

The same Case after a Verb as before it.

¶ V. Any Verb may have the same case after it as before it ; *when both words refer to the same thing ;* as,

Ego sum discipulus,	I am a scholar.
Tu vocaris Joannes,	You are named John.
Illa incedit regina,	She walks as a queen.
Scio illum haberi sapientem,	I know that he is esteemed wise.
Scio vos esse discipulos,	I know that you are scholars.

So *Redeo iratus, jaceo supplex ; Evadent digni,* they will become worthy ; *Rempublicam defendi adolescens ; nolo esse longus,* I am unwilling to be tedious ; *Malim videri timidus, quam parum prudens,* Cic. *Non licet mihi esse negligenti,* Cic. *Natura dedit omnibus esse beatis,* Claud. *Cupio me esse clementem ; cupio non putari mendacem ; Vult esse medium,* sc. *se,* He wishes to be neuter, Cic. *Disce esse pater ; Hoc est esse patrem ?* sc. *eum,* Ter. *Id est, dominum, non imperatorem esse ;* Sallust.

Obs. 1. This rule implies nothing else but the agreement of an adjective with a substantive, or of one substantive with another ; for those words in a sentence which refer to the same object, must always agree together, how much soever disjoined.

Obs. 2. The verbs which most frequently have the same case after them as before them, are,

1. Substantive and neuter verbs ; as, *Sum, fio, forem,* and *existo ; eo, venio, sto, sedeo, evado, jaceo, fugio, &c.*

2. The passive of verbs of naming, judging, &c. as, *Dicor, appellor, vocor, nominor, nuncupor,* to which add, *videor, existimor, creor, constituor, salutor, designor, &c.*

These and other like verbs, admit after them only the nominative, accusative, or dative. When they have before them the genitive, they have after them an accusative ; as, *Interest omnium esse bonos,* scil. *se ;* It is the interest of all to be good. In some cases we can use either the nom. or acc. promiscuously ; as, *Cupio, dici doctus* or *doctum,* sc. *me dici ; Cupio esse clemens, non putari mendax ; vult esse medius.*

Obs. 3. When any of the above verbs are placed between two nominatives of different numbers, they commonly agree in number with the former ; as, *Dos est decem talenta,* Her dowry is ten talents, Ter. *Omnia pontus erant,* Ovid. But sometimes with the latter ; as, *Amantium iræ amoris integratio est,* The quarrels of lovers is a renewal of love, Ovid. So when an adjective is applied to two substantives of different genders, it commonly agrees in gender with that substantive

ftantive which is moft the fubject of difcourfe; as, *Oppidum eft appellatum Pofidonia*, Plin.　Sometimes, however, the adjective agrees with the nearer fubftantive; as, *Non omnis error ftultitia eft dicenda*, Cic.

Obf. 4. When the infinitive of any verb, particularly the fubftantive verb *effe*, has the dative before it, governed by an Impeiſonal verb, or any other word, it may have after it either the dative or the accufative; as, *Licet mihi effe beato*, I may be happy; or *licet mihi effe beatum, me* being underſtood; thus, *licet mihi* (me) *effe beatum.* The dative before *effe* is often to be fupplied; as, *Licet effe beatum,* One may be happy, *fcil. alicui* or *homini.*

Obf. 5. The poets ufe certain forms of expreſſion, which are not to be imitated in profe; as, *Rettulit Ajax Jovis effe pronepos*, for *Se effe pronepotem*, Ovid. Met. xii. 141.　*Cum pateris fapiens emendatufque vocari*, for *te vocari fapientem*, &c. Horat. Ep. 1. 16 30.　*Acceptum refero verfibus effe nocens;* Ovid.　*Tutumque putavit jam bonus effe focer;* Lucan.

Obf. 6. The verb *to be* in Englifh, has always a nominative cafe after it; as, *It was I:* unleſs it be of the infinitive mode; as, *I took it to be him.* We often ufe however this impropriety in common converfation, *It is me, It can't be me, It was him;* for, *It is I, It cannot be I, It was he.*

GOVERNMENT.

I. The GOVERNMENT of SUBSTANTIVES.

VI. / One Subftantive governs another in the genitive, *(when the latter Subftantive fignifies a different thing from the former) ;]* as,

Amor Dei, the love of God.　　*Lex naturæ,* The law of nature.
Domus Cæsǎris, The houfe of Cæfar, *or* Cæfar's houfe.

Obf. 1. When one fubftantive is governed by another in the genitive, it expreſſes in general the relation of property or poſſeſſion, and therefore is often elegantly turned into a poſſeſſive adjective; as, *Domus patris*, or *paterna*, a father's houfe; *Filius heri* or *herilis*, a mafter's fon: and among the poets, *Labor Herculeus*, for *Herculis; Enfis Evandrius*, for *Evandri.*

Obf. 2. When the fubftantive noun in the genitive fignifies a perfon, it may be taken either in an active or a paſſive fenfe; thus, *Amor Dei*, The love of God, either means the love of God towards us, or our love towards him: So *caritas patris*, fignifies either, the affection of a father to his children, or theirs to him. But often the fubftantive can only be taken either in an active or in a paſſive fenfe; thus, *Timor Dei*, always implies *Deus timetur;* and *Providentia Dei, Deus providet.* So *Caritas ipfius foli*, affection to the very foil, Liv. ii. 1.

Obf. 3. Both the former and latter fubftantive are fometimes to be underſtood; as, *Hectoris Andromǎche*, fcil *uxor; Ventum eft ad Veftæ*, fcil. *ædem* or *templum; Ventum eft tria millia*, fcil. *paffuum*, three miles.

Obf. 4. We find the dative often ufed after a verb for the genitive,

particularly

particularly among the poets ; as, *Ei corpus porrigitur*, His body is extended ; Virg. Æn. vi. 596.

Obf. 5. Some fubftantives are joined with certain prepofitions ; as, *Amicitia, inimicitia, pax, cum aliquo ; Amor in*, vel *erga, aliquam ; Gaudium de re ; Cura de aliquo ; Mentio illius*, vel *de illo ; Quies ab armis ; Fumus ex incendiis ; Prædator ex fociis*, for *fociorum*, Salluft, &c.

Obf. 6. The genitive in Latin is often rendered in Englifh by feveral other particles befides *of* ; as, *Defcenfus Averni*, the defcent *to* Avernus ; *Prudentia juris*, fkill *in* the law.

/SUBSTANTIVE PRONOUNS are governed in the genitive like fubftantive nouns ; as, *pars mei*, a part of me.|

So alfo adjective pronouns when ufed as fubftantives, or having a noun underftood ; as, *Liber ejus, illius, hujus*, &c. The book of him, or his book, fc. *hominis :* The book of her, or her book, fc. *feminæ*. *Libri eorum*, v. *earum*, their books ; *Cujus liber*, the book of whom, or whofe book ; *Quorum libri*, whofe books, &c. But we always fay, *meus liber*, not *mei* ; *pater nofter*, not *noftri* ; *fuum jus*, not *fui*.

When a paffive fenfe is expreffed, we ufe *mei, tui, fui, noftri, veftri, noftrum, veftrum ;* but we ufe their poffeffives, when an active fenfe is expreffed ; as, *Amor mei*, The love of me, that is, The love wherewith I am loved : *Amor meus*, My love, that is, the love wherewith I love. We find however the poffeffives fometimes ufed paffively, and their primitives taken actively ; as, *Odium tuum*, Hatred of thee, Ter. Phorm. v. 3. 27. *Labor mei*, My Labour, Plaut.

The poffeffives *meus tuus, fuus, nofter, vefter*, have fometimes nouns, pronouns, and particles after them in the genitive ; as, *Pectus tuum hominis fimplicis*, Cic. Phil. ii. 43. *Nofter duorum eventus*, Liv. *Tuum ipfius ftudium*, Cic. *Mea fcripta timentis*, &c. Hor. *Solius meum peccatum corrigi non poteft*, Cic. *Id maxime quemque decet, quod eft cujufque fuum maxime.* Id.

The reciprocals *SUI* and *SUUS* are ufed, when the action of the verb is reflected as it were, upon its nominative : as, *Cato interfecit fe, Miles defendit fuam vitam : Dicit fe fcripturum effe.* We find however *is* or *ille* fometimes ufed in examples of this kind ; as, *Deum agnofcimus ex operibus ejus*, Cic. *Perfuadent Rauracis, ut una cum iis proficifcantur*, for *una fecum*, Cæf.

VII./If the latter Subftantive have an Adjective of praife or difpraife joined with it, they may be put in the genitive or ablative ;| as;

Vir fummæ prudentiæ, or *fummà prudentià*,   A man of great wifdom.
Puer probæ indolis, or *probà indole*,   A boy of a good difpofition.

Obf. 1. The ablative here is not properly governed by the foregoing fubftantive, but by fome prepofition underftood ; as *cum, de, ex, in*, &c. Thus, *Vir fummà prudentià*, is the fame with *vir cum fumma prudentia*.

Obf.

Obf. 2. In some phrases the genitive is only used ; as, *Magni for-mica laboris*, The laborious ant ; *Vir imi subsellii, homo minimi pretii*, a person of the lowest rank. *Homo nullius stipendii*, a man of no experience in war ; Salluft. *Non multi cibi hospitem accipies, sed multi joci*, Cic. *Ager trium jugerum.* In others only the ablative ; as, *Es bono animo*, Be of good courage. *Mira sum alacritate ad litigandum*, Cic. *Capite aperto est*, His head is bare ; *obvoluto*, covered. *Capite et supercilio semper est rasis*, Id. *Mulier magno natu*, Liv. Sometimes both are used in the same sentence ; as, *Adolescens eximiâ spe, summæ virtutis*, Cic. The ablative more frequently occurs in profe than the genitive.

Obf. 3. Sometimes the adjective agrees in cafe with the former substantive, and then the latter substantive is put in the ablative : thus, we fay, either, *Vir præstantis ingenii*, or *præstanti ingenio ;* or *Vir præstans ingenio*, and sometimes *præstans ingenii.* Among the poets the latter substantive is frequently put in the accufative by a Greek construction, *secundum*, or *quod ad* being underftood by the figure commonly called *Synecdöche ;* as, *Miles fractus membra*, i. e. *fractus* secundum *or* quod ad *membra*, or *habens membra fracta,* Horat. *Os humerofque deo fimilis*, Virg.

Adjectives taken as Substantives.

VIII. An Adjective in the neuter gender without a fubftantive governs the genitive ; as,

Multum pecuniæ, Much money. *Quid rei est ?* What is the matter ?

Obf. 1. This manner of exprefiion is more elegant than *Multa Pecunia*, and therefore is much ufed by the beft writers ; as, *Plus eloquentiæ, minus fapientiæ, tantum fidei, id negotii ; quicquid erat patrum, reos diceres*, Liv *Id loci ; Ad hoc ætatis*, Salluft.

Obf. 2. The adjectives which thus govern the genitive like substantives, generally fignify quantity ; as, *multum, plus, plurimum, tantum, quantum, minus, minimum, &c.* To which add, *hoc, illud, istud, id, quid, aliquid, quidvis, quiddam*, &c. *Plus* and *quid* almoft always govern the genitive, and therefore by fome are thought to be substantives.

Obf. 3. *Nihil*, and thefe neuter pronouns *quid, aliquid, &c.* elegantly govern neuter adjectives of the firft and second declenfion in the genitive ; as, *nihil finceri*, no fincerity ; but feldom govern in this manner adjectives of the third declenfion, particularly thofe which end in *is* and *e* ; as, *Nequid hoftile timerent*, not *hoftilis :* we find however *quicquid civilis*, Liv. v. 3.

Obf. 4. Plural adjectives of the neuter gender alfo govern the genitive, commonly the genitive plural ; as, *Angufta viarum, Opaca locorum, Telluris operta, loca* being underftood. So *Amara curarum; acuta belli*, fc. *negotia*, Horat. An adjective indeed of any gender may have a genitive after it, with a fubftantive underftood ; as, *Amicus Cæfaris, Patria Ulyffes, &c.*

P 2

Opus and *Usus.*

IX. *Opus* and *Usus*, signifying *need*, require the ablative ; as,

Est opus pecuniâ, There is need of money ; *Usus viribus,* Need of strength.

Obf. 1. *Opus* and *usus* are substantive nouns, and do not govern the ablative of themselves, but by some preposition, as *pro* or the like, understood. They sometimes a'so, although more rarely, govern the genitive ; as, *Lectionis opus est,* Quinct. *Operæ usus est,* Liv.

Obf. 2. *Opus* is often construed like an indeclinable adjective ; as, *Dux nobis opus est,* We need a general, Cic. *Dices nummos mihi opus esse,* Id. *Nobis exempla opus sunt,* Id.

Obf. 3. *Opus* is elegantly joined with the perfect participle ; as, *Opus maturato,* Need of haste ; *Opus consulto,* Need of deliberation ; *Quid facto usus est ?* Ter. The participle has sometimes a substantive joined with it ; as, *Mihi opus fuit Hirtio convento,* It behoved me to meet with Hirtius, Cic.

Obf. 4. *Opus* is sometimes joined with the infinitive, or the subjunctive with *ut,* as, *Siquid forte fit, quod opus sit sciri,* Cic. *Nunc tibi opus est, ægram ut te adsimules,* Plaut. *Sive opus est imperitare equis,* Horat. It is often placed *absolutely,* i. e. without depending on any other word ; as, *sic opus est ; si opus sit,* &c.

II. Government of Adjectives.

1. *Adjectives governing the Genitive.*

X. Verbal adjectives, or such as signify an affection of the mind, govern the genitive ; as,

Avidus gloriæ, Desirous of glory.   *Ignarus fraudis,* Ignorant of fraud. *Memor beneficiorum,* Mindful of favours.

To this rule belong, I. Verbal adjectives in AX ; as, *capax, edax, ferax, tenax, pertinax,* &c. and certain participial adjectives in NS and TUS ; as, *amans, appetens, cupiens, insolens, sciens ; consultus, doctus, expertus, insuetus, insolitus,* &c. II. Adjectives expressing various affections of the mind ; 1. Desire ; as, *avarus, cupidus, studiosus,* &c. 2. Knowledge, ignorance and doubting ; as, *callidus, certus, certior, conscius, gnarus, peritus, prudens,* &c. *Ignarus, incertus, inscius, imprudens, imperitus, immemor, rudis ; ambiguus, dubius, suspensus,* &c. 3. Care and diligence, and the contrary ; as, *anxius, curiosus, solicitus, providus, diligens ; incuriosus, securus, negligens,* &c. 4. Fear and confidence ; as, *formidolosus, pavidus, timidus, trepidus ; impavidus, interritus,*

tus, intrepidus. 5. Guilt and innocence ; as, *noxius, reus, suspectus, compertus ; innoxius, innocens, infons.*

To thefe add many adjectives of various fignifications ; as, *æger animi ; ardens, audax, averfus, diverfus, egregius, erectus, falfus, felix, feffus, furens, ingens, integer, lætus, præftans animi ; modicus voti ; integer vitæ ; feri ftudiorum,* Hor. But we fay *æger pedibus, ardens in cupiditatibus, præftans doctrinâ, modicus cultu ; Lætus negotio, de re,* or *propter rem,* &c. and never *æger pedum,* &c.

Obf. 1. Verbals in NS are ufed both as adjectives and participles ; thus, *patiens, algoris,* able to bear cold ; and *patiens algorem,* actually bearing cold. So *amans virtutis,* and *amans virtutem : doctus grammaticæ,* fkilled in grammar ; *doctus grammaticam,* one who has learned it.

Obf. 2. Many of thefe adjectives vary their conftruction, as, *avidus in pecuniis,* Cic. *Avidior ad rem,* Ter. *Jure confultus & peritus,* or *juris,* Cic. *Rudis literarum, in jure civili,* Cic. *Rudis arte, ad mala,* Ovid. *Doctus Latinè, Latinis literis,* Cic. *Affuetus labore, in omnia,* Liv. *menfæ berili,* Virg. *Infuetus moribus Romanis,* in the dat. Liv. *Laboris, ad onera portanda,* Cæf. *Defuetus bello, & triumphis,* in the dat. or abl. rather the dat. Virg. *Anxius, folicitus, fecurus, de re aliqua ; diligens, in, ad, de,* Cic. *Negligens in aliquem, in* or *de re : Reus de vi, criminibus,* Cic. *Certior factus de re,* rather than *rei,* Cic.

Obf. 3. The genitive after thefe adjectives is thought to be governed by *caufâ, in re,* or *in negotio,* or fome fuch word underftood ; as, *Cupidus laudis,* i. e. *caufâ* or *in re laudis,* defirous of praife, that is, on account of, *or* in the matter of praife. But many of the adjectives themfelves may be fuppofed to contain in their own fignification the force of a fubftantive ; thus, *ftudiofus pecuniæ,* fond of money, is the fame with *habens ftudium pecuniæ,* having a fondnefs for money.

XI. Partitives, and words placed partitively, comparatives, fuperlatives, interrogatives, and fome numerals, govern the genitive plural ; as,

Aliquis philofophorum,	Some one of the philofophers.
Senior fratrum,	The elder of the brothers.
Doctiffimus Romanorum,	The moft learned of the Romans.
Quis noftrum ?	Which of us ?
Una mufarum,	One of the mufes.
Octavus fapientum,	The eighth of the wife men.

Adjectives are called *Partitives,* or are faid to be placed *partitively,* when they fignify a part of any number of perfons or things, having after them, in Englifh, *of* or *among ;* as, *alius, nullus, folus,* &c. *quis* and *qui,* with their compounds : alfo Comparatives, Superlatives, and

fo

ſome Numerals ; as, *unus, duo, tres ; primus, fecundus,* &c. To theſe add *multi, pauci, plerique, medius.*

Obſ. 1. Partitives, *&c.* agree in gender with the ſubſtantive which they have after them in the genitive ; but when there are two ſubſtantives of different genders, the partitive, *&c.* rather agrees with the former ; as, *Indus fluminum maximus,* Cic. Rarely with the latter ; as, *Delphinus animalium velociffimum,* Plin. The genitive here is governed by *ex numero,* or by the ſame ſubſtantive underſtood in the ſingular number ; as, *Nulla fororum,* ſcil. *foror,* or *ex numero fororum.*

Obſ. 2. Partitives, *&c.* are often otherwiſe conſtrued with the prepoſitions *de, e, ex,* or *in ;* as, *Unus de fratribus ;* or by the poets, with *ante* or *inter ;* as, *Pulcherrimus ante omnes,* for *omnium,* Virg. *Primus inter omnes,* Id.

Obſ. 3. Partitives, *&c.* govern collective nouns in the genitive ſingular, and are of the ſame gender with the individuals of which the collective noun is compoſed ; as, *Vir fortiffimus noſtræ civitatis.* Cic. *Maximus ſtirpis,* Liv. *Ultimos orbis* Britannos, *Horat.* od. i. 35. 29.

Obſ. 4. Comparatives are uſed, when we ſpeak of two ; Superlatives when we ſpeak of more than two ; as, *Major Fratrum,* The elder of the brothers, meaning *two ; Maximus fratrum,* The eldeſt of the brothers, meaning *more than two.* In like manner, *uter, alter, neuter,* are applied with regard to two ; *quis, unus, alius, nullus,* with regard to three or more ; as, *Uter veſtrum,* Whether *or* which of you *two ; Quis veſtrum,* Which of you *three :* but theſe are ſometimes taken promiſcuouſly the one for the other.

2. *Adjectives governing the Dative.*

XII. Adjectives ſignifying profit or diſprofit, likeneſs or unlikeneſs, &c. govern the dative ; as,

Utilis bello,	Profitable for War.
Perniciofus reipublicæ,	Hurtful to the commonwealth.
Similis patri,	Like to his father.

Or thus, *Any adjective may govern the dative in Latin, which has the ſigns TO or FOR after it in Engliſh.*

To this rule belong

1. Adjectives of profit or diſprofit ; as, *Benignus bonus, commodus, felix, fructuofus, profper, faluber.*——*Calamitofus, damnofus, dirus, exitiofus, funeſtus, incommodus, malus, noxius, perniciofus, peſtifer.*

2. Of pleaſure or pain ; as, *Acceptus, dulcis, gratus, gratiofus, jucundus, lætus, fuavis.*——*Acerbus, amarus, infuavis, injucundus, ingratus, moleſtus, triſtis.*

3. Of friendſhip or hatred ; as, *Addictus, æquus, amicus, benevolus, blandus, carus, deditus, fidus, fidelis, lenis, mitis, propitius.*——*Adverfus, æmulus, afper, crudelis, contrarius, infenfus, infeſtus, infidus, immitis, inimicus, iniquus, invifus, invidus, iratus, odiofus, fufpectus, trux.*

4. Of clearneſs or obſcurity ; as, *Apertus, certus, compertus, confpicuus, manifeſtus,*

manifestus, notus, perspicuus.——Ambiguus, dubius, ignotus, incertus, obscurus.

5. Of nearness, as, Finitimus, propior, proximus, propinquus, socius, vicinus.

6. Of fitness or unfitness, as, Aptus, appositus, accommodatus, habilis, idoneus, opportunus.——Ineptus, inhabilis, importunus, inconveniens.

7. Of ease or difficulty, as, Facilis; levis, obvius, pervius.——Difficilis, arduus, gravis, laboriosus, periculosus, invius. To these add such as signify propensity or readiness; as, Pronus, proclivis, propensus, promptus, paratus.

8. Of equality or inequality, as, Æqualis, æquævus, par, compar, suppar.——Inæqualis, impar, dispar, discors. Also of likeness or unlikeness, as, Similis, æmulus, geminus.——Dissimilis, absonus, alienus, diversus, discolor.

9. Several adjectives compounded with CON, as, Cognatus, concolor, concors, confinis, congruus, consanguineus, consentaneus, consonus, conveniens, contiguus, continuus, continens, contiguous; as, Mari aër continens est, Cic.

To these add many other Adjectives of various significations, as, Obnoxius, subjectus, supplex, credulus, absurdus, decorus, deformis, præsto, indecl. at hand, secundus, &c.—particularly.

Verbals in BILIS and DUS govern the dative, as,

Amandus vel amabilis omnibus,   To be loved by all men.

So Mors est terribilis malis; Optabilis omnibus pax; Adhibenda est nobis diligentia, Cic. Semel omnibus calcanda est via lethi, Hor. Also some participles of the perfect tense; as, Bella matribus detestata, hated by, Hor.

Verbals in DUS are often construed with the prep. a; as, Deus est venerandus & colendus a nobis, Cic. Perfect participles are usually so; as, Mors Crassi est a multis defleta, rather than, multis defleta, Cic. A te invitatus, rogatus, proditus, &c. hardly ever tibi.

Obs. 1. The dative is properly not governed by adjectives, nor by any other part of speech; but put after them, to express the object to which their signification refers.

The particle to in English is often to be supplied; as, Similis patri, Like his father, to being understood.

Obs. 2. Substantives have likewise sometimes a dative after them; as, Ille est pater, dux, vel filius mihi, He is father, leader, or son to me: so, Præsidium reis, decus amicis, &c. Hor. Exitium pecori, Virg. Virtutibus hostis, Cic.

Obs. 3. The following adjectives have sometimes the dative after them, and sometimes the genitive; Affinis, similis, communis, par, proprius, finitimus, fidus, conterminus, superstes, conscius, æqualis, contrarius, and adversus;

verſus ; as, *Similis tibi*, or *tui* ; *Superſtes patri* or *patris* ; *Conſcius facinori* or *facinoris*. *Conſcius* and ſome others frequently govern both the genitive and dative ; as, *Mens ſibi conſcia recti*. We ſay, *Similes, diſſimiles, pares, diſpares, æquales, communes, inter ſe : Par & communis cum aliquo. Civitas ſecum ipſa diſcors ; diſcordes ad alia*. Liv.

Obſ. 4. │Adjectives ſignifying uſefulneſs, or fitneſs, and the contrary, have after them the dative or the accuſative with a prepoſition ;│ as,

Utilis, inutilis, aptus, ineptus, accommodatus, idoneus, habilis, inhabilis, ctportūnus, conveniens, &c. alicui rei, or *ad aliquid*. Many other adjectives governing the dative are likewiſe conſtrued with prepoſitions; as, *Attentus quæſitis*, Hor. *Attentus ad rem*, Ter.

Obſ. 5. Of adjectives which denote friendſhip or hatred, or any other affection of the mind towards any one. I. Some are uſually conſtrued with the dative only ; as, *Affabilis, arrogans, aſper, carus, difficilis, fidelis, inviſus, iratus, offenſus, ſuſpectus*, ALICUI. II. Some with the prepoſition IN and the accuſative ; as, *Acerbus, animatus, beneficus, gratioſus, injurioſus, liberalis, mendax, miſericors, officioſus, pius, impius, prolixus, ſeverus, ſordidus, torvus, vehemens*, IN ALIQUEM. III. Some either with the dative, or with the accuſ. and the prepoſition IN, ERGA, *or* ADVERSUS going before ; as, *Contumax, criminoſus, durus, exitiabilis, gravis, hoſpitalis, implacabilis*, (and perhaps alſo *inexorabilis & intolerabilis,*) *iniquus, ſævus*, ALICUI or in ALIQUEM. *Benevolus, benignus, moleſtus*, ALICUI or ERGA ALIQUEM. *Mitis comis* ; IN, or ERGA ALIQUEM, and ALICUI. *Pervicax* ADVERSUS ALIQUEM. *Crudelis* IN ALIQUEM ; ſeldom ALICUI. *Amicus, æmulus, infenſus, infeſtus*, ALICUI, ſeldom IN ALIQUEM. *Gratus* ALICUI, or IN, ERGA, ADVERSUS ALIQUEM. We ſay *alienus alicui* or *alicujus* ; but oftener *ab aliquo*, and ſometimes *aliquo* without the prepoſition.

AUDIENS is conſtrued with two datives ; as, *Regi dicto audiens erat*, he was obedient to the king; not *regis* ; *Dicto audiens fuit juſſis magiſtratuum*, Nep. *Nobis dicto audientes ſunt*, not *dictis*, Cic.

Obſ. 6. Adjectives ſignifying motion or tendency to a thing, have uſually after them the accuſative with the prepoſition *ad* or *in*, ſeldom the dative ; as,

Pronus, propenſus, proclivis, celer, tardus, piger, &c. ad iram, or *in iram.*

Obſ. 7. │*Propior* and *proximus*, in imitation of their primitive *prope*, often govern the accuſative│ as, *Propior montem*, ſcil. *ad*, Sall. *Proximus finem*, Liv.

Obſ. 8. *IDEM* ſometimes has the dative, chiefly in the poets ; as, *Invitum qui ſervat, idem facit occidenti*, Hor. *Jupiter omnibus idem*, Virg.
                                                                                    Eadem

Eadem illis cenfemus, Cic. But in profe we commonly find, *idem qui, et, ac, atque*, and alfo *ut, cum*; as, *Peripatetici quondam iidem erant qui Academici*, Cic. *Eft animus erga te, idem ac fuit*, Ter. *Dianam & Lunam eandem effe putant*, Cic. *Idem faciunt, ut, &c.* *In eodem loco mecum*, Cic. But it would be improper to fay of the fame perfon or thing under different names, *idem cum*; as, *Luna eadem eft cum Diana*.

We likewife fay, *alius ac, atque* or *et*; and fo fometimes *fimilis & par*.

3. *Adjectives governing the Ablative.*

XIII. (Thefe adjectives, *dignus, indignus, contentus, præditus, captus,* and *fretus* ; alfo *natus, fatus, ortus, editus,* and the like, govern the ablative ;(as,

Dignus honore,	Worthy of honour.	*Captus oculis,*	Blind.	[ftrength.
Contentus parvo,	Content with little.	*Fretus viribus,*	Trufting	to his
Præditus virtute,	Endued with virtue.	*Ortus regibus,*	Defcended of kings.	

So *generatus, creatus, cretus, prognatus, oriundus, procreatus regibus*.

Obf. 1. The ablative after thefe adjectives is governed by fome prepofition underftood; as, *Contentus parvo,* fcil. *cum*; *Fretus viribus,* fcil. *in, &c.* Sometimes the prepofition is expreffed; as, *Ortus ex concubina*, Salluft. *Editus de nympha*, Ovid.

Obf. 2. (*Dignus, indignus,* and *contentus,* have fometimes the genitive after them) as, *dignus avorum*, Virg. So *Macte efto*, or *macti eftote virtutis* or *virtute*, Increafe in virtue, *or* Go on and profper; *Juberem macte virtute effe*, fc. *te*, Liv. ii. 12. In the laft example *macte* feems to be ufed adverbially.

4. *Adjectives governing the Genitive or Ablative.*

XIV. (Adjectives of plenty or want govern the genitive or ablative ;(as,

Plenus iræ or *irâ*, Full of anger. *Inops rationis* or *ratione*, Void of reafon.

So *Non inopes temporis, fed prodigi fumus*, Sen. *Lentulus non verbis inops*, Cic. *Dei plena funt omnia*, Cic. *Maxima quæque domus fervis eft plena fuperbis*, Juv. *Res eft foliciti plena timoris amor*, Ovid. *Amor & melle & felle eft fæcundiffimus*, Plaut. *Fæcunda virorum paupertas fugitur*, Lucan. *Omnium confiliorum ejus particeps*, Curt. *Homo ratione particeps*, Cic. *Nihil infidiis vacuum*, Id. *Vacuas cædis habete manus*, Ovid.

Some of thefe adjectives are conftrued, 1. with the genitive only; as, *Benignus, exfors, impos, impotens, irritus, liberalis, munificus, prælargus*.

2. With the ablative only: *Beatus, differtus, frugifer, mutilus, tentus, diftentus, tumidus, turgidus*.

3. With the genitive more frequently: *Compos, confors, egenus, exhæres, expers, fertilis, indigus, parcus, pauper, prodigus, fterilis*.

4. With

4. With the ablative more frequently : *Abundans, cassus, extorris, foetus, frequens, gravis, gravidus, jejunus, liber, locuples, nudus, oneratus, onustus, orbus, pollens, solutus, truncus, viduus,* and *captus.*

5. With both promiscuously : *Copiosus, dives, facundus, ferax, immunis, inanis, inops, largus, modicus, immodicus, nimius, opulentus, plenus, potens, refertus, satur, vacuus, uber.*

6. With a preposition ; as, *Copiosus, firmus, paratus, imparatus, inops, instructus, à re aliqua ;* for *quod ad rem aliquam attinet,* in, or with respect to any thing. *Extorris ab solo patrio,* banished ; *Orbus ab optimatibus concio,* Liv. So *pauper, tennis, facundus, modicus, parcus in re aliqua. Immunis, inanis, liber, nudus, solutus, vacuus a re aliqua. Potens ad rem, & in re.*

GOVERNMENT of VERBS.

§ 1. VERBS *governing only one Case.*

1. *Verbs which govern the Genitive.*

XV. *Sum,* when it signifies possession, property, or duty, governs the genitive ; as,

Est regis, It belongs to the king ; It is the part or property of a king.

So *Insipientis est dicere, non putârum,* It is the part or property of a fool, &c. *Militum est suo duci parere,* It is the part or duty of soldiers, &c. *Laudare se vani ; vituperare stulti est,* Sen. *Hominis est errare ; Arrogantis est negligere quid de se quisque sentiat,* Cic. *Pecus est Melibœi,* Virg. *Hæc sunt hominis ;* Ter. *Pauperis est numerare pecus,* Ovid. *Temeritas est florentis ætatis, prudentia senectutis,* Cic.

¶ *Meum, tuum, suum, nostrum, vestrum,* are excepted ; as,

Tuum est, It is your duty. *Scio tuum esse,* I know that it is your duty.

Obs. 1. These possessive pronouns are used in the neuter gender instead of their substantives, *mei, tui, sui, nostri, vestri.* Other possessives are also construed in this manner ; as, *Est regium, est humanum,* the same with *est regis, est hominis. Et facere et parti fortia, Romanum est.* Liv. ii. 12.

Obs. 2. Here some substantive must be understood ; as, *officium, munus, res, negotium, opus, &c.* which are sometimes expressed ; as, *Manus est principum ; Tuum est hoc munus,* Cic. *Nequiquam officium liberi esse hominis puto,* Ter. In some cases the preceding substantive may be repeated ; as, *Hic liber est* (liber) *fratris.* In like manner, some substantive must be supplied in such expressions as these ; *Ea sunt modo gloriosa, neque patrandi belli,* scil. *causâ* or *facta,* Sall. *Nihil tam æquandæ libertatis est,* for *ad æquandam libertatem pertinet,* Liv.

OM.

Obf. 3. We fay, *Hoc eft tuum munus,* or *tui muneris :* So *mos eft* vel *fuit,* or *moris,* or *in more,* Cic.

XVI. *Misereor, miseresco,* and *satago,* govern the genitive ; as,

Miserere civium tuorum,	Pity your countrymen.
Satagit rerum suarum,	{ He has his hands full at home, or has enough to do about his own affairs.

Obf. 1. Several other verbs among the poets govern the genitive by a Greek conftruction, particularly fuch as fignify fome affection of the mind ; as, *Ango, decipior, desipio, discrucior, excrucio, fallo & fallor, fastidio, invideo, lætor, miror, pendeo, studeo, vereor ;* as, *Ne angas te animi,* Plaut. *Laborum decipitur,* Hor. *Discrucior animi,* Ter. *Pendet mihi animus, pendeo animi* vel *animo ;* but we always fay, *Pendemus animis,* not *animorum,* are in fufpence, Cic. *Justitiæ prius mirer,* Virg. In like manner, *Abstineo, desino, desisto, quiesco, regno :* likewife, *adipiscor, condico, credo, frustror, furo, laudo, libero, levo, participo, prohibeo :* as, *Abstineto irarum ; Desine querelorum ; Regnavit populorum,* Hor. *Desistere pugnæ,* Virg. *Quarum rerum condixit,* Liv.

But all thefe verbs are for the moft part differently conftrued ; thus, *Angor, desipio, discrucior, fallor, animo. Hoc animum meum excruciat. Fastidio, miror, vereor, aliquem* vel *aliquid. Lætor aliquâ re.* Some of them are joined with the infinitive ; or with *quod, ut, ne,* apd the fubjunctive.

In like manner we ufually fay, *Desino aliquid,* & *ab aliquo,* to give over ; *Desisto incepto, de negotio, ab illa mente ; Quiesco a labore ; Regnare in equitibus, oppidis,* fc. *in,* Cic. *Per urbem,* Virg. *Adipisci id ; Frustrari in re ; Furere de aliquo,* Cic.

Obf. 2. The genitive after verbs, in the fame manner as after adjectives, is governed by fome fubftantive underftood. This fubftantive is different according to the different meaning of the verbs : thus, *Misereor fratris,* fcil. *causâ, Angor animi,* fcil. *dolore,* or *anxietate.*

2. *VERBS governing the Dative.*

XVII. Any verb may govern the dative in Latin, which has the figns TO or FOR after it in Englifh ; as,

Finis venit imperio,	An end is come to the empire, Liv.
Animus redit hoftibus,	Courage returns to the enemy, Id.
Tibi feris, tibi metis,	You fow for yourfelf, you reap for yourfelf, Plaut.

So, *Non nobis folum nati fumus,* Cic. *Multa malè eveniunt bonis,* Id. *Sol lucet etiam fceleratis,* Sen. *Hæret lateri lethalis arundo,* Virg.

But as the dative after verbs in Latin is not always rendered in

Englifh

Englifh by *to* or *for*; nor are thefe particles always the fign of the dative in Latin, it will be neceffary to be more particular.

I. *Sum*, and its compounds govern the dative; (except *poffum*) as,

Præfui exercitui,	He commanded the army.
Adfuit precibus,	He was prefent at prayers.

¶ EST taken for *Habeo, to have*, governs the dative of a perfon; as,

Eft mihi liber,	A book is to me, that is, I have a book.
Sunt mihi libri,	Books are to me, i. e. I have books.
Dico libros effe mihi,	I fay that I have books.

This is more frequently ufed than *habeo librum*; *habeo libros.* In like manner DEEST inftead of *careo*; as, *Liber deeft mihi*, I want a book; *Libri defunt mihi*; *Scio libros deeffe mihi*, &c.

II. Verbs compounded with SATIS, BENE, and MALE, govern the dative; as,

Satisfacio, fatisfio, benefacio, benedico, benevolo, malefacio, maledico, tibi, &c.

III. Many verbs compounded with thefe nine propofitions, AD, ANTE, CON, IN, INTER, OB, PRÆ, SUB, and SUPER, govern the dative; as,

1. *Accedo, accrefco, accumbo, acquiefco, adno, adnato, adequito, adhæreo, adfifto, adftipulor, advolvor, affulgeo, allabor, allaboro, annuo, appareo, applaudo, appropinquo, arrideo, afpiro, affentior, affideo, affifto, affuefco, affurgo.*
2. *Antecello, anteeo, antefto, anteverto.*
3. *Colludo, concino, confono, convivo.*
4. *Incumbo, indormio, indubit, inhio, ingemifco, inhæreo, infideo, infidior, infifto, infifto, infideo, infulto, invigilo, illacrymo, illudo, imminteo, immorior, immoror, impendeo.*
5. *Intervenio, intermico, intercello, intercido, interjaceo.*
6. *Obrepo, oblucteor, obtrecto, obftrepo, obmurmuro, occumbo, occurro, occurfo, obfto, obfifto, obvenio.*
7. *Præcedo, præcurro, præeo, præfideo, prælucco, prætiteo, præfto, prævaleo, præverto.*
8. *Succedo, fuccumbo, fufficio, fuffragor, fubcrefco, fuboleo, fubjaceo, fubrepo.*
9. *Supervenio, fupercurro, fuperfto.* But moft verbs compounded with SUPER govern the accufative.

IV. Verbs govern the dative, which fignify,

1. ¶ To profit or hurt; as,

Proficio,

Proficio, prosum, placeo, commodo, prospicio, caveo, metuo, timeo, consulo, for *prospicio.* Likewise, *Noceo, officio, incommodo, displiceo, insidior.*

2.¶ To favour or assist, and the contrary ¶ as,

Faveo, gratulor, gratificor, grator, ignesco, indulgeo, parco, adulor, plaudo, blandior, lenocinor, palpor, assentor, subparasitor. Likewise, *Auxilior, adminiculor, subvenio, succurro, patrocinor, medeor, medicor, opitulor.* Likewise, *Derogo, detraho, invideo, æmulor.*

3.¶ To command and obey, to serve and resist, as,

Impero, præcipio, mando, moderor, for *modum, adhibeo.* Likewise *Pareo, ausculto, obedio, obsequor, obtempero, moremgero, morigeror, obsecundo.* Likewise, *Famulor, servio, inservio, ministro, ancillor.* Likewise, *Repugno, obsto, reluctor, renitor, resisto, refragor, adversor.*

4.¶ To threaten and to be angry ¶ as,

Minor, comminor, interminor, irascor, succenseo.

5.¶ To trust ; ¶ as, *Fido, confido, credo, diffido.*

¶ To these add *Nubo, excello, hareo, supplico, cedo, despero, operor, prævaricor, prevaricor, recipio,* to promise ; *renuncio; respondeo,* to answer or satisfy ; *tempero, studeo, vaco,* to apply ; *convicior.*

Exc. *Jubeo, juvo, lædo,* and *offendo,* govern the accusative.

Obf. 1. Verbs governing the dative only are either neuter verbs, or of a neuter signification. Active verbs governing the dative have also an accusative expressed or understood.

Obf. 2. Most verbs governing the dative only, have been enumerated, because there are a great many verbs compounded with prepositions, which do not govern the dative, but are otherwise construed ; and still more signifying advantage or disadvantage, &c. which govern the accusative ; as, *Levo, erigo, alo, nutrio, amo, diligo, vexo, crucio, aversor,* &c. *aliquem,* not *alicui.*

Obf. 3. Many of these verbs are variously construed ; particularly such as are compounded with a preposition ; as,

Anteire, antecedere, antecellere, præcedere, præcurrere, præire, &c. alicui, *or* aliquem, *to go before, to excel.*

Acquiescere, rei, re, *v.* in re. Adequitare portæ ; Syracusas.

Adjacere, mari, *v.* mare, *to lie near.*

Adnare navibus, naves, ad naves, *to swim to.*

Adversari ei, *rarely* eum, *to oppose.*

Advolvi genibus, genua, ad genua, *to fall at one's knees.*

Advolare ei, ad eum ; rostra, *to fly up to.*

Adflare rei *v.* homini ; rem *v.* hominem ; aliquid alicui, *to breathe upon.*

Adulari ei, *v.* cum, *to flatter.* Allabi oris ; aures ejus, Virg ad exta, Liv.

Apparere

Apparere consuli, *to attend;* ad solium Jovis; Res apparet mihi, *appears.*
Appropinquare Britanniæ, portam, ad portam, *to approach.*
Dominari cunctis oris, *Virg.* in cætera animalia, *to rule over,* Ovid.
Congruere alicui, cum re aliqua, inter se, *to agree.*
Fidere, confidere alicui rei, aliqua re, in re, *to trust to or in.*
Ignoscere mihi, culpæ meæ, mihi culpam, *to pardon me* or *my fault.*
Impendere alicui, aliquem, in aliquem, *to hang over.*
Incessit cura, cupido, timor ei, eum, *v.* in eum, *seized.*
Incumbere toro; gladium, in gladium, *to fall upon;* labori, ad laudem,
    ad studia, in studium, curam, cogitationem, &c. *to apply to.*
Indulgere alicui, id ei; nimio, vestitu, *to indulge in.* Ter.
Inhiare auro, bona ejus, *to gape after.* Innasci agris, in agris, *to grow in.*
Inniti rei, re, in re; in aliquem, *to depend on.*
Insultare rei & homini, *v.* hominem; fores; patientiam ejus, in mi-
    seriam ejus; bonos, *to insult over.*
Latet res mihi, *v.* me, *is unknown to me.* Mederi ei; cupiditates, *to cure.*
Ministrare ei, *to serve;* arma ei, *to furnish.*
Moderari animo, gentibus; navim, omnia, *to rule.*
Nocere ei, *rarely* eum, *to hurt,* Plaut.
Nubere alicui; in familiam; nupta ei & cum eo, *to marry,* Cic.
Obrepere ei & eum, *to creep upon;* in animos; ad honores.
Obstrepere auribus & aures. Obtrectare ei laudibus, ejus, *to detract from.*
Obumbrat sibi vinea; solem nubes, *shades.* Palpari alicui & aliquem.
Pascisci alicui, cum aliquo; vitam ab eo, *Sall.* vitam pro laude, *Virg.*
Præstolari alicui & aliquem, *to wait upon.*
Procumbere terræ; genibus ejus, *Ovid.* ad genua, *Liv.* ad pedes, *to fall.*

To these may be added verbs, which, chiefly among the poets, govern the dative, but in prose are usually construed with a preposition;
as, 1. *Contendo, certo, bello, pugno, concurro, soeo, alicui,* for *cum aliquo;*
2. *Distare, dissentire, discrepare, diffidere, differre rei alicui,* for *a re aliqua.*
We also say, *Contendunt, pugnant, distant,* &c. *inter se;* and *contendere,*
pugnare contra & *adversus aliquem.*

Obs. 4. Many verbs vary both their signification and construction;
as, *Timeo, metuo, formido, horreo tibi, de te,* & *pro te,* I am afraid for
you, *or* for your safety; but *timeo, horreo te,* v. *a te,* I fear or dread
you as an enemy: So *Consulo, prospicio, caveo tibi,* I consult *or* provide
for your safety; but *consulo te,* I ask your advice; *prospicio hoc,* I foresee
this: *Studere aliquid,* to desire; *alicui,* to favour; *alicui rei, rem,* &
in re, to apply to a thing. So, *Æmulor tibi,* I envy; *te,* I imitate;
Ausculto tibi, I obey or listen to; *te,* I hear; *Cupio tibi,* I favour, *rem,*
I desire; *Fænero,* & *-or tibi,* I lend you on interest; *abs te,* I borrow;
Metuisti, ne non tibi istuc fæneraret, should not return with interest,
or bring usury, *Ter.* And thus many other verbs, which will be
afterwards explained.

Obs. 5. Verbs signifying *Motion* or *Tendency* to a thing
are construed with the preposition *ad;* as,

Eo, vado, curro, propero, feſtino, pergo, fugio, tendo, vergo, inclino, &c. *ad locum, rem,* v. *hominem.* (Sometimes however in the poets they are conſtrued with the dative; as, *It clamor cœlo,* for *ad cœlum,* Virg.

3. *Verbs governing the Accuſative.*

XVIII. A Verb ſignifying actively governs the accuſative; as,

Ama Deum, Love God. *Reverere parentes,* Reverence your parents.

Obſ. 1. Neuter verbs alſo govern the accuſative, when the noun after them has a ſignification ſimilar to their own; as,

Ire iter or *viam; Pugnare pugnam* or *prœlium: Currere curſum; Canere cantinelam; Vivere vitam; Ludere luſum; Sequi ſectam: Somniare somnium,* &c. or when they are taken in a metaphorical ſenſe; as, *Corydon ardebat Alexin,* ſcil. *propter,* i. e. *vehementer amabat,* Virg. *Currimus œquor,* ſcil. *per,* Id. So, *Comptos arſit adulteri crines,* Hor. *Saltare Cyclopa,* olet hircum; *Sulcos et vineta crepat mera,* Hor. *Vox hominem ſonat: Sudare mella,* Virg. *Si Xerxes Helleſponto juncto, et Athone perfoſſo, maria ambulaviſſet, terramque navigaſſet,* ſc. *per,* Cic. Or when they have a kind of active ſenſe; as, *Clamare aliquem nomine,* Virg. *Callere jura; Mœrere mortem; Horret iratum mare,* Hor.

Sometimes inſtead of the accuſative neuter verbs have an ablative; as, *Ire itinere; dolere dolore, vicem ejus; gaudere gaudio; mori* v. *obire morte; vivere vitâ; ardet virgine,* Horat. *Ludere eleam,* v. *â; manare, pluere, rorare, ſtillare, ſudare, aliquid* vel *aliquo. Erubeſcere jura,* Virg. *origine,* Tacit. *equo vehi,* Curt.

Obſ. 2. Several verbs are uſed both in an active and neuter ſenſe; as,

Abhorrere famam, *to dread infamy,* Liv. a litibus; ab uxore ducenda, *to be averſe from:* Id. a meis moribus abhorret, *is inconſiſtent with,* Cic.

Abolere monumenta viri, *to aboliſh,* Virg. Iis Cladis Caudinæ nondum memoria aboleverat, *was not effaced from, they had not forgotten,* Liv.

Adolere penates, *to burn, to ſacrifice to,* Virg.

Ætas adolevit; adolevit ad ætatem, *Plaut.*

Declinare ictum, *to avoid;* loco; agmen aliquo, *to remove.*

Degenerare animos, *to weaken;* patri, *to degenerate from;* a virtute majorum.

Durare adoleſcentes labore, *to harden;* Res durat ad breve tempus, *endures;* In ædibus durare nequeo, *ſtay* or *remain,* Plaut.

Inclinare culpam in aliquem, *to lay;* Hos ut ſequar inclinat animus, *inclines;* acies inclinat, *vel* inclinatur, *gives away.*

Laborare arma, *to forge;* morbo, a dolore, e renibus, *to be ill;* de re aliqua, *to be concerned.*

Morari iter, *to ſtop;* in urbe, *to ſtay;*

ftay; Hoc nihil moror, *I do not mind.*
Properare pecuniam hæredi, *Hor.*
in orbem; ad unam fedem, *Ovid.*
Quadrare acervum, *to fquare*, Hor.
aliquid ad norman; alicui, in aliquem, ad multa, *to fit.*

Suppeditare copiam dicendi, *to furnifh*; Sumptus illi, *vel* illi fumptibus, *Terent.* fuppeditat ei ratio, *is afforded*; Manubiæ in fundamenta vix fuppeditárunt, *were fufficient*, Liv.

Obf. 3. Thefe accufatives, *hoc, id, quid, aliquid, quicquid, nihil, idem, illud, tantum, quantum, multa, pauca,* &c. are often joined with neuter verbs, having the prepofitions *circa* or *propter* underftood; as, *Id lacrimat, Id fuccenfet,* Ter.

Obf. 4. The accufative is often underftood. *Tum prora avertit, fc. fe,* Virg. *Flumina præcipitant, fc. fe,* Id. *Quocunque intenderat fc. fe,* turned or directed himfelf, *Salluft.* Obiit, fc. *mortem,* Ter. *Cur faciam vitulá, fc. facra,* Virg. Or its place fupplied by an infinitive or part of a fentence; as, *Reddes dulce loqui, reddes ridere decorum*; for *dulcem fermonem, decorum rifum,* Hor.

XIX. *Recordor,* memĭni, *reminifcor,* and *oblivifcor,* govern the accufative or genitive; as,

Recordor lectionis or *lectionem,*	I remember the leffon.
Oblivifcor injuriæ or *injuriam,*	I forget an injury.

Obf. 1. Thefe verbs are often conftrued with the infinitive or fome part of a fentence; as, *Memini videre virginem,* Ter. *Oblitus eft, quid paulo ante præfuiffet,* Cic.

Obf. 2. *Memini,* when it fignifies to *make mention,* is joined with the genitive, or the ablative with the prepofition *de*; as, *Memini alicujus,* vel *de aliquo.* So *recordor,* when it fignifies to recollect; as, *Velim fcire ecquid de te recordere,* Cic.

4. *VERBS governing the Ablative.*

XX. Verbs of plenty and fcarcenefs for the moft part govern the ablative; as

Abundat divitiis,	He abounds in riches.
Caret omni culpa,	He has no fault.

Verbs of plenty are, *Abundo, affluo, exubĕro, redundo, fuppedito, fcateo,* &c.; of want, *Careo, egeo, indĭgeo, vaco, deficior, deftituor,* &c.

Obf. 1. *Egeo* and *indigeo* frequently govern the genitive; as, *Eget æris,* He needs money, Hor. *Non tam artis indigent, quam laboris,* Cic.

Obf. 2. The ablative after thefe verbs is governed by fome prepofition underftood; and fometimes we find it expreffed; as, *Vacat a culpa,* he is free from fault, Liv.

XXI.

XXI. *Utor, abutor, fruor, fungor, potior, vescor,* govern the ablative ; as,

Utitur fraude, He uses deceit.   *Abutitur libris,* He abuses books.

To these add, *gaudeo, creor, nascor, fido, vivo, victito, consto, laboro,* for *male me habeo,* to be ill ; *pascor, epulor, nitor, &c.*

Obf. 1. *Potior* often governs the genitive ; as, *Potiri urbis,* Sall. And we always say *Potiri rerum,* to possess the chief command ; never *rebus, imperio* being understood.

Obf. 2. *Potior, fungor, vescor, epulor,* and *pascor,* sometimes have an accusative ; as, *Potiri urbem,* Cic. *Officia fungi,* Ter. *Munera fungi,* Tacit. *Pascuntur silvas,* Virg. And in ancient writers *utor, abutor,* and *fruor;* as, *Uti confilium,* Plaut. *Operam abutitur,* Ter. *Depafco* and *depafcor* always take an accusative ; as, *Depafcitur artus.* Virg.

§ 2. VERBS *governing two Cafes.*

1. *Verbs governing two Datives.*

XXII. *Sum* taken for *affero (to bring)* governs two datives, the one of a person, and the other of a thing ; as,

Eft mihi voluptati,   It is, or brings a pleasure to me.

Two datives are also put after *habeo, do, verto, relinquo, tribuo, fore, duco,* and some others ; as,

Ducitur honori tibi, It is reckoned an honour to you. *Id vertitur mihi vitio,* I am blamed for that. So, *Mifit mihi muneri ; Dedit mihi dono ; Habet fibi laudi ; Venire, occurrere auxilio alicui,* Liv.

Obf. 1. Inftead of the dative, we often use the nominative, or the accufative ; as, *Eft exitium pecori,* for *exitio ; Dare aliquid alicui donum,* or *dono ; Dare filiam ei nuptam,* or *nuptui.* When *dare* and other active verbs have two datives after them, they likewife govern an accufative either expreffed or underftood ; as, *Dare crimini ei,* fc. *id.*

Obf. 2. The dative of the perfon is often to be fupplied ; as, *Eft exemplo, indicio, præfidio, ufui, &c.* fcil. *mihi, alicui, hominibus,* or fome fuch word. So, *ponere, opponere pignori,* fc. *alicui,* to pledge. *Canere receptui,* fc. *fuis militibus,* to found a retreat ; *Habere curæ, quæftui, odio, voluptati, religioni, ftudio, ludibrio, defpicatui,* &c. fc. *fibi.*

Obf. 3. To this rule belong forms of naming; as, *Eft mihi nomen Alexandro,* my name is Alexander ; or with the nominative, *Eft mihi nomen Alexander;* or more rarely with the genitive, *Eft mihi nomen Alexandri.*

2. *VERBS governing the Accusative and the Genitive.*

XXIII. Verbs of accusing, condemning, acquitting, and admonishing, govern the accusative of a person with the genitive of a thing ; as,

Arguit me furti,	He accuses me of theft.
Meipsum inertiæ condemno,	I condemn myself of laziness.
Illum homicidii absolvunt,	They acquit him of manslaughter.
Monet me officii,	He admonishes me of my duty.

Verbs of accusing are, *Accūso, ago, appello, arcesso, anquīro, arguo, defĕro, insimulo, postŭlo, alligo, astringo ;* of condemning, *Damno, condemno, infamo, noto ;* of acquitting, *Absolvo, libĕro, purgo ;* of admonishing, *Moneo, admoneo, commonefacio.*

Obs. 1. Verbs of accusing and admonishing, instead of the genitive, frequently have after them an ablative, with the preposition *de* ; as, *Monere aliquem officii,* or *de officio; Accusare aliquem furti,* or *de furto. De vi condemnati sunt,* Cic.

Obs. 2. *Crimen* and *caput* are put either in the genitive or ablative ; but in the ablative usually without a preposition ; as, *Damnare, postulare, absolvere eum criminis,* v. *capitis* ; & *crimine,* v. *capite* ; also *Absolvo me peccato,* Liv. And we always say, *Plectere, punire aliquem capite,* and not *capitis,* to punish one capitally, *or* with death.

Obs. 3. Many verbs of accusing, &c. are not construed with the acc. of a person, and the gen. of a thing, but the contrary ; thus we say, *Culpo, reprehendo, taxo, traduco, vitupero, calumnior, criminor, excuso,* &c. *avaritiam alicujus,* and not *aliquem avaritiæ.* We sometimes also find *accuso, incuso,* &c. construed in this manner ; as, *Accusare inertiam adolescentium,* for *adolescentes inertiæ,* Cic. *Culpam arguo,* Liv. We say, *Agere cum aliquo furti,* rather than *aliquem,* to accuse one of theft, Cic.

Obs. 4. Verbs of accusing and admonishing sometimes govern two accusatives, when joined with *hoc, illud, istud, id, unum, multa,* &c. as *Moneo, accuso te illud.* We seldom however find, *Errorem te moneo,* but *erroris,* or *de errore ;* except in old writers ; as, Plautus.

XXIV. Verbs of valuing, with the accusative, govern such genitives as these, *magni, parvi, nihili* ; as,

Æstimo te magni,	I value you much.

Verbs of valuing are, *Æstimo, existimo, duco, facio, habeo, pendo, puto, taxo.* They govern several other genitives ;

as, *tanti, quanti, pluris, majoris, minoris, minimi, plurimi, maximi, nauci, pili, assis, nihili, teruncii, hujus.*

Obf. 1. *Æstimo* fometimes governs the ablative; as, *Æstimo te magno, permagno, parvo,* fcil. *pretio:* and alfo *nihilo.* We likewife fay, *Pro nihilo habeo, puto, dico.*

Obf. 2. *Æqui* and *boni* are put in the genitive after *facio* and *confulo;* as, *Hoc confulo boni, æqui bonique facio,* I take this in good part.

Obf. 3. The genitive after all thefe verbs is governed by fome fubftantive underftood; as, *Arguere aliquem furti,* fcil. *de crimine furti; Æstimo rem magni,* fcil. *pretii,* or *pro re magni pretii; Confulo boni,* i. e. *ftatuo* or *cenfeo effe factum,* or *munus boni viri,* or *animi; Munere aliquem officii,* i. e. *officii causâ,* or *de re* or *negotio officii.*

3. *VERBS governing the Accufative and the Dative.*

XXV. Verbs of comparing, giving, declaring, and taking away, govern the accufative and dative; as,

Compăro Virgilium Homero,	I compare Virgil to Homer.
Sum cuique tribuito,	Give every one his own.
Narras fabulam furdo,	You tell a ftory to a deaf man.
Eripuit me morti,	He refcued me from death.

Or rather,—ANY ACTIVE VERB MAY GOVERN THE ACCUSATIVE AND THE DATIVE, (*when together with the object of the action, we exprefs the perfon or thing with relation to which it is exerted*) as,

Legam lectionem tibi, I will read the leffon to you. *Emit librum mihi,* He bought a book for me. *Sic vos non vobis fertis aratra boves,* Virg. *Paupertas fæpe fuadet mala hominibus,* advifes men to do bad things, Plaut. *Imperare pecuniam, frumentum, naves, arma aliquibus,* to order them to furnifh, Cæf.

Obf. 1. Verbs of comparing and taking away, together with fome others, are often conftrued with a prepofition; as, *Comparare unam rem cum aliâ, & ad aliam,* or *comparare res inter fe : Eripuit me morti, morte, a* or *ex morte: Mittere epiftolam alicui,* or *ad aliquem : Intendere telum alicui,* or *in aliquem : Incidere æri, in æs,* or *in ære:* and fo in many others.

Obf. 2. Several verbs governing the dative and accufative, are conftrued differently; as,

Circumdare mœnia oppido, or *oppidum mœnibus,* to furround a city with walls.

Intercludere commeatum alicui, or *aliquem commeatu,* to intercept one's provifions.

Donare, prohibere rem alicui, or *aliquem re,* to give one a prefent, to hinder one from a thing.

Muctare hoftiam Deo, or *Deum hoftiâ,* to facrifice.

Impertire

Impertire falutem alicui, or *aliquem falute,* to falute one.

Interdixit Galliam Romanis, or *Romanos Galliâ,* he debarred the Romans from Gaul.

Induere, exuere veftem fibi, or *fe vefte,* to put on, to put off one's cloaths.

Levare dolorem alicui; dolorem alicujus; aliquem dolore, to eafe one's diftrefs.

Minari aliquid alicui, or fometimes *alicui aliquo,* Cic. to threaten one with any thing; *Cafari gladio,* Sall.

Gratulor tibi banc rem, hac re, in, pro, & de hac re, I congratulate you on this. *Mittus Tullo devictes hoftes gratulatur,* Liv.

Reftituere alicui fanitatem, or *aliquem fanitati,* to reftore to health.

Afpergere labem alicui or *aliquem labe,* to put an affront on one; *aram fanguine. Litare Deum facris,* & *facra Deo,* to facrifice.

Excufare fe alicui & apud aliquem, de re; valetudinem ei.

Exprobrare vitium ei v. in eo, to upbraid.

Occupare pecuniam alicui, & *apud aliquem,* i. e. *pecuniam fænori locare,* to place at intereft, Cic.

Opponere fe morti, & *ad mortem. Renunciare id ei,* & *ad eum,* to tell.

Obf. 3. Verbs fignifying motion or tendency to a thing, inftead of the dative, have an accufative after them, with the prepofition *ad;* as,

Porto, fero, lego, as, præcipito, tollo, traho, duco, verto, incito, fufcito; alfo *hortor,* and *invito, v co, provoco, animo, ftimulo, confuro, laceffo;* thus, *Ad laudem milites hortatur; Ad prætorem hominem traxit,* Cic. But after feveral of thefe verbs, we alfo find the dative; as, *Inferre Deos Latio,* for *in Latium,* Virg. *Invitare aliquam hofpitio,* or *in hofpitium,* Cic.

Obf 4. The accufative is fometimes underftood; as, *Nubere alicui,* fcil. *fe; Cedere alicui,* fcil. *locum; Detrahere alicui,* fcil. *laudem; Ignofcere alicui,* fcil. *culpam.* And in Englifh the particle *to* is often omitted; as, *Dedit mibi librum,* He gave me a book, *for* to me.

4. *VERBS governing two Accufatives.*

XXVI. Verbs of afking and teaching govern two accufatives, the one of a perfon, and the other of a thing; as,

Pofcimus te pacem,	We beg peace of thee.
Docuit me grammaticam,	He taught me grammar.

1. Verbs of afking which govern two accufatives are, *Rogo, oro, exoro, obfecro, precor, pofco, repofco, flagito,* &c. Of teaching, *Doceo, edoceo, dedoceo, erudio.*

Obf. 1. *Celo* likewife governs two accufatives; as, *Celavit*

vit me hanc rem, He concealed this mater from me ; or otherwise, *celavit hanc rem mihi,* or *celavit me de hac re.*

Obf. 2. Verbs of afking and teaching are often conftrued with a prepofition ; as, *Rogare rem ab aliquo ; Docere aliquem de re,* to inform ; but we do not fay, *docere aliquem de grammatica,* but *grammaticam,* to teach. And we always fay, with a prepofition, *Peto, exigo a v. abs te ; Percontor, fcitor, fcifcitor, ex* or *a te,* or *te* without the prepofition ; *Interrogo, confulte te de re ; Ut facias te clfaro ; Exoret pacem divûm,* for *divos,* Virg. *Inftruo, inftituo, formo, informo aliquem artibus,* in the abl. without a prep. *Imbuo cum artibus,* in v. *ab artibus.* Alfo *inftruo ad rem,* v. *in re, ignorantiam alicujus. Erudite aliquem artes, de* v. *in re, ad rem. Formare ad ftudium, mentem ftudiis, ftudia ejus.*

Obf. 3. The accufative of the thing is not properly governed by the verb, but by *quod ad* or *fecundum* underftood.

5. *VERBS governing the Accufative and the Ablative.*

XXVII. Verbs of loading, binding, cloathing, depriving, and fome others, govern the accufative and the ablative; as,

Onerat naves auro,	He loads the fhips with gold.

Verbs of loading are, *Onero, cumulo, premo, opprimo, obruo :* Of unloading, *levo, exonero,* &c. Of binding, *aftringo, ligo, alligo, devincio, impedio, irretio, illaqueo,* &c. Of loofing, *folvo, exfolvo, libero, laxo, expedio,* &c. Of depriving, *privo, nudo, orbo, fpolio, fraudo, emungo :* Of cloathing, *veftio, amicio, induo, cingo, tego, velo, corono,* & *calceo :* Of uncloathing, *exuo, difcingo,* &c.

Obf. 1. The prepofition, by which the ablative is governed after thefe verbs, is fometimes expreffed ; as, *Solvere aliquem ex catenis,* Cic. Sometimes the ablative is to be fupplied ; as, *Complet naves,* fc. *viris,* mans the fhips, *Virg.*

Obf. 2. Several of thefe verbs likewife govern the genitive ; as, *Adolefcentem fua temeritatis implet,* Liv. And alfo vary their conftruction ; as, *Induit, exuit fe veftibus,* or *veftes fibi.*

The CONSTRUCTION of PASSIVE VERBS.

XXVIII. When a verb in the active voice governs two cafes, in the paffive it retains the latter cafe ; as,

Accufar furti,	I am accufed of theft.
Virgilius comparatur Homero,	Virgil is compared to Homer.
Docear grammaticam,	I am taught grammar.
Navis oneratur auro,	The fhip is loaded with gold.

So *Scio homines accufatum iri furti ; ——Eos emptum iri morti, morte, a*

vd

vel ex morte;——pueros doctum iri grammaticam;——rem celatum iri mihi vel me; me celotum iri de re, &c.

Sometimes the active has three cafes, and then the paffive has the two laft cafes; as, *Habetur ludibrio iis.*

Obf. 1. Paffive verbs are commonly conftrued with the ablative and the prepofition *a*; as,

Tu laudaris a me, which is equivalent to, *Ego laudo te. Virtus diligitur a nobis: Nos diligimus virtutem. Gaudeo meum factum probari a te,* or *te probare meum factum:* And fo almoft all active verbs. Neuter and deponent verbs alfo admit this prepofition; as, *Mare a fole collucet,* Cic. *Phalaris non a paucis interiit,* Id. So *Cadere ab hofte; Ceffare a praeliis; Mori ab enfe; Pati, furari, aliquid ab aliquo,* &c. Alfo *Venire ab hoftibus,* to be fold; *Vapulare ab aliquo, Exulare ab urbe.* Thus likewife many active verbs; as, *Sumere, petere, tollere, pellere, expectare, emere,* &c. *ab aliquo.*

The prep. is fometimes underftood after paffive verbs; as, *Deferor conjuge,* Ovid. *Defertus fuis,* fc. *a,* Tacit. *Tabula diftinguitur unda, qui navigat,* fc. *ab unda,* is kept from the water by a plank, *Juvenal.*

The prepofition PER is alfo ufed in the fame fenfe with A; as, *Per me defenfa eft refpublica,* or *a me; Per me reftitutus; Per me v. a me factum eft,* Cic. But PER commonly marks the inftrument, and A the principal efficient caufe; as, *Res agitur per creditores a rege,* fc. *a rege* vel *a legato ejus,* Cic. Fam. i. 1.

Obf. 2. Paffive verbs fometimes govern the dative, efpecially among the poets; as,

Neque cernitur ulli, for *ab ullo,* Virg. *Vix audior ulli,* Ovid. *Scriberis Vario,* for *a vario,* Hor. *Honefta bonis viris quaeruntur,* for *a viris,* Cic. VIDEOR, to feem, always governs the dative; as, *Videris mihi,* You feem to me: But we commonly fay, *Videris a me,* You are feen by me; although not always; as, *Nulla tuarum audita mihi, neque vifa fororum,* for *a me,* Virg.

Obf. 3. *Induor, amicior, cingor, accingor,* alfo *exuor* and *difcingor,* are often conftrued with the accufative, particularly among the poets, though we do not find them governing two accufatives in the active voice; as, *Induitur veftem,* or *vefte.*

Obf. 4. Neuter verbs are for the moft part only ufed imperfonally in the paffive voice; unlefs when they are joined with a noun of a fimilar fignification to their own; as, *Pugna pugnata eft,* Cic. *Bellum militabitur,* Horat. Paffive imperfonal verbs are moft commonly applied either to a multitude, or to an individual taken indefinitely; as, *Statur, fletur, curritur, vivitur, venitur, &c. a nobis, ab illis, &c.* We are ftanding, weeping, &c. *Bene poteft vivi a me, vel ab aliquo,* I or any perfon may live well. *Provifum eft nobis optime a Deo; Reclamatum eft ab omnibus,* all cried out againft it, Cic.

They alfo govern the fame cafes, as when ufed perfonally; as, *Ut majoribus natu affurgatur, ut fupplicum mifereatur,* Cic. Except the accufative: For in thefe phrafes, *Itur Athenas, pugnatum eft biduum, dormitur totam noctem,* the accufative is not governed by the verb, but by the

the prepofitions *ad* and *per* underftood. We find, however, *Tota mihi dormitur hyems, Noctes vigilantur amarae; Oceanus raris ab orbe noftro navibus aditur*, Tacit.

The CONSTRUCTION of IMPERSONAL VERBS.

XXIX. An imperfonal verb governs the dative; as,

Expĕdit reipublicæ, It is profitable for the ftate.

Verbs which in the active voice govern only the dative, are ufed imperfonally in the paffive, and likewife govern the dative; as,

Favetur mihi, I am favoured, and not *Ego faveor*. So *Nocetur mihi, imperatur mihi, &c.* We find however, *Hæc ego procurare imperor; Ego cur invideor*, for *imperatur, invidetur mihi*, Hor.

Obf. 1. Thefe verbs, *Poteft, cœpit, incipit, definit, debet,* and *folet*, are ufed imperfonally, when joined with imperfonal verbs; as,

Non poteft credi tibi, You cannot be believed; *Mihi non poteft noceri*, I cannot be hurt; *Negat jucundè poffe vivi fine virtute*, Cic. *Per virtutem poteft iri ad aftra*. *Aliorum laudi & gloriæ invideri folet*, The praife and glory of others ufe to be envied, Id. *Neque a fortiffimis infirmiffimo generi refifti poffe*, Salluft.

Obf. 2. Various verbs are ufed both perfonally and imperfonally; as, *Venit in mentem mihi hæc res*, vel *de hac re*, vel *hujus rei*, fcil *memoria*; This thing came into my mind. *Eft curæ mihi hæc res* vel *de hac re*. *Doleo* vel *dolet mihi, id factum effe*.

Obf. 3. The neuter pronoun *it* is always joined with imperfonal verbs in Englifh; as, *It rains, it fhines, &c.* And in Latin an infinitive is commonly fubjoined to imperfonal verbs, or the fubjunctive with *ut*, forming a part of a fentence which may be fuppofed to fupply the place of a nominative; as, *Nobis non licet peccare*, the fame with *peccatum; Omnibus bonis expedit rempublicam effe falvam*, i. e. *Salus reipublicæ expedit omnibus bonis*, Cic. *Accidit, evĕnit, contigit, ut ibi effemus*. Thefe nominatives, *hoc, illud, id, idem, quod,* &c. are fometimes joined to Imperfonal verbs; as, *idem mihi licet*, Cic. *Eadem licent*, Catull.

Obf. 4. The dative is often underftood; as, *Faciat quod libet*, fc. *fibi*, Ter. *Stat cafus renovare omnes*, fc. *mihi*, I am refolved, Virg.

EXC. I. *REFERT* and *INTEREST* require the genitive; as,

Refert patris, It concerns my father. *Intereft omnium*, It is the intereft of all.

¶ But *mea, tua, fua, noftra, veftra*, are put in the accufative plural neuter; as,

Non mea refert, It does not concern me.

Obs. 1. Some think *mea, tua, sua,* &c. to be in the ablat. sing. fem. We say either *cujus interest,* and *quorum interest;* or *cuja interest,* from *cujus, -a, -um.*

Obs. 2. *Refert* and *interest* are often joined with these nominatives, *Id, hoc, illud, quid, quod, nihil,* &c. also with common nouns; and with these genitives, *Tanti, quanti, magni, permagni, parvi, pluris; as, Hoc parvi refert; Illud mea magni interest,* Cic. *Usque adeo magni refert studium,* Lucret. *Incessus in gravida refert,* Plin.

They are frequently construed with these adverbs, *Tantum, quantum, multum, plus, plurimum, infinitum, parum, maxime, vehementer, minime,* &c. as, *Faciam, quod maxime reipublicæ interesse judicabo,* Cic. Sometimes instead of the genit. they take the accusative with the prep. *ad;* as, *Quid id ad me, aut ad meam rem refert, Persæ quid rerum gerant?* Of what importance is it, &c. Plaut. *Magni ad honorem nostrum interest,* Cic. rarely the dative; as, *Dic quid referat intra naturæ fines viventi.* &c. Hor. Sometimes they are placed absolutely; as, *Magnopere interest opprimi Dolobellam,* it is of great importance, Cic. *Permultum interest, qualis primus aditus sit,* Id. *Adeone est fundata leviter fides, ut ubi sim, quam qui sim, magis referat,* Liv. *Plurimum enim intererit, quibus artibus, aut quibus hunc tu moribus instituas,* Juv.

Obs. 3. The genitive after *refert* and *interest* is governed by some substantive understood, with which the possessives *mea, tua, sua, &c.* likewise agree; as, *Interest Ciceronis,* i. e. *est inter negotia Ciceronis: Refert patris,* i. e. *refert se hæc res ad negotia patris:* So *interest mea, est inter negotia mea.*

EXC. II. These five, *MISERET, POENITET, PUDET, TÆDET,* and *PIGET,* govern the accusative of a person, with the genitive of a thing; as,

Miseret me tui, I pity you.	*Tædet me vitæ,* I am weary of life.
Pænitet me peccati, I repent of my sin.	*Pudet me culpæ,* I am ashamed of my fault.

Obs. 1. The genitive here is properly governed either by *negotium* understood, or by some other substantive of a signification similar to that of the verb with which it is joined; as, *Miseret me tui,* that is, *negotium* or *miseratio tui miseret me.*

Obs. 2. An infinitive or some part of a sentence may supply the place of the genitive; as, *Pænitet me peccasse,* or *quod peccaverim.* The accusative is frequently understood; as, *Scelerum si bene pænitet,* scil. *nos,* Horat.

Obs. 3. *Miseret, pænitet,* &c. are sometimes used personally, especially when joined with these nominatives, *hoc, id, quod,* &c. as, *Ipse sui miseret,* Lucr.; *Nonne hæc te pudent,* Ter. *Nihil, quod pænitere possit, facias,* for *cujus te pænitere possit,* Cic.

We sometimes find *miseret* joined with two accusatives; as, *Menedemi vicem miseret me,* scil. *secundum* or *quod ad,* Ter.

Obs. 4. The præterites of *miseret, pudet, tædet,* and *piget,* when used

in the paſſive form, govern the ſame caſes with the active ; as, *Miſe-*
ritum eſt me tuarum fortunarum, Ter.   We likewiſe find *miſereſcit* and
miſeretur uſed imperſonally ; as, *Miſereſcit me tui,* Ter. ; *Miſereatur te*
fratrum ; Neque me tui, neque tuorum liberorum miſereri poteſt, Cic.

EXC. III. *DECET, DELECTAT, JUVAT,* and
OPORTET, govern the accuſative of a perſon, with the
infinitive ; as,

Delectat me ſtudere,	It delights me to ſtudy.
Non decet te rixari,	It does not become you to ſcold.

Obſ. 1. Theſe verbs are ſometimes uſed perſonally ; as, *Parvum*
parva decent, Hor.   *Eſt aliquid, quod non oporteat, etiamſi liceat,* Cic.
Hæc facta ab illo oportebant, Ter.

Obſ. 2. *Decet* is ſometimes conſtrued with the dative ; as, *Ita nobis*
decet, Ter.

Obſ. 3. *Oportet* is elegantly joined with the ſubjunctive
mode, *ut* being underſtood ; as,

Sibi quiſque conſulat oportet, Cic.   Or with the perfect participle,
eſſe or *fuiſſe* being underſtood ; as, *Communicatum oportuit ; manſum*
oportuit ; Adoleſcenti morem geſtum oportuit, The young man ſhould have
been humoured, Ter.

Obſ. 4. *Fallit, fugit, præterit, latet,* when uſed imperſonally, alſo
govern the accuſative with the infinitive ; as, *In lege nullâ eſſe ejuſmodi*
caput, non te fallit ; De Dionyſio fugit me ad te antea ſcribere, Cic.

NOTE, *Attinet, pertinet,* & *ſpectat,* are conſtrued with *ad ; Ad rem-*
publicam pertinet, me conſervari, Cic.   And ſo perſonally, *Ille ad me*
attinet, belongs, Ter.   *Res ad arma ſpectat,* looks, points, Cic.

The CONSTRUCTION of the INFINITIVE.

XXX. One verb governs another in the infinitive ; as,

Cupio diſcere,	I deſire to learn.

Obſ. 1. The infinitive is often governed by adjectives ;
as, *Horatius eſt dignus legi,* Quinctil.   And ſometimes depends on a ſubſtantive ; as, *Tempus equûm fumantia ſolvere*
colla, Virg.

Obſ. 2. The word governing the infinitive is ſometimes underſtood ;
as, *Mene incepto deſiſtere victam,* ſcil. *decet,* or *par eſt,* Virg.   *Videre eſt,*
one may ſee.   *Dicere non eſt,* ſcil. *copia,* or *facultas,* Horat.   And
ſometimes the infinitive itſelf is to be ſupplied ; as, *Socratem fidibus*
docuit, ſcil. *canere,* Cic.   So *Diſcere, ſcire fidibus.*

Obſ. 3. The infinitive was not improperly called by the ancients
Nomen verbi, The name or noun of the verb ; becauſe it is both joined
with an adjective like a ſubſtantive ; as, *Velle ſuum cuique eſt,* Every
one has a will of his own ; and likewiſe ſupplies the place of a noun,

not only in the nominative, but alſo in all the oblique caſes; as, 1. In the nominative, *Latrocinari, fraudare, turpe eſt*, Cic. *Dixiſſe fideliter artes emollit mores*, Ovid. 2. In the genitive, *Peritus cantare*, for *cantandi*, or *cantûs*, Virg. In the dative, *Paratus ſervire*, for *ſervitati*, Sall. 4. In the accuſative, *Da mihi fallere*, for *artem fallendi*, Horat. *Quod faciam ſupereſt, præter amare, nihil*, Ovid. 5. In the vocative, *O vivere noſtrum, ut non ſentientibus effluis!* for *vita noſtra*. 6. In the ablative, *Dignus amari*, for *amore*, or *qui ametur*, Virg.

Obſ. 4. Inſtead of the infinitive, a different conſtruction is often uſed after verbs of *doubting, willing, ordering, fearing, hoping;* in ſhort, after any verb which has a relation to futurity; as, *Dubitat ita facere*, or more frequently, *an num*, or *utrum ita facturus ſit; Dubitavit an faceret necne; Non dubito quin fecerit. Vis me facere*, or *ut faciam. Metuit tangi*, or *ne tangatur. Spero te venturum eſſe*, or *fore ut venias. Nunquam putavi fore ut ad te ſupplex venirem*, Cic. *Exiſtimabant futurum fuiſſe ut oppidum amitteretur*, Cæſ.

Obſ. 5. *To*, which in Engliſh is the ſign of the infinitive, is omitted after *bid, dare, need, make, ſee, hear, feel*, and ſome others; as, *I bid him do it:* and in Latin may often be rendered otherwiſe than by the infinitive; as, I am ſent to complain, *Mitter queſtum*, or *ut querar, &c.* Ready to hear, *Promptus ad audiendum;* Time to read, *Tempus legendi;* Fit to ſwim, *Aptus natando;* Eaſy to ſay, *Facile dictu;* I am to write, *Scripturus ſum;* A houſe to let, *or more properly*, to be let, *Domus locanda;* He was left to guard the city, *Relictus eſt ut tueretur urbem.*

To in Engliſh is often taken abſolutely; as, *To confeſs the truth; To proceed; To conclude;* that is, *That I may confeſs the truth, &c.*

The CONSTRUCTION of PARTICIPLES, GERUNDS, and SUPINES.

XXXI. Participles, Gerunds, and Supines, govern the caſe of their own verbs; as,

Amans virtutem, Loving virtue.   *Carens fraude*, Wanting guile.

Obſ. 1. Paſſive participles often govern the dative, particularly when they are uſed as adjectives; as,

Suſpectus mihi, Suſpected by me; *Suſpectiores regibus*, Sall. *Inviſus mihi*; hated by me, or hateful to me: *Indies inviſior*, Suet. *Occulta, et maribus non inviſa ſolum, ſed etiam inaudita ſacra*, unſeen, Cic.

EXOSUS, PEROSUS, and often alſo PERTÆSUS, govern the accuſative; as, *Tædas exoſſi jugales*, Ovid. *Plebs conſulum nomen haud ſecus quam regum peroſa erat*, Liv. *Pertæſus ignaviam ſuam; ſemet ipſi* diſpleaſed with, Suet. *vitam*, weary of, Juſtin. *levitatis*, Cic.

Verbals in BUNDUS govern the caſe of their own verbs; as, *Gratulabundus patriæ*, Juſt. *Vitabundus caſtra beſtiarum*, Liv. So ſometimes alſo nouns; as, *Juſtitia eſt obtemperatio ſcriptis legibus*, Cic. *Ink n. conſult*

consult, Sall. *Domum reditionis spe sublatâ*, Cæf. *Spectatio lusû*, Plaut.

Obf. 2. Thefe verbs, *do, reddo, volo, curo, facio, habeo, comperio*, with the perfect participle, from a periphrafis fimilar to what we ufe in Englifh ; as, *Compertum habeo*, for *comperi*, I have found, Sall. *Effectum dabo*, for *efficiam ; Inventum tibi curabo, et adductum tuum Pamphilum*, i. e. *inveniam* et *adducam*, Ter. Sometimes the gerund is ufed with *ad* ; as, *Tradere ei gentes diripiendas*, or *ad diripiendum*, Cic. *Rogo, accipio, do aliquid utendum ; or ad utendum ; Mifit mihi librum legendum*, or *ad legendum*, &c.

Obf. 3. Thefe verbs, *curo, habeo, mando, loco, conduco, do, tribuo, mitto*, &c. are elegantly conftrued with the participle in *dus* inftead of the infinitive ; as, *Funus faciendum curavi*, for *fieri*, or *ut fieret : Columnas ædificandas locavit*, Cic.

The CONSTRUCTION of GERUNDS.

XXXII. Gerunds are conftrued like fubftantive nouns ; as,

Studendum eft mihi,   I muft ftudy.   *Aptus ftudendo*, Fit for ftudying.
Tempus ftudendi,   Time of ftudy. *Scio ftudendum effe mihi*, I know that
                                    I muft ftudy.

But more particularly ;

I. The Gerund in DUM with the verb *eft* governs the dative ; as,

Legendum eft mihi, I muft read.   *Moriendum eft omnibus*, All muft die. So *Scio legendum effe mihi ; moriendum effe omnibus*, &c.

Obf. 1. This gerund always imports obligation or neceffity ; and may be refolved into *oportet, neceffe eft*, or the like, and the infinitive or the fubjunctive, with the conjunction *ut* ; as, *Omnibus eft moriendum*, or *Omnibus neceffe eft mori*, or *ut moriantur* ; or, *Neceffe eft ut omnes moriantur*. *Confulendum eft tibi a me*, I muft confult for your good ; for *Oportet ut confulam tibi*, Cic.

Obf. 2. The dative is often underftood ; as, *Orandum eft, ut fit mens fana in corpore fano*, fc. *tibi*, Juv. *Hic vincendum, aut moriendum*, *lites, eft*, fc. *vobis*, Liv. *Deliberandum eft diu, quod ftatuendum eft femel* fc. *tibi* vel *alicui*, P. Syr.

II. The gerund in *DI* is governed by fubftantives or adjectives as,

Tempus legendi, Time of reading. *Cupidus difcendi*, Defirous of learning.

Obf. This gerund is fometimes conftrued with the genitive plural ; as, *Facultas agrorum condonandi*, for *agros*, Cic. *Copia fpectandi comœdiarum*, for *comœdias*, Ter. But chiefly with pronouns ; as, *In caftra venerunt fui purgandi causâ*, Cæf. *Veftri adhortandi caufâ*, Liv. *Ejus videndi cupidus*, fc. *fœminæ*, Ter. The gerund here is fuppofed to govern the genitive like a fubftantive noun.

III. The gerund in *DO* of the dative cafe is governed by adjectives fignifying ufefulnefs or fitnefs; as,

Charta utilis fcribendo,	Paper ufeful for writing.

Obf. 1. Sometimes the adjective is underftood; as, *Non eft folvendo*, fcil. *par*, or *habilis*, He is not able to pay. *Is finis cenfendo factus eft.* Liv.

Obf. 2. This gerund is fometimes governed alfo by verbs; as, *Adeffe fcribendo*, Cic. *Aptus habendo enfem*, for wearing; Virg.

IV. The gerund in *DUM* of the accufative cafe is governed by the prepofitions *ad* or *inter* / as,

Promptus ad audiendum,	Ready to hear.
Attentus inter docendum,	Attentive in time of teaching.

Obf. This gerund is alfo governed by fome other prepofitions; as, *Ante domandum*, Virg. *Ob abfolvendum*, Cic. *Circa movendum*, Quinctil. Or it depends on fome verb going before, and then with the verb *effe* governs the dative cafe; as, *Scio moriendum effe omnibus*, I know that all muft die. *Effe* is often underftood.

V. The gerund in *DO* of the ablative cafe is governed by the prepofitions, *a, ab, de, e, ex,* or *in*; as,

Pœna a peccando abfterret,	Punifhment frightens from finning.

* Or without a prepofition, as the ablative of manner or caufe; as,

Memoria excolendo augetur,	The memory is improved by exercifing it.
Defeffus fum ambulando,	I am wearied with walking.

Obf. The gerund in its nature very much refembles the infinitive. Hence the one is frequently put for the other; as, *Eft tempus legendi*, or *legere:* only the gerund is never joined with an adjective, and is fometimes taken in a paffive fenfe; as, *Cum Tifidium vocaretur ad imperandum*, i. e. *ut ipfi imperaretur*, to receive orders, Sall. *Nunc ades ad imperandum, vel ad parendum potius, Sic enim antiqui loquebantur*, Cic. i. e. *ut tibi imperetur. Urit videndo*, i. e. *dum videtur.* Virg.

The gerund in Englifh becomes a fubftantive, by prefixing the article to it, and then it is always to be conftrued with the prepofition *of;* as, *He is employed in writing letters,* or, *in the writing of letters:* but it is improper to fay, *in the writing letters, or in writing of letters.*

Gerunds

Gerunds turned into participles in dus.

XXXVI. Gerunds governing the accusative are elegantly turned into participles in *dus*, which, like adjectives, agree with their substantives in gender, number, and case ; as,

<table>
<tr><td align="center">By the Gerund.</td><td></td><td align="center">By the Participle or Gerundive.</td></tr>
</table>

By the Gerund.		By the Participle or Gerundive.
Petendum est mihi pacem,	} or more frequently {	*Pax est petenda mihi.*
Tempus petendi pacem,		*Tempus petendæ pacis.*
Ad potendum pacem,		*Ad petendam pacem.*
A petendo pacem,		*A petenda pace.*

Obf. 1. In changing gerunds into participles in *dus*, the participle and the substantive are always to be put in the same case in which the gerund was ; as,

Genitive; *Inita sunt consilia urbis delendæ, civium trucidandorum, nominis Romani extinguendi,* Cic.

Dat. *Perpetiendo labori idoneus,* Colum. *Capeßendæ reipublicæ habilis* Tac. *Area firma templis ac porticibus sustinendis,* Liv. *Oneri ferendo est,* sc. *aptus* v. *habilis,* Ovid. *Natus miseriis ferendis,* Ter. *Literis landis vigilare,* Cic. *Locum oppido condendo capere,* Liv.

Acc. and abl. *Ad defendendam Romam ab oppugnanda Capua duces Romanos abstrahere,* Liv. *Orationem Latinam legendis nostris efficies pleniorem,* Cic.

Obf. 2. The gerunds of verbs which do not govern the accusative, are never changed into the participle, except those of *medeor, utor, abutor, fruor, fungor,* and *potior*; as, *Spes potiundi urbe,* or *potiundæ urbis :* but we always say, *Cupidus subveniendi, tibi,* and never *tui.*

The CONSTRUCTION of SUPINES.

1. *The Supine in* um.

XXXVII. The supine in *um* is put after a verb of motion ; as,

Abiit deambulatum,	He hath gone to walk.

So, *Ducere cohortes prædatum,* Liv. *Nunc venis irrisum dominum? Quod in rem tuam optimum factu arbitror, te id admonitum venio,* Plaut.

Obf. 1. The supine in *um* is elegantly joined with the verb *eo,* to express the signification of any verb more strongly ; as, *It se perditum,* the same with *id agit,* or *operam dat, ut se perdat,* He is bent on his

own deſtruction, Ter. This ſupine with *iri* taken imperſonally, ſupplies the place of the infinitive paſſive; as, *An credebas illam ſire
tuâ operâ iri deductum domum?* Which may be thus reſolved, *An
credebas iri (a te, vel ab aliquo) deductum* (i. e. ad deducendum) *illam
domum*, Ter.

Obſ. 2. The ſupine in *um* is put after other verbs beſides verbs of
motion; as, *Dedit filiam nuptum*; *Cantatum provocemus*, Ter. *Revoca-
tus defenſum patriam*; *Diviſit copias hiematum*, Nep.

Obſ. 3. The meaning of this ſupine may be expreſſed by ſeveral
other parts of the verb; as, *Venit oratum opem*: or, 1. *Venit opem
orandi cauſâ*, or *opis orandæ*. 2. *Venit ad orandum opem*, or *ad orandam
opem*. 3. *Venit opi orandæ*. 4. *Venit opem oraturus*. 5. *Venit qui*, or
ut opem oret. 6. *Venit opem orare*. But the third and the laſt of theſe
are ſeldom uſed.

2. *The ſupine in* u.

XXXVIII. The ſupine in *u* is put after an adjective noun; as,

Facile dictu,   Eaſy to tell, or to be told.

So *Nihil dictu fædum, viſuque hæc limina tangat; intra quæ puer eſt*,
Juv. *Difficilis res eſt inventu verus amicus*; *Fas* v. *nefas eſt dictu*; *Opus
eſt ſcitu*, Cic.

Obſ. 1. The ſupine in *u*, being uſed in a paſſive ſenſe, hardly ever
governs any caſe. It is ſometimes, eſpecially in old writers, put after
verbs of motion; as, *Nunc obſonatu redeo*, from getting proviſions, Plaut.
Primus cubitu ſurgat (villicus.) from bed. *poſtremus cubitum eat*, Cato.

Obſ. 2. This ſupine may be rendered by the infinitive or gerund
with the prepoſition *ad*; as, *Difficile cognitu, cognoſci*, or *ad cognoſcen-
dum*; *Res facilis ad credendum*, Cic.

Obſ. 3. The ſupines being nothing elſe but verbal nouns of the
fourth declenſion, uſed only in the accuſative and ablative ſingular,
are governed in theſe caſes by prepoſitions underſtood; the ſupine in
um by the prepoſition *ad*, and the ſupine in *u* by the prepoſition *in*.

The CONSTRUCTION of INDECLINABLE WORDS.

1. The CONSTRUCTION of ADVERBS.

XXXIX. Adverbs are joined to Verbs and
Participles, to adjectives, and to other adverbs; as,

Bene ſcribit, He writes well.   *Fortiter pugnans*, Fighting bravely.
Servus egregiè fidelis, A ſlave re-   *Satis bene*, Well enough.
markably faithful.

Obſ.

OBS. 1.   Adverbs are sometimes likewise joined to substantives ; as,

Homerus planè orator ; planè nofter, verò Metellus, Cic. So, *Hodie manè ; cras manè, heri manè ; hodie vefperi,* &c. *tam manè, tam vefperè.*

OBS. 2.   The adverb for the most part in Latin, and always in English, is placed near to the word which it modifies or affects.

OBS. 3.   Two negatives, both in Latin and English, are equivalent to an affirmative ; as,

Nec non fenferunt, Nor did they not perceive, i. e. *Et fenferunt,* And they did perceive ; *Non poteram non exanimari metu,* Cic. Examples however of the contrary of this sometimes occur in good authors, both English and Latin. Thus two or three negative participles are placed before the fubjunctive mode to exprefs a ftronger negation. *Neque tu haud dicas tibi non prædictum,* And do not fay that you were not forewarned, Ter.

But what chiefly deferves attention in Adverbs, is the degree of comparifon and the mode with which they are joined. 1. *Apprimè admodum, vehementer, maximè, perquam, valdè oppidò,* &c. and *per* in compofition, are ufually joined to the pofitive ; as, *Utrique noftrum gratum admodum feceris,* You will do what is very agreeable to both of us, Cic. *perquam puerile,* very childifh ; *oppidò pauci,* very few ; *perfacile eft,* &c. In like manner, *Parum, multum, nimium, tantum, quantum, aliquantum ;* as, *In rebus apertiffimis nimium longi fumus ; parum firmus, multum bonus,* Cic. Adverbs in *um* are fometimes alfo joined to comparatives ; as, *Forma viri aliquantùm amplior humanâ,* Liv.

QUAM is joined to the pofitive or fuperlative in different fenfes ; as, *Quam difficile eft !* How difficult it is ! *Quam crudelis,* or *Ut crudelis eft !* How cruel he is ! *Flens quam familieriter,* very familiarly, Ter. So *quam feverè,* very feverely, Cic. *Quam latè,* very widely, Caf. *Tam multa, quam,* &c. as many things as, &c. *Quam maximas poteft copias armat,* as great as poffible, Sall. *Quam maximas gratias agit, quam primum, quam fæpiffimè,* Cic. *Quam quifque peffimè fecit, tum maximè tutus eft,* Sall.

FACILE, for *haud dubiè,* undoubtedly, clearly, is joined to fuperlatives or words of a fimilar meaning ; as, *Facilè doctiffimus, facilè princeps,* v. *præcipuus.* LONGE, to comparatives or fuperlatives, rarely to the pofitive ; as, *Longè eloquentiffimus Plato,* Cic. *Pedibus longè melior Lycus,* Virg.

2. CUM, when, is conftrued with the indicative or fubjunctive, oftener with the latter ; DUM, whilft, or how long, with the indicative ; as, *Dum hæc agentur ; Ægroto, dum anima eft, fpes effe dicitur,* Cic. *Donec eris felix, multos numerabis amicos,* Ovid. DUM and DONEC, for *ufque ux,* until, fometimes with the indicative and fometimes with the fubjunctive ; as, *Operior, dum ifta cognofco,* Cic. *Haud definam,*

donec perfecero, Ter. So QUOAD, for *quamdiu, quantum, quatenus*, as long, as much, as far as; thus, *Quoad Catilina fuit in urbe; Quoad tibi æquum videbitur; quoad possem & liceret; quoad progredi potuerit amentia*, Cic. But QUOAD, until, oftener with the subjunctive; as, *Thessalonicæ esse statueram, quoad aliquid ad me scriberes*, Cic. but not always; *Non faciam finem rogandi, quoad nunciatum erit te fecisse*, Cic. The pronoun *ejus*, with *facere* or *fieri* is elegantly added to *quoad*; as, *Quoad ejus facere poteris; Quoad ejus fieri possit*, Cic. *Ejus* is thought to be here governed by *aliquid* or some such word understood. *Quoad corpus, quoad animam*, for *secundum*, or *quod attinet ad corpus* vel *animam*, as to the body or soul, is esteemed by the best grammarians not to be good Latin.

3. POSTQUAM or POSTEAQUAM, after, is usually joined with the Indic. ANTEQUAM, PRIUSQUAM, before; SIMUL, SIMULAC, SIMUL, ATQUE, SIMUL UT, as soon as; UBI, when, sometimes with the Ind. and sometimes with the Subj. as, *Antequam dico* or *dicam*, Cic. *Simulac persensit*, Virg. *Simul ut videro Curionem*, Cic. *Hæc ubi dicta dedit*, Liv. *Ubi semel quis pejeraverit, ei credi postea non oportet*, Cic. So NÆ, truly; as, *Næ ego homo sum infelix*, Ter. *Ne tu, si id fecisses, melius famæ consuluisses*, Cic. But NE, not, with the Imperative, or more elegantly with the subjunctive; as, *Ne jura*, Plaut. *Ne post conferas culpam in me*, Ter. *Ne tot annorum felicitatem in unius horæ dederis discrimen*, Liv.

4. QUASI, CEU, TANQUAM, PERINDE, when they denote resemblance, are joined with the Indicative; *Fuit olim, quasi ego sum, senex*, Plaut. *Adversi rupto ceu quondam turbine venti confligunt*, Virg. *Hæc omnia perinde sunt, ut aguntur.* But when used ironically, they have the subjunctive; as, *Quasi de verbo, non de re laboretur*, Cic.

5. UTINAM, O SI, UT for *utinam*, I wish, take the Subjunctive; as, *Utinam ea res ei voluptati sit*, Cic. *O mihi præteritos referat si Jupiter annos*, Virg. *Ut illum dii deæque perdant*, Ter.

6. UT, when or after, takes the indicative; as, *Ut discessit, venit*, &c. ¶ Also for *quam* or *quomodo*, how! as, *Ut valet! Ut falsus animi est! Ut sæpe summa ingenia in occulto latent!* Plaut. ¶ Or when it simply denotes resemblance; as, *Ut tute es, ita omnes censes esse*, Plaut. ¶ In this sense it sometimes has the subjunctive; as, *Ut sementem feceris, ita metes*, Cic.

7. QUIN for CUR NON, takes the Indic. as, *Quin continetis vocem indicem stultitiæ vestræ?* Cic. ¶ For IMO, nay or but, the Indic. or Imp. rat. as, *Quin est paratum argentum; quin tu hoc audi*, Ter. ¶ For UT NON, QUI, QUÆ, QUOD NON, or QUO MINUS, the Subjunctive; as, *Nulla tam facilis, res, quin difficilis fiet quum invitus facies*, Ter. *Nemo est, quin malit; Facere non possum, quin ad te mittam*, I cannot help sending; *Nihil abest, quin sim miserrimus*, Cic.

The GOVERNMENT of ADVERBS.

XL. Some Adverbs of time, place, and quantity, govern the genitive; as,

Pridie ejus diei,	The day before that day.
Ubique gentium,	Every where.
Satis est verborum,	There is enough of words.

1. Adverbs of time governing the genit. are, *Interea, postea, inde, tunc*; as, *Interea loci,* in the mean time; *Postea loci,* afterwards; *inde, loci,* then; *tunc temporis,* at that time. 2. Of place, *Ubi* and *quo,* with their compounds, *ubique, ubicunque, ubivis, ubiubi,* &c. Also *Eo, huc, uccine, unde, usquam, nusquam, longe, ibidem :* as, *Ubi, quo, quovis,* &c. Also *usquam, nusquam, unde, terrarum,* vel *gentium ; longè gentium ; ibi- dem loci, eo audaciæ, vecordiæ, miseriarum,* &c. to that pitch of bold- ness, madness, misery, &c. 3. Of quantity, *Abunde, affatim, largi- er, nimis, satis, parum, minimè*; as, *Abundè gloriæ, affatim diviniarum, largiter auri, satis loquentiæ, sapientiæ parum est illi* vel *habet,* He has enough of glory, riches, &c. *Minimè gentium,* by no means.

Some add *ergo* and *instar*; as, *Ergo virtutis,* for the sake of virtue, Cic. *Instar montis,* like a mountain, Virg. : But these are properly nouns

Obs. 1. These adverbs are thought to govern the genitive, because they imply in themselves the force of a substantive; as, *Potentiæ glo- riæque abundè adeptus,* the same with *abundantiam gloriæ :* or *res, locus,* or *negotium* and a preposition, may be understood; as, *Interea loci,* i. e. *inter ea negotia loci ; Ubi terrarum,* for *in quo loco terrarum.*

Obs. 2. We usually say, *pridie, postridie ejus diei,* seldom *diem*; but *pridie, postridie Kalendas, Nonas, Idus, ludos Apollinares, natalem ejus, absolutionem ejus,* &c. rarely *Kalendarum,* &c.

Obs. 3. *En* and *ecce* are construed either with the nom- native or accusative; as,

En hostis, or *hostem ; Ecce miserum hominem,* Cic. Sometimes a da- tive is added; as, *Ecce tibi Strato,* Ter. *Ecce duas* (scil. aras.) *tibi Daphni,* Virg. In like manner is construed *hem* put for *ecce* ; as, *Hem tibi Davum,* Ter. But in all these examples some verb must be un- derstood.

XLI. Some derivative adverbs govern the case of their primitives; as,

Omnium optimè loquitur,	He speaks the best of all.
Convenienter naturæ,	Agreeably to nature.
Venit obviam ei,	He came to meet him.
Proximè castris or *castra,*	Next the camp.

The CONSTRUCTION of PREPOSITIONS.

1. *PREPOSITIONS governing the Accusative.)*

AD astra,) *to the stars;* religari ad asserem, *to be bound to a plank;* ad diem veniam, solvam, &c. *at* or *on;* ad portam, ostium, fores, *at. before;* ad urbem, Tiberim, *near, at;* ad templa supplicatio, *in;* ad summum, *at most,* or *to the top;* ad summam, *on the whole;* Cic.; ad ultimum, extremum, *at last, finally;* ad v. in speciem, *to appearance;* mentis ad omnia capacitas; annus fatalis ad interitum; lenius ad severitatem, *for, with respect to,* Cic.; ad vivum, *sc.* corpus, *to the quick;* ad judicem agere, *before;* nihil ad Cæsarem, *in comparison of;* numero ad duodecim, *to the number of:* omnes ad unum, *to a man;* ad hoc, *besides;* ad vulgi opinionem, *according to;* homo ad unguem factus, *an accomplished man;* herbæ ad unam messe, *by the light of,* Virg. ad tempus venit, *at;* Ira brevis est & ad tempus, *for;* ad tempus consilium capiam, *according to;* Cic.; ad decem annos *after;* annos ad quinquaginta natus, *about:* Cic. nebula erat ad multum diei, *for a great part of the day;* Liv.; ad pedes jacēre, provolvi, procumbere, & ad genua; ad manus esse, *at;* ad manus venire, *to come to a close engagement;* ad libellam deberi, *to a farthing, no more and no less;* ad amussim, *exactly;* ad hæc visa auditaque, *upon seeing and hearing these things,* Liv.

AD seems sometimes to be taken adverbially; as, Ad duo millia cæsa sunt; ad mille hominum amissum est; ad ducenti perierunt, *about,* Liv.

APUD forum, *at;* apud me cœnabis, *at my house;* apud senatum, judices, v. aliquem dicere, *before;* apud majores nostros, *among;* apud Xenophontem, *in the book of;* Est mihi fides, vel valeo, apud illum, *I have credit with him;* facio te apud illum deum, Ter.

ANTE diem, focum, &c. *before.*

ADVERSUS, v. -um; CONTRA hostes, *against;* adversus infimos justitia est servanda, *towards;* adversum hunc loqui, *to,* Ter. Lerina adversum Antipolim, *over against,* Plin.

CIS vel CITRA flumen, *on this side;* citra necessitatem, *without;* Ede citra cruditatem, bibe citra ebrietatem, Senec.

CIRCUM & CIRCA regem, *about;* Varia circa hæc opinio, Plin.

ERGA amicos, *towards.* EXTRA muros; Extra jocum, periculum noxiam, sortem, *without;* nemo extra te, *besides;* extra conjurationem, *not concerned in,* Sall.

INFRA tectum, *below the roof.*

INTER fratres, *among;* inter & super cœnam, *during the time of;* inter hæc parata, *during these preparations;* Sall. Inter tot annos, *in;* Cic. Inter diem, *whence,* interdiu, *in the day time;* inter se amant, *they love one another;* Quasi non nôrimus nos inter nos, Ter.

INTRA privatos parietes, intra paucos annos, *within;* intra famum est, *less than report.* Quinct.

JUXTA macellum, *near the shambles.*

OB lucrum, *for gain;* ob oculos, *before;* ob industriam, *for* de industria, *on purpose,* Plaut.

PENES quem, *or* quem penes,

is

in the power of ; Penes te es ? *Are you in your senses ?* Hor.

PER agros, *through* ; per vim, per scelus, *by* ; per anni tempus, per ætatem licet, *for, by reason of.*

PONE caput, *behind.*

POST hoc tempus, *after* ; poſt tergum, *behind* ; poſt homines natos, poſt hominum memoriam, *ſince the world began.*

PRÆTER te nemo, *no body beſides, or except* ; præter caſam fugere, *beyond* ; præter legem, morem, æquum & bonum, ſpem, opinionem, &c. *contrary to, againſt, beyond* ; præter cæteros excellere, lamentari, *above* ; præter ripam ire, *along, near* ; præter oculos, *before,* Cic.

PROPTER virtutem, *for, on account of* ; propter aquæ rivum, *near, hard by,* Virg.

SECUNLUM facta & virtutes tuas, *according to* ; Ter. ſecundum littus, ſecundum aurem vulneratus eſt, *near to* ; in actione ſecundum vocem, vultus plurimum valet ; ſecundum patrem tu es proximus, *after, next to* ; Prætor ſecundum me decrevit, ſententiam dedit. *for, in my favour,* Cic.

SECUS viam, *by, along.*

SUPRA terram, *above.*

TRANS mare, *over, beyond.*

ULTRA oceanum, *beyond.*

To prepoſitions governing the accuſative are commonly added CIRCITER, PROPE, USQUE & VERSUS ; as Circiter meridiem, *about mid-day* ; prope muros, *near the walls* ; uſque Puteolos, Tharſum uſque, *as far as* ; Orientem verſus, *towards the eaſt.* But in theſe *ad* is underſtood ; which we find ſometimes expreſſed ; as, Prope ad annum, Nep. Ab ovo uſque ad mala, Hor. Ad oceanum verſus, Cæf. In Italiam verſus, Cic.

/PREPOSITIONS governing the Ablative.)

A patre,)ab omnibus, abs te, *by or from* ; a puero, *vel* pueris, a pueritia, incunabulis, teneris unguibus, &c. *from a child, ever ſince childhood* ; ab ovo uſque ad mala, *from the beginning to the end of ſupper* ; a manu, *ſc.* ſervus, *an amanuenſis or clerk* ; ad manum, *a waiting man* ; a pedibus, *a footman* ; a latere principis, *an attendant.* So a ſecretis, rationibus, conſiliis, cyathis, &c. *a ſecretary, accountant, &c.* ; fores a nobis, *for noſtræ.* Injuria ab illo, *for illius,* Ter. a cœna, *after* ; Secundus, tertius a Romulo ; ictus ab latere, *on or in* ; a ſenatu ſtare. *for, in defence of* ; ab oculis doleo, Plaut. ab ingenio impactus, a pecunia & militibus imparatus, *as to,* *with reſpect to,* Cic. Eſt calor a ſole ; omiſſiores ab re, *too careleſs about money* ; a villa mercenarium vidi, Ter.

ABSQUE cauſa, *without* ; abſque te eſſet, recte ego mihi vidiſſem, *i. e.* ſi tu non eſſes, niſi tu eſſes, *but for you, had it not been for you,* Ter. Abſque *is chiefly uſed by comic writers* ; fine, *by orators.*

CLAM patre & patrem, *without the knowledge of.*

CORAM omnibus, *before, in preſence of.*

CUM exercitu, *with* ; teſtis mecum eſt annulus, *in my poſſeſſion,* Ter. cum prima luce, *at break of day* ; cum imperio eſſe, *in* ; cum primis, in primis, *in the firſt place*; cum metu dicere, cum lætitia vivere, cum cura, &c. Cic.

S

Cic. *We say*, mecum, tecum, secum, nobiscum, vobiscum ; *rarely* cum me, cum te, &c. *and* quocum *or* cum quo, quibuscum *or* cum quibus.

DE lana caprina rixantur, *about, concerning;* De tanto patrimonio nihil relictum est, *of;* de loco superiore, *from;* de die, *by day;* de nocte, *by night;* de integro, *anew, afresh;* de *v.* ex improviso, *unexpectedly;* de *v.* ex industria, *on purpose;* de meo, *at my expense;* Id de lucro putato esse, *clear gain;* Ter. de *v.* ex compacto agere, *by agreement;* de transverso, *cross-wise, athwart;* de *v.* ex ejus sententia, consilio, *according to;* qua *v.* hac de causa, *for;* homo de plebe ; templum de marmore, *of;* de scripto dicere, *to read a speech;* de Filio emit, *from,* Cic. De servis fidelissimus ; de ipsius exercitu non amplius hominum mille cecidit, Nep. Robur de exercitu, Liv. Adolescens de summo loco, Plaut. De procul aspicere, Id.

E foro, Ex ædibus, *from, out of;* e contrario, *v.* contraria parte, *on the contrary;* e regione, *over against;* e republica, e re alicujus, *for the good of;* statim e somno, ex fuga, ex tanta properantia, aliud ex alio malum, *from, after;* e vestigio, *out of hand, immediately;* poculum ex auro ; ex equo pugnare, *on horseback;* facere pugnam ex commodo, *on advantageous ground,* Sall. diem ex die expectare, *from day to day, day after day;* ex ordine, *in order;* magna ex parte, *for the most part;* ex supervacuo, *superfluously;* ex tua dignitate *v.* virtute, ex decreto senatûs, e natura, *according to;* so vulgus ex veritate pauca, ex opinione multa æstimat ; ex *v.* de mo-

re, ad *v.* in morem alicujus : Ex animo, *from the heart;* Insolentia ex prosperis rebus, e via languere, ex doctrina nobilis, *on account of;* ex usu est tibi, *of advantage;* ex eo die, *since,* ex amicis certis certissimus, *of or among;* ex pedibus laborare, *to be ill of the gout,* Cic. E re nata, *as the matter stands,* Ter. Commenta mater est, esse ex alio viro, nescio quo, puerum natum, *by.* Id.

PRO gloria certare, *for;* Rati noctem pro se, *favourable to them;* Sall. Hoc est pro me, Cic. pro templo, tribunali, concione, rostris, castris, foribus, *before;* pro sua dignitate, sapientia, &c. pro potestate cogere, pro tempore, re, loco, suo jure, *according to;* est pro prætore, pro te molam, comes facundus pro vehiculo est, *for, instead of;* pro viribus, pro parte virili, pro sua quisque parte *v.* facultate, *to one's ability or power;* Parum tibi pro eo, quod a te habeo, reddidi, *in comparison of, considering,* Cic. pro' ut, pro eo ac, pro eo ut mereor, *as I deserve;* pro se quisque, uterque, &c. *for his own part;* pro rata parte, pro portione, *in proportion;* pro cive se gerit; agere pro victoribus; pro suo uti; pro rupto fædus habet, *for, as;* so pro certo, infecto, comperto, nihilo, concesso, &c. habeo, duco. Pro occiso, relictus est, Cic.

PRÆ se pugionem tulit, *before;* speciem præ se boni viri fert, *pretends to be,* Ter. præ lacrymis non possum scribere, *for, because of;* illum præ me contempsi, *in comparison of:* So the *adv.* præut; *as,* præut hujus rabies quæ dabit, Ter.

PALAM populo, omnibus, *before, with the knowledge of.*

SINE labore, *without*; sine ulla causa, pompa, molestia, querela, impensa, &c.; homo sine reside, spe, fortunis, sede, &c. Cic.

Capulo TENUS, *up to the hilt.* *Tenus* is construed with the genitive plural, when the word wants the sing.; as, *Cumarum tenus*, as far as *Cumæ* : or when we speak of things, of which we have by nature only two;) as, Oculorum, aurium, narium, la-brorum, lumborum, crurum tenus, *up to:* *We also find* Corcyræ tenus, & ostiis tenus, Liv. Colchis tenus, Flor. Pectoribus tenus, Ovid.

To prepositions governing the abl. is commonly added PROCUL ; as, *Procul domo*, far from home; but here *a* is understood, which is also often expressed; as, *Procul a patria*, Virg. *Procul ab ostentatione.* Quinct. *Culpa est procul a me*, Ter.

3. PREPOSITIONS governing the Accus. and Abl.)

XLIV. The prepositions *in, sub, super,* and *subter,* govern the accusative, when motion to a place is signified; but when motion or rest in a place is signified, *in* and *sub* govern the ablative; *super* and *subter* either the accusative or ablative.

IN when it signifies *into,* governs the accusative; when it signifies *in* or *among,* it governs the ablative;) as,

IN urbem ire, *into*; amor in patriam, in te benignus, *towards*; in lucem, *until day*; in eanr sententiam, *to that purpose, on that head*; in rem tuam est, *for your advantage*; in utramque partem disputare, *on both sides, for and against*; litura in nomen, *on,* Cic. potestas in filium, *over*; in aliquem dicere, *against*; mirum in modum, *after*; in pedes stare, in aurem dormire, *on*; in os laudare, *to, before*; in *v.* inter patres lectus, *into the number of*; in vulgus probari, spargere, &c. *among*; crescit in dies in singulos dies, omnes in dies, *every day*; in diem posterum, proximum, decimum, *against*; in diem vivere, *to live from hand to mouth, not to think of to-morrow*; Est in diem, *till* happen some time after, Ter. Induciæ in duos menses datæ, in hunc diem, annum, &c. *for*; Ternis assibus in pedem, *v.* in singulos pedes; transegit, *He bargained for three shillings a foot, or for every foot*; So in jugerum, militem, capita, naves, &c. In medimna singula, H. S. quinos denos dedisti, Cic.

IN portu navigo, in tempore, *in*; esse in potestate, *v.* in potestatem, honore *vel* honorem, mente *v.* mentem: in manu *v* manibus esse; habere, tenere, *in one's power, on hand*; in amicis, *among*; in oculis, *before*: Occisus est in provinciam, *for in* provincia, Sall. In pueritia, adolescentia, senectute, absentia, *for* puer *or* pueri, *when a*

key

boy or *bys*, &c. Hoc in tempore, Nep. In loco fratris diligere, *for* ut fratrem, Ter. SUB terras ibit imagno, sub aspectum cadit, *under*; sub ipsum funus, *near*, *just before*. Hor. sub lucem, ortum lucis, noctem, vesperam, brumam, *i. e.* incipiente luce, &c. *at the dawn of day, &c.*; sub idem tempus, *about*; sub eas literas recitatæ sunt tuæ, sub festos dies, *after*, Cic.

SUB muro, rege, pedibus, &c. *under*; sub urbe, *near*, Ter. sub ea conditione, *v. -em on or with*. SUPER Numidiam, *above, beyond*; super ripas, *upon*; super hæc; super morbum etiam fames affixit, *besides*, Liv. super arbore, fronde super viridi, *upon*; super hac re scribere, his accensa super, *concerning*; alii super alios trucidantur, Liv. Super cœnam, super vinum & epulas, *for* inter, *during*, Curt. Nec super ipse suâ molitur laude laborem, *for*, Virg. SUBTER terram *vel* terra, *under*.

Obs. 1. Prepositions in English have always after them the accusative or objective case. And when prepositions in English or Latin do not govern a case, they are reckoned adverbs.

Such are *Ante, circa, clam, coram, contra, infra, intra, juxta, palam, pone, post, propter, secus, subter, super, supra, ultra*. But in most of these the case seems to be implied in the sense; as, *Longo post tempore venit*, sc. *post id tempus*. *Adversus, juxta, propter, secus; secundum, & clam*, are by some thought to be always adverbs, having a preposition understood when they govern a case. So other adverbs also are construed with the acc. or abl. as, *Intus cellam*, for *intra*, Liv. *Intus templo divum*, sc. *in*, Virg. *Simul his*, sc. *cum*, Hor.

Obs. 2. A and E are only put before consonants; AB and EX, usually before vowels, and sometimes also before consonants; as,

A patre, e regione: ab initio, ab rege; ex urbe, ex parte: abs before *q* and *t*; as, *abs te, abs quivis homine*, Ter. Some phrases are used only with *e*; as, *e longinquo, e regione, e vestigio, e re mea est*, &c. Some only with *ex*; as, *Ex compacto, ex tempore, magna ex parte*, &c.

Obs. 3. Prepositions are often understood; as, *Devenere locos*, scil. *ad*; *It portis*, sc. *ex*, Virg. *Nunc id prodeo*, scil. *ob* vel *propter*, Ter. *Maria aspera juro*, scil. *per*, Virg. *Ut se loco movere non possent*, scil. *e* vel *de*, Cæs. *Vina promens dolio*, scil. *ex*, Hor. *Quid illi facias? Quid me fiet*, sc. *de*, Ter. And so in English, *Shew me the book; Get me some paper*, that is, *to me, for me*. We sometimes find the word to which the preposition refers, suppressed; as, *Circum Concordiæ*, sc. *ædem*, Sall. *Round St. Paul's*, namely, *church*; *Campum Stellatem divisit extra sortem ad viginti millibus civium*, i. e. *civium millibus ad viginti millia*, Suet. But this is most frequently the case after prepositions in composition; thus, *Emittere servum*, scil. *manu*, Plaut. *Evomere virus*, scil. *ore*, Cic. *Educere copias*, scil. *castris*, Cæs.

XLV. A prepofition in compofition often governs the fame cafe, as when it ftands by itfelf; as,

Adeamus fcholam,   Let us go to the fchool.
Exeamus fcholâ,   Let us go out of the fchool.

Obf. 1. The prepofition with which the verb is compounded, is often repeated; as, *Adire ad fcholam; Exire e fchola; Adgredi aliquid,* or *ad aliquid; ingredi orationem* vel *in orationem; inducere animum, & in animum; evadere undis & ex undis; decedere de fuo jure, decedere viâ* vel *de via; expellere, ejicere, exterminare, extrudere, exturbare urbe, & ex urbe.* Some do not repeat the prepofition; as, *Affari, alloqui, allatrare aliquem,* not *ad aliquem.* So *Alluere urbem; accolere flumen; circumvenire aliquem; præterire injuriam; abdicare fe magiftratu,* (alfo *abdicare magiftratum*); *tranfducere exercitum fluvium,* &c. Others are only conftrued with the prepofition; as, *Accurrere ad aliquem, adhortari ad aliquid, incidere in morbum, avocare a ftudiis, avertere ab incepto,* &c.

Some admit other prepofitions; as, *Abire; demigrare loco;* & *a, de, ex loco; abftrahere aliquem a, de,* vel *e confpectu; Defiftere fententiâ, a* vel *de fententia, Excidere manibus, de* vel *e manibus,* &c.

Obf. 2. Some verbs compounded with *e* or *ex* govern either the ablative or accufative; as,

Egredi urbe or *urbem,* fc. *extra; egredi extra vallum,* Nep. *Evadere infidiis* or *infidias. Patrios excedere muros,* Lucan. *Scelerata excedere terrâ,* Virg. *Elabi ex manibus; pugnam, vincula,* Tac.

Obf. 3. This rule does not take place, unlefs when the prepofition may be disjoined from the verb, and put before the noun by itfelf; as, *Alloquor patrem,* or *loquor ad patrem.*

3. The Construction of Interjections.

XLVI. The interjections *O, heu,* and *proh,* are conftrued with the nominative, accufative, or vocative; as,

O vir bonus or *bone!* O good man! *Heu me miferum!* Ah wretched me!

So, *O vir fortis atque amicus!* Ter. *Heu vanitas humana!* Plin. *Heu miferande puer!* Virg. *O præclarum cuftodem ovium* (ut aiunt) *lupum!* Cic.

XLVII. *Hei* and *væ* govern the dative; as,

Hei mihi! Ah me!   *Væ vobis!* Wo to you!

Obf. 1. *Heus* and *ohe* are joined only with the vocative; as, *Heus Syre,* Ter. *Ohe libelle!* Martial. *Proh* or *pro, ah, vah, hem,* have generally either the accufative or vocative; as, *Proh hominum fidem!* Ter. *Proh Sancte Jupiter!* Cic.: *Hem aftutias!* Ter.

Obf. 2. Interjections cannot properly have either concord or government. They are only mere founds excited by paffion, and have no juft connection with any other part of a fentence. Whatever cafe

therefore

therefore is joined with them, must depend on some other word understood, except the vocative, which is always placed absolutely: thus, *Heu me miserum !* stands for *Heu ! quam me miserum sentio ! Hei mihi !* for *Hei ! malum est mihi ! Proh dolor !* for *Proh ! quantus est dolor !* and so in other examples.

The CONSTRUCTION of CIRCUMSTANCES.

The circumstances, which in Latin are expressed in different cases, are, 1. The *Price of a thing.* 2. The *Cause, Manner,* and *Instrument.* 3. *Place.* 4. *Measure* and *Distance.* 5. *Time.*

1. PRICE.

XLVIII. The price of a thing is put in the ablative ; as,

Emi librum duobus assibus,	I bought a book for two shillings.
Constitit talento,	It cost a talent.

So *Asse carum est ; vile viginti minis ; auro venale,* &c. *Nocet empta dolore voluptas,* Hor. *Spem pretio non emam,* Ter. *Plurimi auro veneunt honores,* Ovid.

¶ These genitives *tanti, quanti, pluris, minoris,* are excepted ; as,

Quanti constitit, How much cost it ? *Asse et pluris,* A shilling and more.

Obs. 1. When the substantive is added, they are put in the ablative ; as, *parvo pretio, impenso pretio vendere,* Cic.

Obs. 2. *Magno, permagno, parvo, paululo, minimo, plurimo,* are often used without the substantive ; as, *Permagno constitit,* scil. *pretio,* Cic. *Heu quanto regnis nox stetit una tuis ?* Ovid. Fast. ii. 812. We also say, *Emi carè, cariùs, carissimè ; bene, meliùs, optimè ; malè, pejùs, viliùs, vilissimè ; Valde carè æstimas : Emit domum prope dimidio cariùs, quam æstimabat,* Cic.

Obs. 3. The ablative of price is properly governed by the preposition *pro* understood, which is likewise sometimes expressed ; as, *Dum pro argenteis decem aureus unus valeret,* Liv.

2. MANNER and CAUSE.

XLIX. The cause, manner, and instrument are put in the ablative ; as,

Palleo metu,	I am pale for fear.
Fecit suo more,	He did it after his own way.
Scribo calamo,	I write with a pen.

So *Ardet dolore ; pallescere culpâ ; æstuare dubitatione ; gestire voluptate vel secundis rebus : Confectus morbo ; affectus beneficiis, gravissimo supplicio ; insignis pietate ; deterior licentiâ : Pietate filius, consiliis pater, amore frater ;* hence *Rex Dei gratiâ. Paritur pax bello,* Nep. *Procedere vento gradu ; Acceptus regio apparatu : Nullo sono convertitur annus,* Juv. *Jam veniet tacito curva senecta pede,* Ovid. *Percutere securi, defendere saxis, configere sagittis,* &c.

Obf. 1. The ablative is here governed by fome prepofition underftood. Before the manner and caufe, the prepofition is fometimes expreffed ; as, *De more matrum locuta est,* Virg. *Magno cum metu ; Hac de caufa : Præ mærore, formidline, &c.* But hardly ever before the inftrument ; as, *Vulnerare aliquem gladio,* not *cum gladio* ; unlefs among the poets, who fometimes add *a* or *ab* ; as, *Trajectus ab enfe,* Ovid.

Obf. 2. When any thing is faid to be in company with another, it is called the ablative of CONCOMITANCY, and has the prepofition *cum* ufually added ; as, *Obfedit curiam cum gladiis : Ingreffus est cum gladio,* Cic.

Obf. 3. Under this rule are comprehended feveral other circumftances, as the matter of which any thing is made, and what is called by grammarians the ADJUNCT, that is, a noun in the ablative joined to a verb or adjective, to exprefs the character or quality of the perfon or thing fpoken of ; as, *Capitolium faxo quadrato conftructum,* Liv. *Floruit acumine ingenii,* Cic. *Pollet opibus, valet armis, viget memoriâ famâ nobilis,* &c. *Æger pedibus.* When we exprefs the matter of which any thing is made, the prepofition is ufually added ; as, *Templum de marmore,* feldom *marmoris* ; *Poculum ex auro factum,* Cic.

3. PLACE.

The circumftances of place may be reduced to four particulars. 1. The place *where,* or *in which.* 2. The place *whither,* or *to which.* 3. The place *whence,* or *from which.* 4. The place *by* or *through which.*

AT or IN a place is put in the genitive ; unlefs the noun be of the third declenfion, or of the plural number, and then it is expreffed in the ablative.

TO a place is put in the accufative ; FROM or BY a place, in the ablative.

But thefe cafes will be more exactly afcertained by reducing the circumftances of place to particular queftions.

1. *The Place* WHERE.

L. When the queftion is made by *Ubi ?* Where ? the name of a town is put in the genitive ; as,

Vixit

| *Vixit Romæ,* | He lived at Rome. |
| *Mortuus eſt Londini,* | He died at London. |

¶ But if the name of a town be of the third declenſion or plural number, it is expreſſed in the ablative; as,

| *Habitat Carthagine,* | He dwells at Carthage. |
| *Studuit Pariſiis,* | He ſtudied at Paris. . |

Obſ. 1. When a thing is ſaid to be done, not in the place itſelf, but in its neighbourhood or near it, we always uſe the prepoſition *ad.* or *apud;* as, *Ad* or *apud Trojam,* At *or* near Troy.

Obſ. 2. The name of a town, when put in the ablative, is here governed by the prepoſition *in* underſtood; but if it be in the genitive, we muſt ſupply *in urbe,* or *in oppido.* Hence, when the name of a town is joined with an adjective or common noun, the prepoſition is generally expreſſed: thus, we do not ſay, *Natus eſt Romæ urbis celebris:* but either *Romæ in celebri urbe,* or *in Romæ celebri urbe,* or *in Roma celebri urbe,* or ſometimes *Romæ celebri urbe.* In like manner, we uſually ſay, *Habitat in urbe Carthagine,* with the prepoſition. We likewiſe find, *Habitat Carthagini,* which is ſometimes the termination of the ablative, when the queſtion is made by *ubi?*

2. *The Place* WHITHER.

LI. When the queſtion is made by *Quo?* Whither? the name of a town is put in the accuſative; as,

| *Venit Romam,* | He came to Rome. |
| *Profectus eſt Athenas,* | He went to Athens. |

Obſ. 1. We find the dative alſo uſed among the poets, but more ſeldom; as, *Carthagini nuncia mittam,* Horat.

Obſ. 2. Names of towns are ſometimes put in the accuſative, after verbs of telling and giving, where motion to a place is implied; as, *Romam erat nunciatum,* The report was carried to Rome, Liv. *Hæc nunciant domum Albani,* Id. *Meſſanam litteras dedit,* Cic.

3. *The Place* WHENCE.

LII. When the queſtion is made by *Unde?* Whence? or *Qua?* By *or* through what place? the name of a town is put in the ablative; as,

Diſceſſit

| *Discessit Corintho,* | He departed from Corinth. |
| *Laodiceâ iter faciebat,* | He went through Laodicea. |

When motion *by* or *through* a place is signified, the prepofition *per* is commonly ufed ; as, *Per Thebas iter fecit,* Nep.

Domus and *Rus.*

LIII. *Domus* and *rus* are conftrued the fame way as names of towns ; as,

Manet domi,	He ftays at home.
Domum revertitur,	He returns home.
Domo arceffitus fum,	I am called from home.
Vivit rure, or more frequently *ruri,*	He lives in the country.
Rediit rure,	He is returned from the country.
Abiit rus,	He is gone to the country.

Obf. 1. *Humi, militiæ,* and *belli,* are likewife conftrued in the genitive, as names of towns ; thus,

Domi et militiæ, or *belli,* At home and abroad. *Jacet humi,* He lies on the ground.

Obf. 2. When *Domus* is joined with an adjective, we commonly ufe a prepofition ; as, *In domo paterna,* not *domi paternæ* ; So, *Ad domum paternam : Ex domo paternâ.* Unlefs when it is joined with thefe poffeffives, *Meus, tuus, fuus, nofter, vefter, regius,* and *alienus* ; as, *Domi meæ vixit,* Cic. *Regiam domum comportant,* Sall.

Obf 3. When *domus* has another fubftantive in the genitive after it, the prepofition is fometimes ufed and fometimes not ; as, *Deprehenfus eft domi, domo,* or *in domo Cæfaris.*

LIV. To names of countries, provinces, and all other places, except towns, the prepofition is commonly added ; as,

When the queftion is made by

Ubi ? *Natus in Italia, in Latio, in urbe, &c.*
Quo ? *Abiit in Italiam, in Latium, in,* or *ad urbem, &c.*
Unde ? *Rediit ex Italia, e Latio, ex urbe, &c.*
Qua ? *Tranfit per Italiam, per Latium, per urbem, &c.*

Obf. 1. A prepofition is often added to names of towns ; as, *In Roma* for *Romæ ; ad Romam, ex Roma, &c.*

Peto always governs the accufative as an active verb,
without

without a prepofition; as, *Petivit Egyptum*, He went to Egypt.

Obf. 2. Names of countries, provinces, &c. are fometimes conftrued without the prepofition like names of towns; as, *Pompeius Cypri vifus eft*, Cæf. *Cretæ juffit confidere Apollo*, Virg. *Non Lybiæ*, for *in Lybia*; *non antè Tyro*, for *Tyri*. Id. Æn. iv. 36. *Venit Sardiniam*, Cic. *Romæ, Numidiæque facinora ejus memorat*, Sall.

4. MEASURE and DISTANCE.

LV.] Meafure or diftance is put in the accufative, and fometimes in the ablative;] as,

Murus eft decem pedes altus,	The wall is ten feet high.
Urbs diftat triginta millia, or *triginta millibus paffuum*,	The city is thirty miles diftant;
Iter, or *itinere unius dici*,	One day's journey.

Obf. 1.] The accufative or ablative of meafure is put after adjectives and verbs of dimenfion;] as, *Longus, latus, craffus, profundus*, and *altus : Patet, porrigitur, eminet, &c.* The names of meafure are *pes, cubitus, ulna, paffus, digitus*, an inch; *palmus*, a fpan, an hand-breadth, &c. The accufative or ablative of diftance is ufed only after verbs which exprefs motion or diftance; as, *Eo, curro, abfum, difto, &c.* The accufative is governed by *ad* or *per* underftood, and the ablative by *a* or *ab*.

Obf. 2. When we exprefs the meafure of more things than one, we commonly ufe the diftributive number; as, *Muri funt denos pedes alti*, and fometimes *denûm pedum*, for *denorum*, in the genitive, *ad menfuram* being underftood. But the genitive is only ufed to exprefs the meafure of things in the plural number.

Obf. 3. When we exprefs the diftance of a place where any thing is done, we commonly ufe the ablative; or the accufative with the prepofition *ad*; as, *Sex millibus paffuum ab urbe confedit*, or *ad fex millia paffuum*, Cæf. *Ad quintum milliarium* v. *milliare confedit*, Cic. *Ad quintum lapidem*, Nep.

Obf. 4.] The excefs or difference of meafure and diftance is put in the ablative;] as,

Hoc lignum excedit illud digito. Toto vertice fupra eft, Virg. *Britannia longitudo ejus latitudinem ducentis quadraginta milliaribus fuperat.*

5. TIME

5. TIME.

LVI. When the queſtion is made by *Quando?* When? time is put in the ablative ; as,

Venit horâ tertiâ,	He came at three o'clock.

¶ When the queſtion is made by *Quamdiu?* How long? time is put in the accuſative or ablative, but oftener in the accuſative ; as,

Manſit paucos dies,	He ſtaid a few days.
Sex menſibus abfuit,	He was away ſix months.

* *Or thus*, Time *when* is put in the ablative, time *how long* is put in the accuſative.)

Obſ. 1. When we ſpeak of any precife time, it is put in the ablative ; but when continuance of time is expreſſed, it is put for the moſt part in the accuſative.

Obſ. 2. All the circumſtances of time are often expreſſed with a prepoſition ; as, *In praſentia*, or *in praſenti*, ſcil. *tempore*; *in* vel *ad praſens*; *Per decem annos* ; *Surgunt de noſte* ; *ad horam deſtinatam* ; *Intra annum* ; *Per idem tempus, ad Kalendas ſoluturos ait*, Suet.   The prepoſition *ad* or *circa* is ſometimes ſuppreſſed, as in theſe expreſſions, *hoc, illud, id, iſthuc, ætatis, temporis, horæ, &c.* for *hac ætate, hoc tempore, &c.*   And *ante* or ſome other word ; as, *Annos natus unum & viginti*, ſc. *ante*.   *Siculi quotannis tributa conferunt, ſc. tot annis, quot* vel *quotquot ſunt*, Cic.   *Prope diem*, ſc. *ad* ſoon ; *Oppidum paucis diebus, quibus eò ventum eſt, expugnatum, ſc. poſt eos dies*, Cæſ.   *Ante diem tertium Kalendas Maias accepi tuas literas*, for *die tertio ante*, Cic.   *Qui dies futurus eſſet inante diem octavum Kalendas Novembris*, Id.   *Exante diem quintum Kal. Octob.* Liv.   *Lacedæmonii ſeptingentos jam annos amplius unis moribus et nunquam mutatis legibus vivunt, ſc. quam per*, Cic.   We find, *Primum ſtipendium meruit annorum decem ſeptemque*, ſc. *Atticus* ; for *ſeptemdecim annos natus*, ſeventeen years old, Nep.

Obſ. 3. The adverb *ABHINC*, which is commonly uſed with reſpect to paſt time, is joined with the accuſative or ablative without a prepoſition ; as, *factum eſt abhinc biennio* or *biennium*, It was done two years ago.   So likewiſe are *poſt* and *ante* ; as, *Paucos poſt annos:* but here, *ea* or *id* may be underſtood.

COMPOUND SENTENCES.

A compound ſentence is that which has more than one nominative, or one finite verb.

'A compound ſentence is made up of two or more ſimple ſentences or *phraſes*, and is commonly called a *Period*.

The

The parts of which a compound sentence confiſts, are called *Members* or *Clauſes*.

In every compound sentence there are either several subjects, and one attribute, or several attributes, and one subject, or both several subjects and several attributes : That is, there are either several nominatives applied to the same verb, or several verbs applied to the same nominative, or both.

Every verb marks a judgment or attribute, and every attribute muſt have a subject. There muſt therefore be in every sentence or period as many prepoſitions, as there are verbs of a finite mode.

¶ Sentences are compounded by means of relatives and conjunctions ; ſas,

> *Happy is the man who loveth religion and practiſeth virtue.*

The CONSTRUCTION of RELATIVES.

LVII. ſThe relative *Qui, Quæ, Quod,* agrees with the antecedent in gender, number, and perſon ; and is conſtrued through all the caſes, as the antecedent would be in its place ; ſas,

	Singular.	Plural.
Vir qui,	The man who.	*Viri qui.*
Fæmina quæ,	The woman who.	*Fæminæ quæ.*
Negotium quod,	The thing which.	*Negotia quæ.*
Ego qui ſcribo,	I who write.	*Nos qui ſcribimus.*
Tu qui ſcribis,	Thou who writeſt.	*Vos qui ſcribitis.*
Vir qui ſcribit,	The man who writes.	*Viri qui ſcribunt.*
Mulier quæ ſcribit,	The woman who writes.	*Mulieres quæ ſcribunt.*
Animal quod currit,	The animal which runs.	*Animalia quæ currunt.*
Vir quem vidi,	The man whom I ſaw.	*Viri quos vidi.*
Mulier quam vidi,	The woman whom I ſaw.	*Mulieres quas vidi.*
Animal quod vidi,	The animal which I ſaw.	*Animalia quæ vidi.*
Vir cui paret,	The man whom he obeys.	*Viri quibus paret.*
Vir cui eſt ſimilis,	The man to whom he is like.	*Viri quibus eſt ſimilis.*
Vir a quo,	The man by whom.	*Viri a quibus.*
Mulier ad quam,	The woman to whom.	*Mulieres ad quas.*
Vir cujus opus eſt,	The man whoſe work it is.	*Viri quorum opus eſt.*

Vir quem miſĕror,
  cujus miſereor vel *miſcreſco,*   ⎱   The man whom I pity.
  cujus me miſeret,   ⎰
  cujus vel *cuja intereſt, &c.*   whoſe intereſt it is, &c.

¶ If no nominative come between the relative and the verb, the relative will be the nominative to the verb. ¶

But

But if a nominative come between the relative and the verb, the relative will be of that cafe, which the verb or noun following, or the prepofition going before, ufe to govern.

Thus the conftruction of the relative requires an acquaintance with moft of the foregoing rules of fyntax, and may ferve as an exercife on all of them

Obf. 1. The relative muft always have an antecedent expreffed or underftood, and therefore may be confidered as an adjective placed between two cafes of the fame fubftantive, of which the one is always expreffed, generally the former ; as,

Vir qui (vir) *legit* ; *vir, quem* (virum) *amo :* Sometimes the latter; as, *Quam quifque nôrit artem, in hac* (arte) *fe exerceat,* Cic. *Eunuchum, quem dedifti nobis, quas turbus dedit,* Ter. fc. *Eunuchus.* Sometimes both cafes are expreffed; as, *Erant omnino duo itinera, quibus itineribus domo exire poffent,* Cæf. Sometimes, though more rarely, both cafes are omitted; as, *Sunt, quos hoc genus minime juvat,* for *funt homines, quos homines, &c.* Hor.

Obf. 2. When the relative is placed between two fubftantives of different genders, it may agree in gender with either of them, though moft commonly with the former ; as,

Vultus quem dixere chaos, Ovid. *Eft locus in carcere, quod Tullianum appellatur,* Sall. *Animal, quem vocamus hominem,* Cic. *Cogito id quod res eft,* Ter. If a part of a fentence be the antecedent, the relative is always put in the neuter gender ; as, *Pompeius fe afflixit, quod mihi eft fummo dolori,* fcil. *Pompeium fe afflixere,* Cic. Sometimes the relative does not agree in gender with the antecedent, but with fome fynonimous word fupplied ; as, *Scelus qui* for *fceleftus,* Ter. *Abundantia earum rerum, quæ mortales prima putant,* fcil. *negotia,* Sall. *Vel virtus tua me vel vicinitas,* quod *ego in aliqua parte amicitiæ puto, facit ut te moneam* fcil. *negotium,* Ter. *In omni Africa, qui agebant* ; for *in omnibus Afris,* Salluft. Jug. 89. *Non diffidentiá futuri, quæ imperaviffet,* for *quod,* Ib. 100.

Obf. 3. When the relative comes after two words of different perfons, it agrees with the firft or fecond perfon rather than the third ; as, *Ego fum vir, qui facio,* fcarcely *facit.* In Englifh it fometimes agrees with either ; as, *I am the man, who make,* or *maketh.* But when once the perfon of the relative is fixed, it ought to be continued through the reft of the fentence ; thus it is proper to fay,

T

" I am

" I am the man, who takes care of your interest," but if
I add, " at the expense of my own," it would be improper. It ought either to be, " his own," or " who take."
In like manner, we may say, " I thank you, who gave,
who did love," &c.   But it is improper to say, " I thank
thee, who gave, who did love :" it should be, " who
gavest, who didst love."   In no part of English syntax are
inaccuracies committed more frequently than in this. Beginners are particularly apt to fall into them, in turning
Latin into English.   The reason of it seems to be our applying *thou* or *you*, *thy* or *your*, promiscuously, to express
the second person singular, whereas the Latins almost always expressed it by *tu* and *tuus*.

Obs. 4.   The antecedent is often implied in a possessive
adjective ; as,

Omnes laudare fortunas meas, qui haberem gnatum tali ingenio præditum,
Ter.   Sometimes the antecedent must be drawn from the sense of the
foregoing words ; as, *Carne pluit, quem imbrem aves rapuisse feruntur ;*
i. e. *pluit imbrem carne, quem imbrem, &c.* Liv.   *Si tempus est ullum
jure hominis necandi, quæ multa sunt,* scil. *tempora,* Cic.

Obs. 5.   The relative is sometimes entirely omitted ; as, *Urbs antiqua fuit : Tyrii tenuere coloni,* scil. *quam* or *eam,* Virg.   Or if once expressed, is afterwards omitted, so that it must be supplied in a different
case ; as, *Bocchus cum peditibus, quos filius ejus adduxerat, neque in priore
pugna adfuerant, Romanos invadunt ;* for *quique in priore pugna non adfuerant,* Sall.   In English the relative is often omitted, where in Latin
it must be expressed ; as, *The letter I wrote,* for *the letter which I wrote ;
The man I love,* to wit, *whom.*   But this omission of the relative is
generally improper, particularly in serious discourse.

Obs. 6.   The case of the relative sometimes seems to depend on that
of the antecedent ; as, *Cum aliquid agas eorum, quorum consuesti,* for *quæ
consuesti agere,* or *quorum aliquid agere consuesti,* Cic.   *Restitue in quem me
accepisti locum,* for *in locum, in quo,* Ter. And. iv. 1. 58.   But such examples rarely occur.

Obs. 7.   The adjective pronouns *ille, ipse, iste, hic, is,* and *idem,* in
their construction, resemble that of the relative *qui ;* as, *Liber ejus,*
His or her book ; *Vita eorum,* Their life, when applied to men ; *Vita
earum,* Their life, when applied to women.   By the improper use of
these pronouns in English, the meaning of sentences is often rendered
obscure.

Obs. 8.   The interrogative or indefinite adjectives, *qualis, quantus,
quotus, &c.* are also sometimes construed like relatives ; as, *Facies quæ
qualem decet esse sororum,* Ovid.   But these have commonly other adjectives either expressed or understood, which answer to them ; as,
Tanta est multitudo, quantum urbs capere potest : and are often applied to
different substantives ; as, *Quales sunt cives, talis est civitas,* Cic.

Obs.

Obf. 9. The relative *who* in Englifh is applied only to perfons, and *which* to things and irrational animals; but formerly *which* was likewife applied to perfons; as, *Our Father which art in heaven :* and *whofe*, the genitive of *who*, is alfo ufed fometimes, though perhaps improperly, for *of which*. *That* is ufed indifferently for perfons and things. *What*, when not joined with a fubftantive, is only applied to things, and includes both the antecedent and the relative, being the fame with *that which*, or *the thing which*; as, *This is what he wanted*; that is, *the thing which he wanted*.

Obf. 10. The Latin relative often cannot be tranflated literally into Englifh, on account of the different idioms of the two languages; as, *Quod cum ita effet*, When that was fo; not, Which when it was fo, becaufe then there would be two nominatives to the verb *was*, which is improper. Sometimes the accufative of the relative in Latin muft be rendered by the nominative in Englifh; as, *Quem dicunt me effe?* Who do they fay that I am? *not whom*. *Quem dicunt adventare?* Who do they fay is coming?

Obf 11. As the relative is always connected with a different verb from the antecedent, it is ufually conftrued with the fubjunctive mode, unlefs when the meaning of the verb is expreffed pofitively; as, *Audire cupio, quæ legeris*, I want to hear, what you have read; that is, what perhaps or probably you may have read : *Audire cupio, quæ legifti*, I want to hear, what you *(actually or in fact)* have read.

To the conftruction of the Relative may be fubjoined that of the ANSWER TO A QUESTION.

The anfwer is commonly put in the fame cafe with the queftion; as,

Qui vocare? Geta, fc. *vocor. Quid quæris? Librum*, fc. *quæro. Quotâ horâ venifti? Sextâ.* Sometimes the conftruction is varied; as, *Cujus eft liber? Meus*, not *mei. Quanti emptus eft? Decem offulus. Damnalufne es furti? Imo alio crimine.* Often the anfwer is made by other parts of fpeech than nouns; as, *Quid agitur? Statur*, fc. *a me, a nobis. Quis fecit? Nefcio : Aiunt Petrum feciffe. Quomodo vales? Bene, male. Scripfiftine? Scripfi, ita, etiam, immo*, &c. *An vidifti? Non vidi, non, minime*, &c. *Charea tuam veftem detraxit tibi? Fortaffe. Et id eft inutus? Factum.* Ter. Moft of the Rules of Syntax may thus be exemplified in the form of queftions and anfwers.

The CONSTRUCTION of CONJUNCTIONS.

LVIII. The conjunctions *et*, *ac*, *atque*, *nec*, *neque*, *aut*, *vel*, and fome others, couple like cafes and modes; as,

Honora patrem et matrem,	Honour father and mother.
Nec legit nec fcribit,	He neither reads nor writes.

Obf.

Obf. 1. To this rule belong particularly the copulative and disjunctive conjunctions ; as likewife, *quam, nifi, præterquam, an* ; and alfo adverbs of likenefs, as, *ceu, tanquam, quafi, ut, &c.* as,

Nullum præmium a vobis pofeulo, præterquam hujus diei memoriam, Cic· *Gloria virtutem tanquam umbra fequitur.* Id.

Obf. 2. Thefe conjunctions properly connect the different members of a fentence together, and are hardly ever applied to fingle words, unlefs when fome other word is underftood. Hence if the conftruction of the fentence be varied, different cafes and modes may be coupled together ; as,

Intereft mea et reipublicæ ; Conftitit affe et pluris ; Sive es Romæ, five in Epiro ; Decius cum fe devoveret, et in mediam aciem irruebat, Cic. *Vir magni ingenii fummæque induftriâ ; Neque per vim, neque infidiis,* Sall. *Tecum habita, & nôris, quam fit tibi curta fupellex,* Perf.

Obf. 3. When *et, aut, vel, five,* or *nec,* are joined to different members of the fame fentence, without connecting it particularly to any former fentence, the firft *et* is rendered in Englifh by *both* or *likewife* ; *aut* or *vel,* by *either* ; the firft *five,* by *whether* ; and the firft *nec,* by *neither* ; as,

Et legit, et fcribit : fo *tum legit, tum fcribit* ; or *cum legit, tum fcribit,* He both reads and writes ; *Sive legit, five fcribit,* Whether he reads or writes : *Jucere quâ vere, quâ falfa ; Increpare quâ confules ipfos, quâ exercitum,* to upbraid both the confuls and the army, Liv.

LIX. Two or more fubftantives fingular coupled by a conjunction, (as, *et, ac, atque, &c.)* have an adjective, verb, or relative plural ;) as,

Petrus et Joannes, qui funt docti,   Peter and John, who are learned.

Obf. 1. If the fubftantives be of different perfons, the verb plural muft agree with the firft perfon rather than the fecond, and with the fecond rather than the third ; as, *Si tu et Tullia valetis, ego et Cicero valemus,* If you and Tullia are well, I and Cicero are well, *Cic.* In Englifh the perfon fpeaking ufually puts himfelf laft : thus, *You and I read ; Cicero and I are well :* but in Latin the perfon who fpeaks is generally put firft : thus, *Ego et tu legimus.*

Obf.

Obf. 2. If the fubftantives are of different genders, the adjective or relative plural muft agree with the mafculine rather than the feminine or neuter ; as, *Pater et mater, qui funt mortui :* but this is only applicable to beings which may have life. The perfon is fometimes implied ; as, *Athenarum et Cratippi, ad quos, &c. Propter fummam doctoris auctoritatem et urbis, quorum alter,* &c. Cic. Where *Athenæ* & *urbs* are put for *the learned men* of Athens. So in fubftantives ; as, *Ad Ptolemæum Cleopatramque reges legati miſſi,* i. e. the king and queen, Liv.

Obf. 3. If the fubftantives fignify things without life, the adjective or relative plural muft be put in the neuter gender ; as, *Divitiæ, decus, gloria, in oculis fita funt,* Sall.

The fame holds, if any of the fubftantives fignify a thing without life ; becaufe when we apply a quality or join an adjective to feveral fubftantives of different genders, we muft reduce the fubftantives to fome certain clafs, under which they may all be comprehended, that is, to what is called their *Genus.* Now the *Genus* or clafs which comprehends under it both perfons and things, is that of fubftances or beings in general, which are neither mafculine nor feminine. To exprefs this the Latin grammarians ufe the word *Negotia.*

Obf. 4. The adjective or verb frequently agrees with the neareft fubftantive or nominative, and is underftood to the reft ; as,

Et ego et Cicero meus flagitabit, Cic. *Sociis et rege recepto,* Virg. *Et ego in culpa fum, et tu,* Both I am in the fault, and you ; or, *Et ego et tu es in culpa,* Both I and you are in the fault. *Nihil hic nifi carmina, defunt ;* or *nihil hic deeft nifi carmina. Omnia, quibus turbari folita eras - civitas, domi difcordia, foris bellum exortum ; Duo millia et quadringenti capi,* Liv. This conftruction is moft ufual, when the different fubftantives refemble one another in fenfe ; as, *Mens, ratio, et confilium, in fenibus eft,* Underftanding, reafon, and prudence is in old men. *Quibus ipfe meique ante Larem proprium veftor,* for *veftimur,* Horat.

Obf. 5. The plural is fometimes ufed after the prepofition *cum* put for *et* ; as,

Remo cum fratre Quirinus jura dabunt, Virg. The conjunction is frequently underftood ; as, *Dum ætas, metus, magifter probibebant,* Ter. *Frons, oculi, vultus fæpe mentiuntur,* Cic.

The different examples comprehended under this rule are commonly referred to the figure *Syllepfis.*

LX. The conjunctions *ut, quo, licet, ne, utinam,* and *dummodo,* are for the moft part joined to the fubjunctive mode ; as,

T 2

<table>
<tr><td>Lego ut discam,</td><td>I read that I may learn.</td></tr>
<tr><td>Utinam saperes,</td><td>I wish you were wise.</td></tr>
</table>

Obf. 1. All interrogatives, when placed indefinitely, have after them the fubjunctive mode.

Whether they be adjectives; as, *Quantus, qualis, quotus, quotuplex, uter;* Pronouns, as, *quis & cujus;* Adverbs, as, *Ubi, quo, unde, qua, quorfum, quamdiu, quamdudum, quampridem, quoties, cur, quare, quamobrem, num, utrum, quomodo, qui, ut, quam, quantopére;* or Conjunctions, as, *ne, an, anne, annon:* Thus, *Quis eft?* Who is it? *Nefcio quis fit;* I do not know who it is. *An venturus eft? Nefcio, dubito, an venturus fit. Viden' ut alta ftet nive candidum Soracte?* Hor. But thefe words are fometimes joined with the indicative; as, *Scio quid ego,* Plaut. *Haud fcio an amat,* Ter. *Vide avaritia quid facit,* Id. *Vides quam turpe eft,* Cic.

¶ In like manner the relative QUI in a continued difcourfe; as, *Nihil eft quod Deus efficere non poffit. Quis eft, qui utilia fugiat?* Cic. Or when joined with QUIPPE or UTPOTE; *Neque Antonius procul aberat, utpote qui fequeretur,* &c. Sall. But thefe are fometimes, although more rarely, joined with the Indicative. So *Eft qui, funt qui, eft quando* v. *ubi,* &c. are joined with the indicative or fubjunctive.

NOTE, *Haud fcio an recte dixerim,* is the fame with *dico, affirmo,* Cic.

So in Englifh, *if, though, unlefs, except, whatever, whether, or;* alfo *fo, before, ere, till,* &c. have after them the fubjunctive mode; as, *If* thou *let* this man go; *If* thou *be* the Son of God; *Although* my houfe *be* not fo; *Though* he *flay* me; *Though* he *fall,* &c. *Unlefs* he *wafh* his feet; I will not let thee go *except* thou *blefs* me; *Except* it were given from above; *Whether* it *were* I *or* they; *Whofoever* he be; *Whatever* be our fate, &c. So likewife *that,* expreffing the motive or end; *left,* and *that* annexed to a command preceding; and *if* with *but* following it; as, Let him that ftandeth take heed *left* he *fall;* Beware *that* thou bring not my fon thither; *If* he *do but* touch the hills, they fhall fmoke.

The nominative cafe following the verb fometimes fupplies the place of *if,* or *though;* as, " Ha[illegible]e done this, he had efcaped," i. e. if he had done this; " Charm he never fo wifely," or rather, ever fo wifely, i. e. *how* wifely *foever,* for, *though* he charm, &c.

Obf. 2. When any thing doubtful or contingent is fignified, conjunctions and indefinites are ufually conftrued with the fubjunctive; but when a more abfolute or determinate

minate fenfe is expreffed, with the indicative mode ; as, *If he is to do it ; Although he was rich,* &c.

Obf. 3. ETSI, TAMETSI, and TAMENETSI QUANQUAM, in the beginning of a fentence, have the indicative ; but elfewhere, they alfo take the fubjunctive ; ETIAMSI and QUAMVIS commonly have the fubjunctive, and UT, although, always has it ; as, *Ut quæras, non reperies,* Cic. QUONIAM, QUANDO, QUANDO-QUIDEM, are ufually conftrued with the indicative ; SI, SIN, NE, NISI, SIQUIDEM ; QUOD, and QUIA, fometimes with the indicative, and fometimes with the fubjunctive. DUM, for *dummodo,* provided, has always the fubjunctive ; as, *Oderint dum metuant,* Cic. And QUIPPE, for *nam,* always the indic.; as, *Quippe vetor fatis.*

Obf. 4. Some conjunctions have their correfpondent conunctions belonging to them ; fo that, in the following member of the fentence, the latter anfwers to the former : thus, when *etfi, tametfi,* or *quamvis,* although, are ufed in the former member of a fentence, *tamen,* yet, *or* neverthelefs, generally anfwers to them in the latter. In like manner, *Tam—quam ; Adeo* or *ita,—ut :* in Englifh, *As,—as* or *fo ;* as, *Etfi fit liberalis, tamen non eft profufus,* Although he be liberal, yet he is not profufe. So *prius* or *ante,—quam.* In fome of thefe, however, we find the latter conjunction fometimes omitted, particularly in Englifh.

Obf. 5. The conjunction *ut* is elegantly omitted after thefe verbs, *Volo, nolo, malo, rogo, precor cenfeo, fuadeo, licet, oportet, neceffe eft,* and the like ; and likewife after thefe imperatives, *Sine, fac,* or *facito ;* as, *Ducas volo hodie uxorem ; Nolo mentiare ; Fac cogites,* Ter. In like manner *ne* is commonly omitted after *cave ;* as, *Cave facias,* Cic. *Poft* is alfo fometimes underftood ; thus, *Die octavo, quam creatus erat,* Liv. iv. 47. fcil. *poft.* And fo in Englifh, *See you do it ; I beg you would come to me,* fc. *that.*

Obf. 6. *Ut* and *Quod* are thus diftinguifhed : *ut* denotes the final caufe, and is commonly ufed with regard to fomething future ; *quod* marks the efficient impulfive caufe, and is generally ufed concerning the event or thing done ; as, *Lego ut difcam,* I read that I may learn ; *Gaudeo quod legi,* I am glad that *or* becaufe I have read. *Ut* is likewife ufed after thefe intenfive words, as they are called, *Adeo, ita, fic, tam, talis, tantus, tot, &c.*

Obf. 7. After the verbs *timeo, vereor,* and the like, *ut* is taken in a negative fenfe for *ne non,* and *ne* in an affirmative fenfe ; as,

Timeo ne faciat, I fear he will do it ; *Timeo ut faciat,* I fear he will
not

not do it. *Id paves ne ducas tu illam, tu autem ut ducas*, Ter. *Ut fit vitalis, metuo*, Hor.   *Timeo ut frater vivat*, will not ;—*ne frater moriatur*, will.   But in some few examples they seem to have a contrary meaning.

The CONSTRUCTION of COMPARATIVES.

LXI. The comparative degree governs the ablative ; as,

Dulcior melle, sweeter than honey. *Præstantior auro*, better than gold.

Obs. 1. The sign of the ablative in English is *than*. The positive with the adverb *magis*, likewise governs the ablative ; as, *Magis dilecta luce*, Virg.

The ablative is here governed by the preposition *præ* understood, which is sometimes expressed ; as, *Fortior præ cæteris*. We find the comparative also construed with other prepositions ; as, *Immanior ante omnes*, Virg.

Obs. 2. The comparative degree may likewise be construed with the conjunction *quam*, and then, instead of the ablative, the noun is to be put in whatever case the sense requires ; as,

Dulcior quam mel, scil. *est*. *Amo te magis quam illum*, I love you more than him, that is, *quam amo illum*, than I love him. *Amo te magis quam ille*, I love you more than he, i. e. *quam ille amat*, than he loves. *Plus datur a me quam illo*, sc. *ab*.

Obs. 3. The conjunction *quam* is often elegantly suppressed after *amplius* and *plus* ; as,

Vulnerantur amplius sexcenti, Cæf. scil. *quam*. *Plus quingentos colaphos infregit mihi*, He has laid on me more than five hundred blows, Ter. *Castra ab urbe haud plus quinque milliæ passuum locant*, sc. *quam*, Liv.

Quam is sometimes elegantly placed between two comparatives ; as,

Triumphus clarior quam gratior, Liv. Or the prep. *pro* is added ; as, *Prælium atrocius, quam pro numero pugnantium editur*, Liv.

The comparative is sometimes joined with these ablatives, *opinione, spe, æquo, justo, dicto* ; as,

Credibili, opinione major, Cic. *Credibili fortior*, Ovid. Fast. iii. 618. *Gravius æquo*, Sall. *Dicto citius*, Virg. *Majora credibili tulimus*, Liv. They are often understood ; as, *Liberius vivebat, sc. justo*, too freely, Nepos.

Nihil is sometimes elegantly used for *nemo* or *nulli* ; as,

Nihil vidi quilquam alius, for *neminem*, Ter. *Crasso nihil perfectius*, Cic. *Asperius nihil est humili, cum surgit in altum*. So *quid nobis laberi-*
esius,

sius, for *quis*, &c. Cic. We say, *inferior patre nulla re*, or *quam pater*. The comparative is sometimes repeated or joined with an adverb; as, *Magis magisque*, *plus plusque*, *minus minusque*, *carior cariorque*; *Quotidie plus, indies magis, semper candidior candidiorque*, &c.

Obf. 4. In Englifh, the relative *who* after *than* is always put in the accufative cafe; as, He is a man, *than whom* there is none better: but here if we fubftitute a pronoun in place of the relative, the pronoun muft be put in the nominative; as, there is none better than *he*, not, than *him*. In like manner, it is improper to fay, He is better than *me*, than *us*, than *her*, than *them*, &c. It fhould be, He is better than *I*, than *we*, than *fhe*, than *they*, &c. the auxiliary verb being underftood to each of them.

Obf. 5. The relation of equality or famenefs is likewife expreffed in Englifh by conjunctions; as, *Eft tam doctus quam ego*, He is as learned as I. *Animus erga te idem eft ac fuit. Ac* and *atque* are fometimes, though more rarely, ufed after comparatives; as, *Nihil eft magis verum atque hoc*, Ter.

Obf. 6. The excefs or defect of meafure is put in the ablative after comparatives; and the fign in Englifh is *by*, expreffed or underftood: (or more fhortly, the difference of meafure is put in the ablative); as,

Eft decem digitis altior quam frater, He is ten inches taller than his brother, *or* by ten inches. *Altero tanto major eft fratre*, i. e. *duplo maminor*, a foot and a half lefs; *Altero tanto, aut fefquimajor*, as big again, *or* a half bigger, Cic. *Ter tanto pejor eft; Bis tanto amici funt inter fe, quam prius*, Plaut. *Quinquies tanto amplius, quam quantum licitum fit civitatibus imperavit*, five times more, Cic. To this may be added many other ablatives, which are joined with the comparative, to increafe its force; as, *Tanto, quanto, quo, eo, hoc, multo, paulo, nimio*, &c. thus, *Quo plus habent, eo plus cupiunt*, The more they have, the more they defire. *Quanto melior, tanto felicior*, The better, the happier. *Quoque minor fpes eft, hoc magis ille cupit*, Ovid. Faft. ii. 766. We frequently find *multo, tanto, quanto*, alfo joined with fuperlatives; *Multo pulcherrima ●am haberemus*, Sall. *Multoque id maximum fuit*, Liv.

The Ablative Absolute.

LXII. A Subftantive and a participle are put in the ablative, when their cafe depends on no other word; as,

Sole

| *Sole oriente, fugiunt tenebræ,* | { The sun rising, or while the sun riseth, darkness flies away. |
| *Opere peracto, ludemus,* | { Our work being finished, or when our work is finished, we will play. |

So, *Dominante libidine, temperantiæ nullus est locus ; Nihil amicitiâ præstabilius est, exceptâ virtute ; Oppressâ libertate patriæ, nihil est quod speremus amplius ; Nobilium vitâ victuque mutato, mores mutari civitatum puto,* Cic. *Parumper silentium et quies fuit, nec Etruscis, nisi cogerentur, pugnam inituris, et dictatore arcem Romanam respiciente, ut ab augurebus simul aves rite admisissent, ex composito tolleretur signum,* Liv. *Bellice, depositis clypeo paulisper et hastâ, Mars edes,* Ovid. Fast. iii. 1.

Obs. 1. / 'This ablative is called *Absolute*, because it does not depend upon any other word in the sentence. /

For if the substantive with which the participle is joined, be either the nominative to some following verb, or be governed by any word going before, then this rule does not take place : the ablative absolute is never used, unless when different persons or things are spoken of ; as, *Militis, hostibus victis, redierunt.* The soldiers, having conquered the enemy, returned. *Hostibus victus,* may be rendered in English several different ways, according to the meaning of the sentence with which it is joined ; thus, 1. *The enemy conquered,* or *being conquered ;* 2. *When* or *after the enemy is* or *was conquered :* 3. *By conquering the enemy :* 4. *Upon the defeat of the enemy, &c.*

Obs. 2. /The perfect participles of deponent verbs are not used in the ablative absolute ; /as, *Cicero locutus hæc consedit,* never *his locutis.* The participles of common verbs may either agree in case with the substantive before them, like the participles of deponent verbs, or may be put in the ablative absolute, like the participles of passive verbs ; as, *Romani adepti libertatem floruerunt ;* or *Romani, libertate adeptâ, floruerunt.* But as the participles of common verbs are seldom taken in a passive sense, we therefore find them rarely used in the ablative absolute.

Obs. 3. / The participle *existente* or *existentibus* is frequently understood ;/ as, *Cæsare duce,* scil. *existente. His consulibus,* scil. *existentibus. Invitâ Minervâ,* sc. *existente,* against the grain ; *Crassâ Minervâ,* without learning, Hor. *Magistrâ ac duce naturâ ; vivis fratribus ; te hortatore ; Cæsare impulsore, &c.* Sometimes the substantive must be supplied ; as, *Nondum comperto, quam regionem hostes petiissent,* i. e. *cum nondum compertum esset,* Liv. *Tum denmum*

rum palam facto, fc. *negotio*, Id. *Excepto quod non fimul
effes, cætera letus*, Hor. *Parto quod avebas*, Id. In fuch
examples *negotio* muft be underftood, or the reft of the
fentence conſidered as the fubſtantive, which perhaps is
more proper. Thus we find a verb ſupply the place of a
ſubſtantive; as, *Vale dicto*, having ſaid farewell, Ovid.

Obf. 4. We ſometimes find a Subſtantive plural joined
with a participle ſingular; as, *Nobis preſentæ*, Plaut. *Ab-
ſente nobis*, Ter. We alſo find the ablative abſolute, when
it refers to the ſame perſon with the nominative to the
verb; as, *me duce ad hunc voti finem, me milite, veni*, Ovid.
Amor. ii. 12. 12. *Laetos fecit ſe conſule faſtos*, Lucan. v.
384. *Populo ſpectante fieri credam, quicquid me conſcio faciam*,
Senec. de Vit. Beat. c. 20. But examples of this conſtruction rarely occur.

Obf. 5. The ablative called *abſolute* is governed by
ſome prepoſition underſtood; as, *a, ab, cum, ſub*, or *in*.
We find the prepoſition ſometimes expreſſed; as, *Cum diis
juvantibus*, Liv. The nominative likewiſe ſeems ſometimes
to be uſed abſolutely; as, *Pernicioſa libidine pauliſper uſus,
infirmitas naturæ accuſatur*, Salluſt. Jug. 1.

Obf. 6. The ablative abſolute may be rendered ſeveral
different ways; thus, *Superbo regnante*, is the ſame with
cum, dum, or *quando Superbus regnabat. Opere peracto*,
is the ſame with *Poſt opus peractum*, or *Cum opus eſt peractum*. The preſent participle, when uſed in the ablative
abſolute, commonly ends in *e*.

Obf. 7. When a ſubſtantive is joined with a participle
in Engliſh independently on the reſt of the ſentence, it is
expreſſed in the nominative; as, *Illo deſcendente*, He de-
ſcending. But this manner of ſpeech is ſeldom uſed except in poetry.

APPENDIX

APPENDIX to SYNTAX.

I. Various Signification and Construction of VERBS.

[The verbs are here placed in the same order as in Etymology.]

FIRST CONJUGATION.

ASPIRARE ad gloriam & laudem, *to aim at*; in curiam, *to defire to be admitted*, Cic.; equis achillis, *to wish for*; labori ejus, *to favour*; amorem dictis, fe ei, *to infufe*, Virg.

DESPERARE fibi, de fe; falutem, faluti, de falute, *to defpair of.*

LEGARE aliquem ad alium, *to fend us an ambaffador*; aliquem fibi, *to make his lieutenant*; pecuniam alicui, *i. e.* teftamento relinquere. *N. B.* Publice *legantur* homines; qui inde *legati* dicuntur: privatim *allegantur*; unde *allegati.*

DELEGARE æs alienum fratri, *to leave him to pay*; laborem alteri, *to lay upon*; aliquid ad aliquem, *i. e.* in eum transferre, Cic.

LEVARE metum ejus & ei, eum metu, *to eafe.*

MUTARE locum, folum, *to be banifhed*; aliquid aliqua re; bellum pro pace, *to exchange*; veftem, *i. e.* fordidam togam induere. Liv. veftem cum aliquo, Ter. fidem, *to break.*

OBNUNCIARE comitiis *vel* concilio, *i. e.* comitia aufpiciis impedire, *to hinder, by telling bad omens, and repeating thefe words* ALIO DIE; Confuli *v.* magiftratur; *i. e* prohibere ne cum populo agat, Cic.

PRONUNCIARE pecuniam pro reo, *to promife*; aliquid edicto, *to order*; fententias, *to fum up the opinions of the fenators*, Cic.

RENUNCIARE aliquid, de re, alicui, ad aliquem, *to tell*; confulem, *to declare, to name*; vitæ, amicitiam ei, *to give up*; muneri, hofpitio, *to refufe*; repudium ei, *to divorce.*

OCCUPARE aliquem, *to feize*; fe in aliquo negotio, *to be employed*; fe ad negotium, *Plaut.* pecunium alicui *v.* apud aliquem grandi fœnore, *to give at intereft*, Cic. occupat facere bellum, tranfire in agrum hoftium, *begins firft, anticipates*, Liv.

PRÆOCCUPARE faltum, portas Ciliciæ, *to feize beforehand*, Nep.

PRÆJUDICARE aliquem, *to condemn one from the precedent of a former fentence or trial*, Cic.

ROGARE aliquem id, & de ea re; id ab eo; falutem, & pro falute, Cic. legem, *to propofe*; hence, UTI ROGAS, dicere, *to pafs it*; militem facramento, *to adminifter the military oath*; Roget quis? *if any one fhould afk.* Comitia rogandis confulibus, *for electing*, Liv.

ABROGARE legem, *feldom* legi, *to difannul a law, to repeal, or to change in part*; multum, *to take off a fine*; imperium ei, *to take from.*

ABROGARE id fibi, *to claim.*

DEROGARE aliquid legi, *v.* de lege, *to repeal or take away fome claufe of a law*; lex derogatur, Cic. fidem ei, *v.* de fide ejus, *to hurt one's credit*; ex æquitate; fibi, alicui, *to derogate or take from.*

ERO-

EROGARE pecuniam in classem, in vestes, *to lay out money on.*

IRROGARE multam ei, *to impose.*

OBROGARE legi, *to enact a new law contrary to an old.*

PROROGARE imperium, provinciam alicui, *to prolong;* diem ei ad solvendum, *to put off.*

SUBROGARE aliquem in locum alterius, *to substitute;* legi, *to add a new clause,* or *to put one in place of another.*

SPECTARE orientem, ad orientem, *to look towards;* aliquem ex censu, animum alicujus ex suo, *to judge of.*

SUPERARE hostes, *to overcome;* montes, *to pass;* superat pars cæpti, sc. operis, *remains;* Captæ superavimus urbi, *survived,* Virg.

TEMPERARE iras, ventos, *to moderate;* orbem, *to rule;* mihi sibi, *to restrain, to forbear;* alicui, *to spare;* cædibus, a lacrymis, *to abstain from.*

VACARE curâ, culpâ, morbo, munere militiæ, &c. a labore, *to be free from;* animo, sc. in, *to be at ease;* philosophiæ, in v. ad rem, *to apply to;* vacat locus, *is empty;* si vacas, v. vacat tibi, *if you are at leisure.*

VINDICARE mortem ejus, *to revenge;* ab interitu, exercitum fame, *to free;* id sibi, & ad se, *to claim;* libertatem ejus, *to defend;* se in libertatem, *to set at liberty.*

DARE animam, *to die;* animos, *to encourage;* manus, *to yield;* manum ei, *to shake hands;* Plaut. jura, *to prescribe laws;* literas alicui ad aliquem, *to give one a letter to carry to another;* terga, fugam, v. se in fugam, in pedes, *to fly;* hostes in fugam, *to put to flight;* operam, *to endeavour;* operam philosophiæ, literis, palæstræ, *to apply to;* operam honoribus, *to seek,* Nep. veniam ei, *to grant his request,* Ter.

gemitus, lacrymas. amplexus, cantus, ruinam, fidem, jusjurandum, &c. *to groan, weep, embrace, sing, fall, &c.* cognitores honestos, *to give good vouchers for one's character,* Cic. aliquid mutuum, v utendum, *to lend;* pecuniam fœnori, & collocare, *to place at interest;* se alicui ad docendum, Cic. multum suo ingenio, *to think much of;* se ad aliquid, *to apply to;* se auctoritati senatûs, *to yield;* fabulam, scripta foras, *to publish;* Cic. effectum, *to perform;* senatum, *to give a hearing of the senate;* actionem, *to grant leave to prosecute;* præcipitem, *to tumble headlong;* aliquid paternum, *to act like one's father;* lectos faciendos, *to bespeak;* Ter. litem secundum aliquem, *to determine a law-suit in favour of one;* aliquem exitio, morti, neci, letho, *rarely* lethum alicui, *to kill;* aliquid alicui dono, v. muneri. *to make a present;* crimini, vitio, laudi, *to accuse, blame, praise;* pænas, *to suffer;* nomen militiæ, v. in militiam, *to list one's self to be a soldier;* se alicui, *to be familiar with,* Ter. Da te mihi hodie, *be directed by me,* Id. aures, *to listen;* oblivioni, *to forget;* civitatem ei, *to make one free of the city;* dicta, *to speak,* verba alicui, *to impose on, to cheat;* se in viam, *to enter on a journey;* viam ei, *to give place;* jus gratiæ, *to sacrifice justice to interest;* se turpiter, *to make a shabby appearance;* fundum vel domum alicui, mancipio, *to convey the property of, to warrant the title to;* Vitaque mancipio nulli datur, omnibus usu, Lucr. servos in quæstionem, *to give up slaves to be tortured;* primas, secundas, &c. (sc. partes) actioni, *to ascribe every thing to delivery;* Cic. Dat ei bibere, Ter. comas diffundere ventis, *to let them flow loose,* Virg. Da mihi v. nobis, *to!*

tellus, Cic. Ut res dant se, *as matters go*; solertem dabo, *I'll warrant him expert*, Ter.

SATISDARE judicatum solvi, *to give security that what the judge has determined shall be paid*, Cic.

STARE' contra aliquem; ab, cum, *v.* pro aliquo, *to side with, to be of the same party*; judicio ejus, *to follow*; in sententia; pacto, conditionibus, conventis, *to stand to, to make good an agreement*; re judicatâ, *to keep to what has been determined*; stare, *v.* constare animo, *to be in his senses*: Non stat per me quo minus pecunia solvatur, *It is not owing to me that*, &c. multorum sanguine ea Pænis victoria stetit, *cost*, Liv. Mihi stat herem morbum desinere, *I am resolved*, Nep.

ADSTARE mensæ, *to stand by*; ad mensam, in conspectu.

CONSTARE ex multis rebus, animo et corpore, *to consist of*; secum, *to be consistent with*, Cic. liber constitit *v.* stetit mihi duobus assibus, *cost me*; non constat ei color, *his colour comes and goes*: auri ratio constat, *the sum is right*. Constat, *imperf. It is evident, certain, or agreed on*; mihi, inter omnes, de hac re.

EXTARE aquis, *to be above*, Ovid. ad memoriam posteritatis, *to remain*, Cic. sepulchra extant, Liv.

INSTARE victis, *to press on the vanquished*; rectam viam, *to be in*

the right way: currum Marti, *to make speedily*, Virg.; instat factum, *insists that it was done*, Ter.

OBSTARE ei, *to hinder*.

PRÆSTARE multa, *to perform*; alicui, *v.* aliquem virtute, *to excel*; silentium ei, *to give*; auxilium, *to grant*, Juv. impensas, *to defray*; iter tutum, *to procure*; se incolumem, *to preserve*; se virum, *i. e.* præbere, exhibere; amorem, *v.* benevolentiam alicui, *to shew*; culpam, *v.* damnum, *i. e.* in se transferre, *to take on one's self*; præstabo de me; eum facturum, *I will be answerable*. In iis rebus repetendis, quæ mancipi sunt, is periculum judicii præstare debet, qui se nexu obligavit, *In recovering, or in an action to recover those things which are transferable, the seller ought to take upon himself the hazard of a trial*, Cic. *N. B.* Those things were called, Res mancipi, *(contracted for* mancipii, *i. e.* quas emptor manu caperet,) *the property of which might be transferred from one Roman citizen to another; as houses, lands, slaves*, &c.

Præstat, *imperf. i. e. it is better*: Præsto esse alicui, *adv. to be present, to assist*; Libri prostant venales, *the books are exposed to sale*.

ACCUBARE alicui in convivio, *to recline near*; apud aliquem. Incubare ovis & ova, *to sit upon*; stratis & super strata.

SECOND CONJUGATION.
Verbs in BEO.

HABERE spem, febrim, finem, bonum exitum, tempus, consuetudinem, voluntatem nocendi, opus in manibus, *v.* inter manus, *to have*; gratiam & gratum, *to have a grateful sense of a favour*; judicium, *to hold a trial*; honorem ei, *to honour*; in oculis, *to be fond of*, Ter.: fidem alicui, *to trust or be-* *liem*: curam de *v.* pro eo; rationem alicujus, *to pay regard to, to allow one to stand candidate for an office*; rationem, *v.* rem cum aliquo, *to have business with*; satis, *to be satisfied*; orationem, concionem ad populum, *to make a speech*; aliquem odio, in odium, *to hate*; ludibrio, *to mock*; id religioni, *t-*

have a *scruple about it* : So, habère aliquid quæstui, honori, prædæ, voluptati, &c. *sc.* sibi ; se bene *v.* graviter, *to be well or ill* ; se parcè & duriter, *to live*, Ter. aliquid compertum, cognitum, perspectum, exploratum, certum *v.* procerto, *to know for certain* ; aliquem contemptui, despicatui, -um, *v.* in despicatum, *to despise* ; excusatum, *to excuse* ; susque deque, *to scorn, to slight* ; Ut res se habet, *stands, is* ; rebus ita se habentibus, *in this state of affairs* ; Hæc habeo, *v.* habui dicere de, &c. Non habeo necesse scribere, quid sim facturus, Cic. Habe tibi tuas res, *a form of divorce.*

ADHIBERE diligentiam ; celeritatem, vim, severitatem in aliquem, *to use* ; in convivium *v.* consilium, *to admit* ; remedium vulneri, curationem morbo, *to apply* ; vinum ægrotis, *to give* ; aures versibus, *to bear with taste* ; cultum & preces diis, *to offer*, Cic. Exhibere molestiam alicui, *to cause trouble.*

MITTERE legatum, *to send far, to pass* ; regem, *to chuse* ; aliquem salvere, *to wish one health* ; esse bono animo, &c. Uxorem suas res sibi habere jussit, *divorced*, Cic.

DOCEO te hanc rem, & de hac re. Doctus, *adj.* utriusque linguæ ; Latinis & Græcis literis ; Latinè & Græcè ; ad militiam.

MISCERE aliquid alicui, cum aliquo, ad aliquid ; vinum aquâ, Plin. cuncta sanguine, Tacit. sacra profanis, Hor. humana divinis, Liv.

VIDERE rem *v.* de re ; sibi, de isthoc, *to take care of*, Ter. plus, *to be more wise*, Cic. De hoc tu videris, *consider, be answerable for*, Cic. Videor videre, *methinks I see* ; visus sum audire, *methought I heard* ; mihi visus est dicere, *he seemed* ; Quid tibi videtur? *What*

think you? Si tibi videtur, *if you please* ; videtur fecisse, *guilty*, &c.

INVIDERE honorem ei, *v.* honori ejus ; ei *vel* eum, *to envy.*

PROVIDERE & prospicere id, *to foresee* ; ei, *to provide for* ; in posterum ; rei frumentariæ, rem *v.* de re.

SEDERE ad dextram ejus ; in equo, *to ride* ; toga bene sedet, *fits* ; Sedet hoc animo, *is fixed*, Virg.

ASSIDERE ei ; Adherbalem, *to sit by*, Sal. Assidet insano, *is near or like to*, Hor.

DISSIDERE cum aliquo, *to disagree.*

INSIDERE equo, & in equo, *to sit upon* ; locum, Liv. in animo, memoriâ, *to be fixed.*

PRÆSIDERE urbi, imperio, *to command*, Cic. exercitum, Italiam, Tacit.

SUPERSEDERE labore, litibus ; pugnæ, loqui, *to forbear, to give over.*

PENDERE promissis, ab *v.* ex aliquo, *to depend* ; de, ex, ab & in arbore ; Opera pendent interrupta, Virg.

IMPENDET malum nobis, nos, *v.* in nos, *threatens.*

SPONDERE & despondere filiam alicui, *to betroth.*

DESPONDERE domum alicujus sibi, *to be sure of*, Cic. animo & -is, *to promise, to hope* ; animum & -os, *to despair* ; Liv.

RESPONDERE ei, literis ejus, his, ad hæc, ad nomen, *to answer* ; votis ejus, *to satisfy his wishes* ; ad spem.

SUADERE ei pacem, *v.* de pace ; legem, *to speak in favour of.*

DOLERE casum ejus ; de, ab, ex, in, pro re ; dolet mihi cor, *v.* hoc dolet cordi meo ; caput dolet a sole.

VALERE gratiâ apud aliquem, *to be in favour with one*, lex valet, *is in force* ; quid verbum valeat,
non.

non video, *signifies*; valet decem talent..o *oftener* talentis, *is worth*; vale *vel* valeas, *farewel*; *or ironically, away with you.*

EMINERE aliqua re *vel* in aliqua re, inter omnes; super cætera, Liv. super utrumque. Hor. se de eminet, *to excel*; ex aqua, *v.* aquam, super undis, *to be above.* Imminere alicui, *to hang over, to threaten*; in occasionem, exitio alicujus, *to seek, to watch for.*

TENERE promissum; se domi, oppido, castris, *sc.* in, *to keep*; modum, ordinem, *to observe*; rem, dicta, lectionem, *to understand, to remember*; linguam, *but not* suam, silentium, se in silentio, *to be silent*; ora, *to keep the countenance fixed*; secundum locum imperii, *to hold*, Nep. jura civium, *to enjoy* Cic. causam, *to gain*; mare, *to be in the open sea, to hold, to be master of*; terram, portum, metam, montes, *to reach*; risum, lachrymas, *to restrain*; se ab accusando, quin accuset, Cic. Ventus tenet, *blows*; teneri legibus jurejurando, &c. *to be bound by*; leges tenent eum, *bind*; teneri in manifesto furto, *to be seized*; tenet fama, *prevails.*

ABSTINERE maledictis, *v. a, to abstain*; publico, *to live retired*, Tacit. animum a scelere, ægrum a cibo, *to keep from*; jus belli ab aliquo, *not to treat rigorously*, Liv. Id ad me, ad religionem, &c. pertinet, *concerns me*; crimen ad te pertinet, Cic. But it is not proper to say, Liber ad me, ad fratrem pertinet, *for* meus, fratris est, *belongs to*; venæ ad vel in omnes corporis partes pertinent, *reach.*

SUSTINERE personam judicis, nomen consulatûs, *to bear the character*; assensionem, *v.* se ab assensu, *to withhold assent*; rem in noctem, *to defer.*

MANERE apud aliquem; in castris; ad urbem; in urbe; proposito, sententiâ, in sententiâ, statu suo, &c. adventum hostium, *to expect*, Liv. promissis, *to stand to, to keep*, Virg. Omnes una manet nox, *awaits*, Horat. Manent ingenia senibus, modo permaneat studium & industria, Cic. Munera vobis certa manent, Virg.

MERERE laudem; bene, male de aliquo; stipendia, equo, pedibus, *to serve as a soldier*; fustuarium, *to be beaten to death.*

HÆRERE lateri; tergis *v.* in terga hostium. Liv. curru, Virg. alicui in visceribus, Cic. Hæret mihi aqua, *I am in doubt*; Vide, ne hæreas, *lest you be at a loss*, Cic.

ADHÆRERE & adhærescere justitiæ; ad turrim; in me. Inhærere rei, & in re.

MOVERE castra, *to decamp*; bella, *to raise*; aliquem tribu, *to remove a Roman citizen from a more honorable to a less honorable tribe*; e senatu, *to degrade a senator*; risum *vel* jocum alicui, *to cause laughter*; stomachum ei, *to trouble*, Cic.

FAVETE ore, *vel* linguis, *sc.* mihi, *attend in silence, or abstain from words of a bad omen.*

Cavere aliquid, aliquem, *vel* ab aliquo, *to guard against, to avoid*; alicui, *to provide for, to advise as a lawyer does his client*; aliquid alicui, Cic. sibi ab aliquo *vel* per aliquem de re aliqua, *to get security on*; mihi prædibus & chirographo cautum est, *I have got security by bail and bond*; veteranis cautum esse volumus, Cic. Cave facias, *sc.* ne, *see you don't do it*; mihi cavendum, *vel* mea cautio est, *I must take care.*

CONNIVERE ad fulgura, Suet. *to wink*; in hominum sceleribus, *to take no notice of*, Cic.

THIRD

THIRD CONJUGATION.

Verbs in IO.

FACERE initium, finem, pausam, finem vitæ ; pacem, amicitiam ; testamentum, nomen, fossam, pontem in flumine, in Tiberim, *to make* ; divortium cum uxore, Cic. bellum regi, Nep. se hilarem, *to shew*, Ter. se divitem, miserum, pauperem, *to pretend*, Cic. æs alienum, *v.* contrahere, conflare, *to contract debt* ; animos, *to encourage* ; damnum, detrimentum, jacturam, *to lose* ; naufragium, *to suffer* ; sumptum, *to spend* ; gratum alicui, *to oblige* ; gratiam delicti, *to pardon a fault* ; gratiam legis, *to dispense with* ; justa vel funus alicui, *to perform one's funeral rites* ; rem, *to make an estate* ; pecuniam, divitias ex metallis ; fœdus, *v.* inire, icere, ferire, percutere, jungere, sancire, firmare, &c. *to make a league* ; moram alicui, *to delay* : verba, *to speak* ; audientiam sibi, Cic. negotium, et facessere, *to trouble* ; aliquid missum, *to pass over* : aliquem missum, *to dismiss* or *excuse* ; ad aliquid, *rarely* alicui, *to be fit or useful* ; ratum, *to ratify* ; planum, *to explain* ; palam suis, *to make known* ; Nep. stipendium pedibus, *v.* equo, & merere, *to serve in the army* ; sacra, sacrificium, *v.* rem divinam, *to sacrifice* ; reum, *to impeach* ; fabulam, carmen, versus, &c. *to write a play*, &c. copiam consilii ei, *to offer advice* ; copiam *vel* potestatem dicendi legatis, *to grant leave* ; fidem, *to procure* or *give credit* ; periculum, *to make trial* ; potestatem sui, *to expose himself*, Nep. aliquem loquentem, *v.* loqui, *to suppose or represent*, Cic. piraticam, *sc.* rem, *to be a pirate* ; argentariam, medicinam, mercaturam, &c. *to be an*

usurer, *a physician*, &c. versuram, *to contract a new debt to discharge an old one, to borrow money at great interest*, Cic. cum *v.* ab aliquo, *to side with* ; contra *v.* adversus, *to oppose* ; nomen *v.* nomina, *to borrow money*, and also, *to settle accounts*, i. e. rationes acceptarum, *sc.* pecuniarum & expensarum inter se conferre ; nomen in litura, *to write it where something was before*, Cic. pedem, *v.* pedes, *to trim the sails*, Virg. Fac ita esse, *suppose it is so* ; obvius fieri alicui, *to meet* ; ne longum, *v.* longa faciam, ut breve faciam, *not to be tedious* ; equus non facit, *will not move*, Cic. Fac velle, *sc.* me, *suppose me to be willing*, Virg. Æn. iv. 540.

AFFICERE aliquem laude, honore, præmio, & ignominiâ, pœnâ, morte, leto, &c. *to praise, honour*, &c. *to disgrace, punish*, &c. Affectus ætate, morbo, *weakened*.

CONFICERE bellum, *to finish* ; orationes, *to compose*, Nep. cibum, *to chew* ; argentum, *to raise, to get* : also *to spend*, Cic. ; cum aliquo de re, *to conclude a bargain* ; exercitus hostium, *to destroy* ; alterum Curiatium, *to kill*, Liv. Qui stipendiis confectis erant, i. e. emeriti, *had served out their time*, Cic.

DEFICERE animo, *to faint* ; ab aliquo, *to revolt* ; tempus deficit mihi *vel* me, *fails* : Defici viribus, ratione, &c. *to be deprived of.*

INFICERE se vitro, *to stain* : Infectus, part. *stained* ; infectus, adj. *not done.* Inficior, -atus, -ari, *to deny.*

OFFICERE alicui, *to hinder or hurt* ; Diogeni apricanti, *to stand betwixt him and the sun* ; auribus, visui, *to stop or obstruct* : Umbra terræ soli officiens noctem efficit, Cic.

PRÆFICERE

Præficere aliquem exercitui, *to set over*. Proficere alicui, *to profit, to do good*; in philosophia, & progressus facere, *to make progress*.

Reficere muros, templa, ædes, rates, res, *to repair*; animum, vires, saucios, se, jumenta, *to refresh, to recover*.

Sufficere laboribus, ictibus, *to be able to bear*; arma v. vires alicui, *to afford*; Valerius in locum Collatini suffectus est, *was substituted*, Liv. Filius patri suffectus, Tacit. Oculos suffecti sanguine & igne, *sc.* secundum, *having their eyes red and inflamed*, Virg.

Satisfacere alicui, in v. de aliqua re, *to satisfy*; fidei, promisso, *to perform*.

Jacere aliquem in præceps; contumelias in eum, *to throw*; fundamenta, & ponere, *to lay*; talos, *to play at dice*; anchoram, *to cast*.

Adjicere, *to add*; oculos alicui rei, *to covet*; animum studiis, *to apply*; sacerdotibus creandis, Liv.

Conjicere se in pedes, v. fugam, *to fly*; cætera, *to conjecture*.

Injicere manus ei, *to lay on*: spem, ardorem, suspicionem, pavorem, alicui, *to inspire*; admirationem sui cuivis ipso aspectu, Nep.

Objicere se hostibus, in v. ad omnes casus, *to oppose* or *expose*: crimen ei, *to lay to one's charge*.

Rejicere tela in hostes, *to throw back*; judices, mala, *to reject*; rem ad senatum, Romani, *to refer*; rem ad Idus Febr. *to delay*, Cic.

Subjicere ova gallinæ, *to set an hen*; se imperio alicujus, *to submit*; testamenta, *to forge*; testes, *to suborn*; partes v. species generibus, ex quibus emanant, *to put or class under*; aliquid ei, *to suggest*: libellum ei, i. e. in manus

dare: odio civium, *to expose*: bona Pompeii v. fortunas hastæ vel voci & sub voce præconis, *to expose to public sale*, Cic. sub hasta venire, *to be sold*, Liv.

Trajicere copias v. exercitum, fluvium, Hellespontum, vel trans fluvium, *to transport*: Marius cum parva navicula in Africam trajectus est, *passed or sailed over*. Trajectus ferro, *pierced*.

Capere conjecturam, consilium, dolorem, fugam, specimen, spem, sedem, &c. *to guess, consult, grieve, fly, essay, hope, sit, &c.* augurium, v. auspicium, & agere, *to take an omen*: exemplum de aliquo: locum castris: terram, *to alight*: insulam, summa, *sc.* loca, *to reach*: spolia ex nobilitate, *to gain*, Sall. de republica nihil præter gloriam, Nep. magistratum, *to receive or enjoy*: virginem Vestalem, *to chuse*: amentiam, spiritus, superbiam alicujus, *to bear, to contain*: aliquem, consilio, perfidia, *to catch*: nec te Troja capit, Virg. Ædes vix nos capiunt, *the house hardly contains us*: Altero oculo capitur, *blind of one eye*: capitur locis, *he is delighted with*, Virg.

Accipere pecuniam, vulnus, cladem, injuriam ab aliquo, *to receive*: Orbis terrarum divitias accipere nolo pro patriæ caritate, Nep. binas literas eodem exemplo, *two copies of the same letter*, Cic. clamorem, de Socrate, *to hear*: id in bonam partem, *to take in good part, to understand in a good sense*: omnia ad contumeliam, aliter, aliorsum ac, atque, Ter. rudem, v. rude donari, *to be discharged as a gladiator*; aliquem bene v. male, *to treat*: eum male acceptum in Mediam hiematum coegit redire, *roughly handled*, Nep. rogationem, *to approve the bill*;

hill; nomen, i. e. ad petendum admittere, *to allow to stand candidate*; omen, *to esteem good*; satisfactionem *v.* excusationem, Cæf. Acceptus plebi, apud plebem, *popular.*

CONCIPERE verba juramenti, *to prescribe the form of an oath*; conceptis verbis jurare: inimicitias cum aliquo, *to bear enmity to one*: aquam, *to gather, to form the head of an aquæduct*, Frontinus.

EXCIPERE cum hospitio, *to entertain*; fugientes, *to catch*; extremum spiritum cognatorum; sanguinem paterâ, *to keep or gather*; notis, & scribere, *to write in short hand*; motus futuros, *to perceive*; Hos homines excipio, *I except*; virtutem excipit immortalitas; turbulentior annus excepit, *succeeded*; sic excepit regia Juno, *replied*, Virg.

INCIPERE, occipere, *to begin.* Percipere fructus, *to reap.*

PRÆCIPERE futura, *to foresee*; gaudia, spem victoriæ, *to anticipate*; pecuniam mutuam, *to take before the time*, Cæf. lac, *to dry up*, Virg. alicui id, *v.* de ea re, *to order*; artem ei, *to teach.*

RECIPERE aliquid, *to receive*; urbem, *to recover*; eum tectis, *to entertain*; se *v.* pedem, *to retreat*; se domum, *to return*; se, mentem, animum, *to come to one's self again, to recover spirits*; in se, *to take charge*; alicui, *to promise*; se ad frugem, *to amend*; senem seffum, *to give a seat to*, Cic.

RAPERE *vel* trahere in pejorem partem, *to take a thing in the worst sense*; in jus, *to bring before a judge*; partes inter se, *to share*, Liv. Sub divum, *to reveal*, Horat.

U O.

EXUERE vestes sibi, se vestibus; jugum sibi, se jugo, *to cast off*; fidem, sacramentum, *to break*; mentem, *to change*, Virg. hostem castris, *to beat from.*

RUERE ad interitum, in ferrum: cæteros, Ter. spumas, *to drive or tofs*, Virg.

LUERE pœnas capitis, *to suffer*; æs alienum, *to pay*, Curt. culpam suam *vel* alterius, morte, sanguine, *to expiate, to atone or suffer for.*

FLUERE amicitiæ remiffione usûs, *to drop gradually*, Cic.

STATUERE stipendium iis de publico, *to appoint*; exemplum in hominem, *vel* -ne, *to make one a public example*; aliquem capite in terram, *to set or place*, Ter.

CONSTITUERE coloniam, *to settle*; agmen paulisper, *to make to stop or halt*, Sall. in digitis, *to count on one's fingers*, Cic. urbem, *to build*, Ovid. Is hodie venturum ad me conftituit domum, *appointed, resolved*, Ter. Si utilitas amicitiam conftituit, tollet eadem, *makes, conftitutes*, Cic. Corpus bene conftitutum, *a good conftitution*, Id.

DESTITUERE aliquem, *to forsake*; spem, *to deceive*; propositum, *to give over*, Ovid. deos pactâ mercede, *to defraud*, Hor.

INSTITUERE aliquem secundum hæredem filio, *to appoint*, Cic. collegium fabrorum, sacra, *to institute, to found*, Plin. aliquem doctrinâ, Græcis literis, *to instruct*; naves, *to build*, Cæf. sermonem, *to enter upon*, Id. animum ad cogitandum, *to settle*; antequam pro Murœna dicere instituo, *I begin*, Cic.

PRÆSTITUERE petitori, qua actione illum uti oporteat, *to prescribe to the prosecutor what form of process he should use*, Cic. tempus ei, *to determine.*

RESTITUERE exules; virginem suis, *to restore*; oppida vicosque, *to repair*; aciem inclinatam, *to rally*; prœlium, *to renew*, Liv.

SUBSTITUERE aliquem in locum ejus, pro altero, *to substitute or put in the place of*, Cic.

STRUERE

STRUERE epulas, *to prepare*;
insidias, mendacium, *to contrive*;
odium, crimen alicui, vel in aliquem, *to raise against*.

B O.

SCRIBERE sua manu, bene,
velociter, epistolam alicui, v. ad
aliquem; bellum, v. de bello; milites, *to enlist*; supplementum militibus, *to recruit them*; hæredem,
to make one his heir; dicam ei, *to
commence an action against one*; nummos,
to give a bill of exchange; de rebus
suis scribi cupivit, Cic. Decemvir.
legibus scribendis, Liv.

ASCRIBERE aliquem civitati, in
civitatem. v. æ, *to make free*.

DESCRIBERE aliquem, *to describe
and not to name*; partes Italiæ, pecuniam, populum ordinibus, *to
distribute, to divide*; vectigal civitatibus, i. e. imperare; jura, i. e.
dare v. constituere; censores bi-
nos in singulas civitates, i. e. facere, Cic.

INSCRIBERE literas alicui, *to
direct a letter*; librum, *to entitle* or
name; ædes mercede, *to put a ticket
on one's house to let*, Ter.

PROSCRIBERE bona alicujus,
ædes suas, auctionem, *to publish to
be sold, to set to sale*; aliquem, *to
banish, to outlaw*.

RESCRIBERE alicujus literis v.
ad literas, alicui ad aliquid, *to
write an answer*; pecuniam, *to pay
money by bill*; legionem ad equum,
to set foot soldiers on horseback, Cæs.

SUBSCRIBERE exemplum litera-
rum, *to write below*; causæ, *to join
or take part in an accusation*; Cæsaris iræ, *to favour*, Ovid.

C O.

DICERE aliquid, v. de aliqua
re, ex aliquo loco. alicui, ad v.
apud aliquem; in aliquem, *against*;
ad aliquid, *in answer to*; sententiam, *to give an opinion*; jus, *to ad-*

minister justice, *to pronounce sentence*;
multam ei, *to amerce* or *fine*; diem
ei, *to appoint a day for his trial before the people*; prodicere, *to put it
off*; causam, *to plead*; testimonium,
to give evidence; non idem loqui est
ac dicere, *to harangue*, Cic. sacramento; *seldom* sacramentum, *to
take the military oath*.

ADDICERE aliquid ei, *to call out
at an auction, to sell*; servituti, v. in
servitutem. *to sentence or adjudge to
bondage*; bona, *to give up the goods
of the debtor to the creditor*; se alicui,
to devote himself to one's service: aves
non addixerunt, v. abdixerunt, *the
birds did not give a favourable omen*;
pretio addictam habere fidem, *to
be corrupt*, Cic.

CONDICERE operam alicui, *to
promise assistance*; cœnam alicui, v.
ad cœnam, *to propose supping with
one without invitation*.

EDICERE alicui, *to order*; de-
lectum, *to appoint a levy*; prædam
militibus, *to promise by an edict*;
justitium, diem comitiis, vel comitia consulibus creandis, *to appoint*.

INDICERE bellum, justitium, *to
proclaim war*; legem sibi, *to appoint*,
Cic. cœtus in domos tribunorum,
to summon, Liv. indicare. *to shew*;
Indictus, an adj. *not said*; causâ
indictâ, v. non cognitâ condem-
nari, *to be condemned without being
heard*; me indicente, hæc non
fiunt, *not telling*, Ter.

INTERDICERE alicui, aliquid v.
aliqua re; foeminis usum purpuræ,
to forbid or *debar from*; ei aquâ &
igne, v. aquam et ignem, *to banish*;
malè rem gerentibus bonis pater-
nis interdici solet, Cic. interdici
non poterat socero gener, *discharged
the company of*, Nep.

PRÆDICERE alicui aliquid, de
aliqua re, id in hac re, *to foretell,
to forewarn*.

DUCERE

DUCERE in carcerem *v.* vincula, *to lead*; exercitum, *to command*; spiritum, animam, vitam, *to breathe, to live*; fossam, murum, sulcum, *to make* or *draw*; bellum, *to prolong*, also *to carry on*, Virg. ætatem, diem, *to spend*; uxorem, *to take a wife*; in jus, *to summon before a judge*; aliquem, & vultum alicujus, ære, ex ære, de auro, marmore, &c. *to make a statue*; genus, nomen ab *v.* ex aliquo, *to derive*; omnia pro nihilo, infra se; id ei laudi, laudem, *v.* in laudem, *oftener the first*, *to reckon it a praise to him*; in conscientiam, *to impute to a consciousness of guilt*; in gloria, Plin. in crimen, Tacit. centesimas, *sc.* usuras, *vel* fœnus centesimis, *to compute interest at one for the hundred a month*; or *at* 12 *per cent. per annum*; binis centesimis fœnerari, *to take* 24 *per cent. per annum*, Cic. ducere longas voces in fletum, *to draw out*, Virg. ordines, *to be a centurion*, Liv. ilia, *to pant like a broken winded horse*, Hor.

ADDUCERE aliquem in judicium, ad arbitrium meum, *to bring to a trial*; in suspicionem regi, Nep. arcum, *to draw in*; habenas, *to straiten the reins*.

CONDUCERE aliquem ex loco, *to convey*; navem, domum, coquos, *to hire*; columnam faciendam, *to engage to make at a certain price*: Conducit hoc tuæ laudi, in *v.* ad rem, *is of advantage*.

DEDUCERE naves, *to launch*; classem in prælium, *to bring*, Nep. equites, *to make to alight*, Liv. cum domum, *to accompany, to carry home*; de sententia, Cic. coloniam, *to transplant*; lacum, *to drain*.

EDUCERE gladium e vagina, *to draw*; florem Italiæ, *to lead out*; copias in aciem, Cic. filium, *to educate*, *oftener* educare; in astra, *to extol*, Hor. cœlo, Virg.

INDUCERE tenebras clarissimis rebus, *to bring on*, Cic. animum, *v.* in animum, *to persuade himself*; scuta pellibus, *to cover*, Cæs. soleas pedibus, *v.* in pedes, *to put on*; colorem picturæ, *to varnish*, Plin. nomina, *to cancel* or *rase*, *to rub out*.

OBDUCERE exercitum, *to lead against*; callum dolori, *to blunt it*; sepulchrum sentibus, *to cover*.

REDUCERE aliquem in memoriam alicujus, *vel* alicui aliquid in memoriam, *to bring back to one's remembrance*; in gratiam cum aliquo, *to reconcile*; Vallis reducta, *retired* or *low*.

PRODUCERE testes, *to bring out*; funus, *to attend*; sermonem in noctem, *to prolong, to continue*; rem in hiemem, *to defer*; servos vendendos, *to bring to market*.

SUBDUCERE se a custodibus, *to steal away*; naves, *to draw up on shore*; cibum ei & deducere, *to take from*; summam, rationes, *to reckon, to cast up accounts*.

PARCERE sibi, labore, *to spare*, &c. a cædibus, *to forbear*; aurum natis, Virg.

ASSUESCERE rei alicui, *v.* re aliqua, in *v.* ad hoc, *to be accustomed*; mentem pluribus & assuefacere, Hor. Amnis bella, Virg. *to accustom*. So insuesco rei *v.* re; insuevit hoc me pater, Hor.

SCISCERE legem, *to vote, to decree*: hence plebiscitum.

ASCISCERE regium nomen, *to assume*; socios sibi, ad societatem sceleris, *to associate*; ritus peregrinos, *to adopt*.

CONSCISCERE mortem *v.* necem sibi, *to kill one's self*; fugam sibi, *to flee*, Liv.

DISCERE aliquid ab aliquo, *v.* apud aliquem, ex aliqua re, *or without* ex: Dediscere, *to forget what he hath learned*; Ediscere, *to get by heart*.

DESCENDERE

DESCENDERE de palatio, præsidio, ædibus; in forum, curiam, campum; ad accusandum, ad omnia, ad extrema, *to have recourse to*, Cic.

D O.

LUDERE aleâ, v. -am, *to play at dice*; par impar, *at even and odd*; operam, *to lose one's labour*.

ALLUDERE alicui, ad aliquem: Colludere ei, cum eo: illudere ei, eum, in eum, in eo; id, *to mock*.

EVADERE insidias, -iis, vel ex, *to escape*; in muro, *to mount*: Hæc quorsum evadant, nescio, *to what they will turn out*: Clarus evasit, *became*.

CEDERE multa multis de suo jure, Cic. Bona creditoribus, *to yield*, whence cessio bonorum; alicui loco, de, a, ex loco, v. locum, *to give place*; vitâ, e vitâ decedere, *to die*; foro, *to turn bankrupt*; Hæreditas cedit mihi, *falls to*; Cedit in proverbium, *becomes*.

ACCEDERE oppidum, -do, ad v. in oppidum, *to approach*; ad conditiones, *to agree to*; Ciceroni, sententiæ, v. ad sententiam ejus, *to agree with*; ad Ciceronem, *to go to*; ad rempublicam, *to bear the quæstorship, or the first public office*; ad amicitiam Philippi, *to gain the friendship of*, Nep. Ad hæc mala hoc mihi accedit etiam, *added*, Ter. Robur accessit ætati, Cic. Animi accessere hosti, Liv. Ad corporis firmitatem plura animi bona accesserant, Nep. Accedit plurimum pretio; huc, eo, accedit quod, *is added*.

ANTECEDERE alicui rei; aliquem, *rarely* alicui, *to excel*.

CONCEDERE ei aliquid & de aliquo; paullum de suo jure; tempus ad rem, *to grant*; ab oculis, ad dextram, in exilium, in hiberna, *to retire, to go*: fato, naturæ, vitâ, *to die*; in sententiam ejus, *to come*

into one's measures; in conditiones, *to agree to*, Liv.

DISCEDERE transversum, & latum unguem, v. digitum a re, *to depart in the least*.

INTERCEDERE legi, *to give a negative against, to oppose a law*; pecuniam pro aliquo, *to become surety*: Intercedit mihi tecum amicitia vel inter nos, *there is*, &c.

SUCCEDERE ei, in locum ejus, *to succeed*; muro, v. murorum; ad urbem; sub primam aciem; in pugnam, *to come up to*.

CADERE altè, ab alto, in terram, *to fall*; causâ, formulâ, in judicio, & litem perdere, *to lose one's cause, to be cast*; in v sub sensum, oculos, potestatem, &c. in morbum, & incidere, Cic. Non cadit in virum bonum mentiri, *is incapable of*, Cic. Homini lachrymæ cadunt, quasi puero, gaudio, Ter.

ACCIDERE genibus, v. ad genua, *to fall at*; auribus v. ad aures, *to come to*; alicui, casu, præter opinionem, *to happen*; accidit in te istud verbum, *applies*, Ter.

TENDERE vela, *to stretch*; insidias, retia, plagas, &c. *to lay snares*; arcum, *to bend*; iter, cursum, *to direct*; ad altiora, in cœlum, *to aim at*; extra vallum, st. tabernaculum, *to pitch a tent*: Manibus tendit divellere nodos, *tries*, Virg.

ATTENDO te, Cic. tibi, Plin. de hac re, ad hanc rem, *to take heed*; animum ad rem; res hostium, Sall.

CONTENDERE nervos, omnibus nervis, *to exert one's self*; aliquid ab aliquo, *to ask earnestly*; inter se: amori, poet. *for* cum amore, *to strive*: causas, sc. inter se, *to compare*, Cic. Aliquid ad aliquid, cum aliquo, & alicui.

COMPREHENDERE naturam rerum, *to understand*: rem pluribus

& luculentioribus verbis, *to express*; aliquem, humanitate, amicitia, *to gain*; rem fictam, *to discover*.

INTENDERE animum rei, ad &c. in rem, *to apply*: Intendi animo in rem, Liv. Vocem, nervos, *to exert*; arcum, *to bend*; actionem *v.* litem alicui *vel* in aliquem, *also* impingere, *to raise a law-suit against one*; telum ei, *v.* in eum, *to shoot at*; manum *v.* digitum in aliquid, *to point at*: aliquo, *sc.* ire, *to go to*; officia, *to overdo, to do more than is required*, Sall.

OBTENDERE velum rei, *v.* rem velo, *to cover, to veil*.

PENDERE pecuniam, *to pay*; poenas, *to suffer*; id parvi, *to value it little*.

SUSPENDERE aliquem arbori, de, in, *v.* ex arbore, *to hang*; expectatione, *vel* suspensum detinere, *to keep in suspense*; aedificium, *to arch a house*; naso adunco, *to sneer at*, Horat.

ABDERE se literis, in literas, *to hide or shut up one's self among books*, se domum, rus, &c. domo, Virg. in silvas, tenebras; &c.

CONDERE urbem, *to build*; fructus, *to lay up*; in carcerem, *to imprison*; carmen, *to compose*; lumina, *to close*, Ovid. Jura, *to establish*; terrâ, sepulchro, in sepulchro, *to bury*.

DEDERE se alicui, in ditionem alicujas, ad aliquem, *to surrender*; Deditus praeceptori, & studiis, *fond of*; vino epulisque, *engaged in*, Nep. deditâ operâ, *on purpose*.

EDERE librum, & in lucem, *publish*; ovum, *to lay*; sonos, cantus, risus, gemitus, questus, hinnitum, pugnam, stragem, *to sound, sing, &c.* munus gladiatorium, *to exhibit a show of gladiators*; nomen, *to mention*; foetus, *to bring forth*; extremum spiritum, *to die*; exempla cruciatús in aliquem, *to inflict exemplary torture*.

OBDERE pessulum foribus, *to bolt the door*.

PRODERE arcem hostibus, *to betray*; aliquid posteris, *v.* memoriae, *to hand down*; genus ab aliquo, *to derive*: flaminem, interregem, *to appoint*; aliquot dies nuptiis, *to put off*, Ter exemplum, *to give to posterity*, Liv.

REDDERE animum, se sibi, *to revive*; animam *v.* vitam, *to die*; Latinè, verbum verbo, *to translate*; matrem, i. e. referre, *to resemble*; epistolam alicui, *to deliver*.

SUBDERE calcar equo, *to spur*; spiritus alicui, *to encourage*.

CREDERE rem: homini, *to believe*; aliquid alicui, *to trust*; pecuniam ei per syngrapham, *to lend on bond or bill*; rumoribus credi non oportet: Itaque credo, si, &c. *I suppose*, Cic.

FUNDERE aquam, *to pour out*; hostes, *to rout*.

EFFUNDERE fruges, copiam oratorum, *to produce*; aerarium, *to spend*; odium, i. e. dimittere, *to drop*, gratiam collectum, i. e. perdere: omnia, quae tacuerat, *to tell*.

G O.

JUNGERE se cum aliquo, alicui, & ad aliquem, dextram dextrae: equos currui: amnem ponte, *to make a bridge*.

ADJUNGERE accessionem aedibus, *to build an addition to one's house*: animum ad studia, *to apply*.

STRINGERE cultrum, gladium, ensem, *to draw*: frondes, *to lop off*: glandes, baccas *to beat down*: rem, *to waste one's fortune*, Hor. littus, *to touch, to brush or graze upon*, Virg.

TANGERE rem acu, *to hit the nail on the head*.

ATTINGERE Britanniam navibus, *to reach*: reges, res summas, *to mention*, Nep. Aliquem cognatione,

cognatione, affinitate, *to be related to:* forum, *to reach manbood*, Cic. Res non te attingit, *concerns*.

FINGERE orationem. *to polish:* oratorem, *to form:* se ad arbitrium alterius, *to adapt:* Vultus a mente fingitur, lingua fingit vocem, Cic. Sui cuique mores fingunt fortunam, Nep.

FRANGERE nucem *to break;* navem, *to suffer sbipwreck:* fœdus, fidem, *to violate:* sententiam ejus, *to refute*, Cic. hostem. *to subdue.*

AGERE gratias *to give thanks:* vitam, *to live:* prædas, *to plunder:* fabulam, *to act a play:* triumphum de aliquo, ex aliqua re, *to triumph:* nugas, *to trifle:* ambages, *to beat about the busb:* stationem, custodiam urbis, *to be on guard:* rimas, *to chink, to leak, to be rent:* causam, *to plead:* de re, *to speak:* radices, *to take root:* cuniculos, *to undermine:* undam, *to raise a steam:* animam, *to be at the last gasp:* alias res, *to be inattentive:* festum diem, natalem, ferias, &c. *to keep, to observe:* actum, v. rem actam, *to labour in vain:* censum, & habere, *to make a review of the people, their estates, &c.* forum, *to hold a court to try causes:* lege in aliquem, & cum aliquo, *to go to law with one: bence* actor, *a plaintiff:* in hereditatem, *to claim:* cum populo, *to treat with, to lay before:* decimum agit annum, *he is ten years old:* id agitur, *that is the question:* libertas agitur, v de libertate, *is at stake:* actum est de libertate, *is lost:* actum est, ilicet, *all is over:* actum est de pace, *was treated about:* cum illo bene actum est, *he bas been lucky or well used:* hoc age, *mind what you are about.* Civitas læta agere, *for erat*, Salust.

ADIGERE milites sacramento, ad v. in jusjurandum, in sua verba, per jusjurandum, *to force to*

enlist: arbitrum, i. e. agere v. cogere aliquem ad arbitrum, *to force to submit to an arbitration*, Cic.

COGERE copias, *to bring together:* ad militiam, *to force to enlist:* senatum, *to assemble:* in senatum, sc. minis, pignoribus captis, &c. *to force to attend:* agmen, *to rally to bring up:* lac, *to curdle:* jus civile diffusum & dissipatum, in certa genera cogere, *to digest, to arrange.*

EXIGERE foras, *to drive out, to divorce:* aliquid ab aliquo, *to require:* sarta tecta, sc. et, i. e. sarta et tecta, ut sint bene reparata, *to require that the public works be kept in good reparation*, Cic. supplicium, de aliquo, *to inflict:* sua nomina, *to demand or call in one's debts:* ævum, vitam, annos, *to spend:* aliquid ad normam, *to try or examine;* columnam ad perpendiculum, *to apply the plummet, to see if it be straight:* monumentum, *to finish.* Hor. tempus & modum, *to settle* Virg. comœdiam, *to disapprove, to hiss off*, Ter.

REDIGERE aliquid in memoriam alicujus, *to bring back:* pecuniam ex bonis venditis, *to raise money:* hostes sub imperium, *to reduce.*

LEGERE oram, littus, *to coast along:* vela, *to furl the sails:* halitum, *to catch one's breath:* milites, *to enlist:* aliquem in senatum, in Patres, *to chuse:* sacra, *to steal, to commit sacrilege:* Hor.

H O.

TRAHERE obsidionem, bellum, *to prolong:* purpuras, *to spin:* aliquid in religionem, *to scruple:* navem remulco, *to tow.*

DETRAHERE aliquem, *to draw down:* alicui, v. de aliquo, de fama, *to detract from, to lessen one's fame:* aliquid alicui, *to take by force:* laudem, v. de laudibus:

novem

novem partes multæ, *to take from the fine*, Nep.

EXTRAHERE diem, *to spin out, to spend*; certamen, bellum, judicium, *to prolong*.

VEHERE, vehens, invehens, invectus curru, quadrigis, &c. *riding in a chariot*; invehi in portum ex alto, *to enter*; in aliquem, *to inveigh against*; provehi longiùs, *to proceed too far*.

LO.

CONSULERE rem *v*. de re, *to consult about*; eum', *to ask his advice*; ei, *to consult for his good*; de salute sua; gravius in aliquem, *to pass a severe sentence against*; in commune, publicum, medium, *to provide for the common good*; verba boni, *to take in good part*; ego consulor, *my advice is asked*; mihi consulitur, *my good is consulted*; mihi consultum ac provisum est, *for a time, I have taken care*, Cic.

APPELLERE classe in Italiam, vel classem, *to land on*; se aliquò, Ter. ad villam nostram navis appelletur, Cic. animum ad philosophiam, *to apply*.

ANTECELLERE ei, *rarely* eum: excellere aliis, super, inter, præter alios aliqua re, *v*. in re, *to excel*.

TOLLERE animos suos, *to take courage*; animos alicui, *to encourage*; aliquem laudibus, & laudes ejus in astra, *to extol*; inducias, *to break a truce*; clamores, *to cry*; filium, *to educate*; de *vel* e medio, *to kill*.

MO.

ADIMERE claves uxori, *to divorce*; annulum *v*. equum equiti, *to take away from a knight the ring or horse given him by the public, to degrade*.

DIRIMERE litem, controversiam, *to determine*.

EXIMERE aliquem servitio, noxæ, e vinculis, a culpa, de nu-

W

mero proscriptorum, obsidione, *to free*; de dolio, *to draw out*; diem dicendo, *to waste in speaking*.

INTERIMERE se, *to kill*.

REDIMERE captivos, *to ransom*; pecuaria de censoribus, *to take or farm the public pastures*.

SUMERE in manus; diem, tempus ad deliberandum; exemplum ex *v*. de eo, *to take*; pœnas, supplicium de aliquo, *to punish*: pecunias mutuas, *to borrow*; togam virilem, *to put on the dress of a man*; sibi inimicitias, *to get ill will*; operam in re, *vel* in rem insumere, *to bestow pains*; sumo tantum, *vel* hoc mihi, *I take this upon me*.

PREMERE caseum, *to make cheese*; vocem, *to be silent*; dolorem corde, *to conceal*; vestigia ejus, *to follow*; littus, *to come near*; pollicem, *to save a gladiator*; librum in nonum annum, *to delay publishing*, Hor.

EXPRIMERE succum, *to press out*; risum alicui; pecuniam ab aliquo, *to force from*; effigiem, *to draw to the life*; verbum verbo, de verbo, e verbo, ad verbum, de Græcis, &c. *to translate word for word*.

IMPRIMERE aliquid animo, in animo, *v*. in animum, *to imprint*.

REPRIMERE se, & reprendere *v*. retinere, *to check*.

NO.

PONERE spem in homine *v*. re, & habere; castra, *to pitch*; vitem, *to plant*; vitam, *to die*; ova, *to lay*; insidias alicui; panem convivis, *not* ante; personam amici, *to lay aside the character of a friend*; præmia, *to propose*; pocula, *to stake or lay*; studium, tempus, multum operæ in aliqua re, *to employ, to bestow*: aliquid in laude, in vitiis, in loco beneficii, *to reckon*; ferocia corda, *to lay aside*;

aliquæ

aliquem in gratiam *v.* gratia, i. e. efficere gratiosum apud alterum, Cic. : ventos, *to calm* : hominem coloribus, faxo, *to paint, engrave,* Hor. - pecuniam in fœnore, *to lay out at interest* : templa, *to build,* Virg. Venti posuere, *are hush'd,* Virg. Pone esse victum eum, Ter. Positum sit, *suppose, grant,* Cic.

COMPONERE carmen, literas, &c. *to compose* : lites, *to settle* : bellum, *to finish by treaty* : parva magnis, dicta cum factis, *to compare* : manus manibus, *to join,* Virg.

DEPONERE *v.* ponere togam prætextam, *to lay aside the dress of a boy* : imperium & demittere, *to lay down a command.*

EXPONERE rem, *to set forth* or *explain* : frumentum, *to expose to sale,* Cic. pueros, fœtus, *to leave to perish,* Liv. exercitum, *sc.* in terram, *to land.*

IMPONERE onus alicui *v.* in aliquem : aliquem in equum, *to set upon* : personam *v.* partes duriores ei, *to lay a task* or *duty on one* : alicui, *to impose on, to deceive,* Nep. honorem ei, *to confer* : vadimonium ei, *to force to give bail* : Nep. manum summam *v.* extremam rei alicui, in aliqua re, *to finish* : pontem flumini, *to make a bridge,* Curt. Hoc loco libet interponere, *to insert,* Nep.

OPPONERE se periculis & ad pericula, *to expose* : pignori, *to pledge* : manum fronti, ante oculos, *to put,* Ovid.

PROPONERE aliquid sibi facere, exempla ei ad imitandum, *to propose, to set before* : edicta, legem in publicum, i. e. publice legenda affigere : congiarium, *to promise a largess, a gift of corn or money.*

SUPPONERE ova gallinæ, *to set a hen* : testamentum, *v.* subjicere, *to forge.*

CANERE aliquem, *to praise* :

signa, classicum, bellicum, i. e. ad arma conclamare, *to sound an alarm, to give the signal for battle* : receptui, *rarely* -um, *to sound a retreat* : tibia, *to play on the pipe* : ad tibiam, *to sing to it* : palinodiam, *to utter a recantation.*

STERNERE lectos, *to spread* or *cover the couches* : equos, *to harness* : viam, *to pave* : æquora, *to calm,* Virg.

PO.

CARPERE agmen, *to cut off the rear* : somnos, quietem, *to sleep* : viam, iter, *to go,* Virg. opera alterius, *to censure* : labores, virtutes, *to diminish* or *obscure,* Hor.

RUMPERE fidem, fœdus, amicitiam, *to violate* : vocem *v.* silentium, *to speak,* Virg.

ERUMPERE ex tenebris, castris, &c. se portis, *to break out* : stomachum in aliquem, *to vent passion* : nubem, *to break,* Virg.

RO.

QUÆRERE bonam gratiam sibi, *to seek* or *gain,* Cic. sermonem, *to beat about for conversation,* Ter. rem mercaturis faciendis, *to make a fortune by merchandise* : ex aliquo; & in aliquem, de re aliqua per tormenta, *to put to the rack* : in dominum de servo quæri noluerunt Romani, Cic.

ANQUIRERE aliquid, *to search after* : aliquem capitis, *v.* -te, *to accuse* or *try for a capital crime.*

GERERE res, *to perform* : negotium male, *to manage* : consulatum, *to bear, to manage* : se bene vel male, *to behave* : exercitum, *to conduct,* Sallust. morem ei, vel morigerari, *to humour* : civem, se pro cive, personam alicujus, *to pass for, to bear the character of* : inimicitias vel simultatem cum aliquo, *to be at enmity* or *variance with.*

INGERERE

INGERERE convicia ei, in eum, *to inveigh against.*

SUGGERERE aliquid, ei, *to suggest, to hint,* sumptus his rebus, *to supply or afford:* Horatium Bruto, *to chuse in place of, to put after,* Liv.

SERERE crimina in eum, *to raise, to spread accusations.*

CONSERERE manus, manu, certamen, pugnam, cum hostibus, inter se, *to engage.*

ASSERERE aliquid, *to affirm;* aliquem manu, ab injuria, in libertatem, *to free;* in servitutem, *to reduce;* divinam majestatem, *to claim.*

TO:

PETERE aliquid alicui; id ab eo, *rarely* cum; in beneficii gratieque loco, Cic. *to ask;* urbem Romam, murum, montes, *to go to, to make for;* aliquem sagittá, lapide, *to aim at;* consulatum, poenas ab aliquo, & repetere, *to punish.*

COMPETERE animo, *to be in one's senses;* in eum competit actio, *an action lies against him,* Cic.

REPETERE res, *to demand restitution;* bona lege, v. prosequi lite, *to recover by law;* castra, oppidum, huc, *to return to;* aliquid memoriá, *to call to mind;* alté, *to trace from the beginning.* Mihi nihil suppetit, multa suppetunt, *I have;* si vita suppetet, *if life shall remain,* Cic.

MITTERE alicui, v. ad aliquem; in suffragia, *to send the people to vote;* aulæum, mappam, *to drop the curtain;* talos, *to throw the dice;* senatum, *to dismiss;* timorem, *to lay aside:* in acta, *to register, to record;* sanguinem, vel emittere, *to let blood;* noxam, *to forgive;* signa timoris, *to shew;* vocem, *to utter, to speak;* habenas, v. remittere, *to slacken;* manu et emittere, *to free a slave;* filium emancipare, *to free a son from the power of his father;* sub jugum, *to make to pass under the yoke;* inferias

manibus diis, *to sacrifice to the infernal gods;* rem, v. de re, *to omit;* mitto rem! *I say nothing of fortune,* Ter. in possessionem bonorum, *to give the possession of the debtor's effects;* misit orare, ut venirem; i. e. aliquem ad orandum, Ter.

AMITTERE litem, v. causam; vitam, fidem, lumina, aspectum, *to lose,* Cic.

ADMITTERE in cubiculum, *to admit;* equum immittere, & permittere, *to gallop;* delictum in se, *to commit a fault;* aves non admiserunt, *have not given a favourable omen,* Liv.

COMMITTERE facinus, *to commit;* se alicui, v. in fidem alicujus, *to entrust;* prælium, *to engage;* exercitum pugnæ, rem in casum ancipitis eventûs prælii, *to risk a battle,* Liv. iv. 27. aliquem cum aliquo, homines inter se, *to set at variance, or by the ears;* rem eó, *to bring to that pass;* gladiatores, pugiles, Græcos cum Latinis, *to match or pair;* committere; ut, *to chafe;* incommoda sua legibus & judiciis, *to seek redress by law.*

COMPROMITTERE. Candidati compromiserant, H. S. quingenis in singulos apud M. Catonem depositis, petere ejus arbitratu, ut qui contra fecisset, ab eo condemnaretur, *made a compromise or agreement,* &c.

DIMITTERE exercitum, *to disband;* uxorem, & repudiare, nuntium v. repudium ad eam remittere, *to divorce.*

PROMITTERE id ei, *to promise;* capillum, barbam, *to let grow,* Liv.

PERMITTERE alicui, *to allow;* divis cetera, *to leave,* Horat. se in fidem v. fidei ejus; vela ventis; equum in hostem; rem suffragiis populi, *to let the people decide;* tribunatum vexandis consulibus, *to give up, to employ,* Liv.

REMITTERE

REMITTERE animum, *to ease*; calces, tela, *to throw back*; ex pecunia, de supplicio, tributo, &c. *to abate*; debitum, iras alicui, *to give up, to forgive*; justicium, *to discontinue*; pugnam, *to slacken*; remittit explorare, *neglects*, Salluſt.

SUBMITTERE faſces populo, *to lower*; ſe v. animum, *to ſubmit, to humble*; percuſſores alicui, *to ſuborn aſſaſſins*.

TRANSMITTERE in Africam, neut. *to paſs over*.

VERTERE in fugam, *to put to flight*; terga, *to fly*; ab imo, *to overthrow*; ſolum, *to go into baniſhment*; id ei vitio, v. crimini, & in crimen, *to blame*; in ſuperbiam, *to impute*; Platonem, Latinè Græca, Græca vel ex Græcis in Latinum, *to tranſlate*; pollicem, *to doom a gladiator to death by turning up the thumb*; terram, *to plough*; crateram, *to empty*, Virg. Stilum, *to correct*, Horat. Salus vel cauſa in eo vertitur, *depends*; fortuna verterat, Liv. Annus vertens, *a whole year*, Nep. Res bene vertat, Di bene vertant, *proſper*.

ANIMADVERTERE id, *to obſerve*; in eum verberibus, morte, &c. *to puniſh*.

ADVERTERE agmen urbi, *to bring up to*, Virg. oras, *to arrive at*; aures, mentes, animum, v animo ad aliquid, monitis, *to attend to*; in aliquem, oftener animadvertere, *to puniſh*.

ANTEVERTERE ei, *to come before*; damnationem veneno, *to prevent*; rem rei, *to prefer*, Plaut.

INTERVERTERE pecuniam alicujus, & aliquem pecuniâ, *to embezzle, to cheat*; candelabrum, *to ſteal, to pilfer*; promiſſum & receptum, ſc. Dolobellæ conſulatum, intervertit, ad ſeque tranſtulit, *treacherouſly withheld*, Cic.

PRÆVERTERE, & -ti, dep. ventos curſu, *to outſtrip*; deſiderium plebis, *to prevent*; metum ſupplicii morte voluntariâ, Liv. Aliquid alicui rei, *to put before*, Id.

SISTERE vadimonium; ſe in judicio, *to appear in court at one's trial*; nec ſiſti poſſe, *nor could the ſtate be ſaved*, Liv.

ASSISTERE ei, *to ſtand by*; ad fores; contra, ſuper eum.

CONSISTERE in digitos, *to ſtand on tiptoe*; in anchoris, ad anchoram, *to ride at anchor*; frigore, *to be frozen*; Ovid. Spes in velis conſiſtebat, *depended on*; virtus in actione conſiſtit, Cic.

INSISTERE jacentibus, *to ſtand upon*; veſtigiis ejus; viam, v. viâ; in re. aliqua, in rem, v. rei; in dolos, negotium, Plaut. *to inſiſt upon, to urge*.

OBSISTERE ei, *to ſtop, to oppoſe*.
RESISTERE ei, *to reſiſt*.
SUBSISTERE, *to ſtand ſtill*; ſumptui, *to bear*.

VO.

SOLVERE pecuniam ei, *to pay*; verſurâ, *to pay debt by borrowing from another*, Ter. Fidem, *to break a promiſe*, or according to others, *to perform*, Ter. And. IV. I. 19. litem æſtimatam, *to pay the fine impoſed on him*, Nep. Votum, *to diſcharge*; obſidionem urbis, v. urbem obſidione, *to raiſe a ſiege*; navem, e portu, *to ſet ſail*; epiſtolam, v. reſignare, *to break open*; aliquem legibus, legum vinculis, *to free from*; ſolvitur in ſomnos, Virg. Oratio ſoluta, i. e. libera, numeris non aſtricta & devincta, *proſe*; ſolve metus, *diſmiſs*, Virg.

DISSOLVERE ſocietatem, *to break*.

RESOLVERE vocem, v. ora, *to break ſilence*, Virg. jura, *to violate*; vectigal, *to take off taxes*, Tacit. In pulverem, *to reduce to*.

FOURTH

FOURTH CONJUGATION.

AUDIRE aliquem, aliquid ex *v* ab aliquo, *to hear from one*; de aliquo, *about one*, also *from one*, *as*, sæpe hoc audivi de patre, *for* ex patre, Cic.   Audire bene *v.* malè apud socios, ab omnibus, *to be well spoken of*, *to have a good character*; rexque paterque audisti, *have been called*, Hor.   Antigonus credit de suo adventu esse auditum, Nep.

VENIRE ad finem, aures, pactionem, certamen, manus, nihilum, &c. in suspicionem, odium, gratiam, &c. in jus, *to go to law*, Liv. in circulum, *into a company*, Nep.   Hæreditas ei venit, *he has succeeded to an estate*; ei usu venit, *happened*, Nep.   Quod in buccam venerit, scribito, *occurs*, Cic.

ADVENIRE & adventare ei, urbem, ad urbem, *to come to*.

ANTEVENIRE aliquem, & antevertere, Sall. rei, Plaut. tempus, consilia & itinera.

CONVENIRE in colloquium; fratrem, *to meet with*, *to speak to*; ego et frater conveniemus, copiæ convenient, *will meet together*; convenit mihi cum fratre de hac re, inter me et fratrem, inter nos; hæc fratri mecum conveniunt.   *I and my brother are agreed*; sævis inter se convenit ursis, Juv. Ipsi secum non convenit, *vel* ipse, *he is inconsistent*; pax convenit, *vel* conventa est, *is agreed upon*; rem conventuram putamus, Cic. conditiones non convenerunt; mores conveniunt, *agree*; calcei pedibus *v.* ad pedes conveniunt, *fit*, *fuit*; hoc in illum convenit : Catilinam interfectum esse convenit, *ought to have been slain*, Cic.   Convenire in manum, *the usual form of marriage*, named Coempto, *whereby women were called* matresfamilias.

SENTIRE sonorem, colorem, &c. *to perceive*; cum aliquo, *to be of one's opinion*; bene *vel* malè de eo, *to think well or ill of him*.

CONSENTIRE tibi, tecum, inter se; alicui rei, de *v.* in aliqua re; ad aliquid peragendum, *to agree*; So dissentire; *et* ab aliquo, *to disagree*; nè vita orationi dissentiat. Senec.

DEPONENT VERBS.

PROFITERI philosophiam, *to profess*, *to teach publicly*; se candidatum, *to declare himself a candidate for an office*; pecunias, agros, nomina, &c. apud censorem, *to give an account of*, *to declare how much one has*; indicium, *to promise to make a discovery*.

LOQUI cum aliquo, inter se; *sometimes* alicui, ad *v.* apud aliquem; aliquid, de aliqua re.

SEQUI feras; sectam Cæsaris, *to be of his party*, Cic.   Assequi, consequi, *to overtake*; gloriam, *to* attain.   Consequi hereditatem, *to get*; Cic.

PROSEQUI aliquem amore, laudibus, &c. *to love*, *praise*, &c.

NITI hastâ, in cubitum, *to lean*; ejus consilio, in eo, *to depend on*; ad gloriam, ad *v.* in summa, *to aim at*; in vetitum, in adversum, contra aliquem, pro aliquo, *to strive*; gradibus, *to ascend*.

UTI eo familiariter, *to be familiar with one*; ventis adversis, *to have cross winds*; honore usus, *one who has enjoyed a post of honour*.

IRREGULAR VERBS.

ESSE magni roboris, v. -no, -re ; ejus opinionis, v. ea opinione ; in maxima spe : in timore, luctu, opinione, itinere, &c. cum telo, in *vel* cum imperio ; magno periculo, v. in periculo ; in tuto ; apud se, *in his senses* ; sui juris, v. mancipii, sui potens, v. in sua potestate ; *to be at his own disposal* : Res est in vado, *is safe*, Ter. Est animus, *sc.* mihi, *I have a mind*, Virg. Est ut, cur, quamobrem, quod, quin, &c. *There is cause* ; bene, male est mihi, *with me* ; nihil est mihi tecum, *I have nothing to do with you* : Quid est tibi, *sc.* rei, *What is the matter with you ?* Ter. Cernere erat, *one might see* ; religio est mihi id facere, *I scruple to do it* ; si est, ut facere velit, ut facturus sit, ut admiserit, &c. *for* si velit, &c. Ter. Est ut viro vir latins ordinet arbusta fulcis, *it happens*, Hor. Certum est facere, *sc.* mihi, *I am resolved*, Ter. Non certum est, quid faciam, *I am uncertain*, Id. Cassius quaerere solebat, Cui Bono fuerit : Omnibus bono fuit, *it was of advantage*, Cic.

ADESSE pugnae, in pugna, ad exercitum, ad tempus, in tempore, cum aliquo, *to be present* ; alicui, *to favour, to assist* ; scribendo, v. esse ad scribendum; *to subscribe one's name to a decree of the senate*, Cic. consilio utrique, *to be a counsellor to*, Nep.

ABESSE domo, urbe, a domo, ab signis, *to be absent* ; alicui, v. deesse, *to be wanting, not to assist* ; a sole, *to stand out of the sun* ; sumptus funeri defuit, *he had not money to bury him*, Liv. abesse a persona principis, *to be inconsistent with the character*, Nep. Paulum v. parum abfuit quin urbem caperent, quin occideretur, &c. *they were near taking*, &c. Tantum abest ne enervetur oratio, ut, &c. *is so far from being*, &c. Cic. Tantum abfuit a cupiditate pecuniae, a societate sceleris, &c. Nep.

INTERESSE convivio, v. in convivio, *to be at a feast* ; anni decem interfuerunt, *intervened* ; stulto intelligens quid interest, Ter. Hoc. dominus & pater interest, Id. Inter hominem & belluam hoc interest, Cic. *differ in this, this is the difference* ; multum interest, utrum, *it is of great importance.* Pons inter eos interest, *is between*, Cic.

PRAEESSE exercitui, *to command* ; comitiis, judicio, quaestioni, *to preside in or at.*

OBESSE ei, *to hurt, to hinder.*

SUPERESSE, *to be over and above* ; alicui, *to survive* ; modo vita supersit, *sc.* mihi, *if I live* ; superest, ut, *it remains, that.*

IRE ad arma, ad saga, *to go to war* ; in jus, *to go to law* ; pedibus in sententiam alicujus, *to agree with* ; viam v. via ; res bene eunt Cic. Tempus, dies, mensis it, *passes.*

ABIRE magistratu, *to lay down an office* ; a conspectu, *to retire from company* ; in ora hominum, *to be in every body's mouth* ; ab emptione, *to retract his bargain* ; decem menses abierunt, *have past*, Ter. Non hoc tibi sic abibit, i. e. non feres hoc impune, Ter. Abi in malam rem, *a form of imprecation.*

ADIRE periculum capitis, *to run the hazard of one's life.*

EXIRE vita, e, v. de vita, *to die* ; aere alieno, Cic. Verbum exit ex ore, Id. tela, *to avoid*, Virg. Tempus induciarum cum Vejenti populo exierat, *had expired*, Liv.

INIRE magistratum ; suffragium,

gium, rationem, consilium, pugnam, viam, &c. *to enter upon; to begin*; gratiam ejus, apud eum, cum
vel ab eo; *to gain his favour :* Ineunte æstate, vere, anno, &c. *in the
beginning of; but we seldom say,* Ineunte die, nocte, &c. Ab ineunte
ætate, *from our early years.*

OSIRE diem edicti, vel auctio-
nis, judicium, vadimonium, *to be
present at*; provinciam, domos nostras, *to visit; to go through,* Cic. negotia, res, munus, officium, lega-
tionem, sacra, *to perform*; pugnas,
Virg. mortem, vel morte; diem
supremum, v. diem, *to die.*

PRÆIRE alicui, *to go before*; verba, carmen, vel sacramentum alicui,
to repeat or read over before; alicui
voce, quid judicet, *to prescribe* or
direct by crying, Cic.

PRODIRE in publicum, *to go a-
broad*; non præterit te, *you are not
ignorant,* Cic. Dies induciarum
præteriit, *is past,* Nep.

REDIRE in gratiam cum aliquo,
to become friends again; ad se, *to come
to himself, to recover his senses.*

SUBIRE murum, vel -o; ad montes, *to come up to*; laborem vel -i,
onus, pœnam, periculum, crimen,
to undergo; spes, timor subiit animum, *came into.*

VELLE aliquem, sc. alloqui
vel conventum, *to desire to speak
with*; alicui, ejus causâ, *to wish
one's good*; tibi consultum volo;
nihil tibi negatum volo, *I wish to
deny,* Liv. Quid sibi vult? *What
does he mean?* Volo te hoc facere,
hoc a te fieri; si quid recte cura-
tum velis; illos monitos etiam atque etiam volo, sc. esse, *I will ad-
monish them again and again,* Cic.
nollem factum, *I am sorry it was
done*; nollem huc exitum, sc. esse
a me, *I wish I had not come out here,*
Ter.

FERRE legem, *to propose* or

make; privilegium de aliquo, *to
propose* or *pass an act of impeachment
against one,* Cic. rogationem ad
populum, *to bring in a bill*; conditiones ei, *to offer terms*; suffragium,
to vote; sententiam, *to give an opinion*; centuriam, tribum, *to gain
the vote of*; perdere, *to lose it*; victoriam ex eo; omne punctum,
omnia suffragia, *to gain all the votes*;
repulsam, *to be rejected*; fructum
hoc fructi, *to reap,* Ter. lætitiam
de re, *to rejoice*; præ se, *to pretend*
or *declare openly*; alienam personam; *to disguise one's self*; in oculis,
to be fond of, Ter. manus in prælia,
to engage, Virg. acceptum et ex-
pensum; *to mark down as received
and spent or lent, as* Dr *and* Cr, Cic.
animus, opinio fert, *inclines*; tempus, res, causa fert, *allows, requires.*

CONFERRE benevolentiam alicui, in vel erga aliquem, *to shew*;
beneficia; culpam in eum, *to confer, to lay*; operam; tempus, studium ad vel in rem, & impendere,
to apply; capita inter se, consilia
sua, *to lay their heads together, to
consult*; signa, arma, manus, *to engage*; omne bellum circa Corin-
thum, Nep. pedem; *to set foot to
foot*; rationes, *to cast up accounts*;
castra castris, *to encamp over against
one another*; se in, vel ad urbem,
to go to; tributa, *to pay*; se alicui,
vel cum aliquo, *to compare*; neminem cum illo conferendum pietate
puto, Cic. Hæc conferunt ad a-
liquid; oratori futuro, serve, *are
useful to,* Quinct.

DEFERRE situlam vel sitellam,
to bring the ballot-box; aliquid ad
aliquem, *to carry word, to tell*;
rarely alicui; causam ad patronos;
honores ei; gubernacula reipublicæ
in eum; summam rerum ad eum,
to confer; in beneficiis ad æra-
rium, *to recommend for a public service,* Cic. aliquem ambitûs, de
ambitu,

ambitu, nomen alicujus ad prætorem, apud magistratum, *to accuse of bribery*; primas, *sc.* partes ei, *to give him the preference*, Cic.

DIFFERRE *vel* transferre rem in annum; post bellum, diem solutionis, *to put off*; rumores, *to spread*; ab aliquo, alicui, inter se, moribus, *to differ in character*; amore, cupiditate, doloribus, differri, *to be distracted or torn asunder*, Cic. & Ter.

EFFERRE fruges, *to produce*; verba, *to utter*; verbum de verbo expressum, *to translate*, Ter. pedem domo, *to go out*; corpus amplo funere, & cum funere, *to bury*; ad honorem, ad cœlum laudibus, *to raise, to extol*; foras peccatum, *to divulge*.

INFERRE bellum patriæ; vim, manus, necem alicui, *to bring upon*; signa, se, pedem, *to advance*; litem, vel periculum capitis alicui, vel in aliquem, *to bring one to a trial for his life*.

OFFERRE se morti, ad mortem, in discrimen, *to expose, to present*.

PREFERRE legem, *to carry through, to pass it*.

PRÆFERRE facem ei, *to carry before*; salutem reipublicæ suis commodis, & anteferre, anteponere, *to prefer*. Prælatus equo, *riding before*.

PROFERRE imperium, pomœrium, terminos, *to enlarge*; in medium, in apertum, in lucem, *to publish*; nuptias, diem, *to delay*; diem Ilio, *to defer the destruction of*, Hor.

REFERRE alicui, *to answer*; se, gradum *v.* pedem, *to retreat*; gratiam alicui, *to make a requital*; par pari, Ter. victoriam ab, *vel* ex aliquo, et reportare, *to gain*; institutum, *to renew*; judicia ad equestrem ordinem, *to restore to the Equites the right of judging*; aliquid, de aliqua re, ad senatum, ad consilium, ad sapientes, ad populum, *to lay before*; aliquid in tabulam, codicem, album, commentarium, &c. *to mark down*; aliquid acceptum alicui, & in acceptum, *to acknowledge one's self indebted*; pecunias acceptas & expensas, nomina vel summas in codicem accepti et expensi, *to mark down accounts*; alienos mores ad suos, *to judge of by*; in *v.* inter ærarios, *to reduce to the lowest class*; in numerum deorum, in vel inter deos, & reponere, *to rank among*; pugnas, res gestas, *to relate*; patrem ore, *to resemble*; amissos colores, *to regain*, Horat.

TRANSFERRE rationes in tabulas, *to post one's books, to state accounts*; in Latinam linguam, *to translate*; verba, *to use metaphorically*; culpam in eum & rejicere, *to lay the blame on him*.

II. FIGURES of SYNTAX.

A *Figure* is a manner of ſpeaking different from the ordinary and plain way, uſed for the ſake of beauty or force.

The figures of *Syntax* or *Conſtruction* may be reduced to theſe three, *Ellipſis, Pleonaſm,* and *Hyperbaton.*

The two firſt reſpect the conſtituent parts of a ſentence; the laſt reſpects only the arrangement of the words.

I. ELLIPSIS.

ELLIPSIS is when one or more words are wanting to complete the ſenſe, as, *Aiunt, ferunt, dicunt, perhibent,* ſcil. *homines : Dic mihi, Damœta, cujum pecus ;* that is, *Dic* (tu) *mihi, Damœta,* (eum hominem) *cujum pecus* (eſt hoc pecus). *Aberant bidui,* ſc. *iter* vel *itinere. Decies ſeſtertiûm,* ſc. *centena millia. Quid multa ?* ſc. *dicam. Antiquum obtines,* ſc. *morem,* v. *inſtitutum,* Plaut. *Hodie in ludum occœpi ire literarium, ternas jam ſcio,* ſc. *literas,* i. e. AMO, Id. *Triduo abs te nullas acceperam,* ſc. *literas,* i. e. *epiſtolam,* Cic. *Brevi dicam,* ſc. *ſermone :* So. *Complecti, reſpondere,* &c. *brevi. Dii meliora,* ſc. *faciant : Rhodum volo, inde Athenas,* ſc. *ire,* Id. *Bellicum,* v. *claſſicum canere,* ſc. *ſignum,* Liv. *Civicâ donatus,* ſc. *coronâ ;.* So *obſidionalem, muralem adeptus,* &c. Id. *Epiſtola librarii manu eſt,* ſc. *ſcripta,* Cic. So in Engliſh; " The twelve," i. e. apoſtles ; " the elect," i. e. perſons.

When a conjunction is to be ſupplied, it is called A-SYNDĔTON ; as, *Deus optimus maximus,* ſc. *et ; Sartum tectum conſervare,* i. e. *ſartum et tectum ;* So *Abiit, exceſſit, evaſit, erupit,* Cic. *Ferte citi flammas, date vela, impelite remos,* Virg. *Velis nolis,* ſc. *fiu.*

To this figure may be reduced moſt of thoſe irregularities in Syntax, as they are called, which are variouſly claſſed by grammarians, under the names of ENALLĂGE, i. e. the changing of words and their accidents, or the putting of one word for another ; ANTIPTŌSIS, i. e. the putting of one caſe for another ; HELLENISM or GRÆCISM, i. e. imitating the conſtruction of the Greeks ; SYNĔSIS, i. e. referring the conſtruction, not to the gender or number of the word, but to the ſenſe, &c. thus, *Samnitium duo millia cæſi,* is, *Duo millia* (hominum) *Samnitium* (fuerunt homines);

homines) *cœſi,* Liv. So *Servitia immemores,* Liv. *Monſtrum que,* ſcil. mulier, Hor. *Scelus qui,* ſc. *homo,* Ter. *Omnia Mercurio ſimilis,* ſcil. ſecundum, Virg. *Miſſi magnis de rebus uterque, legati ;* i. e. *Miſſi legati* (et) *uterque* (legatus miſſus) *de magnis rebus,* Horat. *Servitia repudiabat, cujus,* ſcil. ſervitii, Sall. Cat. 51. *Familia noſtra, quorum,* &c. ſc. *hominum,* Sall. *Concurſus populi, mirantium,* Liv. *Illum ut vivat optant,* for *ut ille vivat,* Ter. *Populum late regem;* for *regnantem,* Virg. *Expediti militum,* for *milites ;* *Claſſis ſtabat Rhegii* for *ad Rhegium;* Liv. *Latium Capuaque agro multati,* ſc. *homines,* Id. *Utraque formoſæ,* ſc. *mulieres,* Ovid. *Aperite aliquis oſtium,* Ter. *Senſit delapſus,* for *delapſum;* ſc. ſe eſſe, Virg.

When a writer frequently uſes the Ellipſis, his ſtyle is ſaid to be elliptical or conciſe.

2. PLEONASM.

PLEONASM is when a word more is added than is abſolutely neceſſary to expreſs the ſenſe ; as, *Video oculis,* I ſee with my eyes ; *Sic ore locuta eſt ; adeſt præſens : Nuſquam gentium ; vivere vitam ; ſervire ſervitutem ; Quid mihi Celſus agit ? Fac me ut ſciam,* &c. *Suo ſibi gladio hunc jugulo,* Ter. *Suo ſibi ſucco vivant,* Plaut.

When a conjunction is uſed apparently redundant, it is called POLYSYNDĔTON ; as, *Una Euruſque Notuſque ruunt,* Virg.

When that which is in reality one, is ſo expreſſed as if there were two, it is called HENDIADYS ; as, *Pateris libamus et auro,* for *aureis pateris,* Virg.

When ſeveral words are uſed to expreſs one thing, it is called PERIPHRASIS ; as, *Urbs Trojæ,* for *Troja,* Virg. *Res voluptatum,* for *voluptates,* Plaut. *Uſus purpurarum,* for *purpura ; Genus piſcium,* for *piſces ; Flores roſarum,* for *roſæ,* Hor.

3. HYPERBATON.

HYPERBATON is the tranſgreſſion of that order or arrangement of words which is commonly uſed in any language. It is chiefly to be met with among the poets. The various ſorts into which it is divided, are, *Anaſtrophe, tröphe, Hystěron protěron, Hypallăge, Synchěsis, Tmesis,* and *Parenthěsis.*

1. Anastrŏphe is the inverfion of words, or the placing of that word laft which fhould be firft ; as, *Italiam contra ; His accenfa fuper ; Spemque metumque inter dubii ;* for *contra Italiam, fuper his, inter fpem,* &c. Virg. *Terram fol facit are,* for *arefacit,* Lucret.

2. Hystěron protěron is when that is put in the former part of the fentence, which, according to the fenfe, fhould be in the latter ; as, *Valet atque vivit,* for *vivit atque valet,* Ter.

3. Hypallăge is the exchanging of cafes ; as, *Dare claffibus auftros,* for *dare claffes auftris,* Virg.

4. Synchěsis is a confufed and intricate arrangement of words ; as, *Saxa vocant Itali mediis quæ in fluctibus aras ;* for *Quæ faxa in mediis fluctibus Itali vocant aras,* Virg. This occurs particularly in violent paffion ; as, *Per tibi ego hunc juro fortem caftumque cruorem,* Ovid. Faft. ii. 841. *Per vos liberos atque parentes,* fc. *oro vos per liberos,* &c. Salluft. Jug. 14.

5. Tmesis is the divifion of a compound word and the interpofing of other words betwixt its parts ; as, *Septem fubjecta trioni gens,* for *Septentrioni,* Virg. *Quæ meo cunque animo libitum eft facere,* for *quæcunque,* Ter. *Quem fors dierum cunque dabit, lucro Appone,* Horat.

6. Parenthěsis is the inferting of a member into the body of a fentence, which is neither neceffary to the fenfe, nor at all affects the conftruction ; as, *Tityre, dum redeo, (brevis eft via), pafce capellas,* Virg.

III. Analysis and Translation.

The difficulty of tranflating either from Englifh into Latin, or from Latin into Englifh, arifes in a great meafure from the different arrangement of words which takes place in the two languages.

In Latin the various terminations of nouns, and the inflection of adjectives and verbs, point out the relation of one word to another, in whatever order they are placed. But in Englifh the agreement and government of words

can

can only be determined from the particular part of the sentence in which they stand.   Thus, in Latin, we can either say, *Alexander vicit Darium,* or *Darium vicit Alexander,* or *Alexander Darium vicit,* or *Darium Alexander vicit;* and in each of these the sense is equally obvious: but in English we can only say, *Alexander conquered Darius.* This variety of arrangement in Latin gives it a great advantage over the English, not only in point of energy and vivacity of expression, but also in point of harmony.   We sometimes indeed, for the sake of variety and force, imitate in English the inversion of words which takes place in Latin; as, *Him the Eternal hurl'd,* Milton.   *Whom ye ignorantly worship, him declare I unto you.*   But this is chiefly to be used in poetry.

With regard to the proper order of words to be observed in translating from English into Latin, the only certain rule which can be given, is to imitate the CLASSICS.

The order of words in sentences is said to be either *simple* or *artificial;* or, as it is otherwise expressed, either *natural* or *oratorial.*

The *Simple* or *Natural* order is, when the words of a sentence are placed one after another according to the natural order of syntax.

Artificial or *Oratorial* order is, when words are so arranged, as to render them most striking, or most agreeable to the ear.

All Latin writers use an arrangement of words, which appears to us more or less artificial, because different from our own, although to them it was as natural as ours is to us.   In order therefore to render any Latin author into English, we must first reduce the words in Latin to the order of English, which is called the *Analysis* or *Resolution* of sentences.   It is only practice that can teach one to do this with readiness.   However, to be a beginner, the observation of the following rule may be of advantage.

Take *first* the words which serve to introduce the sentence, or show its dependence on what went before; *next,* the nominative, together with the words which it agrees with or governs; *then,* the verb and adverbs joined with

it.

it ; and *laſtly*, the caſes which the verb governs, together with the circumſtances ſubjoined, to the end of the ſentence ; ſupplying through the whole the words which are underſtood.

If the ſentence is compound, it muſt be reſolved into the ſeveral ſentences of which it is made up ; as,

Vale igitur, mi Cicero, tibique perſuade eſſe te quidem mibi cariſſimum ; ſed multo fore cariorem, ſi talibus monumentis præceptiſque lætabēre, Cic. Off. lib. 3. fin.

Farewell then, my Cicero, and aſſure yourſelf that you are indeed very dear to me ; but ſhall be much dearer, if you ſhall take delight in ſuch writings and inſtructions.

This compound ſentence may be reſolved into theſe five ſimple ſentences ; 1. *Igitur*, mi (fili) *Cicero*, (tu) *vale*, 2. *et* (tu) *perſuade tibi* (ipſi) *te eſſe quidem* (filium) *cariſſimum mibi :* 3. *ſed* (tu perſuade tibi ipſi te) *fore* (filium) *cariorem* (mihi in) *multo* (negotio,) 4. *ſi* (tu) *lætabere telibus monumentis,* 5. *et* (ſi tu lætabere talibus) *præceptis.*

1. Fare *(you)* well then, my *(ſon)* Cicero, 2. and aſſure *(you)* yourſelf that you are indeed *(a ſon)* very dear to me : 3. but *(aſſure you yourſelf that you)* ſhall be *(a ſon)* much dearer *(to me,)* 4. if you ſhall take delight in ſuch writings, 5. and *(if you ſhall take delight in ſuch)* inſtructions.

It may not be improper here to exemplify *Analogical Analyſis* as it is called, or the analyſis of words, from the foregoing ſentence *Vale igitur*, &c. thus,

Vale, ſcil. *tu ;* Fare *(thou)* well : Second perſon ſing lar of the imperative mode, active v ice, from the neuter verb, *Valeo, valui, valī-tum, valēre,* to be in health, of the ſecond conjugation, not uſed in the paſſive. *Vale* agrees in the ſecond perſon ſingular with the nominative *tu,* by the third rule of ſyntax.

Igitur, then, therefore, a conjunction, importing ſome inference drawn from what went before.

Mi, Voc. ſing. maſc. of the adjective pronoun, *meus, -a, -um,* my ; derived from the ſubſtantive pronoun *Ego*, agreeing with *Cicero*, by Rule 2. *Cicero, voc.* ſing. from the nominative *Cicero, -ōnis,* a proper noun of the third declenſion.

Et, and, a copulative conjunction, which connects the verb *perſuade* with the verb *vale*, by Rule 60. We turn *que* into *et*, becauſe, *que* never ſtands by itſelf.

Perſuade, ſcil. *tu*, perſuade thou, ſecond perſon ſingular of the imperative active, from the verb *perſua-deo, ſi, ſum, dēre,* to perſuade ; compounded of the prepoſition *per*, and *ſuadeo, -ſi, -ſum,* to advise : uſed imperſonally in the paſſive ; thus, *Perſuadetur mibi*, I am perſuaded ; ſeldom or never *Ego perſuadeor*. We ſay however in the third perſon, *Hoc perſuadetur mibi*, I am perſuaded of this.

Tibi,

Tibi, dat. fing. of the perfonal pronoun *tu*, thou ; governed by *perfuade*, according to Rule 17. *Te*, accufative fing. of *tu*, put before *effe*, according to Rule 4.

Effe, prefent of the infinitive, from the fubftantive verb *fum*, *fui* *effe*, to be.

Quidem, Indeed, an adverb, joined with *cariffimum* or *effe*.

Cariffimum, accufative fing. mafc. from *cariffimus*, -a, -um, very dear, deareft, fuperlative degree of the adjective *carus*, -a, -um, dear : Comparative degree *carior*, *carior*, *carius*, dearer, more dear : agreeing with *te* or *filium* underftood, by Rule 2. and put in the accufative by Rule 5.

Mibi, to me, dat. fing. of the fubftantive pronoun *Ego*, I : governed by *cariffimum*, by Rule 12.

Sed, but, an adverfative conjunction, joining *effe* and *fore*.

Fore, the fame with *effe futurum*, to be, or, to be about to be, infinitive of the defective verb *forem*, -res, -ret, &c. governed in the fame manner with the foregoing *effe*, thus, *te fore*, Rule 4. or thus, *effe fed fore*. See Rule 60.

Multo fcil. *negotio*, ablat. fing. neut. of the adjective *multus*, -a, -um, much, put in the ablative, according to obfervation 6. Rule 61. But *multo* here may be taken adverbially in the fame manner with *much* in Englifh.

Cariorem, accuf. fing. mafc. from *carior*, -or, -us, the comparative of *carus*, as before : agreeing with *te* or *filium* underftood. Rule 2. or Rule 5.

Si, If, a conditional conjunction, joined either with the indicative mode, or with the fubjunctive, according to the fenfe, but oftener with the latter. See Rule 60. obf. 2.

Lætabëre, Thou fhalt rejoice, fecond perfon fingular of the future of the indicative, from the deponent verb *lætor*, *latatus*, *latāri*, to rejoice : Future, *læt-abor*, -abëris or -abëre, *ābitur*, &c.

Talibus, ablat. plur. neut. of the adjective *talis*, *talis*, *tale*, fuch ; agreeing with *monumentis*, the ablat. plur. of the fubftantive noun *monumentum*, -ti, neut. a monument or writing ; of the fecond declenfion ; derived from *moneo*, -ui, -itum, -ëre, to admonifh ; here put in the ablative, according to Rule 49. *Et*, a copulative conjunction, as before.

Præceptis, a fubftantive noun in the ablative plural, from the nominative *præceptum*, -ti, neut. a precept, an inftruction ; derived from *præcipio*, -capi, -ceptum, -cipëre, to inftruct, to order, compounded of the prepofition *præ*, before, and the verb *capio*, *cëpi*, *captum*, *capëre*, to take. The *a* of the fimple is changed into *i* fhort ; thus, *præcipio*, *præcipis*, &c.

The learner may in like manner be taught to analize the words in Englifh, and in doing fo, to mark the different idioms of the two languages.

To this may be fubjoined a *Praxis*, or Exercife on all the different parts of grammar, particularly with regard to the inflexion of nouns and verbs, in the form of queftions, fuch as thefe, Of Cicero ? *Cicerōnis*. With Cicero ? *Cicerōne*. A dear fon ? *Carus filius*. Of a dear fon ?

fon ? *Cari filii.* O my dear fon ? *Mi* or *meus care fili.* Of dearer fons ? *Cariōrum filiōrum,* &c.

Of thee ? or of you ? *Tui.* With thee or you, *te :* Of you ? *Vestrum* or *vestri.* With you ? *Vobis.*

They fhall perfuade ? *Perfuadebunt.* I can perfuade ? *Perfuadeam,* or much more frequently *poffum perfuadere.* They are perfuaded ? *Perfuadetor,* or *perfuafum eft illis,* according to the time expreffed. He is to perfuade ? *Eft perfuafurus.* He will be perfuaded ? *Perfuadebitur,* or *perfuafum erit illi.* He cannot be perfuaded ? *Non poteft perfuaderi illi.* I know that he cannot be perfuaded ? *Scio non poffe perfuaderi illi ;* that he will be perfuaded ? *Ei perfuafum iri, &c.*

When a learner firft begins to tranflate from the Latin he fhould keep as ftrictly to the literal meaning of the words as the different idioms of the two languages will permit. But after he has made farther progrefs, fomething more will be requifite. He fhould then be accuftomed, as much as poffible, to transfufe the beauties of an author from the one language into the other. For this purpofe it will be neceffary that he be acquainted, not only with the idioms of the two languages, but alfo with the different kinds of ftyle adapted to different forts of compofition, and to different fubjects ; together with the various turns of thought and expreffion which writers employ, or what are called the figures of words and of thought ; or the *Figures of Rhetoric.*

IV. Different kinds of STYLE.

The kinds of Style *(genera dicendi)* are commonly reckoned three ; the low, *(humile, fubmiffum, tenue) ;* the middle, *(medium, temperatum, ornatum, floridum) ;* and the fublime, *(fublime, grande.)*

But befides thefe, there are various other characters of ftyle ; as, the *diffufe* and *concife ;* the *feeble* and *nervous ;* the *fimple* and *affected,* &c.

There are different kinds of ftyle adapted to different fubjects and to different kinds of compofition ; the ftyle of the Pulpit, of the Bar, and of Popular affemblies ; the ftyle of Hiftory, and of its various branches, Annals, Memoirs or Commentaries, and Lives ; the ftyle of Philofophy, of Dialogue or Colloquial difcourfe, of Epiftles, and Romance, &c.

There

There is also a style peculiar to certain writers, called their *Manner* ; as, the *style* of Cicero, of Livy, of Sallust, &c.

But what deserves particular attention is the difference between the style of poetry and of profe. As the poets in a manner paint what they describe, they employ various epithets, repetitions, and turns of expreffion, which are not admitted in profe.

The firft virtue of style *(virtus orationis)* is perfpicuity, or that it be eafily underftood. This requires, in the choice of the words, 1. *Purity*, in oppofition to barbarous, obfolete, or new coined words, and to errors in Syntax : 2. *Propriety*, or the felection of the beft expreffions, in oppofition to vulgarifms or low expreffions : 3. *Precifion*, in oppofition to fuperfluity of words or a *loofe ftyle*.

The things chiefly to be attended to in the ftructure of a fentence, or in the difpofition of its parts, are, 1. *Clearnefs*, in oppofition to *ambiguity* and *obfcurity* : 2. *Unity* and *Strength*, in oppofition to an *unconnected, intricate*, and *feeble* fentence : 3. *Harmony*, or a mufical arrangement, in oppofition to *harfhnefs* of found.

The moft common defects of style *(vitia orationis)* are diftinguifhed by various names ;

1. A BARBARISM is when a foreign or ftrange word is made ufe of ; as, *croftus*, for *agellus* ; *rigorofus*, for *rigidus* or *feverus* ; *alterare*, for *mutare*, &c. Or when the rules of Orthography, Etymology, or Profody are tranfgreffed ; as, *charus*, for *carus* ; *flavi*, for *fleti* ; *tibĭcen*, for *tibīcen*.

2. A SOLECISM is when the rules of Syntax are tranfgreffed ; as, *Dicit libros lectos iri*, for *lectum iri* : *We was walking* for *we were*. A barbarifm may confist in one word, but a folecifm requires feveral words.

3. An IDIOTISM is when the manner of expreffion peculiar to one language is ufed in another ; as an *Anglicifm* in Latin, thus, I am to write, *Ego fum fcribĕre*, for *ego fum fcripturus* ; It is I, *Eft ego*, for *Ego fum* : Or a *Latinifm*, in Englifh, thus, *Eft fapientior me*, He is wifer than me, *for than I* ; *Quem dicunt me effe ?* Whom do they fay that I am ? for *who*, &c.   4. TAUTOLOGY

4. TAUTOLOGY is when we either uselessly repeat the same words, or repeat the same sense in different words.

5. BOMBAST is when high founding words are used without meaning, or upon a trifling occasion.

6. AMPHIBOLOGY is when by the ambiguity of the conſtruction, the meaning may be taken in two different ſenſes ; as in the anſwer of the oracle to Pyrrhus, *Aio te, Æacide, Romanos vincere poſſe.* But the Engliſh is not ſo liable to this as the Latin.

V. FIGURES of RHETORIC.

Certain modes of ſpeech are termed *Figurative,* becauſe they convey our meaning under a borrowed form, or in a particular dreſs.

Figures *(figuræ* or *ſchemäta)* are of two kinds ; figures of words, *(figuræ verborum,)* and figures of thought, *(figuræ ſententiarum.)* The former are properly called *Tropes ;* and if the word be changed the figure is loſt.

1. TROPES or FIGURES of WORDS.

A *Trope (converſio,)* is an elegant *turning* of a word from its proper ſignification.

Tropes take their riſe partly from the barrenneſs of language, but more from the influence of the imagination and paſſions. They are founded on the relation which one object bears to another, chiefly that of reſemblance or ſimilitude.

The principal tropes are the *Metaphor,, Metonymy, Synecdoche,* and *Irony.*

1. METAPHOR *(tranſlatio)* is when a word is tranſferred from that to which it properly belongs, to expreſs ſomething to which it is only applied from ſimilitude or reſemblance ; as, a *hard* heart ; a *ſoft* temper ; he *bridles* his anger ; a *joyful* crop ; *ridet* ager, the field *ſmiles,* &c. A metaphor is nothing elſe but a ſhort compariſon.

We likewiſe call that a metaphor, when we ſubſtitute one object in the place of another, on account of the cloſe reſemblance between them ; as when, inſtead of *youth,* we

ſay,

fay, *the morning* or *'spring time of life* ; or when, in' fpeaking of a family connected with a common parent, we ufe
the expreffions which properly belong to a tree, whofe
trunk and branches are connected with a common root,
When this allufion is carried on through feveral fentences, or through a whole difcourfe, and the principal
fubject kept out of view, fo that it can only be difcovered
by its refemblance to the fubject defcribed, it is called an
ALLEGORY.   An example of this we have in Horace;
book I. ode 14. where the republic is defcribed under the
allufion of a fhip.

An ALLEGORY is only a continued metaphor.   This
figure is much the fame with the *Parable*, which fo often
occurs in the facred fcriptures ; and with the *Fable*, fuch
as thofe of Æfop.   The *Ænigma* or *Riddle* is alfo confidered as a fpecies of the Allegory ; as likewife are many
Proverbs (*Proverbia* v. *Adagia ;)* thus, *In fylvam ligna
ferre,* Horat.

Metaphors are improper, when they are taken from low
objects ; when they are forced or far fetched.; when they
are mixed or too far purfued ; and when they have not
a natural and fenfible refemblance ; or are not adapted
to the fubject of difcourfe, or to the kind of compofition,
whether poetry or profe.

When a word is very much turned from its proper fignification, it is called *Catachrefis (abufio ;)* as, *a leaf of
paper, of gold, &c. the empire* flourifhed ; *parricida*, for any
murderer ; Vir *gregis ipfe caper,* Virg.   *Altum* ædificant
caput, Juv. *Hunc vobis deridendum* propino, for *trado,* Ter.
Eurus per Siculas equitavit *undas,* Hor.

When a word is taken in two fenfes in the fame
phrafe, the one proper and the other metaphorical, it is
called *Syllepfis (comprehenfio ;)* as *Galathæa thymo mihi
dulcior Hyblæ,* Virg. *Ego Sardois videar tibi. amarior her-
bis,* Id.

2. METONYMY *(mutatio nominis)* is the putting of
one name for another.   In which fenfe it includes all
other tropes ; but it is commonly reftricted to the following particulars ; 1. When the caufe is put for the effect ;
or the inventor, for the thing invented ; or the author,
for

for his works ; as, *Boum labores,* for *corn* ; *Mars,* for *war* ; thus, *Æquo marte pugnatum est,* with equal advantage; Liv. *Ceres,* for *grain* or *bread* ; *Bacchus,* for *wine* ; *Venus,* for *love* ; *Vulcanus,* for *fire* ; thus, *Sin, Cerere & Baccho friget Venus,* Ter. *Furit Vulcanus* Virg. So, a *general* is put for his *army* ; *Cicero, Virgil,* and *Horace,* for their *works* : *Moses* and the *Prophets,* for their *books* ; a beautiful *Raphael, Titian, Guido Rheni, Rembrant, Rubens, Vandyke, &c.* for their pictures. 2. When the effect is put for the cause ; as, *Pallida mors, Pale* death, because it makes pale ; *atra cura, &c.* 3. The container, for what is contained, and sometimes the contrary ; as, *Hausit pateram,* for *vinum,* Virg. *He loves his bottle,* for *drink : Secundam mensam servis dispertiit,* i. e. *fercula in mensa,* Nep. So *Roma,* for *Romani ; Europe,* for *the Europeans ; Heaven,* for the Supreme Being ; *Secernit Europen ab Afro,* for *Africa ; In arduos tollor Sabinos,* for *in agrum Sabinorum ; Incolumi Jove,* for *Capitolio ; Janus,* for the temple of Janus, Hor. *Proximus ardet Ucalĕgon,* for *domus Ucalegontis,* Virg. So *Sergestus,* for *his ship,* Id. Æn. v. 272. 4. The sign, for the thing signified ; as, The *crown,* for *royal authority ; palma* or *laurus,* for *victory ; cedant arma togæ,* that is, as Cicero himself explains it, *bellum concedat paci. Ferri togæque consilia,* consultations about war and peace, *Stat. Sylv.* v. 1. 82. 5. An abstract, for the concrete ; as, *Scelus,* for *scelestus,* Ter. *Audacia,* for *audax,* Cic. *Custodia,* for *custodes,* Virg. *Servitus,* for *servi ; nobilitas,* for *nobiles ; juventus,* for *juvenes ; vicinia,* for *vicini ; vires* for *strong men,* Hor. *Furta,* for *stolen oxen,* Ovid. Fast. i. 560. 6. The parts of the body, for certain passions or sentiments, which were supposed to reside in them ; thus, *cor,* for *wisdom* or *address* ; as, *habet cor, vir cordatus,* a man of sense, *Plaut.* But with us the *heart* is put for courage or affection, and the *head* for wisdom ; thus, *a stout heart ; a warm heart ; a sound head, &c.* So, *to have a well hung tongue,* for *to speak with ease, &c.*

When we put what follows, to express what goes before, or the contrary, it is called *Metalepsis,* (*transmutatio ;*) thus, *desiderari,* to be desired or regretted, for *to be dead,*

lost,

loft, or *abfent* : So *Fuimus Troes, & ingens gloria Dardaniæ*, i. e. are no more. *Virg. Æn.* ii. 325.

3. SYNECDOCHE (*Comprehenfio* or *conceptio*) is a trope by which a word is made to fignify more or lefs than in its proper fenfe ; as, 1. When a *genus* is put for a *fpecies*, or a whole for a part and the contrary ; thus, *Mortales*, for *homines* ; *fumma arbor*, for *fumma pars arboris* ; *priufquam pabula guftaffent Trojæ, Xanthumque bibiffent*, for *partem pabuli*, & fluminis *Xanthi*, Virg. *Nat uncta* carina, for *navis* ; *centum puppes*, a hundred fail, or a hundred fhips ; *tectum*, the roof, for the whole houfe ; *capita* or *animæ*, for *homines* ; *ungula*, for *equus* or *equi*, Horat. Sat. i. 1. 114 ; the door or even the threfhold, for the houfe or temple, *tum foribus divæ*, for *in templo divæ*, Virg. *Tempe*, for any beautiful vale, &c. 2. When a fingular is put for a plural, and the contrary ; thus, *Hoftis, miles, pedes, eques*, for *hoftes*, &c. *It is written in the prophets*, for in a book of fome one of the prophets ; *millies*, a thoufand times, for many times. 3. When the materials are put for the things made of them ; as, *Æs* or *argentum*, for money ; *æra*, for vafes of brafs trumpets, arms, &c. *ferrum*, for a fword ; *taurus*, for a bull's hide, Virg. *Duft thou art*, i. e. made of duft, &c.

When a common name is put for a proper name, or the contrary, it is called *Antonomafia (pronominatio ;)* as, the *Philofopher*, for *Ariftotle* ; the *Orator*, for *Demofthenes* or *Cicero* ; the *Poet*, for *Homer* or *Virgil* ; the *Wife man*, for *Solomon* ; *Aftu*, for *Athens* ; *Urbs*, the city or town, for the capital of any country ; *Pænus*, for *Hannibal* ; a *Nero*, for a cruel prince ; *Mæcēnas*, for a patron of learning ; as, *Sint Mæcenates non deerunt, Flacce, Marones*, i. e. *fint munifici patroni, non deerunt boni poetæ*, Martial. viii. 56. 5.

An *Antonomafia* is often made by a *Periphrăfis* ; as, *Pelŏpis parens*, for *Tantălus* ; *Anўti reus*, for *Socrates* ; *Trojani belli fcriptor*, for *Homer* ; *Chironis alumnus*, for *Achilles* ; *Potor Rhodăni*, for *Gallus* ; *Jubæ tellus*, for *Mauritania*, Horat. &c. or by a patronymic noun ; as *Anchifiădes*, for *Æneas* ; *Tyndăris, -ĭdis*, for *Helēna*, &c. or by an epithet ; as, Impius *reliquit*, for Æneas, Virg. fometimes

e noun added ; as, *Fatālis et incestus judex,*
for *Paris,* Hor.

'is when one means the contrary of what is
n we say of a bad poet, *he is a Virgil ;* or of a
on, *Tertius e cœlo cecidit Cato.*

thing is said by way of bitter railery, or in an
ner, it is called a SARCASM ; as, *Satia*
yrē, Justin. Italiam *metire jacens,* Virg.

ffirmation is expressed in a negative form, it
ŏTES. ; as, *He is no fool,* for *he is a man of*
milis mulier, for *nobilis,* or *superba ; non in-*
for *decoro,* Horat. When a word has a
rary to its original sense, it is called *Anti-*
uri sacra *fames,* for *execrabilis,* Virg. *Pontus*
mine dictus, i. e. *hospitalis,* Ovid.

thing sad or offensive is expressed in more
it is called EUPHEMISMUS ; as, *Vitâ func-*
uus ; conclamare suos, to give up for lost,
for *abeant ; mactare* or *ferire,* for *occidere ;*
rvi Milonis, quod suos quisque servos in tali re
i. e. *Clodium interfecerunt,* Cic. This figure
ne with the *Periphrāsis.*

HRäSIS, or *Circumlocution,* is when several
ployed to express what might be expressed in
is done either from necessity, as in translating
uage into another ; or to explain what is ob-
finitions ; or for the sake of ornament, par-
oetry, as in the descriptions of evening and

explaining an obscure word or sentence by a
e enlarges on the thought of the author, it is
hrase.

rd imitates the sound of the thing signified,
nomatopœia, (nominis fictio ;) as, the *whistling*
ng of streams, *buz* and *hum* of insects, *hiss* of
But this figure is not properly a trope.

imes difficult to ascertain to which of the
d tropes certain expressions ought to be re-
n such cases minute exactness is needless. It
know in general that the expression is

There

There are a great many tropes peculiar to every language which cannot be literally expressed in any other. These therefore, if possible, must be rendered by other figurative expressions equivalent : and if this cannot be done, their meaning should be conveyed in simple language ; thus, *Interiore notâ Falerni*, with a glass of old *Falernian wine* : *Ad umbilicum ducere*, to bring to a conclusion, Horat. These and other such figurative expressions, cannot be properly explained without understanding the particular customs to which they refer.

2. REPETITION OF WORDS.

Various repetitions of words are employed for the sake of elegance or force, and are therefore also called *Figures of words*. Rhetoricians have distinguished them by different names according to the part of the sentence in which they take place.

When the same word is repeated in the beginning of any member of a sentence, it is called ANAPHŎRA ; as, *Nihilne te nocturnum præsidium palatii, nihil urbis vigiliæ*, &c. Cic. *Te dulcis conjux, te solo in littore secum, Te veneniente die, te descendente canebat*, Virg.

When the repetition is made in the end of the member, it is called EPISTRŎPHE or *conversio* ; as, *Pænos Populus Romanus justitiâ vicit, armis vicit, liberalitate vicit*, Cic. Sometimes both the former occur in the same sentence, and then it is called SYMPLŎCE or *Complexio* ; as, *Quis legem tulit? Rullus. Quis*, &c. *Rullus*, Cic.

When the same word is repeated in the beginning of the first clause of a sentence, and in the end of the latter, it is called EPANALEPSIS ; as, *Vidimus victoriam tuam præliorum exitu terminatam ; gladium vaginâ vacuum in urbe non vidimus*, Cic. pro Marcello.

The reverse of the former is called ANADIPLŌSIS or *Reduplicatio* ; as, *Hic tamen vivit : vivit ! imo in senatum venit*, Cic.

When that which is placed first in the foregoing member, is repeated last in the following, and the contrary, it is called EPANŎDOS or *Regressio* ; as, *Crudelis tu quoque mater ; Crudelis mater magis an puer improbus ille ? Improbus ille puer, crudelis tu quoque mater*, Virg.

The passionate repetition of the same word in any part of a sentence is called EPIZEUXIS ; as, *Excitate, excitate eum ab inferis*, Cic. *Fuit, fuit ista virtus, &c.* Id. *Me, me : adsum qui feci, in me convertite ferrum*, Virg. *Bella, horrida bella*, Id. *Ibimus, ibimus*, Hor.

When we proceed from one thing to another, so as to connect by the same word the subsequent part of a sentence with the preceding, it is called CLIMAX or *Gradatio* ; as, *Africano virtutem industria, virtus gloriam, gloria æmulos comparavit*, Cic.

When the same word is repeated in various cases, moods, genders, numbers, &c. it is called POLYPTŌTON ; as, *Pleni funt omnes libri, plenæ fapientium venes, plena exemplorum vetuftas*, Cic. *Littora littoribus contraria, fluctibus undas imprecor, arma armis*, Virg. To this is ufually referred what is called SYNONYMIA, or the ufing of words of the same import, to exprefs a thing more ftrongly : as, *Non feram, non patiar, non finam*, Cic. *Promitto, recipio, fpondeo*, Id. And alfo EXPOLI-TIO, which repeats the fame thought in different lights.

When a word is repeated the fame in found, but not in fenfe, it is called ANTANACLASIS ; as, *Amari jucundum eft, fi curetur ne quid infit amari*, Cic. But this is reckoned a defect in ftyle, rather than a beauty. Nearly allied to this figure is the PARONOMASIA or *Agnomi-natio*, when the words only refemble one another in found ; as, *Civem bonarum artium, bonarum partium ; Conful pravo animo & parvo ; De oratore arator factus*, Cic. *Amantes funt amentes*, Ter. This is alfo called a PUN.

When two or more words are joined in any part of a fentence in the fame cafes or tenfes, it is called HOMOIOPTŌTON, i. e. *fimiliter cadens* ; as, *Pollet auctoritate, circumfluit opibus, abundat amicis*, Cic. If the words have only a fimilar termination, it is called HOMOIOTE-LEUTON, i. e. *fimiliter definens* ; as, *Non ejufdem eft facere fortiter, & vivere turpiter*, Cic.

3. FIGURES OF THOUGHT.

It is not eafy to reduce figures of thought to diftinct claffes, becaufe the fame figure is employed for feveral different purpofes. The principal are the *Hyperbŏle*, *Pro-fopopeia*, *Apoftrŏphe*, *Simĭle*, *Antithĕfis*, &c.

1. HYPERBOLE is when a thing is magnified above the truth ; as, when Virgil fpeaking of *Polyphēmus* fays, *Ipfe arduus, altaque pulfat fidera*. So, *Contracta pifces æ-quora fentiunt*, Hor. When an object is diminifhed below the truth, it is called *Tapeinōfis*. The ufe of extravagant Hyperboles forms what is called *Bombaft*.

2. PROSOPOPEIA, or *Perfonification*, is when we af-cribe life, fentiments, or actions, to inanimate beings, or to abftract qualities ; as, *Quæ (patria) tecum, Catilina, fic agit*, &c. Cic. *Virtus fumit aut ponit fecures*, Hor. *Arbore nunc aquas culpante*, Id.

3. APOSTROPHE, or *Addrefs*, is when the fpeaker breaks off from the feries of his difcourfe, and addreffes himfelf to fome perfon prefent or abfent, living or dead, or to inanimate nature, as if endowed with fenfe and reafon. This figure is nearly allied to the former, and

therefore

therefore often joined with it ; as, *Trojaque nunc ftares,*
Priamique arx alta maneres, Virg.

4. SIMILE, or *Comparifon,* is when one thing is illuf-
trated or heightened by comparing it to another ; as, *Alex-*
ander was as bold as a lion.

5. ANTITHESIS, or *Oppofition,* is when things contrary or different are contrafted, to make them appear in
the more ftriking light ; as, *Hannibal was cunning, but Fa-*
bius was cautious. Cæfar beneficiis ac munificentiâ magnus ha-
bebatur, integritate vitæ Cato, &c. Sall. Cat. 54. *Ex hac parte*
pudor pugnat, illinc petulantia, &c. Cic. Similar to this
figure is the *Oxumöron,* i. e. *acute dictum ;* as, *Amici ab-*
fentes adfunt, &c. Cic. *Impietate pia eft,* Ovid. *Num capti*
potuere capi, Virg.

6. INTERROGATION, (Græc. *Erotēfis,*) is a figure
whereby we do not fimply afk a queftion, but exprefs fome
ftrong feeling or affection of the mind in that form ; as,
Quoufque tandem, &c. Cic. *Creditis avectos hoftes ?* Virg.
Heu ! quæ me æquora poffunt accipere, Id. Sometimes an
anfwer is returned, in which cafe it is called *Subjectio ;* as,
Quid ergo ? audaciffimus ego ex omnjbus ? minime, Cic.
Nearly allied to this is *Expoftulation,* when a perfon pleads
with offenders to return to their duty.

7. EXCLAMATION ; (*Ecphonēfis*) as, *O nomen dulce*
libertatis ! &c. Cic. *O tempora, O mores !* Id. *O patria !*
O Divûm domus Ilium ! &c. Virg.

8. DESCRIPTION, or *Imagery,* (*Hypotypofis,*) when
any thing is painted in a lively manner, as if done before
our eyes. Hence it is alfo called *Vifion ;* as, *Videor mihi*
hanc urbem videre, &c. Cic. in Cat. iv. 6. *Videre magnos jam*
videor duces, Non indecoro pulvere fordidos, Hor. Here a
change of tenfe is often ufed, as the prefent for the paft, and
conjunctions omitted, &c. Virg. xi. 637. &c.

9. EMPHASIS is when a particular ftrefs is laid on
fome word in a fentence ; as, Hannibal *peto pacem,* Liv.
Proh ! Jupiter, ibit HIC *!* Virg.

10. EPANARTHOSIS, or *Correction,* is when the fpeaker
either recals or corrects what he had laft faid ; as *Filiam*
habui, ah ! quid dixi habere me ? imò habui, Ter.

11. PARALEPSIS, or *Omiffion,* is when one pretends to
omit or pafs by, what he at the fame time declares.

12. APARITH.

12. Aparithmēsis, or *Enumeration,* is when what might be expreſſed in a few words, is branched out into ſeveral parts.

13. Synathroismus, or *Coacervatio,* is the crowding of many particulars together ; as,

$$\text{——————————— } \textit{Faces in caſtra tuliſſem,}$$
Impleſſemque foros flammis, natumque, patremque
Cum genere extinxem, memet ſuper ipſa dediſſem. Virg.

14. *Incrementum,* or CLIMAX in ſenſe, is when one number riſes above another to the higheſt ; as, *Facinus eſt vincire civem Romanum, ſcelus verberare, parricidium necare,* Cic. When all the circumſtances of an object or action are artfully exaggerated, it is called Auxēsis, or *Amplification.* But this is properly not one figure, but the ſkilful employment of ſeveral, chiefly of the Similè and the Climax.

· 15. Transition (*metabäſis*) is when a ſpeech is abruptly introduced ; or when a writer ſuddenly paſſes from one ſubject to another ; as, Horat. Od. ii. 13. 13. In ſtrong paſſion, *a change of perſon* is ſometimes uſed ; as, Virg. Æn. iv. 365. &c. xi. 406, &c.

· 16. Suspensio, or *Suſtentatio,* is when the mind of the hearer is long kept in ſuſpenſe ; to which the Latin inverſion of words is often made ſubſervient.

17. Concessio is the yielding of one thing to obtain another ; as, *Sit fur, ſit ſacrilegus,* &c. *at eſt bonus imperator,* Cic. in Verrem, v. 1. Prolepsis, *Prevention or Anticipation,* is when an objection is ſtarted and anſwered. Anacoinōsis or *Communication,* is when the ſpeaker deliberates with the judges or hearers ; which is alſo called *Diaporēſis* or *Addubitatio.* Licentia, or the pretending to aſſume more *freedom* than is proper, is uſed for the ſake of admoniſhing, rebuking, ·and alſo flattering ; as, *Vide quam non reformidem,* &c. Cic. pro Ligario. Aposiopēsis, or *Concealment,* leaves the ſenſe incomplete ; as, *Quos ego ———ſed præſtat motos componere fluctus,* Virg.

18. Sententia, (*gnome,*) a ſentiment, is a general maxim concerning life or manners, which is expreſſed in various forms ; as, *Otium ſine literis mors eſt,* Seneca. *Adeo in teneris aſſueſcere multum eſt,* Virg. *Probitas laudatur*

Y

&

& alget ; Misera est magni custodia census ; Nobilitas sola est atque unica virtus, Juv.

As most of these figures are used by orators, and some of them only in certain parts of their speeches, it will be proper that the learner know the parts into which a regular formal oration is commonly divided. These are, 1. The *Introduction*, the *Exordium or Prœmium*, to gain the good will and attention of the hearers ; 2. The *Narration* or *Explication* : 3. The argumentative part, which includes, *Confirmation* or proof, and *Confutation* or refuting the objections and arguments of an adversary. The sources from which arguments are drawn, are called *Loci*, topics ; and are either intrinsic, or extrinsic ; common or peculiar, 4. The *Peroration, Epilogue*, or *Conclusion*.

The QUANTITY of SYLLABLES.

The quantity of a syllable is the space of time taken up in pronouncing it.

That part of grammar which treats of the quantity and accent of Syllables, and of the measures of verse, is called *PROSODY*.

Syllables, with respect to their quality, are either *long* or *short*.

A long syllable in pronouncing requires double the time of a short ; as, *tĕndĕrĕ*.

Some syllables are *common* ; that is, sometimes long, and sometimes short ; as the second syllable in *volucris*.

A vowel is said to be long or short by nature, which is always so by custom, or by the use of the poets.

In polysyllables or long words, the last syllable except one is called the *Penultima*, or, by contraction, the *Penult*, and the last syllable except two, the *Antepenultima*.

When the quantity of a syllable is not fixed by some particular rule, it is said to be long or short by *authority*, that is, according to the usage of the poets. Thus *le* in *lĕgo* is said to be short by authority, because it is always made short by the Latin poets.

In most Latin words of one or two syllables, according to our manner of pronouncing, we can hardly distinguish

by

by the ear a long fyllable from a fhort.   Thus le in *lĕgo* and *lēgi* feem to be founded equally long ; but when we pronounce them in compofition, the difference is obvious ; thus, *perlĕgo, perlēgi ; relĕgo, -ĕre ; relēgo, āre,* &c.

The rules of quantity are either *General* or *Special.* The former apply to all fyllables, the latter only to fome certain fyllables.

GENERAL RULES.

I. A vowel before another vowel is fhort ; as, *Mĕus, alĭus :* fo *nĭhil ; h* in verfe being confidered only as a breathing.   In like manner in Englifh, *crĕate, bĕhave.*

Exc. 1.   *I* is long in *fīo, fīebam, &c.* unlefs when followed by *r ;* as, *fĭĕri, fĭĕrem ;* thus,
Omnia jam fient, fĭĕri quæ poffe negabam, *Ovid.*

Exc. 2. *E* having an *i* before and after it, in the fifth declenfion, is long ; as, *specĭēi.* So is the firft fyllable in *āer, dīus, ēheu,* and the penultima in *aulāi, terrāi, &c.* in *Pompēi, Cāi,* and fuch like words ; but we fometimes find *Pompei* in two fyllables, *Horat. Od.* II. 7.

Exc. 3. The firft fyllable in *ohe* and *Diana* is common ; fo likewife is the penult of genitives in *ius ;* as, *illīus, unīus, &c.* to be read long in profe. *Alīus,* in the genit. is always long, as being contracted for *aliius ; alterĭus,* fhort.

In Greek words, when a vowel comes before another, no certain rule concerning its quantity can be given.
Sometimes it is fhort : as, Danăe, Idĕa, Sophĭa, Symphonĭa, Simŏis, Hyades, Phăon, Deucalĭon, Pygmalĭon, Thebăis, &c.
Often it is long ; as, Lycāon, Machāon, Didymāon ; Amphīon, Arīon, Ixīon, Pandīon ; Nāis, Lāis, Achāïa ; Brisēis, Cadmēis ; Latōus, & Latōis, Myrtōus, Nerēius, Priamēius ; Achelōius, Minōius ; Archelāus, Menelāus, Amphiarāus ; Ænēas, Penēus, Epēus, Acrisionēus, Adamantēus, Phœbēus, Gigantēus ; Darīus, Basilīus, Eugenīus, Bacchīus ; Caffiopēa, Cæfarēa, Chæronēa, Cytherēa, Galatēa, Laodicēa, Medēa, Panthēa, Penelopēa ; Clīo, Enyo, Elegīa, Iphigenīa, Alexandrīa, Thalīa, Antiochīa, idololatrīa, litanīa, polĭtīa, &c. Lāertes, Dēïphŏbus, Dēïanīra, Trōes, herōes, &c.
Sometimes it is common ; as, Chorea, platea, Malea, Nereïdes, canopeum, Orion, Geryon, Eos, cōus, &c. So in foreign words, Michael, Ifrael, Raphael, Abraham, &c.
The accufative of nouns in *eus* is ufually fhort ; as, *Orphĕa, Salmonĕa, Caph"rĕa, &c.* but fometimes long ; as, *Idomĕnēa, Ilionēa,* Virg.

Inftead

Instead of *Elegia, Cytherea,* we find *Elegīa, Cythērēa,* Ovid. But the quantity of Greek words cannot be properly understood without the knowledge of Greek.

In English, a vowel before another is also sometimes lengthened; as, *science, idea.*

II. A vowel before two consonants, or before a double consonant is long *(by position, as it is called)*; as,

ārma, fāllo, āxis, gāza, mājor; the compounds of *jugum* excepted; as, *bijŭgus, quadrijŭgus, &c.*

When the foregoing word ends in a short vowel, and the following begins with two consonants or a double one, that vowel is sometimes lengthened by position; as

 Ferte citi flammas, date vela, scandite muros, Virg.
But this rarely occurs.

¶ A vowel before a mute and a liquid is common;

as the middle syllable in *volucris, tenebræ,* thus,

 Et primò similis volŭcri, mox vera volŭcris. *Ovid.*
 Nox tenĕbras profert, Phœbus fugat inde tenĕbras. *Id.*

But in prose these words are pronounced short. So *peragro, phare-tra. podagra, chiragra, celebris, latebra, &c.*
To make this rule hold, three things are requisite. The vowel must be naturally short, the mute must go before the liquid, and be in the same syllable with it. Thus, *a* in *patris* is made common in verse, because *a* in *pater* is naturally short, or always so by custom: but *a* in *matris, acris,* is always long, because long by nature or custom in *mater* and *acer.* In like manner the penult in *salubris, ambulacrum,* is always long; because they are derived from *salus, salūtis,* and *ambulatum.* So *a* in *arte, abluo, &c.* is long by position, because the mute and the liquid are in different syllables.

l and *r* only are considered as liquids in Latin words; *m* and *n* do not take place except in Greek words.

III. A contracted syllable is long; as,

Nil, for *nihil; mī,* for *mihi; cōgo,* for *coago; aliŭs,* for *alius; tibīcen,* for *tibiicen; īt,* for *iit; sēdes,* for *si audes; nōlo,* for *non volo; bīgæ,* for *bijūgæ, scīlicet,* for *scire licet, &c.*

IV. A diphthong is always long; as,

Aurum, Cæsar, Eubæa, &c. Only *præ* in composition before a vowel is commonly short; as, *præire, præustus;* thus;

             Nec

Nec totâ tamen ille prior præeunte carinâ.   *Virg.*
Stipitibus duris agitur sudibusque præustis.   *Id.*
But it is sometimes lengthened ; as,

———————cum vacuus domino præiret Arion   *Statius.*

In English we pronounce several of the diphthongs short, by sinking the sound of one vowel; but then there is properly no diphthong.

SPECIAL RULES.

I. Concerning the FIRST and MIDDLE SYLLABLES.

Preterites and Supines of two Syllables.

V. Preterites of two syllables lengthen the former syllable ; as, *Vēni, vīdi, vīci.*

Except *bĭbi, scĭdi* from *scindo, fĭdi* from *findo, tŭli, dĕdi,* and *stĕti* which are shortened.

VI. Supines of two syllables lengthen the former syllable ; as, *Vīsum, cāsum, mōtum.*

Except *sătum,* from *sĕro ; cĭtum,* from *cieo ; lĭtum,* from *lĭno ; sĭtum,* from *sĭno ; stătum,* from *sisto ; ĭtum,* from *eo ; dătum,* from *do ; rŭtum,* from the compounds of *ruo ; quĭtum,* from *queo ; rătus,* from *reor.*

Preterites which double the first syllable.

VII. Preterites which double the first syllable, have both the first syllables short ; as,

Cĕcĭdi, tĕtĭgi, pĕpŭli, pĕpĕri, dĭdĭci, tŭtŭdi : except *cēcīdi,* from *cædo ; pĕpēdi,* from *pēdo ;* and when two consonants intervene ; as *fĕfelli, tĕtendi, &c.*

INCREASE of NOUNS.

A noun is said to increase, when it has more syllables in any of the oblique cases than in the nominative ; as, *rex, rēgis.* Here *re* is called the *increase* or *crement,* and so through all the other cases. The last syllable is never esteemed a crement.

Some nouns have a double increase, that is, increase by more syllables than one ; as, *iter, itĭnĕris.*

A noun in the plural is said to increase, when in any case it has more syllables than the genitive singular ; as, *gener, genĕri, genĕrōrum.*

Nouns

Nouns of the firſt, fourth, and fifth declenſions, do not increaſe in the ſingular number, unleſs where one vowel comes before another ; as, *fructus, fructui ; res, rēi ;* which fall under Rule I.

Third Declenſion.

VIII. Nouns of the third declenſion which increaſe, make *a* and *o* long ; *e, i,* and *u* ſhort ; as,

Pietātis, honōris ; muliĕris, lapĭdis, murmŭris.

The chief exceptions from this rule are marked under the formation of the genitive in the third declenſion. But here perhaps it may be proper to be more particular.

A.

A noun in A ſhortens *atis* in the genitive ; as, *dogma, -ătis ; poema, -ătis.*

O.

O ſhortens *ĭnis,* but lengthens *ēnis* and *ōnis ;* as, *Cardo, -ĭnis ; Virgo -ĭnis ; Anio, -ēnis ; Cicero, -ōnis.* Gentile or patrial nouns vary their quantity. Moſt of them ſhorten the genitive ; as, *Macedo, -ŏnis ; Saxo, -ōnis :* Some are long ; as, *Sueſſiones, Vettōnes. Brittones* is common.

I. C. D.

I ſhortens *-ĭtis ;* as, *Hydromĕli, -ĭtis. Ec* lengthens *-ēcis ;* as, *Halec, -ēcis.* A noun in D ſhortens the crement ; as, *David, -ĭdis.*

L.

Maſculines in AL ſhorten *ălis,* as, *Sal, -sălis ; Hannibal, -ălis ; Haſdrubal, -ălis ;* but neuters lengthen it ; as *animal, -ālis.*

Sōlis from *ſol* is long ; alſo Hebrew words in *el ;* as, *Michael, -ēlis.* Other nouns in L ſhorten the crement ; as, *Vigil, -ĭlis ; conſul, -ŭlis.*

N.

Nouns in ON vary the crement. Some lengthen it ; as, *Helthon, -ēnis ; Chiron, ōnis.* Some ſhorten it ; as, *Memnon, -ŏnis ; Actaeon, -ŏnis.*

EN ſhortens *inis ;* as, *flumen, ĭnis ; tibīcen, -ĭnis.* Other Nouns in N lengthen the penult. AN *ānis ;* as, *Titan, -ānis :* EN ; *ēnis* as, *Siren, -ēnis :* IN *īnis ;* as, *delphin, -īnis :* YN *ȳnis ;* as, *Phorcyn, ȳnis.*

R.

1. Neuters in AR lengthen *aris ;* as, *calcar, -āris.* Except the following, *bacchar, -ăris ; jubar, -ăris ; nectar, -ăris :* Alſo the adjective *par, păris,* and its compounds, *impar, ăris, diſpar, -ăris, &c.*

2. The following nouns in R lengthen the genitive, *Nar, nāris,* the name of a river ; *fur, fūris ; ver, vēris :* Alſo *Recimer, -ēris ; Byzer, -ēris ; Ser, Sēris ; Iber, -ēris,* proper names.

3. Greek nouns in TER lengthen *teris ;* as, *crater, -ēris ; character, -ēris.* Except *ather, -ĕris.*

4. OR lengthens *oris ;* as, *amor, -ōris.* Except neuter nouns ; as, *marmor, ŏris ; aequor, -ŏris :* Greek nouns in *tor ;* as, *Hector, -ŏris ; Actor, -ŏris ; rhetor, -ŏris,* Alſo *arbor, -ŏris,* and *memor, -ŏris.*

5. Other

5. Other nouns in R shorten the genitive ; AR *aris*, masc.; as, *Cæsar*, *-ăris* ; *Hamilcar*, *-ăris* ; *lar*, *lăris*. ER *eris* of any gender ; as, *ver*, *aëris* ; *mulier*, *-ĕris*, *cadāver*, *-ĕris* ; *iter*, anciently *itiner*, *itinĕris* ; *verbĕris*, from the obsolete *verber*. UR *uris* ; as, *vultur*, *-ŭris* ; *murmur*, *-ŭris*. YR *yris* ; as, *Martyr*, *-ў̆ris*.

A S.

1. Nouns in A S, which have *atis*, lengthen the crement ; as, *pietas*, *-ātis* ; *Mæcēnas*, *-ātis*. Except *anas*, *-ătis*.

2. Other nouns in AS shorten the crement ; as, Greek nouns having the genitive in *ădis*, *ătis*, and *ănis* ; thus, *Pallas*, *-ădis* ; *artocreas*, *eătis* ; *Melas*, *-ănis*, the name of a river. So *vas*, *vădis* ; *mas*, *măris* : But *vas*, *vāsis*, is long.

E S.

ES shortens the crement ; as, *miles*, *-ĭtis* ; *Ceres*, *-ĕris*, *pes*, *pĕdis*.

Except *locŭples*, *-ētis* ; *quies*, *-ētis* ; *mansues*, *-ētis* ; *hæres*, *-ēdis* ; *merces*, *-ēdis*.

I S.

Nouns in IS shorten the crement ; as, *lapis*, *-ĭdis* ; *Sanguis*, *-ĭnis* ; *Phyllis*, *ĭdis*.

Except *Glis*, *glīris* ; and Latin nouns which have *ītis* ; as, *lis*, *lītis* ; *dis*, *dītis* ; *Quiris*, *-ītis* ; *Samnis*, *-ītis* : But *Charis*, a Greek noun, has *Charĭtis*.

The following also lengthen the crement : *Crenis*, *-īdis* ; *Psophis*, *-īdis* ; *Nesis*, *-īdis*, proper names. And Greek nouns in *is*, which have also *in* ; as, *Salămis*, or *in*, *Salamīnis*.

O S.

Nouns in OS lengthen the crement ; as, *nepos*, *-ōtis* ; *flos*, *flōris*.

Except *Bos*, *bŏvis* ; *compos*, *-ŏtis* ; and *impos*, *-ŏtis*.

U S.

US shortens the crement ; as, *tempus*, *-ĕris* ; *tripus*, *-ŏdis*.

Except nouns which have *ūdis*, *ūris*, and *-ūtis* ; as, *incus*, *ūdis* ; *jus*, *jūris* ; *salus*, *-ūtis*. But *Ligus* has *Ligŭris* ; the obsolete *pecus*, *pecŭdis* ; and *intercus*, *-ŭtis*.

The neuter of the comparative has *ōris* ; as, *melius*, *-ōris*.

Y S.

YS shortens, *ydis* or *ydos* ; as, *chlamys*, *-ŷ̆dis*, or *-ŷ̆dos* : and lengthens *ynis* ; as, *Trachys*, *-ȳnis*.

B S. P S. M S.

Nouns in S, with a consonant going before, shorten the penult of the genitive ; as, *cælebs*, *-ĭbis* ; *inops*, *-ŏpis*, *hiems*, *hiĕmis*.

Except *Cyclops*, *ōpis* ; *cops*, *sēpis* ; *gryps*, *grŷpis* ; *Cercops*, *ōpis* ; *plebs*, *plēbis* ; *hydrops*, *-ōpis*.

T.

T shortens the crement ; as, *caput*, *-ĭtis*.

X.

1. Nouns in X, which have the genitive in *gis*, shorten the crement;

ment; as, *conjux*, -*ŭgis*; *remex*, -*ĭgis*; *Allobrox*, -*ŏgis*; *Phryx*, *Phrўgis.* But *lex*, *lēgis*; and *rex*, *rēgis*, are long; and likewise *frūgis.*

2. EX shortens *icis*; as, *vertex*, -*ĭcis*: except *vibex*, -*īcis.*

3. Other nouns in X lengthen the crement; as, *pax*, *pācis*; *radix*, -*īcis*; *vox*, *vōcis*; *lux*, *lūcis*; *Pollux*, *ūcis*, &c.

Except *făcis*, *nĕcis*, *vĭcis*, *prĕcis*, *calĭcis*, *cilĭcis*, *pĭcis*, *fornĭcis*, *nĭvis*, *Cappadŏcis*, *dŭcis*, *nŭcis*, *crŭcis*, *trŭcis*, *onўchis*, *Erўcis*, *mastyx*, -*ўchis*, the rosin of the *lentiscus*, or mastich-tree, and many others, whose quantity can only be ascertained by authority.

4. Some nouns vary the crement; as, *Syphax*, -*ācis*, or -*ăcis*; *Sandyx*, -*ĭcis*, or -*īcis*, *Bebryx*, -*ўcis*, or *ўcis.*

Increase of the Plural Number.

IX. Nouns of the plural number which increase, make *A*, *E*, and *O*, long; but shorten *I*, and *U*; as,

musārum, *rērum*, *dominōrum*; *rēgĭbus*, *portŭbus*: except *bōbus* or *būbus*, contracted for *bŏvĭbus.*

INCREASE OF VERBS.

A verb is said to increase, when any part has more syllables than the second person singular of the present of the indicative active; as, *amas*, *amāmus*, where the second syllable *ma* is the *increase* or *crement*; for the last syllable is never called by that name.

A verb often increases by several syllables; as, *amas*, *amābāmĭni*; in which case it is said to have a *first*, *second*, or *third increase.*

10. In the increase of verbs, *a*, *e*, and *o*, are long, *i* and *u*, short; as,

Amāre, *docēre*, *amātōte*; *legĭmus*, *sŭmus*, *volŭmus.*

The poets sometimes shorten *dĕdĕrunt* and *stĕtĕrunt*; and lengthen *rīmus*, and *rītis*, in the future of the subjunctive; as——*transcrītis aquas*, Ovid. All the other exceptions from this rule are marked in the formation of the verb.

The first or middle syllables of words which do not come under any of the foregoing rules, are said to be long or short by *authority*; and their quantity can only be discovered from the usage of the poets, which is the most certain of all rules.

REMARKS

REMARKS on the Quantity of the PENULT of Words.

1. Patronymics in *IDES* or *ADES* ufually fhorten the penult ; as, *Priamĭdes, Atlantiădes,* &c.   Unlefs they come from nouns in *eus ;* as, *Pelīdes, Tydīdes,* &c.

2. Patronymics, and fimilar words, in *AIS, EIS, ITIS, OIS, OTIS, INE,* and *ONE,* commonly lengthen the penult ; as, *Achāis, Ptolemāis, Chrysēis, Ænēis, Memphītis, Latŏis, Icariōtis, Nerīne, Arifīōne.*   Except *Thebăis,* and *Phocăis ;* and *Nereis,* which is common.

3. Adjectives in *ACUS, ICUS, IDUS,* and *IMUS,* for the moft part fhorten the penult ; as, *Ægyptiăcus, academĭcus, lepĭdus, legitĭmus ;* alfo fuperlatives ; as, *fortifsĭmus, &c.*   Except *opācus, amīcus, aprīcus, pudīcus, mendīcus, poftīcus, fīdus, infīdus,* (but *perfĭdus,* of *per* and *fĭdes,* is fhort,) *bīmus, quadrīmus, patrīmus, matrīmus, opīmus ;* and two fuperlatives, *īmus, prīmus.*

4. Adjectives in *ALIS, ANUS, ARUS, IVUS, ORUS, OSUS,* lengthen the penult ; as, *dotālis, urbānus, avārus, æftīvus, decōrus, arenōfus.*   Except *barbărus, opipărus.*

5. Verbal adjectives in *ILIS* fhorten the penult ; as, *agĭlis, facĭlis, &c.*   But derivatives from nouns ufually lengthen it ; as, *anīlis, civīlis, herīlis,* &c.   To thefe add, *exīlis, fubtīlis ;* and names of months, *Aprīlis, Quinctīlis, Sextīlis :* Except *humĭlis, parĭlis ;* and alfo *fimĭlis.*   But all adjectives in *atilis* are fhort ; as, *verfătĭlis, volatĭlis, umbratĭlis,* &c.

6. Adjectives in *INUS* derived from inanimate things, as plants, ftones, &c. alfo from adverbs of time, commonly fhorten the penult ; as, *amaracĭnus, crocĭnus, cedrĭnus, fagĭnus, oleagĭnus ; adamantĭnus, criftallĭnus, craftĭnus, priftĭnus, peremdĭnus,* &c.

Other adjectives in *INUS* are long ; as, *agnīnus, auftrīnus, bīnus, clandeftīnus, Latīnus, marīnus fupīnus, vefpertīnus,* &c.

7. Diminutives in *OLUS, OLA, OLUM ;* and *ULUS, ULA, ULUM,* always fhorten the penult ; as, *urceŏlus, filiŏla, mufæŏlum ; lectŭlus, ratiuncŭla, corcŭlum,* &c.

8. Adverbs in *TIM* lengthen the penult ; as, *oppidātim, virītim, tribūtim.*   Except *affătim, perpĕtim,* and *ftătim.*

9. Defideratives in *URIO* fhorten the antepenultima,
which

which in the fecond and third perfon is the penult ; as,
esŭrio, esŭris, esŭrit.   But other verbs in *urio* lengthen that
fyllable ; as, *ligūrio, ligūris ; fcatūrio, fcatūris,* &c.

PENULT of PROPER NAMES.

The following proper names lengthen the penult.   Ahdēra, Abȳdus
Adōnis, Æfōpus, Ætōlus.   Ahāla, Alarīcus, Alcīdes, Amȳclæ,
Andronīcus, Anūbis, Archimēdes, Ariarāthes, Ariobarzānes, Ariftī-
des, Ariftobūlus, Ariftogīton, Arpīnum, Artabānus ; Brachmānes,
Bufīris, Buthrōtus ; Cethēgus, Chalcēdon, Cleobūlus, Cyrēne, Cy-
thēra, Curētes ; Darīci, Demonīcus, Diomēdes, Diōres, Diofcūri ;
Ebūdes, Eriphȳle, Eubūlus, Euclīdes, Euphrātes, Eumēdes, Eurīpus,
Euxīnus ; Gargānus, Gætūlus, Granīcus ; Heliogabālus, Henrīcus,
Heraclīdes, Heraclītus. Hippōnax, Hifpānus ; Irēne ; Lacȳdas, La-
tōna, Leucāta, Lugdūnum, Lycōras ; Mandāne, Mausōlus, Maxi-
mīnus, Meleāger, Mefsāla, Mefsāna, Milētus ; Nasīca, Nicānor,
Nicētas ; Pachȳnus, Pandōra, Pelōris, & us, Pharsālus, Phœnīce,
Polītes, Polyclētus, Polynīces, Priāpus ; Sarpēdon, Serāpis, Sinōpe,
Stratonīce, Suffētes ; Tigrānes, Theffalonīca ; Verōna, Veronīca.

The following are fhort :   Amāthus, Amphipōlis, Anabāfis, Anti-
cȳra, Antigōnus, & -ne, Antilōchus, Antiōchus, Antiōpa, Antipas,
Antipāter, Antiphānes, Antiphātes, Antiphila, Antiphon, Anȳtus,
Apūlus, Areopāgus, Arimīnum, Armēnus; Athēfis, Attālus, Attīca;
Bitūrix, Bruēterī ; Calāber, Callicrātes, Calliftrātus, Candāce, Can-
tāber, Carneādes, Cherīlus, Chryfōftōmus, Cleombrōtus, Cleomē-
nes, Corȳcos, Conftantinopōlis, Cratērus, Cratȳlus, Cremēra, Cruf-
tumēri, Cybēle, Cyclādes, Cyzīcus; Dalmātæ, Damōcles, Dardānus,
Dejōces, Dejotārus, Democrītus, Demīpho, Didȳmus, Diogēnes,
Drepānum, Dunmōrix ; Empedōcles, Ephēfus, Evergētes, Eumēnes,
Eurymēdon, Euripȳlus ; Fucīnus; Geryōnes, Gyārus ; Hecȳra, He-
liopōlis, Hermiōne, Herodōtus, Hefiōdus, Hefiōne, Hippocrātes,
Hippotāmos, Hypāta, Hypānis ; Icārus, Icētas, Illȳris, Iphītus, If-
mārus, Ithāca ; Laodīce, Laomēdon, Lampsācus, Lamȳrus, Lapīthæ,
Leucrctīlis, Libānus, Lipāre, v. -a, Lyfimāchus, Longimānus ; Ma-
rāthon, Mænālus, Marmarīca, Maffagētæ, Matrōna, Megāra, Meli-
tus, & -ta, Metropōlis, Mutīna, Mycōnus ; Neōcles, Nerītos, No-
rīcum ; Omphāle ; Patāra, Pegāfus, Pharnāces, Pufiftrātus, Poly-
dāmas, Polyxēna, Porsēna, *or* Porfenna, Praxitēles, Puteōli, Pylā-
des, Pythagōras ; Sarmātæ, Sarsina, Semēle, Semirāmis, Sequāni,
& -a, Seriphos, Sicōris, Socrātes, Sodōma, Sotādes, Spartācus, Spo-
rādes, Strongȳle, Stymphālus, Sybāris ; Taygētus, Telegōnus, Te-
lemāchus, Tenēdos, Tarrāco, Theophānes, Theophīlus, Tomȳris ;
Urbīcus ; Venēti, Vologēfus, Volūfus ; Xenocrātes, Zoīlus, Zopȳrus.

The penult of feveral words is doubtful : thus, *Batāvi,* Lucan. *Ba-
tăvi,* Juv. & Mart. *Fortŭītus,* Horat. *Fortuītus,* Mart. Some make
fortuitus of three fyllables ; but it may be fhortened like *gratuītus,* Stat.
Patrimus, matrimus, præftolor, &c. are by fome lengthened, and by
fome fhortened ; but for their quantity, there is no certain authority.

H. FINAL

II. FINAL SYLLABLES.

A.

XI. *A* in the end of a word declined by cafes is fhort ; as, *Musă, templă, Tydeă, lampădă.*

Exc. The ablative of the firft declenfion is long ; as, *Musā, Æneā ;* and the vocative of Greek nouns in *as,* as, *O Æneā, O Pallā.*

A in the end of a word not declined by cafes is long ; as, *Amā, fruftrā, prætereā, ergā, intrā.*

Exc. *Ită, quiă, ejă, pofteă, pută,* (adv.) are fhort ; and fometimes, though more rarely, the prepofitions *contră, ultră,* and the compounds of *ginta ;* as, *trigintă, &c.* *Contra* and *ultra,* when adverbs, are always long.

E.

XII. *E* in the end of a word is fhort ; as,

Natĕ, fedilĕ, patrĕ, currĕ, nempĕ, antĕ.

Exc. 1. Monofyllables are long ; as, *mē, tē, sē ;* except thefe enclitic conjunctions, *quĕ, vĕ, nĕ ;* and thefe fyllabical adjections, *ptĕ, cĕ, tĕ ;* as, *fuaptĕ, hujufcĕ, tutĕ ;* but thefe may be comprehended under the general rule, as they never ftand by themfelves.

Exc. 2. Nouns of the firft and fifth declenfion are long ; as, *Calliŏpē, Anchisē, fidē.* So *rē-,* and *diē,* with their compounds, *quarē, hodiē, pridiē, poftridiē, quotidiē :* Alfo Greek nouns which want the fingular, *Cetē, melē, Tempē ;* and the fecond perfon fingular of the imperative of the fecond conjugation ; as, *Docē, manē ;* but *cave, vale,* and *vide,* are fometimes fhort.

Exc. 3. Adverbs derived from adjectives of the firft and fecond declenfion are long ; as, *placidē, pulchrē, valdē,* contracted for *validē :* To thefe add *fermē, ferē,* and *ohē ;* alfo all adverbs of the fuperlative degree ; as *doctiffimē, fortiffimē :* But *benĕ* and *malĕ* are fhort.

I.

XIII. *I* final is long ; as, *Dominī, patrī, docerī.*

Exc. 1. Greek vocatives are fhort ; as, *Alexĭ, Amaryllĭ.*

Exc. 2. The dative of Greek nouns of the third declenfion which increafe, is common ; as *Palladi, Minoĭdi.*

Mihi,

Mihi, tibi, sibi, are also common : so likewise are *ibi, nisi, ubi, quasi ;* and *cui,* when a dissyllable, which in poetry is seldom the case. *Sicubi* and *necubi* are always short.

O.

XIV. *O* final is common ; as, *Virgo, Amo, quando.*

Exc. 1. Monosyllables in *o* are long ; as, *o, do, flo, pro :* The dative and ablative sing. of the second declension is long : as, *libro, domino :* Also Greek nouns, as, *Dido,* and *Atho* the genit. of *Athos,* and adverbs derived from nouns ; as, *certo, falso, paulo.* To these add *quo, eo,* and their compounds, *quovis, quocunque, adeo, ideo ;* likewise, *illo, idcirco, citro, intro, retro, ultro.*

Exc. 2. The following words are short ; *Ego, scio, cedo,* a defective verb, *homo, cito, illico, immo, duo, ambo, modo,* with its compounds, *quomodo, dummodo, postmodo :* but some of these are also found long.

Exc. 3. The gerund in DO in Virgil is long ; in other poets it is short. *Ergo,* on account of, is long ; *ergo,* therefore, is doubtful.

U and Y.

XV. *U* final is long ; *Y* final is short ; as, *Vultu : Moly.*

B, D, L, M, R, T.

XVI. *B, D, L, R,* and *T,* in the end of a word, are short ; as,

Ab, apud, semel, precor, caput.

The following words are long, *sal, sol, nil ; par* and its compounds, *impar, dispar, &c. ; far, lar, Nar, cur, fur ;* also nouns in *er* which have *ēris* in the genitive ; as, *Cratēr, vēr, Ibēr ;* likewise *aēr, æthēr :* to which add Hebrew names ; as, *Job, Daniēl, David.*

M final anciently made the foregoing vowel short : as, *Militum octo,* Ennius. But by later poets, *m* in the end of a word is always cut off, when the next word begins with a vowel ; thus, *milit' octo ;* except in compound words ; as, *circumago, circumeo.*

C, N.

XVII. *C* and *N,* in the end of a word, are long ; as,

Ac,

Ac, sic, nōn. So Greek nouns in *n*; as, *Titān, Sirēn, Salamīn; Æneān, Anchisēn, Circēn; Lacedæmon,* &c.

The following words are short, *nĕc* and *donĕc; forsitān, in, forsăn, tamĕn, ăn, vidĕn;* likewise nouns in *en* which have *ĭnis* in the genitive; as, *carmĕn, crimĕn;* together with several Greek nouns; as, *Iliŏn, Pylŏn, Alexĭn.*

The pronoun *hic* and the verb *fac* are common.

AS, ES, OS.

XVIII. *AS, ES,* and *OS,* in the end of a word, are long; as, *Mās, quiēs, bonōs.*

The following words are short, *anăs, ĕs,* from *sum,* and *penĕs; ŏs,* having *ossis* in the genitive, *compŏs,* and *impŏs;* also a great many Greek nouns of all these three terminations; as, *Arcăs* and *Arcădăs, heröăs, Phrygĕs, Arcadĕs, Tenĕdŏs, Melŏs, &c.* and Latin nouns in *es,* having the penult of the genitive increasing short; as, *Alĕs, hebĕs, obsĕs.* But *Cerēs, pariēs, ariēs, abiēs,* and *pēs* with its compounds, are long.

IS, US, YS.

XIX. *IS, US,* and *YS,* in the end of a word, are short; as,

Turrĭs, legĭs, legĭmŭs, annŭs, Capўs.

Exc. 1. Plural cases in *is* and *us* are long; as, *Pennīs, librīs, nobīs, omnīs,* for *omnes, fructūs, manūs:* also the genitive singular of the fourth declension; as, *portūs.* But *bus* in the dat. and abl. plur. is short; as, *floribŭs, fructibŭs, rebŭs.*

Exc. 2. Nouns in *is* are long, which have the genitive in *ītis, īnis,* or *entis;* as, *līs, Samnīs, Salamīs, Simoīs.* To these add the adverbs *gratīs* and *forīs;* the noun *glīs,* and *vīs,* whether it be a noun or a verb; also *is* in the second person singular, when the plural has *ītis;* as, *audīs, abīs, possīs. Ris* in the future of the subjunctive is common.

Exc. 3. Monosyllables in *us* are long; as, *grus, sūs:* also nouns which in the genitive have *ūris, ūdis, ūtis, untis,* or *ŏdis;* as, *tellūs, incūs, virtūs, amathūs, tripūs.* To these add the genitive of Greek nouns of the third

Z

declension;

declenfion ; as, *Clius, Sapphûs, Mantûs ;* alfo nouns which have *u* in the vocative ; as, *Panthûs.*

Exc. 4. *Tethys* is fometimes long, and nouns in *ys*, which have likewife *yn* in the nominative ; as, *Phorcȳs, Trachȳs.*

¶ The laft fyllable of every verfe is common ;

Or, as fome think, neceffarily long on account of the paufe or fufpenfion of the voice, which ufually follows it in pronunciation.

The QUANTITY of DERIVATIVE and COMPOUND Words.

1. DERIVATIVES.

XX. Derivatives follow the quantity of their primitives ; as,

ămicus,	*from*	ămo.	Decŏro, *from*	decus, -ŏris.
Auctiōnor,		auctio, -ōnis.	Exŭlo,	exul, -ŭlis.
Auctōro,		auctor, -ōris.	Păvidus,	păveo.
Audītor,		audītum.	Quirīto,	Quiris, -ītis.
Aufpĭcor,		aufpex, ĭcis.	Radīcĭtus,	radix, -īcis.
Çaupōnor,		caupo, -ōnis.	Sofpĭto,	fofpes, -ĭtis.
Compĕtītor,		compĕtītum.	Nātura,	nātus.
Cornīcor,		cornix, -īcis.	Māternus,	māter.
Cuftōdio,		cuftos, -ōdis.	Lĕgebam, &c.	lĕgo.
Decōrus,		decor, -ōris.	Lēgeram, &c.	lēgi.

EXCEPTIONS.

1. *Long from fhort.*

Dēni, *from*	dĕcem.	Sufpīcio, *from*	fufpĭcor.	Mōbĭlis, *from*	mŏveo.
Fōmes,	fŏveo.	Sēdes,	sĕdeo.	Hūmor,	hŭmus.
Hūmanus,	hŏmo.	Sēcius,	sĕcus.	Jūmentum,	jŭvo.
Rēgula,	rĕgo.	Pēnuria,	pĕnus.	Vox, vōcis,	vŏco, &c.

2. *Short from long.*

Arena *and* ărifta, *from*	ārco.	Lŭcerna,	*from*	lūceo.
Nŏta, *and* nŏto,	nōtus.	Dux, -ŭcis,		dūco.
Vădum,	vādo.	Stăbilis,		ftābam.
Fĭdes,	fīdo.	Dĭtio,		dis, dītis.
Sŏpor,	sōpio.	Quăfillus,		quālus. &c.

2. COMPOUNDS.

XXI. Compouds follow the quantity of the fimple words which compofe them ; as,

Dēdūco,

Dēdūco, of *dē* and *dūco*. So, *prōf ĕro*, *antĕfĕro*, *consōlor*, *dēnŏto*, *dĕpecŭlor*, *deprāvo*, *despĕro*, *despūmo*, *desquāmo*, *enōdo*, *ērŭdio*, *exūdo*, *exăro*, *expăvco*, *incēro*, *inhŭmo*, *inveſtīgo*, *prægrăvo*, *prænăto*, *rĕgĕlo*, *appăro*, *appāreo*, *concăvus*, *prægrăvis*, *dēsŏlo*, *suffŏco* & *suffōco*, *diffĭdit* from *diffindo*, and *diffīdit* from *diffīdo*, *indĭco* and *indīco*, *permănet* from *permăneo*, and *permānet* from *permāno*, *effŏdit* in the present, and *effōdit* in the perfect ; so *exĕdit* and *exēdit* ; *devĕnit* and *devēnit* ; *devĕnīmus* and *devēnimus* ; *reperīmus* and *reperĭmus* ; *effŭgit* and *effūgit*, &c.

The change of a vowel or diphthong in the compound does not alter the quantity ; as, *incĭdo* from *in* and *cădo* ; *incīdo*, from *in* and *cædo*, *suffŏco*, from *sub* and *faux*, *faucis*. Unleſs the letter following make it fall under ſome general rule ; as, *ādmitto*, *pērcello*, *dĕoſculor*, *prŏhibeo*.

Exc. 1. *Agnĭtum*, *cognĭtum*, *dējĕro*, *pējĕro*, *innŭba*, *prŏnŭba*, *maledĭcus*, *veridĭcus*, *nihĭlum*, *semisŏpītus* ; from *nōtus*, *jūro*, *nūbo*, *dīco*, *hīlum*, and *sōpio* : *ambītus*, a participle from *ambio*, is long ; but the ſubſtantives *ambĭtus* and *ambĭtio* are ſhort. *Connŭbium* has the ſecond ſyllable common.

Exc. 2. The prepoſition *PRO* is ſhort in the following words : *prŏfundus*, *prŏfugio*, *prŏfugus*, *prŏnĕpos*, *prŏneptis*, *prŏfeſtus*, *prŏfari*, *prŏfiteor*, *prŏfānus*, *prŏfecto*, *prŏcella*, *prŏtervus*, and *prŏpāgo*, a lineage ; *pro* in *prōpāgo*, a vineſtock or ſhoot, is long. *Pro* in the following words is doubtful : *propago*, to propagate ; *propīno*, *profundo*, *propello*, *propulſo*, *procūro*, and *Proſerpīna*.

Exc. 3. The inſeparable prepoſitions *SE* and *DI* are long ; as, *sēpăro*, *dīvello* : except *dĭrĭmo*, *dĭſertus*. *Re* is ſhort ; as, *rĕmitto*, *rĕf ĕro* : except in the imperſonal verb *rēfert*, compounded of *res* and *fero*.

Exc. 4. *E, I, O*, in the end of the former compounding word are uſually ſhortened ; as, *trĕcenti*, *nĕſas*, *nĕque*, *patĕfacio*, &c. *Capricornus*, *omnĭpotens*, *agrĭcŏla*, *ſignĭfĭco*, *bĭformis*, *alĭger*, *Trĭvia*, *tubĭcen*, &c. *duŏdĕcim*, *hŏdie*, *ſacrŏſanctus*, &c. But from each of theſe there are many exceptions. Thus *i* is long when it is varied by caſes ; as; *quīdam*, *quīvis*, *tantīdem*, *cīdem*, &c. And when the compounding words may be taken ſepa-
rately ;

rately ; as, *ludīmagiſter*, *lucrīfacio*, *sīquis*, &c.   *Idem* in the maſc. is long, in the neuter ſhort ; alſo *ubīque*, *ibīdem*. But in *ubivis* and *ubicunque*, the *i* is doubtful.

A C C E N T.

Accent is the tone of the voice with which a ſyllable is pronounced.

In every word of two or more ſyllables, one ſyllable is ſounded higher than the reſt, to prevent monotony, or an uniformity of ſound, which is diſagreeable to the ear.

When accent is conſidered with reſpect to the ſenſe, or when a particular ſtreſs is laid upon any word, on account of the meaning, it is called *Emphāſis*.

There are three accents, diſtinguiſhed by their different ſounds ; *acute*, *grave*, and *circumflex*.

1. The *acute* or *ſharp* accent raiſes the voice in pronunciation, and is thus marked ['] ; as, *próſero*, prófer.

2. The *grave* or *baſe* accent depreſſes the voice, or keeps it in its natural tone ; and is thus marked [`] as *doĉtè*, This accent properly belongs to all ſyllables which have no other.

3. The *circumflex* accent firſt raiſes, and then ſinks the voice in ſome degree on the ſame ſyllable ; and is therefore placed only upon long ſyllables. When written, it has this mark, made up of the two former [^] ; as *amāre*.

The accents are hardly ever marked in Engliſh books, except in dictionaries, grammars, ſpelling-books, or the like, where the acute accent only is uſed

The accents are likewiſe ſeldom marked in Latin books, unleſs for the ſake of diſtinction ; as in theſe adverbs, *aliquà*, *continuò*, *doĉtè*, *unà*, &c. to diſtinguiſh them from certain caſes of adjectives, which are ſpelt in the ſame way. So *poëtâ*, *gloriâ*, in the ablative : *fruĉtûs*, *tumultûs*, in the genitive : *noſtrûm*, *veſtrûm*, the genitive of *nos* and *vos* : *ergò*, on account of; *occīdit*, he ſlew ; *Pompīli*, for *Pompilii* ; *amâris*, for *amaveris*, &c.

VERSE.

V E R S E.

A Verse is a certain number of long and short syllables disposed according to rule.

It is so called, because when the number of syllables requisite is completed, we always *turn* back to the beginning of a new line.

The parts into which we divide a verse, to see if it have its just number of syllables, are called *Feet*.

A verse is divided into different feet, rather to ascertain its measure or number of syllables, than to regulate its pronunciation.

F E E T.

Poetic feet are either of two, three, or four syllables. When a single syllable is taken by itself, it is called a *Cæsura*, which is commonly a long syllable.

1. *Feet of two syllables.*

Spondēus, consists of two long ;	as, *ōmnēs*.
Pyrrhichius,	two short ; as, *dĕŭs*.
Iambus,	a short and a long ; as, *ămāns*.
Trochæus,	a long and a short ; as, *sērvŭs*.

2. *Feet of three syllables.*

Dactylus,	a long and two short ; as, *scrībĕrĕ*.
Anapæstus,	two short and a long ; as, *pĭĕtās*.
Amphimăcer,	a long, a short, and a long ; as, *chărĭtās*.
Tribrăchys,	three short ; as, *dŏmĭnŭs*.

The following are not so much used.

Moloffus,	*dĕlēctănt*.	Antifpaftus,	*ālĕxăndĕr*.
Amphibrachys,	*bĕnŏrĕ*.	Ionicus minor,	*prŏpĕrābănt*.
Bacchīus,	*dŏlōrēs*.	Ionicus major,	*cālărĭbus*.
Antibacchīus,	*pēllūntŭr*.	Pæon primus,	*tēmpŏrĭbŭs*.
		Pæon secundus,	*pŭtēntĭă*.
		Pæon tertius,	*ănĭmātŭs*.
3. *Feet of four syllables.*		Pæon quartus,	*cĕlĕrĭtās*.
Proceleufmaticus,	*hŏmĭnĭbŭs*.	Epitrītus primus,	*vŏluptātēs*.
Difpondeus,	*ōrātōrēs*.	Epitritus secundus,	*pænĭtentēs*.
Dijambus,	*ămænĭtās*.	Epitritus tertius,	*difcōrdĭās*.
Choriambus,	*pōntĭfĭcēs*.	Epitritus quartus,	*fŏrtūnātŭs*.
Ditrochæus,	*căntĭlēnă*.		

SCANNING.

SCANNING.

The meafuring of verfe, or the refolving of it into the feveral feet of which it is compofed, is called *Scanning*.

When a verfe has juft the number of feet requifite, it is called *Verfus Acatalectus* or *Acatalecticus*, an Acatalectic verfe : If a fyllable be wanting, it is called *Catalecticus* ; if there be a fyllable too much, *Hypercatalecticus*, or *Hypermeter*.

The afcertaining whether the verfe be complete, defective, or redundant, is called *Depofitio* or *Claufula*.

DIFFERENT KINDS OF VERSE.

1. HEXAMETER.

The Hexamēter or heroic verfe confifts of fix feet. Of thefe the fifth is a dactyle, and the fixth a fpondee; all the reft may be either dactyles or fpondees; as,

Lūdĕrĕ | quæ vēl- | lēm cǎlǎ- | mō pēr- | mīsĭt ǎ- | grēftī. *Virg.*
Infān- | dūm Rē- | gīnǎ, jǔ- | bēs rěnŏ- | vārě dŏ- | lōrēm. *Id.*

A regular Hexameter line cannot have more than feventeen fyllables, or fewer than thirteen.

Sometimes a fpondee is found in the fifth place, whence the verfe is called *Spondaic* ; as,

Cārǎ Dē- | ūm sŏbŏ- | lēs mā- | gnūm Jŏvĭs | īucrē- | mēntūm. *Virg*

This verfe is ufed, when any thing grave, flow, large, fad, or the like, is expreffed. It commonly has a dactyle in the fourth place, and a word of four fyllables in the end.

Sometimes there remains a fuperfluous fyllable at the end. But this fyllable muft either terminate in a vowel, or in the confonant *m*, with a vowel before it; fo as to be joined with the following verfe, which in the prefent cafe muft always begin with a vowel; as,

Omnĭǎ | Mērcūrĭ- | ō sĭmĭ- | lĭs vō- | cēmquě cŏ- | lōrēmque
Et flavos crines ———   *Virg.*

Thofe Hexameter verfes found beft, which have dactyles and fpondees alternately; as,

    Ludere quæ vellem calamo permifit agrefti. *Virg.*
    Pinguis et ingratæ premeretur cafeus urbi. *Id.*

Or which have more dactyles than fpondees ; as,

    Tityre ju patulæ recubans fub tegmine fagi.

It

It is esteemed a great beauty in an Hexameter verse, when by the use of dactyles and spondees, the sound is adapted to the sense; as,

> Quadrupedante putrem sonitu quatit ungula campum. *Virg.*
> Illi inter sese magna vi brachia tollunt. *Id.*
> Monstrum horrendum, informe, ingens, cui lumen ademptum.
> Accipiunt inimicum imbrem, rimisque fatiscunt. *Id.*

But what deserves particular attention in scanning Hexameter verse is the CÆSURA.

Cæsura is, when after a foot is completed, there remains a syllable at the end of a word to begin a new foot; as,

> At rē-gīnă gră-vī jăm-dudum, &c.

The *Cæsura* is variously named according to the different parts of the hexameter verse in which it is found. When it comes after the first foot, or falls on the third half-foot, it is called by a Greek name, *Triemimĕris :* When on the fifth half foot, or the syllable after the second foot, it is called *Penthemimĕris :* When it happens on the first syllable of the fourth foot, or the seventh half-foot, it is called *Hephthemimĕris :* and when on the ninth half-foot, or the first syllable of the fifth foot, it is called *Enněemimĕris.*

All these different species of the *Cæsura* sometimes occur in the same verse; as,

> Illĕ lă-tūs nĭvĕ-ūm mōl-lī fūl-tūs hyă-cīnthō. *Virg.*

But the most common and beautiful *Cæsura* is the penthemim; on which some lay a particular accent or stress of the voice in reading an hexameter verse thus composed, whence they call it the *Cæsural pause ;* as,

> Tityre dum rede- O, brevis est via, pasce capellas. *Virg.*

When the *Cæsura* falls on a syllable naturally short, it renders it long; as, the last syllable of *fultus* in the foregoing example.

The chief melody of an hexameter verse in a great measure depends on the proper disposition of the *Cæsura.* Without this a line consisting of the number of feet requisite will be little else than mere prose; as,

> Rōmæ mœnĭă tērrŭĭt īmpĭgĕr Hānnĭbăl ārmīs. *Ennius.*

The

The ancient Romans in pronouncing verse paid a particular attention to its melody. They not only observed the quantity and accent of the several syllables, but also the different stops and pauses which the particular turn of the verse required. In modern times we do not fully perceive the melody of Latin verse, because we have now lost the just pronunciation of that language, the people of every country pronouncing it in a manner similar to their own. In reading Latin verse, therefore, we are directed by the same rules which take place with respect to English verse.

The tone of the voice ought to be chiefly regulated by sense. All the words should be pronounced fully; and the cadence of the verse ought only to be observed, so far as it corresponds with the natural expression of the words. At the end of each line there should be no fall of the voice, unless the sense requires it; but a small pause, half of that which we usually make at a comma.

2. PENTAMETER.

The Pentameter verse consists of five feet. Of these the two first are either dactyles or spondees; the third always a spondee; and the fourth and fifth, an anapæstus; as,

Nātŭ- | ræ sĕquĭ- | tūr sē- | mĭnă quīf- | quĕ sŭæ.   *Propert.*
Cārmĭnĭ- | būs vī- | vēs tēm- | pŭs ĭn ōm- | nĕ mĕīs.   *Ovid.*

But this verse is more properly divided into two hemisticks or halves; the former of which consists of two feet, either dactyles or spondees, and a Cæsura; the latter, always of two dactyles and another Cæsura: thus,

Nātŭ- | ræ sĕquĭ- | tūr | sēmĭnă | quīfquĕ sŭ- | æ.
Cārmĭnĭ- | būs vī- | vēs | tēmpŭs ĭn | ōmnĕ mĕ- | īs.

The Pentameter usually ends with a dissyllable, but sometimes also with a polysyllable.

3. ASCLEPIADEAN.

The Asclepiadēan verse consists of four feet; namely, a spondee, twice a choriambus, and a pyrrhichius; as,

Mæcē- | nās ătăvīs | ēdĭtĕ rē | gĭbŭs.   *Hor.*

But this verse may be more properly measured thus; In the first place, a spondee; in the second, a dactyle; then a cæsura; and after that two dactyles; thus,

Mæce- | nas ata- | vis | edite | regibus.

4. GLYC-

4. GLYCONIAN.

The Glyconian verse has three feet, a spondee, choriambus, and Pyrrhichius; as,

Nāvīs | quæ tĭbĭ crē- | dĭtŭm. *Horat.*

Or it may be divided into a spondee and two dactyles; thus,

Navis | quæ tibi | creditum.

5. SAPPHIC *and* ADONIAN.

The Sapphic verse has five feet, viz. a trochee, spondee, dactyle, and two trochees; thus,

Intĕ- | gĕr vī- | tæ, fcĕlĕ- | rīfquĕ | pūrŭs. *Horat.*

An Adonian verse consists only of a dactyle and spondee; as,

Jŭpĭtĕr | ūrgĕt. *Horat.*

6. PHERECRATIAN.

The Pherecratian verse consists of three feet, a spondee, dactyle, and spondee; thus,

Nīgrīs | æquŏră | vēntīs. *Horat.*

7. PHALEUCIAN.

The Phaleucian verse consists of five feet; namely, a spondee, a dactyle, and three trochees; as,

Sūmmām | nēc mĕtŭ- | ās dĭ- | ēm, nĕc | ŏptĕs. *Martial.*

8. *The* GREATER ALCAIC.

The greater Alcaic, called likewise *Dactylic*, consists of four feet, a spondee or iambus, iambus and cæsura, then two dactyles; as,

Vīrtūs | rĕpūl- | fæ | nēfcĭă | fōrdĭdæ. *Horat.*

9. ARCHILOCHIAN.

The Archilochian iambic verse consists of four feet. In the first and third place, it has either a spondee or iambus; in the second and fourth, always an iambus; and in the end, a Cæfura; as,

Nēc fŭ- | mĭt, aūt | pōnĭt | fĕcŭ- | rēs. *Horat.*

10. *The*

10. *The* LESSER ALCAIC.

The leſſer Dactylic Alcaic conſiſts of four feet, namely, two dactyles and two trochees ; as,

     Arbĭtrĭ- | ū pŏpŭ- | lārĭs | aūræ.   *Horat.*

Of the above kinds of verſe, the firſt two take their names from the number of feet of which they conſiſt. All the reſt derive their names from thoſe by whom they were either firſt invented, or frequently uſed.

There are ſeveral other kinds of verſe, which are named from the feet by which they are moſt commonly meaſured ; ſuch as the dactylic, trochaic, anapeſtic, and iambic. The laſt of theſe is moſt frequently uſed.

11. IAMBIC.

Of Iambic verſe there are two kinds. The one conſiſts of four feet, and is called by a Greek name *Dĭmĕter ;* the other conſiſts of ſix feet, and is called *Trĭmĕter.* The reaſon of theſe names is, that among the Greeks two feet were conſidered only as one meaſure in iambic verſe ; whereas the Latins meaſured it by ſingle feet, and therefore called the dimeter *quaternarius,* and the trimeter *ſenarius.* Originally this kind of verſe was purely iambic, *i. e.* admitted of no other feet but the iambus ; thus,

    Dimeter, Inār- | sĭt æ- | ſtŭō- | sŭīs.   *Horat.*
    Trimeter, Sŭīs | ĕt ī- | psă Rō- | mă vī- | rĭbūs | rŭīt.   *Id.*

But afterwards, both for the ſake of eaſe and variety, different feet were admitted into the uneven or odd places ; that is, in the firſt, third, and fifth places, inſtead of an iambus, they uſed a ſpondee, a dactyle, or an anapæſtus, and ſometimes a tribrachys. We alſo find a tribrachys in the even places, *i. e.* in the ſecond place, and in the fourth ; for the laſt foot muſt always be an iambus ; thus,

    Dimeter, Cānĭdĭ- | ă trā- | ctāvīt | dăpēs.   *Horat.*
       Vĭdē- | rĕ prŏpĕ- | rāntēs | dŏmūm.   *Id.*
    Trimeter, Quōquō | ſcĕlē- | ſtī rŭi- | tis aūt | cūr dēx- | tĕrīs.   *Id.*
       Păvĭdūm- | quĕ lĕpŏ- | r' aūt ād | vĕnām | lăquĕō | grŭēm.   *Id.*
       Alĭtĭ- | bŭs āt- | quĕ cănĭ- | bŭs hŏmĭ- | cīd' Hē-ctŏrēm.

In comic writers we ſometimes find an iambic verſe conſiſting of eight feet, therefore called *Tētrameter* or *Octonarius.*

FIGURES in SCANNING.

The several changes made upon words to adapt them to the verse, are called *Figures in Scanning.* The chief of these are the *Synalœpha, Ecthlipsis, Synærésis, Diærésis; Systōle,* and *Diastōle.*

1. SYNALOEPHA is the cutting off of a vowel or diphthong, when the next word begins with a vowel; as,

> Conticuere omnes, intentique ora tenebant. *Virg.*

to be scanned thus,

Cōntĭcŭ- | ĕr' ōm- | nēs ĭn- | tēntĭ- | qu' ōră tĕ- | nēbānt.

The *Synalœpha,* is sometimes neglected; and seldom takes place in the interjections, *ó, heu, ah, proh, væ, vah, hei;* as,

> O pater, ô hominum, Divûmque æterna potestas. *Virg.*

Long vowels and diphthongs, when not cut off, are sometimes shortened; as,

> Insulæ Ionio in magno, quas dira Celæno. *Virg.*
> Credimus? an, qui amant, ipsi sibi somnia fingunt. *Id.*
> Victor apud rapidum Simoënta sub Ilio alto.
> Ter sunt conati imponere Pelio Ossam.
> Glauco et Panopeæ, et Inoo Melicertæ.

2. ECTHLIPSIS is, when *m* is cut off, with the vowel before it in the end of a word, because the following word begins with a vowel; as,

> O curas hominum! O quantum est in rebus inane! *Pers.*

thus,

O cŭ- | răs hŏmĭ- | n', ō quān- | t' ēst ĭn | rēbŭs ĭn- | ānē.

Sometimes the Synalœpha and Ecthlipsis are found at the end of the verse; as,

> Sternitur infelix alieno vulnere, cœlumque
> Adspicit, et dulces moriens reminiscitur Argos. *Virg.*
> Jamque iter emensi, turres ac tecta Latinorum
> Ardua cernebant juvenes, murosque subibant. *Id.*

These verses are called *Hypermetri,* because a syllable remains to be carried to the beginning of the next line; thus, *qu' Adspicit; r' Ardua.*

3. SYNÆRESIS is the contraction of two syllables into one, which is likewise called *Crasis;* as, *Phæthon* for *Phaethon.*

So *ëi* in *Thefei, Orphëi, deinde, Pompei;* *üi* in *huic, cui;* *öi*, in *proinde;* *ëä*, in *aureâ;* thus,

> Notus amor Phædræ, nota eft injuria Thefei.   *Ovid.*
> Proinde tona eloquio, folitum tibi.   *Virg.*
> Filius huic contrâ, torquet qui fidera mundi.   *Id.*
> Aureâ percuffum virgâ, verfumque venenis.   *Id.*

So in *antehac, eadem, alvearia, deeft, deerit, vehemens, anteit, eodem, alveo, graveolentis, omnia, femianimis, femihomo, fluviorum, totius, promontorium,* &c. as,

> Unâ eâdemque viâ fanguifque animufque ferentur.   *Virg.*
> Seu lento fuerint alvearia vimine texta.   *Id.*
> Vilis amicorum eft annona, bonis ubi quid deeft.   *Hor.*
> Divitis uber agri, Troiæque opulentia deerit.   *Virg.*
> Vehemens et liquidus puroque fimillimus amni.   *Hor.*
> Te femper anteit dira necefitas.   *Alcaic. Hor.*
> Uno eodemque igni, fic noftro Daphnis amore.   *Virg.*
> Cum refluit campis, & jam fe condidit alveo.   *Id.*
> Inde ubi venêre ad fauces graveolentis Averni.   *Id.*
> Bis patriæ cecidere manus : quin protinus omnia.   *Id.*
> Cædit femianimis Rutulorum calcibus arva.   *Id.*
> Semihominis Caci facies quam dira tenebat.   *Id.*
> Fluviorum rex Eridanus, campofque per omnes.   *Id.*
> Magnanimofque duces, totiufque ex ordine gentis.   *Id.*
> Inde legit Capreas, promontoriumque Minervæ.   *Ovid.*

To this figure may be referred the changing of *i* and *u* into *j* and *v*, or pronouncing them in the fame fyllable with the following vowel; as in *genva, tenvis; arjetat, tenvia, abjete, pitvita; parjetibus, Nafidjenus;* for *genua, tenuis,* &c. as,

> Propterea qui corpus aquæ naturaque tenvis.   *Lucr.*
> Genva labant, gelido concrevit frigore fanguis.   *Virg.*
> Arjetat in portas & duros objice poftes.   *Id.*
> Velleraque ut foliis depectant tenvia Seres.   *Id.*
> Ædificant, fectâque intexunt abjete coftas.   *Id.*
> Præcipuè fanus, nifi cum pitvita molefta eft.   *Hor.*
> Parjetibufque premunt arctis, & quatuor addunt.   *Virg.*
> Ut Nafidjeni juvit te cœna beati.   *Hor.*

4. DIÆRESIS divides one fyllable into two; as, *aulii*, for *aulæ; Tröia*, for *Trojæ; Persëus*, for *Perfeus; miliius*, for *milvus; foliiit*, for *folvit; voliiit*, for *volvit; aqiiæ, siietus, siiafit, siievos, relanguiit, reliqiias*, for *aquæ, fuetus,* &c. as,

Aulai

Aulai in medio libabant pocula Bacchi. *Virg.*
Stamina non ulli dissoluenda Deo. *Pentam. Tibullus.*
Debuerant fusos evolüisse suos. *Id. Ovid.*
Quæ calidum faciunt aquæ tactum atque vaporem. *Lucr.*
Cum mihi non tantum furesque feræque sūctæ. *Horat.*
Atque alios alii inrident, Veneremque süadent. *Lucr.*
Fundat ab extremo flavos Aquilone Sũevos. *Lucan.*
Imposito fratri moribunda relangüit ore. *Ovid.*
Reliqūas tamen esse vias in mente patenteis. *Lucr.*

5. Systŏle is when a long syllable is made short; as the penult in *tulerunt*; thus,
Matri longa decem tulĕrunt, fastidia menses. *Virg.*

6. Diastŏle is when a syllable usually short is made long; as the last syllable in *amor*, in the following verse;
Confidant, si tantus amōr, et mœnia condant. *Virg.*

To these may be subjoined the *Figures of diction*, as they are called, which are chiefly used by the poets, though some of them likewise frequently occur in prose.

1. When a letter or syllable is added to the beginning of a word, it is called Prosthĕsis; as, *gnavus*, for *navus*; *tetŭli*, for *tuli*. When a letter or syllable is interposed in the middle of a word, it is called Epenthĕsis; as, *relligio*, for *religio*: *induperator*, for *imperator*. When a letter or syllable is added to the end, it is called Paragōge; as, *dicier* for *dici*.

2. If a letter or syllable be taken from the beginning of a word, it is called Aphærĕsis; as, *natus*, for *gnatus*; *tenderant*, for *tetenderant*. If from the middle of a word, it is called Syncŏpe; as, *dixti*, for *dixisti*; *desim*, for *desrum*: If from the end, Apocŏpe; as, *viden'*, for *videsne*; *Antōni*, for *Antonii*.

3. When a letter or syllable is transposed, it is called Metathĕsis; as, *pistris*, for *pristis*; *Lybia*, for *Libya*. When one letter is put for another, it is called Antithĕsis; as, *faciundum*, for *faciendum*; *olli*, for *illi*; *vultis*, for *vultis*.

Different kinds of Poems.

Any work composed in verse is called a *Poem*, (*Poema* or *Carmen.*)

Poems are called by various names, from their subject, their form, the manner of treating the subject, and their style.

1. A poem on the celebration of a marriage is called an Epithalamium; on a mournful subject, an Elegy or Lamentation; in
praise

praife of the Supreme Being, a HYMN; in praife of any perfon or thing, a PANEGYRIC or ENCOMIUM; on the vices of any one, a SATIRE or INVECTIVE; a poem to be infcribed on a tomb, an EPITAPH, &c.

2. A fhort poem adapted to the lyre or harp, is called an ODE, whence fuch compofitions are called *Lyric poems:* A poem in the form of a letter is called an EPISTLE; a fhort witty poem, playing on the fancies or conceits which arife from any fubject, is called an EPIGRAM; as thofe of Catullus and Martial. A fharp, unexpected, lively turn of wit in the end of an epigram, is called its *Point.* A poem expreffing the moral of any device or picture, is called an EMBLEM. A poem containing an obfcure queftion to be explained, is called an ÆNIGMA or RIDDLE.

When a character is defcribed fo that the firft letters of each verfe, and fometimes the middle and final letters exprefs the name of the perfon or thing defcribed, it is called an ACROSTIC; as the following on our Saviour:

<pre>
I nter cuncta micans I gniti fidera cæl I,
E xpellit tenebras E toto Phœbus ut orb E;
S ic cœcas removet JESVS caliginis umbra S,
V ivificanfque fimul V ero præcordia mot V
S olem juftitiæ S efe probat effe beati S.
</pre>

3. From the manner of treating a fubject, a poem is either *Exegetic, Dramatic,* or *Mixt.*

The *Exegetic,* where the poet always fpeaks himfelf, is of three kinds; Hiftorical, Didactic, or Inftructive, (as the Satire or Epiftle); and Defcriptive.

Of the *Dramatic,* the chief kinds are COMEDY, reprefenting the actions of ordinary life, generally with a happy iffue; and TRAGEDY, reprefenting the actions and diftreffes of illuftrious perfonages, commonly with an unhappy iffue. To which may be added *Paftoral poems* or BUCOLICS, reprefenting the actions and converfations of fhepherds; as moft of the eclogues of Virgil.

The *Mixt* kind is where the poet fometimes fpeaks in his own perfon, and fometimes makes other characters to fpeak. Of this kind is chiefly the EPIC or HEROIC poem, which treats of fome one great tranfaction of fome great illuftrious perfon, with its various circumftances; as the wrath of Achilles in the *Iliad* of Homer; the fettlement of Æneas in Italy in the *Æneid* of Virgil; the fall of man in the *Paradife Loft* of Milton, &c.

4. The ftyle of poetry, as of profe, is of three kinds, the fimple, ornate, and fublime.

COMBINATION of VERSES in poems.

In long poems there is commonly but one kind of verfe ufed. Thus Virgil, Lucretius, Horace in his Satires and Epiftles, Ovid in his Metamorphofes, Lucan, Silius Italicus,

icus, Valerius Flaccus, Juvenal, &c. always ufe Hexameter verfe : Plautus, Terence, and other writers of Comedy,
generally ufe the Iambic, and fometimes the Trochaic.   It
is chiefly in fhorter poems, particularly thofe which are called Lyric poems, as the odes of Horace and the Pfalms of
Buchanan, that various kinds of verfe are combined.

A poem which has only one kind of verfe, is called by
a Greek name, Monocŏlon, fc. *poema* v. *carmen* ; or
Monocōlos, fc. *ode* ; that which has two kinds, Dicōlon ;
and that which has three kinds of verfe Tricōlon.

If the fame fort of verfe return after the fecond line, it is
called Dicolon Distrŏphon ; as when a fingle Pentameter is alternately placed after an Hexameter, which is
named *Elegīac verfe*, (carmen Elegiăcum,) becaufe it was
firft applied to mournful fubjects ; thus,

> Flebilis indignos, Elegëia, folve capillos ;
> Ah ! nimis ex vero nunc tibi nomen erit.   *Ovid.*

This kind of verfe is ufed by Ovid in all his other works
except the Metamorphofes ; and alfo for the moft part by
Tibullus, Propertius, &c.

When a poem confifts of two kinds of verfe, and after
three lines returns to the firft, it is called *Dicolon Triftrŏ-
phon* ; when after four lines, *Dicolon Tetraftrŏphon* ; as,

> Auream quifquis mediocritatem
> Diligit, tutus caret obfoleti
> Sordibus tecti ; caret invidendâ
> Sobrius aulâ.   *Horat.*

When a poem confifts of three kinds of verfe, and after
three lines always returns to the firft, it is called *Tricolon
Triftrophon* ; but if it returns after four lines, it is called
Tricolon Tetraftrophon ; as when after two greater dactylic
alcaic verfes are fubjoined an archilochian iambic and a
leffer dactylic alcaic, which is named *Carmen Horatianum*,
or Horatian verfe, becaufe it is frequently ufed by Horace ;
thus,

> Virtus recludens immeritis mori
> Cœlum, negatâ tentat iter viâ ;
> Cœtufque vulgares, et udam
> Spernit humum fugiente pennâ.

Any one of these parts of a poem, in which the different kinds of verse are comprehended, when taken by itself, is called a *Strophe*, *Stanza*, or *Staff*.

Different Kinds of Verse in Horace and Buchanan.

I. Odes and Psalms of one kind of Verse.

1. *Asclepiadēan*, See N° 3. page 270. Hor. I. 1. IV. 8. III. 30.——Buch. Pſ. 28, 40, 80.

2. *Choriambic Alcaic Pentameter*, conſiſting of a ſpondee, three choriambuſes, and a pyrrhichius or iambus : Hor. I. 11, 18. IV. 10.

3. *Iambic trimĕter*, N° 11.—Hor. Epod. 17.——Buch. Pſ. 25, 94, 106.

4. *Hexameter*, N° 1. Hor. Satires and Epiſtles.——Buch. Pſ. 1, 18, 45, 78, 85, 89, 104, 107, 132, 135.

5. *Iambic Dimĕter*, N° 12. — Buch. Pſ. 13, 31, 37, 47, 52, 54, 59, 86, 96, 98, 117, 148, 149, 150.

6. The *Greater Dactylic Alcaic*, N° 8.—Buch. Pſ. 26, 29, 32, 49, 61, 71, 73, 143.

7. *Trochaic*, conſiſting of ſeven trochees and a ſyllable ; admitting alſo a tribrachys in the uneven places, i. e. in the firſt, third, fifth, and ſeventh foot ; and in the even places, a tribrachys, ſpondee, dactyl, and anapeſtus.—Buch. Pſ. 105, 119, 124, 129.

8. *Anapeſtic*, conſiſting of four anapeſtuſes, admitting alſo a ſpondee or dactyl ; and in the laſt place, ſometimes a tribrachys, amphimăcer, or trochee.—Pſ. 113.

9. *Anacreontic Iambic*, conſiſting of three iambuſes and a ſyllable ; in the firſt foot it has ſometimes a ſpondee or anapeſtus, and alſo a tribrachys.—Pſ. 131.

II. Odes and Psalms of two kinds of verſe following one another alternately.

1. *Glyconian* and *Asclepiadēan*, N° 4. and 3.—Hor. I. 3. 13, 19, 36. III. 9, 15, 19, 24, 25, 28. IV. 1, 3.—— Buch. Pſ. 14, 35, 43.

2. Every firſt line, *(Dactylico-Trochaic,)* conſiſting of the firſt four feet of an hexameter verſe, then three trochees or a ſpondee for the laſt ; every ſecond verſe *(Iambic Archilochian)* conſiſting of an iambus or ſpondæus, an iambus, a cæſura, and then three trochees.—Hor. I. 4.   3. The

3. The first line, *Hexameter ;* and the second, *Alcmanian Dactylic,* consisting of the four last feet of an hexameter. Hor I. 7, 28. Epod. 12.——Buch. Pf. 4. 111.

4. Every first line, *Ariftophanic,* consiftng of a choriambus, and bacchīus or amphimacer : Every second line, *Choriambic Alcaic,* consisting of epitrītus fecundus, two choriambufes, and a bacchīus. Hor. I. 8.

5. The first line, *(Trochaic),* consisting of three trochees and a cæfura ; or of an amphimacer and two iambufes. The second line, *Archilochian Iambic,* N° 9. Hor. II. 18.

6. The first line, *Hexameter ;* the second *(Dactylic Archilochian),* two dactyls and a cæfura. Hor. IV. 7.—Buch. Pf. 12.

7. The first line, *Iambic Trimeter ;* and the second, *Iambic Dimeter,* N° 11.—Hor. Epod. 1, 2, 3, 4, 5, 6, 7, 8, 9, 10.——Buch. Pf. 3, 6, 10, 21, 22, 27, 34, 38, 39, 41, 44, 48, 53, 62, 74, 76, 79, 87, 92, 110, 112, 115, 120, 127, 133, 134, 139, 141.

8. The first line, *Iambic Dimeter ;* the second *(Sapphic)* consists of two dactyls, a cæfura, and four iambufes, admitting alfo a fpondeus, &c. But this verfe is commonly divided into two parts ; the firft, the latter part of a pentameter, N° 2. and the second, iambic dimeter, N° 11. Hor. Epod, 11.

9. The first line, *Hexameter ;* the second, *Iambic Dimeter.* Hor. Epod. 14, 15.——Buch. Pf. 81.

10. *Hexameter,* and *Iambic Trimeter.* Hor. Epod. 16. Buch. Pf. 2, 20, 24, 57, 60, 69, 83, 93, 95, 97, 108, 109, 118, 126, 136, 147.

11. The first line, *Sapphic,* N° 5. and the second, *Iambic Dimeter,* N° 11. Buch. Pf. 8.

12. *Sapphic* and *Glyconian.* Buch. Pf. 33, 70, 121, 142.

13. *Iambic Trimeter* and *Pentameter.* Buch. Pf. 36, 63.

14. The first line, *Hexameter ;* and the second line, the three last feet of an hexameter, with a long fyllable cr two fhort fyllables before. Buch. Pf. 68.

15. *Hexameter* and *Pentameter,* or *Elegiac* verfe. Buch. Pf. 88, 114, 137.

16. The firft line, *(Trochaic),* three trochees and a fyllable, admitting fometimes a fpondee, tribrachys, &c. The second line, *Iambic Dimeter,* N° 11. Buch. Pf. 100.

A a 2

III. Odes

III. ODES and PSALMS of two kinds of verfe, and three or four lines in each ftanza.

1. The three firft lines, *Sapphic*, and the fourth, *Alo-nian*, N° 5. Horat. Carm. I. 2, 10, 12, 20, 22, 25, 30, 32, 38. II. 2, 4, 6, 8, 10, 16. III. 8, 11, 14, 18, 20, 22, 27. IV. 2, 6, 11. *Carmen Secul.*——Buch. Pf. 5, 17, 51, 55, 65, 67, 72, 90, 101, 103.

2. The three firft lines, *Afclepiadēan*, and the fourth, *Glyconian*. Hor. Carm. I. 6, 15, 24, 33. II. 22. III. 10, 16. IV. 5, 12.——Buch. Pf. 23, 42, 75, 99, 102, 144.

3. The two firft lines, *Ionic Trimeter*, confifting of three *Ionici minores*; the third line, *Ionic Tetrameter*, having one *Ionicus minor* more. Hor. III. 12.

4. The two firft lines have four trochees, admitting, in the fecond foot, a fpondee, dactyl, &c. The third line, the fame; only wanting a fyllable at the end. Buch. Pf. 66.

5. The three firft lines, *Glyconian*, No 4. admitting alfo a fpondee, or iambus in the firft foot; the fourth line, *Pherecratian*, N° 6. Buch. Pf. 116, 122, 128.

IV. ODES and PSALMS of three kinds of verfe, and three or four lines in each ftanza.

1. The two firft lines, *Afclepiadēan*, N° 3. the third line, *Pherecratian*, N° 6. and the fourth, *Glyconian*, N° 4. Hor. Carm. I. 5, 14, 21, 23, III. 7, 13. IV. 13.——Buch. Pf. 9, 64, 84, 130.

2. The firft two lines, *the Greater Dactylic Alcaic*, N° 8. The third, *Archilochian Iambic*, N° 9. The fourth, *the Leffer Alcaic*, N° 10. Hor. Carm. I. 9, 16, 17, 26, 27, 29, 31, 34, 35, 37. II. 1, 3, 5, 7, 9, 11, 13, 14, 15, 17, 19, 20. III. 1, 2, 3, 4, 5, 6, 17, 21, 23, 26, 29. IV. 4, 9, 14, 15.——Buch. Pf. 7, 11, 15, 19, 30, 46, 50, 56, 58, 77, 82, 91, 123, 125, 140, 146.

3. The firft line, *Glyconian*; the fecond, *Afclepiadēan*; the third a fpondee, three choriambufes, and an iambus or pyrrhichius. Buch. Pf. 16.

4. The firft line, *Hexameter*; the fecond, *Iambic Dime-ter*; and the third, two dactyls and a fyllable; Hor. Epod. 13.——Buch. Pf. 138. Sometimes the two laft verfes are joined in one or inverted; as, Buch. Pf. 145.

ENGLISH

ENGLISH VERSE.

The quantity of fyllables in Englifh verfe is not precifely afcertained. With regard to this we are chiefly directed by the ear. Our monofyllables are generally either long or fhort, as occafion requires. And in words of two or more fyllables, the accented fyllable is always long.

Of Englifh verfe there are two kinds, one named *Rhyme*, and the other *Blank verfe*.

In rhyme the lines are ufually connected two and two, fometimes three and three in the final fyllables. Two lines following one another thus connected, are called a *Couplet*, three lines, a *Triplet*.

In blank verfe fimilarity of found in the final fyllables is carefully avoided.

In meafuring moft kinds of Englifh verfe we find long and fhort fyllables fucceeding one another alternately ; and therefore the accents fhould reft on every fecond fyllable.

The feet by which Englifh verfe is commonly meafured, are either *Iambic*, *i. e.* confifting of a fhort and a long fyllable ; as, *alòft*, *crĕātĕ* : or *Trochaic*, *i. e.* confifting of a long and a fhort fyllable ; as, *hŏlў*, *lòftў*. In verfes of the former kind the accents are to be placed on the even fyllables ; in the latter, on the odd fyllables. But the meafure of a verfe in Englifh is moft frequently determined by its number of fyllables only, without dividing them into particular feet.

I. Iambic measure comprifes verfes,

1. Of *four fyllables*, or of *two feet* ; as,
    With ravifh'd ears,.
    The monarch hears.   *Dryden.*

2. Of *fix fyllables*, or of *three feet* ; as,
    Aloft in awful ftate,
    The godlike hero fat.   *Dryden.*

3. Of *eight fyllables*, or of *four feet* ; as,
    While dangers hourly round us rife,
    No caution guards us from furprife.   *Francis' Horace.*

4. Of *ten fyllables*, or of *five feet*, which is the common meafure of heroic and tragic poetry ; as,

Poetic

> Poetic fields encompass me around,
> And still I seem to tread on Classic ground;
> For here the Muse so oft her harp has strung,
> That not a mountain rears its head unsung.   *Addison.*

Obs. 1. In measures of this last sort, we sometimes find the last line of a couplet or triplet stretched out to twelve syllables, or six feet, which is termed an *Alexandrine* verse: thus,

> A needless Alexandrine ends the song,
> Which, like a wounded snake, drags its slow length along, *Pope.*

> Waller was smooth; but Dryden taught to join }
> The varying verse, the full resounding line, }
> The long majestic march, and energy divine. }   *Pope.*

We also find the last verse of a triplet stretched out to fourteen syllables, or seven feet, but then it has commonly an Alexandrine verse before it; thus,

> For thee the land in fragrant flow'rs is drest; }
> For thee the ocean smiles, and smooths her wavy breast, }
> And heav'n itself with more serene and purer light is blest. } *Dryden.*

Sometimes also when there is no Alexandrine before it; thus,

> At length by fate to power divine restor'd, }
> His thunder taught the world to know its lord, }
> The god grew terrible again, and was again ador'd. }   *Rowe.*

Obs. 2. The more strictly iambic these verses are, the more harmonious. In several of them, however, particularly in those of ten syllables, we often meet with a trochee, and likewise a spondee, instead of an iambus. Verses of heroic measure sometimes also admit a dactyle, or an anapestus, in place of the iambus; in which case a verse of five feet may comprehend eleven, twelve, thirteen, and even fourteen syllables; thus,

> 1   2 3   4   5   6   7   8 9   10 11 12 13   14
> And many an humorous, many an amorous lay.

> 1   2   3   4 5   6   7   8   9 10 11   12
> Was sung by   many a Bard on many a day.

This manner of writing every syllable fully is now generally used by the best poets, and seems much more proper than the ancient custom of cutting off vowels by an apostrophe. Our language abounds too much in consonants of itself: the elision of vowels therefore should be avoided as much as possible, and ought only to be admitted where it is absolutely necessary; as, *o'er* for *over*; *e'er* for *ever*, &c. The same observation may be applied to every kind of measure.

II. TROCHAIC MEASURE comprises verses,

1. Of *three syllables*; as,

> Dreadful gleams,
> Dismal screams, &c.   *Pope.*

2. Of

2. Of *five syllables*; as,

> In the days of old,
> Stories plainly told,
> Lovers felt annoy.

3. Of *seven syllables*; as,

> ·Faireſt Piece of well form'd earth,
> Urge not thus your haughty birth.   *Waller.*

Theſe are the meaſures which are moſt commonly uſed in Engliſh poetry, eſpecially thoſe of ſeven, eight, and ten ſyllables.

We have another meaſure very quick and lively, and therefore much uſed in ſongs, which may be called *Anapeſtic* meaſure, *i. e.* a verſe conſiſting of feet of three ſyllables, two ſhort, and one long, in which the accent reſts upon every third ſyllable. Verſes of anapeſtic meaſure conſiſt of two, three, or four feet; that is, of ſix, nine, or twelve ſyllables; thus,

> Let the lóud trumpets fóund,
> 'Till the róofs all aróund,
> The ſhrill échoes rebóund.   *Pope.*

> From the pláins, from the wóodlands, and gróves,
> How the níghtingales wárble their lóves!   *Shenſtone.*

> May I góvern my páſſions with ábſolute ſwáy,
> And grow wíſer and bétter, as lífe wears awáy.   *Id.*

In this meaſure, a ſyllable is often retrenched from the firſt foot; as,

> The ſwórd or the dárt
> Shall pierce my ſad héart.   *Addiſon.*

> Ye ſhépherds ſo chéarful and gáy,
> Whoſe flócks never cárelefsly róam, &c.

> I vów'd to the múſes my tíme and my cáre,
> Since néither could wín me the ſmíles of the fáir.   *Shenſtone.*

Theſe meaſures are variouſly combined together in *Stanzas*, particularly in ſhort poems; for generally in·longer works the ſame meaſure is always obſerved.

Stanzas are compoſed of more or fewer verſes, and theſe variouſly diverſified, according to the nature of the ſubject, and the taſte of the poet. But when they are ſtretched out to a great length, and conſiſt of verſes of many different meaſures, they are ſeldom agreeable.

Such poems as conſiſt of Stanzas, which are not confined to a certain number of verſes, nor the verſes to a certain

number

number of syllables, nor the rhymes to a certain diſtance,
are called *Irregular*, or *Pindaric odes*. Of this kind are
ſeveral of the poems of Cowley. But in the odes of later
authors, the numbers are exact, and the ſtrophes regular.

 Stanzas of four lines are the moſt frequent, in which the
firſt verſe anſwers to the third, and the ſecond to the fourth.
There is a ſtanza of this kind, confiſting of verſes of eight
and of ſix ſyllables alternately, which is very often uſed,
particularly in ſacred poetry. Here for the moſt part the
ſecond and fourth lines only rhyme together ; as,

When all thy mercies, O my God,
   My riſing ſoul ſurveys :
Tranſported with the view, I'm loſt,
   In wonder, love, and praiſe.　　*Addiſon.*

Sometimes alſo the firſt and third lines anſwer to one
another ; as,

Keep ſilence, all created things,
   And wait your Maker's nod :
The muſe ſtands trembling while ſhe ſings
   The honours of her God.　　*Watts.*

This ſtanza is uſed in place of what anciently was comprehended in two verſes, each confiſting of fourteen ſyllables, having a pauſe after the eighth ſyllable.

 Several of theſe meaſures are often varied by double endings, that is, by putting an additional ſhort ſyllable at the
end of the verſe ; as,

 1. *In heroic meaſure, or verſes of ten ſyllables, both in blank
verſe and ryhme.*

In Blank verſe.

'Tis heav'n itſelf that points out an hereafter.　　*Addiſon.*
 In Rhyme, where it is called Double Rhyme.
   The piece, you think, is incorrect ? Why, take it,
   I'm all ſubmiſſion ; what you'd have it, make it.　　*Pope.*

 2. *In verſes of eight ſyllables.*
   They neither added nor confounded,
   They neither wanted nor abounded.

 3. *In verſes of ſix ſyllables.*
   'Twas when the ſeas were roaring,
   With hollow blaſts of wind,
   A damſel lay deploring,
   All on a rock reclin'd.　　*Gay.*

4. *In*

4. *In verses of seven syllables.*

> As Palemon, unsufpecting,
> Prais'd the fly mufician's art;
> Love, his light difguife rejecting,
> Lodg'd an arrow in his heart.   *Shenstone.*

5. *In verses of three syllables.*

> Glooms inviting,
> Birds delighting.   *Addifon.*

6. *In the Anapeftic meafure.*

> Ah! friend, 'tis but idle to make fuch a pother.|
> Fate, fate has ordain'd us to plague one another. *Shenstone.*
> Now with furies furrounded,
> Defpairing, confounded.   *Pope.*

Double rhyme is ufed chiefly in poems of wit and humour, or in burlefque compofitions.

Verfes with double endings, in blank verfe, moft frequently occur in tragic poetry, where they often have a
fine effect; thus,

> I here devote thee for my prince and country;
> Let them be fafe, and let me nobly perifh.   *Thomfon.*
> The dropping dews fell cold upon my head,
> Darknefs inclos'd, and the winds whiftled round me.   *Otway.*

APPENDIX

APPENDIX I.

Of *Punctuation, Capitals, Abbreviations, Numerical Characters,* and the *Division* of the *Roman Month.*

The different divisions of discourse are marked by certain characters called *Points*.

The points employed for this purpose are the *Comma* (,), *Semicolon* (;), *Colon* (:), *Period*, Punctum, or full stop (.).

Their names are taken from the different parts of the sentence which they are employed to distinguish.

The *Period* is a whole sentence complete by itself. The *Colon*, or member, is a chief constructive part, or greater division of a sentence. The *Simicolon*, or half member, is a less constructive part, or subdivision, of a sentence or member. The *Comma*, or segment, is the least constructive part of a sentence in this way of considering it. For the next subdivision of a sentence would be the resolution of it into *Phrases* and *Words*.

To these points may be added the *Semiperiod* or less point, followed by a small letter. But this is of much the same use with the Colon, and occurs only in Latin books.

A simple sentence admits only of a full point at the end; because its general meaning cannot be distinguished into parts. It is only in compound sentences that all the different points are to be found.

Points likewise express the different pauses which should be observed in a just pronunciation of discourse. The precise duration of each pause, or note, cannot be defined. It varies according to the different subjects of discourse, and the different turns of human passion and thought. The period requires a pause in duration double of the colon, the colon double of the semicolon ; and the semicolon, double of the comma.

There are other points which, together with a certain pause, also denote a different modulation of the voice, in correspondence with the sense. These are the *Interrogation* point (?) the *Exclamation* or *Admiration* point (!) and the *Parenthesis* (). The first two generally mark an elevation of the voice, and a pause equal to that of a semicolon,

colon, a colon, or a period, as the sense requires. The *Parenthesis* usually requires a moderate depression of the voice, with a pause somewhat greater than a comma. But these rules are liable to many exceptions. The modulation of the voice in reading, and the various pauses, must always be regulated by the sense.

Besides the points, there are several other *marks* made use of in books, to denote references and different distinctions, or to point out something remarkable or defective, &c. These are, the *Apostrophe* ('); *Asterisk* (*); *Hyphen* (-); *Obelisk* (†); *Double Obelisk* (‡); *Parallel Lines* (‖); *Paragraph* (¶); *Section* (§); *Quotation* (" "); *Crotchets* [ ]; *Brace* (}); *Ellipsis* (. . . or —); *Caret* (‸); which last is only used in writing.

References are often marked by letters and figures.

Capitals, or large letters, are used at the beginning of sentences, of verses, and of proper names. Some use them at the beginning of every substantive noun. Adjectives, verbs, and other parts of speech, unless they be emphatical, commonly begin with a small letter.

Capitals, with a point after them, are often put for whole words; thus, A. marks *Aulus*, C. *Caius*, D. *Decimus*, L. *Lucius*, M. *Marcus*, P. *Publius*, Q. *Quinctius*, T. *Titus*. So F. stands for *Filius*, and N. for *Nepos*; as, M. F. *Marci Filius*, M. N. *Marci Nepos*. In like manner, P. C. marks *Patres Conscripti*; S. C. *Senatûs Consultum*; P. R. *Populus Romanus*; S. P. Q. R. *Senatus Populusque Romanus*; U. C. *Urbs Condita*; S. P. D. *Salutem plurimam dicit*; D. D. D. *Dat, dicat, dedicat*; D. D. C. Q. *Dat, dicat, consecratque*; H. S. written corruptly for L. L. S. *Sestertius*, equal in value to two pounds of brass and a half; the two pounds being marked by L. L. *Libra, Libra*, and the half by S. *Semis*. So in modern books A. D. marks *Anno Domini*, A. M. *Artium Magister*, Master of Arts; M. D. *Medicinæ Doctor*; LL. D. *Legum Doctor*; N. B. *Nota Bene*, &c.

Sometimes a small letter or two is added to the capital; as, Etc. *Et cætera*; Ap. *Appius*; Cn. *Cneius*; Op. *Opiter*; Sp. *Spurius*; Ti. *Tiberius*; Sex. *Sextus*; Cos. *Consul*; Cos. *Consules*; Imp. *Imperator*; Impp. *Imperatores*.

In

In like manner, in Englifh, Efq; *Efquire;* Dr *Debtor* or *Doctor;* Acct. *Account;* MS. *Manufcript;* MSS. *Manufcripts;* Do. *Ditto;* Rt Hon. *Right Honorable, &c.*

Small letters are likewife often put as abbreviations of a word; as, i. e. *id eft;* h. e. *hoc eft;* e. g. *exempli gratia;* v. g. *verbi gratia.*

Capitals were ufed by the ancient Romans, to mark numbers. The letters employed for this purpofe were C. I. L. V. X. which are therefore called *Numerical Letters.* I. denotes *one*, V. *five*, X. *ten*, L. *fifty*, and C. *a hundred.* By the various combination of thefe five letters, all the different numbers are expreffed.

The repetition of a numerical letter repeats its value. Thus, II. fignifies *two;* III. *three;* XX. *twenty;* XXX. *thirty;* CC. *two hundred, &c.* But V. and L. are never repeated.

When a letter of a lefs value is placed before a letter of a greater, the lefs takes away what it ftands for from the greater; but being placed after, adds what its ftands for to the greater; thus,

IV.	Four.	V.	Five.	VI.	Six.
IX.	Nine.	X.	Ten.	XI.	Eleven.
XL.	Forty.	L.	Fifty.	LX.	Sixty.
XC.	Ninety.	C.	A hundred.	CX.	A hundred and ten.

A *thoufand* is marked thus, cɪɔ, which in later times was contracted into ᴍ. *Five hundred* is marked thus, ɪɔ. or, by contraction, ᴅ.

The annexing of ɔ to ɪɔ. makes its value ten times greater; thus, ɪɔɔ. marks *five thoufand;* and ɪɔɔɔ. *fifty thoufand.*

The prefixing of c, together with the annexing of ɔ to the number of cɪɔ. makes its value ten times greater; thus, ccɪɔɔ. denotes *ten thoufand;* and cccɪɔɔɔ. *a hundred thoufand.* The ancient Romans, according to Pliny, proceeded no farther in this method of notation. If they had occafion to exprefs a larger number, they did it by repetition; thus, cccɪɔɔɔ, cccɪɔɔɔ. fignified *two hundred thoufand &c.*

We fometimes find *thoufands* expreffed by a ftraight line
drawn

drawn over the top of the numerical letters. Thus, $\overline{\text{III}}$. denotes *three thousand*; $\overline{\text{X}}$ *ten thousand*.

But the modern manner of marking numbers is much more simple, by these ten characters or *figures*, which, from the ten fingers of the hands, were called *Digits*; 1 *one*, 2 *two*, 3 *three*, 4 *four*, 5 *five*, 6 *six*, 7 *seven*, 8 *eight*, 9 *nine*, 0 *nought*, *nothing*. The first nine are called *Significant Figures*. The last is called a *Cypher*.

Significant figures placed after one another increase their value ten times at every remove from the right hand to the left ; thus,

8 Eight.   85 Eighty-five.   856 Eight hundred and fifty-six.   8566 Eight thousand five hundred and sixty-six.

When cyphers are placed at the right hand of a significant figure, each cypher increases the value of the figure ten times ; thus,

1 One.   10 Ten.   100 A hundred.   1000 A thousand.
2 Two.   20 Twenty.   200 Two hundred.   2000 Two thousand.

Cyphers are often intermixed with significant figures, thus, 20202, *Twenty thousand two hundred and two.*

The superiority of the present method of marking numbers over that of the Romans, will appear by expressing the present year both in letters and figures, and comparing them together; CIƆ,IƆCCXCVIII. or M,DCCXCVIII. 1798.

As the Roman manner of marking the days of their months was quite different from ours, it may perhaps be of use here to give a short account of it.

Division of the Roman Months.

The Romans divided their months into three parts, by *Kalends*, *Nones*, and *Ides*. The first day of every month was called the *Kalends ;* the fifth day was called the *Nones ;* and thirteenth day was called the *Ides ;* except in the months of March, May, July, and October, in which the nones fell upon the seventh day, and the ides on the fifteenth.

In reckoning the days of their months, they counted **backwards**. Thus, the first day of January was marked

Kalendis

Kalendis Januariis or *Januarii*, or by contraction, *Kal. Jan.* The laft day of December, *Pridie Kalendas Janua- rias* or *Januarii*, fcil. *ante.* The day before that, or the 30th day of December, *Tertio Kal. Jan.* fcil. *die ante;* or, *Ante diem tertium Kal. Jan.* The twenty-ninth day of December, *Quarto Kal. Jan.* And fo on, till they came back to the thirteenth day of December, or to the ides, which were marked *Idibus Decembribus,* or *Decem- bris:* The day before the ides, *Pridie Idus Dec.* fcil. *ante:* The day before that, *Tertio Id. Dec.* and fo back to the nones, or the fifth day of the month, which was mark- ed, *Nonis Decembribus* or *Decembris:* The day before the nones, *Pridie Non. Dec. &c.* and thus through all the months of the year.

In *Leap-year,* that is, when February has twenty-nine days, which happens every fourth year, both the 24th and the 25th days of that month were marked, *Sexto Ka- lendas Martii* or *Martias;* and hence this year is called *Biffextilis.*

> Junius, Aprilis, Septemque, Novemque tricenos;
> Unum plus reliqui; Februus tenet octo viginti;
> At fi biffextus fuerit, fuperadditur unus.
> Tu primam menfis lucem dic effe kalendas.
> Sex Maius, nonas October, Julius, et Mars,
> Quatuor at reliqui; dabit idus quilibet octo.
> Omnes poft idus luces dic effe kalendas,
> Nomen fortiri debent a menfe fequenti.

Thus, the 14th day of *April, June, September,* and *October,* was marked XVIII. Kal. of the following month; the 15th, XVII. Kal. &c. The 14th day of *January, Au- guft,* and *December,* XIX. Kal. &c. So the 16th day of *March, May, July,* and *October,* was marked XVII. Kal. &c. And the 14th day of February, XVI. Kal. Martii or Martias. The names of all the months are ufed as Subftantives or Adjectives, except *Aprilis,* which is ufed only as a Subftantive.

APPENDIX

APPENDIX II.

Containing RULES from RUDDIMAN's Grammar, which will be found explained in the Pages of this Book that are marked before each Rule.

I. Concerning the GENDER of NOUNS.

Names of Trees. See page 12.

1. Arbor femineis dabitur : fed mas *oleafter*,
Et *rhamnus :* petit hic potiùs *cytifufque rubufque* :
Hic quandoque *larix, lotus* volet, atque *cupreffus :*
Hoc quod in *um, fuberque, filer* dant, *robur acer*que.

Nouns in A *of the firft declenfion.* p. 13. and 18.

2. Hæc dat A quod primæ eft : fed neutrum *Pafcha* requirit.
Hadria mas æquor, pariterque *cometa, planeta :*
Mafcula & interdum *talpam damam*que videbis.

Nouns in US *and* OS. p. 27. 39. and 48.

4. Hæc *domus & vannus,* pro fructu *ficus & alvus ;*
Sic *humus* atque *manus,* pofcunt : *acus* addito quartæ,
Porticus atque *tribus.* Capit hoc *virus pelaguf*que.

Nomen in OS Græcum, quod in US mutare Latini
Sæpè folent, normam fequitur plerumque virilem :
Femineum fed multa petunt : ut *abyffus, eremus,*
*Antidotuf*que, *pharus, dialectus, carbafus :* adde
Ex *odos & phthongos* genitum, quæque à generali
Voce genus plantæ & gemmæ capiunt muliebre.

Hic aut hæc donat *balanus, fpecus,* atque *phafelus,*
Barbitus, atque *penus, groffus :* fed *grus, atomuf*que
Femineum potiùs cupiunt ; *colus* adde, virile
Quod rarò invenies : muliebre at contrà *camelus*
Eft ubi nonnunquam videas. Vult hic dare *vulgus,*
Sed magis hoc. Ternæ *fpecus & penus* addito neutris.

B b 2

Nouns

Nouns of the Third Declension in O. p. 30. and 31.

7. Hic dat O : femineis *halo* cum *caro* dantur & *echo* ;
   Quæque in IO, seu sint verbo, seu nomine nata,
   Rem (numeris demptis) aliquam sine corpore signant.
   Adjice femineis DO, GO : sed mascula *cudo*,
   Harpago, sic *ordo*, simul *udo*, *tendo*, *ligoque*.
   Rariùs hæc *margo*, vati est, hic sæpe *cupido*,
   Arrhabo cum *cardo*, muliebria vix imitanda.

C and *L*. p. 32. rule 3.

9. Quod fit in L, vel T, C, vel M, neutralibus adde :
   Mascula *sol*, *mugil*, seu *sal*, quod rarius hoc vult.

N. p. 32. rule 4.

10. Masculeum capit N.   Finita in MEN dato neutris,
    Quæque secunda creat, cum *gluten* & *inguen* & *unguen* :
    Addideris *pollen*.   *Sindon* petit hæc, & *aedon* ;
    Alcyonem junges, data postea queis comes *icon*.

AR and *UR*. p. 33. rule 5.

11. Postulat AR neutrum : sed masculeum *salar* optat.
    Hoc dat UR.   Hic *furfur* capiet, cum *vulture turtur*.

ER and *OR*. p. 33. rule 6.

13. ER capit hic.   Neutrum plantæ fructusve requirunt :
    At *tuber* hic fructus ; *tuber* quemcunque tumorem
    Significans neutrale petit ; cumque *ubere spinther*,
    *Ver*que, *cadaver*, *iter*.   Dabit hic aut hæc tibi *linter*.
    Hic dat OR.   Hæc *arbor* : *cor*, *ador*que hoc, *marmor*
        & *æquor*.

AS. p. 34. rule 7.

15. AS petit hæc.   Neutrum est *vas*, *vasis*, queisque Pelasgi
    Dant *atis* in patrio : quibus *antis* masculo sunto.

ES. p. 35. rule 8.

16 Hæc dabit ES.   Capient *ales* hic hæcve, *palumbes*,
   Atque *dies* : sed mas proles : mas *poples* & *ames*,

Fomes,

Fomes, pes, paries, palmes, cum *limite stipes,*
Queis addes *trames, termes,* cum *gurgite cespes ;*
Et quæ fonte fluunt Graio ; fed neutra capeſſunt
Hippomanes, panaces, nepenthes, fic *cacoethes.*

IS. p. 36. rule 9.

17. IS dabo femineis.   Sunt maſcula *piſcis* & *axis,*
Glis, callis, vermis, vectis, menſis, cucumiſque,   -
Mugilis & *poſtis* cum *fanguine faſcis* & *orbis,*
Fuſtis item *collis, cauliſque* & *follis* & *enſis,*
Serpentemque notans *cenchris,* cum *vomere, torris,*
In NIS finitum Latium, *lapis, unguis, aqualis.*
Hic aut hæc *finis, clunis,* cum *torque canalis,*
Dant *ſcrobis,* ac *anguis : corbis* muliebre præoptat ;
Maſculeo potiùs gaudent *pulvis, cinis, amnis.*

OS. p. 38. rule 10.

19. Os maribus detur.   Sunt neutra *chaos, melos, os, os,*
Poſtulat hæc *arbos, cos, dos,* & origine Græcâ
Orta *eos, arctos, perimetros* cum *diametro.*

US. p. 38. rule 11.

20. Poſtulat US neutrum, quoties id tertia flectit.
Femineum voluere *palus, fubfcufque faluſque,*
Quæque *fenex, juvenis,* cum *fervio,* nomina formant,
Et *Virtus, incus.*   At maſcula funt *lepus* & *mus,*
Et *pus* compoſitum : petit at muliebre *lagopus.*

ÆS and *AUS.* p. 39. rule 13.

21. Æs neutrale petit : *laus, fraus,* muliebria funto.

S with a confonant before it, p. 40. rule 14.

22. S dato femineis, fi confona ponitur ante.
Maſcula fed *pons, fons, mons, feps,* dum denatat an-
        guem ;
Et queis P præit S polyfyllaba, *forcipe* dempto,
Denſque,   chalybs, cum *gryphe, rudens,* quod rariùs
      hæc vult.

Hic

Hic aut hæc *serpens* dat, *scrobs, stirps* truncus, *adepsque.*
Dans *animans* genus omne, tamen muliebre præoptat.

X. p. 41. rule 16.

23. Hæc petit X.   *Ax, ex* maribus polyfyllaba junge :
Dic tamen hæc *fornax, fmilax, carex,* velut *halex,*
Et cum prole *panax,* & *forfex* atque *fupellex.*
Mafcula funto *calix, phœnix,* pro *vermeque bombyx,*
Et *coccyx, fornix,* & *onyx* vas, aut lapis unde
Vas fit ; *oryx, tradux, grex* his adjunge *calyx*que.
Femineo interdum data *tradux* cum *grege* cernes.
Hæc modò femineis, maribus modò juncta videbis ;
Calx pro parte pedis metâve laboris & *hyftrix,*
Imbrex ; fardonychem jungas, *rumicem, filicem*que *:*
Hic magè vult *cortex* & *obex,* cum *pumice, varix :*
Hæc potiùs *limax, lynx,* & cum *fandice perdix :*
Atriplici neutrum meliùs dabo quàm muliebre.

II.   RULES Concerning the OBLIQUE CASES.

The Accufative Singular of the Third Declenfion, p. 43.

Finit in EM quartus.   Petit *im* fibi *ravis, amuffis,*
*Vis cucumif*que fimul, *tuffis, fitis* atque *finapis,*
Cannabis & *gummis, buris,* conjunge *mephitim.*
Adde urbes, aliofque locos, amnefque, deofque,
IS quibus eft recto : fed & hæc dant *in* quoque quarto.

Sæpiùs *im, turris, puppis,* cum *refte fecuris :*
Em, fed & *im* quandoque, volunt fibi *febris aqualis,*
Et *navis, pelvis, clavis ;* fic *lens, ftrigilif*que,
*Sementif*que, *cutis.*   Cumulant his plura vetufti.

Impurè in patrio cafu crefcentia Græcâ,
Sæpe & *Tros, Minos, heros,* quartum per *a* formant :
EUS *ea* vult.   Vix *em* dato *Pan,* cumque *æthere delphin.*

Ablative Singular. p. 44.

Sextus *e* vult : quibus at rectus per E clauditur : dant,
(Propria ni fuerint :) AL & AR neutralia junge.
Deme *jubar, fal, far, par* fixum, *nectar* & *hepar,*
Sed folet has leges migrare licentia vatum.

I quoque

I quoque dant *in* & *im* tantum facientia quarto.
Cannabis at *Bætis*, *Tigris*, voluiftis utrumque.
Ym quibus in quarto eft, *ye* dant, aut *m* modo demunt.
Dant *e* vel *i* fexto, queis quartus in *em* vel in *im* fit.
Excipe fed *reftis*, quod *e* femper, cum *cute*, donat.
I magè *fementis*, *ftrigilis* petit atque *fecuris*.
Quod fimul *im* vel *idem* format, capit *i* fibi rarò.

Hæc quoque dant *e* vel *i* : *finis*, cum *rure fupellex*,
Occiput & *vectis* : per UBI cum quæritur, urbes,
Et *pugil* & *mugil*, jungas.   Per *e* fæpiùs effer,
I raro, *civis*, *claffis*, *fors*, *anguis*, & *imber*,
Unguis, *avis*, *poftis*, *fuftis*, fimul *amnis* & *ignis*.
Ufus plura tulit prifcus, quæ refpuit ætas
Cultior.   *I* tantum fexto retineto *canalis*.

Genitive Plural. p. 45.

Præbet *ium* patrius, fi fextus in *i* fuit antè.
Tolle *vigil*, *vetus*, *uber*, *inops*, *fupplexque memorque*,
Mugilis & *confors*, quibus & *pugil* & *celer* adde ;
Atque gradus medios ; (fed *ium plus* pofcit.)   Adhæ-
  rent
His compofta *genus*, *capio*, *facio*que *caput*que.

Sextus *e* fi tantum dederit, capit *um* genitivus.
AS fed *ium* Latiale petit : polyfyllaba deme,
Queis magis *um* placuit.   Sed *ium* quærentibus adde
Nomen in IS vel in ES non crefcens : jungito & NS :
Tolle *parens*, *vates*, *panis*, *juveni*fque, *cani*fque.

Donat *ium Samnis*, *linter*, *caro*, *dos*, & *os offis*,
Glis, *nix*, *nox*que *cohors*, *mus*, *faux*, *uter* : adde *Qui-*
  ritem,
Atque *larem*, *litem*, *cotem*, *cor* ; compofitumque
Uncia, quod fimul *as* genuit : monofyllaba junge
Confora quæ duplex claudit.   *Bos* rite *boum* dat.

Dative Plural of the fourth Declenfion, p. 48.

Partus ŭBUS, *fpecus*, *artus*, *acus*, dant & *lacus*, *arcus*,
Atque *tribus* : fed utrumque *genu*, *portu*fque, *veru*que,
III. RULES

III.   RULES concerning ADJECTIVES.

Adjectives wanting the POSITIVE. p. 71.

Hæc viduata gradu funt pauca fequentia primo ;
Ultimus, ulterior ; prior, & primus ; propiorque,
Proximus ; ocyor atque *ocyſſimus* adjiciantur :
Deterior jungi quibus & *deterrimus* ambit.

Adjectives wanting the COMPARATIVE. p. 71
Nuperus, orba gradu medio, *novus* ac *meritus* funt ;
Par, facer, invictus, perfuaſus, & *inclytus* adde.

Adjectives wanting the SUPERLATIVE. p. 71.

Hæc fuperante carent : *fatur,* & *diuturnus,* & *ingens,*
Atque *fenex, juvenis, adolefcens, pronus, opimus ;*
Et finita BILIS propè cuncta, vel ILIS, & ALIS :
Cum multis aliis quæ nunc perfcribere longum eft.

Adjectives wanting the POSITIVE *and* SUPERLATIVE. p. 71.
Anterior folum, *fequior, fatior*que leguntur.

IV.   RULES concerning VERBS.

VERBS *of the* FIRST CONJUGATION *wanting both* PRE-
TERITE *and* SUPINE. p. 108.

———————— *Labo, nexo,* cum *plico* nil dant.

VERBS *of the* SECOND CONJUGATION *wanting the* SU-
PINE. p. 108.

Quod dat UI neutrum, *timeo, fileoque,* fupina
Nulla dabunt. *Valeo, placeo, caret* & *licet* aufer,
Paret, item *jaceo, caleo, noceo, doleo*que ;
Queis *coalet, latet* atque *meret* fociabis, *oletque.
Arceo quod fimplex nefcit, dant nata fupinum :
Quod retinent *taceo, lateo,* fobolique recufant.
———————————— Viduata fupinis
Si capiunt *urget,* cum *fulget, turget,* & *alget.*

VERBS *of the* SECOND CONJUGATION *wanting both* PRE-
TERITE *and* SUPINE. p. 111.

Nil formant *lactet, livet, fcateo*que *renidet,*
Mœret, avet, pollet, flavet, cum *denfeo glabret.*

                                                 VERBS

Verbs *of the* Third Conjugation *wanting the* Supine ; *and some also the* Preterite. p. 113.

SCO. p. 114.

——————————————— *Disco* -
Vult *didici* primam geminans : sic *posco, popofci ;*
Difpefcit, compefcit UI dant : cuncta supinis
Orba.   Nihil *glifco,* nihil Inceptiva crearunt.

UO. p. 113.

Nulla, supina dabunt *metuo, pluo, congruo,* sicut
Annuo, cum fociis ; quibus *ingruo, refpuo* junges.

DO. p. 116.

Tundo facit *tutudi, tunfum* compoftaque *tufum.*
Et *cado* vult *cecidi cafum ;* fed nata supinum
(Incido si demas, *recido,* simul *occido,)* fpernunt.
Præterito.DI *ftrido, rudo,* dant, abfque supinis,
Sidoque, fed foboli *fedeo* dat mutuo *fedi.*

GO. p. 118.

——————————————— Nil *vergo* capeffit.
XI *clango, ningo,* dat et *ango,* supinaque nulla.

Verbs *of the* Fourth Conjugation *wanting the* Supine
p. 124.

Cæcutit, geftit, glocit, & *dementit, inepit,*
Nulla supina dabunt, cum *profilit* atque *ferocit.*

DEPONENT VERBS *wanting the* Participle Perfect, p. 128.

Nil formant *vefcor, liquor, medeor, reminifcor,*
*Irafcor, ringor, prævertor, diffiteor*que :
Queis demum adjungas *divertor, deque fetifcor.*

Verbs wanting the firft perfon fingular. p. 134.
Dor, furo, for, der, fer, vix unquam fufcipit ufus.

V. RULES

V.   RULES concerning the QUANTITY of SYL-LABLES, &c.

I.   Concerning FIRST and MIDDLE SYLLABLES.

A vowel before another.   p. 253.
Vocalem breviant aliâ subeunte Latini.
Ni capit *r, fio* produc : & nomina quintæ
E servant longum, si præsit *i*, ceu *speciei.*
Anceps *ius* erit patrio : sed protrahe *alïus,*
Alterius brevia tantùm ; commune sit *ohe,*
Pompei, Cai, produc, conformia jungens.
Dianam varia : longa *aër, dius,* & *eheu,*
Et patrius primæ cum sese solvit in *ai.*
Hîc Græci variant, nec certâ lege tenentur.

A vowel before a mute and a liquid.   p. 254.

Si mutæ liquida est subjuncta in syllaba eâdem,
Quæ brevis antevenit vocalis, redditur anceps.
Hanc tamen in profa semper breviare memento.
Sunt *l, r,* liquidæ, queis rarò jungimus *m, n.*

Contracted Syllables and Diphthongs.   p. 254.
Vocalem efficiet semper contractio longam.
Diphthongum produc in Græcis atque Latinis ;
In Græcis semper : at PRÆ composta sequente
Vocali brevia ; veluti *præit* atque *præustus.*

Preterites and Supines.   p. 255.
Præterita assumunt primam dissyllaba longam.
Tolle *bibit, scidit,* & *fidit,* ac *tulit,* ortaque *do, sto.*
Præteritum geminans primam, breviabit utramque,
Ut *pario, peperi ;* vetet id nisi consona bina.
At quod *cædo* creat tardat, ceu *pedo,* secundam.
Cuncta Supina tenent primam dissyllaba longam :
Præter nata *sero, cieo, lino,* cum *sino, sisto,*
Quæ breviant ; *eo, doque, ruo, queo* junge, *reorque.*
Cætera præsentis mensuram verba reservant.
Excipe sed *posui positum, genui genitum*que,
Et *potui ;* quæ dant quoque *solvo* & *volvo* supina.

Præ

.Præ *tum* vocalem polyfyllaba cuncta fupina.
Producunt, *atum*, quibus, *etum* finis, & * utum :*
Ivi præterito veniens fociabis & *itum.*
Cætera corripies in *itum* quæcunque refidunt.

II. FINAL SYLLABLES.

A *in the end of a word.* p. 261.

Cafibus A flexum brevia.　Sed protrahe fextum,
Et quintum, Græco quando hic de nomine in AS fit.
Cafibus haud flexum produc.　*Ita,* cum *quia,* & *eja,*
Et *putà* non verbum fubduxeris, *hallequeluja.*
Curta quoque interdum, *contra, ultra,* & *ginta* creata.

E *in the end of a word.* p. 261.

E brevia.　Primæ produc, et nomina quintæ
Cum natis.　Addes pluralia cuncta : fecundæ
Induperativum focians.　Monofyllaba, demptis
Encliticis ac fyllabicis, quoque longa repones.
Adde à mobilibus flexûs quæcunque fecundi
Manârunt, fummique gradûs adverbia quævis.
Sed *benè* cum *malè* corripies, *infernè, fupernè,*
Productis *ferme* atque *ferè* jungantur, & *ohe.*

I *in the end of a word.* p. 261.

I longum pono.　Vocitantem corripe Græcis.
His tamen at ternus dabitur crefcentibus anceps.
Sic variato *mihi, tibi* cum *fibi :* fed magè curtis
Vult *ibi,* vultque *cui, nifi,* mox *ubi,* cum *quafi,* jungi.
Sicuti fed breviant, cum *necubi, ficubi,* vates.

O *in the end of a word.* p. 262.

O commune loces.　Dabis at monofyllaba longis,
Græcaque ceu *Dido,* ternum fextumque fecundæ,
Et patrium Græcum, atque adverbia nomine nata,
Quò jungens & *eò.*　Variant at *denuò, ferò,*
Mutuò, poftremò, verò ; modò fed breve pones,
Sæpiùs *ambo, duo, fcio* corripe, & *illicò* & *imò,*
Et *cedo da* fignans, *ego* queis *homo,* cum *citò* junge.
Sunt aliis variata Gerundia, longa Maroni.
Ergô pro caufa produc : fecus editur anceps.

C c

U and Y *in the end of a word.*   p. 262.

U femper longis, fed Y raptis jungere opartet.

B, D, L, M, R, *and* T, *in the end of a word.*   p. 262.
Corripe B Latium : peregrinum at tendere malim.
D breve ponatur.   Variare at Barbara poffis.
L breve fit.   Cum *fol, fal, nil,* tolluntur Hebræa.
M nunc vocalis perimit : rapuêre vetufti.
R brevies.   Produc cujus dat patrius *eris ;*
Addito *Iber, aër, æther.*   Sit *Celtiber* anceps.
At *par, far, lar, Nar,* quoque *cur, fur,* adjice longis.
T breve femper erit nifi quondam fyncopa tardet.

C *and* N *in the end of a word.*   p. 262.

C produc, præter *nec, donec :* fed variabis
Hic benè pronomen : *fac* verbum jungimus ifti.
N produc.   Demas EN *inis* dans, quæque priore
Græca per ON cafus numero tenuêre fecundæ ;
Et quartum cafum, fi fit brevis ultima recti.
Sin quoque pluralis ternæ conjunge Pelafgum :
Forfitan, in, forfan, tamen, an viden' infuper addens.

AS, ES, *and* OS, *in the end of a word.*   p. 263.

AS produc.   Patrio fed *adis* quod flectit, *anafque,*
Sit breve : plurales ternæ quibus addito quartos.
Ponitur ES longum.   Pluralia corripe Græca
Quæ crefcunt ; velut *es* de *fum ; penes* additur illi ;
Cum neutris ; & queis patrii penultima curta eft
Ternæ.   Tolle *Ceres, paries, aries, abies, pes.*
OS produc.   Patrius brevis eft, & *compos* & *impos,*
Ofque offis prabens.   Rectos breviato fecundæ.
(*O* nifi det patrius :) neutra his dein addito Graiûm.

IS, US, *and* YS, *in the end of a word.*   p. 263.

IS brevio.   Verùm plurales protraho cafus ;
ISque quod in patrio mutatur in *itis* & *inis,*
Aut *entis ; gratifque foris, glis, vis* quoque, nomen
Seu verbum fuerit : ficut & perfona fecunda
Protrahit IS, quoties *itis* plurale reponit.
In fubjunctivi *ris* eft commune futuro.

US correpta datur.   Monofyllaba cum genitivis
Ternæ vel quartæ produc : numerique fecundi
In quarta primum, quartum, quintumque ; & in *uris*,
Dumve in *utis* patrius, vel in *udis*, & *untis*, *odi*fve eft ;
Aut quintus fit in *u*, longus tum rectus habetur.
Ergo produces venerabile nomen Iesus.

YS junges brevibus.   *Tethys* reperitur at anceps.
Longaque funt rectis aliter quæ cafibus yn dant.

The laft Syllable of a verfe. p. 264.
Ultima cujufque eft communis fyllaba verfûs.

III.   The Quantity of Derivatives and Compounds.

1. *The Quantity of Derivatives.* p. 264.

Derivata tenent menfuram primigenorum :
Orta tamen brevibus, *fufpicio*, *regula*, *fedes*,
Seciùs, *humanus*, *penuria*, *mobilis*, *humor*,
Jumentum, *fomes*, primam producere gaudent.
Corripiunt fed *arifta*, *vadum*, *fopor* atque *lucerna*,
Duxque ducis, *ftabilif*que, *fides*, *ditio*que, *quafillus*,
Nata licet longis ; quæ pluraque fuggeret ufus.

2. *The Quantity of Compouuds.* p. 264.

Simplicium fervant legem compofta fuorum,
Quamvis diphthongus vel vocalis varietur.
At breviant *nihilum* cum *pejero*, *degero*, nec non
Veridicus, fociis junctis, & *femifopitus*.
Cognitus his addes, velut *agnitus*, *innubus*, atque
Pronubus : at longis *ambitus* mobile junges,
Imbecillus item : fed *connubium* variabis.
Quam disjuncta dabat menfuram præpofitura,
Juncta tenet : fubiens illam nifi litera mutet.
Eft pro breve in Græcis, pro longum ritè Latinis.
At rape quæ *fundus*, *fugio*, *neptif*que *nepof*que,
Eft *feftum*, *fari*, *fateor*, *fanum*que creârunt.
Huic *profectò* addes, pariterque *procella*, *protervus*.
Atque *propago* genus, *propago* protrahe vitis.
Propino varia, verbum *propago*, *profundo :*
Cum *pello*, *curo*, genitis, *Proferpina* junge.

Se produc & di, præter *dirimo* atque *difertus*.
Eft re breve : at viduum perfonis protrahe *refert*.
Pars fi componens fini prior *i* vel *o* donat, ˙.
Sit breve : *vaticinor* monftraverit, *Arctophylax*que.
I quibus eft flexu mutabile jungito longis,
Quæque queunt fenfu falvo divellier, addens
De quibus aut Crafis aliquid vel Syncopa tollit.
Idem mafculeum produc, & *ubique* & *ibidem* ; -
Huic dein agglomerans turbæ compofta *diei*.
His *intro*, *retro*, *contra*que & *quando* creata
(*Quandoquidem* excepto) bene junxeris, atque *alioquin*,
Quæque per *o* magnum fcribuntur nomina Graiis.

FIGURES of PROSODY.

Synalæpha and *Ecthlipfis*. p. 275.

Vocalem *Synalæpha*, *Ecthlipfis* & *m* quoque tollit,
Altera cùm voci eft vocalis prima fequenti.

Synærěfis and *Diærěfis*. p. 276.

Syllaba de binis conflata *Synærefis* efto.
Diftrahit in geminas refoluta *Diærefis* unam.

Syftŏlè and *Diaftŏlè*. p. 277.

Syftola præcipitat vocales ritè trahendas.
Protrahit huic adverfa *Diaftola* corripiendas.

Figures of DICTION. p. 277.

PROSTHESIS *apponit capiti*, *fed* APHÆRESIS *aufert*.
SYNCOPA *de medio tollit*, *fed* EPENTHESIS *addit*.
Abftrahit APOCOPE *fini*, *fed dat* PARAGOGE.
Conftringit CRASIS, *diftracta* DIÆRESIS *effert*.
Litera fi legitur tranfpofta, METATHESIS *exit*.
ANTITHESIN *dices*, *tibi litera fi varietur*.

F I N I S.